D1150697

BACK TO THE

V☉RTEX

THE UNOFFICIAL AND UNAUTHORISED
GUIDE TO DOCTOR WHO 2005

BACK TO THE

V RTEX

THE UNOFFICIAL AND UNAUTHORISED
GUIDE TO DOCTOR WHO 2005

BY J SHAUN LYON

First published in England in 2005 by
Telos Publishing Ltd
61 Elgar Avenue, Tolworth, Surrey, KT5 9JP, England
www.telos.co.uk

Telos Publishing Ltd values feedback. Please e-mail us with any comments you may have about this book
to: feedback@telos.co.uk

ISBN: 1-903889-78-2 (paperback)
ISBN: 1-903889-79-0 (hardback)
Text © 2005 J Shaun Lyon
Foreword © 2005 Philip David Segal
Afterword © 2005 Rob Shearman

All other contributions are copyright their respective owners and are used with permission. Please see the
index to illustrations which forms an extension to this copyright notice.

Limited edition hardback cover © 2005 Lee Binding

The moral rights of the author have been asserted.

Font design by Comicraft. Copyright © 1998 Active Images/Comicraft
430 Colorado Avenue # 302, Santa Monica, Ca 90401
Fax (001) 310 451 9761/Tel (001) 310 458 9094
WEB: www.comicbookfonts.com; EMAIL: orders@comicbookfonts.com

Internal design, typesetting and layout by Arnold T Blumberg & ATB Publishing Inc
www.atbpublishing.com

Printed and bound in England
Antony Rowe Ltd, Bumper's Farm Industrial Estate,
Chippenham, Wiltshire, SN14 6LH

1 2 3 4 5 6 7 8 9 10 11 12 13 14 15

British Library Cataloguing in Publication Data.
A catalogue record for this book is available from the British Library.

This book is sold subject to the condition that it shall not by way of trade or otherwise, be lent, resold,
hired out or otherwise circulated without the publisher's prior written consent in any form of binding or
cover other than that in which it is published and without a similar condition including this condition
being imposed on the subsequent purchaser.

TABLE OF CONTENTS

This book is dedicated to

Chad Jones
Robert Franks
and
Robbie Bourget

and is in memory of my friend
Michael Mason

With grateful thanks to
Steve Tribe and Paul Engelberg
for time well spent

FOREWORD

Once again the good Doctor returns to see another day, and that's a good thing, not just for mankind but for all *Doctor Who* fans around the world – because he is no longer just a phenomenon, but a true cultural icon.

I've had the pleasure of being Shaun Lyon's friend for ten years and know how dedicated he is to preserving the history of *Who* and the world of our time traveller, not just for today, but forever! Shaun, along with many dedicated, passionate Whovians, have kept the candle burning even when here in the US, the numbers of fans dwindled down to what seemed like a handful.

Back to the Vortex is in some ways a vital document that also happens to be pure fun as well. Books like *Back to the Vortex* create road markers for future generations who want to know more about our beloved Time Lord and his impact on society. Clearly from the very beginning, it was intended that the Doctor's exploits be a way to take us to significant events in human history. Now, decades later, the view from that first window has clearly expanded with great effect ... think of the countless galaxies, life forms, languages and science we have visited and explored because of all those timely adventures in the TARDIS.

Forty two years later, *Doctor Who* is more relevant than ever, and his current and future exploits will lay the foundation for yet another generation of fans to journey through time and space with one of the most unique characters ever created.

I'm proud of Shaun for taking the plunge and I know you will enjoy his unique perspective and genuine affection for this material. Enjoy ... I did!

Philip David Segal
Producer, Doctor Who *(1996)*
Los Angeles, July 2005

INTRODUCTION

Doctor Who is back. Four simple words with a definite and genuine history behind them ... a history of scepticism, regret, determination, frustration, and an endless supply of faith. Four words that fans heard over and over again for fifteen years, with growing degrees of disbelief and disappointment, but all the while longing for the day when it would come true. And in 2005, it did just that. Doctor Who had beaten the odds on many occasions, and the same could be said about its 'afterlife' – a well-received television film, an audio series, countless books and merchandise. In the early 21st Century, Doctor Who did so again: an 'antiquated' television series, best (if in some respects unfairly) remembered for wobbly sets, occasional overacting and pepperpot-shaped nasties, was being reimagined for a modern audience. Would it work? Would its production staff and writers and directors get it right? Most importantly, would the public buy it?

In retrospect, the answer was a resounding yes! ... but for eighteen months, between the announcement of the series's return and the transmission of the first episode, it was the proverbial million-dollar-question. And therein lies the reason why you hold in your hands Back to the Vortex ...

You might be asking yourself the following question: 'Why a book about a British television series written by someone who doesn't live in Britain and wasn't involved in its production?' That's a fair question, and it has a very simple answer: perspective. Doctor Who Magazine and SFX and Dreamwatch and the Doctor Who Confidential documentaries and the Daily Mirror and the Sun are all terrific sources for facts and figures and gossip and glimpses behind the scenes. They'll tell you everything about what it was like being there, during the production, and how it all came down. What they miss, however, is the perspective gained from being on the opposite side of the fence. Books on the Watergate era can tell you all about the shady dealings of Richard Nixon and the break-in at the Watergate Hotel, but not necessarily about what was racing through the minds of the public at the time, about the general consciousness of those who watched it unfold. News footage can give you a play-by-play view of Neil Armstrong's first steps on the moon or of Churchill's greatest speeches or of the coronation of Queen Elizabeth II ... but seldom does news footage show you what it felt like to be an 'ordinary' person, watching history unfold on those key days.

Back to the Vortex is different, because it is written purely from the perspective of the Doctor Who fan from the outside looking in, watching events unfold during this unique era in our history (which would go both for it being the Information Age as well as the New Age of Doctor Who; both are equally relevant, considering how much the former has contributed to the Doctor Who experience for so many fans abroad). I like to think of it as 'what you've seen is what you get'; it's told as it happened, from the point-of-view of the audience, relying solely upon our eyes and ears – what we've seen and heard – rather than inside information or scripts. It's a journey along a slightly different road from the one you might be used to, and one I've taken from my own particular perspective: as editor of a Doctor Who website with a rather large online readership – and resultant reader contributions to match – I've kept up with news about Doctor Who on a daily basis. I've therefore been witness to the coverage of these strange and wonderful events as they've happened: the night of Lorraine Heggessey's announcement that the show was coming back; the frenetic hype around Christopher Eccleston's casting; the giddy anticipation of waiting for that first transmission day. In 2005, in the era of the Internet, the miles that separated me from the United Kingdom were as irrelevant as the steps from my office to the front door; through email, discussion forums, instant messaging and the like (not to mention some wonderful friends in the UK and elsewhere who kept me in the loop), the *Doctor Who* world is closer together than ever before, and we fans are a part of that. Many of us watched these events unfold together, through the newspapers and magazines, the Internet discussions and the television broadcasts, a collective community enjoying the anticipation as much as the actual show itself.

At the end of the day, the general viewing public watches *Doctor Who* and moves on, whereas we, the fans of the series, are the ones who hold it near and dear to our hearts. I have no doubt there will be official reference books and behind-the-scenes tomes and future *Doctor Who Magazine* archive specials, and I welcome those publications with anxious glee. But they're just not telling the story that I wanted to tell; that's what you will find here, in the pages of this book.

Because *Back to the Vortex* is nothing more than that, a story. It's not a behind-the-scenes archive of dates and times and places and names, and there is no hasty gossip from the set, no BBC News-style investigation, no vicious tell-all accounts. It's merely an archive of information crossed with a fond salute to the new television series, a medley of articles and memories to be cherished (and collected in one place) rather than forgotten. It's also a look at the series with a critical eye, examining its successes and flaws, its internal continuity and sense of scale in the larger world. And with, I might add, not just one eye, but an entire collection of them, from a multi-national and multicultural perspective that showcases viewers from the five countries that enjoy significant fan activity for this series: the United Kingdom, Canada, the United States, Australia and New Zealand – a microcosm of *Doctor Who* fans around the world who have anxiously awaited this day, the day they could share in those four immortal words: *Doctor Who is back.*

So, come along and join me on a date with *Doctor Who* ...

J Shaun Lyon
Los Angeles
June 2005

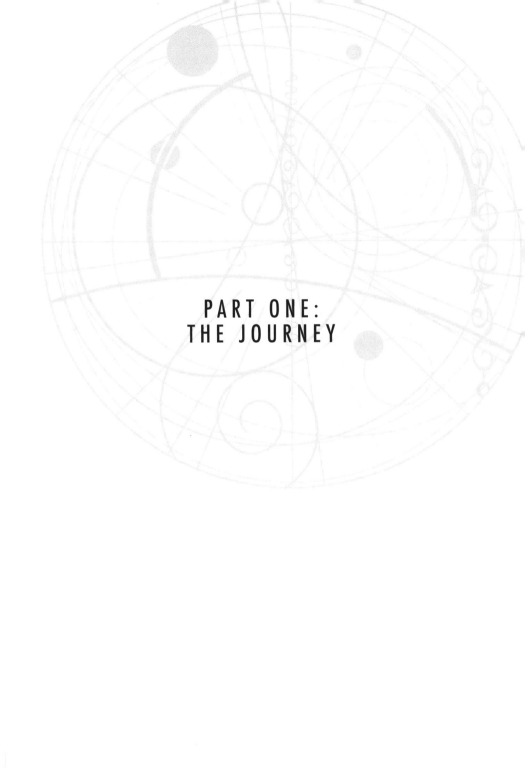

PART ONE:
THE JOURNEY

CHAPTER ONE:
SINCE LAST WE MET

'There are worlds out there where the sky is burning, and the sea's asleep, and the rivers dream; people made of smoke and cities made of song. Somewhere there's danger, somewhere there's injustice, somewhere else the tea's getting cold. Come on, Ace, we've got work to do.'

From 'Survival' by Rona Munroe

When those immortal words were spoken in December 1989, during the final televised episode of the original *Doctor Who*, they marked the end of one era and the beginning of another: the long wilderness years of the classic BBC science fiction series had begun.

The three-part television serial 'Survival' at the end of *Doctor Who's* twenty-sixth season had brought some semblance of closure to the programme, as the venerable Time Lord (Sylvester McCoy) returned his teenage companion Ace (Sophie Aldred) back home to her birthplace, the London suburb of Perivale, while combating his dreaded nemesis, the fiendish Time Lord known as the Master (Anthony Ainley). With the Master's dastardly plan vanquished, the Doctor and Ace headed to their trusted TARDIS for further adventures in time and space ... and the viewers went along with them in their imaginations.

It marked the start of something that *League of Gentlemen* writer and star Mark Gatiss, a long-time fan and subsequent contributor to the series, would later describe as *Doctor Who's* 'interregnum', a fifteen-year stretch that saw the once mighty British icon relegated to television's past, perhaps never to return.

As the Doctor and Ace turned and headed away, there was no announcement of a new series in the autumn, no trace of a reprieve for the wanderer from Gallifrey. *Doctor Who* had effectively been cancelled after twenty-six years of adventures, seven actors in the lead role, a whirlwind of companions, friends, villains and adversaries, and countless feats of compassion and heroism. It had become more than just a television series; it was a BBC icon, a reminder of glory days on the channel ... and it was leaving the telly for good. Fans cried out, the media reacted – although probably not in quite the same fashion they would have if, say, it had happened ten years before – and then, somehow, after the hype died down and the furore subsided, the audience moved on.

While *Doctor Who* stayed on the fringes of British consciousness, the world of television changed. Rumours of new episodes and specials rose and fell around anniversary dates, never quite materialising. Movie plans were announced, then scrapped. But *Doctor Who* lived on through various media – audio, novel, novella, short fiction, fan fiction, and finally, a new TV film co-produced with American companies that made a surprisingly big and positive impact on British television but fell short of resulting in a new series. Companies came forward to carry the flame with licensed material, while others found ways that did not infringe copyright to create their own original works related at least tangentially to the series that *Doctor Who* fans had so enjoyed.

In short, *Doctor Who* lived on, well past its prime, sometimes showing only so much as a heartbeat ... but it was there, bridging the years between television series. Enduring. *Surviving*.

And what a decade-and-a-half it was.

THE ADVENTURES OF VIRGIN PUBLISHING

With stories it branded 'too broad and too deep for the small screen', Virgin Publishing picked up the torch in 1991 eighteen months after the final broadcast of the original *Doctor Who* series, with an all-new range of adventures published in novel form, branded *The New Adventures*. Kicking off the range, John Peel's *Timewyrm: Genesys* followed on directly from 'Survival', with the seventh Doctor and Ace together in the TARDIS. From then on, they faced countless adventures together including: a world in which Hitler won World War II (*Timewyrm: Exodus*, 1991), a cyberpunk-fantasy future world where danger lurked in the heart of the mass transit system (*Transit*, 1992), an alternate universe where the Silurians ruled the Earth (*Blood Heat*, 1993), and a return to the television series's medieval planet of Peladon (*Legacy*, 1994).

The Doctor and Ace were joined in their travels by intrepid archaeologist Bernice Summerfield (introduced in Paul Cornell's *Love and War*, 1992) and 30th Century soldiers Chris Cwej and Roslyn Forrester (from Andy Lane's *Original Sin,* 1995). Ace departed the Doctor's company first in *Love and War*, returned a few books later in Peter Darvill-Evans's *Deceit* (1993) three years older and toughened by Dalek wars, and then finally departed for good in *Set Piece* (1995) by Kate Orman. Bernice married interstellar rogue Jason Kane in the fiftieth Virgin novel, Paul Cornell's *Happy Endings* (1996), while Roz was killed in action at the end of *So Vile a Sin* (1997) by Ben Aaronovitch and Kate Orman. In the meantime, we met new civilisations, faced old enemies and even took a trip to the Doctor's ancestral home of Lungbarrow on Gallifrey ... where we learned that his family and his parentage – and his secrets – were far more complex than realised. Toward the end of the range, there was a novel called *Damaged Goods* (1996), from the pen of a man named Russell T Davies ... and we'll be hearing more about him later.

Meanwhile, Virgin also dipped into the past with their *Missing Adventures* series. These 33 novels covered all six earlier Doctors and their companions (strangely omitting the savage Leela but introducing its own original companions as well). Also published from 1994 to 1997 were a series of five *Decalog* short fiction anthologies (the fourth and fifth of which had only a tangential connection to *Doctor Who*), a special novel called *Who Killed Kennedy?* (1996), and a series of hardcover and paperback non-fiction books including a trilogy of large format books *The Sixties* (1992), *The Seventies* (1994) and *The Eighties* (1996) by David J Howe, Stephen James Walker and Mark Stammers.

BBV PRODUCTIONS

In 1993, independent producer Bill Baggs entered the fray with original video dramas 'borrowing' *Doctor Who* concepts (at least in essence, if not in name). *Summoned by Shadows* starred Colin Baker and Nicola Bryant as 'the Stranger and Miss Brown', a wayward adventurer and his travelling companion who bore more than a passing resemblance to the actors' TV characters, the sixth Doctor and Peri. The adventures of this Stranger continued in several videos featuring other regular and semi-regular *Doctor Who* cast members such as Sophie Aldred, Caroline John, Michael Wisher and Louise Jameson, and it eventually became apparent by *Eye of the Beholder* (1995) that the lead character was not a version of the Doctor after all.

BBV also released on video a series continuing the adventures of Caroline John's original *Doctor Who* series character, Dr Liz Shaw, working for a new organisation called PROBE

(1994-1996); a three-part serial using the sinister plastic baddies the Autons (1997-1999); a comedy story starring Sylvester McCoy with the enigmatic title *Do You Have a Licence To Save This Planet?* (2001); a drama called *Cyberon* (2000) (featuring monsters akin to the Cybermen); and a stand-alone thriller, *The AirZone Solution* (1993), which featured no fewer than four TV Doctors, Colin Baker, Jon Pertwee, Peter Davison, Sylvester McCoy, along with Nicola Bryant (all in new, specially-written roles).

Meanwhile, BBV's foray into the audio medium was even more extensive. Their series of original dramas released on CD began in 1998 with two characters, the Professor and Ace, played by Sylvester McCoy and Sophie Aldred. When BBC Worldwide expressed concern over these productions (as the characters were an obvious play on the two leads from *Doctor Who*) the names were changed to the Dominie and Alice. Other entries in the series included two focusing on a character called the Wanderer (again, effectively the Doctor under a different name), played by Nicholas Briggs; two featuring the Stranger (again played by Colin Baker); and two featuring the Mistress (Lalla Ward, effectively reprising her TV role of Romana) and K-9 (voiced, as in most of his TV appearances alongside Tom Baker's Doctor, by John Leeson). The inclusion of K-9 in these plays was just the first of a number of instances of BBV entering into agreements with the creators of non-BBC-owned *Doctor Who* characters to use them in their dramas. Familiar adversaries that made return appearances in this way were the Zygons, the Krynoids, the Wirrn, the Sontarans and even the Rani (a role resumed by the delightfully devious Kate O'Mara). The audio line also featured several 'stand alone' science fiction stories, including *Punchline* (2000) starring Sylvester McCoy (in a role that, again, was effectively the seventh Doctor in all but name) and written by Jeremy Leadbetter, a pseudonym for Rob Shearman. The company ceased producing new material in 2002.

THE VISUAL ARTS

The *Doctor Who* mythos lived on in the world of multimedia. Video productions appeared more frequently as independent filmmakers arranged for licences to use elements from *Doctor Who* which the BBC did not own themselves. The film *Wartime* (1987) was the first of these spin offs; John Levene reprised his series role as Sergeant Benton in a story written by Andy Lane and Helen Stirling. *Shakedown: The Return of the Sontarans* (1994), written by original series veteran writer and script editor Terrance Dicks, and directed by Kevin Davies, featured series veterans Carole Ann Ford and Sophie Aldred and *Blake's 7* stars Jan Chappell and Brian Croucher in an original story that pitted the crew of a solar yacht against the Sontarans and the Rutans. *Downtime* (1995) brought back the Brigadier (Nicholas Courtney), Sarah Jane Smith (Elisabeth Sladen), Victoria Waterfield (Deborah Watling), Professor Travers (Jack Watling), the alien Yeti and their masters the Great Intelligence, and introduced Beverley Cressman as Kate Lethbridge-Stewart, daughter of the Brigadier, in a story written by Marc Platt ('Ghost Light') and directed by original series director Christopher Barry. (Both *Shakedown* and *Downtime* were, in fact, accepted as part of the series' official 'canon' when they were novelised as part of Virgin Publishing's *Doctor Who* novels range.) *Mindgame* (1998), written by Terrance Dicks, and *Mindgame Trilogy* (1999), by Dicks, Miles Richardson and Roger Stevens, featured a Sontaran and a Draconian as well as Sophie Aldred playing an Ace-like character. Reeltime Pictures released a successful line of interview recordings under the *Myth Makers* title (which began in 1984), as well as several documentary productions including *Lust in Space* (1998), *I Was a Doctor Who Monster* (1996), *Who On Earth Is Tom*

Baker? (1991), *Where On Earth Is ... Katy Manning* (1998) and *K9 Unleashed* (2000) and other documentaries filmed at various conventions, including reuniting the cast of the original series story 'The Daemons' for *Return to Devil's End* (1993). Other documentaries included *The Doctors: 30 Years of Time Travel and Beyond* (1995), *Bidding Adieu* (1996), *Who is Tom Baker* (1997) and Paul McGann speaking in *Big Finish TalksBack: In Conversation with the Eighth Doctor* (2002). Not to be outdone, the BBC sponsored its own documentary to celebrate the series in 1993, *Thirty Years in the TARDIS* (later extended with the words 'More Than ...' added to the front for the video release) was directed by Kevin Davies.

THE DARK DIMENSION

In 1992, aware that the following year would see *Doctor Who's* thirtieth anniversary, BBC Enterprises became involved in plans to produce a special film – possibly to be marketed on a direct-to-video basis – to celebrate the event. Adrian Rigelsford and Jo McCaul's script for *The Dark Dimension* would have united all five living Doctors – Jon Pertwee, Tom Baker, Peter Davison, Colin Baker and Sylvester McCoy – as well as Ace and the Brigadier ... if it had been made.

Many behind the scenes issues prevented it from getting off the ground. The complicated relationship between the BBC and its commercial arm, BBC Worldwide, did not allow the latter to focus on production, as it was geared solely toward revenue generation. Meanwhile, issues with the actors who would potentially return to their roles arose, as several were concerned that their involvement would comprise no more than a cameo appearance. The final straw came as plans for a forthcoming *Doctor Who* television series being negotiated with American networks (plans that would eventually result in the one-off TV film in 1996) required that the project be halted. So *The Dark Dimension* never really got off the starting blocks, and aside from a script and some initial design thoughts, no real progress had been made on the production.

DIMENSIONS IN TIME

The thirtieth anniversary year of *Doctor Who* did, however, see the broadcast of *Dimensions in Time*, a light hearted feature with a charitable purpose, written by David Roden and former series producer John Nathan-Turner. The two-part skit was originally produced for the BBC's annual *Children in Need* telethon; the first part was broadcast during the telethon itself, and the second as part of the following day's *Noel's House Party*, a Saturday evening light entertainment show presented by Noel Edmonds. Jon Pertwee joined Edmonds on the *House Party* set for *Children in Need* to watch the first part on Friday November 26. A marriage of characters from both *Doctor Who* and popular long-running soap *EastEnders*, the special featured appearances by Pertwee, Tom Baker, Peter Davison, Colin Baker and Sylvester McCoy as various facets of the Doctor (with Tom Baker's sequences recorded separately), and guest appearances by former *Doctor Who* actors Sophie Aldred (Ace), Nicola Bryant (Peri), Nicholas Courtney (Brigadier Lethbridge-Stewart), Carole Ann Ford (Susan), Richard Franklin (Mike Yates), Louise Jameson (Leela), Caroline John (Liz Shaw), Bonnie Langford (Mel), John Leeson (K9), Kate O'Mara (the Rani), Elisabeth Sladen (Sarah Jane Smith), Sarah Sutton (Nyssa), Lalla Ward (Romana) and Deborah Watling (Victoria). The *Doctor Who* element of *Children in Need* that year was marked with a multi-Doctor *Radio Times* cover.

At the conclusion of the first episode, viewers were asked to make a selection between two *EastEnders* characters, Mandy and Big Ron, who would aid the Doctor in the second episode (in what amounted to nothing more than a cameo of a few seconds in length). Mandy eventually won out, and the alternative version with Big Ron was never publicly shown. The story was never repeated, and due to the complicated and charitable nature of its origin (and the contracts written as such), will most likely never see the light of day on an official BBC release.

THE 1996 DOCTOR WHO TV MOVIE

In 1996, it seemed that the prayers of *Doctor Who* fans everywhere had been answered. BBC Television, in cooperation with Universal Television and FOX, brought actor Paul McGann to the role of the Doctor for *Doctor Who*, a television movie that debuted in May 1996. McGann, a critically acclaimed film, television and stage actor who had appeared in such productions as *Withnail and I* (1987), *Paper Mask* (1990), *Alien3* (1992) and *The Three Musketeers* (1993), was cast under the auspices of producer Philip David Segal, who had been working first for Steven Spielberg's Amblin Entertainment and then as head of production at Lakeshore Television in America. Segal had fought for years to bring *Doctor Who* to American shores (a quest later recounted in his book *Regeneration* co-written with Gary Russell, released by Harper Collins). He and his production team cast Daphne Ashbrook, seen previously in an appearance in *Deep Space Nine* and later in the popular FOX television series *The OC*, as the Doctor's newest companion, surgeon Grace Holloway, while Canadian actor Yee Jee Tso would play streetwise teenager Chang Lee. Rounding out the cast was well-known American actor Eric Roberts, playing the Doctor's arch enemy, the Master. Of great importance was the return to the role of Sylvester McCoy, the seventh Doctor, who would participate in the first ten minutes of the film, leading to an archetypical regeneration sequence in which he transformed into the likeness of McGann.

The film was intended as a possible 'backdoor pilot' for the return of *Doctor Who* as a regular television series, but it was simply not to be. Ratings were extremely good in the UK, with over nine million viewers. A confluence of circumstances prevented any significant viewing figures in America, however, thus ending any possibility of American funding and killing the future of the project.

Nevertheless, the television movie made an extraordinary impact on *Doctor Who* fans worldwide. McGann's incarnation of the Doctor was generally accepted by them as a *bona fide* one, and this would later prove to be the launching point for the actor's return to the role in original audio and Internet-broadcast dramas.

BBC BOOKS

In June 1997, BBC Books started publishing original *Doctor Who* fiction after Virgin Publishing's licence to do so ended the month before. BBC Books chose to kick off their range with a celebratory novel called *The Eight Doctors* by Terrance Dicks. A series of novels in two ranges then ensued: one the continuing adventures of the eighth Doctor (as played on television by Paul McGann), and the other a series of past Doctor adventures featuring the first seven Doctors and their respective companions.

The eighth Doctor novels brought forth many original characters and developments over the years, including a teenage orphan from the streets of London (Sam Jones), a 1960s stalwart English layabout (Fitz Kreiner), the first-ever companion to become a living TARDIS (the short-lived Compassion, aka Laura Tobin), a 21st Century go-getter (Anji Kapoor), and a rogue con-artist and stowaway aboard the TARDIS (Trix MacMillan). Within the series, a new breed of enemy was created: Faction Paradox, a cult of former Time Lords and time travellers who perfected themselves by changing time to create the ultimate paradox. The Doctor prevented Faction Paradox from securing their ultimate objective, but in the process, he was forced to destroy his home planet Gallifrey. Having no memories of anything prior to that event, the Doctor wandered alone on Earth throughout the 20th Century, until he was reunited with his TARDIS and then continued his adventures. BBC Books's specific eighth Doctor series came to a close in 2005 with Lance Parkin's *The Gallifrey Chronicles*.

The past Doctor novels also brought forth some interesting developments, sometimes filling in the blanks between stories that on first glance appeared to be continuous, allowing no adventures between them. Terrance Dicks's novel *Players* (1999) was the first in print to postulate a time period between the end of the era of the second Doctor (Patrick Troughton) and the beginning of that of the third (Jon Pertwee), when all evidence on screen at the end of the 1969 story 'The War Games' demonstrated a sudden and swift decision by the Time Lords to banish him to Earth. Meanwhile, BBC Books also published some original non-fiction (including the first edition of *The Television Companion* (1998), a guide to the entire series by David J Howe and Stephen James Walker now published by Telos Publishing, as well as Gary Gillatt's book of critical analysis, *Doctor Who From A to Z* (1998) and the fortieth anniversary book *The Legend* (2003, reprinted in 2005) by range editor/consultant Justin Richards) and several paperback collections of short fiction under the series title *Short Trips* (1998-2000).

BIG FINISH PRODUCTIONS

In 1999, the Doctor entered another realm of adventures courtesy of Big Finish Productions, an independent audio company owned by entrepreneur Jason Haigh-Ellery. Under the aegis of Gary Russell, a long-time fan and *Doctor Who* novelist for both Virgin and BBC Books, a successful line of audio adventures was created that starred 'classic' series cast members. The range kicked off with *The Sirens of Time*, a serial that brought the fifth, sixth and seventh Doctors (Peter Davison, Colin Baker and Sylvester McCoy) together in a single production for the first time, and future instalments saw the return of familiar companion characters including Nyssa (Sarah Sutton), Turlough (Mark Strickson), Peri (Nicola Bryant), Melanie (Bonnie Langford) and Ace (Sophie Aldred).

In addition, many other original series actors returned to familiar and not-so-familiar roles: Nicholas Courtney once again appeared as Brigadier Lethbridge-Stewart; Lalla Ward reprised her character of Romana, now promoted to President of Gallifrey; Louise Jameson recreated the savage Leela, still accompanied by the robot dog K-9 portrayed by John Leeson; Elisabeth Sladen added weight to her role of Sarah Jane Smith in a separate series of audio stories; Geoffrey Beevers once again became the Master (which he had first played in 1979's 'The Keeper of Traken' as a decaying, decrepit shell of the Doctor's former foe); Terry Molloy returned as the villainous Davros, the creator of the Daleks; and other instalments, both standard as well as a 'What If?' series generically called *Doctor Who Unbound*, brought back original series veterans Carole Ann Ford, Wendy Padbury, Anneke Wills, Deborah Watling, Caroline John and William Russell, generally in new roles. Finally, original series star Katy

Manning played Iris Wildthyme, a renegade Time Lady and old flame of the Doctor's, first introduced by writer Paul Magrs in the BBC Books range, who appeared in a number of the Big Finish audio dramas.

Actors popular from other series and genres also appeared in this version of *Doctor Who*, including *Babylon 5*'s Peter Jurasik, *Blake's 7* alumni Gareth Thomas, Sally Knyvette, Stephen Greif, Michael Keating and Jacqueline Pearce, comedy actor Christopher Biggins, actors Eleanor Bron, Bill Oddie, Philip Madoc, Michael Praed, Don Warrington, Nickolas Grace, Graeme Garden, Martin Jarvis and Caroline Munro – and even radio DJ Tony Blackburn, playing himself! (Plus, an up-and-coming actor named David Tennant... but more about him later.)

The range expanded further in 2001 when Paul McGann returned to the role of the eighth Doctor. Cast alongside him was stage actress India Fisher as a new companion, Charley Pollard, a self-styled Edwardian adventuress. Big Finish's *Doctor Who* range also introduced other new companions: Maggie Stables as university professor Evelyn Smythe to accompany the sixth Doctor; Caroline Morris as Erimem, whose destiny as a future Pharaoh was cut short during the Doctor's brief visit to ancient Egypt, to travel with the fifth Doctor; Philip Olivier as Hex to join the seventh Doctor and Ace; and Conrad Westmass as C'rizz, a reptilian alien regular to accompany the eighth Doctor and Charley. Big Finish also enjoyed success with a *Dalek Empire* audio series, a series of UNIT adventures, and a series based around the Doctor's home planet Gallifrey.

THE CURSE OF FATAL DEATH

In 1999, the producers of Comic Relief UK commissioned a special sketch for the Red Nose Day charity drive. *Doctor Who and the Curse of Fatal Death* was a parody written by established TV writer Steven Moffat. Familiar *Black Adder* and *Mr Bean* star Rowan Atkinson was cast as the Doctor, with Julia Sawalha (Saffron from the hit comedy series *Absolutely Fabulous* (1992-), and earlier a star of the children's TV series *Press Gang*, 1989-1993) joining him as assistant Emma, both facing the dastardly deeds of the Master (in this incarnation, played by big-screen star Jonathan Pryce). During the course of the special, the Doctor encountered the dank sewers of the planet Terserus and the might of the evil Daleks, until a sudden accident caused him to regenerate through the rest of his life cycles ... first into actor Richard E Grant, then comedy actor Jim Broadbent, then international star Hugh Grant, and finally into the body of a woman, played by Joanna Lumley, well known from *Absolutely Fabulous* and also from her role in the cult show *Sapphire and Steel* (1979-1982).

The special was released on video in 1999 (along with a semi-spoof documentary and sketches from *French and Saunders*, *The Victoria Wood Show* and *Lenny Henry*), with all proceeds going to Comic Relief.

BBC VIDEO AND AUDIO

Between 1983 and 2003, BBC Video issued every complete *Doctor Who* story on VHS videotape and even released special compilations of stories that (due to their original tapes being wiped or lost over the years) were incomplete ('The Tenth Planet', 'The Reign of Terror', 'The Ice Warriors'), some with linking narration ('The Invasion'), some even 'reconstructed' ('Shada', never completed for broadcast due to strike action at the BBC). BBC Worldwide later shifted its focus toward DVD, releasing a handful of stories before focusing solely on the DVD range once the VHS collection had been completed. The DVD range included a special release called *Lost in Time*, which held the 'orphan' episodes that existed as the sole evidence of early 1960s stories otherwise lost from view. (Although the DVD releases elsewhere in the world tended to follow behind the BBC's releases in the UK, BBC America did release a special box set of its own, a six-DVD collection of stories which comprised Season 16, *The Key to Time*. As of writing, the latter stories have yet to be released on DVD in the UK or elsewhere.)

In 1999, the BBC Radio Collection (now known as BBC Audio) began releasing soundtrack recordings of *Doctor Who* episodes that did not exist in their entirety visually. Since all *Doctor Who* episodes existed on audio (thanks to several prescient fans of the series in its early years, who had made off-air recordings), the BBC issued these recordings with linking narration from several actors who had been involved with them, Frazer Hines, William Russell, Peter Purves, Anneke Wills and Wendy Padbury. The range has also included other items such as documentaries and specials, MP3-CD versions of some of the soundtrack recordings, and dramatic readings of novelisations by several *Doctor Who* stars including Colin Baker, Peter Davison and William Russell.

TELOS PUBLISHING

In late 2001, Telos Publishing, a company formed by David J Howe and Stephen James Walker, previously best known for their non-fiction *Doctor Who* books, started publishing original hardcover *Doctor Who* fiction in novella format. Boasting collectable, high-quality book design – including signed and numbered deluxe editions with full colour frontispiece illustrations – and contributions from established names in the science fiction, fantasy and horror genres, the range was launched with *Time and Relative* by novelist Kim Newman (with an introduction by BBC Books's consulting editor Justin Richards). Other books in the range were written both by established *Doctor Who* writers, such as Keith Topping, Dave Stone, Kate Orman and Jonathan Blum, Simon A Forward and former series script editor Andrew Cartmel, and by writers new to the *Doctor Who* genre but well known in their own circles, like Louise Cooper, Simon Clark and Paul McAuley. The books featured introductions by other prominent writers including Storm Constantine, John Ostrander, Stephen Laws and Neil Gaiman. One entry in the series, Mike Tucker and Robert Perry's *Companion Piece*, introduced a one-shot companion of its own, named Cat.

The novellas were highly acclaimed: *Time and Relative* was voted the best *Doctor Who* book of 2001 by readers of *Doctor Who Magazine*; Kate Orman and Jon Blum's *Fallen Gods* won the Aurealis Award for Best Novel in Australia in 2003; and Simon A Forward's *Shell Shock* won publishing industry awards for both its design and production.

Telos's licence to publish the novellas was not renewed by BBC Worldwide, and the range came to an end early in 2004 with Simon Clark's *The Dalek Factor*, a book that returned the Daleks to print after a gap of six years.

Telos has continued to explore the *Doctor Who* genre with several factual books, including an updated edition of *The Television Companion* (2003), a revised compilation of the Howe/Stammers/Walker behind-the-scenes Handbook reference guides called simply *The Handbook* (2005), and *Howe's Transcendental Toybox* (2003) by David J Howe and Arnold T Blumberg, considered the definitive guide to *Doctor Who* collectibles. And, of course, the book you're reading at this very moment ...

DOCTOR WHO SPIN-OFFS AND RELATED PROJECTS

After the success of the Faction Paradox mythos created by writer Lawrence Miles for the BBC's range of *Doctor Who* novels, Miles developed his ideas further, eventually spinning them off into their own projects. BBV Productions released, in 2001 and 2002, six original audio plays featuring new characters in situations surrounding the Faction Paradox's 'Eleven Day Empire'. Magic Bullet Productions later took over the licence, planning to release a new series of audios starting in 2005. Mad Norwegian Press, owned by writer Lars Pearson, started publishing original Faction Paradox fiction, producing a series of books that began in 2002 with the publication of the anthology/encyclopedia hybrid *The Book of the War* edited by Miles, followed by a series of novellas, and a short-lived comic book. Mad Norwegian also produced several well-received volumes of its *I, Who* book series, large-format reference books summarising the *Doctor Who* audios and books released to date.

Virgin Publishing, BBC Books and, later, Big Finish Productions all produced several series of *Doctor Who* licensed fiction anthologies featuring the first eight Doctors and their companions and nemeses: the previously-mentioned *Decalog* and long-running *Short Trips* collections. Several fan publishers, meanwhile, contributed their own high-profile volumes, raising money for charitable funds and featuring the support (and short fiction) of established *Doctor Who* writers and, in some cases, the actors themselves, including the *Perfect Timing* and *Perfect Timing 2* books (1998/1999, edited by Helen Fayle, Julian Eales and Mark Phippen), *The Cat Who Walked Through Time* (2001, edited by Alryssa and Tom Kelly), *LifeDeath* (2001, edited by Kereth Cowe-Spigai and Patrick Neighly), *Walking in Eternity* (2001, edited by Julian Eales) and *Missing Pieces* (2001, edited by Mark Phippen and Shaun Lyon). Writer Jim Mortimore self-published his own *Doctor Who* novel, *Campaign* (2000), after a dispute with BBC Books, for whom it had originally been written. Jean-Marc and Randy Lofficier released *Doctor Omega* (2003) through Black Coat Press, an adaptation of a 1906 French science fiction novel by Arnould Galopin that was eerily similar to *Doctor Who* (with some of the most coincidental items embellished even further by the Lofficiers).

Alan Stevens's Magic Bullet audio imprint also developed a *Kaldor City* audio series, which started in 2001. *Kaldor City* was created by writer Chris Boucher, using the name of a fictional city first mentioned in the *Doctor Who* story 'The Robots of Death' and later the setting for his 1999 BBC past Doctor novel *Corpse Marker*. The series saw actor Russell Hunter reprising his role of Commander Uvanov from 'The Robots of Death'. Another star of the audio series was Paul Darrow, best known as Avon on *Blake's 7*, here playing a man named Kaston Iago, while Scott Fredericks reprised the character of Carnell that he had played in the 'Weapon' episode of *Blake's 7*. As the series progressed, another element from *Doctor Who* was introduced, that of the alien Fendahl from another of Boucher's televised stories, 'Image of the Fendahl'. In effect, the *Kaldor City* series married *Doctor Who* and *Blake's 7* into one universe.

In 1996, as Virgin's licence to publish *Doctor Who* fiction was not renewed by BBC Worldwide, the publisher kept its *New Adventures* line going, focusing on the further exploits of ex-companion Bernice Summerfield. Twenty-three novels were published in this series until the reins were picked up by Big Finish, who first issued a series of six audios featuring actress Lisa Bowerman as Bernice (with guest appearances – in new roles – by Elisabeth Sladen, Richard Franklin, Nicholas Courtney and Colin Baker, and adapted from the published novels). Subsequently, the audio series was continued with original adventures, and Big Finish also launched a series of books and short story collections about Summerfield's ongoing quests as an adventurer, a mother and the colleague of the mysterious Irving

Braxiatel (played by Miles Richardson on audio.)

Other spin off material came from Comeuppance Comics which, in 2003, began publishing a limited series based on the adventures of Miranda, the Doctor's adopted daughter, a character established by writer Lance Parkin in the 2001 BBC Books novel *Father Time*. (To date, however, the series has seen only three issues published.)

Independent audio productions abounded: Mark J Thompson's MJTV Productions created a running series of plays, *Soldiers of Love*, utilising both *Doctor Who* and *Blake's Seven* actors; Cineffigy Studios released two audios, *Augury* and *Cairo Dawn*, featuring the vocal talents of Sarah Sutton, Louise Jameson, Wendy Padbury and Mark Strickson; and Peter Trapani produced a short-lived audio series called *Layton's Mission* featuring Anneke Wills.

Telos Publishing invested in its own spin-off novella series in 2003 with *Time Hunter*, which built on the successful characters of Daniel O'Mahony's 2003 *Doctor Who* novella *The Cabinet of Light* and features time-travelling characters Honoré Lechasseur and Emily Blandish, as well as occasional characters and monsters from the *Doctor Who* television series. As an adjunct to the *Time Hunter* range, Keith Barnfather's Reeltime Pictures produced and released in 2004 a DVD drama called *Daemos Rising*. This was written by David J Howe, and starred Miles Richardson as ex-UNIT operative Douglas Cavendish and Beverley Cressman reprising her *Downtime* role as Kate Lethbridge-Stewart, in a new adventure featuring the Daemons from the *Doctor Who* story 'The Daemons', and based on concepts being explored in the *Time Hunter* series.

THE BBC GOES ONLINE

Throughout the first few years of the 21st Century, BBC Online (later renamed BBCi, then simply bbc.co.uk) spent considerable amounts of money developing its brand-specific products, including the BBC Cult section devoted to popular television series. One of these sections was an extensive *Doctor Who* website, which slowly grew from a rarely-updated archive of photos into an active, highly productive medium that branched out with several original productions and projects.

Death Comes to Time (2001) was the first of the BBCi 'webcasts', audio productions married to artwork (occasionally animated with Flash technology, but only for illustrative effect). The production received an extensive amount of coverage in the UK press, noting that *Doctor Who* was 'returning' (and failing to recognise the audios that had been available for several years), and even overseas, such as in the pages of the popular American magazine *Entertainment Weekly*. Producer Dan Freedman, who doubled as writer for the serial (under the pseudonym Colin Meek), and script editor Nev Fountain led a team of production staff and actors, including: Sylvester McCoy and Sophie Aldred, reprising their roles as the Doctor and Ace; *Buffy the Vampire Slayer* perennial Anthony Stewart Head; *Blake's 7* actress Jacqueline Pearce; and well-known stage and screen actor and writer Stephen Fry. The success of the project ensured future productions, which continued with *Real Time* in 2002, this time produced for BBCi by Big Finish Productions and starring Colin Baker as the Doctor with his audio companion Maggie Stables (as Evelyn), and finally an adaptation of the late Douglas Adams's screenplay 'Shada' in 2003, a *Doctor Who* serial infamously aborted midway through production in the late 1970s due to a BBC industrial strike. The script was rewritten to accommodate the audio medium and to include Paul McGann as the Doctor instead of the original's Tom Baker, while allowing him to unite with original series veterans Lalla Ward (as

Romana) and John Leeson (as K-9), and also featured appearances by actors James Fox, Andrew Sachs (of *Fawlty Towers* fame) and Susannah Harker.

BBCi also began a range of photo novels, using off-air photographs taken during the original series's run, to recapture part of the magic of the episodes of *Doctor Who* no longer resting comfortably in the BBC archives. In the 1960s, photographer John Cura was contracted to take these photo stills, or telesnaps, of the television screen, during the broadcast of numerous different TV productions, to allow a visual record of a director's or artist's work; these were, after all, the days before the advent of commercial video recorders. During *Doctor Who's* interim years, some fans took up the task of marrying together their narrated TV soundtrack recordings with the relevant photographs into what would become known as 'telesnap reconstructions'. In 2005, BBC Audio recognised the potential involved in this with the first release in their *Doctor Who: Reconstructed* multimedia CD range. Complementing this on BBCi was another range of e-books: revised and updated versions of out-of-print Virgin Publishing novels from the early-to-mid 1990s, accompanied by original illustrations and notes from the authors.

Another popular feature at the BBCi site for a time was the TARDISCam, a series of video selections featuring clips from classic *Doctor Who* adventures accompanied by new material created by the BBC Visual Effects department under the supervision of Mike Tucker and Nick Sainton-Clark. The TARDISCam clips were later included in several of BBC Video's DVD releases.

THE SCREAM OF THE SHALKA

On the heels of their successes with various audio webcasts streamed over their website, BBCi put plans in motion for a fully-animated original *Doctor Who* production. *Scream of the Shalka* by Paul Cornell was broadcast in November 2003, in what was intended to be the first of several highly anticipated animated serials. Actor Richard E Grant, best known for his role in *Withnail and I* (1986), was cast as the ninth Doctor while Sophie Okonedo, later a 2004 Academy Award nominee for her role in the film *Hotel Rwanda*, featured as his new companion, bartender Alison Cheney. In a casting coup, the legendary thespian Sir Derek Jacobi (who had played an 'unbound' Doctor on audio the year before) portrayed the Master in the animated serial, while Craig Kelly (Vince in Russell T Davies's drama *Queer as Folk*), Diana Quick and others joined the cast. Famed animators Cosgrove Hall (*DangerMouse*) crafted the design of the serial, while Cornell himself would later novelise the story for BBC Books in 2004 (along with a 'making-of' journal included in the volume).

For a while, it seemed that the future of *Doctor Who* lay in the success of *The Scream of the Shalka* to continue the mythos in future instalments. As the clock ticked down toward that November 2003 launch date, no-one could have guessed that the online animated serial would be the only one of its kind. However, there was later at least one additional story utilising this incarnation of the Doctor, Cavan Scott and Mark Wright's *Feast of the Stone*, published as a short story by BBCi.

FILM RUMOURS

Rumours about a *Doctor Who* film adaptation first surfaced around 1986, as Coast to Coast Productions (later Green Light, then Lumiere Pictures) purported to hold the rights. By the end of the 1980s, the rumours went as far as the casting of the Doctor's assistant – actress Caroline Munro. Nothing was to come of this, however, and the story behind several of the film projects that surfaced during this time and leading up to the eventual production of the 1996 *Doctor Who* television film starring Paul McGann was chronicled in Jean-Marc Lofficier's 1997 book *The Nth Doctor* published by Virgin Books (subsequently reissued in 2003 by iUniverse).

Toward the end of the 1990s, it was suggested on many occasions that BBC Films currently held the rights, and the intention, to produce a *Doctor Who* film. Rumours persisted for several years that the film was in various stages of production, even going so far as to suggest that actors were being looked at to star in the film. When no progress was made or announced by 2003, BBC1 Controller Lorraine Heggessey took it upon herself to investigate the rights situation ...

CHAPTER TWO:
EXPECT ... THE UNEXPECTED!

For years, rumours persisted that *Doctor Who* would eventually return to television. When and where would be anyone's guess... but in the meantime BBC Worldwide, the commercial arm of the BBC, ensured that there were books, CDs and other items available with the *Doctor Who* name on, and in some cases this resulted in a significant income from the licensing deals. The series, while well past its peak of popularity, nevertheless remained a treasured memory with the British public, while overseas, countless reruns on television and satellite broadcasts in America, Canada, Australia and New Zealand continued unabated. Memories held fast – after all, over nine million people in the UK had tuned into the 1996 television movie with Paul McGann – and while a section of the public considered *Doctor Who* a triviality, a product of its time, there was a sizeable proportion that believed a revival would happen. At some point.

When it did, almost no one saw it coming.

For years, there were rumours that a sea change of attitudes toward the *Doctor Who* brand was occurring within the confines of the BBC. Some years were good, others bad; years went by in which no-one wanted to talk about the show, and others in which there were positive feelings and good possibilities, all unfulfilled. In the wake of the ultimate failure of the 1996 *Doctor Who* TV movie to go from a backdoor pilot film to series status, the late 1990s were awash with stories and counter-stories about bids and proposals that had made their way to the desks of BBC executives, only to be met with slammed doors and a lack of progress. Names were bandied about as possible new producers, but nothing concrete came about. The success of Virgin Publishing and then BBC Books in developing a monthly release of novels, and Big Finish in creating a monthly audio CD line, as well as the BBCi webcast *Death Comes to Time*, were mere flashes of hope that someone, somehow, would recognise the unique value of the *Doctor Who* franchise as a viable TV series.

In May 2003, early signs that things were about to change were on the horizon. In a letter to Ian Wheeler, coordinator of the world's largest *Doctor Who* fan group, the *Doctor Who* Appreciation Society, Lorraine Heggessey, the Controller of BBC1, responded to ongoing calls for the return of the show: '*Doctor Who* is a classic BBC format, beloved by millions, myself included! If there was a refreshing, affordable treatment for a new series available and we could navigate ourselves around some potentially troublesome rights issues, then I would consider reviving the series. It's only a wish, there is nothing substantial to back things up, so I don't want to raise false hopes with die-hard fans! Suffice to say that *Doctor Who* has its fans among my commissioning team, most of whom spent the 70s behind the sofa on Saturday evenings too!'

Wheeler noted that he found Heggessey's honesty in her reply refreshing. 'It means we can enjoy the anniversary without worrying about whether there will or will not be a new series this year.' Wheeler apparently believed that something regarding the series would happen soon ... but, in fact, restoration was closer than he, or anyone, had thought.

Things were indeed changing within the BBC. In late May, an Australian fan named Chris Thomas had e-mailed BBC Director General Greg Dyke about reviving the series. To Thomas's surprise, he received a reply, not from Dyke but from Nathan Johnston of BBC Information, who replied in Dyke's stead with some optimism: 'Lorraine Heggessey has revealed that discussions are taking place at present regarding the possible revival of *Doctor Who*,' Johnston noted in his letter. 'I must point out, however, that nothing definite has been decided upon as yet, and there are certain issues, such as copyright, which must be dealt with before any further action can be taken.'

There had been an assumption that the production of new *Doctor Who* episodes for television had been impeded by what were generically referred to as 'rights issues'. Speculation persisted for a long time that the BBC had sold some or all of the rights to *Doctor Who* on television to FOX or maybe Universal in 1996 when they made the television film with Paul McGann, or that the rights were tied up with the production of a new feature film. On 21 August, the editors of the BBC's *Doctor Who* website published an article addressing these so-called rights issues with a statement about who actually owned *Doctor Who* according to the people who should know, the BBC Rights Group. According to that statement, rights to the basic property were still owned jointly by the BBC and BBC Worldwide (the latter owning the key trademarks internationally), with most of the writers of the original stories retaining the dramatic rights to the various characters they had created (a notable exception being the Daleks, which were jointly owned by the estate of Terry Nation and the BBC.) They also acknowledged that the rights that were acquired by the American producers during the licensing of the 1996 TV movie had now reverted back to the BBC, and that the BBC did plan to develop a film, but the project was still in its very early stages. They concluded the report with a very interesting comment: 'So, the BBC could commission a new *Doctor Who* series for TV if it wanted to.'

On 26 August, the BBC1 Controller gave an interview to the *Guardian* for an article entitled 'Jury's out on *Fame Academy*', in which she discussed the BBC1 series *Fame Academy* and also hinted about a possible future for the *Doctor Who* series when she revealed she'd like to bring it back to its traditional Saturday evening slot on the network. 'I would like to resurrect *Doctor Who*,' Heggessey said, 'but the rights situation is too complicated to do that at the moment. Maybe that will happen one day.' Heggessey indicated that her plans to overhaul BBC1's Saturday night schedule might include what the reporter described as her '*Doctor Who* initiative'. The BBC *Doctor Who* site covered this *Guardian* report, adding that they had recently looked into the rights concerning *Doctor Who* (referring to their August 21 article) and discovered that there was nothing to prevent the show's return. The *Daily Express* reported on 2 September that there were still implications from the Controller's statements, acknowledging the so-called rights issues. But the newspaper also called upon her to investigate further, noting that other information indicated these rights issues didn't exist at all.

By the time these statements had been made, however, Heggessey was already working behind the scenes to make it happen. In early September, Russell T Davies had been approached by Heggessey, Jane Tranter, BBC Controller of Drama, and Julie Gardner, BBC Wales's Head of Drama, with an offer he couldn't refuse.

Tranter had, in fact, made comments earlier in the year that noted her own disposition toward having *Doctor Who* back as a Saturday night staple. A 16 March 2003 article in the *Observer* that quoted both Tranter and Heggessey, asked them what their 'fantasy' ideas of Saturday television would be. While Tranter noted that she had a horror of 'relentlessly pretentious middle-class wank, drama all about people having writer's block, that absolutely nobody watched,' she did note that she would: '... like to do a modern version of *Doctor Who* starring someone like Judi Dench, go into an entertainment show like *Pop Idol*, then *Casualty* at 8pm, and at 9pm, I'd like to run a made-for-television Saturday-night movie of the week. Maybe like *Edge of Darkness*, but run over two nights.' While Lorraine Heggessey had been more broad-based about her ideas toward the return of the classic science-fiction serial, Tranter's interest in the same cannot be overlooked.

Davies had long been interested in the idea of a possible revival for *Doctor Who*. In the end, though, the project came to him in a roundabout way. Tranter had met with Gardner in early September and offered her the opportunity to make *Doctor Who*; Gardner later reflected in an interview with *Doctor Who Magazine* (issue 354) that she immediately knew they had been thinking of Davies to take creative control of the series. As she later described it, she couldn't wait long enough to find a land line to phone Davies, so she used her mobile. 'I phoned Russell and said, "Oh my God, they want you to do *Doctor Who* ... with me!" And he just laughed this huge laugh.' Davies, needless to say, replied positively. From that brief moment, a new *Doctor Who* series was born.

In the week immediately prior to the announcement of *Doctor Who*'s return, the BBC was buzzing with rumours, with conflicting statements to employees in various departments that something was imminent, versus other whispers of rumours to be discounted. Being involved in the transmission of *Doctor Who* news over the Internet, this author's first indication was on 22 September, when a strange e-mail appeared in my inbox from someone calling himself Stop Press: 'TV show back in production. Russell T Davies is writing 8 x 50-minute episodes. Tentatively scheduled for transmission next September. Casting *has* begun, but no details at present. Likely to "officially leak" within the next week. Enjoy being one of the first to know.' Later that week, my phone rang with news that there was something about to happen, a major announcement that could come as early as the weekend. On 25 September, author Mark Campbell was given a tip from a friend at BBC Wales that Heggessey was about to give an interview regarding *Doctor Who* and the ramifications would be tremendous; he'd been asked to talk about the announcement she was to make on their radio news programme *Good Morning Wales* on Friday morning, and it all had something to do with Russell T Davies. At the same time, Clayton Hickman, editor of *Doctor Who Magazine*, was given a heads-up to be ready to make an appearance on a weekend news programme, again because of a statement Heggessey would give that would be released this week.

When Lorraine Heggessey spoke, it often made the headlines. In October 2000, Heggessey became Controller of BBC1, the first woman to hold the position. During her time with the network, Heggessey oversaw a comprehensive analysis of the BBC1 schedule, including the network's rebranding, moving around various programmes to different times and reviving a flagging drama genre, as well as invigorating new fact-based programming on the channel including documentaries on art and culture. Originally a television producer creating current affairs and fact-based programmes for the BBC, Channel 4 and ITV, she had worked as producer of *Panorama*, a long-running current affairs series for the BBC, as well as *This Week* on ITV. She was also the founding editor of *Biteback*, a right-to-reply programme aired on BBC television, and series producer of *The Underworld*, which featured the very first interview with a notorious criminal. She had come to the new position at BBC1 after spending time as Head of Children's Production from 1997 to 1999, and then as BBC Productions Director of Programmes and Deputy Chief Executive from October 1999. Now, as Controller of one of the most respected and popular television networks in the world, Lorraine Heggessey would be listened to. That's why the statement she made to the London *Daily Telegraph* on 25 September 2003 was so important to *Doctor Who* fans worldwide.

That's when the world of *Doctor Who* changed forever.

'*Doctor Who* ready to come out of the Tardis for Saturday TV series' was the headline for a story run by the *Telegraph*, written by media editor Tom Leonard and appearing in the 26 September 2003 edition. The *Telegraph* article, which was first of many on the story, said that 'in a move that heralds the most eagerly anticipated comeback in television history, BBC1 said yesterday that it is developing a new series of the sci-fi classic.' Lorraine Heggessey was quoted as saying, 'Worldwide has now agreed that, as they haven't made the film and I've been waiting for two years, it's only right that BBC1 should have a crack at making a series,' referring to the infamous tie-up of film rights that had prevented anything from happening before. The *Guardian* newspaper, meanwhile, also ran a piece entitled 'Who? The Doctor comes back' by Rebecca Ellinor, in which Mal Young, Controller of Continuing Series at the BBC, was quoted as saying, '*Doctor Who* is a much-loved, truly iconic piece of TV history. It's time to crank up the TARDIS and find out what lies in store for the Doctor, and we're thrilled to have a writer of Russell's calibre to take us on this journey.' However, as he noted later to the *Irish Examiner*, 'We're at the very early stages of development and further details, including casting, will not be available for some time.'

In a twist of irony – one that would be repeated many times going forward – the story about the relaunch appeared on the newspapers' websites just after midnight London time, hours before their respective print editions would be released; press embargoes occasionally prevented stories of this type from appearing until a certain date, but 12:01am lives up to the letter of that law, if not the spirit. Because of the nature of international time zoning, the British public had mostly gone to sleep by the time the story broke, but fans in North America, Australia and New Zealand celebrated the news for hours before their UK counterparts knew what had happened.

The articles noted specifically that the new series would be in the hands of Russell T Davies, creator of several pieces of controversial television including Channel 4's *Queer as Folk* about gay life in Manchester, and *Bob and Rose*, an ITV drama that told the tale of a homosexual man falling for a straight woman. Of course, what they neglected to mention was Davies's long admiration for the programme, which was well-known to the Powers That Be at the BBC, or the *Doctor Who* novel he had written for Virgin Publishing. Heggessey noted that Davies wanted to introduce the character to a modern audience, but (in response to crass questions from some journalists) she did not expect a gay Doctor. She also made it clear that Davies was chosen because he was an absolute *Doctor Who* fanatic (of course, probably being a television producer also helped a great deal). 'I grew up watching *Doctor Who*,' Davies told the *Telegraph*, 'hiding behind the sofa like so many others. He's had a good rest and now it's time to bring him back. The new series will be fun, exciting, contemporary and scary.'

When Davies later spoke to the official *Doctor Who* website in December 2003 about his reactions to being asked to executive produce the new series, he noted he: '... was delighted. To be absolutely honest, I was busy – making *Mine All Mine* – and I presumed the phone call was about a vague, tentative chat with the BBC. So I ignored it! (You can waste your whole life in TV just chatting about projects, so I refuse chat-meetings.) It took me a couple of weeks to realise that this wasn't chat, this was real, and mine.'

BBC News confirmed the story at 04:00 GMT on Friday, 26 September, in a news story entitled simply '*Doctor Who* returns to TV', accompanied by a photo of Tom Baker. The news story mentioned that the series revival would be produced by BBC Wales, and quoted their Head of Drama, Julie Gardner, as stating: 'It will be a thrill to work with [Davies] on such a landmark TV series. This is very early days and it is unlikely anything will be on screen for at least two years but it is very exciting and I can't wait to get started.' The news story was then picked up and carried across most major news services in Europe and North America, even reaching the cover section of CNN.com and other popular news outlets. By midday on 26 September, an official BBC press release had been issued, stating that 'No budget has been set for the new series; the number of episodes and their duration is under discussion. It will be a family show, but no details are available as to when it will be scheduled.'

Of course, at the time, it was far too early to speculate on who might play the Doctor, or which of his famous adversaries would feature; the on-screen debut of the new series was still many months away, and was noted by several sources not to be due until, at the earliest, 2005. One report, also in the *Telegraph*, had already noted that it would be limited to one six-part series, a notion that didn't bear out in the long run. Heggessey herself confirmed later (in early October) that when it returned to television, it would run in the traditional Saturday evening time slot, and that she was proposing to run polls in the UK TV listings magazines to find out which *Doctor Who* stories were the public's favourite for a potential series of 'classic' repeats. By this point, an eight- or twelve-episode season seemed more likely than a six-parter.

The crazed atmosphere continued in the press. Simon Jeffrey penned an article for the *Guardian* expressing some sentiments he'd picked up on the Internet about the return of the show, and who the Doctor might eventually be. 'Who should star in the new series – and should be an assistant – is likely to become a topic of hot dispute among the Whovians,' he wrote. 'Alan Davies is an early favourite, and has the slightly wild hair the role seems to require. But Richard E Grant played the doctor with élan in the show's recent Internet version. Believe it or not, there are places online where people get together to discuss this kind of thing.'

The immediate reaction from within fandom was sheer elation. 'Well, it seems that the day that we've been eagerly waiting to hear about for the last thirteen years or so is finally here – an announcement from the BBC to indicate that the Doctor will once again be adventuring through time and space in a new series of *Doctor Who*,' wrote Chuck Foster of the *Doctor Who* Appreciation Society. 'There seems to be every intention for this project to go ahead and for us to see the series hit the screens in 2005, and we're very optimistic that this will be a successful venture and not fall to the wayside as [did] the other attempts to resurrect the series during the '90s. However, it is of course still early days. We would urge everybody to show their enthusiasm for the venture and welcome the developments as and when they are revealed.' Popular and fan-created websites all across the Internet showed interest; Drew 'Moriarty' McWeeny, one of the principal correspondents of the *Ain't It Cool News* website (the legendary movie gossip site run by film critic Harry Knowles) said, prior to the BBC News confirmation, 'For now, take all of this with a grain of salt, but I sure hope it happens for the fans who have kept hope alive all this time ...' The series was featured on the 26 September BBC *Wales Today* news programme, stressing that the show would be an in-house production from BBC Wales and emphasising quite strongly that Davies was a Welshman.

Doctor Who Magazine editor Clayton Hickman did indeed appear on Radio 4 on Saturday morning, 27 September, on the *Today* programme, along with the *Evening Standard*'s John Lyttle. Hickman revealed on the programme that Davies's favourite for the role of the new Doctor was actor Bill Nighy. 'I think certainly, the way Russell has spoken, he really wants to take it back to basics and make it into a family show that kids can really relate to,' Hickman said. 'Russell favours Bill Nighy, but I'm not sure I should have said that.' The *Daily Mail* later picked up on this in their 'Wicked Whispers' column by noting that neither Alan Davies nor Richard E Grant were Davies's choice to play the Time Lord. 'While the BBC brass would prefer either of two Scots – campy Alan Cumming or austere Ian Richardson – the *Queer as Folk* writer's favourite is craggy Bill Nighy, currently appearing under a ton of make-up in the bloodless vampire flick *Underworld*.'

Misinformation abounded, in a heady time full of speculation. On 27 September, the *League Online* website, a website devoted to the band the Human League, claimed that lead singer Philip Oakey would be offered the part. Their article stated that the Human League would possibly be offered the opportunity to update the '... world-famous theme tune. There is no other electronic band who could do justice to this classic theme than the Human League who are the UK's premier electronic pioneers. It would be fitting for them to provide a new version of Ron Grainer's famous music.' In fact, Oakey himself was said to be a massive *Doctor Who* fan; and the instrumental B-side of The Human League's single 'Boys and Girls' (1981) had been entitled 'Tom Baker'. And, from one quarter, disinformation abounded too: Tom Baker himself gave an interview that day noting that cross-dressing actor and comedian Eddie Izzard was the likely choice for the role. During an interview with BBC Radio Five Live, he said that Izzard: '... has an alien quality. Eddie Izzard is so mysterious and strange. He seems like he has lots of secrets. You always feel Eddie Izzard knows something you don't, or has been somewhere you haven't been.' Baker later stated on BBC London News on 1 October that Izzard would, in fact, be the new Doctor, the actor's sense of humour shining through as always; he noted he was 'sworn to secrecy' but then later 'outed' Izzard. When asked about rumours surrounding another actor, he was more flippant: 'Oh Christ, no, not Richard E Grant.' It took about a week until Baker was finally ready to set the record straight, as he did for the *Telegraph* in a phone interview in which he stated, 'I went on the radio last week and told someone it would be Eddie Izzard. I have been putting the word around that it's him, with Sue MacGregor as his assistant. Sue MacGregor is a joke, but Eddie Izzard would be politically interesting ...'

Several web services, including the Ananova news service, stated that '*Jonathan Creek* star Alan Davies is the bookies' favourite to become the new *Doctor Who*' and said that the William Hill betting agency had made Davies the 8/1 favourite to land the role, followed by Richard E Grant, Sean Pertwee (the son of third Doctor actor Jon Pertwee), Patrick Stewart and *Cold Feet* star James Nesbitt. The William Hill spokeswoman Jennie Prest said: 'Amazingly it is 14 years since the last series, but everyone remembers who was Doctor Who when they were a kid! Every time the actor was replaced there was intense excitement about who would be the next one, and this time it is just the same!!' Other actors making the list in various places were Hugh Grant, Jonathan Pryce, Timothy Spall, Stephen Fry, Ian McKellen, Michael Caine, and even Lenny Henry (said to have 33/1 odds to become the first black Doctor in the show's history). Henry had played the Doctor in a comedy sketch in 1985 (later issued on the *Doctor Who and the Curse of Fatal Death* video release). William Hill later removed the betting pool from their servers.

These were only a few of the potential Doctors being touted by the British press in the days following the official announcement of the new series. Some of the longer shots included Australian journalist, writer and actor Chris Thomas, who actually launched a minor press campaign in Australia to become the new Doctor. 'I know it's a long shot but when you get one chance to fulfil your ultimate ambition, then surely it's worth doing all you can to pursue it?' he was quoted as saying, in local newspapers. 'There are bound to be howls of protest from some quarters when they hear an Australian wants to take on the part but it's simply a matter of doing it with a British accent. Besides, Sylvester McCoy had a notable Scottish lilt when he played the role.' His campaign lasted only a few short weeks, but one must admire the tenacity! The *Sun* on 5 October claimed *This Life* actor Andrew Lincoln was on the BBC's wish list of actors, while a few weeks later, on 25 October, the *Daily Mirror*, quoting a 'BBC insider', suggested that *EastEnders* actor Shane Richie was on an unofficial shortlist of five. In fact, there was a significant amount of casting speculation from a variety of quarters in the wake of the announcement, as publicists and agents scrambled to get their clients' names in the press.

Eddie Izzard was one of the first to stand up to discount the rumours of his interest. Discussing the subject with Radio 1, he said that Tom Baker mentioning him: '....was fantastic, it's a wonderful honour. I hadn't considered it, I didn't even know [the series] was happening, and I don't think the BBC would want me. They'd probably rather spit on me and slap me about with fish.' Izzard had been on tour in America, and hadn't yet heard of the revival of the series. 'I think the BBC would say, "Well we want someone simpler and safer." I think my breasts are too dangerous.'

Later, on BBC1's *Friday Night with Jonathan Ross* programme on 17 October, Alan Davies also took the opportunity to discredit the press: 'Well, now you see, that's just paper talk ... No. Sadly, I'm not the new Doctor Who,' he said. 'I haven't been asked. Two years ago it was in the *News of the World*, God bless 'em. They said I was signed up under a massive deal.' Davies mentioned that many of his friends had become so wound up with the idea that he was going to be the new Doctor, they'd started contacting him asking him if they could play Daleks or Cybermen. But Davies was very kind about his namesake, Russell T Davies, the new man in charge. 'I would do *Doctor Who* because Russell T Davies is writing it. He's Britain's nicest man and best writer and he wrote *Bob and Rose* [in which Alan Davies starred], so I sent him an e-mail saying if you're really stuck and you can't get who you want, I'll fill in but I'm not wearing that hat.' In early November, Alan Davies took the opportunity to address comments made toward him by Matthew Norman of the *Guardian*, who had launched a 'campaign' to prevent him from being the Doctor: 'The *Doctor Who* thing was all paper talk cooked up by people who, like yourself, have to fill a certain amount of space each week, and sometimes find it a bit of a struggle. So a "campaign" is hardly necessary.'

The rumours about casting began to calm down, with the news reports around the end of 2003 focusing on only a few candidates, the most prominent being Bill Nighy, whom television presenter Richard Bacon described as a 'shoo-in' for the job, in fact quoting Mark Gatiss. *The Times*, in an article on 5 October called 'New Dr Who located on planet of the character actors' by Arts Editor Richard Brooks, noted that the BBC would in fact approach Nighy ('one of Britain's most sought-after character actors') to play the role. 'Nighy, who played the crusading newspaper editor in the BBC's hit political thriller *State of Play*, is said by friends to be very interested in the role.' Of course, *The Times* report did note that speculation had 'been rife' over who would assume the part. 'All the gossip has shown just how much interest there is in the Time Lord and his enemies, the Daleks. Yet the speculation has been wide of the mark.'

Speculation was indeed at the forefront of press attention, especially in a little snippet from the *Guardian* printed on 7 October in their 'Diary' feature. After a note that Alan Davies had been involved in an incident at a St Martin's Lane hotel the night before, it had this little pearl of wisdom: 'Meanwhile, rumours that Christopher Eccleston is interested and has put feelers to the BBC remain unconfirmed after his agent resolutely refuses to return our call.'

The press roundabout continued on other fronts. The *Telegraph*'s letters page on 27 September printed a slight rebuttal on its coverage. 'Sir – You report (News, Sept 26) that the appointment of Russell T Davies as writer of the new *Doctor Who* is likely to "alarm purists", because Mr Davies once wrote a Channel 4 drama about some gay men,' wrote Ian Wheeler of the *Doctor Who* Appreciation Society. 'Do you expect a Doctor Who dressed in pink, mincing about and saying, Shut that TARDIS door? Mr Davies is a fine writer who has contributed to many excellent television dramas. His skills as a writer are obvious to all. *Doctor Who* is in safe hands.' The *Daily Mirror* columnist Sue Carroll reported this later in her column, adding her own thoughts: 'He can be Graham Norton as far as I'm concerned, provided the show looks as if it's been filmed in a sandpit up the M25, the walls are wobbly and the Daleks still can't get up a flight of stairs.'

On 28 September, the current reigning Doctor, Paul McGann, weighed in with his own impressions. 'I think it's high time that Doctor Who was a woman,' he told writer Elizabeth Day in an article that appeared in the *Sunday Telegraph*. 'There is nothing in the stories to say that the Time Lord can't be female. I'd like to see somebody really scary, Amazonian, highly intelligent and gorgeous in the role: someone who could be a complete handful. Rachael Stirling [the actress daughter of Dame Diana Rigg] could do it because she's got great charisma. Dame Maggie Smith would be brilliant. I'd like to see the Doctor as diva, rather than being played by some dippy, wide-eyed girl.' McGann later noted that he felt the Doctor had for too long been played as a very heavy, melancholic man with Victorian gravitas, and suggested a black actor like Chjwetel Ejiofor (*Dirty Pretty Things*) take the role. 'The producers of the ninth series [sic] should cast their net slightly wider than the usual white male, but it'll probably end up going to James Nesbitt, the star of *Cold Feet*, because his stock is so high at the moment and he'll be a ratings winner.' The subject also came up in the article regarding the gender of the Doctor. Writer and publisher David Howe told Day that the storylines should come first, and that there was no reason for making the Doctor a woman or making him gay. 'It is a family show and there is no place for overt sexual relations. I'd like to see someone unknown in the role. *Doctor Who* is big enough as a brand to survive without a big name.' Quoted in the same article, Sophie Aldred, who had played Ace in the original series opposite Sylvester McCoy, said she'd rather the Doctor remain male. 'I'm very old school and I don't think they should really change anything. I'm afraid I'm terribly sexist and I'm sure my feminist character wouldn't approve.' She noted that if they had to cast a female actor, it would have to be 'someone stronger' like Judi Dench or Helen Mirren ... but then she noted that she'd like to see her co-star McCoy make a comeback.

The impact of the announcement of the new series was felt across Britain. Jon Culshaw from the BBC's comedy impressions show *Dead Ringers* appeared frequently as Tom Baker and at one point parodied the forthcoming series as a makeover/reality TV show, with the first episode ending as the Doctor regenerated into *Changing Rooms* designer Linda Barker. BBC *SouthEast Today* ran a story on 29 September featuring a rundown of the top three locations used in the area on the original show, chatting with *Doctor Who Magazine*'s Clayton Hickman about his thoughts on the new series. The 29 September *Independent* asked the big question 'Are you looking forward to *Doctor Who*'s return?' to such notables as Colin Baker (who described the news as 'a cautious pleasure'), Clayton Hickman ('dancing on the desks'), Mark Gatiss ('simultaneously sick with excitement and trepidation'), *Dead Ringers*'s Jon Culshaw ('delighted, but don't Americanise it too much'), Kylie Minogue's tour set designer William Baker ('ecstatic') and British Medical Association Press Officer Linda Millington ('we're short of doctors, does he know of an intergalactic planet with a surplus of GPs?'). *Doctor Who* even made *The Sunday Times* editorials section on 28 September, which featured a cartoon of a BBC man ordering a Dalek to 'Exterminate Alastair Campbell' (a reference to Prime Minister Tony Blair's political adviser, who had been involved in a dispute with the BBC over coverage of the war in Iraq).

In short, it was a very exciting week for *Doctor Who* aficionados. But not everyone was convinced. 'Rejoice, rejoice – but with reservations,' wrote Brian Logan in his 29 September article, 'The spirit of wobbliness' for the *Guardian*, noting the celebrative air surrounding the announcement, as well as the anxiety that went along with it. The portents, he said, were good. 'The series is to be scripted by Russell T Davies, the creator of Channel 4's *Queer as Folk*, the programme that turned the Doctor's robot dog K-9 into a gay icon. That show's main character selected his sexual partners according to their knowledge of *Doctor Who* – which seems to me eminently sensible. Davies says the character was semi-autobiographical: he's a fan, with respect for the series's traditions.' Logan discussed the names being touted for the lead role, male and female, black and white, even the comments about a possible gay Doctor. 'No wonder fans are restive. Because these are issues that strike at the heart of the paradox of *Doctor Who* fandom. On the one hand, we like to argue that the series's unique virtue (in contrast to the dreaded *Star Trek*) is the anarchic flexibility of its format. One bloke, one time machine, anything can happen. But we reserve the right ruthlessly to circumscribe that flexibility.'

Logan also took issue with what he called the 'ghastly Americanised version' of the series from the 1996 television film, often overlooking the achievement of first bringing back the show when no-one else was looking. As that first weekend came to an end, it was obvious that the initial giddiness – *Doctor Who* is back! The long night is finally over! – was making way for trepidation and concern. Would, in fact, it be any good? Would it still be a family programme, aired on Saturday nights, or would the sensibilities of the 1960s and 1970s be replaced with the flash and glamour of the 21st Century? 'An educational sci-fi series in which an old man and a teenage girl travel through time in a police telephone box?' wrote Logan. 'In 2003, it would never get past the focus groups.' In fact, as Logan wrote, if the show were to be a success, it would have to bring back the elements that made it so ... not the wobbly sets but, as he called it, 'the spirit of wobbliness, the primacy of imagination over special effects.'

Not everyone who had fond memories of *Doctor Who* from the early days was sceptical. 'I think its wonderful, I'm really thrilled,' Verity Lambert, the first producer of the original *Doctor Who* series, told interviewer Joey Donovan on his *American Who* Internet radio programme. Lambert also imparted some advice to her latest successor:: 'Well, I think that I always felt that you had to play it for real, you know, that camping it up wasn't right. And I think that that's the advice. I mean, it just has to be believable.' Lambert was quite taken with the idea of Bill Nighy in the role (though made note that Alan Davies was, in her mind, too young.)

Within the course of one week, *Doctor Who* had gone from an embattled forty-year-old programme that had been off the air for fifteen years, to one of the most anticipated events forthcoming from British television. And while the papers and the news media swarmed over the story with the fervour often shown a major political firestorm, there were other signs of life left in the old science-fiction legend. Big Finish Productions had just had its licence to publish *Doctor Who* audios extended to 2007. The *Scream of the Shalka* webcast would begin transmission on the official *Doctor Who* website at BBCi very shortly. Meanwhile, plans continued apace for the celebration of the show's fortieth anniversary, due on 23 November. The anniversary celebrations would include a major BBC-sponsored event at the end of October in London: the Panopticon 2003 convention at the Hilton Metropole, an event that ironically featured almost no word of a new series and none of the advance coverage that many attendees expected. (The beautiful, slick press packages given to attendees, while neglecting to mention the recent new series announcement, were probably printed some time before.) That same anniversary would feature a series of three specially commissioned, collectible front covers on the BBC's listings magazine *Radio Times* (and a pullout *Doctor Who* special in the same edition).

Doctor Who Magazine was not to be left out. Though lead time for production is a fact of life when dealing with the print medium, issue 336 of the long-running publication owned by Panini featured a flashy 'Stop Press' type embellishment on the front cover ... '*Doctor Who* set for BBC TV Comeback: The news we've all been waiting for' with an accompanying brief article in which Davies offered his own thoughts. Davies spoke for the first time about the circumstances surrounding his meeting with Lorraine Heggessey and Jane Tranter, although he also mentioned that the meeting, and the significant press coverage that followed the announcement, were likely to be all that would happen for quite a while. 'I'm currently committed to a Red Production Company drama for TV,' Davies said, referring to *Mine All Mine*, in production for ITV for Spring 2004, 'and have to complete that before meetings can start.' Davies noted that the plan was to produce the show at BBC Wales, as had been noted in the press, with three executive producers: himself, Julie Gardner and Mal Young. 'Although I've yet to work out the exact details of my commitment, the BBC is absolutely dedicated to the programme's future,' Davies noted, a ray of realistic optimism through all the hype. Though the power of the Internet connected the series's fans together in those first heady days, there was nothing like reading the words of the show's new captain in print in the pages of the official magazine to make things seem that much more real.

This time it was happening. *Doctor Who* was coming back to television as a regular series for the first time since late 1989, when the Doctor and his assistant Ace had trotted off in search of new adventures. The BBC had officially said it, the press knew all about it, *Doctor Who Magazine* had reported it, and the public was excited about it.

Now, all they had to do was *make* it.

CHAPTER THREE:
THE EXECUTIVE THREE

If anyone was up to the challenging task of bringing back a cultural icon like *Doctor Who*, it was Russell T Davies.

As Davies told *Doctor Who Magazine* in November 2003, making the series would be a great responsibility. 'Marvellous,' he said, in response to being asked how it felt to bring the Doctor back to television. 'It's all a bit surreal, suddenly I've got an inbox offering me police boxes and Nimons.' Of course, as he noted, it was a bit early for all that; he'd have several other projects to take part in before he sat down with anyone to discuss plans for the new series. Davies said he treated the event with caution. 'Right now, all your options are open. Anything could happen.'

Anything usually *did* happen with Davies. Born the same year *Doctor Who* first appeared on television, 1963, Russell Davies hailed from Swansea, the 'golden coast of Wales' on the Gower peninsula and hometown of such notables as actress Catherine Zeta-Jones and poet Dylan Thomas. Davies – who later adopted the 'T' as his middle initial to distinguish himself from BBC radio presenter Russell Davies – studied at Oxford, graduating with a degree in English Literature in 1984. All the while, Davies had remained a fan and admirer of the *Doctor Who* series. In an interview given in March 2005 to the *Media Guardian*, he noted how delighted he had been by it: 'When I was eight, walking home from school down Hendrefoilan Avenue, I always used to think, "I could turn round the corner and the TARDIS would be there – and I would run inside and I would fight alongside the Doctor." It was the one programme that encouraged you to make up stories. The TARDIS could land in the everyday world and no other science-fiction programme would do that. You were never going to be a member of the crew on the *Enterprise* when you were eight years old: it was in the future and they were the navy. Even if we don't get an audience, I hope there will be some eight-year-olds sitting there thinking the same thing. That's when I fell in love with it. I was transfixed.'

In a later interview given in 2005 to the *Independent*, Davies gave some off-the-cuff answers to questions posed about his early life. 'You wouldn't know it,' he said, 'but I'm very good at ... drawing. One of my very first jobs was as a cartoonist for BBC Wales.' He said that as a child he wanted to be 'a teacher, because my mother and father, and then both my sisters, were teachers.' And his favourite kind of art, well ... 'I've got an autographed print of Charlie Brown and the Kite-Eating Tree, signed by Charles M Schulz. One of the greatest artists ever.'

Perhaps most tellingly, Davies told the *Independent* that the best invention ever was: '... the word processor and all its descendants. Allows infinite rewriting, 'cos that's where the real work is done.' How apropos for a writer/producer who would one day be responsible for the revival of one of the world's most beloved series.

Having an early interest in film and television, Davies joined BBC Television on staff as a floor manager and production assistant, before taking a BBC directors' course in the 1980s. He wasn't totally enamoured by staying behind the camera at first, though; in 1987, he presented one episode of *Play School*, a BBC show for pre-school children, before making 'a hasty move behind the scenes' according to *Doctor Who Magazine*. Davies soon realised his talents lay in production. From 1988, he worked for BBC Manchester's Children's Department, including spending four years as producer of *Why Don't You...?* – an activity-based show transmitted over the summer holiday weeks that discussed what children should be doing *instead* of sitting at home watching television! (This series also marked the television debuts of a couple of young lads from Newcastle later to become better known as Ant and Dec ...) He had been invited to join the Department by producer Edward Pugh, who had spotted Davies's talent when he was working on *Why Don't You...?* in Cardiff. After Davies's contract at Cardiff finished, Pugh had offered him a job in Manchester, where further editions of the programme were to be made. It was an offer Davies had quickly accepted.

It was while producing *Why Don't You...?* that Davies first took a substantial interest in writing for the television medium – indeed, he did his level best to turn *Why Don't You...?* into something more than a mildly educational kids series. 'I'd already changed *Why Don't You...?* from a magazine show into a drama, with the gang and their sheep fighting a supercomputer,' he told bbc.co.uk's *Dark Season* mini-site in 2004. In 1989, he penned the comedy-dubbed version of *The Flashing Blade* for the Saturday morning series *On the Waterfront*, while in 1990 he created *Breakfast Serials*, a half-hour television series for children, which featured segments including storytelling, comedy and science fiction. Davies was the producer as well as writer of *Breakfast Serials*, and one of his duties as producer was to provide the BBC's *Radio Times* listings magazine with descriptions of the show for its billings. Davies took great delight in amusing himself by providing the magazine with completely spurious listings that bore no relation to the transmitted programmes.

His first major television drama, *Dark Season*, was a six-part science fiction adventure series for children that aired on BBC1 in 1991. Davies had written the first episode on spec (using *The Adventuresome Three* as the provisional title), and then used the BBC's internal mail system to send it to the Head of Children's Programming at the time, Anna Home, who immediately commissioned the serial for later in the year. 'I owe Anna Home everything,' he later told the CenturyFalls.co.uk fansite. 'I wouldn't be writing now if it wasn't for her.' *Dark Season*, an early critical favourite in Davies's repertoire, featured the acting debut of Kate Winslet, later nominated four times for the Academy Award for Best Actress and/or Supporting Actress, as well as appearances by former *Doctor Who* guest stars Jacqueline Pearce ('The Two Doctors') and Cyril Shaps ('The Androids of Tara', 'The Tomb of the Cybermen',' etc). Davies also novelised the serial, the BBC-published book being advertised at the end of each episode's transmission.

In 1992, Davies left the BBC for Granada Television. He immediately went to work on ITV's long-running children's hospital drama *Children's Ward*, on which he served as both writer and producer for three years. The series had been co-created by Paul Abbott, another writer who would go on to a high profile career in adult television drama, and with whom Davies became good friends. In 1996, an episode of the series penned by Davies during his final season on the show won a BAFTA Children's Award for Best Drama. In 1992, the director of *Dark Season*, Colin Cant, wrote to Davies explaining that he had been assigned a new children's serial to direct for the BBC but that he thought the script was terrible, and that he wondered if Davies had anything better he could possibly replace it with. Davies wrote the first episode, which was quickly commissioned, and the full serial, *Century Falls*, was transmitted to great acclaim in early 1993, increasing Davies's good reputation amongst telefantasy fans. *Century Falls* was, however, much darker in tone than its predecessor, and perhaps indicated that Davies was beginning to outgrow children's drama.

While working for Granada, Davies wrote in 1993 the first episode of the fourth season of the quiz show *Cluedo*, 'Finders Keepers', as well as continuing work there on a daytime soap opera, *Families*, which – continuing his association with future Hollywood stars – featured a young Jude Law. By the time he departed *Children's Ward*, he was already writing for such series as *The House of Windsor* (having penned a 1994 episode, 'I've Managed to Track Down Royston Bloat') and both creating and writing for the soap *Revelations*, which starred Judy Loe and Gary Cady.

Davies went on to work on a variety of projects through the next few years: scripting Channel 4's *Springhill* (1996); writing one episode of Paul Abbott's ITV drama *Touching Evil* ('Amathus, Part One') (1997); and, for a brief period, working as a storyliner on ITV's popular soap *Coronation Street*. 'Briefly,' he told BBC *Breakfast* in an interview on 11 March 2005, 'a storyliner is a marvellous job, a complicated job, in which the writer comes up with the stories, but then the storyliners have to hammer that into shape, into five episodes a week. It's quite a science, in a way, because if you've got a big story, for Deirdre, she can't be in every scene, or she'd die of exhaustion. You weave them together ... you plan literally how many days the actors are working, how many sets you've got. So, it's the science of putting the show together with the art of telling a good story. It's a lovely job.' Davies did, in fact, love working on soaps, as he told BBC *Breakfast*: 'Absolutely loved it ... Just teamwork, really. I only actually spent one story block on *Coronation Street*, and the stuff you learn off the writers in there like John Stevenson, it was ... miraculous!'

Davies was also commissioned to write for *The Grand* (1997-1998), a period drama set in a hotel aired on ITV; in fact, several of the series's other staff, including the creator and head writer left the production, and Russell stepped up to the challenge by writing all of the scripts for the series. One episode of *The Grand* told the story of Clive, a repressed homosexual struggling to deal with his sexuality in the 1920s. Davies later wrote in an article for the *Guardian*: 'The Granada executives, Gub Neal and Catriona MacKenzie, were then appointed as heads of drama at Channel 4. Catriona pointed out that the Clive script was better than anything else I'd written. In essence, she was saying, "Go gay!", but a lot more elegantly than that. The idea was enough. Go gay.' At the conclusion of that production, Davies left Granada Television to work with the independent Red Production Company, although he later wrote for *Coronation Street* again, for the direct-to-video special *Viva Las Vegas* (1997).

His association with Red Productions led to his first major commercial success. This was Channel 4's *Queer as Folk* (1999), a saucy look at gay life in Manchester, commissioned by those very executives who had encouraged him to 'Go gay'. The series caused considerable controversy when its first episode depicted a twentysomething clubgoer seducing an underage boy. Davies's passion for *Doctor Who* was quite obvious by this point, as *Queer as Folk*'s lead character, Vince (Craig Kelly), was portrayed as a video-collecting *Doctor Who* fan, who discovers in the middle of a sexual encounter that the man he's brought home with him turns out to be a bigger fan than he is. *Queer as Folk* brought extensive accolades; so extensive that, two years later, the American cable network Showtime bought the rights to film a new version, albeit moving the Manchester locale to Pittsburgh, Pennsylvania, and changing the lead's *Doctor Who* fixation to a passion for comic books. Meanwhile, Davies's original went to a second, shorter series that tied up the events of the first. 'My heart wasn't in it,' he wrote in the *Guardian* article. 'I didn't want this to continue. A story should tell the one, special time in a character's life. Invent new stories, and you're saying that all their times are special, and I don't believe that ... So I wrote a short sequel and finished the lives of Stuart (Aiden Gillen) and Vince. Plenty of people hate that ending, but for once I'm not allowing any doubters. I love it. And anyone else who loves it has the ride of their life. If you get left behind, tough. Right at the end, they become mythologised, and fictionalised, and they're frozen in a moment from which they could never return. The end.'

Davies followed up *Queer as Folk* by creating *Bob and Rose*, a six-part series starring Alan Davies as a gay man and Lesley Sharp as a straight woman, the former of which, to his complete surprise, falls in love with the latter. *Bob and Rose* aired on ITV in 2001, and meanwhile Davies wrote 'Rest in Peace', an episode of the BBC One series *Linda Green* – again for Paul Abbott – before turning his attention to scripting *The Second Coming* (2003), which starred future Doctor Christopher Eccleston, who had previously auditioned for the role of Stuart in *Queer as Folk* before admitting that he was too old for the part and recommending Aiden Gillen to the production team. *The Second Coming*, a play about the second coming of Christ, had been commissioned and then rejected by successive Heads of Drama at Channel 4, and had also been turned down by the BBC. It was eventually picked up by ITV and brought both writer and star some rather pointed critical acclaim. It won Davies a Royal Television Society Award, and allowed him to take forward two further projects: *Mine All Mine* (2004), a further ITV production filmed in and taking place in his native Swansea; and *Casanova* (2005), a lavish costume drama featuring Peter O'Toole and David Tennant as old and young versions of the titular lothario that had been languishing in development for some time at London Weekend Television (LWT) before being picked up for BBC Wales by Julie Gardner, after she moved from LWT to become Head of Drama at BBC Wales. In May 2003, Davies was announced by Celador Films as providing the screenplay for a film version of the 2001 *Who Wants To Be A Millionaire?* cheating scandal (in which Major Charles Ingram apparently cheated at the game by having a 'plant' – a man named Tecwen Whittock – in the audience who coughed at appropriate moments as Ingram debated with himself the possible answers to each question). At the time of writing, this production hasn't yet emerged from the development process.

Throughout what was already a successful career, Davies remained a fan of Britain's most influential and iconic science fiction series. The proof positive had come nearly ten years before any rumbling of his association with the series on television, in the form of a novel called *Damaged Goods*, published in October 1996, for Virgin Publishing's *Doctor Who* range. The book was a gritty look at drug use and alien influences in Margaret Thatcher's Britain, circa 1987, and Davies received much praise from the *Doctor Who* fan community for its realism and depiction of its characters.

In his review of *Damaged Goods* in *Doctor Who Magazine*, Dave Owen called Davies 'a welcome new addition to *Doctor Who* fiction, bringing a lucid, matter-of-fact style of storytelling that has more in common with Stephen Gallagher's modern horror novels than Irvine Welsh's stylised fables.' Owen noted that Davies 'often uses the children's fiction technique of describing what is seen, rather than what is happening, in order to protect the naïve but telegraph to the experienced.'

Davies's novel was actually far ahead of the times as far as *Doctor Who* was concerned. 'Purists might argue that a book full of sex, drugs and squalor can't really be *Doctor Who*,' Owen argued, 'but they would be forgetting that the essence of the series and those like it is in portraying ordinary people's reactions to the unprecedented. It's done so brilliantly here that, much as I abhor scores, rankings and superlatives, I'll admit that *Damaged Goods* is currently my favourite New Adventure.' As Owen later commented on the *Outpost Gallifrey* discussion forum, 'Bless him, he took the trouble of writing to me to thank me for my enthusiasm. That used to be an extremely rare occurrence!'

During his *Doctor Who Magazine* interview in November 2003 with editor Clayton

Hickman, Davies said that he felt that it wasn't just a particular period of *Doctor Who* he was fond of, it was 'the whole thing', demonstrating his very clear belief that the show should be back on television. Of course, it wouldn't be easy: fans had changed over the years, and the Internet was rife with speculation. In the months following the initial announcement, there were rumours that the series would feature either six episodes or twelve, depending on who you listened to. Much of the rumour could be combined together with the notion that it would, in fact, be six two-part stories, each of 45 minutes in length and that Davies wouldn't write all of them – this gossip was, in fact, somewhat closer to the truth. Davies had noted in the November *Doctor Who Magazine* interview that he would write: '... at least six episodes. If there are more, I'll be involved in selecting the new writers, and determining what they're writing.' Davies also noted that he would start work in January 2004 (sixteen months before the first episode premiered).

Davies also spoke to *SFX* magazine in November 2003, clarifying something of how things had progressed since the announcement less than three months earlier. 'Well, I can't say too much and it's television, so anything can go wrong, but at the end of August they approached me!' he said, alluding to the fact that it was Lorraine Heggessey and Jane Tranter who had indeed approached him directly about bringing the Doctor back.

In an interview with the *SFCrowsNest* website, Russell admitted he paused before committing himself to restoring the Doctor to prime-time television, fifteen years on. 'I actually spent three days thinking very seriously about it. I love *Doctor Who,* and part of me thought, "If you love something maybe you should leave it alone." But it was three days of nonsense really, and my friends were slapping me round the head and saying, "Don't be stupid, of course you've got to do it!"'

To do it, however, would mean meeting his own specifications. 'The key word is fun,' Davies told *SFCrowsNest*. 'It's funny, scary, fast-moving, adventurous but above all the new *Doctor Who* is fun. I watch a lot of other science-fiction shows and they tend to be very pious, sombre, dark, even angst-ridden, and that would just die a death on a Saturday evening. People want to be entertained at that time, so *Doctor Who* is fun, fast-paced and takes viewers on a rollercoaster ride.'

But even with verification that it would be the story he wanted to tell, and that he would not have one imposed on him by the BBC, there were worries. 'I worried they meant a cheap pastiche version,' he told the *Media Guardian* on 6 March, 'or an ironic version, but it was the real deal – Saturday night, proper budgets. All those things you think you'd have to fight for. Astonishing.'

In his *SFX* magazine interview, Davies confirmed what he'd told *Doctor Who Magazine*, also mentioning that only after he had started writing in January 2004 would there be any decision on who would take the lead role. In these early days, in fact, it seemed that everything was on the table. 'He's ruling nothing out,' said the *SFX* article. 'If, when he comes to write it, a complete reboot seems the only way around to make a new series work, that's what he'll do, but he has yet to start so that's a "not ruled out" rather than a statement of intent.'

A rethinking and reworking (otherwise known as a reboot) of a popular television series often faces considerable challenges to overcome prior to and during broadcast; *Doctor Who* would be no exception. Late 2003 had seen the re-launch of another legendary science fiction staple, *Battlestar Galactica*, an American television series from the late 1970s, this time produced as a four-hour television miniseries for the US Sci-Fi Channel. *Galactica*, in the hands of television producer Ronald D Moore (*Star Trek: Deep Space Nine*) faced overwhelming scorn from the small but dedicated fan base who objected to his 'reimagining', as he called it, of the tale, with notable twists (such as turning one popular character, Starbuck, into a woman). The miniseries's eventual success (leading to a weekly TV show that gained significant attention and critical acclaim) proved Moore's theories correct: that while the fans themselves can make a great deal of noise, the general public will usually accept an updated version if there is something within the new production that provides originality and spark. Other examples of this in the media abound: the Harrison Ford/Tommy Lee Jones remake of the television series *The Fugitive* as a film, which eventually garnered Jones an Academy Award as Best Supporting Actor, and a nomination for the production as Best Picture of the Year. *A Star Is Born*, the iconic Judy Garland/James Mason film, was not only remade, but was itself a remake of an earlier version. Tim Burton's 2005 film project, *Charlie and the Chocolate Factory* starring Johnny Depp, could theoretically be considered a remake (although, to be fair, it's really a film based on Roald Dahl's classic series of books and not the earlier production that Gene Wilder tiptoed through.) Even Davies's own watershed series *Queer as Folk* was itself remade into a series that, to date, has run four seasons on the Showtime network in America.

In truth, all the indications are that Davies never had any interest in starting *Doctor Who* again from scratch, preferring instead to honour its rich history with a nod, but moving in new directions into the future. In his November interview for *Doctor Who Magazine*, he spent time doing a little foreshadowing for readers on two fronts, regarding the new Doctor and his eventual companion. 'You will love him,' Davies said of the Doctor. 'That's all I'm saying for now, because it's the only thing that matters. You will absolutely love being with him ....' But any major changes would be out; no-one, in fact, was talking about such changes, and this would be the same *Doctor Who* the fans and the general public had always loved. 'I want the Doctor, at least one companion, whose name is probably Rose Tyler. I want the TARDIS, I want it to look like a Police Box, and I want them to fly through the universe and all its history, facing death and danger and braving it out with a fast and funny fighting spirit. That's *Doctor Who*, isn't it?' It was the very first mention of a character name associated with the new series other than (obviously) the Doctor ... Rose Tyler would remain the character's name throughout the casting phase, production and upon final transmission. It should be noted that the name Tyler is much loved by Davies; Mark Benton, who would star as Clive in the first episode of the new series, 'Rose', played the role of Johnny Tyler in *The Second Coming*; Matthew Radford and Amanda Wenban played the roles of Mark and Ruth Tyler, respectively, in Davies's co-produced *Revelations*; it is the surname given to Winnie and her children Bev and Gabriel in his novel *Damaged Goods*; and Craig Kelly and Denise Black played Vince Tyler and his mother Hazel in *Queer as Folk*.

Davies did, however, have his own ideas about exactly where the series should go, and what course it should take. 'If you chase a cult you just become a smaller cult,' he noted during the 8 March 2005 press launch. 'If a cult fan hates this series it means they will only watch it 20 times instead of 30 times. When they brought *Crossroads* back and made it a bit camp it was a turkey of disastrous proportions.' As he told the interviewers from *Televisual* magazine in their March 2005 edition, he and Julie Gardner would have a 'tone meeting' on every episode, out of which came the rule that the TARDIS must return to Earth. 'We need to return to Earth to get an emotional focus on what's going on,' he told *Televisual*. 'If we're on Planet Zog and Zog people are being affected by a monster, we couldn't really give a toss. But if there's a human colony on Planet Zog, then that's more interesting.'

CHAPTER THREE

On 9 November 2003, Davies attended a literary festival in Hull, where he noted that at this point, there was no concrete plan for the series other than an outline. In fact, there was no 'master plan', he said, to bring the show back; it was the circumstances of events, later disclosed as coming together in Heggessey's and Tranter's meeting with him earlier in the year, that had led to the series being rediscovered for British television. Davies did disclose that there would indeed be other writers besides himself and that an initial production meeting scheduled for 8 December would get the ball rolling on what would be thirteen episodes, not six or twelve as previously rumoured, which should include three two-part stories depending on how the budget played itself out.

Davies later denied a set number of episodes to *SFX* magazine in its March 2004 issue (though, to be fair, the interview was most likely conducted at the end of 2003). Asked about the length of the season, Davies commented: 'Until all the money's in place, we can't be certain. This is normal stuff, happens on every show. You never hear about them juggling the ... schedule and budget [for *A Touch of Frost*], do you? But it happens. The *Doctor Who* Magnifying Glass makes this normal process seem so much more significant, turning pores into caverns.'

Most importantly, however, at the Hull event, Davies noted that it was, in fact, Mal Young who should receive proper credit for bringing back the series: nearly every year, Davies noted, Young had been coming up with budgeting plans trying to get the series made.

At one point dubbed the 'most influential man in TV soaps,' Mal Young was the Controller of Continuing Series for the BBC until the end of 2004. The Liverpool-born former graphic designer didn't even get into the television industry until he was 27 years old, and his efforts led him to his first mainline TV job producing the Channel 4 serial *Brookside* (1992-1996). As an executive producer, his responsibilities have included overseeing such BBC series as *Dalziel and Pascoe* (1996), *Doctors* (2000), *Merseybeat* (2001), *Holby City* (2001-2005), *EastEnders* (2003) and *Casualty* (2004-2005). He worked with eighth Doctor Paul McGann on the legal drama *Fish* (2000), and brought *Starsky and Hutch* star David Soul to two episodes of *Holby City* ('Going Gently', 2001, and 'Change of Heart', 2002) after seeing him in a stage performance.

Young was equally enthusiastic about his contribution to the return of *Doctor Who*. He told the BBC staff magazine, *Ariel*, that he had: '... never received so many requests from writers and actors to be involved in a drama series as I have had for *Doctor Who*. Everyone seems to want to be part of bringing back such an iconic series.' Said Davies of Young: 'People shouldn't just judge him by the fact that he produces *Casualty* and *EastEnders* – he also does less mass-market stuff like *Dalziel and Pascoe*, which tends to get overlooked.'

Young and Davies had had several encounters prior to their joint involvement with *Doctor Who*. 'When I worked at Granada in the early 1990s,' Davies told *Doctor Who Magazine* in December 2003, 'I suggested they pitch for [*Doctor Who*] as an independent production, and was laughed out of the room.' But he had a friend who worked as a drama producer at the BBC, he noted, 'and he knew that Mal Young's department was very keen on resurrecting the Doctor.' A meeting was arranged between Davies, Young, and Young's development producer Patrick Spence. This meeting was later blown out of proportion by the newspapers when they got wind of it. 'Nothing was written down, nothing was decided beyond a general agreement that the programme could be great again. It was certainly never called *Doctor Who 2000*.' Two weeks later, as Davies noted, Spence discovered a pending BBC Films script development for *Doctor Who*, and a television series had to be put on hold. 'Over the next few years,' Davies said, 'I'd meet the film people, in passing, and ask how the film was going.' He would be offered other BBC projects, but he refused them, saying: 'If I was going to write for the BBC, it would only be for *Doctor Who* ... I don't think the nagging had that much effect – the programme's return now is entirely down to Lorraine Heggessey's enthusiasm for the show, backed by Jane Tranter and Mal Young.' He did note, however, that his 'nagging' for the series did link his name with it: 'In hindsight, it looks like I had a magnificent master plan, whereas in fact, it was a long, slow accident.'

BBC Radio Wiltshire sat down with Young in early January 2004 to discuss his own thoughts on the series. 'The trick that we have to pull off,' Young said, 'is to stay true to the original spirit of the show and the original character, but make it for the 21st Century and a younger audience now who have been brought up watching some fantastic sci-fi films and TV shows. Television's changed, films have changed, so we have to move with the times.' He echoed earlier sentiments that he didn't want to change the foundation of *Doctor Who*, but that it was probably time for a rethink on some of its trappings. 'Viewers today wouldn't stand for those kind of production values; we need to have filmic values, we need to bring production values to it that they expect now from shows like *Buffy*.' The latter was, of course, a reference to the successful American drama series *Buffy the Vampire Slayer* (1997-2003), the influence of which on the storytelling style of the new show would be significant.

Young noted at the time that he and his colleagues were working on a 'short list' of actors they'd like to see in the role. 'The consideration is that the expectation from the audience will be so high,' he continued, 'that the pressure on the actor, whoever that may be, will be so great to carry off this iconic character that it will have to be someone who can really pull it off ... It's probably not realistic to think that we're going to take a chance on someone whose never worked on television before, they're going to have to know what they're doing.' He also discounted the idea that it would be a woman in the role: 'In my taste I think it would probably be male but ... we'll just leave it open to the best person for the role.'

Moreover, Young echoed Davies's sentiments that this shouldn't be a reboot, but in fact an updated version of *Doctor Who* that continued on from established history. 'There's no point redesigning the wheel,' Young said. 'It's a fantastic character, this Time Lord ... It works, so why change that? ... We'll just make sure the storytelling is pacier, that it can be intelligent ... They'll expect us to do quite heavy, tough and involving stories that a whole family can watch.' Young indicated to BBC Wiltshire that the series would be in production later in 2004, hoping that it would be ready for transmission in 2005 ... 'Which end of 2005, we're not sure yet. We want to get it right, we don't want to set ourselves a deadline and then rush with the script, the casting and the production and not get it right. We're gonna get one go at this, and the interest already from the media this far ahead has proven that we have to get it right – that the pressure will be great. We're taking our time, putting a lot of time and effort into it and all the best talent onto it as possible.'

Young later described what the *real* trick would be: the baddies. *Broadcast* magazine interviewed him in May 2004, and asked him whether or not the Daleks were coming back: 'Yeah, they are, and they're going to be scary. They might be a bit more sophisticated but they're still scary as f– as far as I'm concerned.' The story ended with the following: 'Interview over, Young picks up what he says is "the most valuable thing in this office". It's Russell T Davies's script for the first episode of the new *Doctor Who*.'

Young was also honoured with a special achievement award in May 2004 at the British Soap Awards for his achievements in British television, while *Radio Times*, compiling a list of the top 40 most powerful figures in UK television drama in July 2004, named Young in ninth place; BBC Controller Lorraine Heggessey weighed in at seventh place, while Davies was at number 17 and future Doctor Christopher Eccleston at number 19. Of Young, *Radio Times* said: 'Emblematic of BBC drama's leaner, meaner approach of recent times, Young has eschewed the traditional Oxbridge route to the top, having worked his way up from *Brookside*'s shop floor to be the Beeb's soap tsar. He's been instrumental in transforming *Casualty* and *Holby City* into year-round series, which has provided the major bulwark against ITV1's ratings domination. Says Lucy Gannon, "He's enthusiastic, realistic and has brought a breath of fresh air to the Beeb. A can-do man."' Davies was also given the nod by the magazine: 'If, as numerous executives contributing to this poll suggest, TV is increasingly dominated by writers, Davies is sitting pretty. *Queer as Folk* placed him in an elite group of writers with Paul Abbott and Andrew Davies and, as the main writer of the new *Doctor Who*, his profile looks set to rise even further. "He has a unique voice, can deal equally well with humour and tragedy, and all that he does is suffused with real compassion and humanity," says Jane Tranter.'

At the end of 2004, Young elected to leave the BBC behind, lured away to 19 Television by Simon Fuller, the man behind the international television success story *Pop Idol* (2001-2003). 'The only connection I'd had with [Fuller] was a year before when an agent came to see me about an actor and he said, "Have you ever thought of leaving the BBC? If you ever do, I think we should set you up with Simon Fuller. We'd like to broker a deal between you and Simon, it's a good fit." I thought it was a good deal because we are both populist, we love big audiences and big projects and we like to entertain in big ways. I had always admired what he has done. I thought one day I might go and meet him. I admire anyone who does popular.' Said Alan Yentob, Creative Director and Director of Drama, Entertainment and CBBC at the BBC: 'Mal has made a great contribution to BBC Drama. Over the last seven years he's developed shows which bear testament to his passion and commitment to popular drama. He's now got a new challenge in the USA. We'll miss him but we look forward to working with him in his new role.' Jane Tranter, Controller of Drama Commissioning, also paid kudos to Young in the official BBC statement about his departure: 'Mal Young is one of television drama's best known and [most] highly respected characters. His contribution to popular drama at the BBC has quite simply been immense – there is no doubt that we shall all miss him, but his new venture is a hugely exciting opportunity.' He was succeeded in his post by John Yorke, who took on the Continuing Drama Series portfolio, while Head of Serials Laura Mackie was made Head of Series & Serials, taking on the non-soap opera programmes he had overseen. However, neither Yorke nor Mackie was added to *Doctor Who* as an Executive Producer, the London-based BBC Drama staff seeming content to leave Julie Gardner and BBC Wales to it, though Young's contributions to *Doctor Who* would continue to be felt throughout its first season.

While Young had been a champion of *Doctor Who* at the BBC, the third member of the partnership that would bring this show to television wasn't quite so versed in its rich history. Julie Gardner, like Davies, was a native of Wales. She had been an A Level and GCSE English teacher until she decided she wanted to be involved in the television industry. Her first job in television was as a producer's secretary on *Our Friends in the North*, a major BBC2 drama of 1996, which had co-starred Christopher Eccleston. She later became a script reader in the Serial Drama Department, a script editor and then producer. She joined BBC Wales as Head of Drama (replacing Matthew Robinson, a director of *Doctor Who* in the mid 1980s) in July

2003 after a three-year stint at London Weekend Television, where she had been a development producer, overseeing dramas such as *Me & Mrs Jones* (2002) and a critically acclaimed version of *Othello* (2001) set amid corruption and racism in the Metropolitan police, which again featured Christopher Eccleston in a starring role. She had earlier produced several BBC1 drama series including *The Mrs Bradley Mysteries* (1999) and *Sunburn* (1999). Once in her role at BBC Wales, she commissioned the multiple-personality-disorder drama *May 33rd* (2004), the Richard Briers drama *Dad* (2005) and the Peter O'Toole/David Tennant period piece *Casanova* (2005).

'I've given Julie a crash-course in *Doctor Who*,' Davies told *Doctor Who Magazine*. 'She's a huge *Buffy*, *Angel* and *Smallville* fan, but has only vague *Doctor Who* memories from childhood.' Davies noted that she'd gone off at one point to watch the *Doctor Who* 'classics' such as 'City of Death', 'The Ark in Space' and 'The Dalek Invasion of Earth', '... and she loves it! I get phoned up, to be told how marvellous "The Curse of Fenric" is. Julie turned up at our last meeting armed with a copy of *Doctor Who on Location* [by Richard Bignell] because she wanted to know how many stories had been filmed in Wales!'

'Russell gave me a *Doctor Who* viewing list,' Gardner told Benjamin Cook in *Doctor Who Magazine*, 'which was a cross-section of some of his favourite episodes.' She then spent time 'catching up' to find out everything she could about *Doctor Who*, making notes and taking it in. 'City of Death' was her favourite, she told Cook: 'I love the idea that it's Tom Baker being eccentric, quite dangerous and unpredictable.'

She commented that being asked if she wanted to make *Doctor Who* was 'the most unexpected moment of my career.' She had been asked to a meeting with Jane Tranter in September 2003, and was asked, very bluntly, 'How would you feel about bringing back *Doctor Who*?' according to an interview with Gardner on the documentary series *Doctor Who Confidential*. The very idea had put her off guard ... in a quite delightful way. In fact, she said that she'd laughed: '... because it seemed perfect. I knew as soon as they said *Doctor Who* that they were thinking of Russell.'

'He didn't say yes immediately,' Gardner told Jessica Martin of *SFCrowsNest* in an interview conducted in January 2005, 'but it was so obviously the right fit for everyone that Russell was soon working on the scripts and we were in pre-production.'

Gardner's philosophy behind *Doctor Who*, and the reason it interested her as a project, was the 'dizzying possibilities for storytelling' integral to the series. 'There's no story that can't be told,' she told *SFCrowsNest*. 'It can go anywhere in time and space, and the main characters are an alien and a human, with all the confusion that brings. I can absolutely see why that draws people in. But without the quality of the scripts by Russell and our other writers – Mark Gatiss, Steven Moffat, Robert Shearman and Paul Cornell – we couldn't hope to attract the likes of Simon Callow, Richard Wilson, Penelope Wilton and Simon Pegg as guest artists.'

As she later told *SFX* magazine in April 2004, Gardner had a lot of ideas about what would make this work. 'I want it to be scary and full of adventure for a family audience. The new series will be made with strong effects and high production values. And there will be one demand above any other. It will be beautifully written – however hard we will all have to work.'

Even with the challenges, and her inexperience with the particular genre, Gardner believed that working on *Doctor Who* would be a different sort of dream-come-true. 'Every day you walk on set, you think, "What are we doing?"' she told the *Project: WHO?* radio documentary series. 'Okay, so in that shot, it's the miniature, and then in the next shot, it's the prosthetic, but then it goes CGI – okay what do we go back to? ... It's mad.'

As Davies noted in his regular 'Production Notes' column in *Doctor Who Magazine*, it was rare that their 'executive three,' as he called himself, Julie Gardner and Mal Young, would have time together at ease. In early March 2004, all three found themselves together in Los Angeles, attempting to secure US funding and meet several actors for the role of the Doctor, and the whole thing was still in a state of transition. 'Mal, Julie and I have become so used to the state of flux,' Davies wrote, 'that we've become ... well, flux-like. Fluxish. Fluxescent.'

With a top-notch executive production crew now on board, there were many roads still to chart; already, *Doctor Who* was gaining once again in popularity, while its on-screen debut was still more than a year away. A producer would have to be assigned; writers would have to be contracted; casting would likely take several months. And all that before one second of video would be captured. There was still plenty to do, but of course, this was nothing new to *Doctor Who* fans, who were still captivated by the sudden resurgence the show was making in the press, not only for the new series but also for the fortieth anniversary. Late October 2003 would mark the BBC's official anniversary event, the aforementioned PanoptiCon convention – dubbed *PanoptiCon: 40 Years of a Time Lord* – but there was scarce mention of the new series at the event (and no guests from the new show ... at least, none from the production team). Everything was being kept low key, and for good reason: the show wouldn't premiere until 2005, and there wasn't yet much to say.

The rapid pulse of commentary surrounding Lorraine Heggessey's surprise announcement and the follow-up speculation about who would step into the Time Lord's shoes had momentarily subsided. For a time. As Davies himself had said in *Doctor Who Magazine* in 1999, when taking part in a group discussion with other fans working in the TV industry on how the series might be resurrected, 'God help anyone in charge of bringing it back – what a responsibility!'

CHAPTER FOUR:
FULL SPEED AHEAD

Doctor Who was enjoying a rather lengthy stay in the public eye as 2003 dwindled to a close. By late November, news of the development of the new television series was temporarily overshadowed by the marking of the *Doctor Who* anniversary. On 23 November 1963, *Doctor Who*'s first episode, 'An Unearthly Child', had been transmitted. The series had at one point looked as if it wouldn't continue past its initial block of episodes. But it had, and in fact had transcended every barrier it had crossed: supporting cast and production changes, the departure of its original lead actor (William Hartnell), the move of the BBC channels to colour broadcasting, and so on. Few could have speculated in those early years that *Doctor Who* would have such longevity, but those who recognised it now, forty years hence, were equally expectant of great things from the new production.

Where *Doctor Who* had been nothing more than an afterthought only months before, the fondly but (by the general public) not often remembered by-product of an era long passed, it was now making its way through the newspapers as a major media event. In fact, despite some rather major *Doctor Who*-related developments around that time – such as the discovery of a previously missing episode of the 1965/66 story 'The Daleks' Master Plan', and the uncovering of a near-complete set of off-screen telesnap photographs from another missing serial, 'Marco Polo' – the fortieth anniversary of *Doctor Who* was only tangential to the mix; the new series, after all, was something current and fresh, rife for speculation and discussion. The key, it seemed, was sorting out the differences between the 'new' series and what would become the 'classic' show. 'There'll be at least one important difference ... between the programme's 20th and 21st-Century incarnations,' wrote Matthew Sweet in an article about the series's anniversary in the 16 November edition of the *Independent*. 'The new *Doctor Who* will be one of the BBC's flagship programmes. Davies and his co-conspirator, Mal Young, Controller of Continuing Drama Series, have secured a commitment to five series of 13, 45-minute episodes. They'll be able to afford an expensive actor for the lead role. They'll get billboard ads, *Radio Times* covers and publicity spots across the media. The original programme rarely enjoyed such security.' It was perhaps the first indication that this wasn't just a shot in the dark: that *Doctor Who* did, in fact, have potential as a viable candidate for a lengthy run on British television, and that the BBC had fully committed itself to the show. The article noted the 8 December production meeting in which Davies, Gardner and Young would perhaps shift from a passive to an active role in bringing the Doctor back to television.

WHO WOULD IT BE?

As expected, interest in the question of the choice of actor to portray the good Doctor continued to run high. The 3 November edition of the *Daily Mirror* suggested that Rowan Atkinson should 'expect the call any day now.' 18 November's *Sun* suggested *The Royle Family* star Ricky Tomlinson: 'Royle family slob Ricky Tomlinson wants to be the new Doctor Who. He reckons the Time Lord should be a scouser and says: "I'd be perfect! There are always funny moments and a scouse accent would work well. It instantly makes things funnier ... I've always fancied myself as a bit of an action hero and I'd love to do some Dalek bashing".' The *Sun* article reiterated the press rumours about Rowan Atkinson as well as the earlier reports that Eddie Izzard and Alan Davies might be in the running.

Bill Nighy, meanwhile, continued to be high on everyone's 'short list' of potential Doctors; the rumours that Russell T Davies had felt he was a possible first choice for the role had linked the actor's name to *Doctor Who* for many months. 'I have no idea about that,' Nighy told the *Western Mail* in mid-November. 'No-one's actually asked me. I did hear a rumour, but that's as far as it goes. I don't know if I'd be up for it or not; it would depend on so many things really. And I haven't got around to thinking what kind of a Doctor I would be – except I probably wouldn't wear a scarf.' Nighy appeared on the BBC Radio 4 show *Loose Ends* on 22 November and made it clear: '[I'm] not going to be the new Doctor. Well, no-one has asked me and ... well, no-one has really survived *Doctor Who* ...'

Nor could Anthony Stewart Head escape similar comments, especially after being voted the audience's favourite to play the Doctor in a *Radio Times* poll the same month. Best known as Rupert Giles in the cult TV favourite *Buffy the Vampire Slayer*, and recently known to *Doctor Who* fans for his turn as Grayvorn in the *Doctor Who* audio series *Excelis* and from a brief role in the *Death Comes to Time* webcast, Head beat runners-up Alan Rickman, Stephen Fry, Alan Davies and Ian Richardson in the poll. 'I'm in very good company – good God, I beat Alan Rickman,' Head told *Radio Times*. 'I suppose I would be a logical choice to play the Doctor just because Giles, my character in *Buffy*, has the same light and dark sides and quirkiness as Doctor Who.' Head later gave an interview to the *Daily Express* on 12 December, in which he was more circumspect. 'I suppose I might be considered because of my sci-fi status,' Head was quoted as saying. 'If I did get the part I'd like to take him back to the kind of character that was played by Patrick Troughton. He was the best. He had whimsy but he had a dark side, too, and I think that the subsequent Doctor Whos, there was too much emphasis on whimsy.'

There were other quarters that wanted their say. In a poll carried out by BBC Worldwide, 130 Members of Parliament responded to questions about who they'd most like to see become the next Doctor: actor and writer Stephen Fry came out top. Many MPs showed 'huge enthusiasm for this uniquely British institution' as they voted Fry over Alan Rickman, Bill Nighy, David Jason and former Doctor Tom Baker. They weren't the only ones on the list, either: in all, seventy-eight names were suggested, including Eddie Izzard, Hugh Laurie, singer David Bowie, Zoë Wanamaker, Joanna Lumley, Dawn French, Kate O'Mara, Patricia Routledge ... and even a few non-actors such as Jeremy Paxman (a political interviewer for the BBC), Iain Duncan Smith (ex-leader of the Conservative Party), John Peel (a Radio 1 DJ), and William Hague (another ex-Conservative Party leader). Obviously, the quest for a new Doctor would continue for some time, and the answer was still several months away.

In mid-November, Davies gave an interview to *Radio Times* to clear up some misconceptions and give a bit of insight into the future plans of the series's production team: 'The trick is to make it more real in terms of the very first episode having genuine wonderment. I can fairly confidently predict that there will be a young female companion who will discover that she can explore time and space. If you watch *Doctor Who* you can take that for granted, but it's the most astonishing concept. It's really time to go back to basics on that.' Davies said that he wouldn't exclude historical stories, or in fact, any type of story. 'Why exclude anything? The budget is going to be a determining factor. The 21st Century is going to be the handiest place to be, because it's on our doorstep.' There were copyright issues, he acknowledged, about old monsters, but: 'It'd be nice to bring in one or two moments of old archenemies, just because there's a great audience of dads and mums at home going, "I remember that monster!" You wouldn't bring back Dracula without giving him fangs.' But he promised the sets wouldn't wobble. 'They won't!' he exclaimed. 'I shall lean against them myself, and I'm six foot, six inches. I will personally eliminate wobble.'

ISSUES BEHIND THE SCENES

It was also during November 2003 that the first indications of a possible problem with the use of the classic *Doctor Who* villains, the Daleks, emerged. In the 24 November edition of the *Sun*, the newspaper indicated that the Daleks might not appear in the new series because of 'an ongoing rights issue' between the BBC and the agents of the late creator of the Daleks, Terry Nation. While the BBC jointly owned rights to the Daleks with Nation's estate, the executors were apparently saying no to a deal, said the *Sun*. 'No-one knows exactly why, but Terry fell out with the BBC at some point. He told the executors never to let the BBC use the Daleks again. Fans want to see the Daleks return, but they may be disappointed.'

There had been rumours to this effect for some time, sparked by an earlier change in the state of affairs whereby BBC Worldwide had started to offer for overseas sale packages of 'classic' *Doctor Who* episodes *without* Dalek stories in them; the result being that stations in North America and Australia were being offered renewals of their *Doctor Who* licences, but were unable to show Dalek serials. A report to the fan website *Outpost Gallifrey* by Sue Cowley of BBC Worldwide in early 2003 noted, 'As it currently stands, stories written by Terry Nation cannot be screened on TV anywhere in the world during the latter half of 2003 and beyond. Hence the situation with PBS, and UK Gold's Dalek special is being run rather earlier in the year than might have otherwise been anticipated. This matter relates specifically to stories and situations penned by Terry Nation, and it is not restricted to *Doctor Who*. Neither is it a new or unexpected "problem".' It appears that the 'embargo' was actually due to the fact that negotiations were still ongoing between BBC Worldwide and Nation's agents, Roger Hancock Ltd, over a new deal regarding residual payments for repeats and overseas sales of all BBC programmes scripted by the late writer. This did not, in truth, have any bearing on the use of the Daleks in the new series, as that – like the release of 'classic' *Doctor Who* stories featuring the Daleks on DVD – would be subject to a separately negotiated agreement in any event.

As the anniversary date arrived, there was a new conjunction of past with future. Speaking to the *Liverpool Daily Post*, sixth Doctor Colin Baker, offered his own thoughts on the next incarnation of the Time Lord: 'I think the next Doctor should be a woman – Dawn French. She'd be fabulous, but I don't know if they'd have the bottle to do it this time.' Baker, who played the Doctor from 1984 to 1986, was circumspect on what he felt was the winning combination: quality storytelling with frightening moments to scare the children. 'I don't know if it's a prompted memory, but people still say, "I used to hide behind the sofa." If *Doctor Who* came back, think of all those backs of sofas that have been lonely for so long that are suddenly going to have children behind them again ...'

Not only would the show be scary but, according to Davies, it would be electrifying ... and break some of the stereotypes of the series, including the often mentioned (and arguably exaggerated) clichés of wobbly sets and screaming companions. Davies also reiterated that the TARDIS would stay as it was – in other words, outwardly resembling a 1960s Police Box – but the rest of the show would be brought 'up to date' ... and, perhaps insightful of the challenges to come, he hedged his bets on whether or not the Daleks would be back: 'I love the Daleks, but I wouldn't load the series with lots of old monsters. We want to make brand new ones.'

Davies was also a bit more confrontational when asked about the ongoing rumours of a gay

Doctor. For months, there had been subtle (and sometimes *not* so subtle) comments to the effect that Davies, as an openly gay writer/producer whose body of work had included the sexually themed *Queer as Folk* and *Bob and Rose*, would attempt somehow to project a gay sexuality on the series, and especially on the Doctor. Davies's reply to *TV Times* was matter-of-fact and pointed: 'It's so offensive that, because I'm gay, they say things like that. I was on the radio, and the woman presenter said, "Does this mean the Doctor's going to wear a pink shirt and a chiffon scarf?" How stupid is that?' While these sorts of comments would come up periodically in the early days of the new series production, they would mostly disappear with the announcement of casting in early 2004.

Not that there wouldn't be controversy. Fourth Doctor Tom Baker, weighed in with comments in a 19 November interview, noting how different he thought the new series should be. 'They do have to move on and make it funny and wry. Will there be sexual chemistry between the Doctor and the companion? Will they make the Doctor gay? Black? Or a woman?' Baker noted that he wouldn't play the role of the Doctor again ... 'but if they did bring back the TARDIS they could have me in a glass cage, just moving my eyes ... [the new Doctor] could turn to it and say "What would you do I wonder?" Perhaps I could go back as the Master.'

On 8 December 2003, Davies and Gardner went to meet with Tranter and Young. In Davies's hand was a fifteen-page outline and series overview, explaining the main characters, the stories and the series's overall tone. Also included was a list of writers they would want to work with to develop the storylines into scripts; Gardner later told *Doctor Who Magazine* that they were concerned that some of the writers were not particularly well known in television circles: '... but the BBC just signed up to all the writers that we wanted. They loved every story that Russell had planned.'

In an interview on BBC3's *Liquid News* in early December, immediately prior to the production meeting, Young commented that progress was further along than anyone had originally planned for; Davies had written thirteen storylines, though the comments were misinterpreted widely as news that he was writing the entire series, when in fact he'd simply created the outlines for each, planning a season-wide story arc, but would leave the actual writing of the scripts for several of the stories to writers who had already been contracted and would be announced soon. At the time, Young was cautious on the subject of who would play the Doctor, although there was a 'long short list' of potential Doctors already vetted and casting was in progress. While in retrospect it appears there was never any possibility of a female Doctor being cast for this series, Young did make note at the time of several actresses including Caroline Quentin (*Men Behaving Badly* and *Jonathan Creek*) and Michelle Collins (*EastEnders* and the drama *Sunburn*) who might fit the bill.

Young's comments about thirteen storylines, repeated across the Internet, prompted the editors of the BBC's *Doctor Who* site to contact BBC Publicity for clarification. 'Their response was that Russell T Davies has developed thirteen possible storylines. The keyword here is *possible*. It doesn't mean that thirteen episodes will be made, and it is unlikely that Russell will be writing them all.' However, the need for obscurity would be short lived; as Davies told *Doctor Who Magazine*, 'At the moment, we're planning thirteen episodes, 45 minutes long. This could change, of course – the number of episodes could lessen as soon as the budget becomes more complete.' Davies explained that this block of thirteen episodes would comprise of a few two-parters with cliffhangers, as well as individual stories, that would be set both on Earth and in space: 'I did an interview with *Doctor Who Magazine* a few years ago, where we speculated how *Doctor Who* could return. In that, I said that budgetary restrictions would make the show Earth-bound. Well now we're here, and it's real, and I'm looking at the budget and thinking to hell with it.' In fact, *Doctor Who* would voyage in time and space; present-day Earth would be a 'touchstone', but the series would travel anywhere the stories took it.

Davies was presenting *Doctor Who* as a much broader canvas than anyone could have imagined, given the limited budgets. What he and his fellow executive producers had constantly in mind was the need for *Doctor Who* to find and develop its audience amongst viewers used to the modern-day special effects, sets and costumes of a *Star Trek* series. 'I can certainly tell you,' he told *Doctor Who Magazine*, 'that the BBC talks about this show as a potential long-runner. We aren't looking at a special one-off series for nostalgists only – we all want this show to succeed, to gather viewers, to exhilarate and stimulate and create new memories, and return every year.'

As 2003 ended, there were reflections in the media that such a major event as *Doctor Who*'s fortieth anniversary hadn't been celebrated in as much style as it should have been. 'The milestone could have been marked by screening a different episode nightly for a week,' wrote Charlie Catchpole in the 31 December *Daily Star*. 'Maybe somebody in high places is still embarrassed by the intergalactic hoo-hah over the decision to axe the show toward the end of the Eighties – an awesome example of viewer power that forced the Corporation grudgingly to grant the time-travelling Doctor a brief reprieve.' *Doctor Who* was not only looked upon quite fondly, but was now being defended in the popular media. But there were still some journalists who noted the almost insurmountable odds against reviving a series and doing it well. '*Doctor Who* is, you realise, bigger than any one of his incarnations,' wrote Gareth McLean in the *Guardian* on 31 December. 'He's a great big pop culture artefact in whom thousands of people have an ... investment and about whom they have an opinion. Often, it's quite a fiercely held opinion expressed with pointy fingers and sweaty brow. It makes you consider the task [Davies] has taken on in resurrecting him. Or, indeed, her.'

Her, McLean had written, pointing up the fact that the Doctor could still be a woman. Attention did, in fact, turn again at this time to the question as to who would play the title role, and that of the regular companion. One actor, however, who wouldn't find himself in the running for even a brief spot in the new series was the previous Doctor, Paul McGann.

Hopes for McGann's fans had been raised, ever so slightly, at the end of UK Gold's *Doctor Who@40* anniversary tribute celebration that aired on 22-23 November; among the highlights during the weekend was a ten-minute feature at the end about the future of *Doctor Who* ... which concluded with a number of people recommending Paul McGann for the new series, and McGann saying 'You never know ...' and winking at the camera.

On 16 January, 2004, an 'exclusive' article written by Simon Holden on the UK Teletext service raised some eyebrows and created a whirlwind of new rumours. Holden's article suggested that there would be a 'fleeting appearance' by McGann as the Doctor, shortly before he regenerated into the new incarnation: 'The last Doctor will be regenerated into the new one and have a glamorous female sidekick.' Mal Young had already commented that the Doctor would indeed be regenerated, but had not specifically addressed the question as to whether or not the regeneration would take place on screen. Much of the UK Teletext article was actually extrapolation based on these comments Young had previously made.

In truth, a regeneration scene, showing the transition from McGann into the next Doctor, wasn't even considered for the new series. The case that would later be made was very simple: ten minutes into the 1996 *Doctor Who* telefilm, the lead actor changed ... an interesting moment for fans, but very off-putting to the casual viewer.

McGann himself had recently spoken to *SFX* magazine about the subject: 'I'm not being disingenuous now when I say that I've heard nothing,' he said, in response to reports he was being courted to appear in the series, either in a cameo appearance or as a regular. 'And I'm unlikely to hear anything, except that they'll probably ask me to go back and do the regeneration, which I'd be happy to do ... This is purely, purely rumour, so this could be nonsense, but not only have I heard that David Warner is up for it, but he really wants to do it. And if that's the case, then they should give it to him, because you can't beat that. You can't beat passion.' McGann noted that he would not necessarily possess the same amount of passion that someone like David Warner would bring to the role, simply because he'd done it before. He did indicate, however, that if he could do everything he had wanted to do with the role in 1996, he might be interested. This confirmed what he had said on stage at the PanoptiCon convention the previous year, when his expression of willingness to continue as the eighth Doctor on TV, if asked, had won a rapturous round of applause from the large audience.

Admirers of McGann's portrayal of the Doctor – of whom there were many – pointed out that only once before had the role been recast when the incumbent actor had been both willing and able to continue; this had been when the BBC's then Controller Michael Grade had decided to sack Colin Baker in 1986, effectively making him a scapegoat for the perceived shortcomings of the series at that time, and prompting a huge outcry from fans. Many felt that it was only right and proper that McGann should be allowed the opportunity that had been denied him in 1996 to develop his interpretation of the Doctor on screen, and some even went so far as to start an online petition to campaign for him to be offered the title role in the new series.

Alas, it was not to be; the hunt was on for an actor to play the ninth Doctor, and it wouldn't be anyone who had previously held the role.

Bill Nighy's name appeared again (and would continue do so, in fact, up to and even slightly beyond the actual announcement of the Doctor's casting). Nighy had recently been cast as Slartibartfast in the forthcoming 2005 film adaptation of Douglas Adams's cult classic *The Hitchhiker's Guide to the Galaxy*, but rumours still persisted that he was going to be offered the role of the ninth Doctor. In fact, Nighy's wife, Diana Quick (herself no stranger to *Doctor Who*, having played the role of Prime in *The Scream of the Shalka*), gave a quick comment to a fan, Trevor Dobbin, after a performance of her play *After Mrs Rochester* at the Richmond Theatre over the weekend of 21-22 February. She said that Nighy had already been offered the role but had turned it down. Nighy himself had noted on 5 February at the *Evening Standard* Film Awards that he'd recently played a vampire and a zombie, but 'I've reached that difficult age where I can only play men from different dimensions.' Perhaps he was referring to his *Hitchhiker's Guide* role, perhaps not.

Nighy's name wasn't the only one being bandied about at the beginning of February; so, quite surprisingly, was that of magician Paul Daniels. According to an article published by *The People*, 'TV chiefs have already talked to Daniels, 65, famous for his catchphrase "You'll like it; not a lot, but you'll like it." A source said: "Paul may seem an extraordinary choice, but he would make a very entertaining Time Lord. He may even be able to use his magic to defeat enemies like the Daleks and Cybermen."'

'Not in a million years!' Davies told *SFX* magazine in March 2004 when asked about the casting speculation. 'All this bollocks is just loony agents desperately getting their clients into the papers.' Indeed, rumours were once again flying, and names from the previous year, including Shane Richie, Stephen Fry and Eddie Izzard, started appearing again.

Whoever was eventually chosen to be the lead actor in the new *Doctor Who*, Andy Pryor would have something to do with it. The UK casting newsletter *Professional Casting Review* announced on 23 February that Pryor, whose casting credits include, on film, *Beautiful Thing* (1996), *Trainspotting* (1996) and *Long Time Dead* (2002), and on television, *Linda Green* (2001), *In a Land of Plenty* (2001), *Cutting It* (2002) and *The Long Firm* (2004), would be the casting director for the new series. The article in *PCR* that noted Pryor's assignment also noted, misleadingly, that shooting of the new series was 'anticipated for late spring', which many took to mean that production was further ahead than previously believed and that April or May would be a likely target for the start of recording ... perhaps with the new series debuting on air earlier than expected as well. In truth, camera work was still on target to commence in the summer, July being, in the end, the month that location work actually began.

ENTER PHIL COLLINSON

Casting and production time frames weren't the only issues being looked at while the wheels slowly turned through pre-production. The assembled team of executive producers, now firmly set as Davies, Gardner and Young, would need a day-to-day producer of the series who could both complement their own unique styles and strike out on his or her own. Word of who that might be had filtered out in couched phrases and double talk. As Davies told *SFX* magazine in December, he eventually had chosen a hands-on producer for the series. 'Our lovely Chosen One is still finishing off on another drama. I would tell you, except the moment the name gets announced, the e-mails flood in ... so let's leave the poor soul in peace for now. See how I said all that without giving away their sex? Marvel at my avoidance, marvel at it!'

That producer was, in fact, Phil Collinson, as revealed in the pages of *Doctor Who Magazine* at the end of February 2004. Collinson had been hand-picked by Davies, with whom he had worked previously on *Springhill* (1996); Collinson had been script editor for the second series, where he'd worked with both Davies and another writer, Paul Cornell. ('Russell and I are old friends,' he later said. 'He was one of the first writers I met as a young and terrified script editor for Granada TV!') Prior to *Doctor Who*, Collinson had acted as producer on *Linda Green* (2001) (where he had been reunited with Davies and met writer Paul Abbott, at one point a candidate to pen a script for the series's first season), on *Born and Bred* (2002-) alongside former *Doctor Who* director Chris Clough, and on the first series of *Sea of Souls* (2004), which he had produced for BBC Scotland.

'I am delighted to be joining the team bringing back such an iconic and exciting series,' Collinson told *Doctor Who Magazine*. 'I'm going to relish terrifying a whole new generation and putting such a well-loved character back on our TV screens where he belongs.'

Reaction from Davies was equally ebullient: 'I knew he was clever when he looked at the storyline for the very last episode and said, "I think you've all gone mad." And he was right!'

Collinson became part of a group that was already working at full speed: thirteen episodes, of which Davies would write seven. This number later increased to eight, after it became apparent that Abbott – having been one of the original writers invited to participate in the series' first eyar – would not be able to contribute after all. Collinson later noted to *Doctor Who Magazine* after a month being aboard the production that he was only just starting to realise the enormous task that he'd undertaken:'Special effects, spaceships, monsters and the hopes of so many people to make the show a hit!'

He added, recalling his childhood: 'I loved *Doctor Who*, absolutely loved it. It was the only programme that my whole family watched together, and so that gives it a bit of a halcyon glow for me: dark nights, potted meat sandwiches, Mr Kipling's cakes and *Doctor Who*. My mum tells me that one of my first words was "drashig" [a monster from the 1973 serial 'Carnival of Monsters'].' Collinson also noted that he wanted the series to appeal to the broadest audience, not the fans alone. 'I'm just going to approach it in the way I would any other drama series, though, and make it as beautiful and "produced" as I am able.' He noted that he would handle the day-to-day running of the series, including casting and scripting, working with the executive producers to choose the directors, and managing the budget. As Davies would later tell the *Doctor Who Confidential* documentary series, Collinson would work hands-on with the production, while Davies would stand back and watch it happen.

Collinson certainly had his heart in the right place, when he concluded the *Doctor Who Magazine* interview noting that he wanted *Doctor Who* to be: '... as imaginative and well-loved as it was back in the 1960s and 70s ... I want to introduce a whole new generation to one of the most amazing TV characters ever created. And finally I hope it's a huge and monstrous hit.'

THE WRITERS

While Phil Collinson got up to speed on the production, Davies and the writers he'd asked to join him were facing the challenge of scripting the new series. The BBC staff magazine *Ariel* published the news about the writers of the new series the same day that *Doctor Who Magazine* issue 341 had been released to subscribers. Both journals noted that Davies would pen eight episodes himself, but the other five would be written by Steven Moffat, Paul Cornell, Mark Gatiss and Robert Shearman.

10 December 2003 was the day that Steven Moffat had received the call asking him if he'd be interested in writing for the series. 'My agent rang me about the job just as I was leaving for the Comedy Awards, where we won for *Coupling*,' Moffat told *Doctor Who Magazine* alongside the official announcement. 'I don't need the rest of my life now!' Television was no stranger to Moffat, nor was *Doctor Who*; in 1999, he'd been responsible for the satirical skit *Doctor Who and the Curse of Fatal Death*, produced to raise money for the Comic Relief charity. He was perhaps best known, though, for *Coupling* (2000-), a very popular BBC2 comedy series that won Sitcom of the Year at that award ceremony, and for penning all 43 episodes of the children's drama *Press Gang* (1989-1993). Moffat's other credits included *Stay Lucky* (1989), *Joking Apart* (1991), *Murder Most Horrid* (1991), *The Office* (1996) and *Chalk* (1997), and he'd previously penned the *Doctor Who* short story 'Continuity Errors' for the anthology *Decalog 3: Consequences* published by Virgin in 1996. Moffat was the only writer aside from Davies himself who would pen more than one episode, scripting the two-part story that would comprise episodes nine and ten.

'Every soul on the planet was applying to do it,' Moffat told the *Scotsman* website on 6 June 2004, about his *Doctor Who* commission. But though it was an exciting prospect, he also knew it would be one of the toughest. 'TV doesn't bother trying to target entire families any more. If 10-year-olds aren't talking about the show in the playground on Monday morning then we'll have failed.' Moffat was extremely quiet about specifics during his interview, refusing to give up any details about his scripts, but he did note 21st-Century morality would play a big part in the new series – including sexuality. 'There always was. Patrick Troughton had pretty girl, and boy, assistants, both in skirts. Russell is quite keen on an element of sexiness and, anyway, all TV now is cast with this question high up the list: do we want to go to bed with these characters? But that will never be the central element of *Doctor Who*. The show is still about saving the universe. You can't be thinking about lovey-dovey stuff when there's that level of jeopardy involved.'

'One of the reasons *Doctor Who* survived for so long, and a rival like *Blake's 7* was so risible, is that it was funny,' Moffat opined. 'The Doctor was in on the joke, he knew the show was cheaply made and that some of the storylines were nonsensical.' But humour wasn't the only element that would be necessary. 'I don't think the fact we're in the post-*Star Wars* era is an issue – matching *Buffy* is. *Doctor Who* was never a space opera anyway, it was about horror: dark shadows and creepy monsters lurking just around the corner.'

The Sunday Times profiled Moffat on 9 May 2004, discussing the new series of *Coupling* as well as noting his participation in the forthcoming *Doctor Who* series: 'Not that Moffat need worry about returning to America for work ... he has other projects to keep him busy, like working on the new *Doctor Who*, for instance. He says it will be much like it always was but with more laughs and less shaky walls. "There's no point in doing it if it isn't the same, so it will be the way you remember it when you were 11 – though I'm not sure if Bacofoil will take over the world," says Moffat.' The article notes that Moffat had written a Dalek into the second episode of the fourth series of *Coupling* before he'd even been offered the job on *Doctor Who*.

While he boasted extensive television credits to his name, Moffat was the only one of the four new writers whose repertoire did not include a serious amount of previous *Doctor Who* material. The fact that the other three had all started out as fans contributing to the Virgin and BBC novels ranges and/or Big Finish audio dramas led some other fans to express scepticism that they would be able to write successfully for the TV series itself. What this overlooked was that, quite apart from their *Doctor Who* work, all three already had significant television and/or stage credits to their names.

For many years, Paul Douglas Cornell had been one of the most acclaimed of the *Doctor Who* stable of novelists, in part because he had provided the embryonic Virgin range with two of its early and most significant titles: *Timewyrm: Revelation*, which set the direction for the next few years of the books; and the watershed novel *Love and War*, which introduced the non-television series companion Bernice 'Benny' Summerfield. He'd also written several comic strips for *Doctor Who Magazine*, having previously written for various other comics. Other *Doctor Who* novels included *No Future* (1994) and the landmark *Human Nature* (1995), winner of several awards from the readers of *Doctor Who Magazine*, as well as Virgin's fiftieth 'anniversary' novel, *Happy Endings* (1996), and the book that spun Benny off into her own range, *Oh No It Isn't* (1997). Cornell also wrote for the fifth Doctor in his novel *Goth Opera* (1994), which launched the Missing Adventures range, as well as for the eighth for BBC Books with *The Shadows of Avalon* (2000). On top of this, he has written three audio plays for Big Finish, one with his wife, author Caroline Symcox. More recently, he was the writer on the webcast *Doctor Who* adventure *Scream of the Shalka*, and edited four anthologies: three Bernice Summerfield collections, and one *Doctor Who* collection: *Short Trips: A Christmas Treasury* (2004).

In addition, as previously noted, Cornell was no stranger to television. He had written for, amongst others, *Coronation Street* (1996), *Casualty, Holby City, Doctors, Children's Ward* (1996-1999), *Wavelength* (1996-1997) which he also created, *Love in the 21st Century* (1999) and *Springhill* (1997), as well as a children's series pilot for Nickelodeon called *Chase the Fade*

(1995). Radio credits meanwhile included sketches for *The Z Team* and *Where Were You?* and *Arnold Brown and Company* (1990).

Cornell also wrote the young adult horror novel *Horrorscopes: Leo – Blood Ties*, under the in-house pseudonym Maria Palmer for Mammoth Books in 1995, as well as a novelisation of the supernatural TV drama *The Uninvited* in 1997. *Something More* was his first original science fiction novel, released by Gollancz in 2001, which was followed by *British Summertime* in 2002.

For his *Doctor Who* commission for the 2005 series, Cornell was assigned episode eight, a potentially landmark episode that would delve into Rose Tyler's relationship with her father. 'It's like the completion of my lifetime's ambition,' Cornell wrote on the online *Outpost Gallifrey* Forum, 'but at the same time knowing that if I get sacked, my life will thus be one huge shaggy dog story! I got the call while putting some oven chips in. "You know what this is about," said Russell, after some musings on the niceness of oven chips (he's the most positive man I've ever met). And I whooped a bit.' Cornell noted that writing for the series was much harder than he'd first thought it might be. 'I was writing before the casting, but I had an idea of what Russell wanted the character to be like. It's important to lay some stuff down and then work with it, rather than wait around until you've got all the info. We're working on the character and dialogue in further drafts. And I've been able to read some of Russell's scripts, which helps a lot.

'I think that modern television has demonstrated an appetite for shows like *Who*, whereas in the past it had become the last of its kind. I can't really talk about how it's different from the original (and I can't see the whole picture of that yet), but I do think both the public and *Doctor Who* fans (whose interests really aren't as different as people say they are) will be very, very pleased.'

'Very, very pleased' was also the reaction that most fans had to another of the confirmed list of *Doctor Who* series writers. At the *Doctor Who Magazine* 2002 reader awards ceremony at the PanoptiCon 2003 convention, Robert Shearman had been awarded the prestigious title Best Writer (Books/Comics/Audios) by a virtual landslide. In addition, his 2002 audio, *The Chimes of Midnight* starring Paul McGann and India Fisher, won the award for Best Audio Drama. In fact, Shearman had penned a total of six audio adventures, including *The Holy Terror* (winner of the *Doctor Who Magazine* Best Audio 2000 award), the mini-adventure *The Maltese Penguin* (2002), *Scherzo* (2003), and a different take on the subject, *Deadline* (2003), which starred Sir Derek Jacobi as a man who believes that the *Doctor Who* mythos has come to life. But it was his adventure *Jubilee* (2003), a serial starring Colin Baker, that would win the *Doctor Who Magazine* Best Audio award the following year, and that would particularly attract the attention of Russell T Davies.

As resident dramatist at the Northcott Theatre in Exeter from 1993 to 1994, Shearman was the youngest playwright in Britain ever to be honoured by the Arts Council in this way. He wrote four main house productions for the Northcott, including *The Magical Tales of the Brothers Grimm* (1993) and *Breaking Bread Together* (1994), which was later revived in London. A regular writer for Alan Ayckbourn at the Stephen Joseph Theatre in Scarborough, he has to date written six plays performed there, including *White Lies* (1994), which was also produced in London and Rome, and which won the Young Playwright Award hosted by Wimbledon and Thorndike Theatres; *Fool to Yourself* (1997), recipient of the first Sophie Winter Memorial Trust award; and *Knights in Plastic Armour* (1999). His other plays have included *Couplings*, which won the World Drama Trust Award; *Binary Dreamers*, winner of the Guinness Award for Ingenuity in association with the Royal National Theatre; *Mercy Killings*, which he also directed at Harrogate Theatre; *Shaw Cornered* (2001), for the National Trust; and *Easy Laughter* (1993), winner of *The Sunday Times* Playwriting Award, which has been staged all over Britain and America, most recently by Francis Ford Coppola in Los Angeles. Shearman is also an experienced adaptor for the stage, with versions of *The Mayor of Casterbridge* (1993) and *Great Expectations* (1994) that were critically acclaimed in Exeter, while his *Jekyll and Hyde* recently toured Italy, *Don Quixote* was written to open the Dartford Festival, his version of Thomas Hardy's *Desperate Remedies* (1999) played at Edinburgh, and his open air presentation of *Pride and Prejudice* was produced at Gawsworth Hall. His plays for Radio Four are *About Colin* (2000, and which started life as a stage play in 1998), *Inappropriate Behaviour* (2002, originally a stage play in 2001), *Afternoons with Roger* (2003) (long-listed for the 2004 *Sony* Awards for Best Radio Play) and *Forever Mine* (which debuted in 2004). *Teacher's Pet*, *Odd*, and *Toward the End of the Morning* followed in 2005, the latter (among others) directed by actor Martin Jarvis.

Shearman's accomplishments haven't been limited to the stage and audio, either. He was the writer for the second series of BBC1's *Born and Bred* (2003) and has recently penned a new black comedy series for the BBC. *Doctor Who* was a classic case of works in one medium attracting attention for another, as *Jubilee*, featuring an isolated Dalek held captive, was a good starting point for a new television episode ... in this case, 'Dalek', the sixth episode of the new series. But this tale had perhaps the rockiest ride to completion. 'My story has about three or four titles at the moment,' Shearman wrote on the *Outpost Gallifrey* Forum in May 2004. 'There's the one in the original outline document given to me at Christmas. There's the one on my contract. There's the one I originally came up with to tie my first draft on. And, lastly, there's the one I came up with a little while ago, that I *hope* will be the "official" one – Russell quite likes it too, but nothing's been confirmed yet.' In fact, Shearman would write not one television episode, but two ... after a fashion, but that story will be revealed later on.

The final writer chosen by Davies to work on the show was Mark Gatiss, who would be responsible for the first episode to be transmitted that wasn't part of Davies's original setup. Gatiss was also no stranger to British television. He, with Steve Pemberton, Reece Shearsmith and Jeremy Dyson, had risen to prominence at the Edinburgh Fringe Festival as The League of Gentlemen (although Dyson wrote for the group, he did not appear as an actor with them). They later brought their comic stylings to a series called *The League of Gentlemen*, which began life on radio in 1997, before moving to television on BBC2 in 1999, and a cinema film, *The League of Gentlemen's Apocalypse* in 2005. *The League of Gentlemen* was set in the fictional town of Royston Vasey (the real name of famously-crude comedian Roy 'Chubby' Brown), a seemingly picturesque spot populated by dangerous lunatics, social misfits, sinister grotesques and psychopaths, and won the BAFTA award for Best Comedy in 2000 and the *NME* Award for Best Television Programme in 2001.

Gatiss had long been a *Doctor Who* fan himself, penning one of the earliest novels in Virgin's *Doctor Who* range, *Nightshade* (1992), very much an homage to 1950s science fiction in general and to Nigel Kneale's *Quatermass* saga in particular. He later wrote the novel *St Anthony's Fire* (1994) for Virgin and two novels for BBC Books: *The Roundheads* (1997) (an historical tale) and *Last of the Gaderene* (2000), a present-day UNIT story. Big Finish also enjoyed both sides of Gatiss's talents, as both writer and actor. Their first *Doctor Who* release, *The Sirens of Time* (1999), featured Gatiss's vocal talents, while their second boasted Gatiss's own script, *Phantasmagoria* (1999). Gatiss also penned an homage to *War of the Worlds* entitled *Invaders from Mars* (2002) and could be heard in supporting roles in such audios as *Oh No It Isn't* (1998), *Just War* (1999), *The Mutant Phase* (2000), *Sword of Orion* (2001), *The Stones of Venice* (2001), *Excelis Decays* (2002) and *Sympathy for the Devil* (2003). Gatiss also penned several screenplays for BBV Productions for their direct-to-video specials, including *The Zero Imperative* (1994), *The Devil of Winterbourne* (1995), *The Ghosts of Winterbourne* (1996) and *Unnatural Selection* (1996), also starring in each. His additional writing credits have included: a trio of sketches in which he also appeared for a 1999 *Doctor Who* documentary: *The Kidnappers, The Pitch of Fear* and *The Web of Caves*; the 2000 remake of *Randall and Hopkirk (Deceased)*; and a spoof documentary called *Global Conspiracy* (2004) for the BBC DVD release of the 1974 *Doctor Who* story 'The Green Death'. He's also appeared on screen in *In the Red* (1998), *Now You See Her* (2001), *Spaced* (2001), *Legend of the Lost Tribe* (2002), *Bright Young Things* (2003), *Catterick* (2004), *Nighty Night* (2004), *Shaun of the Dead* (2004), *Agatha Christie: A Life in Pictures* (2004), *Marple: The Murder at the Vicarage* (2004) and *Funland* (2005), among others. In addition, he appeared as Paterson in the 2005 BBC4 live television dramatisation of *The Quatermass Experiment*.

Gatiss spoke to Radio 4's programme *Front Row* in early March 2004 about his plans to write for the new *Doctor Who* TV series: 'Russell T Davies said to me the other day that he worked it out in his head that he's always regarded it as a science fiction,' Gatiss told presenter Mark Lawson, 'but what *Doctor Who* always did best was horror, and I think that's absolutely true. From arctic bases besieged by monsters to Cybermen on the moon, it's the creeping unknown, it's the shadows and the hand at the end of the episode; it's all horror.' While he noted that the new producers of *Doctor Who* would love to get back to 'proper scares', they also had a mainstream audience to deliver to. However, Gatiss himself would get to write the season's 'ghost story', the episode transmitted with the title 'The Unquiet Dead', set in the 1860s.

But Gatiss was tight lipped in his *Front Row* interview: 'I can't give too much away. I think ... being in a position of a viewer as well, I want people just to hear the thing at the end that says, "And next week; 'Doctor Who and the Android Invasion'", which just makes you go "WOW!" because you didn't know too much in advance.' He had his own thoughts on the Doctor, and how he should be portrayed: 'I've got a first script to go on, which Russell's written, and ... there are certain things that are essentially Doctor-ish, which you're never going to lose ... At the same time, you want to make it distinctive, and I think, particularly, what we're trying to do, this time, is make him a really vibrant, incredibly exciting character; the sort of person you just want to be with.'

Gatiss was later interviewed for a BBC press release issued in early 2005 that explored his thoughts about his story after it had been completed. 'The original idea came from Russell T Davies, but it was ideal for me – a Victorian ghost story set at Christmas with the dead coming back to life!' He noted he'd always enjoyed possession stories. 'Alan Bennett once said that we all have only a few beans in the tin to rattle, and I do tend to keep coming back to the idea of things being possessed. They're always my favourite kind of stories and it really must scare me on some basic level, the concept of being occupied by other entities.' But what really appealed to him was the idea of writing an historical story: 'Part of the fun of those historical adventures was seeing a Fifties police public call box standing on a Chinese plain in 2000 BC.'

'Being asked to write for the new series was the best present I've ever had,' Gatiss added. 'But having wanted the show to return for so long, it was also a bit daunting and I think we all ran around like headless chickens for a while. But then you just have to get on with it and the hard work really starts, but it's always a joy because of the love and loyalty we have for the show.'

While Moffat, Cornell, Shearman and Gatiss were the four writers selected, they weren't the only ones approached. Harry Potter creator/author J K Rowling 'turned down the chance to bring some magic to the new *Doctor Who* series' according to a *Doctor Who Magazine* 'Production Notes' column written by Davies; a story later picked up by the *Daily Record* on 4 May 2004. The *Doctor Who Magazine* feature explained that the BBC wanted her to write an episode, but that she was too busy writing the sixth Harry Potter novel, due out in 2005. 'I asked J K Rowling if she would like to write an episode for the new series,' Davies told *Doctor Who Magazine*, 'but unfortunately she had to turn it down. She told me she was absolutely charmed to have been asked but was so busy at the moment she just couldn't accept. It was slightly disappointing to say the least.'

There were others who weren't approached, but quietly signalled their interest. Posting on his web blog in late December 2003, popular comics writer and novelist Neil Gaiman (*American Gods*, *Sandman*), when asked if he'd write an episode if he was approached, noted, 'If I have time, certainly. (It took five years to find time to write a *Babylon 5* episode, of course ...)' Gaiman was familiar with *Doctor Who*, and had penned the foreword to Telos Publishing's novella *Eye of the Tyger* by science fiction novelist Paul McAuley. Also, in *SFX*'s March 2004 issue, writer Christopher Priest was said to have been sounded out about writing an episode; he had previously penned two stories, 'Sealed Orders' and 'The Enemy Within', for the original series in the late 1970s, both of which had ultimately been discarded before going into production.

'We only wanted to bring back *Doctor Who* if we could have the best talent around,' Mal Young told *Ariel* when the announcement about the final list of writers had gone out. 'Russell T Davies was always everyone's first choice, but now we're thrilled that Julie Gardner has been able to assemble a truly stellar team of writing talent to support Russell and enable us to keep the high standard of writing required, right across the series.'

Julie Gardner agreed: 'Finding writers for the new series of *Doctor Who* has been one of the best jobs I've ever had. The talent available was exceptional. The team, led by Russell, is passionate about bringing the Doctor back to our screens. For many months to come we'll all be burning the midnight oil to make the new series the best it can be.' Davies himself noted that he believed that he had: '... the best people in the business now working on the best show. They'll be writing stories ranging across the whole of time and space. The Doctor and Rose already have the best allies on their journey – brilliant writers with brilliant scripts. It's an honour to work with these people who are so talented; they shouldn't be allowed to travel together!'

Reactions from the fan community were bountiful. 'What a great writing team. Four people whose writing I really, really respect,' wrote Andy Frankham on the *Outpost Gallifrey* Forum. 'I'm utterly delighted by this,' said Ian Potter. 'These are all hugely creative people who love *Doctor Who*, and know what was wonderful about it and what wasn't, who are like us but brilliant, and who have created wonderful things of their own in TV, radio, [printed] fiction and theatre. They're coming together to bring *Doctor Who* back to the general public!' 'For anyone who was a kid in the late '80s/early '90s, the list looks especially cool – it's odd to think the people behind *Press Gang* and *Century Falls*, which I watched pretty much at the same time as I got into *Doctor Who*, are now writing the show,' wrote Jon de Burgh Miller (author of the *Doctor Who* novel *Dying in the Sun*.) Novelist Craig Hinton defended the choices as being far more than writers commissioned for the *Doctor Who* works known to fandom: 'Considerably more. These writers cover the whole spectrum of writing – plays, audios, comics, books, TV drama ... how many more credentials do you want? ... These are writers with experience, who also happen to know and love the series.' Fellow writer Jim Sangster noted: 'These are people who are currently writing (or have recently written) for some of the Beeb's top shows. They understand the format of modern serial drama and ... have the added attribute of having wildly different but equally passionate ideas about what *Doctor Who* is, which is an exciting thing to bring in to the mix.' John Dorney wrote, very matter of fact, 'I am happy beyond belief. Such a great line up. Something for everyone. Don't like everything done by all of them, but I'm not the total arbiter of taste. I've thoroughly enjoyed enough by all five that I think we're on a winner.'

CASTING RUMOURS INTENSIFY

As news of the new writers filtered out, press interest in the series was renewed, culminating in an article by Ben Dowell entitled 'Drop the dead Daleks, it's Dr. Who the sex machine' in the 7 March 2004 *Sunday Times*. The article seemed poised to engender a sense of panic among fans, as certain aspects of the Doctor's character were brought under scrutiny. 'I have a philosophy – I can do what I want,' Russell T Davies was quoted as saying. 'The purists may be up in arms, but there are more things to worry about in life. There is no pure *Doctor Who*. He is 41 years old – it is the only way to do it, to change.' The article noted that the Doctor might, in fact, 'lose his ascetic character', and pointed to several ways in which this could occur, including losing the signature look of the character (the 'frilly, flamboyant image usually topped off with an eccentric old-fashioned coat'). Besides regurgitating the names Bill Nighy and Eddie Izzard as candidates to play the role, the article raised two points that immediately set off warning signs for many fans: the sex life of the assistant, Rose Tyler, whom *The Sunday Times* described as 'a feisty young woman who talks to the Doctor about Dirty Den and the plot of *EastEnders* ... [and who] engages in flirty sexual banter with him and talks about her sex life with her boyfriend'; and the suggestion that two of the icons of the series, the Daleks and the established theme tune, might not be featured. *The Sunday Times* article was the first to mention the presence of the series's first returning monsters, which it noted as 'likely to be shop dummies ... [the Autons, who] will launch an attempt to conquer the world by terrorising a London housing estate'. It also settled into the comfort zone of readers expecting to see the blue TARDIS Police Box. 'The series, to be screened later this year on BBC1,' the article continued, 'will consist of episodes longer than they used to be. They will be self-contained, rather than cliffhangers to be resolved the following week.'

Unfortunately, the article also misquoted a representative of the *Doctor Who* Appreciation Society. 'I have met Russell and I am a huge fan of him and his writing. But I am very cautious about this,' the article quoted David Bickerstaff of the DWAS as saying. 'Time Lords don't have sex at all. We don't even know how they reproduce – it could be a matrix on Gallifrey (the Doctor's home planet), it could be chemical, we just don't know.' Ian Wheeler, coordinator of the DWAS, later issued a rebuttal: 'The article says that DWAS could be "the Doctor's greatest foe" because we are a "group of fans who adhere to the character's original persona". Both of these things are untrue – we support *Doctor Who* in all its forms and are very supportive of the new series. In addition, my DWAS colleague, David Bickerstaff, has been misquoted in the article. For example, it says that he claims to have met Russell Davies when he did in fact say no such thing.' *The Times* article also quoted Colin Baker as saying, 'Never pay attention to what the fans say. You have to appeal to a new audience. Love is a human emotion and the Doctor isn't human. We were always told there is one golden rule: no hanky-panky in the TARDIS.' Colin Baker spoke at a *Doctor Who* convention the weekend after *The Sunday Times* article appeared, claiming that the writer of the article had misinterpreted his comments. According to Baker, what he said was that the new series should not be made *solely* to appeal to existing fans; however, he mentioned that the journalist's opening comments were akin to, 'Looks like the Doctor's going to be gay in this new series, doesn't it?' Bickerstaff himself said, 'I now open the pages of *The Sunday Times* to find me being mis-quoted. The *Doctor Who* Appreciation Society is committed to promoting and enthusing, we are definitely NOT the "new foes", and I have every faith in Russell and his team. In fact I don't know where the reporter got the impression that DWAS was opposed to the new production team, I did nothing but sing their praises.'

Toward the middle of March 2004, the casting process was wrapping up, though that didn't stop the *Western Mail* from speculating that Bill Nighy would soon be cast in the role. The same *Western Mail* article, published on 13 March, also mentioned Robert Lindsay (*Citizen Smith, My Family, Hornblower*) and Paul Bettany (*Master and Commander: The Far Side of the World*) as contenders for the role. The article quoted Anthony Wainer of the *Doctor Who* Appreciation Society: 'I understand they are desperately keen to have Bill Nighy, but he's doing *The Hitchhiker's Guide To The Galaxy* and I think there is some delay in the announcement because they are trying to tie up schedules or speed his contract up so that he can do all that filming and then play the Doctor.' While this wasn't exactly correct, Wainer did note that fans were, on the whole, quite positive about the new series and delighted with the quality of its writing team, though Paul Murphy, editor of *TV Quick*, believed: 'There will be diehards who complain because it does not feature in their version of how *Doctor Who* should be. But if you don't like it get off your backside and do something about it. The new writers are people who quite cheerfully admit they are fans. Mark Gattis [sic] is a huge fan. He got off his backside and worked himself into a position where he can do something about it.'

Whoever would be cast in the role, they would have big shoes to fill ... and not just those of the Doctor. Saturday nights were to be the BBC's new focus, according to the *Guardian* on 16 March: BBC1 Controller Lorraine Heggessey was said to be turning 'to tried and tested talent to win the Saturday night ratings battle.' Among the series mentioned at the time were *Strictly Come Dancing*, a revamped celebrity version of the classic ballroom dancing show (which would be hosted by entertainer Bruce Forsyth), *EastEnders, Fame Academy* and *Doctor Who*. 'We are trying to grow the next generation of shows, but it is really difficult to get entertainment right,' Heggessey told the *Guardian*. 'The only way we are going to do that is through a process of trial and error. We would love to guarantee that every one will be a hit but sometimes it takes two or three times to get it right. We are trying to ring the changes and we want to bring freshness into the early evening.' The actor in the title role would also very likely face the Daleks, according to a 17 March Teletext report: 'The negotiations are going well,' Davies is quoted as saying, 'and I expect a positive result ... The estate is protecting an important property, after all, and I can appreciate why they are being so careful.' BBC News issued a slightly different take on this subject on 18 March, a BBC spokesperson noting, 'We are negotiating to feature the Daleks in the new series, but no deal has yet been made ... Negotiations are going on all over the place about the monsters, including the Daleks. We are just waiting to see what comes out.' The official *Doctor Who* website followed this up: 'Cult did its own bit of checking, and was told the same by Publicity. They stressed, however, that they, "could not confirm the Daleks, or any other monsters for the new series."'

For a time, it appeared that Bill Nighy was indeed the man who would take the Doctor into the 21st Century. The rumours had persisted since the autumn; the tabloids were joined by the mainstream press in touting his name, noting that he'd been one of Davies's favourites for the role. Nighy himself appeared on *Liquid News* on 16 March 2005, talking about the rumours: 'My wife shouted from the kitchen, "Are you going to be *Doctor Who*? – it says in the paper", but that's as near as I ever got ... So I don't know.' When asked again by the reporter, Nighy replied, 'I don't know, I've no idea. You'd have to tell ... ask whoever, I don't know, who wrote the story.'

Was Nighy being genuine, or did he really have no idea? An internal BBC memo circulated earlier in the week was said to contain a note that casting was down to 'a short list of three.' Would it be Nighy, or would there be a different man at the helm of the TARDIS?

Four days later, the world would have its answer.

CHAPTER FIVE:
CHRISTOPHER ECCLESTON IS ... DOCTOR WHO!

20 March 2004. An actor had been cast in the role of the Doctor, and although the BBC had attempted to keep things as close to their chest as possible, word had begun to leak out.

No one ever expects groundbreaking news to stay secret for very long. From around Monday 15 March 2004, e-mails containing the name of the series's new lead were being sent around the world; soon thereafter, a fan website called Gallifrey Online posted the name of the actor, and thereby started a tumult of speculation. This revelation caused serious consternation at the BBC, and especially within the new series's production team, because at the time this had come out, the final contracts had yet to be signed. (In fact, several of the new series's writers later confirmed in interviews that they had found out about the casting only a day or two before it was officially announced, and the fan site's ill-considered announcement had caused serious problems behind the scenes.) Obviously, good news travels fast, and word leaped through *Doctor Who* fandom ... Could this be the new man at the helm of the TARDIS?

Friday 19 March passed in the UK; the clock turned to Saturday morning, and the stories finally began to appear on newspapers' websites. So began a weekend flood of publicity culminating in international press coverage and mentions on the BBC's own overnight news broadcasts. Many British fans were asleep, yet those in North America and elsewhere were coming home from the Friday work day and discovering the news ... repeating the experience that had happened the previous September with the announcement of the new series. The new Doctor had been announced.

His name was Christopher Eccleston.

Born on 16 February 1964 in Salford, Lancashire, and trained at the Central School of Speech and Drama in London, the British stage, television and film actor Christopher Eccleston first came to public attention portraying Derek Bentley in the 1991 film *Let Him Have It*, based on the real-life events surrounding the conviction of a slow-witted teenager for the murder of a policeman in England in November 1952, and his subsequent death by hanging in 1953, before his posthumous pardon in July 1998. Eccleston also appeared in episodes of *Casualty* (1990), *Inspector Morse*, *Chancer* and *Boon* (all 1991) and *Poirot* (1992). However, it was a regular role as DCI David Bilborough in the TV series *Cracker* (1993-1994) – culminating in his character's dramatic death early in the second series – that made him a recognisable figure in the UK. He also appeared in the low-budget Danny Boyle film hit *Shallow Grave* (1994), in which he co-starred with another young British actor by the name of Ewan McGregor, and as Drew McKenzie in *Hearts and Minds* (1995). The same year, he won the part of Nicky Hutchinson in the epic BBC drama serial *Our Friends in the North*, and it was the transmission of this production on BBC2 in 1996 that perhaps really established him as a household name in the UK. Also in 1996, he played the title role in *Jude* opposite Kate Winslet, now a star thanks to her role in the movie *Titanic*.

He was originally offered, but did not take, the role of Begbie (eventually played to great acclaim by Robert Carlyle) in the cult favourite film *Trainspotting* (1996). His film career nevertheless took off with a variety of high-profile, but never quite mainstream roles, including in *Elizabeth* (1998), *eXistenz* (1999), *Gone in Sixty Seconds* (2000), *The Others* (2001), *24-Hour Party People* (2002) and another Danny Boyle film, the horror movie *28 Days Later* (2002), which became a cult favourite on both sides of the Atlantic. At the time he was announced as playing the Doctor, there were also rumours that he'd filmed a very brief segment in the then still-to-be-released *Star Wars: Episode III* (2005), as a younger version of Peter Cushing's infamous turn as the sinister Grand Moff Tarkin; a doctored photograph that appeared on the Internet was actually a mock-up, and Eccleston had no part in the film. (The young Tarkin would, in fact, be played by Wayne Pygram of *Farscape* fame, but only for a fleeting moment of screen time at the end of the film.)

Despite his successful film career, Eccleston has continued to appear in a variety of meaty television roles, racking up credits in some of the most challenging and thought-provoking British television dramas of recent years. These have included *Hillsborough* (1997), *Clocking Off* (2000) and *Flesh and Blood* (2002) for the BBC, and a modern version of *Othello* (2001) and the religious telefantasy epic *The Second Coming* (2003), written and produced by Russell T Davies, for ITV. He also found time for the occasional light-hearted role, as guest appearances in episodes of the comedy drama *Linda Green* (2001) and the macabre sketch show *The League of Gentlemen* (2002) have shown.

Eccleston has also done radio drama, most notably *Bayeux Tapestry* (2001) for Radio 4, and stage work, including a starring role in *Miss Julie* at the West End's Haymarket Theatre in 2000.

Eccleston's name had first been suggested for the role not for this production, but in fact a decade before. According to the book *Regeneration: The Story of the Revival of a Television Legend* by Philip Segal with Gary Russell, Eccleston's name had been on a short list of actors whose agents had informed the production team for the 1996 *Doctor Who* television film that their clients would not be averse to committing to television productions lasting several years. However, Eccleston himself later insisted he wasn't interested in the role at that time, and so his involvement never got past this initial stage. Eccleston later admitted that he generally found it hard to get hold of the kind of scripts that interest him, which have been described as earthy, political or challenging.

Eccleston appeared to have found his niche with the role of the enigmatic Time Lord. In Rachel Williams's *Press Association News* article 'Eccleston to Take Control of the TARDIS', the earliest press announcement to be circulated (and seen first on the website of the Scottish newspaper the *Scotsman*), Jane Tranter noted the immediate internal reaction at the BBC: 'We are delighted to have cast an actor of such calibre in one of British television's most iconic roles. It signals our intention to take *Doctor Who* into the 21st Century, as well as retaining its core traditional values – to be surprising, edgy and eccentric. We have chosen one of Britain's finest actors to play what, in effect, will be an overtly modern hero.' In the same article, Davies weighed in with his first public comments about the casting: 'We considered many great actors for this wonderful part, but Christopher was our first choice. This man can give the Doctor a wisdom, wit and emotional range as far-reaching as the Doctor's travels in time and space. His casting raises the bar for all of us. It's going to be a magnificent, epic, entertaining journey, and I can't wait to start.'

Such were the range of emotions and hype around the announcement that there were bound to be errors, and perhaps the most visible one came from the *Daily Mail*. Having been given an apparent false lead about the casting announcement, the *Mail* went forward on the morning of Saturday 20 March with an article in their first edition stating that Bill Nighy had been signed to the role. 'After weeks of negotiations,' they stated, 'BBC executives whittled down the contenders to three, with Nighy finally beating off competition from Richard E Grant and *Jonathan Creek* star Alan Davies.' The *Mail* corrected this article in their second and subsequent editions on the Saturday morning with a new story entitled 'New Dr Who is a Cracker' in the same space, and written by an unidentified 'Daily Mail Reporter', containing details about Eccleston and a photo of Tom Baker. The Nighy story was then picked up sporadically elsewhere, including in a report from Australia in the *Adelaide Sunday Mail*, which on 28 March issued an apology for the erroneous story, blaming the *Daily Mail* for originating the report, which subsequently went into syndication.

The *Daily Mail* later won a 'Shafta Award' at a spoof award ceremony held on 27 April at London's Café de Paris, presented by Capital Radio's Johnny Vaughan, that 'targets the biggest blunders in the UK's media industry.' *Daily Mail* TV editor Tara Conlan was awarded the Michael Fish award for 'best TV prediction' for the report confirming Nighy in the role. 'If only, like the good Doctor himself,' the *Guardian* reported the next day, 'Conlan had been able to travel back in time ... It could have been worse. Well, sort of. The *Daily Star*'s Peter Dyke really put his head on the block when he said the new Doctor Who would be ... Paul Daniels. With Debbie McGee as his assistant, presumably. Where did he magic that one up from?'

Bill Nighy didn't take things too badly, though. He spoke to the *Daily Mail* on 25 March to wish Eccleston well. 'These things happen and sometimes the best man wins,' he said. 'He's taller, stronger and better looking – just. I think a great tradition is in great hands.' Some have read into this comment about the best man winning a tacit admission by Nighy that he had indeed been in the running for the role, as had for so long been rumoured.

There were many other stories and rumours circulating that weekend, and it was simply impossible that all of them would turn out to be true. The *Daily Express* noted that Eccleston had signed a 'three year contract' for £500,000 and that the budget for each episode would be £1 million. The *Daily Record* was, meanwhile, talking about a second season to be broadcast in 2006.

Tom Baker later addressed the Sunday edition of the *Mail* with his thoughts about the casting choice. Baker has long been known for making offbeat comments about his time in *Doctor Who*, and this would be no exception: 'I've never heard of him,' said Baker, 'but I wish him well.' According to the report in the *Mail*, Baker admitted, 'I thought I was the only Doctor Who but there again I never watched it, even when I was in it.' Colin Baker told *Doctor Who Confidential*, 'When I heard it was Christopher Eccleston – that really came out of left field – I was overjoyed,' while his successor Sylvester McCoy noted, simply, 'I'm very excited that he's doing it.' Writer Paul Cornell was even more upbeat. 'I think it's wonderful that we've got such a high calibre actor in the role,' he told *Outpost Gallifrey*. 'Along with everyone else, it was great to get the rush of a "new Doctor day" again. My Dad called to read me out a news item about it, just like he always used to. Chris is going to have to get used to being beloved by parents and small children everywhere!'

Eccleston himself was apparently quite delighted at the opportunity. '*Doctor Who*? And Russell T Davies! Tell me which way to Cardiff because I can't wait,' he told *icWales*, which also quoted Gardner's reaction, the BBC Wales Head of Drama having worked with Eccleston before on *Othello*. 'He is just such a delight to work with,' Gardner said. 'Chris is so professional and hard-working and he's a very writer-friendly actor. He chooses his roles from the best scripts because his work is so important to him. We are very lucky to have such a great actor working with us. He loved the scripts and he loved the character.' Gardner noted for the *Doctor Who Confidential* documentary series: 'We just wanted someone who would be a brilliant actor and would surprise the audience, and not be a predictable choice.'

'We considered many great actors for this wonderful part,' Davies told *icWales*, 'but Christopher was our first choice. Both he and I live in Manchester and we knew each other even before we did *The Second Coming*. He's not just a great actor, he's a lovely man. He's passionate about good writing and he genuinely loves *Doctor Who*.' Davies later spoke to *Doctor Who Magazine*, noting that he: '... couldn't be happier, this is exactly the man we wanted. And you wouldn't believe his passion for the job – it's energised the entire team.'

The feeling was mutual. 'I am a huge fan of his,' Eccleston would say nearly a year later, at the 8 March 2005 press launch of the new series, shortly before its broadcast debut. 'I've tried to capture his speed of thought and the pace of his words, and of course they are his words.' He would note to BBC News that his would be a different sort of portrayal: 'I'm different from the other Doctors. All the others spoke with this RP [received pronunciation – a "proper" form of English] accent – maybe it was that that put me off. I think that it's good that we teach kids that people who speak [with a regional accent] can be heroic too.'

'When Mal Young, Julie Gardner and I first got into the same room together in September, he was the very first name mentioned,' Davies told *SFX* magazine in April 2004. 'And that's a fact. Of course, there were other names, there had to be, but he was first. Who'd have thought we'd actually get him?' Julie Gardner agreed: 'Christopher is, first and foremost, a wonderful actor. He's energetic, passionate, professional and instinctive. And he's got a great sense of humour. He loved the first episode, did an amazing audition, and here we are. I couldn't be more pleased ...'

Rumours flew, especially toward the end of 2004, that Eccleston had himself approached Davies for the role. 'He e-mailed me and said if we were looking for a Doctor Who, he'd be interested,' Davies confirmed to *Radio Times* in March 2005. 'It was gob smacking because you think he's going to be doing Hamlet all the time. Which, come to think of it, he was.' Only episodes one and two of the new series had actually been scripted prior to Eccleston's casting, and while they hadn't been specifically written for him (or anyone, for that matter), it would be easy to slip him into the part. 'I'd established a template for what I wanted, which fitted Chris perfectly. That was a happy accident – we both wanted to strip it down, make it more down-to-earth.'

Eccleston later admitted to *Doctor Who Confidential* that he'd read about the return of the series in the newspapers, and took it upon himself to approach the production team... a group that, in his own words, 'would never have approached me in a million years!'

Davies and Gardner were joined in their accolades by Mal Young. 'His work to date has been impressively eclectic, from messiah to modern-day Iago, but Eccleston's position in this list owes most to the kudos that will come with being the next *Doctor Who*,' Young was quoted as saying by *Radio Times* in its 5 July 2004 edition, in connection with the magazine's list of the top forty most powerful figures in UK television drama, on which Eccleston, three months after this casting announcement, was listed at number 19. 'Very few actors can green-light a project but, because of the amazing response I've had from *Doctor Who*, I'd say he's now one that can.'

BBC News Online conducted a survey of readers concerning the casting. This drew hundreds of responses from Britain and elsewhere. 'A fine choice demonstrating the desire to bring some of the edge back to *Doctor Who*,' said one correspondent. 'Chris is a very versatile and until now cruelly-underrated actor; can't wait to see him confronting Daleks,' responded another. 'Weh-hey! A Doctor Who with sex appeal. I'll be watching!' said a woman from London. In fact, there were several very direct comparisons between Eccleston and Patrick

Stewart, another actor who had a significant heritage to live up to when he took the role of Jean-Luc Picard in *Star Trek: The Next Generation*. Specifically, Stewart had the thankless task of succeeding William Shatner's larger-than-life portrayal of Captain Kirk, and while the Doctor had been seen in multiple incarnations in times past, the transition from 'classic' series to this 'next generation' of *Doctor Who* could be seen as travelling the same uncharted course. Of course, you can't please everyone all the time; the *Daily Record* reported on 22 March that 'outraged' *Doctor Who* fans dressed as Daleks had protested in Southampton, apparently under the impression that the Daleks would not appear in the new series. 'Daleks were infamous for sending children diving behind sofas in the 1960s and 70s,' said fan Chris Balcombe. 'A Doctor Who not facing them is almost unthinkable.' Those sharing Balcombe's view would have a lot more to think about over the coming months ...

On the Internet, most of the reactions were quite jubilant, some even more so than over the original announcement of the new series. When the casting was announced, shortly after midnight, those who had been participating in the *Outpost Gallifrey* Forum watched as the minutes counted down – at one point with nearly 20 posts in the same minute, all expecting the good news. *Radio 5 Live* was the first to break the story that weekend, followed by the leak of the covers of the *Daily Mirror* and an article in the *Daily Express*. 'To those who don't know about Chris Eccleston,' wrote a jubilant Paul Dawson, 'please believe me (us) when I (we) say he is going to be the best Doctor since Tom. Possibly the very best ever. This is the best possible news.' Alan Hayes was a bit more circumspect: 'Good choice. Not necessarily a "Doctorish" actor, but I'm sure he'll do a fine job. Some solid news at last, and it's good.' *Doctor Who* novelist Craig Hinton, however, couldn't contain the emotions many fans were feeling at that moment: 'Magnificent. Absolutely magnificent. I couldn't be happier! I actually started to cry when I heard the news and saw it confirmed.' There were also immediate web searches to see who could be identified as having done the deed of predicting Eccleston the earliest; author Daniel Blythe had first made a comment about Eccleston's appeal even before the airing of the 1996 TV movie, posting in early March 1996 on the *rec.arts.drwho* newsgroup: 'Well, if [McGann] doesn't do any more sequels, then I'd love to see Christopher Eccleston in the part. He could really show us what a "stroppy" Doctor was like!'

But there were also some rather dismayed fans reacting quite harshly to the fact that they'd been robbed of the chance to see Paul McGann return to the role, including a rather sizeable number on the BBCi message boards and the group that had started an online petition. At the *Gallifrey 2004* convention in Los Angeles a month earlier, McGann had again commented that, were the BBC to ask him, he might be up for the role. But McGann had not possessed the same sort of 'wait and see' attitude he'd displayed in the taped segments for UKGold broadcast during the November 2003 anniversary celebrations. Notwithstanding the enormous amounts of speculation over the months as to how likely it was that McGann would be seen in the role in the new series, many had always felt that it was simply not to be; the BBC would likely wish to go in a new direction. With the casting of Eccleston in the role, that new direction was all but assured.

Reactions continued to pour in. Steven Moffat told *Outpost Gallifrey*, 'It's a fantastic casting. Not just because he's a brilliant actor, though clearly he is, but because he'll bring people to the audience, who wouldn't touch the show with a barge pole otherwise. The morning of the announcement, I went into the *Coupling* rehearsals, and the cast – trendy lovelies that they are, hardly the natural *Who* audience – were bouncing around about the news. Clearly rather more excited about that than the fact that a good friend of theirs was now writing it. So I sacked them all.' Mark Gatiss was no less enthusiastic: 'Chris Eccleston's casting is sensational. He's a fantastic actor and a lovely man and is just the right kind of "serious" choice to forever banish those tiresome tabloid stories about various TV weathermen or magicians being chosen as the Doctor. And for those who think he's "too serious" for the part, I'd point to the casting of William Hartnell all those years ago. He was known for a particular type of role and seized upon *Doctor Who* as a chance to show his versatility. Besides, when Chris did a cameo in *The League of Gentlemen*, he told me he was fed up with playing miserable bastards, so this will be just what the Doctor ordered!' Gatiss also said in an early 2005 BBC press release that he thought Eccleston: '... makes a great Doctor, and [Eccleston and Davies are] both clearly men having fun. But that's what Russell said from the start – whatever he's up to, whatever danger he's in, the Doctor's having a good time.'

'About a year or so ago,' commented Rob Shearman, 'my wife and I were spellbound watching *The Second Coming* on TV. "This is by Russell T Davies," I told her – and, in a vain attempt to convince her I was as good a writer by connection, said, "He's a *Doctor Who* fan, you know." My wife – who is not like you or I – grunted non-committally. At the first commercial break, I said, "Wouldn't it be great if this was *Doctor Who*? Back on the telly?" and she grunted again. At the next break I sallied with a "And wouldn't it be great if he was the Doctor?" And, to my surprise, she didn't grunt, but agreed. Because she'd realised as I had that Christopher Eccleston is the perfect choice to play the Doctor. Extraordinary – someone entirely "other", who'll always stand out from the crowd. Charismatic – if he can pull off being a modern day Jesus, you know he can pull off a modern day Time Lord too. Capable of great passion, anger, and warmth. And, obviously, an astonishingly good actor. I can't tell you how delighted I am to be writing for such a talent. And my wife is jolly pleased too.'

Dreamwatch magazine captured other opinions later in April, with former Doctor, Colin Baker, reflecting on the choice ... and the pairing of Eccleston with Davies: 'The combination ... is very exciting indeed, as one of the best pieces of television in the last decade was *The Second Coming*. I couldn't be more pleased; it's as if we had been told that Dennis Potter and Michael Gambon were back working together. If *Doctor Who* is to emerge as the equivalent programme for 2005 as it was in 1963 then this is just the kind of approach that is needed. I hope the budget matches the talent that is being assembled.' Writer and television director Stephen Gallagher, who penned two *Doctor Who* serials, 'Warriors' Gate' and 'Terminus', for the original series, said that it was 'an unexpected choice in the context of Whos-gone-by, but potentially a very, very good one if his selection is a marker of Russell T's intentions for a radical new approach.' And Rockne S O'Bannon, a long-time producer in the science fiction genre whose most recent success was the US/Australia co-produced *Farscape*, noted that the new series would: '... need to both satisfy the memories of fans of the series's previous incarnations and present a genre drama that will have resonance for today's larger audience who has never seen nor heard of *Doctor Who* ... A new *Doctor Who* with the same high imagination quotient and state-of-the-art effects and production design could be the best of all worlds. And who knows the concept of "all worlds" better than the good Doctor? I, for one, can't wait!'

The *Northern Echo* would have none of that, running a story on 5 May called 'The emotional dimension' in which the author bemoaned recent choices of phrase by Eccleston in the press. 'My heart sank when Christopher Eccleston was announced as the new Doctor Who,' she wrote. 'He always makes such heavy weather of everything ... We turn on programmes like *Doctor Who* for a bit of escapism.'

The casting of a new Doctor is never a 'minor' incident to the British press, and Christopher Eccleston's casting was a widely reported media event. Besides the gamut of British press interest, the story was carried far and wide, across Europe, North America and Asia, with reports by everyone from the *New York Times* to the *Sci-Fi Channel* website, *FOX News* and *CNN*, Canada's *Globe and Mail* to the Melbourne *Herald Sun* in Australia, the Yahoo! and America Online services, *Cinescape* magazine and *FilmForce* ... It was truly an international cause for celebration, as a major icon was being repainted with a fresh, new face. To celebrate the momentous event, the BBC Press Office issued a press release noting that Eccleston: '... will take *Doctor Who* into the 21st Century – travelling through time and space, fighting monsters on all fronts, in a fresh and modern approach to the popular science fiction series.' Eccleston himself was quoted in the press release as saying, 'I am absolutely delighted to be playing Doctor Who. I am looking forward to joining forces again with the incredible writer Russell T Davies and taking both loyal viewers and a new generation on a journey through time and space – which way is the TARDIS? I can't wait to get started!' In the wake of all the media attention, BBC Drama published a web page on their 'Drama Faces' site with details of Eccleston's career.

Gardner appeared on the BBC Wales evening news programme on 22 March. When asked what the most enduring element of *Doctor Who* was that she personally wanted to bring back to the show, her considered answer was very simple: 'Fear.' She also confirmed that the production team was working hard to have the series ready by 'early next year,' drawing closer to the rumoured January start than in previous statements. The same day, the *Daily Express* reported that 'NEW Doctor Who Christopher Eccleston has shot to number two in this weeks OK! Celebrity Chart ...' – a chart that measures the amount of press coverage a celebrity receives; only one person had more written about them in the UK newspapers that particular week!

That would be the mere tip of the iceberg as far as press coverage was concerned over the next several weeks. BBC News published an article entitled, 'No more props for "darker" Doctor.' Noting that 'Enthusiasts think he may portray a darker character than many of the previous Doctors, who were often quirky, offbeat and replete with props,' the piece featured comments from Antony Wainer of the *DWAS* and Boyd Hilton, editor of *Heat* magazine. 'I think it's quite exciting,' said Hilton. 'He's one of the best actors of our time, and rather than going for a colourful character actor as they've done in the past, they've gone for a brilliant actor.' Offered Wainer, 'It's about the quality of the writing and the audience expectation, and things that just catch on.'

Eccleston himself was featured in the *Sun,* which claimed the scoop of the first proper interview with the actor on 28 March, one week after the announcement. 'My bony face is like a car crash,' a self-deprecating Eccleston mused. 'I haven't got good looks, just weird looks, enough to frighten the fiercest monster ... I've played a lot of characters who are very troubled and dark, but I can't wait to get into the TARDIS – it's going to be brilliant.'

Doctor Who Magazine rushed into production a brand new cover for issue #342. Noting 'Christopher Eccleston Is The Doctor!', the issue featured a large photo of Eccleston from *The Second Coming* on the front. As Clayton Hickman, *Doctor Who Magazine* Editor, noted when the issue was printed, 'Russell lamented that he'd wanted to tell *Doctor Who Magazine* about the casting personally – not that it really mattered amidst the incredible excitement of that day. The only shame was that our ... front cover wouldn't appear until more than five weeks later.' In fact, a successful stop press meant that the *Doctor Who Magazine* cover appeared within a fortnight of the announcement.

Eccleston continued to make waves in the press. The *Guardian* offered a view about BBC domination of the BAFTA Awards (the annual achievement awards from the British Academy of Film and Television Arts) on 23 March, but noted that Christopher Eccleston was nominated for Russell T Davies's *The Second Coming*, originally broadcast on rival ITV. (His main competition in the papers for the role of the Doctor, Bill Nighy, actually won the award for Best Actor in a TV Drama title, for *State of Play* on BBC1.) The *Guardian* also noted in a separate article that 'When Christopher Eccleston [sic] steps out of the TARDIS next spring, *Doctor Who*, scourge of fibreglass lumps everywhere, will have been off our screens for 16 years.' Besides quotes from Gatiss and *Death Comes to Time* script editor Nev Fountain, the article offered a pointed statement from Hickman: 'The *Doctor Who* mafia. That's why the show's coming back. If it wasn't for all the fans in high places, it would just have faded away.' In the print edition, the piece was accompanied by a caricature of Eccleston stepping into the TARDIS, while in a separate section, 'Diary' columnist Matthew Norman noted his late 2003 'campaign' to prevent Alan Davies from becoming the Doctor, and suggested that there were 'rumours that Christopher Eccleston' was interested. 'At this stage,' Norman noted, 'it's too early to be sure how this uncanny piece of prescience came about.' The paparazzi was also having its due. 'He may be the new Doctor Who,' wrote Fiona Cummins in the *Mirror* on 30 March, 'but Christopher Eccleston was Mr Nobody when he tried to waltz into a nightclub. The 40-year-old was stopped by bouncers who failed to recognise him as the star who's just landed a 1 million pound deal to play the ninth TV Doctor.'

While rumours began to circulate that Eccleston's co-star had been cast and was about to be announced (rumours that proved untrue, as she wouldn't be confirmed until late May – in fact, casting of Rose didn't begin until Eccleston had been signed), the lack of any further significant developments allowed the media to have a field day with *Doctor Who* fandom. Such was the case with a letter written by several Members of Parliament fronted by Tim Collins, then Shadow Education Secretary and a Conservative MP for Westmorland and Lonsdale, who had long been an ardent supporter of *Doctor Who*. The letter, signed by representatives from the Tories, Labour and the Liberal Democrats, noted that 'The multi-million pound new series of *Doctor Who* is weeks away from the start of filming,' and begged former BBC1 Controller Michael Grade – who had recently been rumoured to be on the shortlist for Chairman of the BBC Board of Governors – not to interfere with the series. 'Some ... are concerned,' they wrote, 'that, were you to become BBC Chairman, the project would be derailed – potentially wasting significant sums of licence payers' money. Are you therefore prepared to guarantee that, should you be appointed to the post, you would not interfere in any way with decisions about *Doctor Who*?' Grade was the man behind both the temporary cancellation of *Doctor Who* in 1985, when its originally-planned twenty-third season was pulled from broadcast, and, as previously mentioned, the sacking of Colin Baker from the lead role in 1986. While never a fan of the series, Grade was nevertheless not in a position to pull the plug on the show, even after his eventual installation as Chairman the following month – but it made for good newspaper copy. In a brief chat conducted with the *Sunday Express* on 18 April, he noted: 'I am very pleased that it is coming back to our screens, but I won't be watching it.' At the same time, Grade appeared on Radio 4's *PM* programme and made it clear he couldn't and wouldn't interfere.

Eccleston, meanwhile, avoided much of the spotlight for a while as he took a role in a spring and summer season presentation of a new stage drama called *Electricity*. 'I'm very excited to be playing Doctor Who,' he was quoted as saying in a press release about the play. 'However, at the moment the most important thing to me is *Electricity*, the fantastic new play by Murray Gold that I'm rehearsing at the West Yorkshire Playhouse, a place that I love and one that I hope to work at many times in the future. It's an ensemble piece and a comedy and I'm playing a role unlike anything I've ever done before.' Eccleston received accolades from Charles Spencer for his performance in a review in the *Daily Telegraph* on 1 April: 'Christopher Eccleston, recently announced as the new Doctor Who, offers charismatic value as the truculent Jakey, spending much of the show eating sandwiches on his employer's expensive recliner, and able to turn in a flash from loutish belligerence to sudden glimpses of unexpected charm, decency and wit.'

This wasn't the first time Eccleston had worked on a project with, or affiliated with, composer and playwright Murray Gold. Gold had provided the music for both *The Second Coming* and *Clocking Off* ... and before they knew it, they'd be reunited on *Doctor Who*, as Gold was subsequently confirmed both to write the incidental score for all thirteen episodes and to craft the latest version of the series's signature theme. Gold, born in Portsmouth in 1969, had extensive composer credits in film, television and the theatre, including the score for the BBC production of *Vanity Fair* (1998) for which he secured his first BAFTA nomination; his second came for the highly stylised signature theme and incidental music for Davies's *Queer as Folk* (1999), which won an award from the Royal Television Society in 2000. His other television credits included *Randall and Hopkirk (Deceased)* (2000), *America Beyond the Color Line* (2002) for the PBS public network in America, and *Servants* (2003). His film work has included 'an evocative jazz score' to Jez Butterworth's acclaimed first feature, *Mojo* (1997), as well as scores for the films *Beautiful Creatures* (2000), *Wild About Harry* (2000), *Miranda* (2002) and *Kiss of Life* (2003). *Electricity* won Gold the Michael Imison Memorial Prize for Best New Radio Play in 2002 in a version commissioned by BBC Radio 3. (The late Imison had coincidentally directed for *Doctor Who* many years earlier, on the 1966 story 'The Ark'.) Besides compositions for stage productions *Dr Faustus* and *50 Revolutions*, Gold recently penned the book and lyrics for *Queer as Folk: The Musical*.

Early April saw a new development in Christopher Eccleston's suddenly press-friendly life: his first live interview since the announcement of his taking the role of the Doctor. That honour was granted to the *BBC Breakfast* programme on 2 April, as hosts Bill Turnbull and Sian Williams welcomed Eccleston to their couch. 'I was very excited, particularly because of the writer, who's Russell T Davies, because I've always chosen my work on the strength of the scripts,' Eccleston told his hosts. 'I worked with Russell on *Second Coming* and I do think the most important thing about any television project is the writer and the script, and we've got some fantastic scripts. Very exciting.'

Eccleston noted that this would be a somewhat different take on the Doctor: 'Well, we're not gonna wear scarves and hats ...' In fact, many of the details would come later. 'That's all to be decided – what he's going to look like, what he's going to wear, but I don't think he's gonna be quite as eccentric and as foppish as he was in ... some of his incarnations.' Eccleston confirmed the name of his companion, Rose Tyler, but that she was still to be cast. 'She's going to be much more ... intelligent, sort of ... proactive.' He also spoke about past recollections of *Doctor Who* (he remembered Patrick Troughton and the Sontarans, which he said 'looked like baked potatoes', most of all) and his accent. 'I don't want to sound like a member of the royal family ... nor will ... my accent be as strong as it is now. I think it'll just be my voice ... My accent has been poshed up since I became an actor, so he'll sound like me.' And he offered his own polite comments to Bill Nighy, whom Williams noted 'was saying that you're younger and prettier and better than he is, so you deserve to get the role.' 'I was an usher at the National Theatre when Bill was doing ... some of his fantastic stuff with Anthony Hopkins,' Eccleston noted. 'He's a great actor, Bill ... We like that, us luvvies.'

Perhaps the biggest news that came out of the live interview was Eccleston noting the start of production in July in Cardiff. Previously, there had been only speculation about a start date sometime during the summer; this was the first specific prediction, and would soon prove to be accurate.

While early April turned attentions elsewhere – such as to the question of who would play Rose Tyler – the media kept tabs on Eccleston, who was seen visiting children in the cancer department of St James Hospital in Leeds on 25 April. 'It's an honour just to be here,' Eccleston told *Leeds Today*. 'It's a really nice place and the staff do a great job.' Eccleston had stopped in as a courtesy call while appearing in *Electricity*.

So starved did the British press seem for additional information about Eccleston that they began purloining paragraphs from Eccleston's first interview with *Doctor Who Magazine*. The interview, which appeared in issue 343 published in the final week of April, quoted Eccleston as stating that he would be filming 'seven months of each of the next two or three years and have five months off,' indicative of plans (at the time) for him to stay with the series for the next few years. Eccleston also reiterated that it was Davies that had really attracted him to the role: 'I was asked to audition for the *Doctor Who* film five or six years ago,' he noted, referring to his experience with the 1996 *Doctor Who* TV movie, 'and it was a very firm "No" from me, because really it hadn't resonated with me for a long time ... Russell's talent is to take the work very seriously and to take himself not seriously at all. I think he does have a very big heart and a great deal of love. He does have a social conscience, but he doesn't soap box and he isn't pompous.'

While the *Daily Telegraph* presented extracts from *Doctor Who Magazine*'s interview as its own front-page exclusive, *The Times* quoted selectively from the interview on 29 April in an opinion piece entitled 'The new Dr Who should not exterminate his ratings', in which they pondered the 'darker, more dangerous' and 'melancholy' side of the Doctor. 'Now, to be fair, Eccleston is new to this regeneration business and it must be a change from Grand Prix racing,' quipped the paper, making a link with Formula 1 racing promoter Bernie Ecclestone. 'But he does seem a little weak on the history of his character. We may live in harsh times, but the Doctor has seen an awful lot worse, especially dealing with the Cybermen who, among other crimes, sparked the boom in shoulder pads during the 1980s.' It also noted that perceptions existed that the Doctor had for a long while been a liberal interventionist, taking the word 'Who' as a namesake for the World Health Organisation (WHO), and that what Eccleston dismissed as 'spooky escapism' was, in the journalist's mind, the point of the series. 'Where Eccleston really needs to get his act together, though, is on the question of enemies. The next Doctor Who has expressed a personal sympathy with the Daleks on the basis that they are actually "very vulnerable, strange, frightened creatures."'

Comments on the emotional resonance of the role, as noted originally in the *Doctor Who Magazine* interview, were further recycled, picking up on Eccleston's thoughts as he said the series would address the Doctor's 'loneliness and his place as an outsider,' and noting that modern audiences: '... turn on the television to look into people's souls. That's basically what they're looking for, human feelings and emotions ... the rest, really, is icing. Daleks and all that, is really just icing.' About the character of the Doctor, Eccleston said: 'He's the idealistic, humane alien, isn't he? And this must be something to do with his desire to belong.'

Most of the press outlets that repeated this information didn't mention the original source of the interview quotes, though the BBC's online news service did. So too did the *Guardian* which, on 29 April in Marina Hyde's Friday 'Diary' column, noted the press reports of the past couple of days with a curious eye. 'The casting of the new *Doctor Who* starts to look like some kind of intergalactic conspiracy. You'll recall that Matthew Norman [another Diarist writing for the paper] has responsibilities towards a *Doctor Who*-obsessed small boy, who has met all four living Doctors, but is yet to learn that a certain regular "Diary" feature – "Is there a smugger and more irksome actor in Britain than Christopher Eccleston?" – is likely to prevent an encounter with the latest.' Other press focused on different aspects of the actor in stories published the same day: the *Big News Network* led with a headline, 'New "Dr Who" actor once turned down role,' referring to Eccleston's refusal to audition for the 1996 *Doctor Who* TV film. The ABC news network in Australia noted a 'New face for "Dr Who"' with a simple three-line story about Eccleston, reiterating the 'melancholy side' quote. The *Telegraph* discussed, 'How to play Dr Who: less soul, more hot pants' in its 'Notebook' column, as well as printing a current affairs quiz that included the question, 'Which character did actor Christopher Eccleston say needed more "emotional weight" to the role?'

Eccleston's stock as an actor, already quite high, was nevertheless boosted by his attachment to the role of the Doctor. The *CelebDAQ* website, trending celebrities in much the same way stock exchanges track finances, ranked Eccleston in fourth place of five in their weekly vote for new IPOs (initial public offerings) for the first week of May. (Interestingly, Billie Piper, rumoured at the time to be a possible pick to play the companion, was also listed.) Eccleston had become tabloid fodder – proof positive, if anything could be, that there was a new level of interest in the man – when 2 May's *Sunday Mirror* profiled Clare Calbraith, said at the time to be Eccleston's current girlfriend. 'The pair are smitten after a string of dates and nights together. The actor, 40, swept the pretty brunette off her feet when they met at a theatre while performing in different plays. Pals say the former *Cracker* star has been "like a schoolboy in love" ever since and has hardly let her out of his sight.' The World Entertainment News Network later published a personal note about Eccleston, noting he'd been teased by friends since landing the role; as Eccleston is quoted as saying, 'I've had so many phone messages from mates, all drunk as monkeys, doing the theme tune for me.'

The world had its new Doctor. Christopher Eccleston was an enormously popular choice, judging by the media reaction in the month and a half that followed his announcement, and had won accolades from the production, its writers, the fans and the media. The questions soon on everyone's lips would be: Who would play his companion, Rose Tyler? When would they get started? And when would the Doctor return to the screen? The really hard part was still to come.

CHAPTER SIX:
THE SHAPE OF THINGS TO COME

With the confirmation of Christopher Eccleston as the Doctor, eyes turned to other matters: other casting, writing, and production. From the time the initial media hype died down until the start of production on the new series, there would be a period marked by two major events – the casting of Billie Piper as Rose Tyler and the apparent fiasco of the loss, and eventual restoration, of the dreaded Daleks as villains in the series – as well as months filled with rumour and speculation.

BILLIE PIPER IS ... ROSE TYLER!

Since the debut of *Doctor Who* in 1963, every Doctor has enjoyed the company of travelling companions both to guide him on his journey and to help him fight the good fight ... men and women, human, alien and machine. From the Doctor's own granddaughter to a robot dog; from a Scottish bagpiper to a feisty air hostess; the companions have shared one thing in common: to stand in for the viewer, as their advocate in a world of alien situations and impossible odds. From those assistants who were simple ciphers, to redefined, more worldly roles as time went on, the basic function of the companion never changed; the companion would ask what was going on, because the viewers were asking the same question. Fifth Doctor Peter Davison has noted that he didn't realistically believe that there was a larger role for the assistant: 'I think that the job of the assistant ... is to say "What is it, Doctor?", "Help, Doctor!" and for the Doctor to get them out of trouble. I do think that their job in *Doctor Who* is to get into trouble, if you like, and for the Doctor to get them out.'

Russell T Davies would have none of that. In an interview with *TV Times*, run on 1 December 2003, he noted that the new Doctor would: '... get a *Buffy*-style female sidekick ... a 'modern action heroine. A screaming girly companion is unacceptable now ... I don't mean in terms of women's rights – dramatically, we've got *Buffy the Vampire Slayer* now, so a screaming girly companion would be laughed out of the room.'

From a very early stage, this new companion for the 21st Century had a name: Rose Tyler. She would be strong, energetic, and in fact would eventually share top billing with Christopher Eccleston. Not an easy thing to grasp for a public either used to a companion subservient to the Doctor, or not familiar with the series at all ... but certainly a model for, and a reflection of, the times. Speculation over casting of the role started early, and as with the role of the Doctor, seemingly every press agent in Britain put their clients' names forward.

'The first name to be pulled from the hat of unnecessary conjecture is Rachael Stirling, daughter of Diana Rigg, who cemented her reputation in the BBC landmark drama *Tipping the Velvet*,' said the *Sci-Fi Online* website in December 2003. 'Like so many of the names being batted around for the Doctor, this is almost certainly nothing more than groundless gossip fuelled by grapevine ardour, although the talented young actress could easily fulfill producer Russell Davies's casting brief of "strong and independent" so who knows?' The race to find a companion had officially begun, even if only in the fan media, and it would certainly continue as the press began its own drive to predict which young woman would accompany the Doctor on his new adventures.

Speculation kicked into high gear after the announcement of Eccleston in late March 2004, and in a startlingly ironic twist, one of the first names circulated at the time was actually the woman who would eventually win the role. Actress/singer Billie Piper, according to BBC News, was 'in the running' to play Rose, but at this early juncture, no-one believed a word of it. Could a former pop starlet be interested in the role ... and more importantly, would the production want her? 'It may be that the idea has been mooted,' said Piper's agent to *Radio Times* in their 30 March 2004, edition, 'but it's not a conversation I have had.' The *Radio Times* report noted that an announcement wasn't expected for another two months, according to a BBC spokesperson (who was right on the money as far as timing went). The *Western Daily Press* picked up on the rumours about Piper the next day. 'Billie, married to DJ and TV producer Chris Evans, has told friends she would dearly love to work on the new series of the cult show watched by audiences across the globe,' the report said. 'The BBC remained tight-lipped yesterday but told the *Western Daily Press* it is not ruling Billie out for the part of the Doctor's glamorous sidekick Rose Tyler, despite her limited acting experience.'

Billie Piper, it seemed, was a long shot, so attention began focusing elsewhere. The BBC's *Pure Soap* website pointed toward rumours that Anna Friel, who had played the lesbian character Beth on *Brookside* for several years, was one of the 'names' being looked at for the new series. That spiralled into more than a simple mention later in the month, as the *Daily Express* ran an article entitled 'Who'll Be The Doctor's Girl?' on 24 April: 'Three actresses are vying for the role of Doctor Who's assistant in the £13 million remake of the show,' they claimed. 'Former *Brookside* beauty Anna Friel, *Spooks* actress Keeley Hawes and *Casualty's* Loo Brealey are in the frame to star alongside new Doctor Who, Christopher Ecclestone [sic].' Of course, these stories had to be approached with a degree of scepticism; this report also noted that David Jason (*Only Fools and Horses*, *A Touch of Frost*) and Helen Mirren (*Prime Suspect*) were 'among the big names mentioned as having possible roles.' Friel, Hawes and Brealey rapidly became the popular choices in several newspapers and their websites, all picking up the same news feeds mentioning the three actresses, while Anna Friel also rated a mention as a possible companion in Marina Hyde's 29 April 'Diary' column in the *Guardian*: 'Rumours, then, that Christopher's co-star is to be Anna Friel – latterly of regular "Diary" feature "That Anna Friel's SUCH a pleasure to work with" – seem unfortunate in the extreme. Perhaps it's too soon to take things overly personally, but the second that Bernard Ingham's installed as Davros we'll know something very rum is afoot.' Ingham was best known for acting as Prime Minister Margaret Thatcher's chief press secretary in the 1980s. The speculation went as far as 26 April's *Wales on Sunday* presenting a photo spread with pictures of Friel, Hawes and Brealey.

Another name that had been making the rounds was that of Carla Henry, a young actress who had previously been seen as Donna Clark, the best friend to budding gay youth Nathan Maloney (Charlie Hunnam) in Davies's *Queer as Folk*. Given several indications that Davies was quite comfortable with using both actors and crew that he'd previously worked with, Henry could certainly have been a good fit for the part. Henry was, in fact, seen meeting with Davies in late April at his office, an indication that she could possibly have been under consideration for Rose.

On 24 May 2004, the answer became clear: Billie Piper would join the cast in the role of Rose Tyler, according to press releases and reports in the popular media. While her name had been in the papers as early as September, earlier presumptions that this had been due simply to lobbying by her publicity agent had been unfounded, but her name had recently left the spotlight in favour of others. The *Daily Mail* was first online with the breaking news; in an article entitled 'Evans Moves a Few Rungs Down the Property Ladder', about Piper's entrepreneur husband Chris Evans, it also mentioned the following: 'As well as winning the part of Doctor Who's assistant in the new BBC series, the former pop singer has gained her first starring role in a movie.' The same day's *Media Guardian* also noted: 'BBC drama bosses still want Mrs Chris Evans, aka Billie Piper'. The 25 May edition of the *Independent* stated unequivocally: 'Billie Piper will play Doctor Who's assistant in the new BBC series. The 21-year-old said she was "thrilled" to have landed the role of Rose Taylor [sic]'.

Said the official BBC press release: 'Billie Piper is confirmed to play Rose Tyler, companion to Doctor Who, it was announced today by Julie Gardner, Head of Drama, BBC Wales. The former singer who made her acting debut last year in the critically-acclaimed BBC1 drama serial *Canterbury Tales: The Miller's Tale*, will star alongside Christopher Eccleston in the forthcoming 13-part drama series which returns to BBC1 early next year.' Executive producer Julie Gardner was quoted as saying, 'Billie is beautiful, funny and intelligent. We needed to find a unique, dynamic partner for Christopher Eccleston, and Billie fits the bill perfectly. She will make an extraordinary Rose Tyler. Doctor Who has his new assistant!'

Born on 22 September 1982, Billie Paul Piper was brought up in a Swindon housing estate and began taking dance lessons at age five; by age seven, she was filming soft-drink commercials in America as well as taking a brief film role as an extra in *Evita* (1996) starring Madonna. She won a scholarship to the Sylvia Young Theatre School in London in her teenage years – beating a fellow three hundred hopefuls for a place in the renowned school, which launched the careers of singers Louise Redknapp, Emma Bunton, Nicole and Natalie Appleton and actress Daniella Westbrook among many others over the years – and moved to London to live with her aunt and uncle. 'I was very emotional and homesick,' she later told *HELLO!* magazine. 'I'd only just moved to a new secondary school and had gone through the stage of making all new friends. But I knew I wanted it so badly and if I didn't take the opportunity I'd regret it.' While she filmed several commercials and even had a bit part on *EastEnders*, her first true big break came when she starred in a commercial for *Smash Hits* magazine, becoming a 'spokesmodel' for a year until she was scouted by the head of Virgin Music's Innocent label, who signed her up aged 15.

'Because We Want To' was her first hit, topping the charts in 1998 – making her the youngest female vocalist to hit the exalted top position since Helen Shapiro in 1961. Billie Piper – or simply Billie, as she was generally known during her pop career – was very much in the spotlight; she once performed for American President Bill Clinton, whose appreciation of her talents was enthusiastic. She followed her success up with promotion of her first album, 'Honey to the B' (1999), which went platinum and led her toward a very hectic and busy schedule over the next two years, producing two additional chart-topping hits, 'Girlfriend' and 'Night and Day'. Her second album, 'Walk of Life', came out during the summer of 2000 ... but was accompanied by tabloid gossip, as she collapsed in a bar amidst rumours of burnout and drugs (around the same time she'd split with Richie Neville, formerly of the boy band 5ive) and threats by a stalker after an appearance on the *Pepsi Chart* show. Her career started cooling off, with rumours running rampant that her record label would soon drop her. Late in 2000, after an appearance on a radio show hosted by Chris Evans, the two began dating, and in May of the following year, despite a sixteen year age gap, they married in Las Vegas. After the wedding, Piper disappeared from the music scene. She eventually turned back to acting, and in 2003 starred in *Canterbury Tales: The Miller's Tale*, following this with several film roles, including *The Calcium Kid* (2004), *Bella and the Boys* (2004), *Things To Do Before*

You're 30 (2004) and *Spirit Trap* (2005).

'*Doctor Who* is an iconic show and I am absolutely thrilled to be playing the part of Rose Tyler,' Piper said in the BBC press release. 'I am also looking forward to working with Christopher Eccleston and writer Russell T Davies.'

Davies was equally ebullient: 'The Doctor's companion is one of the most important and cherished roles in the history of TV drama. I'm delighted that someone of Billie's talent is coming on board the TARDIS, to travel through time and space.'

Reaction to Piper's casting was broad; here was a woman often obsessed-over by the tabloids now being given one of the most prominent roles on British television. The *Daily Express* featured a large colour photograph of Piper in their 25 May edition and a teaser on the front page. The *Daily Record* of Scotland said, 'So Billie Piper is to be Doctor Who's new assistant. Pretty young girl hooks up with old weirdo who wonders what planet he's on – inspired stuff. But hasn't she done that already?' (This would be just the first of many such jokes at the expense of Piper's then husband.) 'Dr Who's new buddy ... all the way from planet pop' said the free London newspaper *Metro*.

But the *Daily Express* the following day was very positive about Piper taking the job. 'Just What the Doctor Ordered,' it pronounced. As columnist Marcus Dunk wrote, 'Whether they're escaping from Daleks, combating Sea Devils or helping to save Earth from an intergalactic war, the life of a *Doctor Who* companion has always been fraught with danger and full of adventure. It's safe to say ... that none has been quite as young or as nubile as Billie Piper.' Nicola Bryant, who had played Peri Brown opposite two former Doctors (Peter Davison and Colin Baker), told the *Express* that the benefits of being a *Doctor Who* companion far outweighed the drawbacks. 'It sounds like a cliché,' she said, 'but when you join *Doctor Who* you are entering an extended family and every year I still attend conventions around the world and get incredible fan mail. I'm still in touch with the old Doctors, and some of the assistants are among my closest friends.' Bryant noted that Piper would probably not have to endure some of Peri's more outrageous costumes. 'My first scene had me in a bikini and I seemed to wear revealing clothing for the rest of the series.' And on the budget: 'Their budget will be bigger, too. We had to work very hard because whenever we blew anything up, we were only allowed one take. As an actress, nothing really compares with *Doctor Who* because its appeal is so overwhelming.'

Louise Jameson, who had been cast as Tom Baker's companion Leela with an eye to adding some sex appeal to the show in the 1970s, was more reflective in her comments to the *Daily Express*: 'I wanted Leela to be strong and tough, not some screaming girl who couldn't take the action. But I also had to wear a tight leather costume.' She noted that she'd been very disappointed that her character had left the series by getting married (to another Gallifreyan like the Doctor): 'I'd have preferred to have died trying to rescue the Doctor.' But Jameson was far more positive about the series today: 'What's really incredible about *Doctor Who* is how loyal fans are. When there have been gaps in my work over the years, I've always managed to get work that is a spin-off from those few months of doing *Doctor Who*. I still try to attend conventions and meet the fans of the show whenever I can. Billie should be aware of the huge interest. It can take you by surprise. But she's probably used to coping with the media by now.' The *Mirror* also offered advice from a former companion, Lalla Ward, who had played Romana (and later married Tom Baker): 'Billie should bear in mind that the show is very hard work – and she could easily become typecast. All the girls had the same problem, you came out of it feeling you had to prove you weren't just the Time Lord's floozy.'

Sylvia Young, the founder of the theatre school Piper had attended early in her adolescence, told the *Sunday Express* in late May that Piper was 'brilliant', noting that: '... a drama coach described her as "very talented, indeed potentially brilliant". He went on to say that she had an incredible comedic talent, too. This is one of the hardest kinds of acting, and Billie excelled. She was without doubt of National Theatre quality. From the second she stepped into our school for her first audition, I knew there was something special about her. There wasn't an area she was weak in, she just did very well all round. Teachers always noted her application, her talent and her wide repertoire. We always knew that her real talent lay in acting. She only got into the singing side by mistake.' Young also referred to her as 'Britain's answer to Nicole Kidman.'

Piper was certainly used to massive media attention, but none of that mattered to Davies, who had made a careful and considered choice in casting her, regardless of press reactions . 'It was a long, thorough search to find Billie – despite the fact that the tabloids have been touting her name for months now!' Davies told the official BBC *Doctor Who* website. 'We auditioned all sorts of actors – some famous, some unknown – but we've now met with Billie three times, and she's absolutely perfect, and very close to the description of Rose on the page – I think Billie's 21, and Rose is 19, so that's a great fit! ... Over the course of 13 episodes, Rose will change and grow, and hopefully, we can keep that story going in the years to come.' Davies noted to *Doctor Who Magazine* that it 'wasn't exactly the search for Scarlet O'Hara, but it was close!' He noted that Piper had indeed been on their shortlist for some time, that she was 'perfect – shining and clever and independent,' just like the character he'd envisaged all along.

As Davies told the official site, he didn't want to give too much away at this point; he wanted the viewers to discover it alongside her. 'We should all start this adventure together!' he noted. 'But suffice to say, I think the companion is as pivotal to these adventures as the Doctor himself – Rose can be our eyes, discovering spaceships and alien creatures with awe and wonder, and a vital sense of humour. When I was a kid, I always imagined becoming the companion. Now, at last, I'm close, cos I get to write her!' Davies told *Doctor Who Magazine* that Piper, as well as the other actresses who had auditioned for the role, read parts of episode one, 'Rose', specifically scenes 28, 48, 49 and 75, as well as scene two of episode two, 'The End of the World'. Piper was officially cast on 21 May 2004.

Reactions from *Doctor Who* fans were mixed. For years, there had been occasional press reports about *Doctor Who* companions that were cast purely for their sex appeal; singer Britney Spears's name had been bandied about as often as reports of revivals of the series. 'Stunt casting' in the past had often been a problem, sometimes catastrophic; reaction to the casting of former child star Bonnie Langford as the sixth Doctor's companion had been extremely critical, a problem compounded when the writing and direction had given her somewhat two-dimensional character almost nothing to do. (Langford would prove the critics wrong many years later when her character, Melanie Bush, was revived in the audio dramas range and proved what she could do given the right material.) Piper might have been no exception to this, except for the acclaim she'd won in the recent *Canterbury Tales* series ... but much of fandom wasn't having it.

BBC News and the *Register* both printed reports in late May that judged fan reaction to the casting. '*Doctor Who* fans are apparently beside themselves with excitement at the news that former popstress Billie Piper will become Doctor Who's new assistant for the scheduled return of the roving Time Lord,' the *Register* article noted, quoting DWAS spokesman Antony Wainer: 'She's a very pretty lady, her acting credentials have been proven and she will have a wide appeal.' Both articles discussed fan reaction, referring to the *Outpost Gallifrey* Forum as examples of both schools of thought: fantastic casting versus publicity stunt casting. Stunt casting 'does remain my major worry,' wrote John Dorney, 'because it's easy to forget that some of these naysayers are members of the general public, not just *Who* fans. Some of them will read the news of the casting and dismiss it.' Bob Furnell had a different take: 'I've not seen her acting ... so I really don't have a preconceived notion about her. As long as she is good in the part, plays the role well, and they don't have her sing in the show, I don't have an opinion one way or another.' Paul Hayes was quite optimistic: 'I have to admit that, as for most people in the UK, the memory of her pop career jars a little, but from everything I've read, she's a good actress.'

Yet there would still be lingering questions until Piper actually appeared in the role the following year. As Gary Merchant wrote, 'I have no real problems with Billie Piper as Rose, but assuming she can do the job, I think there's a danger in her acting being overshadowed by the baggage she brings with her, as was the case in the eighties with Bonnie Langford ... I think it's that point which most people are concerned about – it's the Evans connection that the press tend to latch onto here in the UK, which might have a negative effect on Billie, however good she may be as Rose ... Give Billie Piper a chance. By all means criticise all you want after the series is shown, but to lay into her before she's even appeared on a single frame of film is hardly fair.'

Focus on Piper's forthcoming *Doctor Who* role nevertheless encouraged the British tabloids to continue their coverage of her ... mainly in articles focusing on her personal life, which would include stories that her marriage was on the rocks as the production date approached. 'When Billie Piper hooked up with Chris Evans, 16 years her senior, people doubted it would last. Nearly four years down the track, the pair are still together – but could Billie's new-found acting success bring about the end of their relationship?' wrote a columnist for the *Mirror* only a few days prior to the start of production. Piper had been filming *Spirit Trap* in Romania, and the tabloids, always loving a juicy story, took the time to report on Piper's 'disappearance' halfway through with co-star Sam Troughton (the grandson of former *Doctor Who* actor Patrick Troughton). These stories would continue throughout the production of the first season of the new series, including noting Piper's subsequent break-up with Evans around the start of 2005.

However, any misgivings about Piper's acting ability, from both the media and fandom, slowly began to dissipate. 'Give her a chance' was the oft-mentioned phrase; after all, she was one link in a chain that also included Christopher Eccleston, the production team and the writers. Ironically, when the series eventually debuted, Piper would turn out to be one of the most critically acclaimed aspects of it , giving a *tour-de-force* performance and making Rose Tyler one of the best drawn companions to the Time Lord ever to appear.

DELIVERANCE OF THE DALEKS

Very few people would disagree with one fundamental statement: the Daleks helped make *Doctor Who* the institution it is today. In 1963, it was the first appearance of these pepper pot-shaped metal monsters that transformed *Doctor Who* from a Saturday evening lark into must-see television, as all seven actors to portray the Doctor in the original series faced the nasties and helped thwart their goals of universal domination. The Daleks have always been more than just villains; they are the quintessence of evil personified in the *Doctor Who* universe, and perhaps one of the most important icons in the series's long history.

Doctor Who without the Daleks? The concept scarcely bears thinking about.

But a series revival without the Daleks was indeed looming large as the summer of 2004 rolled on. The Daleks are co-owned by the BBC and the estate of the late Terry Nation, the writer/producer who first created them back in 1963 for the seven-part serial that introduced them. Where the Daleks appeared, and how that appearance played out, was often the subject of very complicated negotiations; Virgin Publishing had not been able to secure them for their line of *Doctor Who* novels, but BBC Books later acquired them for two instalments, *War of the Daleks* (1997) and *Legacy of the Daleks* (1998), both penned by a writer Nation had known personally, John Peel. Telos Publishing also managed to gain permission to use the creatures for their final *Doctor Who* novella, Simon Clark's *The Dalek Factor*, in 2004. Big Finish, meanwhile, had acquired the rights to the Daleks for both their *Doctor Who* original audio productions and their own spin-off series, *Dalek Empire*, in a deal separately negotiated with Roger Hancock Ltd – one of whose principal concerns had always been to ensure that, in line with Nation's own wishes during his lifetime, the Daleks were depicted as threatening adversaries, and not made the subject of humour. One Big Finish drama to have featured the Daleks was *Jubilee*, a 2003 adventure that starred Colin Baker as the Doctor. *Jubilee* was written by Rob Shearman, and the story dealt with a lone Dalek isolated from its compatriots, and forced to contend *mano-a-mano* with the Doctor. That story would be the inspiration for Shearman's eventual script for the new series of *Doctor Who*, which he began working on in late 2003. 'I'm a bit of a traditionalist, really,' Shearman wrote on the *Outpost Gallifrey* Forum. 'I think that if you bring back the Daleks to a modern audience, then you should bring back the *Daleks*. Not some strange, unrecognisable spider variant. Not something which feels apologetic. If you think that the show can't resurrect a monster without apologising for it – and I strongly doubt whether "Revenge of the Taran Beast" is on Russell's schedules – then don't resurrect it at all.'

The Daleks were a part of the plan for the new series from day one, and everyone at the time thought it would happen without incident. As previously noted, the first indication that the Daleks might not appear after all was reported on in November 2003 by the *Sun*, indicating 'ongoing rights issues'. That information was brought up again in the 28 March 2004 edition of *Manchester Online*, which noted that the new Doctor might never meet the Daleks: '*Doctor Who* star Christopher Eccleston could be denied a showdown with the dreaded Daleks in his latest role – because of a legal row,' stated the article. 'The Corporation does not own the copyright to the metallic-voiced alien robots and producers have been forced to negotiate with representatives for the late sci-fi writer Terry Nation, who created the Daleks in the 1960s. So far, no agreement has been reached and *Doctor Who*'s Manchester-based writer, Russell T Davies, is battling against his script deadlines as negotiations continue. Mr Davies said: "The estate is protecting an important property, after all, and I can appreciate why they are being so careful."' At the time, however, there was nothing to indicate that negotiations weren't ongoing.

In fact, there was a subtle disconnect behind the scenes. Shearman had been informed that rights to the Daleks had all been worked out, and such stories in the press were only idle speculation. Indeed, the 30 March edition of the *Daily Star* noted that rights issues had been completely resolved; the paper even went so far as to declare the Daleks had been completely redesigned (to look 'more like something out of the *Terminator* movies'). Quoted the *Daily Star* from a BBC source: 'We spared no expense to get the Daleks and we're going to drag them into the 21st Century.' The *Star* was not alone; the *Daily Mail* also included a piece noting that the BBC had apparently come to an agreement within the past week in a deal that paid 'well over the odds' for the 'ratings guarantee' that the Daleks would bring to the new series. In other quarters, however, rights issues continued to be rumoured, as if the Daleks' appearance was nowhere near a done deal. Nearly a month later, the *Daily Express* joined the fray, suggesting that the Daleks would now be able to hover: '... about eight feet above the floor. I know kids were terrified by the old Daleks, but the latest models will have a new generation of children cowering behind their sofa cushions.' Fans of the original series were quick to point out that the Daleks had already achieved flight, in the serial 'Remembrance of the Daleks' transmitted during the twenty-fifth season in 1988. (Indeed, even the second season story 'The Chase' in 1965 had contained a scene implying, but not showing, that a Dalek had ascended a flight of stairs.)

When the *Daily Star* next reported the situation on 4 May 2004, it insisted the rights issues had been sorted out: '*Doctor Who*'s most memorable foes are to return to the BBC in a deal worth £250,000.' Again it was mentioned that the BBC jointly owned the rights to the Daleks with Terry Nation, but that it still needed permission to feature them in the new series. 'Show producers are already having fun giving the Daleks more powers. The formerly floor-bound machines will be able to fly.' The story noted that the Daleks might try to take over London, though at the time, only Shearman's script, which featured one Dalek and took place nowhere near London, had been written. The *Express* also picked up this story, calling it 'ex-tor-tion-ate!' and noting that the deal 'means that the formidable baddies can get ready to terrify an entirely new generation.' Keith Aitken penned an editorial in the *Express* two days later: 'Can't share, I'm afraid, in the hoo-hah over the Beeb shelling out a quarter of a million to the estate of Terry Nation for the right to revive his brilliant creation, the Daleks, in its new version of *Doctor Who*. The BBC knows it wouldn't be *Doctor Who* without Daleks. That's the measure of Nation's genius in rising above his budget to create a monster that, uniquely, didn't look like an actor in a rubber suit, and which is still the scariest sci-fi baddie of all.'

All great stories ... but sadly misinformed. At some point in the spring, prior to the start of production, Shearman was informed that negotiations had failed, and that the production team did not have the rights to the Daleks. Shearman was asked to write a new script, with a new adversary created by Davies, which he began work on while the situation remained out of public view. That changed in the first week of July, when word finally broke that the rights hadn't been secured. 'After lengthy negotiations,' reported a BBC spokesperson, 'the BBC and Terry Nation have been unable to reach an agreement on the terms of the use of the Daleks. The BBC offered the very best deal possible but ultimately we were not able to give the level of editorial influence that the Terry Nation estate wished to have.'

According to BBC News, the Nation estate was 'bitterly disappointed' by the failure to reach a deal, while Tim Hancock of Roger Hancock Ltd stressed that he felt the BBC was trying to: '... ruin the brand of the Daleks. We wanted the same level of control over the Daleks that we have enjoyed for the last 40 years. If the BBC wanted to re-make any of George Lucas's films, you can bet George Lucas would have something to say about it.' Hancock accused the BBC in several reports of putting out misleading information about the reasons a deal had not been made, suggesting that the BBC had attempted recently to commission an animated series about 'gay Daleks' for BBC3. The recent appearance of the Daleks in a Warner Bros live action/animated hybrid film, *Looney Tunes: Back in Action* had been approved by the BBC without consultation with the Nation estate, Hancock noted. 'We want to protect the integrity of the brand,' he told BBC News, and added that the estate would be willing to make a new deal if the BBC accepted the arrangement that had been in place for the previous forty years. The *Manchester Evening News* quoted Hancock as saying, 'Without us the BBC would have screwed up the integrity of the Daleks' image years ago.' Hancock later made an online statement: 'I'm very sorry for *Doctor Who* fans. We accept the Daleks need modernising, and are all for it. All we ask is that they consult us on the designs. But the BBC are not prepared to.'

Davies, naturally, was disappointed, as he told BBC News, but felt that it would not affect the success of the new series: 'We are disappointed that the Daleks will not be included but we have a number of new and exciting monsters. And I can confirm we have created a new enemy for the Doctor which will keep viewers on the edge of their seats.'

In the *Independent* on 3 July, commentator John Walsh noted that it was outrageous that the new series wouldn't feature the Daleks. 'I was one of the original short-trousered *Doctor Who* fans who watched through latticed fingers the first gliding steps of the metal myrmidons, and I'm sorry not to see them return.' As for the reasons, Walsh could only speculate: 'They had other commitments; the timing wasn't right for this stage of their career; they weren't in a good place right now; they were scheduled to appear on Broadway, in a musical called *Hello Dalek*. I pictured them on the phone to their agent, shouting "Neg-o-ti-ate! Neg-o-ti-ate!".'

News of the loss of the Daleks from *Doctor Who* spread like wildfire. The *Express* covered a planned protest march by fans in Southampton, noting that the return of the series without its metal monsters would be a shame: 'While most fans are obviously delighted the series has finally come back, there are fears that it may bear very little resemblance to the original. And the Doctor not facing the Daleks is almost unthinkable.' MP Tim Collins, from whom the media now routinely sought comments regarding big *Doctor Who* events, told the *Sun*, '*Doctor Who* without the Daleks is like fish without chips. It's important the BBC does a deal.' Fellow MP Bob Russell told the East Anglian *Daily Times*: '*Doctor Who* without the Daleks is not going to be impossible, but it will be very difficult. After the Doctor himself and the police phone box, the Daleks are the most obvious part. I think it is very regrettable. You have to bear in mind that the *Doctor Who* series is a massive income earner – it's a very successful international export. So there is a serious side to this, alongside the enjoyment that's gained from the programme.'

The *Sun* gained some prominence in its *Doctor Who* coverage during this time, as it immediately launched a 'campaign' to save the Daleks from being 'exterminated' from the new series. The paper intimated that the BBC were 'desperate for hi-tech versions of the Time Lord's arch-enemies' to appear in the show, but that talks had broken down only the previous Wednesday when Nation's estate demanded control of Dalek storylines and feared producers planned to make the creatures 'too evil.' A BBC 'insider' spoke to the *Sun*, noting: 'It's hard to imagine *Doctor Who* without Daleks but it seems we have no choice. The Nation estate's demands were completely unacceptable. They care a lot about the Daleks. We fear they have been lost forever.' The *Sun* also ran an article, fairly obviously meant either in jest or simply as a space-filler, about 'New Yorkers joining the fight' to get the Daleks back. 'The Daleks hit New York yesterday as the *Sun*'s campaign to save them went global ... Doctor Who's arch enemy rumbled through aptly-named TIMES Square sporting a *Sun* hat and Cross of St George flag.' The *Sun*'s 'campaign' would continue for only a brief time, but the publicity it gained from this would be milked quite extensively for many months to come, and would later lead to often-mentioned claims of 'success' in masterminding the return of the metal villains to the series ... even though all evidence suggests that their campaign had no effect on the ultimate outcome. As production began, and prior to the matter having finally been resolved, there were Dalek sightings around the location shoots ... but these would turn out to be sightings of the *Sun's* own gold Dalek, placed nearby for added publicity. Raymond Cusick, the designer who had created the look of the Daleks in 1963 while working for the BBC, was also sought out by the *Sun* for his views on the situation: . 'It'll be very sad if the Daleks are exterminated. When people remember *Doctor Who*, they remember Daleks, it's as simple as that. Good on the *Sun* for campaigning to bring them back.' The *Western Morning News* meanwhile noted on 6 July that West Country *Doctor Who* fans were 'joining the campaign' to reinstate the Daleks.

A month later, the situation changed again. On 4 August, Mal Young of the BBC and Tim Hancock for Roger Hancock Ltd announced that they had reached an agreement that allowed the Daleks to return to *Doctor Who*. 'I am absolutely delighted that the Terry Nation estate and the BBC have been able to reach agreement on terms for the use of the Daleks in the new *Doctor Who* series,' Hancock said in a BBC press release. 'We look forward to working closely with the production team in the forthcoming months.' Young added, 'As well as coming face-to-face with a number of new and exciting monsters, it's good news that the Doctor will also do battle with his arch enemy, the Daleks, in a series which promises to surprise and entertain a new generation.' Antony Wainer of the *Doctor Who* Appreciation Society told BBC News, '*Doctor Who* without Daleks would be like Morecambe without Wise or Wimbledon without strawberries.'

There were rumours that the whole thing had been a publicity stunt, but these were strongly denied by Davies, the production office and the BBC. While Shearman returned to work on his original script, putting aside the replacement he had been writing, the *Sun* made its first claims of victory in its campaign to bring the Daleks back. The *Guardian*, quite amused by the whole thing, noted, 'Oh Lordy. Stand by for a gloating "It was the *Sun* wot won it" style headline in tomorrow's current bun ... The *Sun* will no doubt be claiming its Save The Daleks campaign – launched last month after the BBC said negotiations with the estate of *Doctor Who* writer Terry Nation to bring the croaky-voiced baddies back had broken down – made all the difference. Maybe they have a point. After all, the impact of plastering a Dalek with *Sun* stickers, a *Sun* hat and a cross of St George flag and wheeling it through New York's Times Square, accompanied by reporter Bryan Flynn, should not be underestimated.'

Whether success had been secured through a publicity campaign by a tabloid newspaper, or through the closed-door dealings between two interested parties, didn't much matter: the Daleks, quintessentially part of *Doctor Who* since its foundation, were back in action.

NEW NAMES JOIN THE PRODUCTION

In the same *Doctor Who Magazine* article that had noted Christopher Eccleston would be playing the ninth Doctor rather than a new character (confirming that there was to be no reboot; this would be a continuation of the mythos), Davies had announced the names of the series's new script editors, Elwen Rowlands, former script editor of *Carrie's War* (2004), and Helen Raynor, who had script edited the BBC's ongoing afternoon soap opera *Doctors* (which started in 2000). As both later told *Doctor Who Magazine*, they would become responsible for everything from keeping track of which episode is at which draft to development of the ideas, the characters and the tone: 'A lot of what a script editor does involves acting as a sounding board, collating everyone's input and then crucially, being a point of contact for the writer.' Rowlands and Raynor split the script editing duties for the first season; Rowlands would work primarily with Davies and Cornell, while Raynor worked with Shearman, Moffat and Gatiss, as well as to a small extent with Davies. 'That said,' Raynor told *Doctor Who Magazine,* 'the order the episodes are being filmed in changed after we'd divvied them up, so Elwen is in fact now across the first four episodes and working flat out, while I've got four episodes back to back at the end of the schedule.' They noted: 'Rob Shearman is chucking the "ooh" moments around like confetti [and] Paul Cornell's episode is so moving it brought a tear to the eye. Mark Gatiss's script has some hilarious moments and the sheer naughtiness of Russell's "Aliens of London" had us chuckling away all day. We wait delivery of Steven Moffat's script with bated breath.'

Other new faces were soon to join the production team. Phil Collinson noted in an interview with *TV Zone* magazine in early May that the new production manager on the series would be Helen Vallis, whose credits included being associate producer on *Hearts of Gold* (2003), *Care* (2000), *Harpur and Iles* (1997) and *Streetlife* (1995). The *Professional Casting Review* newsletter broke the story on 23 May that director Keith Boak would be the 'helmer of the first block', at the time thought to be referring to the first group of episodes recorded (later to be confirmed as episodes one, four and five).

Doctor Who Magazine issue 344 revealed that Lucinda Wright would be the show's costume designer. Wright's credits included *Maisie Raine* (1998), *Fish* (2000), *The Jury* (2002) and *Murphy's Law* (2003) on television, and the film *Deathwatch* (2002). The same issue interviewed incoming production designer Edward Thomas, whose credits included *Darkness Falls* (1999), *The Mystery of Edwin Drood* (1993), *The Last Leprechaun* (1998) and *Merlin: The Return* (1999). As production designer, Thomas noted, 'I will be responsible for the overall look and feel of all 13 episodes ... I will have lots of help in the form of art directors, illustrators, set designers, CGI and a whole host of other creative people who will assist me in introducing a brand new look, whilst retaining a few of the most unforgettable features.'

Award winning comics artist Bryan Hitch, winner of the 2003 *SFX* magazine Reader Award for Best Comic Book, whose work included such titles as *The Authority* (1999-2000), *JLA* (2000-2001) and *The Ultimates* (2003-2004) as well as a one-issue strip for *Doctor Who Magazine* issue 139 (1988), was announced in early June as the concept artist for the series. 'This is entirely thanks to *SFX*,' Davies noted. 'The Head of Drama at the BBC had talked about getting a concept artist right from the start, so we were already beginning to think about it. Then out of the blue Nick Setchfield at *SFX* got in touch, saying that Bryan Hitch had heard about the new series of *Doctor Who* and wanted to help.' Davies noted that he had been an old comics fan, and was certainly a fan of Hitch's work. 'I showed [Julie Gardner and Phil Collinson] the comics, they went mental, we summoned the Hitch, and here we are ... Now Bryan can give us concepts and wild ideas to spark us off in new directions. Thank you *SFX*, it's really appreciated!' The interview Davies gave *SFX* noted that Hitch would be in charge of the signature look of the series and would work alongside Thomas to develop the TARDIS interior as well as the series's aliens and technology.

'Ed [Thomas] and I attached to the project around the same time in very early pre-production and we've both been active on the game for about six weeks to two months,' Hitch noted in an online message a few days later. 'The crew is all set (just about) and major design work with the whole design team has been running about a month. A series this ambitious doesn't get done quickly and something as iconic as the TARDIS design is a lengthy process of approvals (though it actually went swimmingly). And to clarify, as production designer Ed's genius is employed in overseeing and coordinating the overall visual scope of the series from locations, costumes, lighting, set construction and of course design. He's a member of staff, I'm freelance.' Hitch noted he was a consultant who 'rushes into meetings, flings ideas and sketches at anyone and everyone and runs out leaving folks scratching their heads and looking shell-shocked.' Moreover, Hitch mentioned that what he'd seen so far for the new series was beyond anyone's expectations.

Visual effects work was commissioned from the CGI effects house The Mill, announced first on the *Planet Who* website. A 'world leading visual effects company with bases in the globe's most important advertising centres', The Mill is a provider of pioneering visuals including their Oscar-winning work on the film *Gladiator* (2000). Their MillTV subsidiary has worked for years with the BBC and Channel 4 with some of broadcasting's most respected producers and directors, contributing effects to, amongst others, *The Nile* (2004) and a 2004 recreation of the D-Day landings for BBC1. MillTV ultimately created over 1,300 visual effects for the new series of *Doctor Who* over the year prior to transmission, working with a team of ten CGI artists, seven 'flame and shake compositors' and a digital matte painter to create the look, often putting in twelve-hour days, six times per week for eight months to complete their work. 'We saw many visual effects companies while looking for the right people,' Julie Gardner noted on MillTV's website, '[and] were blown away by the level of compassion, commitment and imagination in MillTV's pitch ... The team, led by Will Cohen and Dave Houghton, have worked tirelessly to complete a groundbreaking number of visual effects. The great thing about working with MillTV is that all their painstaking work is undertaken to support the scripts, rather than to dominate the story.' *Media Guardian* also later covered this on 20 July, in an article entitled '*Doctor Who* gets Hollywood Treatment', in which it was noted that the Mill's remit was to 'bedazzle' younger viewers accustomed to the impressive effects featured in such films as *The Matrix* and *Lord of the Rings*. 'Effects that were seen as ground-breaking when *Dr Who* first aired obviously won't cut it with today's audience,' Dave Throssell, the head of The Mill's TV department, told the *Guardian*. 'It will be a tough job because it will demand feature film effects on a TV schedule.' The article noted that the series had been famous for its 'low production values, making a virtue out of its shoestring budget.'

DAVIES SPEAKS TO THE FANS

Davies began penning a series of articles, 'Production Notes', for *Doctor Who Magazine*. Starting in issue 341, Davies immediately shaped the dynamic of his continuing column: 'You will hate this page,' he wrote. 'Maybe not now, but in the months to come, oh yes.' The three reasons he posited: fans would want to know who plays the Doctor, who plays Rose, and were the Daleks coming back. Obviously, these questions would be answered in the popular media ... but it was certainly a great hook to keep readers coming back. At the time, there was still no firm date of production, but the grand chaos that existed behind the scenes was perfectly normal for a television series, according to Davies. He closed his first entry noting three words that would appear in the script for the first episode: *radial, balcony* and *shunt*. Davies would continue this teasing over his series of articles, first bringing up the Moxx of Balhoon as one of the new series's creations, which most readers took to be a joke, as well as revealing individual episode titles – after a spurious debate as to whether or not there would actually *be* episode titles – such as 'Rose' and 'The End of the World'.

The entries in Davies's 'Production Notes' column were refreshing, not only for what they didn't reveal (thus avoiding spoilers), but from the sideline information gleaned from them (and from various other *Doctor Who Magazine* reports) that suggested how events were playing out behind the scenes. Davies noted that Rose Tyler's mother would be named 'Jackie', and would be a prominent character in the series, as well as mentioning a new character named 'Mickey' (later to be revealed as Rose's boyfriend). 'This programme is barmy,' Davies would later note, referring to the intense creativity going on behind the scenes.

Davies's column also continued to reassure fans as much as it gave them new information. For example, in issue 345, Davies got to the point of whether or not to consider the Christopher Eccleston incarnation as the 'ninth Doctor': 'Of course he bloody is! There is no official, co-ordinated BBC policy on this, and never will be; but ... Chris is number nine.' Davies quantified the first series as 'Series One' (rather than 'Season Twenty-Seven', to please the completists), but noted that the episodes had not been assigned individual production codes picking up from the first twenty-six seasons' worth of stories. 'Because the forthcoming series has shifted base to BBC Wales – and on a simpler level, because no one involved in the production would even stop to worry about this – the Production Codes are brand new. They don't continue from the 1996 movie, or the 1989 series. The new series is not called Season Twenty-Seven on any documents, it's Series One. And the first episode is officially episode one, not episode 697.'

IDLE HANDS ARE THE DEVIL'S PLAYTHINGS

Both press and fan interest in the new series continued throughout the spring. The first indication that perhaps things were kicking into high gear came in an interview Gardner gave to *SFX* in April. 'We start filming in the summer,' she noted, confirming earlier rumours that production was going to begin as the weather changed, 'with principal locations and studio work being done in South Wales. Being based in Cardiff offers endless possibilities – urban landscapes, countryside, beaches, historical houses are all within easy reach. There are many decisions to be made before that first camera rolls. We are currently receiving pitches from SFX companies and CGI specialists and we're still in the early stages of meetings with heads of departments.'

With indications that the production was gearing up to begin principal photography, the media circus ramped up for its own challenges ... much of it inventing controversy where none previously existed. The *Daily Telegraph* had its own go at *Doctor Who* fans, bidding Michael Grade to get into a war with fandom in early May, as he'd done in the 1980s, and to offer Eccleston a different job, painting fans as too eager and too obsessed to be of real importance. The *Daily Express* took a different approach, noting that *Doctor Who* would, in fact, be the 'jewel in the crown of the BBC Christmas schedule,' proposing that BBC1 would launch the series early, perhaps on Christmas Day 2004. 'The *Doctor Who* project has lifted off with the kind of momentum no-one could have anticipated,' the *Daily Express* quoted an unnamed source as saying. 'I don't think anyone knew how interested people would be or indeed what a huge fan base there is.'

At such a late date prior to production, both the press and the fan community would be hungry for any news that could be gleaned. Spoilers were rampant. 'In one episode,' wrote a columnist for the *Guardian* on 24 May, 'the members of the Cabinet are displayed, body-snatchers-style, as aliens hiding under human exteriors who only reveal their true selves when they lie.' Many such stories, however, were completely wrong: the *Mirror* reported on the same day that the new Doctor would face an enemy even worse than the Daleks ... in the shape of footballer David Beckham! In an obvious miscommunication mixing up the storylines of 'Rose' (the first episode) and the two-part 'Aliens of London'/'World War Three' (the fourth and fifth episodes), the *Mirror* reported that: '... a lifelike dummy of the 29-year-old football star will lead a horde of waxwork celebs in a raid on Downing Street. Becks, the leader of the sinister celebrity army, will blast everything in his path with a ray gun. BBC bosses are pitting the Time Lord against modern day figures. The models, who appear in an episode called "Aliens of London", are under the control of a deadly extra-terrestrial race known as the Autons.'

With interest running so high, there was no shortage of people who wanted to get in on the act. 'I'd really like to play Doctor Who,' said Jon Culshaw of *Dead Ringers* fame, in an interview with *Radio Times* in May 2004. 'It will be interesting to see how Christopher Eccleston plays the part. He brings a lot of intensity to what he does.' Drummer Joey Jordison of the band Slipknot had grown up watching *Doctor Who* and wanted his band to be given the chance to record the theme tune; the *Sun* even noted that the BBC were apparently interested in getting them involved. 'It turns out the nine-strong nu-metal band are obsessed with the time travelling doctor,' said the paper, which quoted Jordison as saying he was: '... excited *Doctor Who*'s coming back. It's a great show, wild and exciting. I watched it as a kid and it freaked me out. I'm 29 now and it was only a couple of years ago that I figured out what was going on.' The article noted that Slipknot had dedicated a track on their newest album to the show. A few weeks later, however, the music magazine *Kerrang* stated on its website that Slipknot were not in talks to record the theme: '... despite a report in a tabloid last week. The *Sun* "revealed" that the masked metallers were working on a song to be used for the show's comeback at the end of the year, but a spokesperson for the band denied the claims when contacted by *Kerrang*.'

When a television series is close to production, any small event can be seized upon as sufficient proof for any number of things, and dots can be connected without regard for reality. Despite the fact that the start of shooting was still several months away, the UK online gossip column *Popbitch* noted in late May: '*Doctor Who* filming at the IBM offices in Cosham right now, Eccleston running around the quad as I type.' This story had actually been sparked by the recent production by Bill Baggs of a short series of documentary specials about the 'classic' *Doctor Who* series for BBC South's regional news programme, which had involved some location recording in the area A late May report on the *This is Penarth* website featured a similar rumour: Christopher Eccleston had: '... been spotted property shopping in the town. The acclaimed star, who is taking on the title role of the cult science fiction television series, was seen looking at exclusive homes at Penarth Marina on Saturday.' Unlike the *Popbitch* article, there was a bit more reason to believe this one; the article stated that the BBC had a policy of housing its actors close to the location of filming (Penarth being a suburb of Cardiff).

The life of a *Doctor Who* celebrity, even one who hadn't yet recorded one minute of footage, becomes part of the public consciousness. Rumours circulated around this time that Eccleston had quit the production, but of course there was nothing of substance in these reports then. There were also stories about his personal life, including mentions in the *Manchester Evening News* that he had received libel damages over a claim that he'd reacted violently and aggressively toward a suggestion about how he should portray a role. These rumours began to spread in the tabloid press, presenting the actor in a less-than-flattering manner and suggesting that he was somehow reticent to undertake the role of the Doctor. However, Eccleston was very happy to be nearing the start of work on *Doctor Who*, and especially in Wales. 'I can't wait to bring my TARDIS back to Cardiff' was the title of a story in *icWales* on 20 May, in which Eccleston demonstrated his excitement at coming to work in the area: 'I think it's a whole new life for me, a whole new element to my career, and I'm looking forward to working in Cardiff because I worked there 12 years ago. I like the people and I like the place. I think it's good that it has not gone to London or Manchester, that somebody else has got this thing.' For all that, however, Eccleston was a very private individual, reluctant to give interviews about the new series. The *Doctor Who* Appreciation Society printed the following note to its members from Eccleston in early June: 'I won't be giving interviews on *Doctor Who* until I've got something to brag about. But here's a quote: I'm very excited to be the ninth Doctor Who, I want to honour its past but also bring something new, I look forward to the reaction of your readers/members.'

While Eccleston was keeping things rather low key until production began on the series, there were a few reports in late May and early June about his participation in a video for the band I Am Kloot. A report on the *NME* music website explained: 'Eccleston stars in the video to the band's new single "Proof", set for release on June 14 through Echo. A fellow Mancunian, the actor fell for the band during their five-night residency at the city's Night & Day Café last year. They decided to work on the video with mutual friend and filmmaker Krisher Stott.' 'I haven't actually met him,' I Am Kloot frontman John Bramwell told the *Belfast Telegraph* on 28 May. 'He's been to a few gigs and he got in touch. We came up with the idea for the video and we were very flattered he agreed because he's a great actor. In the video, he just stares at the camera and doesn't mime or anything. His expression just changes ever so slightly from tearful to joyous – it's very simple and intense, just small changes and it's fascinating to watch.' The band Orbital also used Eccleston's dulcet tones, sampling from his appearance in *The Second Coming*, on the track 'You Lot', released as the B-side of their single 'One Perfect Sunrise' (2004).

Spoilers – or, as Davies would later call them, Ruiners – attempted to get every piece of every story into the press, even before the series had begun shooting. The tabloids, he noted, were masters of the game, calling in favours and paying top dollar for anything and everything they could get their hands on. The *Daily Star* noted that the series would 'feature historic figures including Shakespeare, Henry VIII and Einstein – who are locked up together inside a Big Brother-style house.' The *Daily Mail* had touted guest appearances by Alfred Molina and *Amélie* star Audrey Tautou, and noted a possible storyline set in France dealing with Joan of Arc. The *Daily Express* repeated that David Jason and Helen Mirren would be appearing. Tabloids played a game of one-upmanship, with every *Doctor Who* report being regurgitated over and over again and frequently making the front page.

During June 2004, *Doctor Who* was very much a part of the public consciousness. '*Doctor Who* is about to become cool,' said the 8 June edition of the web magazine *lowculture*. 'Not the shonky old version where everything was made out of egg boxes and bubble wrap, of course (although we still think that was a little bit cool). We mean the new one, the one they're about to start filming in Wales with Christopher Eccleston and (shriek!) Billie Piper.'

Doctor Who was soon to transform itself from a fondly-remembered, but often misunderstood, family series into a modern adventure series for the 21st Century. It was no longer a target for ridicule in 'lads' magazines', but something to be taken seriously: a flagship BBC series, about to go before the cameras, sporting a leading man and lady with serious star power. People were simply paying more attention. Steven Moffat told the *Paisley Daily Express* he was 'a little embarrassed' that the new series had picked up its first award ... even before it began recording. 'Even before a single frame has been shot, we have already picked up an award for Best New Hope from a science fiction magazine. I did feel slightly embarrassed about receiving it.' Meanwhile, calling the series 'Back in Fashion', the *Western Mail* noted that while the fantastic costumes of yesterday's *Doctor Who* companions might stick in one's mind, 'they do have to compete with the Doctor's multi-coloured scarf.' None of that would necessarily be relevant, especially in light of the simplistic costuming afforded Eccleston and Piper ... but *Doctor Who* being remembered fondly for its costuming?

Hopes were high for the series, as the *Scotsman* noted in early July when it pondered the state of BBC television, and whether or not it was too late to re-establish what had been their stellar Saturday night line up for years: 'The running order of BBC's Saturday evening schedule remains chiselled in my memory. After *Basil Brush* was the exhilarating love/terror of *Doctor Who* – love, for whichever of his female assistants was then custodian of my heart; terror, lest the Cybermen, or the Daleks when we were younger, made an appearance and sent us scuttling behind the sofa.' Time would tell if *Doctor Who* would reinvigorate the BBC Saturday night line-up, as July 2004 approached ... and the cameras began to roll.

CHAPTER SEVEN:
BACK IN BUSINESS

Doctor Who, at long last, was back in production. When Lorraine Heggessey made her statement to the British press in September 2003, the natural enthusiasm and energy to be expected at such a time was tempered with measured optimism and a large dose of reality: all the false starts and promises over the years had taken their toll. The often-promised film adaptation first discussed even before the original series had been cancelled – Coast to Coast Productions, Lumiere Films, Caroline Munro ... all the rumours that had run wild across the planet – had never become a reality. The new series that was supposed to follow the TV movie in 1996 had never materialised.

So it's no surprise that, even after the casting process had been vetted through the popular press, there was still some concern. Would Doctor Who become a reality? Could fate step in and the BBC cancel the production outright? (Of course, that was never a possibility ... but it's difficult to stop speculation when people's hopes had been dashed so often.) No-one, it seemed, would be satisfied until those first images started to appear out of the production – the first glimpse of the Doctor, of the TARDIS, of Rose Tyler.

There were ongoing rumours through the first weeks of July that recording was imminent. Speculation over the date that the series entered actual production – the moment the cameras began to roll – ran rampant. And when those first images started trickling in, it was almost manna from heaven for dedicated Doctor Who fans: the Doctor was, indeed, back in action.

THE FIRST WEEK OF PRODUCTION

Principal photography on the new Doctor Who television series began on location in the streets of Cardiff on Sunday 18 July 2004, with the recording of shots that, according to a report in Doctor Who Magazine, would be for episode four, 'Aliens of London'. Cardiff residents had been warned several days ahead of schedule of the impact the production would have on the community; the NewsWales website ran an article entitled 'Dr Who Causes Traffic Chaos' on 16 July, explaining: 'Cardiff commuters will have to make way for Doctor Who next week as the BBC uses the city's streets for the filming of the new series.' The article noted that, according to their sources, Working Street and St John Street were to be closed on 20 and 21 July to make way for BBC camera crews, but that 'allowances will be made for pedestrians coming from the St David's Hall concerts.' Also, St Mary Street, High Street and Guildhall Place would be closed on 21 and 22 July for night shooting. Retailers in the Cardiff area had also been individually warned in certain places, especially near the sites where recording would actually take place. The BBC News website itself confirmed the commencement of production with a simple note: 'Shoppers in Cardiff will have a sneak preview of life in the fourth dimension as filming of the new Doctor Who series starts this week.'

'Cameras will start to roll on the new Doctor Who series on Monday, an insider has confirmed,' reported the ITV Teletext service on 16 July. The report noted that production staff in the area had been sworn to secrecy, 'not ... allowed to divulge details of plots, characters or even who is writing the music', and said that the first group of episodes entering production would be directed by Keith Boak. In fact, this was one of the first hints that episodes would be produced out of sequence; as viewers would later learn, episodes one, four and five were to enter production at the same time ... and no-one outside the production team would be the wiser for months on exactly what was going on, and when.

But even with the tight security, the location managed to become a haven for *Doctor Who* fans who wanted to be part of the return of their favourite show. Fans from the Cardiff area, and even from elsewhere, decided to make the pilgrimage to the production site – politely, for the most part, and with respect, but carrying their cameras and ready for the action. Those who came at the right times did not leave empty handed. 'After looking at the streets listed as this week's locations on the news page, I popped in to the Cardiff visitor centre in Working Street,' wrote Dave Shuttleworth of Taunton on Monday 19 July, the day after he had journeyed to Cardiff. 'I figured there was no harm in asking whether or not they could confirm that *Doctor Who* was going to be recorded outside their premises and, sure enough, not only are the crew using the street, they're using the visitor centre itself as a location, together with the pub next door.' That pub was the Toad at the Exhibition on Working Street ... though on screen, it would be seen not as a pub but as a police station! 'From there I walked out to the old Cardiff Royal Infirmary, which is a wonderfully ramshackle example of gothic decay – a great location! In the area at the front of the building was a group of about eight or ten extras, dressed as soldiers – camouflage gear, red berets and heavy rifles – together with one man dressed in a smart military uniform, with a cap ... There were various crew types wandering about and an awful lot of lighting/equipment vans and other lorries ... Back round at the front of the building, some set dressing was going on at the hospital gates – a big "metal" arch, painted black, with *Albion Hospital* in gold letters, which were being dirtied down.'

Writer Paul Mount was also present for the start of recording that Sunday. 'I managed to position myself surreptitiously near the main gates to the Hospital (renamed Albion Hospital),' he wrote, 'where a scene with a reporter was being rehearsed/filmed ... There was some reference to a General Asquith, the body being human or alien, and then the roads were closed again as a scene of a military police car and an ambulance driving through the gates was recorded. The general area was "decorated" with London-style bus stops, one of which, I noticed as I walked right past it, was bearing a London street map – the familiar red circle-style London underground symbol. The area was literally packed with people: technicians, production crew, etc, presumably Keith Boak directing from the concourse area inside the gates. There were loads of black-clad police officers brandishing machine guns; the tank had been moved nearer the gates and there were quite a few other vehicles and extras in military uniform. I caught a quick glimpse of the script in the hands of one technician and while I couldn't get close enough to have a good look I could clearly see dialogue and reference to one character speaking – Jackie.'

While initial footage was recorded in Cardiff mostly employing extras, the media continued its barrage of interest in the series's new stars, who were as yet nowhere to be seen. The *Daily Star* filled the gap by running a brief article noting that Billie Piper was interested in playing the tragic '70s porn star Linda Lovelace: 'She's spurred by her sexy role in *The Canterbury Tales*, but husband Chris Evans needs persuading,' the article read. In fact, neither Eccleston nor Piper had been to the location sets in Cardiff; they weren't scheduled to appear until two days later ... but that didn't stop intrepid fans from taking photographs of the location, in some instances encouraged by the crew. The photos included shots of a Saxon APC (military vehicle) of the British Army; the Cardiff Royal Infirmary, whose signs had been replaced to decorate it as the aforementioned Albion Hospital (site of several major sequences in the two-parter 'Aliens of London' and 'World War Three'); St German's Church and the Church of St

James the Great, two impressive buildings in Cardiff; as well as production vehicles and security. Also pictured were actors portraying red-bereted military soldiers, and the windows of the Infirmary blacked out using scaffolding and drapery; these were likely covered to allow night shooting inside the building, perhaps for the scenes featuring the Doctor, Dr Sato and the pig.

At this time, the official *Doctor Who* website began a feature called WhoSpy, which each day displayed one new photograph from the production, allowing fans to get an inside peek at the goings-on on set. This was immediately met with complaint, as the snapshots revealed very arcane information or, quite frequently, nothing at all but coffee cups or piping; this changed later in the course of production as more information was shared. (The site editors revisited their WhoSpy pictures as each episode was transmitted in the UK, clarifying what each photograph was and where and when it was taken.) The WhoSpy feature noted the very first sequence recorded for the new series: scene 21 of episode four, 'Aliens of London', which was shot on Sunday 18 July. The same photograph of the clapperboard confirmed that the series's director of photography would be Ernie Vincze, who had in his career worked on some very prestigious productions such as Stephen Poliakoff's *Shooting the Past* (1999) and, with producer Phil Collinson, *Sea of Souls* (2004); coincidentally, he had also been the cinematographer on the 1974 feature film *Got It Made*, which starred former *Doctor Who* companion Lalla Ward.

Rumours that weekend and on the Monday suggested that there would be some sort of 'official' launch and photo shoot to mark the occasion taking place early in the week. Tuesday 20 July featured exactly that, as *BBC Wales Today* was on hand with a journalist, Rebecca John, for a live on-location set visit in downtown Cardiff in front of the Howells Department Store, which had been redesignated Henrik's (for scenes set at the store in 'Rose'). John introduced an interview recorded the previous day with both Christopher Eccleston and Billie Piper, both of them in clothing they would be wearing during the series – he in a leather jacket, she (at least for the first few episodes) in a sweater. 'Gone are the trademark hats, cloaks and scarves,' the *Wales Today* interviewer noted in the broadcast. Eccleston defended his new wardrobe: 'Well I wouldn't want to put labels on it, I mean, I think in the past, each actor's made specific choices about their costume and I've made mine.'

The *Wales Today* broadcast included the very first shots of Eccleston and Piper together with Russell T Davies; all three were pictured on location in Cardiff as well as in studio, including watching some unidentified video footage. Billie Piper, for one, was very excited, but: '... trying not to feel the pressure but just accepting that ... we're trying to create something new ... with the essence of the old *Doctor Who*, but more contemporary ... Times have moved on, and so have we, and we're going to give it a different approach.' Piper also remarked on her new surroundings: 'I've only been in Cardiff now for a week, so I'm still finding my bearings, and getting used to everything, but, having a great time.' Eccleston seemed equally interested in the work that they were about to embark upon: 'It's escapism, isn't it, and a romp?'

The interview concluded, *Wales Today* then went to a live spot with John meeting Davies in front of the Howells store, where he explained that the sequences being shot were from the first few minutes of 'Rose'. He noted that the series would record approximately ninety-five percent of its footage in Cardiff (although that might subsequently have changed as the series later went on location to Monmouth and Swansea), and that Cardiff would represent itself in the past and present, as well as London and other locales. He also made it clear that the Daleks might not be present (at the time of this interview, their return still had not been officially announced) but that there'd be some new exciting monsters in store. Quite positively, though, Davies waxed on the importance of *Doctor Who* to himself, and to its fans: 'Because it's the best idea ever invented in the history of the world! I really think so. I love it. But, it's great adventure, it tells great stories about the human race, I think, about optimism, and those are good stories to tell in this age.'

That Tuesday featured some daytime recording, specifically shots of Billie Piper inside and leaving the department store (early moments of 'Rose'), as well as some extensive evening recording. London Underground signage, red buses bound for Marble Arch and Victoria, black London taxis, an *Evening Standard* van, a Royal Mail lorry, gas lamps and industrial metal dustbins and a red telephone box ... all were brought in to be used for that evening's work, which would be shot primarily at the Queen's Arcade, a shopping mall in Cardiff. The 20 July location work done here would feature in 'Rose' as the Auton attack in the closing minutes of the episode, including Clive meeting his demise while his family flees, and Jackie Tyler being accosted by the Autons that burst out of the shop windows. The evening's events were further documented by fans who caught part of the action. As David Shaw noted, 'We found the Working Street/St John Street location quite easily, and wandered past the production team vans at 5.30pm.' His daughter: '... was delighted to spot a familiar group of shop-dummy props in the back of one of the trucks, clearly indicating the return of the Autons! ... We tried to keep out of the way and were allowed to wander up and down the street until after 8pm. A few of the workers spoke to us in a friendly manner, and no-one asked us to move away. As darkness fell, the area was closed off by the police with "do not cross" tape, and some extras dressed as firemen arrived. We heard a few rehearsals and shouts of "Quiet Please!" as some scenes were [recorded].' Shaw left, and then returned early in the morning: '... to find the clear-up in full swing. Significantly, there was shattered glass all over the pavement in front of the "Classic Bride" shop, and we watched as the props were systematically removed (all the vehicles had already gone).' Another fan, Anna Roberts, described seeing one scene being recorded of a woman in a jumper and denims: 'The scene consisted of the actress ... walking across the road talking on her mobile, while a couple of the vehicles drove past and the best part of a dozen normally-dressed extras carrying shopping bags milled about. I could hear most of the dialogue, and following a line about where are you, she was talking to somebody she referred to as darling. As best I can remember the dialogue, it was: "I can't hear you, the signal's breaking up. I'm just going to do some late night shopping." Gripping, huh?' A second scene that Roberts watched featured the same actress coming out of the shopping centre.

As viewers would later realise, the actress recording her scenes at the shopping centre was Camille Coduri, playing Jackie Tyler, Rose's long-beleaguered mum. Coduri's appearance in the series would be first announced on 2 August by her own website, which said that she would play Rose's mother in six of thirteen episodes: 'Camille is thrilled to be appearing in the re-launch of the popular family science fiction show, which originally ran from 1963 to 1989 on BBC TV,' the website stated. 'She says she is "having a brilliant time" and that working on the show is "so exciting".'

Coduri's sequences on 20 July included the shooting outside the police station set (the aforementioned back door of the Toad at the Exhibition pub), where she would record her first scene for the series, as well as the use of a local shoe shop on Working Street, turned into 'Classic Brides', a shop that would see Autons in wedding gowns break free and attack her.

Fans Chris Thomas and George Duffield both watched buses and taxis being prepared to slide down the street and, in the case of one of the taxis, smash through a false window placed at the scene, much of it planned to take place near midnight. As another fan, John Smith, noted, 'Elsewhere in the street were warning signs for the London "congestion charge zone", a traffic toll recently imposed on drivers in central London, so it can be assumed that at least some scenes were set in the heart of the city, and in the present day or thereabouts.' This perhaps described items for possible daytime photography later in the week for the sequence in 'Aliens of London', where the Doctor and Rose attempt to get to the site of the alien crash, but to no avail. The details on the police signs, the newspaper kiosks and the Underground markers were all done with great realism, including 'a vendor stand for the *London Evening Standard* (a real newspaper), bearing the headline "Proper Rigmarole".'

Much of the press was aware of the recording taking place in Cardiff and of the presence of the Autons. The *Sun,* for example, noted that the Autons 'terrify the time traveller's helper, played by Billie Piper, when they spring to life as she shops,' and identified their last adversary as Jon Pertwee, the third Doctor. The presence of the Autons was a very big deal to many members of the viewing public, having witnessed their invasion attempts before in two stories, 'Spearhead from Space' and 'Terror of the Autons', in the early 1970s. Now, choreographer Ailsa Berk had put together a new cast of extras to fill the roles of the dreaded plastic villains who would ravage England under a new invasion, and pictures appeared far and wide. The *Daily Star* and the *Mirror* both billed their photos as exclusives.

However, the very first new photos of another classic *Doctor Who* icon appeared online. Taken by diligent fans William Owen and Roger Anderson, and posted on the *Outpost Gallifrey* and *Doctor Who Cuttings Archive* websites, these were images of the Police Box outer form of the TARDIS. They showed the new TARDIS sitting beneath a London bus stop sign, for a scene that was also very likely the first time it was seen on screen in the new series, in the scene just after Rose Tyler leaves the department store during 'Rose'. Many fans commented that the TARDIS appeared very bulky, as if the dimensions were somehow out of kilter with those seen before (while always aware that the size and shape of the TARDIS exterior props had varied slightly over the years during production of the original series). The photos showed the TARDIS being assembled by production crew next to the HSBC Bank building in Cardiff, near the production's first on-location base at the Cardiff Arms car park.

John Smith described the recording that took place the next day, Wednesday 21 July: 'Tonight's shoot on St Mary Street, starting just after 11pm, appeared to be endless re-takes of the same brief scene: Rose leaves Henrik's department store and crosses the street, hurrying but not running, looking nervously behind her. A black cab has to brake to avoid her, and beeps at her. The cab then continues up the street and drives through a puddle. The puddle is obviously important as it was re-filled for every shot! It's what Rose is carrying that makes the shot interesting; it's the severed arm of a shop mannequin ... Onlookers became so familiar with this scene, that doubtless Internet arguments will rage for years over whether [or not] they selected the best take! Techies could be seen working on hinged prosthetic hands, of an obviously Auton design. The TARDIS was built in-situ, in plain view, and it was possible for a short while to get right up close.' Gregory Jones told the *Doctor Who* Appreciation Society that, on the day: 'Howells Department Store was changed to Henrik's and there was a sale sign put up. The windows were being changed. The police station set had been up all day, "Classic Brides" had been taken down.' Jones later noted that he: '... went back to Queens Arcade for 10pm and saw an Auton chase some shoppers. He was wearing a grey suit. Very scary.'

Billie Piper was on hand on Wednesday for her scenes, recorded at Howells and in the street outside, as well as for some evening sequences. Of note was an entire sequence where a burning couch was dropped close to Piper, who fled across the street; the sequence was likely intended for the opening moments of 'Rose' as the Henrik's Department Store building exploded, but was abandoned prior to transmission.

Exterior recording continued on Thursday 22 July, with Anna Roberts watching the crew recording: '... scenes in front of the entrance of Queen's Arcade (used as a location on Tuesday night). It was dressed similarly, with the same vehicles around, but this time the location seemed to be dirtied down with many bin bags and other rubbish scattered around. The scenes included a group of extras running away from Autons. There was then a period when they seemed to be filming closer shots of two Autons in wedding dresses plus other shots around the exterior of the police station.'

While there would be other moments of public and fan excitement at being able to watch recording in progress (most especially when the production later moved to Swansea and Monmouth for exterior shots for 'The Unquiet Dead'), there were also great periods of quiet time as the team moved indoors to the studio, or to locations inaccessible to the public. Recording had begun, and fans and the public had been allowed a unique opportunity to experience the excitement and to feel close to the new series.

THE PRESS, THE FANS

The press jumped on the opportunity afforded them by the first stages of recording being conducted in such a public manner.

The recording of the Autons emerging from the Queen's Arcade and into the streets, and the ensuing on-screen chaos, was covered by the press during the week. The *Daily Star* reported on the first day's recording with the main cast and included a photograph of Piper in her red sweater and one of an Auton mask, while 22 July's *Mirror* had a black-and-white photo of both an adult and a 'child' Auton walking out of the shopping mall. Several papers also began displaying photos of Eccleston and Piper together in costume, including the *Mirror*'s 'Dr Who's World of Leather' picture of Eccleston with the TARDIS prop several days later, although Eccleston himself would not be a part of the location shoot – or indeed record any of his scenes – for another few days. As explained in the *South Wales Echo* on 21July, 'Christopher Eccleston, who plays the new Doctor, will not be at this week's shoot, although his new feisty assistant, Rose Taylor [sic], played by Billie Piper, will be filming in Cardiff.' Eccleston had apparently come to the location for a short photo call, but then left until he would be needed for actual recording several days later. The *Echo* also featured a photograph of Billie Piper (as Rose) in the doorway of the department store with another actress – this was during the sequence at the very start of 'Rose' where as she is about to leave the store, Rose is handed the lottery money – which proved that she was already involved in principal photography.

The sight of the TARDIS was just as powerful for the papers as it had been for the fans. 'As filming for the revival series of *Doctor Who* takes to the city's streets,' said the *South Wales Echo* on 22 July, 'rumours are flying that the traditional exterminating enemy has been replaced by an army of suave but evil mannequins.' The *Echo* also noted the next day that 'Drinkers in Cardiff might have been alarmed to find their favourite watering hole had been take over by the police,' noting that the back door of the Toad at the Exhibition bar in the city centre had been transformed into the front door of the police station that Jackie Tyler would later be seen walking away from. 'Large blue stickers with white lettering reading Police were stuck in the windows of the bar which faces St David's Centre, and a sign hanging from the outside wall was covered with a police banner. Half of the bar was closed on Tuesday and Wednesday evenings, and last night, to accommodate the crew.' The fan interest was also noted on 24 July by the *Manchester Evening News*, which commented: 'It may be forty years since blue police boxes were last seen on the streets, but *Doctor Who* fans were celebrating after catching a glimpse of one still in perfect working order.'

Doctor Who Magazine issue 346 made a timely arrival during the first week of production. This confirmed that Keith Boak was directing episodes one, four and five, hence the cross-purpose recording together of outdoor sequences that would later appear in these episodes. Said Boak, the new series would be: '... powerful, it's emotive, it's sh*t scary, it's chilling, it's fun, it's warm and it's adventurous. All those things pulled together ... All I can hope is that it will be completely different to anything anyone's ever seen on TV before.' The issue also noted the title of episode seven, 'The Long Game', the next screenplay written by Davies, but that it would be a while before further episode titles were revealed. Meanwhile, *TV Zone* magazine, out at the same time, interviewed Davies about the continued swirl of press information, much of it unreliable. 'I did see that one rumour in the *Guardian* about Cabinet members who became alien when they lied, or something,' Davies said, 'which was hardly credible, since the disguise wouldn't last long! It does seem some rumours get so strong that the production team is asked to make an official statement, which I'm absolutely refusing to do. Comment on nonsense, and you give that nonsense an official status. No chance!' Davies himself fudged the details a little, noting there were no current plans for 'pure' historical adventures (i.e. without any science fiction trappings; 'The Unquiet Dead' featured some SF elements) and that Rose didn't have super powers or a secret destiny. 'At least not yet. I just used *Buffy* as an example of a well-written modern leading female role,' he said, referring to the oft-mentioned claims that *Doctor Who* was taking a lesson from the popular vampire serial, *Buffy the Vampire Slayer*. *TV Zone* also interviewed concept artist Bryan Hitch, discussing the influences on his design work (on which he noted that 'everything from blown glass to high architecture has given us ideas ...') and budget restrictions. 'We have all been allowed to think about how it should look,' Hitch said. 'How we want it to be, and then working out a way to do it within budget rather than letting the budget dictate the look ... We are getting pretty close to what we want.'

The arrival of Christopher Eccleston for his first recorded scenes for the series was also subject to the usual media circus. The *Mirror* noted on 27 July that Eccleston had 'traded hats, cloaks and scarves for a leather jacket,' and that the actor had said that the previous costumes were 'a bit foppish for me, a council estate kid.' Photos printed in the *Daily Star* and the *Mirror* saw Eccleston and Piper walking together on the streets of Cardiff, and posing for photographs with onlookers outside local establishments. Eccleston was also the subject of a 29 July article in the *Manchester Evening News*, which noted that he was: '... bringing a no-nonsense attitude to his new role as Doctor Who. The actor, originally from Little Hulton, has swapped the cult Time Lord's dandy scarves and hats for a slick leather jacket and sharp black clothes.' The Doctor's wardrobe makeover was immediately met with controversy amongst fans, views ranging from acceptance to bafflement as to why the character, always very distinctive in his fashion statements, would suddenly abandon that history and move toward commonality. It seemed this was as much a statement of the new series's goals as anything:

that this was indeed a new era, and some of the trappings of the 'classic' series could no longer be relied upon. As Davies later told *SFX* magazine, 'There was no big grandstand moment where we all decided to "jettison the Edwardian" – the whole process is a lot more reasoned than that. It's not a policy, it's a gradual process of elimination. For starters, I was never in favour of an Edwardian look. To be honest, wearing a frock coat now makes you look like John Leslie at the National Television Awards.' Davies was referring to an outfit worn by ex-*Blue Peter* presenter Leslie prior to an emerging scandal about his love life.

Gossip columnists had a field day with the fallout from the first weeks of production. The *Sun* printed photographs of Piper and Noel Clarke (playing her boyfriend Mickey) kissing beside the fountain in 'Rose', while the *Western Mail* reported that Piper had taken a new flat in Cardiff to be close to the production, and that her new neighbour would be singer Charlotte Church. No longer simply a subject for news stories, *Doctor Who* was now becoming a tabloid sensation again.

CAST AND CREW DEVELOPMENTS

Sometimes the most minute information about the new series could be found in the most unlikely places. Documents relating to the renewal of the BBC's Royal Charter contained some information about minority actors in BBC productions, noting that *Doctor Who* would also reflect multicultural life by introducing Mickey: 'The hapless, long-suffering boyfriend of Rose, the Doctor's assistant, provides a major role for an actor from an ethnic minority background.' The *Sun* spilled the beans on 27 July that Mickey would be played by Noel Clarke, best known as Wyman Ian Norris in the BBC drama series *Auf Wiedersehen, Pet*.

At the same time, another casting coup was announced in the pages of the *Daily Telegraph*: former BBC Political Editor Andrew Marr, at the time still in his official role, outed himself as a participant in the series (later known to be in episodes four and five, 'Aliens of London' and 'World War Three'). 'Sunday night, I was standing outside a faked-up Downing Street jabbering away about the whereabouts of the Prime Minister at this time of national emergency, while SAS men, riot police and a tank moved all around,' Marr revealed in his column. 'I've made it at last. For someone of the Patrick Troughton/Jon Pertwee era, this is a bit like being asked to carry a spear in the first performance of a lost Shakespeare play.'

Casting rumours also abounded in July and August, including early reports that John Barrowman had won the role of Captain Jack, a character who would feature in the second half of the first season. Barrowman appeared on BBC Radio Five on 23 August on the Richard Bacon show, initially very cautious about spilling any details, but eventually mentioning that he would start recording the following November, and that his character would be 'something of an intergalactic rogue.'

The BBC in early August confirmed Barrowman's participation, in addition to confirming roles (in 'Aliens of London' and 'World War Three') for Penelope Wilton and Annette Badland. Early September saw the confirmation of Navin Chowdhry, who played Indra Ganesh in 'Aliens of London'; he started two weeks' work on the series on 1 September. Rupert Vansittart and Mark Benton were also mentioned at the time.

Perhaps the biggest casting news of the late summer came on 7 September, when the *Independent* broke the story that esteemed actor Simon Callow would appear in the series (in episode three, 'The Unquiet Dead'), as the famed historical personage Charles Dickens. 'To be honest,' Callow told the newspaper, 'when they sent me the script, my heart sank. As I know all about Dickens, I can say with authority that most attempts to put him on screen are awful – and there are a lot of them. But this script ... is fantastic.' As Davies later told the official *Doctor Who* website, 'It's wonderful to welcome an actor of Simon Callow's calibre on board the TARDIS. As soon as the words "Charles Dickens" first appeared in Mark Gatiss's clever, scary, inventive script, then we knew there was only one actor we wanted to approach. We're genuinely honoured that Simon has accepted, and I know that Chris and Billie are delighted too. This sets the standard for a *Doctor Who* with wonderful casts, exciting scripts and the highest production values.'

Casting wasn't the only information leaking from sources other than the production team; many confirmations were soon to follow, from information on WhoSpy that George Gerwitz would be the series's first assistant director, to revelations from the reliable *Professional Casting Review* that suggested that Joe Ahearne would be the director of the third block of episodes. *Doctor Who Magazine* continued to announce casting and crew information, including the first news of the name of the second director, Euros Lyn, and other positions on the team. The Any Effects website first revealed their own participation in the project; Any Effects would provide the 'physical' effects for much of the series, having previously contributed to productions including *London's Burning* (1988-2003), the *Hornblower* series of TV movies (1998-2003) and *Star Wars Episode II: Attack of the Clones* (2002). Another group, MTFX of Gloucester, would also provide certain special physical effects for the series; their credits included *24 Hour Party People* (2002) and the series *Casualty*, *Hearts of Gold* (2003) and *Inspector Morse*. Despite the many reliable reports now emerging, there were still rumours and idle gossip generated through the press; as Phil Collinson noted in *Doctor Who Magazine*: 'We read the reports of David Jason's casting with some surprise! ... If the right part came along, we would be delighted to approach him. But for the moment, I have to confirm that he's not on board.'

LONDON AND CARDIFF RECORDING

After the initial week's recording, the production moved to London for several sequences. Author and fan Mark Campbell was present to take photographs of the assembly of the TARDIS on the bank of the River Thames, for the night time sequences that would be used in 'Rose', specifically for the scenes shot across the river from the London Eye (and, presumably, for those of the Doctor and Rose at the Eye itself).

Over the second week of recording, 25 to 30 July, various London locales were used, as members of the *Doctor Who* Appreciation Society saw when they were able to take snapshots (although from a more distant vantage place). On 25 July, John Adam Street, near Charing Cross Station, doubled as the exterior of 10 Downing Street, as seen in 'Aliens of London' and 'World War Three', and actor David Verrey was seen on hand by attending fans as Joseph Green, the acting Prime Minister (and Slitheen mastermind). Andrew Marr's scenes were also recorded here as the members of the Government approached the Prime Minister's offices. (The interiors themselves would be recorded later, at Hensol Castle in the Vale of Glamorgan in South Wales.) On the night of 26 July, the sequence was shot in which the Doctor and Rose cross Westminster Bridge from the landing location of the TARDIS to the London Eye.

The crew moved on later in the week to the Brandon Estate in Southwark, where some of the exterior sequences at Rose's flat from all three episodes were shot; fan photographs show the hand-made banners hanging out of windows revelling at the landing of the aliens ('Aliens of London') and the presence of Noel Clarke as Mickey. 'Pretty much everyone else there is a resident of the Estate, renamed for the series but actually the oft filmed Brandon Estate in Southwark,' noted fan Martin Hoscik. Hoscik commented that producer Phil Collinson, whom he met at the location: '... is a nice man, relishing his role and clearly determined to make the best show he can. The whole crew seem relaxed and appear to be enjoying themselves. The impression is of a well prepared team for whom everything is going to plan ... Only one scene's being filmed tonight, the main action sequences were done last night involving what local residents describe as a "military invasion". Several rehearsals later and they film the shot. Eccleston seems to pass Billie the TARDIS key and utters something about heading "into mortal danger".' According to a locations guide on the BBC Wales Southeast website, a council estate in Cardiff, near the Gabalfa roundabout, was used for the stairwell between floors, while St David's Market in the centre of Cardiff was the site of the alley in which the TARDIS landed at the end of 'Rose'. Both these sequences were recorded on later dates.

While some of the production team stayed in London, others moved back to Cardiff for simultaneous recording of different sequences. As fan Andrew Ford noted on 2 August: '[Recording] for the new series of *Doctor Who* commenced this morning at the Heath Hospital in Cardiff.' Heath Hospital is also better known as the University Hospital of Wales in Cardiff, and the sequences recorded that day were of the first appearance of the Autons in the basement of Henrik's Department Store in 'Rose'. 'Location work is occurring throughout today in the hospital's underground, labyrinthine corridors ... The scenes being recorded involved Billie Piper and some latex clad extras. The eyewitness reports [indicated] that the scene (it seemed to be an action/escape scene involving Rose) was recorded a number of times from different angles and in fairly extreme circumstances – it was nearly 90 degrees down there! The location was dressed to look like a factory floor; one of the larger industrial elevators was redressed to look like an old fashioned department store type elevator.'

Back in London on the same day, the second production unit made the papers while recording further sequences. According to the *Daily Star*, 'A *Doctor Who* film crew had more than the Daleks to worry about when it was surrounded by anti-terrorist cops on the River Thames.' The sequence involved the crashed spaceship in the Thames and its recovery at the beginning of 'Aliens of London'. As fan Mark Coupe wrote: 'Apparently there was some kind of flap over the last couple of days, where the crew on *Doctor Who* had been filming some scenes with river police on the Thames, and had somehow drifted into the area around the MI6 building ... and caused anti-terrorist police to be rather concerned! Apparently, the crew from Wales weren't *au fait* with all the river regulations.' The MI6 building is an impressive glass and steel construction on the south bank of the Thames by Vauxhall Bridge.

By 22 August, the production had fully moved back to Cardiff, with all its London location work complete. Fan Jez Connolly spotted Eccleston and Piper preparing for recording at St David's Hall, most likely for the sequences at the end of 'Rose' in the alleyway. 'I saw Christopher reading the script sat on a bench a few yards from the outside of the building,' Connolly wrote. 'He looked deep in thought most of the time; it's a great testament to the people of Cardiff that even though it was a fairly busy street and filming was occurring nobody was interfering or pestering the production team. I sat at a nearby outside café for a while to observe proceedings; the filming was clearly going on inside the building as it had been closed to the public. Round the side of the building I saw three or four vans carrying lighting equipment. Most exciting of all though was one van containing the top section of the TARDIS.

The crew looked pretty relaxed; at one point Christopher appeared out of a people-carrier car and gave the driver a broad grin.'

Doctor Who Magazine clarified the production schedule in early September, noting that the next block, comprising episodes two and three, would be handled by director Euros Lyn. As August came to a close, much of the principal recording on 'Rose', 'Aliens of London' and 'World War Three' (then known simply as 'Aliens of London, Part Two') would be complete.

DALEK FALLOUT

As noted in Chapter 6, an agreement to feature the Daleks in the new series was completed in early August, causing a deluge of press coverage about the return of the popular villains. The *Sun* claimed victory, having championed the cause for several months with repeated appearances of its own Dalek prop at various events – including several on location during production. On 22 July, as the production crew recorded its first Cardiff location sequences for 'Rose', the newspaper's gold Dalek had a close encounter with one of the series's stars. 'Billie recorded a scene getting off the bus and running into Henrik's,' fan Gregory Jones told the *Doctor Who* Appreciation Society, detailing the recording of the sequence at the start of the episode. 'Suddenly the *Sun* pushed a Gold Dalek onto the location and [were] immediately stopped. They took lots of photos of the Dalek on the set. The crowd loved it. Billie ran onto the bus and hid!'

'The *Sun* certainly generated a lot of extra publicity,' *Doctor Who Magazine*'s assistant editor Tom Spilsbury later told *Outpost Gallifrey*. 'If nothing else, the *Sun's* campaign showed that people cared, and the fact that the breakdown of negotiations had been made so public made both the BBC and Hancocks keen to seek a quick resolution! I'm sure that this may well have happened at some point anyway, but the *Sun's* coverage certainly wasn't counter-productive ...'

Word slowly crept out about the production team's plans for the Daleks, now that they were definitely returning. The *Media Guardian*, however, wondered if the whole thing had been a publicity stunt. 'Was this "crisis" just a piece of well-placed PR?' asked columnist Mark Borowski. 'Yes, "our" soaraway *Sun* has been railing against the BBC's inability to come to an agreement with Terry Nation's estate ... And now? Quelle surprise! The publicity has made the forthcoming show as famous as the original, and LOOK OUT! THE DALEKS ARE COMING BACK AFTER ALL!' As previously mentioned, the *Doctor Who* production office and the BBC adamantly denied that it had been planned this way.

'Classic' series personalities associated with the Daleks also reflected on the resurrection of the popular metal meanies. 'I would happily run around as a Dalek again,' veteran *Doctor Who* actor John Scott Martin, who had played Daleks in most of the original series episodes to feature them, told *BBC News* on 8 August. 'It could be difficult at times and I'm not as fit as I used to be, but I'm sure I could do it again.' Director Andrew Morgan, who directed the last televised Dalek serial, 'Remembrance of the Daleks' in 1988, had some important tips for whoever would be looking after their next appearance, as he told *The Times* on 18 August: 'While castors are quite efficient on studio floors, I felt we were courting disaster when one of the 1988 locations for a major battle was to be a cobbled street near Waterloo.' He also mentioned that recent talk that the Daleks would hover wasn't exactly newsworthy: 'Thankfully I was much more successful in a later scene, when I managed to film them going upstairs.'

Details of the Dalek plotline slowly began to leak out throughout August. 'Insiders say the original plan was for a single, rogue Dalek in a plotline similar to the film *Alien*,' noted the *Telegraph*, spoiling details about the sixth episode of the new series, 'before letting loose an entire Dalek army at the end of the series.' The *Mirror*, on the other hand, noted, highly inaccurately as it turned out: 'The BBC may have shelled out a whopping £250,000 for the right to use the Daleks in the new series of *Doctor Who* – but the metal monsters only pop up in one episode. And when the big moment comes, in the eighth instalment, there's only one of them. It turns out he's a bit of an antique who has survived on a space station where he is killing off the crew one by one. And gasp, that's the only time we'll clap eyes on the old-style Daleks.'

The *Sun*, apparently not being aware that the Daleks had hovered in their last serial as Morgan had explained, reported: 'Show bosses are looking at the exterminators being able to climb stairs, fly and hover.' Tim Hancock, who administered the rights on behalf of the Terry Nation estate, commented: 'We all accept that the Daleks were designed in the early sixties and need to be updated. They have got to be able to move, be mobile, but they have also got to retain the initial look of the original Daleks about them.' The *Western Morning News* on 9 August focused on reactions to the return of the Daleks, quoting fan John Swithinbank from Seaton: 'I'm over the moon, really. I have missed them in a way – for years they have been part of my life. I have been interested in them since I was eight years old.' And the *Telegraph* was simply astounded by the whole thing: 'Whoever's in charge of the PR for the new *Doctor Who* series has been doing a knockout job.'

MONMOUTH AND SWANSEA

While production on the series continued in Cardiff, scouts had already found new sites for on-location photography in the area for 'The Unquiet Dead', the first new series adventure set in Earth's history, which would transform 21st Century streets into 19th-Century Cardiff. True to its focus on showcasing Wales, the team found several sites in the towns of Monmouth and Swansea, the latter being Russell T Davies's birthplace.

The first real indication that the towns were being scouted appeared on 11 September on the *This is South Wales* site, part of the syndicated IC network of websites that function alongside counterpart newspapers. *This Is South Wales* reported that Swansea's maritime area would be 'taken back in time and transformed into a scene from 1869 for the star-studded production.' Fake snow would be set to cover the road between Adelaide Street and Pier Street, and along the whole of Cambrian Place, Burrows Place and Gloucester Place, and period costume along with horses and carriages would help bring the scene to life. Simon Callow's recently reported appearance as Charles Dickens would feature prominently in these scenes. 'We have recognised the timeless charm of the Maritime area of Swansea and we would like to shoot some of our scenes there,' a production source told the site. 'The shots are snow scenes and are at night so for one night people will be treated to a Christmas scene outside their windows. We will also introduce horses and carriages, background artists in period costume and the use of braziers to take us back to Christmas 1869. We will be providing alternative parking for residents in a nearby secure car park and although road closures have been agreed and will be implemented, emergency vehicles will have access as normal.' Swansea Councillor Gerald Clement, responsible for local culture, recreation and tourism, commented, 'We are delighted that part of the new *Doctor Who* series will be filmed in Swansea and extremely pleased to be associated with such a high-profile project.'

'From Monday the "old section" of Swansea's Maritime Quarter will be used to film a 19th-Century scene featuring actor Simon Callow as Charles Dickens,' the *icWales* news service reported. 'Artificial snow will be sprayed onto Adelaide Street and Gloucester Place, around Swansea's five-star Morgan's Hotel. And horses and carriageways [sic] will be brought in to add atmosphere to what is intended as a Christmas scene.'

Swansea wasn't the only locale that was about to be taken over for the production. Clive Evans, the series's location manager, had sent a letter explaining the situation in the same terms as the *This Is South Wales* report to residents in the nearby Welsh community of Monmouth; the letter explained that the sequences would involve transforming the streets into a snowy Christmas-time complete with horse-drawn carriages. The letter also noted that emergency access would be available as usual to local residents.

Recording in Swansea began on or around 20 September. 'Just got back from where tonight's [recording] is taking place in Swansea,' noted correspondent John J Moran, who had been one of the fans to locate the production on the streets. 'Several streets had been closed off with a thin layer of snow covering the entire area,' he said, as well as commenting that there were a large number of extras, along with several coaches and horses, on site, and a crane blowing fake snow. Piper and Eccleston had been spied on location recording several scenes, with Piper in period costume and Eccleston in his now-trademark jacket, as well as 'what looked like Simon Callow, in Victorian regalia again, walking from a street, straight towards a close up to a camera in a snow blizzard.'

Fan Ian Golden also watched the recording, revealing that he saw: '... Simon Callow wishing someone Merry Christmas and the Doctor and Rose scene which looks like it's early on in the episode as the Doctor grabs a newspaper. Perhaps he's looking to see what date it is ... or something more mysterious.' Wrote Paul Mount: 'Quite simply it was a breathtaking shoot. The streets looked amazing covered in extremely realistic snow and the attention to detail was quite staggering – extras dressed as Victorian gentlemen and women, street urchins, policemen, draymen, prostitutes, sailors. Simon Callow appeared fairly early in the evening in full Dickensian makeup and sporting a thick beard. His one scene seemed to involve striding along the snowy streets, acknowledging passers-by and crossing in the general direction of a building made up as the Taliesyn Halls, a theatre in 1870s Cardiff (where the story appears to be set).' Unfortunately, at several points, onlookers in the side streets had taken photographs using flashes, which had disrupted recording, prompting one of the producers to ask fan websites to print requests for fellow fans not to use flash when taking photographs. 'If used during takes it can ruin complicated set-ups, and, in particular it can also scare the horses being used in these scenes.'

Many scenes were recorded in Swansea; fans reported seeing several sequences being shot, including the kidnapping of Rose by Sneed and Gwyneth, and the subsequent start of the pursuit by the Doctor and Dickens in his carriage. On 21 September, shooting continued here. 'It was **** cold,' fan Darren Floyd told *SFX* magazine. Said another observer, John Campbell Rees: 'First was a short establishing scene featuring Callow as Dickens being wished a "Merry Christmas" by a passer-by as Dickens walked along a crowded street, in a flurry of acrid fake snow. There were two brief rehearsals of this shot, and then straight to a take. After a short break, the scene was filmed again from the opposite camera angle. With this shot in the can, the action moved a few yards down Gloucester Place to a scene featuring Christopher Eccleston and Billie Piper ... My friend told me that the Lee Electrical vans and a van belonging to Any Effects Limited had been seen parked outside Cardiff's New Theatre on Sunday, 19 September, and it is likely that [recording] inside that Edwardian building, which could easily pass as Victorian, took place on that day. Given the way that Rose is dressed, and the brisk pace Callow's Dickens adopted in his scene, I speculate that the Doctor is taking Rose to see one of Dickens's famed readings, and this was [recorded] at the weekend.' Another observer, Steven Howlett, noted: 'If you look closely, you can make out the addition of some street furniture such as carts, crates and barrels etc. The street lamps are original for this area.'

SFX magazine printed some photographs from the shoot, as did fan sites such as *Outpost Gallifrey*, the *Doctor Who Cuttings Archive* and the *Doctor Who* Appreciation Society, revealing coaches and horses and all sorts of period costumes. *SFX* captured clear images of the undertaker's coach from Sneed and Company, while fan photos showed the snow-blasted streets outside, the Swansea locales passing perfectly for 19th-Century Cardiff. Horse-drawn carriages, period costume and playbills added to the unique Dickensian look of the scene.

It wasn't long before the newspapers began reporting on the action. 'Snow covered the streets of Swansea last night,' said *This is South Wales* on 21 September. 'But this wasn't more bad weather for the city – Time Lord Doctor Who had landed his TARDIS in the Maritime Quarter as part of his latest TV adventure.' The article noted: 'Fake snow covered the road between Adelaide Street and Pier Street, as well as along the whole of Cambrian Place, Burrows Place and Gloucester Place, as the area was transported back to 1869. Horses and carriages helped to bring the scene to life as it went through a 19th Century makeover. Filming lasted for much of the night.' In addition to mentioning Simon Callow's participation in the episode, Mark Gatiss had apparently revealed to several reporters that the story would be transmitted as the third episode, confirming some earlier speculation that it had been the fourth and fifth episodes in production along with 'Rose' early on in Cardiff and London.

Production moved on to Monmouth on 21 September. 'A large crowd of set workers descended on the market town of Monmouth to prepare it for the arrival of the star-studded *Doctor Who* cast,' reported the *Western Daily Press*. 'Old fashioned signs, shop frontages, bales of hay and tons of false snow transformed the square back to Victorian times.' The article quoted location manager Clive Evans, who asserted that it was: '... absolutely perfect because it is charming and dateless. Nowadays it's so hard to find anywhere without a McDonalds coming into view but this is fantastic.'

'Filming in Monmouth took place on Tuesday night and the early hours of Wednesday morning in Beaufort Arms Court in the centre of the town,' reported Roger Anderson. 'There was also a small sequence due to be shot just around the corner outside the Punch House bar in Agincourt Square ... The area of the shoot was cordoned off and many props, such as barrels, braziers and rather a lot of fake snow [were] already in place. A giant crane towered above the scene, in place to shower the location with even more fake snow once [recording] had commenced ... Shortly after our arrival the final work was being done on dressing the area, with 20th Century telephone boxes camouflaged under sacking and a large horse trough with a fake water pump carried out into Beaufort Arms Court.' Anderson also revealed that, ironically, the troubles with reshooting scenes in Swansea ruined by flash photos hadn't been caused by fans, but instead by the paparazzi and press cameras being used with large flash guns ... Britain's tabloids attempting to get the story.

'There were two vantage points [from] where [recording] could be glimpsed,' Anderson continued, 'although with difficulty; one being our initial location at the far end of Agincourt Square. From here I could see through a large door into Beaufort Arms Court itself, but the site of the actual shoot was, I discovered, pretty much obscured. This was even more the case when the crew cleared onlookers away from the side of the Punch House and strung up black material to hide the road and any passing traffic.' Later, near the Beaufort Arms Court, Anderson saw the recording of an old woman dressed in black uttering a blood-curdling moan as she advanced on the camera ... later seen as the opening pre-credit sequence of 'The Unquiet Dead', with actress Jennifer Hill playing the undead Mrs Peace. 'In comparison to my earlier visit to Cardiff in July to see shooting on block one, there seemed to be fewer takes and the pace of filming appeared far quicker,' Anderson revealed. 'During the course of [recording] this scene, two of the stars of the story arrived in costume: Christopher Eccleston ... and Simon Callow ... Callow looked particularly distinguished in his period clothes and cape and this was a good chance to see the actors close up. Eccleston seemed very relaxed and happy to chat and joke with Callow and the crew, even winking at the odd onlooker.' Other sequences recorded at that point included those of the Doctor and Dickens knocking on the door of Sneed and Company, and Dickens later escaping from the undertakers, and presumably also those of Sneed and Company burning to the ground and the Doctor and Rose bidding farewell to Dickens. Photographs confirm the presence of the TARDIS prop in Monmouth, placed in the alleyway where it arrives and departs. Other photographs show the front of the theatre where Dickens performs, as well as the side street where the Doctor and Dickens pursue Sneed's coach, and the front of Sneed's business. Anderson continued: 'I later discovered that this was dressed as "Sneed and Company, Undertakers of 7 Temperance Court, Llandaff". Llandaff (now a suburb of Cardiff) was host to some early experiments with gas in 1767 when the bishop of the diocese conveyed generated gas in tubes, made coke, and purified gas for burning. Certainly by the time the story is set, gas lighting had been installed in the area for some years but was still a "modern" wonder of the time.'

The Swansea and Monmouth shoots were the last of the major on-location sequences to be attended by large numbers of fans and press photographers; there would be several other location shoots, both in Cardiff and in the surrounding countryside, but nothing rivalling the sheer spectacle of a Victorian period piece being shot around a major thoroughfare. Ahead would be many more months of studio-bound and interior work, special effects shots and guest stars galore. *Doctor Who*'s first season was well on its way.

CHAPTER EIGHT:
CARRY ON, DOCTOR!

Few, if any, other television series can boast the level of media and public interest shown in *Doctor Who*; after all, where else than on a *Doctor Who* location would one find dozens of press photographers and fans camped out in freezing cold conditions waiting for a glimpse of an actor on an established television drama series?

This wasn't always the case. During the long history of the 'classic' *Doctor Who* series, the public had gradually grown accustomed to it; it was a Saturday night staple for its first two decades, something taken for granted ... it had to be there, it was *Doctor Who*, and it would *always* be around. Cast changes often made the headlines, especially when one of the actors playing the Doctor departed (as, for example, was the case when Tom Baker, stalwart Doctor of seven years, left the series in 1980), but not to the degree of being a major media event. The latter half of 2004 brought media interest in *Doctor Who* to perhaps an all-time high, arguably eclipsing that shown in any other single television series while in production.

PRESS AND GOSSIP

It began with small mentions in odd places. The *Western Mail* cast an eye on the series in August 2004, shortly after production had begun: '*Doctor Who*: Midnight filming all over Cardiff, snatched sightings of Billie Piper and Christopher Eccleston ... ooh, the excitement of the new BBC Wales series. We can't wait for the first episode.' *Heat* magazine, always keen to cover gossip and rumour about anyone fîted as a 'celebrity' in the growing media obsession with – in particular – female soap stars, ex-soap stars, and anyone deemed remotely newsworthy, posited: 'It's usually the housemates on [*Big Brother*] who end up becoming TV stars when the series finishes, but this year stardom beckons for one of the legendary Superfans on *Big Brother's Little Brother*. Yes, Stuart's superfan Glen Williams, the one with the incredible mop of curly hair, is set to join main stars Christopher Eccleston and Billie Piper to make a key series of *Doctor Who*. Glen has been cast in a 2-part story as the first victim of the new-look veteran *Doctor Who* baddy, the Master.' This was a somewhat typical piece of *Heat* reportage, linking members of the public from reality television series like *Big Brother* with anything that happens to be in the news.

Speculation ran rampant about the series's eventual screen villains. Tom Baker himself wanted to go 'over to the dark side on *Doctor Who*,' or so he told the *Daily Record* (amongst others) in early September: 'If the BBC were brave enough, which they're not, then what they really should do would be to make me the Master. That would be really witty. Heroes always need villains. Superman can't exist without evil and vice versa. So it would be very clever to have this person who was once the hero become the villain, because within life, as well as fiction, we are nowhere without villains. Without them there'd be no newspapers, no film industry, no literature. You absolutely need the dark side.' Baker also had some words for the *Guardian* later in the month, wary that the new series would tackle: '... social issues and romantic encounters. "Romance?" said Baker. "Well, I shouldn't be surprised, really. They'll do anything to make people watch ... [Eccleston] was talking about Earth as if it was important! I was deeply, deeply disappointed. I mean, Christ, the next thing they'll be doing is talking about global warming. Oh, it's so sad, isn't it? I find a fantasy programme's preoccupation with this world so parochial."' Late in September, Baker was reported in the *Sun* saying that he found Eccleston (whom in other interviews he'd said he'd never heard of) was taking the role 'too seriously.' 'Get your head out of your fat bottom,' Baker apparently challenged Eccleston. 'It always sounds very hollow in the mouth of an actor. When actors use words like "challenge" and "serious" you think to yourself, "Oh just shut up."'

In the world of tabloid newspapers and gossip magazines, no stone went unturned; Billie Piper's life was suddenly fair game. The publicity surrounding her started in a somewhat tame fashion: her quest to lose weight and drop a dress size. 'I was brought up on bread and butter,' she told the *Mirror* on 21 September. But then things slowly began to turn ugly, as the gossip columnists got wind of some troubles behind closed doors. 'Chris Evans and Billie Piper are battling to save their marriage,' the *Daily Record* reported on 25 September. 'The pair have admitted to friends that their four-year relationship is in crisis.' Soon, Piper was linked (often inaccurately) to a steady stream of alleged suitors, including Eccleston himself ...

Russell T Davies was also part of the spin cycle. The *Guardian* on 28 September described him as one of the country's top 30 'hottest people, places and things', noting what a national institution he had inherited. 'I can do what I want,' he told the paper. 'The purists may be up in arms but there are more things to worry about in life.' *SFX* magazine also interviewed Davies in September, the executive producer wondering, 'How we could ever go back to a normal show after this. What, film two people just walking down the street?' He said that the most exciting moment in his experience had been the day he first saw the new TARDIS interior. 'I was lucky, 'cause I'd been trapped at home, writing episode seven, and only saw it in studio half-built. So my first sight of it was fully lit, on a glorious wide shot, on the rushes. The second best day of my whole working life.' At around the same time, it was announced that Davies's co-executive producer Mal Young would be leaving the BBC at the end of September, effectively breaking up the 'executive three' that had founded the series the year before.

Meanwhile, Davies and remaining co-executive producer Julie Gardner would have to juggle their work on *Doctor Who* with the production of a lavish three-part adaptation of *Casanova* for BBC Television, to be transmitted first on the digital station BBC3. 'We were keen to do what Russell wanted to do and to enable Julie to continue an ongoing relationship with Russell on *Casanova* and *Doctor Who*,' said Head of Drama Jane Tranter. The production would eventually star as Casanova both Peter O'Toole and, as the younger incarnation of the same character, an actor whose destiny would soon become intertwined with *Doctor Who*, David Tennant. Davies also spent part of the time he worked on *Doctor Who* finalising a new drama series, *Mine All Mine*, a six-part serial that debuted in November 2004 on ITV1 and starred Griff Rhys Jones, Ruth Madoc, Jason Hughes and Joanna Page.

Series writer Mark Gatiss spent some time in the spotlight, too, being interviewed by the *Independent* on 27 October, mostly referring to *The League of Gentlemen* but also mentioning the new series in one paragraph. As Gatiss noted, 'Who would win in a celebrity death match: Daleks or Cybermen? For sheer mobility, you would have to say the Cybermen, but of course the Daleks can now go upstairs. And they have firepower on their side. My sister used to tease me when I was little because she had seen *Doctor Who* from the beginning and used to say that her favourite story was when the Cybermen and the Daleks got together. But I knew they never had.'

The press got its story anywhere it could find it. The 22 October edition of the *Express*: 'Producers of the BBC's new *Doctor Who* series ... have become so paranoid about leaks that they have now resorted to MI5-style measures to ensure secrecy. My sources tell me that each script has been watermarked, individually printed, signed out with a confidentially agreement and tracked to ensure no details filter through. When a member of the production team had his laptop stolen from his car, BBC security went into overdrive to track it down in an all-out bid to protect the storyline information contained in the computer's files. Sadly it seems that even with such measures the leaks just keep on coming ...' The *Guardian* on 27 October: 'Bananas to the BBC's Drama Department, which is working overtime to bring the more far-flung bits of the British Isles to the screen. The Welsh town of Usk is being used to send *Doctor Who* back to Victorian Britain ...' The *Newcastle Chronicle & Journal* on 23 November also featured an interview with Gatiss: 'I've spoken to Chris [Eccleston] and we're going to have a kind of Brown/Blair thing. He's going to retire gracefully after a few years and give it to me. No, I wish that were true. But if I waited as long as Gordon Brown has, it'll never happen!' (This was a reference to press speculation about rivalry between Britain's Prime Minister Tony Blair and his Chancellor of the Exchequer Gordon Brown.)

Through it all, Russell T Davies remained the series's most important and visible emissary... even when everything didn't appear to be coming up roses. 'A lot of the time the actual writing process is as miserable as f**k,' Davies told *The Times* for its 22 November edition. 'Absolutely, this thing will follow me for the rest of my life. But the marvellous thing about writing *Doctor Who* is that I know when I die there are magazines that will report my death.' He remained optimistic, however, about the series's chances up against its expected adversaries, popular light entertainment presenters Anthony McPartlin and Declan Donnelly – better known as Ant and Dec – on ITV1, because it would be telling good stories: 'It's very funny in places. In episode two they go to space for the first time and meet loads of aliens and it's so funny. There is a plot underneath it all and their lives end up in danger, but, my God, it's funny.' Davies also told Radio Five Live on 22 November that the series would debut in the 'new year, probably March, and it's going marvellously.' Davies in this interview appeared a bit more tense and less happy-go-lucky than he had in July when the series's start of production had been featured so visibly on BBC *Wales Today*; but perhaps there was some good news in the *Guardian*, in a story that appeared in their 'Media Monkey' column at the end of November: 'The new *Doctor Who* has passed the fear-factor test. Outgoing drama series boss Mal Young took an episode home to see how the drama, scheduled for a family audience in its old Saturday teatime slot, went down with his seven-year-old step-daughter. Monkey is glad to report that she ended up watching it from behind the sofa.' Good news, indeed.

TO EXTERMINATE, OR NOT TO EXTERMINATE

Issues relating to the Daleks continued to take up column-inches. The *Sun* noted on 23 September that *Doctor Who*'s metal monsters, who had recently been announced as finally being part of the action once again, would return without their famous catchphrase 'Exterminate!': 'BBC chiefs have deemed the aliens' catchphrase too cheesy for modern audiences. A Beeb insider confirmed last night: *Doctor Who* fans may be upset. But although the word may have scared kiddies in 1963, today it would be laughed off screen.' Yet the *Sci-Fi Online* website noted on 4 October, in an article called 'Latest on the Daleks' dialect', that they would *not* abandon their trademark catchphrase. The website also described the new Daleks as appearing not that different from their previous incarnations: '... although a final decision on a colour scheme has apparently yet to be reached. What is clear, however, is that the first Dalek we see will be damaged and covered in gunk, the sole survivor of a forgotten patrol that's killing the unsuspecting crew of a spacecraft.' (The dreaded Internet rumours strike again; there was never any spacecraft involved in the story at any point.) The Dalek design rumours were confirmed as the *Sun* on 1 November published the first shots of the Dalek featured in the episode of the same name. And according to the *Daily Record*, the creatures would have a new catchphrase, 'Levitate!': 'Doctor Who's mortal enemies – with the fearsome cry of exterminate – can fly ... A BBC insider confirmed they can now fly. The Daleks were always the Doctor's scariest enemy – but now they can exterminate from mid-air. The Doctor will have his work cut out dealing with flying Daleks.' As viewers would later discover, the expression used in the series would actually be 'Elevate!', not 'Levitate!'

'I can confirm that the Daleks *will* say exterminate – it would be madness to stop that happening,' producer Phil Collinson told *SFX* magazine in its November 2004 issue, clearing up the confusion. 'I can tell you that the Daleks will be doing things they've never done on screen before ... If ever you've laughed at them, prepare to have the smile frozen on your face.'

THE TRAPPINGS OF SUCCESS

In the same *SFX* article, Collinson noted that, unlike the design of the Daleks, some other aspects of the series would indeed have some changes in store. Pre-titles teaser sequences, long the subject of debate, were being considered. 'All the early episodes have got the potential to do this,' he explained. 'If we sit in the edit and don't like them, we can change our minds at the last minute.'

This wasn't the only potential change to the long-established *Doctor Who* format; for the first time, the companion would receive equal billing. 'Meet the partners in time!' noted the *Manchester Evening News* on 4 October, which explained that unlike in previous years, 'the masterful, male Time Lord and his submissive, female assistant will be history-surfing companions boasting identical billing.' Davies said that the Doctor and Rose would be written as a team, much of it resting on the strength of the actors: 'You couldn't have him as the dominant man and her as the humble assistant in this day and age ... It's magnificent and it's very funny. That's partly because Christopher Eccleston knew he had a reputation as a very serious actor and wanted to do it because he wished to reinvent himself and show how funny he could be. At the same time as being funny, he brings a tremendous weight ... [Billie Piper is] the hardest-working woman I have ever dealt with. People have this preconception about her being a former pop star, but she has an absolutely brilliant future as an actress. The scene where she walks into the TARDIS is beautifully shot and beautifully acted. It's stunning.'

Another break from the series's past would be the lack of cameo appearances from actors who had played former Doctors – long the subject of anniversary celebrations, and certainly a potential *cause célèbre* in the new series. 'I toyed with the idea of giving Tom and Colin [Baker] cheeky little cameo roles as a bit of fun,' Davies told the *Daily Mail*. 'However, even though I admire them both very much, it won't be possible. I thought that if they appeared, it would distract viewers and affect the freshness of the new series.'

BRIEFINGS AND BROADCASTERS

In early September, one of the first pieces of official *Doctor Who* series promotion material was issued for several sales presentations ... and soon made its way into the hands of the press. It was the first official mention of the series airing in 'spring 2005', synching with March 2005 transmission rumours that had now begun to crop up in online circles. The document also noted five actors associated with the series – Eccleston, Piper, Camille Coduri (as Rose's mother), Noel Clarke (as Mickey Smith) and Mark Benton (as Clive). Mark Benton had been rumoured to be in the series for some time, but this was the first official word that he'd been associated with the production.

The press document noted that Rose was a 'shop girl' and that the Doctor could be 'found wanting' when it came to relationships. It stated that the two would witness 'the natural end of the world,' journey 'back to Victorian times for an encounter with Charles Dickens and the mysterious Geith [sic] – gaseous monsters with deadly plans for humanity,' and investigate an alien crash-landing in 2005 that would 'divert attention from a conspiracy that leads to the very heart of the government.' Perhaps of greatest interest, the text of the press document confirmed the involvement of Canadian broadcaster CBC, which it noted had purchased the series ahead of delivery and would be transmitting it shortly after the UK.

On 4 October, CBC itself formally announced in a press release that it had signed an agreement to carry the new series. Slawko Klymkiw, executive programming director of CBC Television, said: 'This was an exciting opportunity for CBC to bring the popular *Doctor Who* to fans – new and old alike – across the country. We are pleased to be working closely with the BBC to bring Canadians this exceptional new series.' Hilary Read, Chief Operating Officer, BBC Worldwide Canada, added: 'The CBC is the perfect partner for this fantastic new production. We're delighted to be bringing such a classic series to new audiences.' While *Doctor Who* carried an international fandom, Davies noted that it was the new audience that he cared about most. 'Someone who has never heard of a TARDIS or a Dalek, whether in Toronto or Swansea, will be able to start with this new series, climb on board with Christopher and Billie, and travel the whole of time and space.'

On the other side of the world, there were rumours that Australian broadcaster ABC was interested in the series and was working to acquire the rights; confirmation of that wouldn't come until the second quarter of the new year, reportedly because ABC wanted to view all thirteen episodes before they purchased it, and remained hesitant about buying it sight-unseen. The same could not be said about Prime TV in New Zealand, which announced on 5 December that it would pick up the series: 'BBC Worldwide announces today the licence of the new series of the cult classic *Doctor Who* to Prime Television New Zealand. Only the second international deal to be finalised, the new series will deliver to Prime Television in the first quarter of 2005.' David Vine, BBC Worldwide Managing Director for Asia Pacific, noted in the Prime TV press release: 'This series has been long anticipated. We are very excited that Prime will bring the new Doctor to New Zealand audiences.' Programming Manager Andrew Shaw meanwhile said he was: '... delighted to have acquired this fantastic new drama from the BBC. *Doctor Who* promises to be an outstanding series. We very much look forward to placing it in our primetime schedule. This series will captivate a whole new generation of fans who have never experienced the legend that is *Doctor Who*.'

American fans, meanwhile, were still clinging to idle speculation that the Sci-Fi Channel or another US broadcaster would pick up the series. It looked as though the BBC was attempting to sell the series in a package: the 'classic' series combined with the new one. Hopes of a possible breakthrough on American broadcast came on 6 October, as the TBI Buyers' Briefing, a weekly information service sent to over 6,000 worldwide TV executives, featured a note that

'BBC scout gets feet under US table: *Doctor Who* US sale being finalised.' The report suggested an impending sale of the new series to the large US television market; BBC Worldwide executive Paul Telegdy said that he was speaking to an 'interested party' and was confident it would be sold to a US network in the near future. 'We're discussing the ratings potential of the show,' Telegdy explained. This sale didn't materialise, however, even though the signs were there that the BBC had been shopping around the series; the previously-held contracts for the 'classic' series with independent stations on the PBS (Public Broadcasting System) network had begun to dry up, with stations being told that no further options for renewal remained on the show. Meanwhile, the presence of the series had begun to pervade the mainstream media; as writer Maureen Ryan said in the 17 December edition of the *Chicago Tribune*: 'I'm sure more alert sci-fi mavens have known about these developments for months, but ... filming has already begun on a new *Doctor Who* series ... I'm hoping the BBC raises the bar with Eccleston's outing as the good Doctor.'

There were also signs of possible investment in new technology, according to the *Brand Republic* in September, which noted that viewers might be able to see the series through pay-per-view on the British Telecom broadband service in the UK: 'Viewers can expect to download a selection of programmes from an archive by typing in a keyword like "Dr Who", giving the viewer complete control of their own schedule.' This appeared to be referring simply to a potential use of the technology rather than to a firm plan ... that is, until much later, during the broadcast of the first season, when the episode 'Dalek' was suddenly made available via streaming RealVideo in what appeared to be the first Internet broadcast of the series.

Attention moved to potential launch dates. A press release from the BBC on 1 December mentioned *Doctor Who* as part of its 'Winter Highlights', setting off a storm of curiosity as to whether the 'winter' moniker meant early in the new year, or perhaps March or April. 'Filming in Cardiff until 2005 for transmission on BBC One' was how the series was described, and while the item intimated an early 2005 time frame, there were still at least six episodes of thirteen that had not as yet gone before the cameras, and the setting of an actual debut date would depend on how quickly the show was completed. Rumours that the BBC had considered a Christmas 2004 launch date proved unfounded as the holiday season came and went; meanwhile, there were additional rumours coming out of the production that, being a bit behind schedule, the team had been asked to stay on through the summer, and that autumn 2005 wasn't outside the realm of possibility. However, none of that would pan out, as all eyes began looking toward the series's eventual debut date; by the end of 2004, speculation had it pegged as the third or fourth week of March, speculation that ultimately proved correct.

CONFIDENTIAL AND PROJECT: WHO?

Broadcast magazine first announced on 7 October 2004 that the BBC would produce a companion series for the new *Doctor Who* season. *Doctor Who Confidential* would be a thirteen-part, half-hour series featuring behind the scenes footage and interviews with cast members from both generations of the timeless classic. BBC3 would broadcast this series, airing each week immediately after the transmission of the counterpart episode on BBC1. Each episode would be based around a particular theme, explained producer Mark Cossey, such as the challenges of creating a new Doctor or of finding his assistant. 'It will have a very entertaining glow to it,' Cossey explained. 'It won't be discussions of technology. We are going for a bigger audience than that.' The series would be co-produced by Gillane Seaborne – who would travel extensively to *Doctor Who* events over the following six months, including the UK-based *Dimensions* convention in November 2004, the *Doctor Who* exhibition in Brighton, and North America's *Gallifrey One* event in Los Angeles in February 2005 – and co-executive produced by Gardner and Russell, and would be in production from October 2004 through April 2005. Seaborne would be joined by several additional producers to tackle individual installments of the series. Each edition would have a title and a theme 'covered by that week's episode [of *Doctor Who*] and looking back at how that theme has been developed in previous episodes with past Doctors,' as well as interviews with Eccleston, Piper, Davies, past Doctors and assistants, licensees and fans. It would cover such topics as 'how the BBC approached the task of bringing back the Doctor', 'making convincing aliens', and 'the role of the TARDIS, and the past times the Doctor has visited'.

'*Confidential* is its own beast,' Cossey told the official *Doctor Who* website several weeks later. 'It will be more observational than the others, more of a documentary but with an entertainment edge. Like *Doctor Who*, we just want to tell a good story and give the audience an insight into the legend that is *Doctor Who*.' Cossey noted that the access of the documentary team to the series's production was extensive, and that each episode would feature exclusive behind-the-scenes material. It was unclear, however, whether or not the material from *Confidential* would make it onto any DVD release. 'While people won't have to wait for DVD extras to see how the show is put together,' Phil Collinson explained in a report in *Doctor Who Magazine*, 'we hope the DVDs will still have extras all of their own!'

In early March 2005, it was announced that the producers of *Confidential* would additionally supply BBC1 with a half-hour special. Entitled *Doctor Who: A New Dimension*, the special, which would air about an hour and a half prior to the launch of the new series, would be a 'primer' for those who might not know the rich history of the series; each Doctor would be profiled, leading up to a sneak preview of the ninth Doctor. *A New Dimension* would also prime the viewing pump early, so to speak, increasing the amount of viewers for the evening to boost ratings for the later airing of 'Rose'.

While the *Confidential* productions would cover the new series on television, *Project: WHO?* would gain access as the BBC's official radio documentary. 'Tying in with transmission of the new BBC1 Saturday night series of *Doctor Who*, this two-part BBC Radio 2 programme takes a look at the *Doctor Who* phenomenon. Why is now the right time for it to return? There will be interviews with the stars and producers of the new series, location and set visits, and interviews with famous people who are fans of *Doctor Who*.' An official press document was released in early February, explaining that the two-part series would 'examine the continuing fascination with one of the BBC's best loved and most enduring characters' and 'why the BBC decided to launch a new television series nearly a decade after the Doctor's last small screen adventure, how the format of the show has been developed and shaped for a new audience, how the character of the Doctor was cast, and how the series will be launched and marketed around the globe.' *Project: WHO?* would be part of Radio 2's 'Countdown to Who?' season commencing in March, which would include a dedicated website and interviews on Steve Wright's weekday afternoon radio show.

CAST AND CREW ADDITIONS CONTINUE

Further developments regarding *Doctor Who*'s personnel, whether cast announcements or crew additions, were followed closely by the media; having an involvement with what would be a BBC flagship series was obviously considered desirable and newsworthy.

The *Doctor Who* Appreciation Society first confirmed several new cast members for an upcoming episode, including Basil Chung and Fiesta Mei Ling as 'an old Chinese couple' and Corey Doabe as a 'spray-painting kid'; these cast members would participate in 'Aliens of London' (with Doabe again seen briefly at the end of 'World War Three'), but as minor players only. On the production side, the DWAS linked several names to the first block of stories, as directed by Keith Boak, including unit manager Lowri Thomas, assistant directors James DaHaviland and Steff Morris, props master Patrick Begley, and sound manager Ian Richardson. The DWAS noted that the action vehicles seen in the Cardiff location shoot photographs from late July and early August outside the 'Albion Hospital' location, had been provided by Millers Action.

Doctor Who Magazine was also a prime source of cast and crew information, noting in its October issue that actor Rupert Vansittart would play the role of General Asquith, and Naoko Mori would play Dr Sato, and that both were in the very first scene shot for the new series. *Doctor Who Magazine* would feature many more reports over the coming months of new actors and crewmembers as the production team allowed their names to be revealed.

Another source of information would be the *Internet Movie Database*. The popular repository of film and television credits would be the first to list many crew members such as makeup artist Davy Jones and assistant director Lloyd Ellis, but was also subject to error and speculation (including false titles and speculative episode transmission dates) as predominantly it was fans who submitted the updates to the online database.

John Barrowman, for whom production hadn't begun yet, as his character Captain Jack would not be needed until late in the season, was interviewed in the October edition of the UK's *Gay Times* magazine, which mentioned his forthcoming appearance as more than a simple guest role: 'Next year will see him appearing in the BBC's new series of *Doctor Who*, as the Doctor's male assistant opposite Christopher Eccleston and Billie Piper,' it said. Barrowman told the magazine that it was: '... a dream come true for me because I watched *Doctor Who* as a kid in Scotland, and used to catch all the marathons on public TV in the States. When I got the news from my agent, I just stood in the street screaming. I mean ... I'll be inside the TARDIS!' Barrowman was keeping busy in the meantime, participating in charity events for World AIDS Day.

The *Sun* scooped other papers on 7 October in confirming that a character called Adam would be played by Bruno Langley, who had appeared in the long-running ITV soap *Coronation Street* playing Todd, a gay teenager. 'Bruno will be a recurring character towards the end of the series,' said the *Sun* report, quoting their usual 'BBC insider'. 'No-one is sure yet if Adam is good or bad. Bruno is really chuffed. It's a great break so soon after he left *Corrie*.'

Other casting reports came in the form of interviews, sometimes without prior notice. 'Standing at just three foot eight inches, Jimmy Vee may be small, but he packs a punch as an alien in the latest series of *Doctor Who*,' said the *Daily Record* on 26 October. 'I play different aliens in it,' Vee told the *Record*. 'It's my biggest part yet and although I'm not yet raking it in, I hope it will lead to bigger things. There are lots of different episodes and everything is top secret.' Similarly the *Mirror* reported that Zoë Wanamaker had been cast in an episode called 'Survivor' as 'the oldest person in the world, who is being kept alive in a desolate and abandoned London by her alien captors.' Viewers would later discover that Wanamaker's contribution came in the second episode, 'The End of the World', and the character, Cassandra, wasn't exactly the one being held captive ...

Sometimes, casting information came right from the source. Having passed on appearing in the series in episode eight (where it appears he might have been considered for the role of Rose's father, Pete Tyler) because of other commitments, actor Simon Pegg eventually was cast in 'The Long Game' playing the mysterious Editor. 'After a slight hiccup in time,' Pegg wrote in an e-mail to the administrators of the *Spaced Out!* website, 'I am now confirmed to appear in *Doctor Who*. I travel to Cardiff to commence filming with Chris Eccleston and Billie Piper this week.' Later in the e-mail, a wry comment from Pegg: 'I am not playing Young Davros.'

On 29 November, it was confirmed that composer Murray Gold, who had previously been announced as developing the signature theme tune for the series, would also be the composer of all the incidental music. Later, in early February 2005, *SFX* magazine accurately noted of the theme music: 'It's not as radical a remix as many thought we might get. The new arrangement updates Delia Derbyshire and Ron Grainer's original, but keeps the basic sounds. Producer Russell T Davies told *SFX* that the production team did consider keeping the 1960s/70s original, but, "When we watched it on the small screen, it just seemed a little bit empty and a bit old."' The new theme tune was delivered to the production team by Gold on 17 January, according to *SFX*, which quoted Davies as saying it was: '... brilliant, absolutely brilliant. I thought the original theme would be perfect though, but the version Murray's done is so faithful.' Although some fans were disappointed that the original Delia Derbyshire arrangement had not been retained, feeling that it was quite simply unbeatable, most were delighted to note that the Gold version would at least bring back the classic 'cliff-hanger screech' used to great effect during the 1970s.

Doctor Who Magazine confirmed the engagement of Joe Ahearne, who had previously been announced by *Professional Casting Review* as the director of block 3, comprising the sixth and eighth episodes, 'Dalek' and 'Father's Day'. The magazine also confirmed in early December the final two directors of the first series; they would be Brian Grant and James Hawes. Grant would direct block 4A which would ultimately be comprised solely of the seventh episode, 'The Long Game', while Hawes would direct Steven Moffat's two-part story, 'The Empty Child' and 'The Doctor Dances', as block 4B. After a long delay, *Doctor Who Magazine* also confirmed that Ahearne would in addition be helming the final three episodes of the series.

LOCATION PRODUCTION CONTINUES

In early October 2004, a new session of location recording was discovered by *Doctor Who* fans taking place at a Cardiff landmark, the Temple of Peace in Cardiff City Centre, a building dating back to the 1930s and dedicated by Lord Davies to the Welsh people. Recording was underway on the episode fans would later realise was 'The End of the World', as 'lots of blue midget aliens and "tree people" having lunch in the catering wagons on Museum Avenue' were spotted, according to fan Mark Davies. Photographs showed several dwarf-sized extras, mostly children, with blue painted skin, along with Jimmy Vee, the actor playing the Moxx of Balhoon, wearing only his prosthetic face mask and large forehead, smoking a cigarette outside his trailer.

On 7 October, the *Newsquest* syndicated news service reported that a security company at a leisure centre in Penarth, south of Cardiff, which had been guarding props and high-tech equipment being used to record the new *Doctor Who* series, was almost broken into by a crowd of thugs. 'Officers were called in to deal with an incident at the Leisure Centre last Friday night,' Huw Smart, inspector at Penarth police station, was quoted as saying. 'There is an ongoing problem of youth annoyance at the Leisure Centre in Cogan. We have arranged for regular patrols of the area.' Penarth was also used for recording on 21 October at Penarth Pier.

Wales continued to be the primary location for recording. In fact, the authorities in Cardiff were hoping the city would become a tourist attraction because of its association with *Doctor Who*. Said Matt Hills in the *Western Mail*: '*Doctor Who* could help Cardiff become the centre of the universe for science fiction buffs around the world, following the sale of international TV rights. Shooting for the eagerly-anticipated new series continued in the capital this week, with dedicated websites excitedly trailing pictures of new aliens and blue-painted dwarves milling around the city centre's Cathays Park ... Cardiff is fast becoming a magnet for British fans of the show, drawn by the prospect of a rare glimpse of *Doctor Who*'s space-and-time-travelling craft the TARDIS, as well as his young assistant Rose ... A similar thing happened with Vancouver when they were filming *The X-Files* there, with tourists who would be science fiction fans going around locations where it was filmed.'

Cardiff's Millennium Stadium was used in late October as the primary location for the recording of the sixth episode, 'Dalek', which took advantage of the long concrete corridors and spiralling staircases. According to the *Planet Who* website, production papers leaked to the press: '... detailed a filming schedule on episode 6 (written by Rob Shearman), and contained several production drawings/concept art [sketches] for the episode. One sketch appeared to show a Dalek hovering high above a workman/security guard surrounded by a high wall. The documents also revealed that the Daleks had acquired jet propulsion.' Use of the Millennium Stadium continued through at least the first week of November, during which it was reported in the *Western Mail* that police were alerted after Daleks were involved in a shootout with armed guards! 'Gunfire and explosions could be heard for miles around as the filming for the new TV series of *Doctor Who* went off with a bang,' reported the *Western Mail* on 2 November. 'Police had a series of calls from passers-by who thought an armed robbery was going on in Cardiff city centre. But the noise was from the special effects on the set of the cult time-travelling show.' A BBC spokesman later told the *Mail* that police had been aware of the recording at the stadium, but locals had not been informed.

There were also sequences recorded in Cardiff along Queen Street in the second week of November, with director Euros Lyn on hand as well as banners and signs for the Henrik's department store. Although rumours were prevalent that they were simple pick-up shots for already recorded episodes, Davies had noted in his 'Production Notes' in an issue of *Doctor Who Magazine* that 'Euros is juggling schedules (just to make life easier, one of his scenes from block two has been recorded in block one, while another will shift to block three.' Quite different from the production of a standard episodic television series, much of *Doctor Who* this time around was being recorded piecemeal, with several episodes before the cameras at any given time. As fan Ian Golden reported on 10 November: 'The day's filming started at 9.30am at the British Gas office in Churchill Way. They were there to shoot just one minute of film, two TARDIS landing shots from different episodes. Billie and Chris were the only two actors present ... For the second bit of the filming, the TARDIS was moved. Only three sides of the TARDIS were built for this scene.' The *Sun* also covered the on-location production, noting that Piper and Eccleston had been seen holding hands (although this was most likely part of the recording session.)

Two weeks later, *SFX* magazine reported sequences being recorded on the streets of Cardiff again, this time on a street in Bute, near Cardiff Bay train station. 'We don't know which episode they're shooting, but because of the presence of soldiers in red caps, our guess is that they're filming pick-up shots for the two-parter "Aliens Of London",' reported the magazine. Their correspondent, Darren Floyd, noted that he had seen Mickey (Noel Clarke) get in a car a few times, and some soldiers walking back and forth ... presumably scenes from an episode yet to be discussed in the press and among fans.

THE LOGO, DESIGN AND BRANDING

The visual elements of *Doctor Who* were always going to be controversial amongst fans who paid attention to these sorts of things. A major discussion point occurred on 18 October, as the series's new logo was revealed. The logo, which very much looked like a still frame from a moving image, had been created 'with widescreen TVs in mind,' explained the *Sci Fi Online* website. 'All the lettering is on one line in square upper-case text, backed by a coloured oval, some lens flare and the hint of printed circuits.' The logo had been created by Louise Hillam, Alison Jenkins and Hywel Roberts from the Graphic Design team at BBC Wales, with Luke Davies and Paul Humphrey at Insect Design working on the background. Within a few days, several viewers had managed to work out the BBC employees' e-mail addresses and had sent disparaging notes through (although nowhere near the massive amounts of threatening e-mail reported in some quarters of the fan press). Some time later, the logo was cause for some newspapers to have a bit of fun. 'Far be it from us to cast aspersions on the hype-tastic new *Doctor Who*, powered by a thousand tabloid Billie Piper stories and the slavering of sci-fi fans everywhere,' the *Guardian* would say on 16 March, 'but isn't there something a little familiar – a little earthbound – about its logo? Are we the only ones to notice the uncanny similarity between the new *Who* signage and the little orange lights that twinkle on taxis? What can it mean? That taxi drivers are like Time Lords in that they both take ages to get anywhere? That their average age is 900 years old? That they won't go south of the river? Or has the new logo been inspired by some BBC execs' favourite mode of transport? There are, as the good Doctor might say himself, no such things as coincidences.'

On 1 November, BBC Worldwide, attending a brand licensing event in London, distributed *Doctor Who* promotional materials including a postcard ... the first piece of stand-alone official promotional material associated with the new series. The postcard featured a photograph of Christopher Eccleston and Billie Piper on the front, in costume and standing in front of the TARDIS. 'The Doctor looks and seems human,' read the back of the postcard. 'He's handsome, sexy and witty, and could be mistaken for just another man in the street. But the Doctor is a Time Lord: a 900 year old alien with 2 hearts, part of a gifted civilisation who mastered time travel. Christopher Eccleston plays the Doctor, and Billie Piper is Rose in the thrilling new series of *Doctor Who*, on BBC TV in Spring 2005. Brace yourself for some exhilarating experiences and deadly confrontations across time and space. The human race will survive – but only with the Doctor's help.'

Design concept illustrations began leaking out over the last few months of 2004. The Bristol-based Pixel Studios posted what it called 'concept art' for the forthcoming series, including pieces resembling the spiders and orbital platform from 'The End of the World' and the TARDIS deep within the Nestene lair in 'Rose'. The images were used 'to help visualise some of the more challenging parts of the scripts', though it's unclear as to whether or not they were actually used by the production team. Concept artist Matthew Savage, later confirmed to be working on the production, posted several designs in his portfolio on his personal website, including some TARDIS elevations and sketch drawings of a possible revamp of the Cybermen.

Overall design was an ongoing process on the new series, especially when it came to the TARDIS. 'The TARDIS has changed over the years, so many times,' production designer Edward Thomas told *Doctor Who Confidential*, 'so I wanted to make it feel as if it had arrived at this juncture in history. So we looked mostly to nature, to organic structures ... Things like coral were quite a nice idea. So the main metal structure of the TARDIS has been covered in this coral-type effect.' Thomas later told the *SFCrowsNest* website in early January 2005: 'To be able to completely re-design the interior of the TARDIS was amazing. Its basic drive mechanism is the same but we've gone for a more organic look using materials such as glass, porcelain and even coral, with a raised central area and a domed roof.' He noted that the roundels remained in the walls, there was still a coat stand in the corner ... but that within the TARDIS console would be seen 'old handbrakes, pressure dials, loose nuts and bolts, an old trim-phone, post-it notes, glass balls, hammers and even a navigation sextant.' As Thomas explained, 'Most long-running series have sets and props they use all the time, but because *Doctor Who* is so varied, changing from week to week, we use things again, which I'm sure they did on the old shows. Technology has moved on but in some ways things haven't changed and the challenges are just as demanding today as they were then.'

The TARDIS interior was actually designed by group effort; the entire design team – Thomas, Savage, Stephen Nicholas, Colin Richmond, Dan Walker, Peter Walpole and Bryan Hitch – contributed towards its ultimate look. The elements within the TARDIS, including the glass panels and walls, consisted of eighty sheets of acrylic vacuum-formed panels, 800 meters of jumbo pipe, fifty sheets of industrial wire mesh and 1500 meters of steelwork. According to the *SFCrowsNest* interview, the TARDIS interior was only one of approximately 650 sets created, from location shots to studio work, for the first series alone.

Some long-time fans were disappointed when the new TARDIS interior was eventually unveiled, feeling that it was too great a departure from the gleaming white, futuristic image established in the 'classic' series. A widely held view was that the original version, as introduced in the very first episode back in 1963, remained the most visually impressive – and, to the puzzlement of some, this view appeared to be shared by key members of the production team, notwithstanding that they had ultimately decided on such a radical departure. Thomas, in an interview in early 2005 with *Televisual* magazine, said: 'Russell and I thought the most powerful TARDIS was the first one, so we kept this in mind, but then went back to nature.'

Physical design wasn't the only area of new creative design work; CGI and miniature photography would add to the mix. 'The kind of things we're doing now couldn't have been done fifteen years ago when the show was last on,' Mike Tucker, who had worked on the original *Doctor Who* series in its final years, told the *SFCrowsNest* site. 'During the last couple of Sylvester McCoy stories, what was then the BBC Video Effects Department was doing some groundbreaking stuff, but it was only after the show came off air that the real digital revolution came along. The gulf between what we can do now and did then is enormous.' Tucker told *Televisual* that the visual effects firm The Mill were animating 'a retro-looking UFO smashing into Big Ben' based on designs by Bryan Hitch, but the moment of impact was best achieved using a miniature. 'You could sit there and hand-animate every single particle of dust, but sometimes it's easier to create miniatures and then just smash them up.'

'With *Doctor Who*, the storytelling was so good we knew it was something we really wanted to do,' Robin Shenfield, chief executive of The Mill, told Stephen Hunt of *SFCrowsNest*. 'The range of effects we're using is quite extraordinary. Everything we do that's cutting edge is in this production.' The Mill's visual effects producer for *Doctor Who*, Will Cohen, noted the extensive effects work to be done on the creatures later revealed as the Gelth, and on the cosmetically enhanced 'last human' Cassandra. The Gelth: '... started off just as ectoplasm but then became faces that had to speak. In another story, one computer-generated character needed four minutes of lip-synching, which is a huge undertaking in a TV project. The series was very stimulating for our team, because we were able to input our own creative ideas, much more so than in film. We were contributing, not just executing.' Will Cohen told *Televisual* that this would be the largest number of effects shots ever pulled together for a UK TV drama; on episode two, 'we refer to it as the "space opera" episode because there are two exterior space-station shots, views from outer space, a lot of green-screen set replacements, animated spiders and loads of particle work with suns expanding.' The first season featured approximately 800 of The Mill's special effects in all, with episode two involving the largest number of these. No other British television production had been as ambitious in scale as the new series of *Doctor Who* would be.

Other technical developments included the use of a high-quality digital alternative to 16mm and Super 16 film, both of which had become the de-facto standard for quality TV production in most of the world; the new series would be shot in widescreen on Digital Betacam, or DigiBeta for short, formatted for PAL-format televisions (the video standard used in the UK), and then 'filmised' in post production to give it a slick 'film look'. According to *Televisual*, the BBC had to turn down a prospective Sony sponsorship deal involving the use of a newer technology, HDCam, both because of the lack of a current high-definition market in the UK, and because negotiations had started far too late to make use of it.

The result of all of this effort was first seen in a brief clip shown at a BBC Winter Highlights promotional event held in early December and then quickly made available to view on the official *Doctor Who* website. A simple teaser trailer, accompanied by the original Delia Derbyshire arrangement of the series's theme tune, it featured the opening montage from 'Rose' (the space-bound shot of the Moon, then focusing on the Earth and down into Rose's flat) along with a brief selection of dialogue (in which the Doctor tells Rose to 'Run for your life!'), and the dematerialising TARDIS. 'It's almost time ...' noted a caption at the beginning of the trailer, followed at the end by the ominous '... but not yet.' While there had been many photographs and news interviews, this was the first true sign that televised *Doctor Who* was soon to appear.

MOMENTS WITH THE PRESS

As 2004 drew to a close, many of the actors associated with the new series started to speak to the press. Noel Clarke discussed the end of *Auf Wiedersehen, Pet* and the beginning of his work on *Doctor Who*. 'It seems to be that whenever they're rehashing a show from 20 years ago, I get a call,' he told *icWales* on December 1. 'I watched both of the series when I was young and to grow up and then be in them is really rare. It's fun and just what you imagine it would be like, especially with *Doctor Who*. When I was little I dreamed about running from monsters and Daleks and 20 years later here I am doing just that. I got really excited when I went inside the TARDIS for the first time.' When asked about Billie Piper, he told the *Daily Express* on 18 December, 'Billie is great, very down to earth. She is a brilliant actress and seriously underrated. So what about the kissing scene? Who doesn't like doing kissing scenes?' And about the relationship between their two characters: 'You want them to get together but you're not sure if they're going to.'

Not sentiments shared by Piper; she felt Rose's attentions lay elsewhere, as she explained to *Marie Claire* magazine in their Christmas issue: 'The great thing about this *Doctor Who* is that as much as it's sci-fi, it's so much about the Doctor's and Rose's dynamic and their journey and about educating each other. About him expanding and challenging her ideas and, you know, just showing her stuff that she would have never seen. And it's her teaching him to be more human and be sympathetic towards things. So they're kind of like a good friendship or a good marriage or whatever. Of course, you desperately want them to get together.' The magazine called the relationship between the Doctor and Rose an 'unspoken sexual frisson', although sex would never come into play. Piper was obviously very enthusiastic about the work she'd done over the course of the past six months, and about her co-star, Christopher Eccleston: 'He's so brilliant. What a top bloke.'

Bruno Langley mentioned that he had nightmares about being chased by Daleks; but it was a price worth paying, as he explained in a BBC press release: 'I couldn't have asked for a better next role because *Doctor Who* is another great institution. I do remember Tom Baker wandering around with his long scarf, but not much else.' Langley also had one of the first glimpses in the series of a flying Dalek. 'Adam says: "Big alien death machine defeated by a flight of steps" then the Dalek says: "Elevate" and starts to fly ... It's probably one of the biggest gags in the series. I was very privileged to be given that line.'

Simon Callow, who had completed his recording on the series earlier in the year, spoke to the *Frank Skinner Show* on ITV about his role in *Phantom of the Opera* and that in the new *Doctor Who* series. 'Once you're in the series you're part of *Doctor Who* forever,' Callow said, noting that fans had turned up during the recording in Wales amidst the paparazzi when he was on location, sometimes at three in the morning (and a few even in costume, he explained, although in truth those were probably the extras!) Callow was excited about the role, in which his character, Charles Dickens, 'teams with the Doctor to save the Earth from alien infestation.' He later told the *SFCrowsNest* website: 'The script very cleverly connects his idealism, which ends up being restored by his experiences, with the Doctor's desire to save the world. Initially, he is shattered by the notion that this realm of the unknown, which he has always dismissed, actually exists, but he then embraces it. As the Doctor tells him, he's not wrong about everything, he just has more to learn.'

The various interviews and press reports added a sense of urgency at the end of 2004, as if the series were closer than had been previously thought. And it wasn't just the fans who were paying attention, but the general public too; Russell T Davies thought that it was really all about them, the viewing public, and capturing their imaginations. 'If we were doing it for nostalgia, just to look back and make a pastiche of what was,' he told ITV1's *The Afternoon Show* in late December, 'I'd think – what was the point of that? I fell in love with that programme when I was eight years old, and it actually made me fall in love with television full stop. And I'm still here, twenty years later. It's aiming for those eight-year-olds who sit there now: who want something like that.' Then, when host Eamonn O'Neal commented that the series would start in March 2005, Davies did not contradict him. Truly, it was almost time ...

CHAPTER NINE:
THE APPROACHING STORM

At last, 2005 arrived. The year that *Doctor Who* would make its celebrated return was here ... but a definite broadcast date had yet to be announced. There were still months to come, press calls and photos and interviews and moments of grandeur in the lead-up to the long-awaited return of one of Britain's most honoured television traditions.

EXPECTATIONS RISE

'Never has a TV series been so shrouded in secrecy,' reported the *Sunday Mirror* on 2 January, 'but soon we'll be able to see how Christopher Eccleston fares as the travelling Time Lord, and whether Billie Piper measures up as his assistant.' The paper was merely stating the obvious: 2005 would be either the year of *Doctor Who*, or its last gasp. Time would tell.

It wasn't as if the series didn't have its air of celebrity. 'Billie Piper is out to prove her mettle as *Doctor Who*'s new sidekick,' proclaimed the *Independent on Sunday* on the same day, calling Piper a 'talent to watch.' Not too coincidentally, her recent work on the film *Spirit Trap* would soon be shown at the prestigious Sundance Film Festival before making its way to Britain and across the United States. In America, fans were already able to tune in to Piper's work in *The Canterbury Tales* as the BBC America network began broadcasting it in early January.

Eccleston, too, had plenty of attention focused upon him. 'Everyone was expecting him to be dour, and he's so funny. I think we can do extraordinary things with it,' Davies told the *Independent on Sunday*. 'It's classy, eccentric, there's a lot of satire, and I think it's going to work.' As writer Mark Gatiss told the *Twitchfilm* website in early January, 'He's brilliant. I think the show will surprise a lot of people and that, particularly, Chris will. He's known for his intensity, his rather scary intensity, which he *does* have as the Doctor. And equally, if you know him in real life, he's a really good laugh and a lovely man and it's that sort of duality that he brings to it. He's like a kind of crazy child, but then when he tells you off you quake in your shoes. It's actually kind of a Tom Baker-ish quality, but in a completely different way.'

The press was beginning to roll out the proverbial welcome mat. The *Guardian* on 9 January called the new series one of its 'fifty must-sees for spring', placing it at the high point of #5 on the list. 'Few people under the age of 30 will remember Tom Baker at his most magnetic, as the Dalek-thwarting Time Lord,' wrote the paper. 'Four decades on from the first shows the BBC is bringing the Doctor back and the signs for success are good, with the brilliant Russell T Davies on writing duty. A massive *Doctor Who* fan of old, he promises "full-blooded drama" and storylines which are "fun, exciting, contemporary and scary", while Christopher Eccleston should have just the right balance of bit-of-rough charm and glowering, Messianic intensity to merit the shabby great coat and (we hope) loop-the-loop scarf. Billie Piper in the role of his assistant, Rose Tyler, will doubtless help keep teenage boys of all ages happy.' Not to be outdone, the Scottish *Sunday Herald* called the series one of its '101 Big Events of 2005': 'Thou shalt watch enraptured as *Doctor Who* returns to the small screen,' commanded the newspaper. 'Fifteen years after it was taken off the air, *Doctor Who* is remembered as a defining piece of cult television ... The brilliant character actor Christopher Eccleston will be the new Doctor – that curious, inscrutable, vaguely unsettling alien time-traveller who defends humanity for his own whimsical reasons.'

Former Doctors weighed in on what they were expecting, too. 'I'll be very interested to see it myself,' Peter Davison said in a syndicated interview in early January. 'Hopefully, it will have more money spent on it than they spent on ours. I remember it as a lot of running up and down corridors. And a lot of acting with people who weren't there because of blue screen.'

The expectations were rising, as production continued and the date of launch fast approached.

THE TITLE GAME

For a television series with so much public attention, the fact that so many of its episode titles were unknown until shortly prior to transmission was a major coup for the production. Russell T Davies had already disclosed the titles 'Rose', 'The End of the World' and 'Aliens of London' in his early 'Production Notes' in *Doctor Who Magazine*, and they'd come to be the expected final titles on their respective episodes. The title 'The Unquiet Dead' for episode three first circulated as a possible title during the summer of 2004, though it wasn't actually confirmed by *Doctor Who Magazine* until January 2005.

'Aliens of London' was originally the title used for episodes four *and* five, with the labels 'Part One' and 'Part Two' appended. In early January 2005, it was reported on Internet forums that the two episodes would have their own titles, and not, as had previously been considered, subtitles. '10 Downing Street' was the chosen title for episode five, though in early March, *SFX* magazine confirmed that it would finally be called 'World War Three'. The same issue noted the title for episode six was 'Dalek', though at one point it was known to be 'Creature of Lies'; the titles 'The Creature Inside' and 'Museum Piece' were never working titles for the episode. (Writer Rob Shearman at one point joked that he'd been tempted to call his replacement script, when the Daleks were not in the picture, 'Absence of the Daleks'.)

'The Long Game' was revealed in *Doctor Who Magazine* by Davies in July 2004, although 'The Companion Who Couldn't' was an early working title. 'Father's Day', meanwhile, was the final title for episode eight, as confirmed in *Radio Times* in the third week of March 2005. The previous working title for the episode, for a long period of time, had been 'Wounded Time'. The title for episodes nine and ten had been revealed by *Doctor Who Magazine* in November 2004 as 'The Empty Child' but, as with the earlier two-parter 'Aliens of London', the second episode eventually gained its own title: 'The Doctor Dances' was revealed by the *Outpost Gallifrey* website in mid-January 2005, as was the title of episode eleven, 'Boom Town'.

'The Parting of the Ways' had been referred to by Davies in his original notes as the title of the last two episodes, but again, with individual titles for each two part story, there was soon a new title for episode twelve. Rumoured to be 'Gamesworld' (or possibly 'Gameshow World') for a considerable amount of time, it was finally announced as 'Bad Wolf' in April 2005 by *Doctor Who Magazine*.

LOCATION RECORDING CONTINUES

The Cardiff branch of the *Doctor Who* Appreciation Society, Timeless, reported some location recording on 9 January. On that day, the two ends of Womanby Street (one in Quay Street and the other opposite Cardiff Castle) were blocked off by traffic cones and security people;

Eccleston and Piper recorded a sequence shortly before 7.00pm in which they ran into an alley off Womanby Street opposite the Gatekeeper pub. 'The alley was dressed with washing hanging to dry from lines between the buildings and looked not unlike the closing credits to 1960s editions of soap opera *Coronation Street*, albeit in colour,' reported fan Timothy Farr. 'This prompted speculation among onlookers that these scenes are intended for the rumoured storyline in which Rose finds herself in a time when her deceased father was still alive. There was one strong overhead light source on set shining into the alley from Womanby Street all evening, suggesting both a moonlit scene and that all shots being recorded were taking place in the alley.' It was assumed that this location work was being completed for episode eight, later revealed to be 'Father's Day', especially after a *Starburst* magazine photo shoot carried shots of a 1980s wedding that appeared to be from the same location. (Photographs on the BBC official site's *WhoSpy* web feature showed flora brought in specifically for the production of the episode, including topiary swans.) It is, however, more likely that the Womanby Street recording was for scenes where the Doctor and Rose arrive in 1940s London in 'The Empty Child'.

13 January was apparently the last day of recording at Cardiff Royal Infirmary, which had experienced a re-dress of the location for the recording of Steven Moffat's wartime two-parter. 'A security guard last night confirmed that it is *Doctor Who*, and that filming had finished for the day – Chris and Billie had already left,' wrote fan Alex Willcox, who revealed that the building had once again been mocked up as Albion Hospital, the site of the alien autopsy in 'Aliens of London'. The next day, Timothy Farr noticed that the production was still recording on City Road in Cardiff. 'An arched sign over the gates, apparently of cast iron, proclaims it as Albion Hospital,' he explained. 'Behind the walls to either side of the gates are gunmetal coloured sheets of corrugated iron. Behind the gates, the low walls along the ramp to the curved double front doors have been surmounted with goldfish bowl gas lamps and reinforced with sandbags. All the windows have diagonal crosses of white tape and a large cloth banner hangs far above the doors covering much of the frontage. It bears the symbol of the Red Cross.' Farr described to *Outpost Gallifrey* an extensive technical process for setting up the shots that would be recorded that night; traffic noise would not be a problem, as no dialogue would be recorded. They would include Eccleston breaking through the gates using his sonic screwdriver (described as a 'pen light') and an eerie sequence marked by a thick fog created by smoke machines: 'The doors of the hospital swing open and a column of figures shamble out, moving at an unnaturally slow, even pace towards the open gates. They all wear primitive gas masks.' The set décor was of such intricate detail, in fact, that much of the design work wouldn't be seen completely on screen.

Several days later, on 18 January, reports came in from several correspondents discussing further location footage shot for Moffat's story. Paul Mount recounted that the 'last scene filmed, several times, showed a dozen or more "zombified" humans in gasmasks ... lots of mist drifting across and a cleverly-placed arc light on the other side of the road cast an extremely spooky shadow of a tree branch right across the building.' 'The Hospital was mocked up with the same Albion Hospital sign used previously,' said Alex Willcox. 'A big Red Cross flag hung from the front of the building, and the windows had crosses of tape over them. A corrugated iron fence had been erected above the outer wall, with KEEP OUT signs, and several wartime posters, about A4 in size ... The first shot recorded was of the Doctor walking up to the gates of Albion Hospital, rattling them and finding them locked. He takes out his sonic screwdriver, which shines a blue light, and the padlock opens. He then opens the gate and walks through.

The camera starts high above the gate and swoops down, taking in the Albion Hospital sign, ending up at ground level as Chris walks into shot.'

Willcox also saw some of the episode's 'zombies' coming out of the doorway. 'There were about two dozen by my reckoning; men, women and children; all in period costume and wearing gas masks. I remember a large chap at the front in a purple tank top, two schoolgirls in brown coats, with satchels, and I think a nurse. They all appeared to have a cut or scar on their right hands. The zombies walked out of the door, and straight down the pathway to the main gates – no other movement or emotion at all.'

The next day, Eccleston was back recording the first of several days' work at the Bistro 10 restaurant in Cardiff Bay. 'The scene I saw being [recorded] involved a fairly lengthy exchange of dialogue between Eccleston and a blonde actress,' reported Matt Hills, 'who were sat facing each other across a swanky restaurant table – Chris seeming to be doing most of the talking. Since he was pretty much stationed in the centre of the restaurant, and since it is entirely glass-fronted, passers-by – and the few fans in attendance – had a perfect view as takes were rehearsed ... What I saw was a tight close-up of Eccleston shot in exact profile, and positioned towards the right-hand side of the frame facing inwards ... The camera stayed on Chris as he spoke, and then very slowly (this was one take, approximately a minute or so long) moved further away and started to circle the table. Eccleston then became more clearly animated and began to gesture as if to emphasise points in an argument or exposition.'

The actress Eccleston was dining with was Annette Badland, previously announced as appearing solely in the 'Aliens of London' two-parter, but now recording separate scenes for her return in the late-season story 'Boom Town', which would pick up on a few disparate plotlines. 'It is beginning to seem as though this season's stories,' Hills continued, 'though distinct, may jigsaw together in extremely crafty ways to create far more than the sum of their parts.'

A week later, on 2 February, there was another spate of outdoor recording in two separate locations: in Cardiff Bay at the Plas Roald Dahl, and at a train station at Barry Island. The Cardiff shooting was an especially public spectacle. 'I arrived outside the new Wales Millennium Centre, and there she was, the old girl herself, the TARDIS, with its white tarpaulin to protect it from the curious,' wrote fan John Campbell Rees. 'I walked towards the waterfront of Cardiff, and could not help but notice where [recording] was taking place. Russell T Davies and Phil Collinson had set up their monitors midway along Bute Crescent, the road that runs along the length of Plas Roald Dahl, and were monitoring the setting up of a scene on the waterfront. This was a few hundred yards from the restaurant where [recording] occurred last week.' Rees noted that it appeared that these three episodes – 'Boom Town' and the two parter begun with 'The Empty Child' – were being recorded simultaneously by director Joe Ahearne. 'The scene was set for Eccleston and Badland to run from the waterfront,' Rees continued, 'along Bute Crescent and down a set of concrete steps into Plas Roald Dahl. As well as the two leads, the scene featured a number of extras who ran around, giving the impression of panic. This scene was rehearsed and then [recorded] twice, before Joe Ahearne was satisfied.'

In every report from the location – including a number from fans over Christmas and well into January and February – Christopher Eccleston's joviality was mentioned. He was described as 'obviously enjoying what he is doing immensely, laughing and joking' with Piper or Davies or the series's guest cast ... a far cry from claims made months later about his being burned out by the production and wanting to leave because of typecasting.

'At 9.00pm,' Rees continued, 'a sequence featuring Billie Piper as Rose was prepared. The last time I had seen Ms Piper in costume, portraying ...Rose Tyler, at the Swansea shoot last September, she looked every inch a Victorian young lady in a long skirt which swept the floor. This time, after discarding a warm sheepskin coat and jogging bottoms, she looked a very modern young woman, in a skirt that barely swept the top of her legs.' The sequence he saw recorded was of Rose running into Plas Roald Dahl.

Alex Willcox reported on another scene: '... featuring the Doctor, Rose, Mickey and Captain Jack all running down the alleyway at the opposite end of the building from the first shot. This scene was recorded several times, with the camera positioned further down the alley each time. I caught a snippet of dialogue shouted by John Barrowman: "... telephone! We'll never get her out. It's teeming!" Shortly after this, Annette Badland was recorded running down the same alley ... The most exciting scene of the day came last. There's a balcony running the length of the rear of the building, and we spotted Chris peering through a French window above this. At the end of the balcony was scaffolding with a ladder down to the ground. Annette Badland ran out [of] the window, along the balcony, over the edge onto the scaffold, down the ladder and in front of the building to the alley we'd previously seen her running down. As she reached the scaffold, Chris came through the same window and shouted "Margaret!" A chap in a suit came out behind him, and the two fought on the balcony. After throwing the other guy off him, Chris followed Badland's route down to the ground.' The recording caused the *icWales* news website to ponder, on 9 February, 'Who could that be rushing around Cardiff Bay? Surely not a Time Lord with the ability to turn back the clock?'

Location work commenced at the Vale of Glamorgan Railway station on Barry Island in early February, but public and press were kept a considerable distance away ... although fan Peter Dickinson did manage to capture with a telescopic lens, pictures of the redesigned station, which included many period signs and authentic-looking railway cars. 'Kill him with war savings!' proclaimed one of the posters, setting the tone for 1940s Britain. Again, not all the period detail apparent here would be fully seen on screen in the transmitted episode.

The final location recording that was witnessed by fans took place on 15 February 2005, amidst a cold snap that chilled both production crew and onlookers alike. Reported Paul Mount, 'The TARDIS is there outside the Millennium Centre ... Further on, on the esplanade of the Bay where a number of restaurants and bars cluster together, the unit's been busy filming outside the long Terra Nova bar. Here Noel Clarke and Billie Piper's stand-in (Billie's sick, apparently) are filming a scene on a bench by the railings overlooking the bay. A couple of rehearsals and the camera turns. Mickey is talking with Rose. A number of pedestrians are passing by. Suddenly, they start looking alarmed, looking up and all around. They start running and screaming, mass panic. Rose jumps up and runs off. Mickey, clearly annoyed, jumps up too. "It's him again, isn't it?" he says (or words very much to that effect). "It's the Doctor. It's always about the Doctor, isn't it? It's never about me!" The scene is recorded again – Noel fluffs his line to the amusement of crew and onlookers. A quick break and the scene's rehearsed and recorded again, this time with the addition of a shower of polystyrene rubble being thrown on the fleeing crowd from the balcony of the Terra Nova bar.'

For all of the location work done, there were many more scenes shot during those months inside the studio. *Doctor Who Magazine* noted that on 7 February, the opening scenes from 'The Empty Child', featuring the TARDIS interior, were shot. Recently the entirety of recording for episode seven, 'The Long Game', had taken place inside the studio. ('Dalek' was shot mostly on location under the Millennium Stadium in Cardiff, even though it was also all interior shots.) Many sequences were recorded inside what became, in effect, the BBC's *Doctor Who* studio: a huge warehouse in Newport, near Cardiff, converted for use. Large swathes of action had been captured away from prying eyes. The TARDIS interior scenes were only one example; other major locales shot fully in-studio included Rose's flat, Captain Jack's spaceship and the inside of Satellite Five.

Throughout eight months of production, *Doctor Who* fans had been treated to 19th-Century Cardiff, Blitz-ravaged London, aliens from the far future and Auton invasions in the present. Unprecedented access to the location recordings had been granted by the production team, with the proviso that the fans stayed out of the way; and to gauge from reports over the months, they'd done so and managed to retain the respect that the production team had for the series's army of devotees.

CAST AND CREW UPDATES

News about casting continued to be reported both in official publications and the press. While *Radio Times* broke news of actress Tamsin Greig appearing in the new series, specifically in 'The Long Game', *Doctor Who Magazine* continued its supply of exclusive casting updates. Popular actor Richard Wilson would also star in the series, in the two-parter begun in 'The Empty Child', playing 'the mysterious Doctor Constantine'. The press also continued to report on the strange role Zoë Wanamaker would play ('a part shrouded in secrecy ... tabloid rumours [about the nature of the part] are completely untrue!')

Cast continued to come and go on their episodes, many of them enjoying being part of the new series. Mark Benton, who had recorded his role some months earlier playing Clive in the episode 'Rose', spoke to the *Designer* magazine website in mid-January: 'I play this *Doctor Who* boffin who's got this website running about the show and Billie Piper comes to find out about it. I guess I play the voice of every *Doctor Who* fan. I'm not saying that every *Doctor Who* fan lives in a shed though. I talk about the Doctor in the way I suppose fans would ... and then I get killed.' Albert Valentine, a seven-year-old actor who guested in 'The Empty Child' and 'The Doctor Dances', was the subject of an article several months later in the *Southland Echo*, noting that he'd spent almost three weeks in January shooting. 'Despite having his dad, Dean, along for the duration of the filming, in Cardiff,' wrote columnist Simon Bishop, 'Albert admitted: "I still missed my mum." ... Says Dean, "It was quite touching at the end of his last scene, because all the crew clapped and congratulated him on doing so well. And we got to keep the special mask that he had to wear for part of the show."' Albert admitted he didn't know too much about *Doctor Who* before gaining the part: 'My mum and dad told me a bit about what he was like. I told my teacher about the part and she thought that it was exciting.'

Doctor Who Magazine confirmed that Joe Ahearne would return to helm episodes twelve and thirteen as the 'sixth block' of recording, but remained close-lipped on who would direct 'block five' (episode eleven, 'Boom Town'); word first broke on the Internet that Ahearne would also direct this episode, bringing his total *Doctor Who* directing contribution to five episodes throughout the first season.

AN UNTAMED PRESS

With so much interest in *Doctor Who* in the months prior to its transmission, it was perhaps inevitable that much 'secret' information would leak via the press and the Internet. It's hard for a small group to keep information secret; it's almost impossible for a production on the scale of a major BBC television series to do so.

Sometimes stories take on a life of their own. The *Mirror*, on 12 January, was one of the first papers to report a story about the series being hit by a shortage of dwarf actors because of the production of two films, Tim Burton's remake of *Charlie and the Chocolate Factory* and the next film in the *Harry Potter* series, *Harry Potter and the Goblet of Fire*. 'It's very difficult to employ persons of restricted growth when, as our producer Phil Collinson says, "Bloody Gringotts and the Chocolate Factory are filming at the same time,"' Davies was quoted as saying. The problem wasn't necessarily in the meaning of this story (while there might have been issues behind the scenes, they were relatively minor, and *Chocolate Factory*, in reality, employed only one dwarf actor, Deep Roy, to play *all* the eccentric Oompa Loompas), but rather in the timing: the story had been gleaned from Davies's 'Production Notes' column in a recent issue of *Doctor Who Magazine*, and had dramatically spiralled out of control. The recording itself – which the press (including even science fiction magazines and journals) reported as being in turmoil from the supposed dwarf shortage during a very recent time period – had actually taken place *months* prior, for 'The End of the World', during August 2004.

Magazines and newspapers often wanted to be first with a story, and everything was suddenly fair game. Suggestions were made by fans, often half-heartedly, that the tabloids were sending spies into the various online discussion communities, purloining information and representing it as factual – suggestions that turned out to be completely true. False information about the episode 'Dalek' taking place on board a space station had made it into the *Mirror* and into the science fiction magazines, after having originated amongst fans online. One rumour in particular made the rounds that a working title for the series's Dalek episode had been 'Cargo'; this was picked up in several places, including in at least one tabloid newspaper, unaware that it had been made up in jest by a fan, Simon Cooper, on the *Outpost Gallifrey* discussion forum. Rumours had a nasty way of spiralling out of control, and there were eyes everywhere. As journalist Tim Rider, who had himself covered the series for the *Daily Star*, explained in a post on the same forum, 'You ARE being watched! I can tell you that this website is regularly monitored by every national newspaper. Why? Because there are genuine *Doctor Who* fans on every national newspaper who care as much for the show as me and you!'

Christopher Eccleston was a target of these so-called 'reports' as late as January 2005, being represented by newspapers and online sources as 'refusing to speak between scenes, and asking his fellow actors and crew members not to talk to him.' He was quoted as stating, 'It brings me out of character.' The problem was, there were no actual authenticated reports of this happening, and in fact everyone who had visited the locations – including anxious fans wanting a glimpse of the new Doctor, and those who had actually posed for photos with the actor – would say quite the opposite ... that Eccleston was a gracious, charming and very positive man who seemed to relish his experience on *Doctor Who*.

And then there were those who might ruin the enjoyment of the forthcoming series for viewers. 'The Ruiners are coming,' proclaimed Russell T Davies in his regular *Doctor Who Magazine* column in early 2005. His piece was accompanied by an artwork sketch of fans reading *Radio Times* and the *Sun* promoting '*Doctor Who* exclusives' and another, with a preview tape of 'Rose', being poked by the devil on her shoulder. 'Believe me, this information is gonna bombard you with such ferocity that the safety and sanctity of "spoiler sections" will become a fond-remembered thing of the past.' These comments were clearly aimed mostly toward the major British media and not fandom, which knew how to keep information under close guard when required; indeed, many fan website editors continued to keep any significant spoilers 'under wraps' right up until the end of the series's UK transmission.

The press onslaught and air of excited anticipation continued through the first two months of the year. Writer Mark Gatiss told *TwitchFilm* that a press junket held on 13 January in Cardiff was 'one of the most exciting days of my entire life.' He also revealed that everyone wanted the series to go on to a second season, but this was still uncertain: 'I mean, thirteen forty-five minute episodes may not sound like a lot, but the thing is that apart from a few two-parters they're all one offs, so you need new sets, new situations, and new casts. It's really exhausting ... Russell said to me, "We've discovered the show that will kill us all." But, god yes. We'd love to continue.' He also explained that he didn't want to end up doing just one episode (a desire that was fulfilled when he was later commissioned for a further episode after the second season was eventually confirmed).

Piper and Eccleston used their celebrity in very positive ways. Piper spoke on 18 January during a radio promotion for the relief programme *Radio Aid*, raising money for victims of the catastrophic tsunamis that had hit parts of Asia at the end of December. Piper confirmed that the series would start, as far as she knew, 'at the end of March', and that she had put forward the 'hoody' she wore in the first two episodes to be auctioned on eBay as part of the aid appeal. Eccleston, meanwhile, was on hand on 27 January to lead the Holocaust Memorial Day services in London, commemorating the sixtieth anniversary of the liberation of the Auschwitz labour camp. Both actors also kept very busy with work, Eccleston narrating a BBC Radio 2 programme, *Sacred Nation*, on 13 February.

MERCHANDISING, MERCHANDISING ...

As one might expect with a popular television series aimed primarily at families, including children, there were indications of some major pushes for tie-in merchandising for the new *Doctor Who*. Character Options, a UK firm that specialises in the manufacture, design and distribution of toys – including the 2004 Christmas 'must-have', the Robosapien – was announced in late January as being the new master licensee for toy products; company representative Jon Diver was quoted in a press release as saying, 'We are delighted with the appointment, and will be producing an innovative range of products to complement the heritage of this property. The footage that we have seen to date is simply awesome.' The first Character Options products planned for release, around the end of 2005, included radio controlled Daleks and a toy version of the Doctor's sonic screwdriver.

On the publishing front, BBC Books announced a trilogy of hardcover novels featuring the ninth Doctor and Rose. *The Clockwise Man* by BBC Worldwide's *Doctor Who* editorial consultant Justin Richards, *Death Players* (later renamed *Winner Takes All*) by BBC Books editor Jacqueline Rayner and *The Monsters Inside* by ex-BBC Worldwide *Doctor Who* range overseer Stephen Cole would deal with a trip to London in the 1920s, a futuristic prison camp and an alien war respectively. Also tying into the series was a factual book, *Monsters and Villains*, written by Richards with contributions from Russell T Davies, which would include descriptions of aliens and nasties both from the 'classic' series and from the new. Other publishers also announced books based on the new series. Pocket Essentials reprinted Mark Campbell's *Doctor Who* guide with updated information on the new series, Telos Publishing announced in late 2004 a title called *Back to the Vortex* by J Shaun Lyon, a more in depth look at the series (and the book you are holding at this moment), and Panini Publishing made known that they would be producing a *Doctor Who* 2006 Annual as well as their licensed series magazine.

Penguin Books negotiated the rights to carry a new line of children's tie-in books. The Amazon.com online bookstore network quickly listed for pre-order a number of Penguin's planned titles, including a *Sticker Guide*, an *Intergalactic Activity Book*, a *Make Your Own TARDIS* book and a postcard book, but the publisher later issued a correction noting that, at the time, the details of their forthcoming range had not been finalised. The initial releases in the range were eventually scheduled to include a *Fun Fax* (a 96 page two-ring binder featuring photographs and facts from the series) as well as the *Sticker Book* and *Activity Book*, while the *Make Your Own TARDIS* book was among other titles apparently held back for later in the year.

Other product ranges to be negotiated included pewter figurines, a 2006 calendar, greetings cards, jigsaw puzzles, a board game, clocks, watches, money banks, radios, talking waste paper bins, first day covers (Scificollector's new series stamp cover had the distinction of being the first item of commercial merchandise to become available), stamp sheets, posters, post cards, button badges and keychains ... It seemed that *Doctor Who* was enjoying something of a resurgence of interest amongst merchandisers.

While Panini's official licensed *Doctor Who Magazine* continued to remain at the forefront of the *Doctor Who* press, an unprecedented amount of access had been given to another genre magazine, *SFX*, which featured in-depth interviews with producers and crew members as well as members of the cast, and many photographs. *SFX* even gave away a poster by respected artist Chris Achilleos (who had painted cover illustrations for many of the Target *Doctor Who* novelisations in the 1970s) depicting the Doctor and Rose surrounded by monsters from the new series, and with a different issue a set of photographic postcards. A *Doctor Who* special edition of *SFX* appeared too, in April 2005. Other UK genre magazines such as *Dreamwatch*, *TV Zone* and *Starburst* also featured the new series on a monthly basis.

As well as their range of novels and other books, BBC Worldwide made plans for some special audio releases (including an extended release of the *Project: WHO?* radio show), and also announced in early March 2005 their DVD release schedule for the new series. There would first be four stand-alone, 'vanilla' DVD releases ('vanilla' being the non-technical term for releases that consist solely of the televised episodes without any notable extras), in May, June, August and September respectively. These would then be followed by a lavish boxed set of the entire first series complete with extras, first rumoured by *DVD Times* magazine as being an October 2005 release, and later confirmed as being available in November. 'The new series promises to be one of the biggest TV events of the year and we are confident of being able to sell half a million units in 2005,' said Matthew Parkes, publicist for *2Entertain*, the company handling *Doctor Who* DVD releases for BBC Worldwide.

A TEAM FOR THE 21ST CENTURY

Subject to an increased amount of attention in the months immediately prior to the series's official launch were Christopher Eccleston and Billie Piper, now inescapably pegged as the Doctor and Rose Tyler. Eccleston told BBC News in early March that it had been easy to become the ninth Doctor: 'I just wanted to work with Russell T Davies. It's a fantastic series and I am proud to be a part of it.'

Piper liked the idea of being a new role model: 'When I was singing I was a role model then and when you are in that position you can do some good.' She didn't want to go back to her singing career, according to the *Mirror,* as she was 'in a great place right now' with new acting projects on the horizon; however, the *Sun* swore in early March she had been planning to relaunch her singing career. 'Billie would love to make a return to the music scene but she has to be happy with what's being offered. She has been having talks with a number of labels ... but hasn't put pen to paper yet. She wants a lot of input in and outside of the studio.' The *Mirror* later countered that Piper: '... laughed at the suggestion that she'll be releasing any more music. She told *3am* this week: "I don't want to sing again. I'm happy acting – it's something I have always wanted to do. I didn't want to do both, I felt that one would suffer as a result, I'd be trying to do too much."'

Eccleston and Piper were now a team in the eyes of the public. Their relationship was a new dynamic. *Sky Showbiz* noted on 10 March that Eccleston had helped Piper 'get over her broken marriage'. As Piper noted to the *Guardian*, 'Christopher and I have shared a lot during the past eight months. We had heavy schedules and personal lives and we're joined at the hip ... We get on famously. It was instant – it just worked straight away ... Me and Chris had a great time while we were together and that's all that concerns me. We're best buddies and always will be.' She was filled with admiration for her co-star: 'I don't know how Chris does it but he did it. It's like playing James Bond, the Doctor, he's established, there's nothing he doesn't know and there's nothing he can't do, as an actor that must be most frustrating.' Eccleston regarded the pair as colleagues on a grand adventure, filled with praise about Piper and about their characters' relationship. 'They love each other,' he told the *Guardian*. 'It's very much love at first sight. It's not a conventional love affair. It's far more mysterious than that.' Piper herself noted that the two characters: '... have a very interesting dynamic and there are times when you can't put your finger on their relationship. But there's lots of holding hands throughout the series.'

All indications were that Eccleston was planning to stay for the duration. He told *Manchester Online* that he would love to see an episode 'set in Salford in the sixties', referring to his home town. He also remained very satisfied that he'd been able to keep his accent in the series: 'It's good that we say to kids: "Actually people who sound like this can also be heroic and very intelligent." It's a good message to send.' He later noted to the same paper that he was prepared for the role and to be identified with it: 'The death scene in *Cracker* has been that for me. But I intend to keep busy and keep doing very different things. If people remember me just for this – I'd be happy to be remembered.'

REFLECTING THE PRODUCTION

Doctor Who was never a sure bet. With such a rich history and unique cultural mindset behind it, it would be easy to believe that it would be an unparalleled success ... but like all popular culture, there are highs and lows; not everything is welcome all of the time. Taking *Doctor Who* into the 21st Century would be a risk, retrospectively seen as either a great success or a colossal failure. It takes a special kind of person to accept that burden, and even more so to carry it out.

'We just don't know what to expect, there is no real yardstick,' Julie Gardner told the press the day after the 8 March launch. 'Of course I'm nervous.' Her thoughts turned back to those early days of production: 'The first day on set was a combination of joy, absolute hysterical laughter, complete fear ... and an anxiety that it's day one, July the 18th, and we're making thirteen episodes, and we're going to be doing this for nine months, working eleven-day fortnights. What a mountain we have to climb.'

'I spent the first three months terrified that the whole thing was going to grind to a halt,' Phil Collinson said on the *Project: WHO?* radio documentary. 'I'd wake up at four o'clock in the morning, and thinking, "Oh my God, did I order that? Did I say that to that person? Is that really going to happen? How the hell are we going to do that?" ... There was a particular day when I walked onto the set, and the green screen was up at one end, because we were on the Platform One interior set, which looks down onto the Earth beyond and the Sun that's exploding – that's all go in CGI – and there was something like eight species of alien, all dressed up. There were about twenty kids all painted blue, several other huge aliens that were props ... there's a big creature that's called the Face of Boe that's basically a huge steam driven tank with a great big face in it ... We had a stuntman who was working with Billie, and I looked around and every single element was there and it was all working, and it was happening, and I think that was the first day when the fear kind of left me.'

The directors weren't spared any of the anxiety ... or the desire to contribute to a cultural icon. 'I was surfing the web in a cafe in Siberia when I read that *Doctor Who* would be returning to our screens,' Euros Lyn told the *Siarc Marw*, a Welsh magazine. 'From that second, I desperately wanted to work on a series which is such an unusual combination of humour, adventure and nonsense ... Of course, as soon as the cameras started turning, there was no time to think of anything but my work. There were a lot of technical challenges – like trying to direct actors in rubber monster suits, or sets that were green screens to be added later by computers. It was an experience to direct actors as talented as Christopher Eccleston, Simon Callow, Billie Piper and Eve Myles – and being able to stand in the TARDIS doorway between takes was exciting, too!'

'I think the biggest challenge for a director working on this,' Joe Ahearne told *Project: WHO?*, 'is just getting through every day. It's a very punishing schedule, and there's a lot of very difficult stuff being done almost every day ... A big challenge for a director is just stamina ... just the sheer amount of it.'

Keith Boak agreed that it took a lot of hard work, and was always a team effort. 'We tie it together as a team,' he told *Doctor Who Magazine*, 'because it's a team process, and there's no way this is a solo effort on anyone's part.'

It was not only a job, but also a grand adventure, as Davies recalled to the *Sunday Telegraph* on 20 March 2005: 'I remember shop-window dummies coming to life. I remember maggots. I remember devils coming out of the sea, an evil plant bigger than a house and a Frankenstein's monster with a goldfish bowl for a head. And if you're somewhere over 35, you might remember the same things. That's *Doctor Who*, the show that burned its way into children's heads and stayed there for ever, as beautiful and vivid as a folk tale. Now the good and constant Doctor is coming back, and I'm one of those in charge of it.' Davies noted that he was 'trapped in the tornado' of the BBC publicity machine selling the series, but that would soon be over. 'The shop-window dummies are back, by virtue of the fact that they are, as *The Simpsons*' Comic Book Guy would say, the Best Idea ... Ever.'

A FOND FAREWELL

Confirming rumours that had surfaced earlier in the year, BBC1 Controller Lorraine Heggessey announced on 14 February that she would leave the BBC soon to become chief executive of Talkback Thames, the company responsible for the production of *The Bill* and *Pop Idol*. Immediately there were suggestions of possible replacements, although it was announced the following month that Jane Tranter would not apply for the job, one which, according to the Media *Guardian*, she had been widely fancied for. The BBC eventually named Peter Fincham, ironically the outgoing chief executive of Talkback Thames, as taking the post – effectively swapping jobs with Heggessey. Newspapers quoted Fincham as saying, 'I'm of that generation that is old enough to remember a world when there was only the BBC to watch, and in our house BBC was the default setting.' He added, 'I grew up with BBC1 and cowered behind the sofa when *Doctor Who* was on,' casually noting his support for the production.

In early March, after the press launch of the series in Cardiff, the *Guardian* weighed in on Heggessey's standing. 'BBC1 Controller Lorraine Heggessey was very much the regal Time Lady at the launch of *Doctor Who* – and deservedly so,' it observed, noting that the paper was sure the series 'will be a huge smash for a Saturday teatime audience, and probably ... the crowning glory of Heggessey's reign at BBC1 ... But will one of her last BBC1 acts be to recommission *Doctor Who* for a second series? Many in the commercial arm of the BBC certainly hope so and executive producer Russell T Davies attested last night that he had already worked out the storylines.' *Guardian* writer Tara Conlan also noted on 15 March that Heggessey 'signed off her valedictory season launch today – defiantly summing up her reign by saying, "I did it my way."' The BBC press office confirmed that Heggessey departed the BBC on 15 April 2005. She left behind an established and sophisticated *Doctor Who* production team. Had it not been for Heggessey's forethought and sense of nostalgia for Saturday nights long past, it is possible that *Doctor Who* might have languished for many years longer.

WORLDWIDE BROADCASTING

As the first trailer for the new series – the aforementioned teaser utilising brief footage shots from 'Rose' – made its way to television for a single 1 January showing, it appeared that a final broadcast date was closer than ever. A few fan websites had begun reporting on an actual date as early as 2004 when, in truth, nothing had been decided until approximately six weeks prior to transmission. (In one instance, a fan website predicted 26 March, then celebrated its 'inside knowledge', when this actually seemed to have been a lucky guess.) Davies warned about this in *Doctor Who Magazine*: 'If you hear anyone, anywhere, quoting sources giving an authoritative date, they are merely guessing and trying to sound important.' Davies's comments were put in perspective by people close to the production sometime later; he'd been referring to speculation in the print magazines and a few websites seeking their own publicity. By now, though, everyone knew it was March. The *Eurovision Song Contest*'s website claimed the BBC would launch the series on the same night as its pre-broadcast show giving viewers the chance to vote for the UK entry. Retailers were under the impression it would be the second Saturday in March, while other rumours speculated that the launch party for the show, prior to any transmission, wouldn't be held until early April. If anything, the disparity of information showed that the actual date of transmission was still in flux.

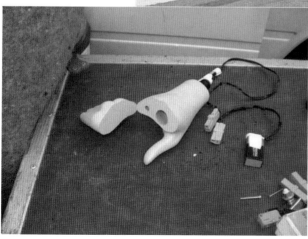

Overseas fans were still awaiting news that their broadcasters would be showing the series. New Zealand's Prime TV network had announced in late December its decision, but confirmation of a broadcaster and an air date in Australia would not come until several months later, as the ABC-TV network finally announced in April 2005 that it would debut the series on 21 May. To differentiate between the 'classic' series and the new show, ABC would run it with a tag line – 'Adventures in the Human Race'. The series would be followed in the schedules by *Very Little Britain* and *The Bill*, two of its most popular programmes, demonstrating the faith ABC had in it.

The BBC Prime satellite network, carried in Europe, Asia and Africa, announced on its FAQ page that it would be carrying neither the new *Doctor Who* series nor the 'classic' episodes, but in April this statement was replaced with confirmation that the network would, in fact, be showing the new series. The Dutch teletext service announced on 22 March that the public channel Nederland 3 would show the series later in the year or early in 2006.

Canada's CBC Television – which had announced during the last quarter of 2004 that it had purchased the series – surprised everyone when on 6 March it aired the first in a new batch of trailers, then on March 8 became the first broadcaster to announce a definite transmission date: CBC would show 'Rose', the first episode, on Tuesday 5 April at 8.00pm, with subsequent episodes to follow on a weekly basis.

Meanwhile, American fans continued to worry about the possibility that no US broadcaster might buy the new series. The *IGN FilmForce* website, long a media and industry gossip network, reported that 'sources close to the US cable network Sci Fi Channel' had informed them they were not in negotiations for it. A long line of potential networks had in fact been in contact with the BBC over the possibility of airing the series. The Bravo network, owned by NBC Universal, had been in touch as early as February 2004, while later in the year, the Sci-Fi Channel, the Arts and Entertainment (A&E) Network and BBC America – a fully owned subsidiary of the Discovery Networks enterprise – had all been approached, to no avail. Later speculation would indicate that one of the possible reasons for the refusal of any American cable network to purchase the show was that it was 'too British' ... not a problem for established fans of the show, but perhaps more so in attracting a new audience. *Doctor Who* as a commodity had been pulled by the syndication rights holders from the stations – affiliates of the public broadcasting network, PBS – still broadcasting the 'classic' episodes in order to prepare a sales package that included the new series as well as the 'classic', so a by-product of these negotiations was that while licensing of the new series was held up, the original began disappearing from the airwaves. A source within BBC America, which syndicated the original *Doctor Who* series in the US, stated, 'Unfortunately, we won't be able to proceed with a renewal of *Doctor Who* at this time. The new series of *Doctor Who* is currently being shopped around to various commercial broadcasters. For this reason, we have been asked not to make any syndication agreements on this title until further notice. Our sales department has been under strong pressure to get this new, glossy series highly placed. Unfortunately, this was a commercial strategy decision, and we do not have enough of an existing PBS user base to bid against cable or the commercial giants, some of which are taking the new series in consideration.' Rumours later grew about a possible American broadcasting deal to be announced in early April, but again this did not materialise.

Attention was focused on the possibility of any further broadcasts of trailers or other materials on the BBC, though expected arrivals of new teasers in early February (as rumoured online) didn't happen. News features on the series, such as a 3 February report and interview about the production on *BBC Wales Today*, where the show's production launch had been covered extensively seven months before, failed to include any new material except brief shots of the TARDIS and a few comments from Davies. Fans wondered how the series could appear in March if, at this point in time, there was so little concrete word from BBC Television on a final air date. Meanwhile, *SFX* magazine released on their website a list of the thirteen episodes that would make up the *Doctor Who Confidential* documentary series, to be narrated by Simon Pegg ... and then was asked to remove it, having posted it prematurely. Was a delay of the debut in the works?

Thankfully not, but the debut was announced very close to the wire. 'The exact date of transmission can't yet be confirmed,' *Doctor Who Magazine* reported in late February, noting that schedules could change up to a fortnight in advance, but 'it is still likely that the new series will begin transmission on Saturday 26 March.' The report stated that both the BBC and BBC Worldwide were said to be 'gearing up for a major launch of the series this spring'. This would include UK press screenings in early March, possibly on 8 March (the date on which the press launch did indeed take place), 'which will coincide with the start of a major television advertising campaign,' with photographs and interviews following in UK newspapers and magazines.

As the press launch date approached, more and more BBC sources began touting the 26 March date. These included the 7 March edition of BBC Radio 4's *Front Row*, which announced the date matter-of-factly after interviewing Davies. The official *Doctor Who* website confirmed the fact with a splash page complete with a countdown clock (which had also appeared on several fan websites the day before). Finally, the BBC Press Office issued a press release on 10 March, two days after the official press launch in Cardiff. Among the items noted in that release were details of forthcoming features on the official BBC *Doctor Who* website, including video and audio clips, desktop wallpapers and photographs, and exclusive games; information about the *Confidential* documentary series and the *Project: WHO?* radio programme; and news of a 19 March *Doctor Who* night on BBC2 that would feature Christopher Eccleston presenting a prize to the winner of a special *Doctor Who*-themed edition of *Mastermind*. And a date: 26 March 2005.

A date that would soon join 23 November 1963 in the annals of *Doctor Who* history.

CHAPTER TEN:
MARCH MADNESS

At last, the new series was about to arrive, the collective hearts of *Doctor Who* fans started palpitating, the press went from overheated to boiling point, and everyone counted the days until the series would begin. Three and a half weeks ... three and a half *long* weeks punctuated by a major *Doctor Who* launch event, an unexpected twist from the Internet, and a barrage of media attention. It was a month no *Doctor Who* fan would ever forget.

THE PRESS LAUNCH

On 8 March 2005, the new series was officially debuted to an invitation-only crowd at the St David's Hotel in Cardiff Bay. On hand were Russell T Davies, Julie Gardner and Mal Young, stars Christopher Eccleston and Billie Piper, BBC1 Controller Lorraine Heggessey, and a diverse gathering of writers, production associates, press reporters and even fans who had been invited to the event. The first episode, 'Rose', was screened, along with a trailer showing highlights from other first series episodes.

This followed on from an event the previous weekend, when Davies and Gardner had attended the BBC Worldwide Brighton Showcase. There, a short sketch written by Davies and featuring the character of the Steward from 'The End of the World', played on this occasion by an actor named Andrew Clover, had featured an assortment of aliens introducing the festivities, and an invasion by a Dalek, arranged by Nick Briggs and Barnaby Edwards. In terms of media attention, however, this had been a much lower-profile event than the official launch, and had garnered little press attention.

The *Guardian* interviewed several past *Doctor Who* luminaries for a 10 March report. 'I'm so pleased,' said former series script editor and writer Terrance Dicks. 'The last *Who*, I hated it. It was aimed at the mid-Atlantic; I've always said it should be made in England. They've kept the feeling of the show. I think Christopher Eccleston is very good. There's a gap in the market for something both good and popular. There's stuff that's critically acclaimed and stuff that's popular, like reality TV. But this does both.' Said Barry Letts, the producer of the series during the Jon Pertwee era, 'I was desperate for it to work and it has. Russell T Davies said what he was doing was carrying on the torch from our time. He's a big fan. It's a relay race, you stagger on for so many years, then pass the baton on when you're exhausted. They've managed to give a few nods to the past, which the old *Doctor Who* fans will appreciate, without making it confusing for anybody coming to it fresh. They've done a brilliant job of updating it.' Tom Spilsbury, deputy editor of *Doctor Who Magazine*, said that he: '... really enjoyed it. Chris and Billie were great. It was great to see everyone else enjoying it. They laughed at the funny bits and were scared by the scary bits. It bodes very well for the series. I think kids will love it. It's exactly the sort of thing I fell in love with as a child. Christopher Eccleston still feels like a Doctor Who. He'll be looked back on by kids in 20 years' time as their Doctor.' Also mentioned were some of the celebrity guests who had turned up for the launch: 'Matt Lucas, from *Little Britain*, [singer] Charlotte Church and [actor] Robson Green. But one unexpected attendee was Beryl Vertue, the stately executive producer of the sitcom *Men Behaving Badly*. Vertue [commented] that her son-in-law, Steven Moffat, had written two episodes of the new *Doctor Who* series and was currently in Australia and desperate for a report about the launch and first episode. Vertue then revealed that in the 1960s she has been the agent of *Who* legend and Daleks' creator Terry Nation when he had negotiated his copyright agreement with the BBC, the one that caused the BBC all that trouble last year when Nation's estate [initially] refused to allow the metallic monsters into the new series. Everyone was all smiles last night, but there must have been times over the last year when the BBC wished it had driven a harder bargain back in 1963.'

The *Sun* sent a Dalek along with Charlotte Church to the press launch. 'Our baddie – who led a successful campaign to reinstate the Daleks after problems with their contracts – rolled up to the bash in Cardiff. But security guards refused to let him in to the screening with stars Christopher Eccleston, Billie Piper and Charlotte, 19. A BBC spokesman said: "I'm sorry, but there is no room for your Dalek."' Church told the *Sun* that she thought the episode was: '... brilliant. I have never seen *Doctor Who* before. I would have been two when it was last on but this was like a mini-movie.'

The *Independent* also revealed that the BBC had invited several MPs to the press launch, and it was a: '... hot ticket – until, that is, the Government decided to hold yet another debate on its draconian anti-terror Bill. Several guests are reported to be gutted, not least the Tory education spokesman, Tim Collins, a lifelong fan who has appeared on TV documentaries about the Time Lord. "Terror debate or not, I'll be very surprised if Tim misses the screening," reckons a colleague. "As for the rest of us, we'll have to decide which is more important: the invasion of the Daleks, or the invasion of al-Qa'ida." Best leave it to your consciences, chaps.'

Nick Setchfield wrote for *SFX*, 'As we walked in, we were greeted by the *Sun's* roving Dalek, amid a gaggle of paparazzi scum. As usual, those present were a mixture of industry professionals, scruffy journalists, leggy PR dollies and premiere-hungry celebs.' *SFX* noted that the screening: '... went better than even Russell T Davies could have expected. Standing at the back of the packed hall alongside executive producer Julie Gardner, Davies watched with the assembled hacks and beautiful people the first new episode of *Doctor Who* in 15 years. People laughed (a lot), people jumped and people applauded.' *Doctor Who Magazine* wrote that, among the comments made at the event, director James Hawes noted that episodes nine and ten would be the scariest in the series and would not be cut by censors (a statement that would prove premature; producer Collinson later gave the press details of a sound effect cut to 'The Empty Child') and that Terrance Dicks commented how Eccleston "could have been terrible, but wasn't."

Following the screening, there was a question and answer session that featured Eccleston, Piper, Davies and Gardner, along with general mingling of the assembled crowds and a party atmosphere that lasted well into the next day.

THE LEAK OF 'ROSE'

One of the problems with any new television show in the Information Age is keeping it under wraps until the final possible moment. That was not achieved with the new series of *Doctor Who*; the show made international headlines because it was unable to stay out of the public eye. Episode one, 'Rose', leaked out onto the Internet three weeks prior to the on-air debut of the series, and three days prior to the press launch event in Cardiff; the circumstances that surrounded this were the subject of considerable controversy.

Using a number of Internet file sharing systems, thousands of fans managed to watch 'Rose' early. There were a number of statements put out about the leaked episode by the BBC, noting that it was somewhat inferior to the final cut, and lacked music, special effects and other finishing touches. (Later evidence would show that, in fact, the leaked episode matched the final transmission version almost perfectly, save for the absence of the proper musical score over the opening and closing credits, the inclusion of some additional music in one scene early in the episode, and some minor changes to the credits list; these differences are covered in more detail in the episode section of this book under 'Rose'.)

It was stated initially that an 'unidentified employee of a foreign broadcaster of the show' had been responsible for the leak. Vicky Thomas, Head of Press, Consumer Publishing at BBC Worldwide, later issued a full statement: 'After a thorough investigation by BBC Worldwide's Canadian broadcast partner, the source of the leak of episode one of the new *Doctor Who* series has been traced to a third party company in Canada which had an early preview copy for legitimate purposes. The individual responsible for the leak has had their employment terminated by that company as a result. BBC Worldwide is considering further legal remedies and takes extremely seriously any unlawful copying or misuse of its copyright material.'

'The pirating of a *Doctor Who* episode on the net before it is even broadcast has put TV downloading into the spotlight,' wrote Darren Waters in the *BBC News* article 'How *Doctor Who* spread on the net'. It wasn't exactly the spotlight the series wanted to be in, however, as the carefully planned unveiling of the first episode as a major event on 26 March became slightly diluted. It wasn't a problem with viewership and ratings, though; it has been proven time and time again that television episode downloads have little impact on the overall viewing figures associated with a broadcast, and especially such a high profile event as the *Doctor Who* debut. (A frequently unspoken but oft-acknowledged theory on this posited that anyone in the UK who had downloaded the episode would likely tune into the broadcast as well, if only to see what had changed.)

The leaked episode prompted a barrage of initial reviews, some positive and some negative. It was widely reported that even Eccleston was not pleased with the early online reactions to the leaked episode, likely brought on by the largely negative reviews posted on such websites as *Ain't It Cool News*. The *Sun* commented that Eccleston warned series fans against watching the downloaded episode: 'It's a rough cut without special effects. Wait to see it in all its glory.'

BBC News covered the leak on both BBC1 and BBC News 24 on 8 March, mentioning these advance reviews. 'There's been a couple of early reviews, and they've ... they've attacked it,' Eccleston noted in an interview taped prior to the day's press launch, 'and it's painful. You accept it, you take it on the chin, but when you've worked it out as we have, with so much love, you hope you'll get some of it back.'

The leak made the news internationally as well. It was a talking point on the American radio programme *Talk of the Nation*, a daily syndicated series on the National Public Radio network. During a story entitled 'Movies, Technology and the Future of Viewing', host Neal Conan mentioned the first episode and that downloaders 'must feel that it's pretty cool to see the new *Doctor Who* three weeks before the BBC airs it,' though the story primarily focused on the transformation of media and the new digital age. NPR was not alone in discussing this for an American audience; digital services such as *Yahoo!* mentioned the leak, demonstrating at least a small ripple in the American consciousness.

All of the attention regarding the leak prompted several media sources to speculate that it might actually have been set up by the BBC itself, to generate yet more publicity. Said *Wired* magazine, 'The pilot episode of the BBC's highly anticipated new *Doctor Who* series may have been intentionally leaked onto file-sharing networks to generate buzz, a source who instructed the network on viral advertising told *Wired* News ... In any case, buzz about the *Doctor Who* episode has certainly paid off, whether the BBC takes credit for it or not. Word about it has reached countless sites, and, more importantly, the episode seems largely well-received.' The *Chicago Tribune* noted: 'Building online buzz by putting full episodes online has become such a hot marketing tool that there's speculation the BBC was behind the recent "unauthorised" online release of an episode of its new *Doctor Who* series. But the BBC denied to *Wired* News that an in-house "viral marketing" plan was responsible for the show's premature online debut.'

These categorical BBC denials that it was somehow involved in the leak didn't slow the questions about it. While it was an unfortunate incident that possibly spoiled that 'magic moment' for a 26 March 2005 premiere for some fans, there was a bright side: after the few initial poor reviews, a much larger amount of positive commentary about the episode reverberated throughout *Doctor Who* fandom and beyond, which in turn seemed to breed even more interest in the show.

As the *Manchester Evening News* noted on 13 March, 'It's a shame that an episode of the new *Doctor Who* series – the first since 1989 – has been leaked onto the Internet in advance of its Easter screening, but surely there is some poetic justice in the sci-fi hero who travels through time and space arriving three weeks ahead of himself.'

THE FIRST REVIEWS COME IN

As noted above, the *Ain't It Cool* website, a major Internet destination for Hollywood film gossip and television commentary, was first on the scene with two reviews of the leaked episode ... both of which were very negative. 'Bottom line: Excrement', one reviewer for *AICN* said. 'It feels nothing, nothing like *Doctor Who*, more like a cheap sitcom.' The other noted: 'The main fault is in the script. Sure, it does a great job in introducing the Doctor and Rose but that's just about all it does.' Word of these initial negative reviews spread quickly throughout *Doctor Who* fandom; the *Guardian* on 8 March mentioned them, and largely ignored the protests that had started to arrive in *AICN's* feedback section, 'Talk Back', pointing out that other initial reviews of the leaked episode on various websites, including *Doctor Who* fan sites, were largely positive. A review by graphic novelist Warren Ellis on his website was pointed to by many in the first few days after the leak as being exemplary of the opposing view: '*Doctor Who* hasn't been this good since the early days of Peter Davison in the role,' Ellis wrote. 'It's nice to have it back, and I'm looking forward to watching it with my daughter when it airs on the BBC in a few weeks.' Another popular media website, *Dark Horizons*, also reviewed the episode on 8 March, the reviewer saying, 'Bottom line, it's very watchable, it's very British, and it's generally very good.'

At about the same time, the UK newspapers began printing their initial reviews, omitting to mention whether these were based on official 'screener' copies, or whether their reviewers had purloined the episode from the illegal download sites. 'It's a funny feeling,' said the reviewer in *The Times*. 'When the dum-de-dum, dum-de-dum starts, and the new-look title sequence begins, the hairs on your arms stand up, and a smile fixes itself, rictus-like, to your face. This warm feeling alone is enough to transport you blithely through the first five minutes of the new *Doctor Who* before any critical faculties kick in. And when they do, you realise that you're enjoying yourself.'

Manchester Online opined: 'This is a bold restating of what *Doctor Who* was always about –

scaring the kids and entertaining families on a Saturday night. Old series monsters the Autons – recreating the famous shop window breakout of their 1970 debut – keep the show in touch with its past, while the energetic direction and decent special effects show off its new coat of paint cheerfully. To coin a phrase – he's back, and it's about time.'

The *Daily Express* commented: 'So much of the BBC's shiny new *Doctor Who* has been lovingly assembled according to a clear philosophy of "if it ain't broke, don't fix it" ... But it comes at a souped-up pace and delights in showing off the results of the huge resources of budget and talent that have been thrown at a programme whose sets were once only out-wobbled by those of *Crossroads*. Between [Eccleston and Piper] they are a revelation ... To be successful *Doctor Who* needs to look brilliant, crack along with never a dull moment, and excite and amuse in equal measure. By the look of the first episode it will do that in spades.'

The *Sun* said: 'The new *Who* doesn't wear a scarf or fancy coat – but from the start Eccleston is outstanding. And the script from *Queer as Folk* writer Russell T Davies is sparky, witty and will please even the most ardent fans.'

The *Daily Telegraph*, meanwhile, was very matter-of-fact: 'The first *Doctor Who* series for 16 years could give the BBC a much-needed hit for its ailing Saturday night schedules if the verdict of critics, fans and children is correct.'

Amid the sudden glut of positive reviews, the *Guardian* took a different approach: 'It is unfair to review a restaurant on opening night, but an event as important as the return of *Doctor Who* after a hiatus of 15 years ... is of such importance to millions of fans around the world that instant judgments are required. The good Doctor is most definitely back ... and many traditionalists are going to greet this radical new version with utter dismay ... As a diehard *Who* fan, I will watch all the remaining episodes wishing, hopefully not totally in vain, that they had laid off the Ritalin.' Interestingly, a mere two days later, perhaps recognising that the tone of their review differed markedly from that of their rivals' pieces, the *Guardian* posted a second and far more upbeat assessment of the new series. 'To the relief of traditionalists,' wrote Owen Gibson, 'the TARDIS, the wry British humour and all the key premises remain. The Daleks also return, although this time they can fly.'

Fan reactions to the early episode leak were mixed, skewing slightly toward positive. 'A triumph, and leaves me incredibly, astonishingly excited to see the rest of the season,' wrote Brett O'Callaghan on the *Outpost Gallifrey* forum.. 'I feel like I'm ten years old again.' 'The Doctor and Rose are going to make a fantastic team,' enthused Matthew Kopelke, 'and I look forward to joining them each week on their adventures. We're certainly going to be in for one hell of a ride, that's for sure.' Todd Green was more excited about what it represented: 'What's really great ... is there wasn't a single thing that made me wince, inwardly or outwardly, or made me feel I would have to apologise for to my wife or non-fan friends.' Others were less than thrilled. 'My disappointments outweigh my satisfactions by quite a ways,' wrote Chris Frame. 'We have to have better, more low key incidental music, and a less frenetic editing pace.' Writer Mark Stevens was more objective about the series, based on this first look: 'Is the new series of *Doctor Who* the saviour of genre TV? If the first episode is anything to go by, the answer is *not quite*, but that's only if we're looking at a bigger picture that includes American TV productions. "Rose" twats the nose of half-arsed in-house Sci-Fi Channel productions, but it still looks like the younger, snotty-nosed sibling of the likes of *Smallville* and *The Dead Zone*. However, this zippy, witty continuation of our favourite show could very well be the saviour of genre TV in the UK – assuming it finds the right audience.'

Q magazine, a popular UK music periodical, published a glowing review of the new series at the end of February. Reviewer Boyd Hilton said: 'The inestimable Christopher Eccleston plays the ninth Doctor ... replete with trendy leather jacket and wry sense of humour.' As for Billie Piper, Hilton opined that: '... the biggest surprise of the show is Billie Piper's performance as the Doctor's assistant Rose Tyler. Not only does Piper prove she can hold her own in the company of esteemed actors, but her feisty cockney character shows real depth. Importantly, Rose's relationship with the Doctor is as an equal, rather than just being there to whimper when the aliens show up.' Hilton commented that the cardboard sets and 'naff looking monsters' of old were a thing of the past, whereas this new modern version possessed 'slick, sharp dialogue' and was: '... as convincing and exciting as anything shown before in a British TV series. This is must-see TV for everyone.'

PRODUCTION WRAPS ... AND SEASON TWO?

Even before the first series had debuted, rumours about a second had already cropped up. An issue of *Doctor Who Magazine* released in early March quoted Julie Gardner as wanting to do a second series with Eccleston, should it be commissioned, and saying that the team were due to have a meeting at the start of February to talk about what they'd do if they got the go-ahead. 'We're already behind [because] to go again with the same number of episodes ... we'd need to start filming at the same time as we did last year. On the first series, we were having those conversations in December [... but] I think there are lessons from the first series that we could implement to speed things up.' Davies, meanwhile, mentioned in his 'Production Notes' column that he and Gardner had discussed his outline for thirteen episodes for series two during a train journey to London: 'If series two ever exists, then these scripts will happen.' Importantly, Davies prefaced this with, 'Of course, series two isn't commissioned yet – I suspect we won't know until a good few weeks into transmission of series one – but we've got to plan ahead regardless.'

Even with no concrete information, there was plenty of speculation ... but there were still spanners to be thrown into the works. The *Sun* said on 2 March that the series was 'over budget and behind schedule', noting that it 'will struggle to meet its scheduled 26 March debut date. A source said: "There were ten extra days of shooting with special effects and that cost a fortune."' And the *Manchester Online* website commented on 10 March that 'a second series is already in development, although Eccleston is undecided about whether he'll return to the role.' Strangely prescient words ...

The end of production on the first series of *Doctor Who* was staggered over the first two weeks of March. Eccleston's final day on the production was 5 March; he had taped two different endings for 'The Parting of the Ways,' including a sequence shot with a minimum amount of crew on the set. Piper's last day on set was 10 March, and the wrap party for cast and crew was held in the evening the same day. Recording continued for several days – including sequences with John Barrowman – with main unit production completed on 14 March. Davies later told *Doctor Who Magazine* that all that was left were some effects shots to complete, which would be finished up in post-production over the next several months.

One final scene, however, would be recorded sometime later: the conclusion of a regeneration sequence (taped in April), the details of which had yet to leak to the press. Only a select few knew that 5 March was not only Christopher Eccleston's last day for the season, but his final day involved in the production of *Doctor Who* altogether – a fact that would remain secret until the end of March.

ADVERTISING HEATS UP

Fans of *Doctor Who* had begun noticing, and complaining about, the absence of BBC promotion for the new series up to a month prior to its debut. False starts were commonplace, such as rumours spread by some websites about trailers airing when no plans for trailers had been made.

Ironically, the jump start began not in the United Kingdom, but in Canada. Hot on the heels of being the first country actually to announce a planned debut date for the series, the CBC Network aired a teaser trailer on 6 March during a broadcast of the film *Harry Potter and the Chamber of Secrets*, displaying the previously announced – but not, at the time, fully confirmed – airdate of 5 April.

Over the 12-13 March weekend in Britain, billboard posters for the new series began showing up all over the country, finally getting the BBC's own promotional campaign under way. These posters showed a press photo of the Doctor and Rose, looking upward toward adventure, smiling all the while, framed with a silhouette of the London skyline; the same image would be used widely across series advertising in both the UK and abroad and was included as a free poster in the May 2005 edition of *Doctor Who Magazine*.

The billboards were only one example of the barrage of advertising that would hit the British public over the next weeks. A series of teasers began running on BBC television at around the same time, the first one to make a notable impact arriving on 8 March ... a simple teaser with Eccleston, at first alone and then with Piper, standing still in the TARDIS console room as the central column of the console bobbed in the traditional fashion, the music stylings of Murray Gold (the new theme arranger) playing in the background. It was a short, five second piece that caused considerable interest, especially insofar as it was one of the first times the interior of the TARDIS had been glimpsed, and certainly the first televised unveiling. The piece ran several times during the evening of 8 March, first immediately prior to *EastEnders* and then at various times throughout that evening on BBC1 and BBC2. An alternate version, which also aired that evening, substituted Piper as a first glimpse, followed by the pairing of the two stars as in the other case.

Another teaser aired for the first time on 12 March. This consisted of another quick snapshot, in which the TARDIS was shown dematerialising in an underground pedestrian walkway that slowly filled with an incoming fireball. It was first shown mid-day during afternoon programmes, and then again before the news that evening prior to the *Comic Relief* telethon (before which one of the earlier teasers of Piper in the control room was also reshown.)

'Do you wanna come with me?' asked Eccleston's Doctor, standing inside the TARDIS doorway, in the first full length trailer, which aired initially on 15 March. '... Because if you do, then I should warn you,' he continued, as viewers saw various TARDIS interior images, 'you're going to see all sorts of things: ghosts from the past, aliens from the future, the day the Earth died in a ball of flame. It won't be quiet, it won't be safe, and it won't be calm. But I tell you what it will be: the trip of a lifetime." The trailer concluded with a montage of clips from future episodes, including a crashing spacecraft, a Victorian street scene, a Dalek and a missile. 'The 'trip of a lifetime' remark would in fact be used quite extensively over the next several weeks as a tagline for the *Doctor Who* series itself. Several versions of this trailer, in both 30-second and 50-second lengths, were shown alongside such programmes as *EastEnders*, *Holby City* and *Mastermind*. Later airings also included an attached mini-trailer for BBC3's *Doctor Who Confidential* documentary series, subtitled: '(No TARDIS Necessary)'.

Piper first spoke in a *Doctor Who* trailer the next day, 16 March: 'I've got a choice,' she said to the camera. 'Stay at home with my mum, my boyfriend, my job ... or chuck it all in for danger, and monsters, and life or death. What do you think?' She then smiled, nodding toward the man standing next to her, the eternally present Doctor. This trailer first aired immediately preceding the children's show *Newsround* during the CBBC strand of programming.

Around the same time, previews for the new series began airing in Canada; in fact, they first appeared on the big screen, as the CBC network, in preparation for the early April premiere of the series there, attached a trailer to film screenings across the nation, first with the Bruce Willis movie *Hostage*.

A new edit of the main Eccleston trailer, now dubbed the 'Trip of a Lifetime' trailer, was shown during late-night BBC1 programming on 18 March, removing all but the specially recorded Doctor scenes in the console room and him running from the fireball and placing his opening sentence, 'Do you wanna come with me?' at the very end. The 15-second insert was also trailed in a box-out during the end credits of a showing of *Dr Who and the Daleks*, a 1960s film adaptation starring Peter Cushing, which aired on BBC2 on Saturday 19 March; that spot featured, in addition, several clips from the first episode, as well as an announcement of the same evening's BBC2 *Doctor Who* night and then, following the film's credits, a trailer for the first part of the forthcoming radio documentary series, *Project: WHO?*, over a Radio 2 caption slide.

BBC2's '*Doctor Who* Night' special began just a few hours later. It featured a slightly re-edited version of *The Story of Doctor Who*, a documentary that had originally aired in late 2003 as part of the celebration of the fortieth anniversary, now noting the development of the new series, and a ten-minute documentary, *Some Things You Need to Know about Doctor Who* hosted by impressionist Jon Culshaw, the evening concluded with the previously-announced special instalment of the knowledge-based quiz series *Mastermind* hosted by John Humphrys, which was won by Norwich resident, and editor of the *Doctor Who* Appreciation Society's monthly newsletter, Karen Davies. 'I wanted to show *Doctor Who* fans are not all nerdy boys, and some of us do have a life,' Davies told the *Norwich Evening News* the next day; she was picked along with three others from over seven thousand applicants to go on the programme. Christopher Eccleston was on hand to present Davies with her award. The *Planet Who* website later revealed that BBC2's *Doctor Who* night pulled in a staggering high of 10.73% audience share, albeit dropping to 7.56% during the *Mastermind* special. With approximately 2.4 million viewers tuning in to *The Story of Doctor Who* documentary, this was proof positive that there was still life in the franchise.

TELEVISION COVERAGE

If the BBC was going to instil *Doctor Who* back into the British consciousness, it would take more than just a few trailers and radio spots ... it would take a significant, concerted effort to promote the series on major television programmes, both news and chat shows. It worked better than anyone at the BBC Press Office could have hoped, with an extensive campaign throughout March leading up to the series's debut.

BBC *Wales Today* again sent reporter Rebecca John to Cardiff on 8 March to cover the new series press launch. She interviewed Davies at the St David Hotel prior to the event, and they discussed the Welsh viewers of the channel being able to recognise quite a few locations in the new series: 'Tons of locations,' Davies confirmed, 'not just Cardiff, but Swansea, Monmouth

... we used just about all of the South Wales coast, like Barry Island ... late at night, they weren't very happy!' John also caught up with Eccleston during the live broadcast, the actor stating that he was very happy, that the group was working very hard, and that he would wrap up his recording the following Saturday, 12 March. Eccleston also mentioned, with a smile, that he'd 'gotten down on his knees and begged' for the role of the Doctor. The BBC *Wales Today* broadcast that day had some sound issues with the live feed from Cardiff, specifically during John's interview with Eccleston, leading anchor Sara Edwards to apologise for the 'obviously intergalactic' interference. 'I shouldn't read anything sinister into it,' Edwards noted, 'but then you never know, the Daleks could be around.'

Later that day, BBC *Northwest Tonight* featured another interview with Eccleston, from their broadcast centre, by anchor Gordon Burns. 'It's been very hard, and it's completely taken over my life,' Eccleston said. 'You can't do anything else when you're shooting thirteen 45-minute episodes of Saturday night high-concept telly.' Eccleston mentioned that the Daleks appeared in episode six, 'but they might appear later as well, who knows?' – an allusion to the two-part season-ender. He was very complimentary toward Piper: 'As well as having a hero in the shape of the Doctor, you have a heroine. The fan base of *Doctor Who* has been predominantly male, and we're hoping we can change that, and for eight and twelve year old girls, they've got somebody.'

The BBC *Breakfast* programme on 9 March featured a lengthy series of segments on the show, including footage from the previous night's press launch and interviews recorded at the event. 'If the kids don't like that,' *Doctor Who Magazine* editor Clayton Hickman said, 'then the kids don't deserve to have any television ever shown to them again!' Retailer Alexandra Loosely-Saul reacted with joyous laughter to the episode screening: 'I feel seven. I absolutely feel seven ... fantastic, absolutely fantastic.' The programme featured extended interviews with Eccleston and Piper, and also focused on the Daleks, interviewing fans from the Hyde Fundraisers group about their charitable work with props and costumes.

Later the same day, CBBC's *Newsround* also featured several clips from the first episode, as well as brief interviews with Eccleston and Piper, accompanied by factoids printed in the lower part of the screen. 'I was quite keen to kind of not focus on what had been done before,' Piper told the programme, 'because this is obviously contemporary *Doctor Who* and things have changed.'

Later in the evening, BBC News's flagship serious news programme, *Newsnight*, got in on the act too, featuring an item on the return of the series. Reporter Stephen Smith arrived in a TARDIS and introduced a montage of clips from the show ... and interviews with children who had no idea what *Doctor Who* actually was. The programme also included a clip of Michael Grade, former BBC1 Controller, speaking in 1986 about 'how few' people actually watched *Doctor Who* ... quite a difference from what would be coming soon. 'I think it looks like an attempt to sort of hark back to a "golden age",' Stuart Prebble, former ITV Chief Executive, told *Newsnight*, 'where we were broadcasting in a four or five channel environment, and the whole family were willing to sit down as a group and watch. Unfortunately, in 2005, very little television viewing is like that.'

Davies was in exuberant form on BBC1's *Breakfast* programme on 11 March, talking about his new production of *Casanova* as well as about *Doctor Who*. During his eight-minute slot, he said that when the chance to do *Doctor Who* came up, 'I had no choice but to work on it because I love it.' And now that it was finished, he felt the same: 'I love it. I'm so proud of it.' A slip of the tongue earlier in the show had seen co-presenter Bill Turnbull refer to him as

'Russell TV Davies', and much fun was made of that when Davies appeared. Quizzed by Turnbull as to what the 'T' stood for, Davies joked 'TARDIS', but then confirmed that it didn't stand for anything; it was to distinguish him from another Russell Davies in the industry. Of course, Davies said it could stand for 'Tussle', while co-presenter Sian Williams cheekily suggested 'Tawdry'. Davies also talked briefly about how much he had learned while working as a storyliner on popular ITV soap *Coronation Street*, and then mentioned that he hoped there would be a second series of *Doctor Who* on the horizon. When Turnbull mentioned he expected to see Davies at next year's BAFTA awards, Davies, joking as ever, self-deprecatingly replied: 'Serving, probably!'

On the rival ITV1 network, GMTV's *Entertainment Today* segment on 11 March featured coverage of the press launch a few days earlier. Presenter Ben Sheppard focused first on the mechanics of a press launch (a location, for example, close to both the press and the production team) and then presented a taped interview with Eccleston and Piper as well as clips and photos of the Autons, the Moxx of Balhoon, the Face of Boe, and so on. Sheppard confirmed the Daleks' forthcoming appearance, all the while playing with a radio controlled gold Dalek!

A lengthy new series clip appeared on the 12 March edition of *Test the Nation*, an entertainment quiz series on BBC1. This was from the scene in the first episode where the Doctor tells Rose to run for her life after helping her to escape. The clip was shown in response to the question, 'Which show connects these three characters ...' with pictures displayed of Piper, Bonnie Langford and Peter Purves. Clips from the original series stories 'The Ark' and 'The Trial of a Time Lord' were also shown. Meanwhile, 12 March's *What the Papers Say* on BBC2 commented on the buzz around the new show, including quotes from the *Sun* and *The Times* – the latter focusing on Rose Tyler attempting to sell her story to the tabloids ... which wouldn't actually happen in the series!

On 13 March BBC3's *60 Seconds* news programme ran a story about Tom Baker winning a recent poll of favourite Doctors, and showed scenes from the first episode of the new series. Even now, *Doctor Who* was much more than simply a television series about to make its heralded return; it was a news story, fodder for journalists as well as entertainment reporters.

BBC Wales's *On Show* anchor Sian Williams interviewed Davies on 17 March about 'one of the biggest television comebacks of all time'. Davies said there was 'nothing wrong with the ratings war,' discussing the potential viewership on the Saturday night of transmission, which was in effect what the programme makers were all after. 'The nervousness comes in on the Monday morning, when you get the ratings ... For the actual programme itself, we've made it as well as we can, and I love it, and we're very, very happy with it.' The full half-hour interview show gave Williams and Davies a chance to explore many facets of the latter's career, including his work on *The Second Coming*, *Queer as Folk* and *Mine All Mine*.

Davies, writer Mark Gatiss ('The Unquiet Dead') and seventies *Doctor Who* producer Philip Hinchcliffe were interviewed on the 17 March edition of *The Culture Show* on BBC2 by commentator (and *Doctor Who* fan) Matthew Sweet, who looked at how the series used to use horror, and asked whether or not it could scare the children of today, as British culture had changed so much since it was last on the nation's screens. Gatiss referred to how well *Doctor Who* exploited neuroses such as whether or not one really could trust those people one thought trustworthy. The show acknowledged that *Doctor Who* had been influenced by various horror types, and Hinchcliffe pointed out that children were encountering these myths and stories for the first time, but conceded that 'a more knowledgeable adult audience

... would ... if they were being unkind ... say we were ripping off Hammer horror, or the Mummy stories, or Frankenstein.' Hinchcliffe further commented: 'You are really showing that there are very dark and powerful forces out there [that can] somehow connect or control the dark forces in man – and that's scary.' Davies observed that there had been a growing sophistication in drama and story-telling, and that although kids would always be scared of the dark and the wardrobe door that might open, story-tellers would be in trouble if they relied just on that; younger audiences wanted more drama, emotion, honesty and truth, and simple pictorial thrills were no longer enough. The new series 'has an amazing velocity to it,' Sweet then told the audience, having seen the first episode at the press launch. 'It's incredibly fast. It's almost like watching the edited highlights of an old *Doctor Who* story. It's amazingly spectacular and [Eccleston's] terrific.' The feature finished with Sweet saying that suddenly *Doctor Who* was 'cool', and asking Davies, 'Can we come out of the closet about being *Doctor Who* fans?' Davies jokingly admonished him by saying, 'You should never have been in there!'

The following day's *Newsnight Review* on BBC2 lent more intellectual credence to *Doctor Who* in an eight minute discussion about the return of the series. Host Mark Lawson was joined by best-selling novelist Ian Rankin, American critic and writer Bonnie Greer, and Professor John Carey, the chief book reviewer for *The Sunday Times*, for a lively – and at times heated – analysis of the first episode. All three men were obviously fond of *Doctor Who*, whereas Greer, admitting she had 'no idea what this is all about', was less than positive. 'It's got something for everyone,' said Rankin. 'They've updated it very well.' Greer, however, opined that the show: '... looks really cheap ... The stories are all over the place. Who is this for? Is it for my generation? Is it for fortysomethings? Is it for babies? ... They haven't made up their mind who they're talking to. That's the big problem for me ... The acting is wonderful, the writing is wonderful, but it looks thin, it just looks cheap.' Carey leapt to the show's defence: 'The cheapness is part of the point. It's very British. The fact that it's done on a shoestring is very important. It's self-mocking. It's not to be taken too seriously. In my opinion, the cheap things were the best things.' However, Rankin was quick to point out that, compared to the early *Doctor Who* serials: '... the effects are not cheap in this. It's a series that's been waiting for digital, the age, to come along.' Carey later noted: 'The further they get away from trying to explain where all the mystery is, the better it is. The empty streets and the cheapness don't matter.' One thing that Greer, Lawson and Rankin were in agreement on was that Eccleston was an excellent choice to play the Doctor, with Lawson saying that he had 'a sense of danger', Greer commenting on his 'incredible face' and Rankin stating that Eccleston was the best Doctor since Patrick Troughton, whom he referred to as the last 'really good, edge-of-craziness Doctor.' Carey, however, said that he found Eccleston 'too ordinary.'

Piper appeared on the chat show *Parkinson* on 19 March on ITV1 and discussed her role on the new series. 'It's like one of those songs you hear at wedding receptions – you don't know how you know the words but you do and you sing along,' she said, regarding her memories of the original series. She went on to describe her character as 'contemporary', adding that she was: '... gutsy, she's ballsy and she goes with her instinct. She hardly ever applies logic and she's just a great girl. She's actually quite good in confrontation, because she'd rather kind of talk her way out of it as opposed to pulling any kind of crazy kick-boxing stunts – she's not too hot on those.' Her character would: '... get up, she goes to work, she comes home. There's nobody really in her life that's challenging her ideas or broadening her horizons, and then suddenly this 900-year-old bloke rocks up in a blue box and he's like "Come with us" and she's like "Yeah!" and she takes off! She's quite ruthless. She just ditches life as she knows it and hops in the old TARDIS.' Piper noted how tough the eleven-day-fortnight shooting schedule had been on her, keeping her and her husband Chris Evans apart, but reasoned that their split would have happened eventually in any event, as she explained that they both 'wanted different things.' But for right now, with the series about to be transmitted, she was happy being in the moment and was anxiously awaiting its start.

Eccleston next appeared on the 21 March instalment of the children's magazine show *Blue Peter* on BBC1. *Blue Peter* had always had a close and special relationship with *Doctor Who*, going back to its early days (when one of its presenters was Peter Purves, who had formerly played Steven Taylor opposite William Hartnell's Doctor), and its current editor Richard Marson was a big fan of the series and one-time contributor to *Doctor Who Magazine*. Piper was supposed to be on the show live along with Eccleston, but was unable to make it as she was unwell. Eccleston emerged from the TARDIS, describing his relationship as the Doctor with his assistant and defending the production values of the original series. Talking about taking over the role, he said he was very excited about it and that he 'felt ready to do something which had that kind of responsibility,' having been an actor for about eighteen years. He also praised the scripts, which he said were 'so strong'. He then talked about the reasons for the Doctor having a battered leather jacket, saying that it was scripted by Davies, who thought it would be good because it was quite practical for a time traveller, and also tough enough to stand up to what was a very physical role. Asked what the hardest thing about making *Doctor Who* was, Eccleston said: 'The fact you don't have any life'. He explained that not only were there the twelve-to-fourteen-hour days of recording, but he then had to learn his lines at night because of his lead role. He said it was an honour and privilege, but echoed earlier sentiments that it 'took over your life'. Also featured on the show were some *Doctor Who* models, including of Eccleston and Piper, made by a viewer, plus a compost bin in the shape of a Dalek, put together by two other viewers.

ITV's *This Morning* programme on 23 March featured easily one of the best, and funniest, interviews with Davies to date. The presenters, Phillip Schofield and Fern Briton, introduced taped interviews with Eccleston and Piper, and then spoke to Davies live in the studio. 'I've been saying I wanted to do [*Doctor Who*] for years and years,' Davies (mis-captioned on screen as 'Russell T Davis') said, 'and eventually someone listened. I think I just wore them down like a dripping tap in the end, and they said "Let's bring it back", and they asked me. I was so happy.' Asked how big a fan he'd been, Davies noted that he really loved the series. 'I should be proud of my fandom, because I really love it, and really thought it had a lot of potential to come back ... We're not recreating that seventies and eighties stuff, because that was beautiful in its time. It is 2005 now.' Davies identified several aliens that appeared in 'The End of the World', including the Steward and Cassandra. How, he was asked, did he come up with aliens with such wonderful names as Hop Pyleen? 'I just sit at home and make them up,' he said, laughing. 'I have a drink, and make them up! ... The Moxx of Balhoon, I think I had too much to drink that day!'

Also on 23 March, BBC2 ran an edition of *The Daily Politics* that featured a ten-minute segment on the new series, with guests including BBC political correspondent Andrew Marr, who had secured a role in the two-part 'Aliens of London'/'World War Three' story, former Shadow Spokesperson for Health and Education and well-known *Doctor Who* supporter Tim Collins MP, and Barry Letts, former producer of *Doctor Who* during the early 1970s. The crux of the feature, although a thinly veiled excuse to talk about *Doctor Who*, was about how the original series, especially in the 1970s, used political comment as the basis for many stories.

Issues of environment, tax and Government bureaucracy were illustrated by way of clips from 'classic' series stories 'The Green Death', 'The Sun Makers' and 'The Happiness Patrol'. Marr confirmed that the episode he was in, featuring aliens taking over MPs, would be transmitted some time between the time of the interview and the general election on 5 May.

The final cast appearance prior to the series's debut was Eccleston's visit to *Friday Night With Jonathan Ross* on 25 March, in which the actor noted that when he was growing up, he didn't want to be the Doctor, but rather, the assistant. About Davies, Eccleston said, 'You get mention of his love of the series in *Queer as Folk* and stuff. There's a real passion in him for the series, he really believes in it as a vehicle for Saturday night television, because it is a fantastic idea: an alien who can travel backward and forward in time.' Eccleston also gave away a previously unreported detail of episode eight, noting that in this story, Rose 'gets to meet the father she never met.' He went on to say that playing the Doctor with a smile, confidence and humour: '... takes the fear factor out of it for kids. If I'm being chased down a corridor, and just before I slam the door I give them the flash of a grin, that invites kids into it ...' 'But not in a Michael Jackson sort of way,' responded Ross, referring in his usual ribald fashion to the singer's then ongoing child molestation trial in America. Ross was also unable to resist commenting on Piper's current marital woes, and quipped his way through some humorous material about the identity of the 'best Doctor'. An extensive, and impressive, montage of clips from forthcoming episodes was shown, many of them previously unseen by the viewing public, and Character Options prototypes of a Christopher Eccleston action figure (one half of a two-way radio set, the other half being a Slitheen) and a sonic screwdriver toy were displayed. All in all, it was a happy segment looking forward to the new series, which was now less than one day away.

RADIO COVERAGE

Television viewers weren't the only ones bombarded with *Doctor Who* content, as radio listeners also had a field day of coverage. On 8 March alone, leading up to the press launch, listeners to BBC Radio 5 Live's breakfast-time show were treated to the new *Doctor Who* series theme tune by Murray Gold, and snippets of the tune were also played on Chris Moyles's breakfast show on Radio 1. Radio 2 meanwhile featured an interview by Johnnie Walker with Davies, conducted over the telephone from the press launch. 'I can remember the days when *Doctor Who* was a tiny little joke,' said Davies, 'and now it's become this extreme monster of a phenomenon!'

The Stuart Maconie programme on Radio 2 on the same date focused on the new theme extensively, including via interview clips. Executive producer Julie Gardner said, 'The original theme music is utterly key to the new series. It's glorious, why would you muck around with that? ... It's the moment again when the hairs on the back of your neck stand up, and it's inconceivable that we wouldn't use that type of theme music on the show.' Said producer Phil Collinson, 'One of the reasons we had thought we might use the original theme tune is that it's magnificent and was never better. What they tried to do with it ... we've never [again] had that spooky, atmospheric, dramatic feel that the original piece of music had.' Gardner agreed: 'What I love about some of the meetings I've done with Murray [Gold] is that he comes to meetings saying, "That theme music is so utterly fantastic. How did they do that?" And that's exciting. When you have a composer of that stature talking with such emotion about a piece of music composed forty years ago ...'

Steve Wright's show on Radio 2 two days later featured a radio trailer for the series as well as an additional interview with Davies. 'I never thought in a million years Chris [Eccleston] would be interested in this,' Davies told Wright, 'but he knows himself that he's got this reputation for being tense and dour and Northern, God bless him, but then he actually e-mailed me to say "Please put me on the list," because I've known him from years back ... I think he'll be a revelation to people.'

Several radio trailers ran on all the BBC's radio networks, including the digital tiers such as BBC7. One variation had a female voice, in hushed tones, saying, 'Coming soon from BBC1 ...' as the echo-treated voice of Eccleston approached as if in a tunnel, complete with the Doctor/Rose exchange from the first episode that ended with 'Run for your life!' Another variation omitted the Doctor's and Rose's voices entirely, retaining only the announcer's 'Coming soon ...' remark along with the opening title music.

BBC Radio 4's *Saturday Review* covered the show on 19 March. Commentator Robert Sandal said that he felt the series may simply be fun for the 'old' viewers rather than looking for 'new' ones. 'I felt slightly uneasy about the casting of Billie Piper in this. She does a very good job ... but I didn't think the relationship between her and the Doctor quite works ... I personally found also that the special effects, which are quite impressive, are competing, with the audience that's going to watch them, with some pretty impressive Hollywood stuff, and I don't think they're quite flashy enough.'

Steve Wright returned to the fray with another instalment on his 21 March show, interviewing Eccleston. The actor recalled that he had: '... read an article about Russell T Davies, who I did *Second Coming* with ... I thought it was an odd career move for Russell [to take on *Doctor Who*], because [he's] associated with more niche, more controversial subject matter, to say the least.' On the subject of new monsters to face, Eccleston commented: 'I think we've got two original villains, the Daleks and the Autons ... Other than that, Russell and the other writers have created an entire gallery of new villains.' He went on to mention various new monsters including Cassandra from 'The End of the World', describing her as being 'from the planet Botox!' Eccleston said that he felt he was somewhat similar to Patrick Troughton, at least facially, but maybe in outlook as well, and talked about political reporter Andrew Marr's cameo appearance.

The barrage of coverage continued as the show's debut date approached. On 18 March, BBC Radio Derby featured interviews with several members of a local fan group, the Derby Whoovers, regarding the new series; they had with them a life size Dalek in the studio. The *Dead Ringers* sketch comedy series announced an evening of fun to be aired on 25 March; host Jon Culshaw, well known for his Tom Baker impressions, hosted. Radio 2 meanwhile featured a *Doctor Who* segment on its comedy programme *The Day the Music Died*, including a *Vision On*-inspired sequence with descriptions of pictures of new *Doctor Who* aliens sent in by musicians. (*Vision On* was a popular children's activity show, aimed mainly at the deaf and hard-of-hearing but also enjoyed by many others, which ran on BBC TV from 1964 until 1976. Much of the music used in it touches chords with the generation of viewers who grew up with it.) BBC Radio Leicester ran a series of interviews during the week prior to the broadcast of 'Rose', the aim being to find Leicestershire's biggest *Doctor Who* fan.

The two episodes of the specially-produced BBC radio documentary series *Project: WHO?* aired on Radio 2 on 22 and 29 March respectively. The series's brief was that it would 'examine how the format of the show has been developed and shaped for a new audience, how the character of the Doctor was cast, and how the series will be launched and marketed around the globe.' *Project: WHO?* was originally to feature narration by Patrick Stewart (*Star Trek: The Next Generation*), but he had to pull out due to a scheduling conflict. Stewart was replaced by Anthony Stewart Head (*Buffy the Vampire Slayer*), himself no stranger to *Doctor Who*, having played roles for both Big Finish Productions (in their *Excelis* audio miniseries) and for BBCi (in the webcast serial *Death Comes to Time*). The opening instalment, 'Bigger on the Inside', took listeners back to the beginning, as Lorraine Heggessey explained how the series was revived. 'This opening programme,' said the press brief, 'considers how the creator of *Queer as Folk* and *The Second Coming* approached the task of re-creating one of the most popular and enduring formats on television.' The concluding chapter, 'Reverse the Polarity': '... considers what makes a perfect television adventure for the Doctor ...' and '... what some have perceived as a renaissance in television science fiction, and asks if fantasy shows are merely the invention of niche television marketing.'

Project: WHO? turned out to be a rather slick production, put together by Radio 2 producer Malcolm Prince. It featured interviews with a large number of notable *Doctor Who* personalities, including: actors Eccleston and Piper; executive producers Davies, Gardner and Young; producer Phil Collinson; BBC1 Controller Lorraine Heggessey; BBC Head of Drama Jane Tranter; director Joe Ahearne; original series actress Elisabeth Sladen and writer Terrance Dicks; writers Paul Cornell, Robert Shearman, and Mark Gatiss; The Mill's chief executive Robin Shenfield and various members of his technical staff; production designer Edward Thomas; visual creative consultant Bryan Hitch; *Doctor Who Magazine* editor Clayton Hickman; Dalek actor/writer Nicholas Briggs; *SFX* editor Dave Golder; *Heat* magazine editor Boyd Hilton; *Outpost Gallifrey* editor Shaun Lyon; and Barry Letts, *Doctor Who*'s producer from 1970 to 1975.

BBC Radio Wales also got into the action with a three-part documentary, *Back in Time*. This series would begin with two episodes broadcast on 26 March ('How Green Was My Tardis') and 2 April ('Who's Next') and conclude with a third instalment ('Dalek Nation') a month later, on 2 May. *Back In Time* and its presenter, producer Julian Carey, looked at links between *Doctor Who* and Wales, peering back into the series's history for connections including the parts of Snowdon that doubled for Tibet ('The Abominable Snowmen'), the giant maggots in Brynmawr ('The Green Death') and Dalek road signs in Llangollen. The programmes featured interviews with *Doctor Who* celebrities from yesteryear and the modern day, including Davies, Gardner, Eccleston, original series stars Sylvester McCoy, Katy Manning and Deborah Watling, production designer Ed Thomas, model effects supervisor Mike Tucker, writers Mark Gatiss and Richard Bignell (author of *Doctor Who On Location*) and actor Nicholas Briggs. They also went behind the scenes on the *Doctor Who* set in Newport, and profiled Terry Nation, creator of the Daleks, who had been born in Cardiff.

Eccleston made the rounds two days prior to transmission on two BBC radio programmes, the Jo Whiley show and the Simon Mayo show. Eccleston's appearance on Jo Whiley's Radio 1 programme consisted mainly of a discussion of the actor's experiences on the series in general; when asked what his favourite monster from the new series was, he claimed it was 'the creatures who come through a crack in time in episode eight', noting that this episode ('Father's Day') was his favourite. He described his character as a 'car crash between me and Russell T Davies,' and reiterated his enjoyment of the Patrick Troughton portrayal of the Doctor (as well as noting that Tom Baker had recently had 'a pop' at him in an interview). Eccleston addressed fan questions at the end of the show, commenting in response to one that he'd likely never attend a convention ... and that he was 'reserving judgement' about doing a second season – one of the first times that he'd hedged his discussion of any future plans, and a foreshadow of events that would come up only a week later. Whiley ended the interview by reading out a message from a woman called Anna who apparently worked on the beginning of the recording the previous year, saying that Eccleston had promised to take the entire crew out to dinner if he ever said a certain phrase. Whiley asked what the phrase was, and Eccleston laughed and replied that it was: 'Trust me, I'm a Doctor!'

On the Simon Mayo show the same day on Radio 5 Live, Eccleston spent the better part of an hour in discussion, beginning with a good-natured argument with the sports correspondent who'd professed he wasn't a *Doctor Who* fan! He variously pondered topics such as James Bond ('I'd be a big eared James Bond!'), the interior of the TARDIS, and how the new series was a 'balancing act', having to appeal across the generations, and how he had to make sure he seemed like a hero so that children would not be frightened by the peril in which the character often finds himself. Eccleston noted that the Doctor was not frightened, 'except for when the Daleks arrive.' He took listener calls (answering one who asked about a second series by saying that it 'depends on ratings') and begged an American listener not to watch the pirated first episode: 'It doesn't show us in our best light and is also illegal!' Such diverse subjects as costumes, production values, and even the production crew – who had worked, as Eccleston said, a 'tough rate' on the show, completing thirteen episodes in eight and a half months, often at fourteen hours days – were brought up in a generally jovial session.

As the hours prior to the new series's broadcast debut counted down, Richard Allinson on Radio 2 asked listeners to nominate their pick for the 'scariest *Doctor Who* monster'; representatives from the *Doctor Who* Appreciation Society appeared on BBC Radio Essex; BBC Radio Wales's *Good Morning Wales* previewed the series; and *Newsbeat* and Chris Moyles both profiled the battle about to be waged, between the Doctor and 'a pair of wisecracking Geordies', Ant and Dec, on ITV ...

COVERAGE IN PRINT

During the weeks leading up to transmission, the press was also flooded with further coverage of the new series, and no stone was left unturned.

Attention focused in some quarters on the personal life of Piper, who appeared semi-clothed in an *Arena* magazine shoot and spoke about her soon-to-be-ex-husband, Chris Evans: 'I always thought it was weird, exes that hung out. But now I'm doing it myself I understand it. We've been through a lot. There's been no pressure. It's almost nicer now because there are no harboured feelings, no resentment. We're still best buds.'

The *icWales* network, meanwhile, noted on 13 March that Eccleston was 'just what the Doctor ordered,' quoting Davies as hitting back at critics who slammed the actor ... and the Doctor's new costume: 'The Doctor has his own identity. After all he has two hearts and is 900 years old. He does not need to wear a silly coat!' Davies also defended his decision to pass Cardiff off as London in various scenes in the forthcoming show: 'We had to base it around London as we are selling the series to America and Australia. We had to set it somewhere which will be recognised by a global audience. However, Cardiff does feature as itself in two episodes and we filmed an earthquake in Cardiff Bay.'

The Daleks were also subject to scrutiny, a *Liverpool Daily Post* article on 2 March noting: 'After giving Doctor Who a lot of bother and forcing Britain's under-10s to quiver behind the sofa, these weird alien invaders became the thing to have, whether in toys, comics, books or on television. They even had their own comic strip series which ran in *TV Century 21* for 104 issues – not bad for what were essentially dustbins on wheels.' *The Times* on 6 March discussed the Daleks being revamped for the new era: 'The upgraded versions take to the air using rocket-boosters, enhancing their ability to exterminate, exterminate. The new Daleks are also bigger than the ones last seen in 1989 and have more lethal weaponry than the old guns that resembled sink plungers. But fans will have to wait: the evil forces do not appear in the first episode, to be shown on BBC1 on Easter Saturday.' The *Guardian* on 9 March asked: 'Why can't Daleks go up stairs?' This article discussed the peril of the classic monsters and how they had been updated for the new series: 'As terrifying as Doctor Who's arch enemies might have seemed, the fact that they could be outwitted by a simple staircase made them a shade less menacing.' Of course, the papers all neglected to mention that this had been something already dealt with in the original series.

Various publications for which *Doctor Who* was not a usual topic of conversation ran articles throughout March. *Attitude* magazine, a publication for 'gay professionals', featured a large article on the show, headlined 'Who's the Daddy', covering the age-old topic of why *Doctor Who* is considered by some to be a 'gay pastime' and discussing the series's appeal in general. *BellaOnline* ran an article on 9 March entitled '*Doctor Who* 101 – A Newbie Viewing Guide to the Classic Series.' This took a light-hearted look at the original series in preparation for the new: 'The special effects were bad even in their own day, thanks to a virtually non-existent budget. Imagine, if you will, creating a green lumpy monster by wrapping someone with green-painted bubble wrap. They did that. Yes, this show was famous for its cheesy effects.' *Digit* magazine, which focused on 3D design, released an edition emblazoned on the front cover with a picture of the new TARDIS exterior and text hinting at secrets revealed inside. Among the stills included within the magazine's pages were an image of the spiders used in 'The End of the World', as well as some from the teaser trailer. Descriptions were also given of other creature designs, including that of Cassandra, the stretched-skin human.

The mainstream press had their own share of *Doctor Who* coverage. The 6 March edition of the *Observer* discussed the obsession of fans with *Doctor Who*, framed in the context of the return of the series; of note, it quoted Davies as saying that there were actually only a few thousand fans that were considered to be 'active or interested', a comment that, judging by the interest shown in the series, was something of an understatement. The same day, *The Times* discussed the relaunch, observing: 'For 25 years, *Doctor Who's* creaky charm captivated a nation. Now Russell T Davies has polished it up, with slick effects and an even slicker script.' The report went on to say that the scripts themselves were: '... slick, witty and, most important of all, fresh. They also have Davies the Mouth's fingerprints all over them. The Doctor's slightly deranged monologue sounds suspiciously like Russell T himself.' On 11 March, the *Scottish Daily Record* poked some fun at the series's new aliens: 'If the sneak preview we had yesterday of the Blue Moxx is anything to go by, the villains in the new version of *Doctor Who* look like they're going to be a bit more menacing than the overgrown pepper pots and extras wearing upturned buckets wrapped in tinfoil that the Time Lord used to battle in the Sixties and Seventies ... Let's just say the following list of forthcoming evil baddies is just informed speculation.' The *Record* then included such items as the 'Teekay Moxx', like the Moxx of Balhoon, only wearing last year's fashions; 'The Dohleks', similar to the Daleks, but not as intelligent ... they have a fatal weakness for doughnuts and Duff beer; the 'Cydermen', crazed monsters from the English West Country; and the 'Eltonjonians', manic, vertically-challenge beings that regard all authority figures as vile pigs and chant: 'Exfoliate, exfoliate!'

The *Radio Times*, always a part of the collective *Doctor Who* mythology from its years of television listings, feature coverage and magazine covers, included a one-page colour article in its 8 March edition, with summaries of the various monsters and cast members to be featured in the early episodes of the new series, as well as quotes from Davies and Gardner. The next week's edition featured more coverage, including the billboard poster photograph that had been seen around the UK and information about the various forthcoming shows that the cast and crew would be interviewed on. A week later, the edition covering the series's on-air debut date would, it was promised, feature a front cover and a special sixteen page supplement detailing 'the characters, monsters and special effects of the new series'. A number of actors appearing in the new series were profiled in the press. These included Jimmy Vee, who was interviewed in the *Daily Record* on 10 March. Vee, who played the Moxx of Balhoon in episode two as well as other various alien roles: '... admitted it was tough filming in the cumbersome costume, which took three hours to put on and featured a 2ft head weighing more than half a stone. Once the outfit was on, Jimmy couldn't go to the toilet for 10 hours and its weight meant the pounds were falling off him. He said: "I must have lost a stone in a week, even though I was drinking to rehydrate constantly. As soon as I got out, I had to eat everything I could get my hands on."' Richard Wilson, who would play Dr Constantine in Steven Moffat's two-part story, was interviewed for the same day's update of *Manchester Online*: 'I play a doctor in an episode set in the Second World War and am in two episodes. I was excited when I was approached to play a part and as soon as I read the script for the episodes they wanted me to feature in I made my mind up that I wanted the role. As well as the kudos of starring in *Doctor Who*, it was also good to play alongside Christopher Eccleston, because although I know him socially I'd never had the opportunity to work with him until now. He's made a very good Doctor Who and has brought a fresh touch to the role.'

The BBC itself added to the hype as its Press Office began issuing a series of online 'press packs' containing various interviews. The first of these, made available on 10 March, focused on discussing Eccleston and Piper. It also covered the revamp of the *bbc.co.uk* official *Doctor Who* website, reporting that it would now include new video and audio and interactive material, and contained quotes from Davies and Eccleston himself. Later instalments would interview various series writers, cast members and production personnel. The BBC's in-house magazine *Ariel* also covered the series's return, occasionally mentioning items that hadn't yet been confirmed to the general public.

And there were spoilers ... lots of spoilers, now commonplace in the UK media. A 'tree person' was featured on the cover of the *Sun* on 10 March; she would later be identified as Jabe, played by Yasmin Bannerman, in the second episode, 'The End of the World'. The *Sun* would also reveal the presence of the Moxx of Balhoon and the Face of Boe in the second instalment and, as was fairly widely reported previously, the Autons in the first. At the same time, a series of press photographs began circulating, some culled from BBC Pictures's official publicity photograph archive; these were embargoed from being used on fan websites, although were quickly swapped by fans in online forums. They included one of the Doctor being held back by Autons, and another of Rose smiling as she stood in front of the TARDIS console. Magazines also began printing some of these photos, mostly from the first two episodes, by agreement with the BBC. Those that saw print at this time included pictures of the Autons and the various aliens from the second story, and one of the Doctor and Rose standing on Platform One overlooking the dying Earth from 'The End of the World'. Plot reports also began appearing in the tabloids; it seemed Davies had predicted correctly that the 'ruiners' were alive and well, ready to spoil the secrets of the first series for the sake of selling newspapers.

By the second week of March, the press barrage had intensified. The 13 March edition of the *Independent* interviewed production designer Edward Thomas, writer Mark Gatiss and Eccleston. 'Towards the end of the last series, I don't know if he was faring well,' said Thomas of the 'classic' *Doctor Who*. 'He had become something of a cartoon character. No doubt that article about why we shouldn't bother to bring him back will be written, but great stories never have a set time.' Gatiss was pleased with Eccleston's performance as the Doctor: 'Chris endows the role with this extraordinary energy. He plays the Doctor with this full-tilt brio that actually frightens me. He also possesses this great credibility. When Christopher Eccleston tells you a Dalek is lethal, you instantly believe it.' Eccleston himself appeared to be enjoying not only the role, but what it represented: 'The Doctor is ... completely non-judgmental. He accepts everything and everyone, whether they're black or blue, gay or straight. If he meets an alien, his first reaction is not revulsion, but joy. He celebrates life in all its forms, shades, colours and creeds. Without being didactic, that's a very strong message.' It was a message carried throughout the series, predominantly in the writing Davies was supervising; as the *Sunday Herald* noted, 'Having dropped hints with the BBC throughout his career, as his knack for writing superior popular television became ever more reliable – *Queer As Folk, Bob And Rose, Mine All Mine* – Davies has finally been given the keys to Doctor Who's TARDIS, the iconic inter-dimensional phone box that has gone unused for far too long.' The *Observer* noted that the BBC was banking on the series to vanquish all opponents and revive family viewing: 'It seems unlikely that a post-Dalek generation would get excited by an army of croaking jelly moulds, but the Doctor will, no doubt, be tackling more blood-curdling foes this time round.'

The 15 March edition of the *Sun* discussed 'Why Wales is so hip it hurts', noting that 'the most anticipated TV series this year will be the new *Doctor Who* – filmed entirely in Wales.' The *South Wales Echo* noted that 'Scary new monsters and Cardiff's Howells department store exploding [are] just some of the treats due for fans of *Doctor Who* in the much-anticipated new series,' and discussed Simon Pegg's involvement in the narration of *Doctor Who Confidential*. The *List*, a Scottish culture magazine, presented a three page feature on the series including interviews, while *This is Gloucester* hoped that the Doctor's latest incarnation would adhere to the principles of the series being family-orientated: 'I know children are more worldly-wise these days, but there are certain standards which must be observed. I would also beware of political correctness. Kids hate being preached at.' The *Newcastle Chronicle & Journal*, however, believed that politics would be much in evidence, reporting that the new series: '... includes a sinister episode where all members of the Cabinet are taken over by aliens. Does the Doctor triumph, or is it possible that the aliens leave of their own accord after encountering [Deputy Prime Minister] John Prescott and deciding to look for a more intelligent life form?'

On 17 March, the *Stage* featured an interview with Penelope Wilton ('Aliens of London'): 'I really have been sworn to secrecy on that project,' she maintained, 'and the director would kill me if I gave away any of the plotlines. But let's just say that I will be using that famous black door at No 10 Downing Street.' *Design Week* covered the 2D and 3D illustration work by the effects company The Mill: 'From an art and design point of view, I think we achieved a huge amount ... and lots of scary animatronic monsters too!' said production designer Edward Thomas. The *Journal* that day called *Doctor Who* its 'programme of the week': 'After 16 years of hard campaigning from true fans, it's about to get a new lease of life. Things may have moved on, but you can bet the Daleks will be there. But will they be able to go upstairs?' *Newsquest Digital Media* proclaimed: 'Christopher Eccleston was always going to be a good Doctor Who ... Eccleston's acting consistently impresses, but he has one other vital attribute to play the good Doctor: wild eyes and a slightly dangerous air.' The *Express* noted that several MPs had already seen a sneak preview of the series: 'Some were granted a private screening of the new show, starring Christopher Eccleston, in Westminster this week. "It's another good example of the perks on offer," says one Parliamentary colleague. "The Doctor has quite a few fans here." Well, at least he knows he'll get a warm welcome if he ever chooses to park his TARDIS on the House of Commons terrace.' The *Metro* claimed that comedian Graham Norton: '... hankered after a role in the new *Doctor Who* series. "I did train as an actor so why don't you want me?" he flounced.' Very prescient words, considering what would happen on the first night of transmission ...

The *Daily Post* discussed the Daleks on 18 March. 'Since my item last week about the return of *Doctor Who*, several people have informed me that the new-look Daleks are much deadlier than their predecessors,' wrote columnist Valerie Hill. 'They now fly around on jet-powered platforms. You can no longer outwit these ruthless, intergalactic, metal tyrants by simply running up a flight of stairs.'

Broadcast asked viewers to: 'Get behind the sofa! Why, is the TV licence detector van outside again? It's much scarier than that – the return of *Doctor Who*. *Doctor Who*? I thought he died out long ago.' *Broadcast* also noted that the Doctor was: '... up against his most fearsome opponents yet. The Master? The Cybermen? Blokes in outsized green rubber outfits waving coat hangers? ... Even worse than that, Ant and Dec!' This was one of the first of many press references to what was looking likely to be the series's time slot competition on ITV1, *Ant & Dec's Saturday Night Takeaway*. *Broadcast* wasn't necessarily convinced that *Doctor Who* would win the ratings war: 'It won't be easy for the Doctor – younger viewers won't have heard of him ... but he's got a secret weapon, Billie Piper.'

Down under, the 18 March edition of the *Daily Telegraph* in Australia lamented the lack of confirmation of a broadcaster (at the time, ABC had yet to make its final announcement): 'The ABC, which has screened BBC shows since January 1965, is yet to buy the new series despite being offered the rights last year.' ABC head of programming Marena Manzoufas was quoted as saying: 'At that stage they hadn't shown it to us and I wanted to see an episode before we bought it. Before we saw it a week-and-a-half ago we were concerned about whether [or not] it would work for a non-*Who* audience. But it's fabulous – even if you're not a *Doctor Who* fan, you can come to it cold and be engrossed in it.'

The amount of press attention and coverage devoted to the new series during the week leading up to its 26 March on-air debut unquestionably reached record proportions for *Doctor Who*. And so, we take a seven-day snapshot look at that final week before transmission:

19 March – The *Daily Telegraph* presented an 'A to Z' of the series by Matthew Sweet (who had presented the *Culture Show* piece on BBC2 the previous evening) and an interview with Mark Gatiss. The *Times* profiled Piper, noting some of her favourite moments from making the new series. The *Express* wondered 'Why Billie has Fallen For A Dalek': 'You'd never guess it in a million light years. But new *Doctor Who* star Billie Piper has admitted to a growing attachment with a Dalek.' Said Piper, 'I had this quite emotional scene with a Dalek. I'm sat there the night before the take thinking, how am I going to tap into my emotions? This is a hunk of junk! And then, I think because it is so beautifully written with human emotion, I am stood there and I am actually feeling for this thing.' The *Telegraph*, in an article referring

mostly to the *Quatermass* serials of the 1950s, called *Doctor Who* its 'spiritual successor'. The *Scotsman* recounted a viewer's tales, remembering back when he was twelve years old, compared to the excitement of today: 'All my adult worries and responsibilities have receded, replaced by an obsessive childish concentration on just one thing: next week, after nine years in televisual limbo, *Doctor Who* is returning to our screens.'

20 March – Welsh Assembly First Minister Rhodri Morgan's close encounter with the *Doctor Who* production was recounted; said BBC News, 'Morgan arrived at BBC Wales's Cardiff studios to appear on the political show *Dragon's Eye* at the same time as a group of extras on the sci-fi series. The mix-up was noticed as he was ushered into a make-up room to become a tree-like sidekick of new monster Jabe. An employee from London has been blamed for the case of mistaken identity.' Morgan apparently thought it was really funny. The *Sunday Mail* quoted several past assistants with some advice for Piper. 'I haven't the foggiest who Billie Piper is but I'd tell her to be careful of turning her role into a romantic one,' said Lalla Ward (who had played Romana and later married Tom Baker). 'You spend two years prancing around with somebody on TV and you end up thinking it's really you.' Said Louise Jameson (Leela), 'Part of *Doctor Who*'s charm is its innocence. It's very important the girl has sex appeal to keep the male viewers interested but it would be a shame to make the story itself sexy'. Deborah Watling (Victoria) meanwhile commented: 'To me, the relationship was always more fatherly. It kept the children interested and made the fathers think they were in with a chance. It's got to have an innocence or you're lost.' The *Independent on Sunday* magazine profiled Piper, noting she was someone 'we underestimate ... at our peril!' The *Observer* and *Independent on Sunday* ran interviews with Eccleston and Piper respectively, while the *Mail* profiled the late Delia Derbyshire, the electronic music pioneer who had arranged the original version of the *Doctor Who* theme tune. The *Observer* commented on the first episode: 'The first story suggests that Davies has found the right balance between respect and renovation. The Internet and the London Eye play significant roles but the TARDIS retains its '50s exterior and an interior representing a '60s idea of the future.' The *Sunday Herald* previewed the series with spoilers, but also noted that Eccleston's casting was: '... as inspired as making Vincent D'Onofrio a cop ... There's already an odd, intense, Tom Bakerish charm, grins flashing at inopportune moments.' The *Sunday Independent (Ireland)* said: 'We should all be grateful for Billie's involvement. Among those tipped for a starring role alongside the Doc during the 15-year gap since the last series was Pamela Anderson. But kick-ass Pam wouldn't have been right as one of the Doc's sidekicks.' And the *Scotsman* bade readers to: '... forget American puppets who need wires to make themselves animated ... forget Spock, whose character is actually the epitome of an eastern seaboard, Ivy League intellectual of the Kennedy era, busy getting the Federation into some galactic Vietnam War. Give me British sci-fi heroes every time – Dan Dare, Jeff Hawke, Jet Morgan, with the eponymous Doctor high on the list ... Like the ancient Greek heroes, Doctor Who was always at the mercy of the Gods and a wayward navigation device in the TARDIS. That's the whole point of heroes – they show you how to deal with an indifferent, even perverse, universe with wit, courage and a stiff upper lip.'

21 March – The *Sun* reported Eccleston as saying that he was 'not completely sure' he wanted to do a second series, citing the fear of typecasting. 'I need to think about it ... It's more than a huge responsibility to shoulder. And no, I don't want to be thought of as the Doctor to the exclusion of everything else I've done or may do in the future. So I'll have to think long and hard about it before I make the final decision to say yes or no. I am keenly aware that the

whole thing could be a poisoned chalice.' Eccleston did note that the show was 'amazing' and 'bonkers' at the same time: 'The first scene had me as the Doctor chasing this very brilliant actor down a street while he was dressed as an alien pig. I thought, "It doesn't get much [more] bonkers than this!" It was such fun to do.' Eccleston told the *Manchester Evening News* that he had been in the acting 'game' for eighteen years and 'won't allow myself to be absorbed completely,' but also revealed that he had met several *Doctor Who* fans and that they'd been kind and generous to him. The *Daily Star*, meanwhile, said that Piper wouldn't be tuning into the debut: 'I'll do what I always do on transmission dates ... go to the pub and get lashed!' The *Mirror* reported that Piper had said she would be 'too critical' and that she would 'be looking for all the things I could have done better.' The actress was quoted by the *Newsquest Media Group* as saying that she hadn't enjoyed her singing career, and *The Times* commented: 'Everyone presumes that the role will finally airlift her out of her previous life and on to the A-list, but I think it's quite a long shot ... In the first episode of the new *Who* at least, Billie underwhelms.'

22 March – The BBC released its second *Doctor Who* press pack, which included information about the visual effects work achieved by The Mill, and profiled Edward Thomas ('I just waded in there because it's *Doctor Who* and it's a legend'), Mike Tucker ('What [Davies has] brought back is *Doctor Who*, but *Doctor Who* re-invented for the mindset and viewing tastes of the 21st Century viewing public') and prosthetics designer Neill Gorton ('When it came back, I just had to be involved.') BBC political reporter Andrew Marr told the *Telegraph* that he had: '... a vanishingly small part in the new run of *Doctor Who*. Thanks to a small miracle of lateral thinking, I play a bat-eared political reporter.' Of course, as he said, he 'would have happily played a cactus on a windowsill or Billie Piper's missing sock' to be on *Doctor Who. icLiverpool* profiled 'the two Merseysiders responsible for the new-look *Doctor Who*,' make-up designers Davy Jones and Linda Davie: 'Davy and Lin are still sworn to secrecy on what happens but are confident that the new Doctor will be a triumph.' Jones was quoted as saying: 'Chris and Billy [sic] have a great chemistry on screen,' while Davies noted that the series was: '... very hip. Both characters are the type of people you'd want to hang out with.' The *Daily Star* asked 'Who's That Girl?', discussing Piper's transformation from a pop star to a *Doctor Who* assistant, while the *Evening Standard* wondered 'Who is this Doctor?', profiling Eccleston. 'When Christopher Eccleston grins at you, it is hard to know whether to smile back at him, or to jump on a chair and scream,' wrote columnist Matthew Sweet. 'It is the eyes. Hypnotic, glittery things that make you ponder two questions: is this a nice man – or is he about to go for my neck?' *Manchester Online* reported that a second series was in the planning stages, 'but can *Doctor Who* defeat his greatest enemy – ITV1 rivals Ant and Dec?' The industry trade paper *Variety* wondered the same thing, saying: 'BBC execs hope *Doctor Who* will play a key role in combating ITV's *Ant & Dec* in the Saturday evening ratings battle, as well as highlighting the quality public service fare that will help the Beeb keep its license fee.' *Louth Today* spilled the beans on the Doctor's latest enemy, 'man-eating wheelie bins' from the first episode. 'But while they note the irony, objectors to the introduction of wheelie bins in Louth say the subject is no laughing matter.' *Radio Times* confirmed that Simon Day would appear in episode two as the Steward, and Sydney Australia's *Daily Telegraph* reported that the ABC network had now seen 'Rose' and 'hopes to buy' the new series. Everyone was talking about the return of the programme, according to *icCoventry*, which went on to say: 'Saturday telly will take a nostalgic turn this coming weekend ... So clear behind the sofa, get in some crumpets, and pile in front of the telly this Saturday for a chance to relive your childhood, and,

of course, to see if the Daleks have finally worked out how to negotiate stairs.'

23 March – ITV announced that it would be moving *Ant & Dec* up 15 minutes to 6.45pm on the schedule, throwing down the gauntlet for a challenge. The *New Statesman* pondered the lack of a regeneration sequence in the new series: '[Davies's] reasons are sound enough. Most of the target audience of children will never have even heard of *Doctor Who*, let alone know that eight actors have played the role since 1966. It would have made a puzzling and slow start.' *Creative Match* analysed the new series's effects: 'After [The Mill's] Academy Award for the effects on *Gladiator* there is no doubt that this will be a more sophisticated treat than the original.' The *Herald* commented on the return, discussing with Mark Gatiss and Phil Collinson the notion of being a *Doctor Who* fan in the modern age. The *Western Mail* printed a guide to the new series's monsters – mostly from 'The End of the World' including the Steward as well as Hop Pyleen and the other incidental creatures – while *BlogCritics* published an interesting account, 'What *Battlestar Galactica* Can Teach *Doctor Who* About Television In The Digital Age', bidding the BBC to pay attention to the recent return of the American cult favourite. Several newspapers ran stories about a mother who said 'her life has been ruined because she is terrified of Daleks' and 'is sent into a blind panic if she even hears the words "exterminate".'

24 March – Former Doctor Sylvester McCoy penned an article for the *Guardian*: 'I was a bit worried that the new series might not work ... But this new version with Christopher Eccleston as the Doctor and Billie Piper as his assistant, Rose, is just wonderful. Part of its charm is the way in which it makes a sly wink to earlier series ... It is very scary, just like in the old days, but now children will be frightened of mannequins. And dustbins.' Actor Paul Kasey is profiled by the *Leicester Mercury*: '... and the chances are, you've never heard of him. That could be about to change.' It notes that Kasey will play four aliens including a Slitheen and an Auton. 'I also play an android robot ... It was also a she. That was fantastic, but really hard to play. The costume was so hard; we were basically built into it. It was a full body costume in lilac and cream. As soon as you were in, you were in for good, although you could take the head off while the crew wasn't working.' *Newsquest Digital Media* profiled Mark Troughton, son of the second Doctor, the late Patrick Troughton, who said he'd be watching this weekend: 'And I'm sure my kids will too.' *BBC News* presented an overview of the many websites, conventions and fan clubs that existed for the series, quoting Ian Chandos of a group called the Sisterhood of Karn: 'We all want a chance to watch the first episode in its entirety then meet up the following week to discuss it. Having said that, we'll probably all be on the phone to each other as soon as it's over.' *Sky News*, the *East Anglian Times*, the *Daily Express* and the *Daily Star* all profiled Piper with the usual comments, while the *Northern Echo* ran a piece on Eccleston: 'You couldn't imagine him welcoming the barrage of press and public recognition that playing the Doctor would bring'. This article again brought up the spectre of a second series without him. The *Spectator* said: 'Davies is such a dedicated *Doctor Who* fan that he even carried on watching in that difficult period after Peter Davison had gone, when it apparently went down and down. If anyone on this planet was ever likely to breathe new life into an ageing Time Lord, then Russell T was surely the man.' The *Sun* said that the Doctor should 'stay in his TARDIS', noting some of the new nasties he would be facing, while the *Daily Star* printed an A to Z of monsters from the past. The *Telegraph* wondered, 'Is Doctor Who gay? ... Perhaps he ought to keep two photographs next to his bed in the TARDIS: one of Scarlett Johansson, say, and one of Justin Timberlake. When he regenerates, all he has to do is look at both of them and discover which one makes his hearts beat faster.' The newspapers began to run

teasers for the Saturday night broadcast. The *South Wales Echo* said 'Get ready to dive behind the sofa again!' *City Life*, a Manchester listings magazine, interviewed Eccleston: 'It was my idea to bring a bit of Northern realism to the whole thing.' *Net4Nowt* analysed the scheduling of the new series: 'By scheduling *Doctor Who* in the prime timeslot of 7.00PM Saturday night, BBC1 is evidently hoping to capture market share from *Ant & Dec* ... An analysis of Internet searches for both "ant and dec saturday night take away" and "new doctor who" suggests that BBC1 has a fighting chance: despite Ant and Dec's solid audience base, [the] share of searches for their show online [has] decreased in the lead-up to the resurrection of *Doctor Who*. The share of Internet searches for the phrase "new doctor who" overtook "ant and dec saturday night take away" two weeks ago, and the phrase is currently receiving 50% more searches than its rival.' The Welsh-language weekly *Golwg* printed a photo of the Doctor and Rose over Cardiff's Millennium Stadium, noting the recent recording and tying in with a larger feature on celebrating the centenary of Cardiff's city status. The *Oxford Dictionary of National Biography*, the principal biographical reference work for the British past, marked the start of the new series by having former Doctor, the late Jon Pertwee, as their featured 'Life of the Day'. The *Daily Record* commented on Piper accidentally swearing on the previous day's Chris Moyles radio show. And the *Croydon Guardian* said it was looking for 'any *Doctor Who* fans planning anything special to mark the Time Lord's return,' wanting to know: 'If you are crazy about the guy from Gallifrey, dotty about Daleks or mad about the Master then we want to hear from you.'

25 March – The day before the debut carried an unbelievable amount of press coverage, befitting such a major television event. The *Evening Gazette* interviewed Mark Gatiss: 'I didn't sleep for a week after the announcement it was coming back. I thought if they don't ask me to write an episode, I'll have to shoot myself. Then Russell called and asked if I would like to do it ... I wanted to avoid my story becoming an exercise in nostalgia for the show. But then Russell gave all of the writers vague storylines to work on. I was hoping I'd get the historical storyline and I did.' *BBC News* noted that 'thanks to *Doctor Who*, blue police boxes topped with flashing police lights became a national icon during the 1960s.' The *Guardian* entered 'the time-warped world of *Doctor Who*'s assistants,' discussing the role of the companions: 'Few appointments carry the gravitas of the role of *Doctor Who*'s sidekick. Its social and cultural significance is perhaps on a par only with discovering which blue-blooded virgin the heir to the throne will choose to be his bride.' Clayton Hickman of *Doctor Who Magazine* told the *Guardian*, 'Russell T Davies is into strong women. If you look at his earlier work, such as *Bob and Rose* and *Queer as Folk*, there's always a woman chaperoning the guys. So I don't think Billie will be hobbling down the corridor in high heels.' The *Sun* noted that Piper was 'out of this world' and called her the 'Babe Of The Week', as well as including news on how the mole who had leaked the first episode in Canada had been 'exterminated'. *Media Guardian* noted the oncoming war between *Doctor Who* and *Ant & Dec's Saturday Night Takeaway*: 'Oxford will be clashing oars with Cambridge this weekend and Ireland will be hoping to defeat Israel in the World Cup qualifier, but the struggle of truly galactic proportions will take place in living rooms across the UK on Saturday night.' *New Musical Express* (NME) called *Doctor Who* 'a classic rock'n'roll star' and noted: 'For the first time ever, *Doctor Who* is about to become cool.' The *Scotsman* reported that there were 237 blue police boxes still scattered throughout Britain, and that the police might even bring them back, especially in the wake of renewed popularity. *Leeds Today* said that it was 'a shame that a whole generation of kids haven't had a Doctor to grow up with, but now that's going to

change.' The *London News Review* opined that 'Rose' was: '... wonderful ... The chief beef is Murray Gold's incidental music. Gold did a fine job of reworking the theme tune ... But his incidental music in "Rose" sounds like bad library CDs from the 1990s.' The *Birmingham Evening Mail* noted: 'People just want to spend Saturday evening in front of their television and not be distracted.' Scotland's *Evening Times* said: 'Scotland fans stuck at home could miss the start of the vital World Cup clash with Italy because of *Doctor Who*. BBC bosses have scheduled coverage of tomorrow's game to begin at 7.45pm – the same time as kick-off ... The move has angered fans who can't make the journey.' The *Daily Star* complained that the Cybermen won't be back: '[They] have been killed off because TV bosses think they are out of date. And in their bid to give the SF series a fresh look, they claim the Time Lord is more likely to go up against iPod-man.' The *Coventry Evening Telegraph* asked, 'Two, four, six, eight, Who do we appreciate?' ... and, of course, the answer was *Doctor Who*. *Newsquest Digital Media* observed: 'Unless you've been hiding behind a sofa for the past month (and be honest, has anyone ever done that?) you'll be aware that a new series of *Doctor Who* is upon us ... As long as [it] can be watched without the aid of nostalgia-tinted glasses, it should be a step in the right direction.' The *Forester* (from the Forest of Dean) noted that the series was shot on location in nearby Monmouth. The *Express and Echo* (Exeter) said: 'Exeter youngsters with an appetite for time travel are appealing to new *Doctor Who* Christopher Eccleston to help them put the finishing touches to a school play based on the famous TV Time Lord. On the eve of the return of the classic BBC series this weekend, children at John Stocker Middle School in St Thomas are rehearsing their own version of the much-loved sci-fi show.' The *Sunderland Echo* interviewed former series star William Russell (one of the first companions) who was delighted at the return of the series. The *Bolton Evening News* dedicated four pages to the series with large photo supplements.

26 March – In the early hours of Saturday, the press had been working overtime to mark the series's return that evening. The morning's *Financial Times* said: 'The BBC's reincarnation of *Doctor Who* is likely to give some middle-aged viewers a rude awakening ... Tonight's Easter weekend resurrection of the Doctor is going to make some uncomfortable viewing for middle-aged fans.' The *Financial Times* also discussed Davies's influences: 'No television drama has ever stoked the imaginations of its fans quite like *Doctor Who* ... As a child, Davies dreamed of discovering the TARDIS somewhere in his hometown of Swansea and running away with the Doctor to frolic in a world of limitless imagination and adventure.' The *Daily Record* reported: 'A fortune is being gambled on tonight's big telly clash – *Doctor Who* versus *Ant & Dec*. Viewers will be torn between Christopher Eccleston and Billie Piper's new adventures in the TARDIS and the Geordies' show featuring [footballer] David Beckham. Bookies have been taking hundreds of bets on the winners, with *Ant & Dec*, who usually get eight million viewers, edging in front.' A spokesman from Ladbrokes, a betting house, told the *Record*, 'Money suggests *Ant & Dec* will take away the highest ratings but we haven't seen such an intense battle for viewers on Saturday night since the finals of *Strictly Come Dancing* and *The X Factor* went head-to-head at the end of last year.' The *Sun* pictured the ghostly Gelth from 'The Unquiet Dead' – 'Talk about grave expectations!' – and called *Doctor Who* 'Best New Series' in its 'What To Watch This Weekend' listings. The *Independent* discussed feminism in *Doctor Who*: 'Reams of wordage have been dedicated to considering the issue of whether Billie Piper will make a properly emancipated assistant to *Doctor Who*, or whether she will descend, as so many have before her, into damsel-on-the-train-track cliché. Less intellectual energy has been spent on considering how it is that while the good Doctor can travel through time and space

with ease, the body that is so marvellously mutable never manages, even briefly, to adopt a new gender.' Director James Hawes, who helmed both episodes written by Steven Moffat to be seen later in the season, told the *Independent*, 'I am not a *Doctor Who* geek. True, I strode off in 1978 from my rural comprehensive to Oxford in a Tom Baker outfit, but I quickly dumped the scarf, got a girlfriend and honestly never gave the Doctor a thought for 20 years.' *The Times* noted that a new sonic screwdriver was to be seen: 'This is a state-of-the-art Merlin's wand. It unlocks the high-tech traps that encompass Doctor Who about the TARDIS.' The *Telegraph* said that, after a long absence, the new series was: '... smack, bang, up-to-date. It works. Thumbs up. Let them live.' The *Telegraph's* reporter observed that that the show's popularity: '... is not for an adult to say. My teenage son twice purred "This is really cool," which augurs well. But he worried that his friends would not watch it. "It's sad watching programmes your parents liked." Do these children have no sense of tradition?' And the *Evening Times* (Glasgow) commented, 'If we can accept Worzel Gummidge as a Time Lord we can easily accept *Shallow Grave* star Christopher Eccleston ...*Doctor Who* has enough character base to be a success with *Buffy*-loving teenagers but perhaps it simply can't appeal to grown-ups who grew up with the original. Back then, the strong storylines and weak special effects prompted the imagination to work overtime. Or perhaps we recall too fondly the time of our lives when we could be so easily terrified. And to overcome that nostalgia is asking a little too much of television.'

Perhaps ... but the print media, joined by their colleagues in broadcasting, had introduced nostalgia into the den of modern British television. *Doctor Who* versus the juggernaut of ITV1 Saturday night, a skirmish between an icon of the past and today's pop culture. It was going to be a weekend to remember.

The trip of a lifetime was about to begin.

CHAPTER ELEVEN:
THE TRIP OF A LIFETIME

S aturday 26 March 2005. *Doctor Who* returned to television with fanfare and pageantry and a much-heralded evening of entertainment starting at 5.25pm with the broadcast of *Doctor Who: A New Dimension* on BBC1. This documentary special, from the producers of the *Doctor Who Confidential* documentaries and narrated by David Tennant, would focus on the series's rich history, giving way to the debut of Graham Norton's *Strictly Dance Fever* leading up to 7.00pm. And when that hour finally came, the trip of a lifetime finally began.

LATE MARCH: 'ROSE'

The image of a police box in a tunnel consumed by fire was suddenly broken by the BBC1 announcer. 'And now,' he said over the image of tap-dancing lads in denim jeans (one of a series of BBC1 idents), 'BBC1 hurtles through space and time. Come with us for the trip of a lifetime ... Aliens, you have been warned. Christopher Eccleston ... is the new ... *Doctor Who!*' And with that, the BBC One ident faded away, to be replaced by the blues of a strangely familiar vortex and the sight of an old friend – a blue London police public call box – hurtling away from us as the music played in earnest.

Doctor Who had been reborn.

'Rose' introduced us to Rose Tyler, a nineteen year old London shop girl who, only through sheer bad luck, must take the lottery money down to the basement, where she encounters moving plastic mannequins and is rescued by a mysterious stranger in a leather jacket. What follows is an amazing adventure alongside the Doctor, as Christopher Eccleston and Billie Piper – unlike previous Doctors and companions in the original BBC series, both given billing on the opening credits – carry the action for forty-five minutes. When it was over, it was immediately followed by *Doctor Who Confidential*, a voiceover at the end of the episode encouraging fans to turn to the digital station BBC3 to watch this official behind-the-scenes documentary.

The opening minutes of 'Rose' were slightly marred by the unplanned intrusion of the voice of another star familiar to UK television audiences, yet one out of his element; BBC3 had left open an audio circuit, so *Strictly Dance Fever*'s presenter Graham Norton's voice carried through as Rose explored the basement of Henrik's. The circuit was eventually closed, however, and the episode carried on without further interruption. 'The Time Lord had Graham Norton breathing down his neck too,' said *BBC News* the following day, 'as a technical problem meant the sound from *Strictly Dance Fever* was briefly played over the opening scenes of *Doctor Who*. "There was a technical problem which was resolved as quickly as possible," a BBC spokesperson said. "We apologise if it affected viewers' enjoyment of *Doctor Who*."' The *Sunday Express* called it 'an embarrassing technical blunder' but it was largely forgotten as the episode got underway. (By way of a side note, the issue did not seem to occur everywhere; viewers in Scotland, for example, did not experience it.)

The debut was greeted by the usual cacophony of praise and concern. 'Trailers suggest some fairly strong production values for future Saturdays,' said the *Observer*, 'so I would have thought the BBC – thanks mainly to producer Russell T Davies who also penned last night's episode – is on to a winner. I for one will be watching.' 'I was hooked from the outset,' wrote a reviewer in the *Guardian*. 'The whole thing was stuffed with in-jokes I wasn't sure I was fully getting, but I laughed anyway.' The *News of the World* called it: 'Quality. Brilliant. After 16 years locked in the warp-shunt fantasies of the plasters-on-specs brigade, Russell T Davies has breathed new life into an old favourite. The Doctor got his girl and BBC1 found itself reacquainted with an old pal.' The *Sunday Telegraph* said: 'The new *Doctor Who* succeeded in establishing its own reality: skewed, sprightly and assured, without ever taking its audience's attention, or goodwill, for granted.' The *Independent* noted that the special effects, 'with which the series has been retrofitted, struck me as being as clunky as ever, and Eccleston's performance was a bit too reminiscent of a nerdy teenager, but it has a real heartbeat ... or perhaps even two.' The *Independent* said that while the series could hardly fail to disappoint: '... amazingly, it didn't. OK, the monster was feeble and the lack of a cliff-hanger ending was a shame. But Christopher Eccleston portrayed a far more complicated Doctor character than we've become used to seeing, certainly since Jon Pertwee – and far more interesting as a result.' The *Sunday Express* said: 'An alien form, called entertainment, has been discovered on Saturday nights. It's a thoroughly bizarre, glossy new concoction called *Doctor Who*.' However, the spoilsports also had their say; the *Daily Mail* opined: 'The much-hyped special effects were considered a prodigious waste of money by the BBC.' The *People* called it: '... poorly cast, badly written, pointlessly northern, relentlessly silly and, fairly crucially, the sci-fi is thoughtless and throwaway.' And *The Sunday Times* thought: 'The current incarnation of the Time Lord has barely moved on and the one thing the future can't afford to be is old-fashioned.'

More appropriately, it was the kids' market – not only a mainstay of *Doctor Who* but its main original target audience – whose eyes the series caught. 'I loved it and will definitely watch it every week,' wrote one teenaged correspondent to CBBC *Newsround*, while another noted that it: '... put me off shopping for life! It was brilliant!' Still another said it: '... was amazing! I was hooked straight away, and I feel it is much better than Ant and Dec,' while one viewer objected to Rose's admitted lack of A-levels: 'Which, frankly, are really important. That really wound me up. Otherwise, I would say it's fantastic!'

Thousands of *Doctor Who* fans experienced this new episode of the series for the first time, with the immediacy of reaction and emotion at their fingertips through the Internet. As such, it became an experience shared alongside fellow British citizens as well as fans around the world who had viewed the downloadable copy weeks prior. 'I can now actually say that I've seen a *Doctor Who* story on its original broadcast,' wrote Claire Chaplin on the *Outpost Gallifrey* Forum, 'which kind of makes Christopher Eccleston my Doctor. This was just perfect in every respect.' Novelist David A McIntee called it: '... a bit of a thin romp, but a good way to introduce the show to a new generation – and clearly a regeneration story as well. The production values were great, but most importantly it was real *Doctor Who*, and Eccleston makes a great Doctor.' 'All the reservations I had before the episode turned out to be groundless,' wrote Jonny Barker. 'Billie was great, I thought the music worked brilliantly (wouldn't listen to it at home but in the context of the episode it was perfect) and the humour was spot on.' Paul Clarke, in his review on the site, said that the episode 'is visually one of the most striking episodes of *Doctor Who* I have ever seen,' and that while it was flawed, it was 'an interesting start to the new series, and one that has tremendous promise.' Comedian/performer Mitch Benn noted that the episode: '... had too much to get done in 45 minutes to allow the story to really take root properly, but by 'eck it succeeded admirably it getting it all done, didn't it? May have to watch it again now ...'

Using the Autons was a good idea, said Adam McGechan on *Roobarb's DVD Forum*: 'First, it's a cool old enemy that old fans will enjoy seeing again. But more importantly, it is a very simple monster – they are living plastic and they want to eat us. Easy. By using a more complex enemy, or inventing a new one, the episode would have got bogged down in explaining their backstory and motives, etc. The Nestene and the Autons don't need any of that.' At the *Behind the Sofa* website, Damon Querry said that he: '... quite enjoyed the dig at Internet geeks who are obsessed with the Doctor, although Clive's website is so badly put together it would never have resulted in such a high search engine rating. Amateurs!' Stuart Ian Burns described the tone as: '... just right. Some will no doubt knock on about the humour, especially in the scene when the Auton arm comes to life and attacks the Doctor without Rose noticing, or the wheelie bin burps, but that's not much better or worse than Jon Pertwee's cleaning lady, or any number of jelly baby scenes. It's an important part of the series and in the [Joss]Whedon age, vital – otherwise it would all look a bit earnest and silly.' Fiona Moore and Alan Stevens offered their views on the message the episode conveyed in reviews for the DWAS's newsletter *Celestial Toyroom* and the *Kaldor City* website: 'The Doctor complains to Rose about how the bulk of people on Earth simply live their lives eating, sleeping and working, not caring about anything outside of this simple, Darwinian daily round, or looking for anything different. At the end of the story, the Doctor offers Rose a choice to come with him, in which the alternative is staying at home, finding a new job in a shop or hospital canteen, taking care of her unintelligent mother and ungrateful boyfriend, and, significantly, she very nearly accepts the second option rather than look for adventure. The story is thus a wake-up call to people who aren't living up to their full potential, or who are not willing to have their preconceptions shaken up or to look beyond the obvious.'

Even 'classic' series stars got in on the act. Sylvester McCoy reviewed the episode for *BBC News*: 'Before I saw the episode I didn't think I would catch the new series, as I am working in the theatre all the time and watching television can be difficult. But I have been captivated by both the new Doctor and his assistant, Rose. I want to learn more about them as the series progresses.' Katy Manning, who played Jo Grant in the 1970s, had some advice for Billie Piper in the Australian Associated Press news: 'She is as good as anybody else, better than some, and she will bring her own magic to it. The key word to this show is truth because you are dealing in totally unreal situations. Truth will get them every time because it should make you laugh, cry, feel afraid. That is what the show is all about.' Sixth Doctor Colin Baker, writing in his regular column in the *Bucks Free Press*, reported that he: '... watched the first episode of the new *Doctor Who* with a mixture of delight and ruefulness. Delight because it is precisely the mix of innovative creativity and connection to the past that the future of the programme needed ... All of which has contributed to a whole fresh and inspiring feel to the programme. The Doctor is back with a vengeance.' And Maureen O'Brien, who had played one of the series's earliest companions, Vicki, told the *Bucks Free Press* on 8 April that she: '... really liked it. They really have something going for them and the casting is perfect. Christopher Eccleston reminds me so much of William Hartnell.'

Much of the attention was focused not only on the first episode itself, but on how it would fare in the larger world: the ratings war. As noted previously, much of the opinion favoured the chances of *Ant & Dec's Saturday Night Takeaway*, the ITV Saturday night light-entertainment spectacular, that *Doctor Who* would face for the first time. By 10am on Sunday 27 March the answer was clear: *Doctor Who*, and its far-reaching impact, had been underestimated. 'Cult sci-fi hero *Doctor Who* won the battle of prime time,' said several sources including *BBC News*, 'as 10 million viewers tuned in to watch the series return after a 16-year absence.' Though *Ant & Dec* had been a proven hit, and football star David Beckham made a special guest appearance that night, *Doctor Who* commanded over ten million viewers and an incredible 43% of the audience share, making it a *bona fide* hit. *Ant & Dec's* ratings were down to seven million. Meanwhile, *Doctor Who* itself wasn't the only BBC hit: over four million viewers had tuned in for the *Doctor Who: A New Dimension* special earlier in the evening, while over 800,000 viewers turned to BBC3 after the episode's transmission to watch the first instalment of *Doctor Who Confidential* – huge ratings for a BBC3 documentary. In fact, the ratings battle itself became news that day; however, the real test would come not from this first episode – which many viewers no doubt tuned into purely out of curiosity – but from whether or not it could hold its own in future weeks.

Jane Tranter, BBC Head of Drama Commissioning, had said that *Doctor Who* was 'probably the riskiest thing I've ever commissioned' because of the costs involved, but had been shocked at how popular the first episode had proved on Saturday night. 'In all honesty I had got myself into proverbial steel jacket as far as *Doctor Who* was concerned. I told myself I'd be completely and utterly thrilled if it got 6.5 million, but there was a little voice inside whispering "4.5 million".' Tranter stated that *Doctor Who's* Audience Appreciation Index (AI) had scored 81 out of 100 for the programme, above the 78 average for the BBC's drama series. Another transmission slot had never been on the cards, she said: 'We wanted it to be early Saturday evening, because that had been the slot before, and Russell had written it with that time in mind. There's something there for every adult to chew on, but also something for children. If you played it at a different time, it's just not going to work.'

Within the first few days after broadcast, the hype surrounding *Doctor Who* once again took on a life of its own. The *Daily Express* printed a photo of a smiling Billie Piper with the caption 'Billie Helps You Know *Who* Win The Ratings War', noting that *Ant & Dec* were 'TV's war casualties'. Claiming that this new Doctor was 'the right prescription', the paper continued: 'The special effects are dazzling, the script by Russell T Davies is sharp and witty ... The opening episode was perfectly in tune with the show's traditions but it could just as easily have stood alone.' Eccleston and Piper were listed as numbers two and three on the weekly *OK Magazine* Celebrity Chart. Calling the series 'a joyful, exuberant reinvention', *The Times* on Monday 28 March congratulated the series on its 'happy landing', as it noted 'new *Doctor Who* wins acclaim – and an audience,' directing readers to the inside headline 'Who's the daddy as 10m find time to see the Doctor'. *The Times* also covered, as did other papers, the death of former Labour premier Jim Callaghan, whose passing was announced on BBC1 straight after the *Doctor Who* episode had aired on Saturday. Monday's *Daily Star* said that the new-look Doctor 'makes dummies out of Ant 'n Dec as the fans go wild for a trip in the TARDIS and another monster showdown'. *The Times* also interviewed Simon Callow, who would be seen in two weeks' time in the third episode, 'The Unquiet Dead'; as Callow told *The Times*, he was: '... not a fan of the Time Lord: "I saw the first episode in 1963 with William Hartnell as the Doctor. It wasn't for me so I missed the entire procession of Doctors that followed."' *Radio Times* continued heavy promotion of the series, printing photos of the monsters that would be seen in the next week's episode, 'The End of the World'. *Heat* magazine observed: 'Now that you've seen the first episode of *Doctor Who*, or made your mind up sight-unseen on whether it's your particular cup of Saturday-evening tea, the nation can divide itself into *Who* people or *Ant* people – so to speak.' Many other online sources and print media ran reviews and features about the series, with the *Daily Record* and *Media Guardian* focusing on the wide variety of merchandise that would see release, including remote controlled monsters, the Doctor's sonic screwdriver, books, birthday cards, watches, clocks, jigsaw puzzles, a Playstation *Doctor Who* themed game and even official *Doctor Who* ringtones. The *Daily Star* previewed 'The End of the World' with selected dialogue from the episode, while the *Daily Express* ran a list of 'ten things you never knew about the Doctors'. The Canadian *News and Star* called the new series a 'triumph', explaining that it: '... has much in common with James Bond. It is a huge challenge to be the next in line to play a part which is an institution where you will be compared mercilessly with all those who have gone before.' The *Hollywood Reporter* in America called the series: '... very much Davies's baby ... But his *Doctor Who* should please dyed-in-the-wool fans and attract new audiences to a children's programme that will please adults too. Davies deals delightfully with the background to the good Doctor's character in a way that should satisfy cultists and also bring newcomers up to speed.' Reviews and stories were carried far and wide, not only in British papers but also international media from as far away as India and Italy, where it was announced that the series would begin airing on the satellite channel Jimmy, owned by Sky Italia. Canada's *TV Guide* magazine carried the series on its front cover, expecting a large viewer turnout for its own series debut in early April.

In the 'real' world, Christopher Eccleston was scheduled to appear on the forthcoming *Heaven and Earth* show the following weekend, while *Newsround Showbiz* and *Blue Peter* prepared behind-the-scenes stories about the series. Fans appeared on the BBC chat shows *Good Morning Wales* and *Radio Five Live* discussing the weekend's debut. The official *Doctor Who* site launched the first of its weekly makeovers, in tune with the broadcast of each episode; the site would focus primarily on the new show, including specially-themed splash pages and video diaries. The BBC's official merchandising website, *BBC Shop*, spilled the beans on new *Doctor Who* DVD releases starting in mid-May, which would feature the new series's episodes, *sans* extra material and fillers, for immediate consumption. The public was now watching; the first episode was a proven success; the media were following suit; and it looked like *Doctor Who* was not only back, but was on its way to becoming a juggernaut.

Then, only a few days after the premiere, the bottom of the *Doctor Who* world dropped out.

CHRISTOPHER ECCLESTON ISN'T DOCTOR WHO

The BBC's Jane Tranter indicated at a BBC press conference on 30 March 2005 that new dramas would face budget cuts, of up to fifteen percent, to pay for 'prestige hits' such as the new *Doctor Who* series. 'Doctor Who and current shows are protected,' Tranter said, 'but we have to find a way of making a certain number of dramas at a lower cost.' The statement was carried in major newspapers such as *The Times*, which went on to say that producers of BBC programmes would be told to squeeze out more minutes of drama a day during film shoots, and actors would face tough salary negotiations. 'Now we've got to start talking to Billie Piper and Chris [Eccleston] about what they want to do,' Tranter said. 'There is a mischievous element to it, in that you can keep regenerating the Doctor.'

They were words that carried portents of what would occur over the next two days. Meanwhile, the *Daily Mirror* ran what appeared to be a speculative article on 30 March as well, reiterating many of the same rumours that had circulated for several months: Christopher Eccleston might leave, Christopher Eccleston was unhappy, Christopher Eccleston wanted out. The rumours were fuelled by Eccleston's own comments; asked directly by reporters on various television programmes, he had seemed evasive about his future with the show, leaving much speculation in his wake. But no-one was aware that these old rumours were part of a much larger story. Noting that Eccleston had not yet committed to a second series – at least 'not yet' as far as it was aware – the *Mirror* announced that actor David Tennant, star of the current three-part BBC serial *Casanova*, was being lined up to play the Doctor only a week after Eccleston's debut on television: 'BBC insiders revealed last night that Paisley-born Tennant, 33, who played young *Casanova* on BBC3, is the man to replace him. Even if Eccleston does decide to stay on for another series, Tennant will have first refusal on the job after he goes.' The *Mirror* quoted a BBC source as saying, 'At the end of this season, you are led to believe that the Doctor could be dead after he's saved his companion Rose – played by Billie Piper – and the Earth from the Daleks. But it turns out that there's a way for Rose to save him and that's how the second season starts. So she gets back to the TARDIS and is able to get the Doctor brought back to life.' The paper hesitated slightly, assuming that if Eccleston *were* to return, there would be no issue. But the paper was also emphatic that Tennant *would* play the Doctor 'at some point – and will be asked to stay for the long haul.'

Both the reports on Tranter's comments and the items in the *Mirror* carried within them the seeds of truth. At the time, it seemed ludicrous to believe that Eccleston, who had appeared so jovial and so supportive of *Doctor Who* to date, was interested in leaving – despite the rumours that there were issues behind the scenes. Fans speculated that this was nothing more than publicity, and would be settled in the days and weeks to come ... but only one day later, the world had its answer: Eccleston was indeed leaving. The *Mirror*, it turned out, had acquired some information that had been known to BBC executives and members of the production team for some time, and had anxiously expected to scoop the BBC in its announcement. While the *Sun* and online press agencies began to reiterate the *Mirror's* report, the BBC, in an apparent effort to scoop the *Mirror* itself, issued a statement through BBC News early on 31 March 2005 – in the usual fashion, shortly after midnight, after much of the British public had retired for the evening – that Eccleston would not return for a second year. 'Eccleston, whose first appearance as the ninth Time Lord attracted around 10 million viewers, feared being typecast,' the report stated. Press Association, the media wire service, noted that Eccleston: '... has quit as Doctor Who after just one series, it was announced tonight. The star, who has appeared in television drama *Cracker* and hit film, *Shallow Grave*, is worried about being typecast. He is also planning new projects and found filming the series gruelling.' Press Association quoted a BBC statement, released several hours later, in which Eccleston himself said, very simply, 'The audience's response for the new *Doctor Who* has been incredible and I am really proud to be part of it and I hope viewers continue to enjoy the series.' The reports also noted that Billie Piper would return to the role of Rose Tyler for the second series.

Although the news reports were definitive on Eccleston's departure – including the actor's own words stating he would leave – they were far more ambivalent about his replacement. 'A BBC spokesman said the Corporation would issue a formal statement later on Thursday,' said BBC News, 'and that it had hoped, rather than expected, that Eccleston would continue in the role. He said that although talks to make David Tennant the tenth Doctor were taking place, other names may be put forward.' It seemed that the BBC was hedging its bets, although the fact that Tennant was being discussed openly suggested there was more to the story than mere rumour. *Media Guardian* in fact suggested that Tennant was 'the only name being looked at'. Tennant himself had briefly mentioned to the press that he was flattered to be suggested but he was not currently in discussions with the BBC about the role, which later was revealed to be part of the smokescreen; as he later said: 'I couldn't possibly comment but there are talks going on. It's very exciting.'

As news slowly crept out about Eccleston's departure, media outlets that had previously ignored the story began reporting it; the BBC morning news programmes and GMTV's *Breakfast* mentioned it, and the tabloids, other newspapers and online wire services started carrying the news. By late in the day, 'Eccleston Quits!' and '*Doctor Who* Quits!' were major headlines in all the national papers, and it was one of the lead stories on the evening news programmes. But the story didn't end there; there was much more to come out. On 4 April, according to BBC News, the BBC 'admitted it broke an agreement' with Eccleston on the subject of his departure from the series. 'The BBC failed to speak to actor Christopher Eccleston before revealing he was going to quit *Doctor Who* after the first series, it has admitted. It was originally claimed the actor feared being typecast if he stayed on. In a statement, the BBC quoted Eccleston as saying "he hoped viewers continued to enjoy the series." But the BBC has admitted it did not consult him about that statement and also broke its agreement not to reveal he planned to film just one series.' Some of the press reports alluded to the fact that it *appeared* as though the BBC were being forced into the admission after an attempt to sideline the *Mirror* in its news reporting. Jane Tranter issued a statement in which she said, 'The BBC regrets not speaking to Christopher before it responded to the press questions on Wednesday 30 March. The BBC further regrets that it falsely attributed a statement to Christopher and apologises to him. Contrary to press statements, Christopher did not leave for fear of being typecast or because of the gruelling filming schedule.' A BBC spokesman who remained anonymous stated that a mutual agreement had been reached between Eccleston and the BBC as far back as January that he would make only one series, and that the information would not be made public until the conclusion of transmission.

THE FALLOUT

With Eccleston's name in the press, there was considerable reaction from all quarters. By 3 April, the news had spread far and wide across the Internet, been reported in many major international publications, and been carried on all of the major news wires, including the Associated Press and Reuters. The *Mirror* stated that Eccleston had been 'ordered back on set to re-shoot crucial final scenes after his decision to quit as *Doctor Who* after just one series.' The paper suggested that, to replace a previously-recorded ending in which the Doctor had escaped the Daleks (revealing their return in the final two-parter): '... BBC1 bosses hastily scheduled a specially re-written climax to pave the way for a new star to take his place in the next series. The alternative ending is believed to show the Doctor disappearing into the ether, watched by his horrified assistant Rose Tyler ...' Said the *Western Mail*, 'The news Christopher Eccleston has quit as Doctor Who just days after the new series started may have come as a shock to fans, but the show's writer says the actor had never intended to stay long term.' The paper quoted Davies as stating: 'This had all been planned. You will see the story [of his departure] unfold on screen and it's brilliant. We've got 13 episodes of the best Doctor in the world – [Eccleston] worked himself to death on the show.' Said a BBC spokesperson, 'We have filmed two different endings for the series finale, but we don't want to give anything away. You'll just have to wait and see.' The BBC's own *Doctor Who* website stated that Eccleston's last appearance would be in the Christmas special still to be recorded – presumably a case of the site editors having been given inaccurate information. Hard facts were in short supply at this time.

Reactions to the news were generally angry in tone. 'Doctor Who Do You Think You Are?' asked the *Sun*, quoting their usual BBC 'insider' as saying, 'The BBC has shot itself in the foot. It spent considerable money and energy on him as the new Doctor.' The *Sun* TV editor Emily Smith footnoted the article stating, 'It's a huge slap in the face for ten million fans who eagerly awaited the big-budget new series ... He's Time Lord-ing it over us.' The *Daily Mail* said that BBC bosses were 'furious over Christopher Eccleston's decision to quit as *Doctor Who* after spending millions on merchandising which carries his image.' The paper suggested that one of Eccleston's friends had intimated the role was 'too effeminate' for the actor and that he had grown uncomfortable playing such a 'fey' Doctor. The *Daily Mail* also discussed the chaos caused by the departure to merchandisers themselves: 'A *Who* collectors item featuring Christopher Eccleston will still be made available for sci-fans – even though the Salford actor may not be in the role by the time they are released.' Both the suggestions that Eccleston did not want to play an 'effeminate' role and that merchandisers were upset were later denied. Said a spokesperson from toy manufacturers Character Options, 'We're going ahead with an image of Christopher Eccleston as Doctor Who which will be available at Christmas. This can always be updated if there is someone else playing the character.' The *Sunday Mirror* said that Eccleston 'had made a gentleman's agreement to stay for at least another series,' according to their own BBC source. 'It leaves a bitter taste in the mouth.' *Newsround* covered the story by noting that the departure 'was a big surprise because the new TV show is proving such a big hit.' In a brief on-set interview with Eccleston, obviously taped prior to the announcement, the actor noted: 'Working six day weeks, fourteen hour days, for nine months and I'm finding ... finding that really tough.' The *Express and Star* called for any potential replacement to have a little more forethought: 'He is worried about typecasting. Which makes one wonder why he took such a high profile job in the first place ... Let's hope that this time the good people at the BBC use their brains and realise it just might be a good idea to sign up the next candidate for more than one series.' Without knowing any *real* reasons why Eccleston had left, the media were grasping at straws.

Once again, despite David Tennant's name being all over the news reports, the speculation business opened up on who the next Doctor would be. All the old names came back out of the woodwork: Bill Nighy, once considered the front-runner before Eccleston's announcement; Richard E Grant; Alan Davies; David Thewlis; even Eddie Izzard. 'Tom Baker said it would be a fun idea,' Izzard told BBC1's *Friday Night with Jonathan Ross*, noting the comments that the former Doctor had made nearly a year and a half prior. He did add, however, 'There isn't enough time and I'm not being asked.' Grant topped a list in a *Sky Showbiz* poll, but didn't seem interested. Anthony Stewart Head, whose most recent association with the series was his narration of the *Project: WHO?* radio documentary, told the *SciFind* website on 3 April: 'I think it is very unlikely that they will ask me as I was the readers' choice in the *Radio Times* and that is enough to put any producer off actually coming to me to ask if I'll do it. I don't know to be honest. I've done one character in a "cult" series [in *Buffy*] and I don't want to get a reputation for doing that. But then never say never.' The *Daily Star* mentioned that Rhys Ifans (*Notting Hill*) might be in the running, but Ifans himself told the *icNews Network* on 8 April, 'I haven't the time.' (The actor at the same time claimed to have just turned down the role of James Bond for the next 007 film.) Septuagenarian actor and comedian Ronnie Corbett (*The Two Ronnies*) put his own name in the running, according to *The Times*, when he said:

'I'd love to be considered for the part. Mind you, the episodes are likely to be somewhat shorter' – a quip referring to his own lack of height. CBBC presenter Devon Anderson created an entire publicity campaign to become the tenth Doctor, describing himself as 'a Doctor for the youth of today.' And TV presenter John Leslie, who had lost his job as presenter on *This Morning* in 2002 following a sex scandal, hoped to audition for the role, said the *Sun*. According to an unnamed 'pal' of the actor, 'There is more chance of him playing one of the monsters.'

The William Hill betting agency wouldn't accept any odds on the casting (though Ladbrokes had mentioned it early on 3 April) because, according to a spokesperson, 'It appears that the BBC has moved quickly to secure David Tennant's services following the departure of Eccleston, and it seems that the role is his should he want it, which makes it impossible for us to open a book.' Suggestions about the Daleks not appearing manifested again, with *Digital Spy* commenting: 'BBC bosses have yet to secure a deal allowing the Daleks to appear in the next series of *Doctor Who*.' Even *Doctor Who* fans themselves became part of the news cycle, when the *Mirror* and the *Daily Record* reported that the *Outpost Gallifrey* discussion forum had been shut down for two days: '... after fans fell out about the show's star quitting the role. Popular online forum *Outpost Gallifrey* was swamped with strongly worded e-mails from fans furious over Christopher Eccleston's shock departure from the programme. As fans accused the actor of using the show to boost his profile, his supporters defended him, leading to bitter clashes on the forum.' The decision to close the forum to allow things to 'cool down' had been taken after some participants started making personal attacks on Eccleston, something that was felt to be unwarranted.

While critical mass approached on the outpouring of emotions, there were a few people who managed to remain objective about the whole deal. 'How dare Christopher Eccleston have a life and ambitions,' wrote director Joe Ahearne in a letter to the *Guardian*. 'So he's pulled off a staggering performance on a punishing schedule (with unfailing good humour and grace on set) revitalising the Doctor for a new generation. He's only done a mere 10 hours of thrilling television. God forbid we should give him a round of applause.'

EARLY APRIL: 'THE END OF THE WORLD'

Despite all the hype and controversy, there were still twelve more episodes in the can and ready to be shown, starting on 2 April with 'The End of the World'. The second instalment of the series continued *Doctor Who's* strong lead over its ITV competition, *Ant & Dec's Saturday Night Takeaway*; *Doctor Who* had been watched (according to initial overnight figures) by over a million more viewers. The *Daily Record* noted that the series had beaten its rival 'despite a 2.6 million drop in viewers.' Several days later, the Broadcasters Audience Research Board, or BARB, released the final viewing figures for the first story, 'Rose', upping the final take to 10.81 million, putting it in third place on the BBC1 chart and seventh overall for the week. The BARB figures, considered the definitive ratings for programmes, exclude repeat and omnibus showings but do include 'timeshifting' figures, in other words, viewers who recorded a programme and watch it within seven days of broadcast. 'Rose' was, in fact, the third most watched non-soap series in the UK in 2005 to date, behind early March's *Comic Relief* and the New Year's Day special of *The Vicar of Dibley*. The *Doctor Who Confidential* series was faring equally well, achieving staggeringly high ratings (for a non-terrestrial channel) on every episode.

Of course, there are those who would look at the glass as half empty. '*Doctor Who* losing viewers,' proclaimed the *icNews Network*. 'Viewing figures for *Doctor Who* have dropped more than two-and-a-half million since Christopher Eccleston announced he was quitting,' said the paper, focusing on the drop in viewership of 2.6 million instead of the fact that the series had still soundly beaten its competition on ITV. BBC reports were quick to point out that they had expected this, and indeed would have been surprised if it *hadn't* happened; new television series often achieve considerably high interest on first glance, and the secret would be to keep the ratings healthy in subsequent weeks. While the drop-off between episodes one and two was considerable, the ratings eventually stabilised throughout the next three months (with the only substantial drop coming in late May, as the two episodes of Steven Moffat's story 'The Empty Child' and 'The Doctor Dances' were affected by schedule changes and a bank holiday weekend respectively). For a complete summary of the ratings for the series, see Appendix B.

As the series continued, so did publicity engagements ... not to mention hype surrounding its cast and crew. On 8 April, Davies and Gardner appeared at the Celtic Film Festival together to answer questions and show clips of the series. Both stated unequivocally that Eccleston's departure at the end of this first series had always been planned, as he was only supposed to do one season, but that his departure at the end would have been an enormous surprise for the audience (a surprise now ruined by the premature leak of the news). Eccleston himself put his name behind a campaign to raise funds for Christie Hospital in Manchester, including starring in a commercial for the facility created by the McCann Erickson agency. 'I am very proud to be able to support this new campaign – and I hope everyone else will too,' Eccleston told the media. There were also reports that he would star as 'an albino killer monk' alongside Tom Hanks in the film version of the popular novel *The DaVinci Code* – reports that proved untrue in May when it was announced that he hadn't won the role. Eccleston would however: become an ambassador for Mencap, a charity for people with learning disabilities (an issue he first became aware of when he researched his role in the 1991 film *Let Him Have It*, and also through a more recent television film, *Flesh and Blood* (2002) where he played a man who found his birth father to be a mentally disabled man); do a voiceover narration for a Channel Four documentary, *Porn Shutdown* (a 'lucid and informative introduction to the California sex industry'); and take part in a televised concert, *A Party To Remember*, to mark the sixtieth anniversary of VE-Day in early May. Billie Piper would continue to be the subject of tabloid reports about her marriage, her social life (including a report in the 6 April *Express* that she 'was spotted in London's Soho in the wee hours trying to negotiate a good deal for a taxi home') and her career. On 24 April the BBC's Ceefax teletext service interviewed Piper, who said she: '... did have an idea of how big [the series] was going to be ... But I made a conscious effort not to think about the sheer amount of work and all the anticipation and expectation surrounding the show. It's only now I'm starting to see it. And it's quite scary.' She also described her close friendship with Eccleston: 'Me and Chris shared a lot together ... The last eight months have been heavy both in terms of schedule and personal life. So we've been forced together and joined at the hip. It's been a very intense relationship.'

Other cast members were thrust into the spotlight. Bruno Langley, whose introduction in the series as Adam (in 'Dalek') was yet to be broadcast, was the subject of several articles throughout April. The actor, who would soon appear as Romeo in the Stafford Festival adaptation of Shakespeare's *Romeo and Juliet*, was profiled in *Buxton Today* in an interview with his sister, Lakshmi, who said that the actor had spent two months filming the episodes in

Cardiff: '... and had an absolutely brilliant time. He got on so well with Christopher, saying he was an amazing actor.' Press Association interviewed Langley in late April: 'When they brought the Dalek onto the set, it was really exciting and everyone was taking photos ... I get the Doctor and Rose into a bit of trouble because I like meddling with things. Him thinking he's a genius gets him into bother.' Langley wryly noted that the door had been left open for him to return ... an event that would happen sometime later. *Heat* magazine also interviewed the actor, with Langley expressing disappointment that Adam and Rose don't hook up as 'certain things get in the way.' Also interviewed was actor Jimmy Vee, who would appear in 'The End of the World' as the Moxx of Balhoon, whose countenance was featured prominently across the press in late March and early April as photos of the episode's aliens were leaked. 'I got the part through a friend that was working on the prosthetics and things for *Doctor Who*,' Vee told the *Wishaw Press*. 'He got a list through for the characters he'd have to make, and a list of what kind of actor they'd need to play each part. He then let them know he knew someone who would be suitable for the part.'. And, as detailed in Chapter 9, young Albert Valentine, who would feature prominently in the two-part story 'The Empty Child' and 'The Doctor Dances' in May, was interviewed by the *Southland Echo* on 5 April.

On UK television, coverage continued unabated. *Russell T Davies: Unscripted*, an hour-long documentary that profiled the series's executive producer, debuted on the BBC4 arts programme *Timeshift* on 11 April. The 12 April issue of the *Guardian* called the production 'a timely tribute to a man who's done more than anyone to drag television drama into the 21st Century,' but said it 'did have a slight whiff of editorial control.' Davies recalled his career being 'one long series of happy accidents' but the *Guardian* noted that his pre-*Queer as Folk* career had been glossed over and there had been no mention of his falling-out with Channel Four. The earlier planned appearance of Eccleston on BBC1's *Heaven and Earth* on Sunday 3 April was delayed (due to the coverage of the death of Pope John Paul II) but eventually aired later that morning on BBC2, while – as previously mentioned – 4 April's edition of *Blue Peter* featured presenters Simon Thomas and Zoe Salmon talking about how to make a Dalek out of a compost bin. Throughout the first week of April, the CBBC channel ran its 'campaign' for presenter Devon Anderson to become the next Doctor, while *Newsround* featured a spot on how Christopher Eccleston's leather jacket had caused a surge in the purchase of similar jackets around the country. Later in the month, chat show hosts Richard Madeley and Judy Finnegan welcomed Sylvester McCoy and Nicholas Briggs, the actor behind the new series's Dalek voices, and on a later edition Billie Piper, to discuss the series on their daytime chat show, along with exclusive previews from the series, while *Blue Peter* returned to *Doctor Who* again on 29 April with a preview spot and clips.

OVERSEAS INTEREST

Attention was now firmly focused on how well the show would do overseas, starting in Canada. Tuesday 5 April marked the debut date for *Doctor Who* on the CBC network, which was met with nearly a million viewers tuning in. 'Compared to the 9.9 million in the UK,' said a statement from the *Doctor Who* Information Network, the national *Doctor Who* club of Canada, 'this number might seem small ... but for Canadian television numbers, and for the CBC, this is HUGE, and exactly where we wanted the show to come in at.' Surprisingly, CBC broadcast the episode in widescreen format, and that wasn't the only surprise – Christopher Eccleston himself introduced the episode (and the series) to audiences in special pre-taped sequences prior to the broadcasts and at the commercial breaks. This continued throughout CBC's transmission.

Prior to transmission, the Canadian *Globe and Mail* ran an article covering the series's return: 'It's a new beginning that will be scrutinised closely by *Doctor Who* fans in Canada – although perhaps not as closely as it was in the UK where the show is an institution. (This is a country that issued a postage stamp in the 1990s featuring a Dalek, a favourite *Doctor Who* villain shaped like a life-sized salt shaker and intent on exterminating everything in its path.)' But as the broadcast occurred, the paper was elated: 'Tonight's first episode of *Doctor Who* is terrific. It's wacky, colourful, lively and vastly entertaining ... In fact, it's a great example of a tired concept being expertly revived and cast.' Canadian viewers agreed: the ratings kept up, with nearly nine hundred thousand tuning in for episode two. Subsequent episodes continued the trend, slightly smaller each week but still mostly holding its massive audience, achieving second place in its time slot across Canada. The ratings effect also boosted the CBC series that followed it on Tuesday nights, *This Is Wonderland*.

Meanwhile, Australian fans also had reason to celebrate: on 5 April, the *Herald Sun* confirmed the ABC network had acquired the series, after much speculation that they had been interested and were in the running. ABC Head of Programming Marena Manzoufas said, 'This is *Doctor Who*, 21st Century-style, and it most definitely will appeal to people who are new to the *Doctor Who* phenomenon, as well as long-term fans. I am in no doubt that a whole new Australian audience will be attracted to the series.' As announced at the end of the month (16 April), the series would debut on Saturday 21 May with the tag line *Adventures in the Human Race* – as detailed in Chapter 9.

Having previously denied it was interested in the series, BBC Prime confirmed in early April that it would indeed carry the show ... at some point. The cable and satellite network widely available throughout Europe, the Middle East and Africa, issued a press statement: 'We will be showing the new series of *Doctor Who* at some point in the future however, we do not currently hold the rights to the series and they are unlikely to be made available until the show has been broadcast in the UK.' New Zealand's PrimeTV also indicated that it was still going to carry the series at some point 'this winter', probably after the Australian ABC broadcasts in either June or July. And after the BBC Showcase event – a trade fair – the BBC announced deals for two other new broadcast outlets. As mentioned previously, the pay-TV channel Jimmy would carry the series in Italy; and at least one episode ('Rose') would be shown on select flights of Thomsonfly airlines.

In America, however, there was no good news on the horizon. Rumours at the beginning of April that the signing up of a broadcaster was in the works ultimately proved unfounded. This led to a dramatic increase in online episode trading using Internet file sharing technology, with tens of thousands of downloads noted for each episode. A representative for BBC America stated that release on DVD would not come any time soon, a guarantee having being made that the series would have to be broadcast before it could be released on DVD (although a certain amount of hedging followed, with several fans reporting that they'd been told by BBC America representatives that the series might be released a year later, if it were not broadcast within that time). Either way, while other countries with substantial *Doctor Who* followings celebrated the return of the series, the world's largest market for *Doctor Who* was missing out.

DAVID TENNANT IS ... DOCTOR WHO!

As soon as his name had been mentioned in the 30 March news report in the *Mirror* and the BBC Press Office release the following day, all eyes focused firmly on David Tennant. The actor, whose work in 2005 had included his star-making appearance in *Casanova*, appeared in 2 April's BBC4 recreation of the cult classic *The Quatermass Experiment*, the first drama production broadcast live on a BBC channel in decades. Said the *Guardian* on 6 April, 'This was a useful dummy run for David Tennant, who is heavily backed to be the next Doctor Who, playing a doctor confronted with a man eating vegetable.' Tennant himself hadn't shied away from the speculation; as he told the *Mirror*, 'It would be a great role to play.' Said the paper, 'There is little doubt that, even as the chaste Doctor, his appeal to female viewers will be as strong as ever ... It was highly unlikely before but if, as expected, the BBC unveils David as its next Doctor Who, it is certain he'll never need to contemplate an alternative career.'

Prophetic words that came to fruition on 15 April, as the BBC – to no-one's surprise – officially announced that David Tennant would take over from the departing Christopher Eccleston for the second series of *Doctor Who*. (Once again, the press release was issued only a few moments after midnight, with night-owl UK fans joining their North American and Australasian cousins in the revelry.) Tennant, the announcement stated, would be seen in the role in 2005's Christmas special – the first real indication that Eccleston would, in fact, leave at the end of the first series rather than in an episode of the next. The press release also indicated, as the Press Office had done when Eccleston was announced to be leaving, that Billie Piper would remain in her role and had already signed on for a second year. 'David Tennant is a great actor who will build on the excellent work already done by Christopher in establishing *Doctor Who* for a new generation,' said Julie Gardner. Tennant's words were effusive: 'I am delighted, excited and honoured to be the tenth Doctor. I grew up loving *Doctor Who* and it has been a lifelong dream to get my very own TARDIS.' Tennant called Davies 'one of the best writers television has ever had' and said he was 'chuffed to bits to get the opportunity to work with him again' as well as expressing his interest in working with Piper. Added Davies, 'Christopher Eccleston's wonderful Doctor has reinvented the role, so that it now appeals to the best actors in the land. I'm already writing David's first new adventure on board the TARDIS!' Davies said that 'regeneration' was an enormous part of the series's mythology. 'I'm delighted that new, young viewers can now have the complete *Doctor Who* experience, as they witness their hero change his face!'

Born in West Lothian, David Tennant had trained early at the Royal Scottish Academy of Music and Drama in Glasgow. He began his career on the stage, performing as part of the Royal Shakespeare Company, including in such roles as Touchstone in *As You Like It* (1996), Romeo in *Romeo and Juliet* (2000), Antipholus of Syracuse in *The Comedy of Errors* (2000) and Captain Jack Absolute in *The Rivals* (2000), and performing at such venues as the Young Vic, the Edinburgh Lyceum, the 7:84 theatre company and Dundee Rep. Tennant had been nominated for a 2003 Laurence Olivier Theatre Award for 'Best Actor of 2002' for his performance in *Lobby Hero* at the Donmar Warehouse and the New Ambassador's Theatres.

A fan of the series, Tennant had narrated *Doctor Who: A New Dimension*, the preview special that had aired on BBC1 prior to the first episode's transmission. He had also played the Caretaker in the official BBC *Doctor Who* website's animated serial *The Scream of the Shalka* (2003) and had appeared in several audios for Big Finish Productions, not only in their *Doctor Who* range but also in their *Dalek Empire*, *Unbound* and *UNIT* spinoffs, and playing the title role in their 2005 adaptation of Bryan Talbot's graphic novel series *Luther Arkwright*.

Tennant's many film and television roles included *Jude* (1996), *Bite* (1997), *Holding the Baby* (1997), *Duck Patrol* (1998), *LA Without a Map* (1998), *The Last September* (1999), *Love in the 21st Century* (1999), *The Mrs Bradley Mysteries* (1999), *Being Considered* (2000), *Randall and Hopkirk (Deceased)* (2000), *Bright Young Things* (2003), *Posh Nosh* (2003), *Spine Chillers* (2003), *The Deputy* (2004) and *Blackpool* (2004). He had achieved acclaim for his roles in *Casanova* and *Quatermass*, and coming up was an appearance as Barty Crouch Jr in *Harry Potter and the Goblet of Fire*, which had commenced principal photography as the announcement of his *Doctor Who* casting was made.

'I was very small, about 3 or 4 I think, and just wanted to be the people on telly telling these wonderful stories,' Tennant told the Portuguese-language website *BrazilInMind*. 'Obviously the idea grew and matured with me but I can't ever remember wanting to do anything else. I've just sort of taken it for granted all my life that that was what I would do.' On how theatrical training has helped his career, he said, 'Drama school is a pretty intense experience and I think it changes who you are. I think I grew up at drama school (which was fairly useful personally as much as professionally) and I certainly got exposed to a huge range of ideas, techniques and practices that I had no previous experience of. I wouldn't have known what I was doing as an actor if I hadn't gone.'

The announcement of Tennant's casting was carried on all major news services, including most of the morning shows and newspapers, on 16 April. Tennant appeared two days later at the awards ceremony of the British Academy of Film and Television Arts (BAFTA), telling BBC News that 'the expectations are fierce.' Asked by *Hello* magazine how long he had signed up for, Tennant was tactful. 'Let's get through one at a time. I'd love to do 100 years but they might sack me.' He noted that everything was 'up for grabs' at this point – his costume, his accent – but that he was looking forward to working with Billie Piper. But all was not completely joyous; the *Daily Mail* reported on 19 April that his salary would be *half* what Eccleston's had been, leading to even more speculation that the dispute between the BBC and the actor had been over money, and more specifically over cost-cutting exercises thrust upon the *Doctor Who* production team with intense pressure. 'There was some relief that Chris went as he was so expensive,' was the *Mail's* quote from 'a BBC source'. 'The show was only going to be recommissioned if the costs were cut.'

Tennant's appearance had yet to be recorded at the time of the official 15 April announcement. His scenes in the TARDIS – the conclusion of a regeneration sequence begun when Eccleston was still involved in the production – would be taped by the series' second unit only a week after the official confirmation, on 21 April, with a minimal production crew that would later edit them seamlessly into the production.

Public interest in David Tennant soon brought him to the attention of the tabloids. The *Daily Star* pointed out his rumoured relationship with actress Sarah Parish (*Cutting It*). The actor told the XFM radio station on 28 April that *Casanova* was in effect his audition for *Doctor Who*, and that he hadn't actually done a specific audition. The *Sunday Mail* discussed Tennant's interest in being the first Doctor to wear a kilt ...'And I intend to speak with a full Scottish lilt when I make it into the TARDIS,' Tennant was quoted as saying. Another Scottish Doctor, Sylvester McCoy, spoke to the *Daily Record* on 29 April: 'It'll be interesting to see if he does it in a stronger Scottish accent than I was allowed to use. Mine had to be a gentle lilt compared to my normal accent.' And while much of the media focused on the new Doctor, a now-familiar name from the recent past spoke to the *Daily Express*: Bill Nighy, once touted as a probable Time Lord, now insisted that he wasn't disappointed not to be named as

Eccleston's successor. 'It was,' as he told the *Express*, 'never to be.'

THE HYPERACTIVE PRESS

For anyone paying attention to the media, it was nearly impossible to avoid minor *Doctor Who* spoilers or rough indications of what was to come. Certain developments would be difficult to keep under wraps; most viewers knew, for example, that the Daleks would feature at some point in the series, and an episode entitled 'Dalek' would be hard to miss. Thanks largely to statements from the BBC's Press Office, many newspapers and magazines (both online and off) kept viewers up to date on the goings-on and future happenings of the series.

The BBC's Press Office put out almost weekly statements throughout April, featuring interviews and behind-the-scenes revelations that were recycled and reused by most of the major print media. As mentioned in Chapter 10, Davies, Gardner, Eccleston and Piper were all profiled and interviewed in the first instalment, while Press Pack Two featured behind-the-scenes articles on the special effects, production design, miniature effects, prosthetics and makeup, and the monsters. Press Pack Three interviewed Simon Callow and writer Mark Gatiss about the making of 'The Unquiet Dead' ('As well as being brilliantly written, Mark's script was obviously the work of someone who knows exactly what Dickens is all about,' said Callow), while the fourth pack featured just one interview, with Penelope Wilton about her time recording 'Aliens of London' and 'World War Three' ('The episodes I'm in are extremely exciting and terribly funny'). Writer Rob Shearman and actors Bruno Langley and Nicholas Briggs were profiled in the fifth pack ('I hope, in the nicest possible way, they manage to traumatise a whole new generation of viewers,' said Shearman, referring to the Daleks), while the sixth previewed 'The Long Game' and interviewed actor Simon Pegg ('The last time I played a bad guy was in *Black Books* and it is always fun to play a bad guy, particularly if they are really smilingly nasty'). Press Pack Seven interviewed writer Steven Moffat ('Comedy is just another sort of drama really, and there's always been comedy in *Doctor Who* to offset its scariness') and actors John Barrowman and Richard Wilson on making 'The Empty Child' and 'The Doctor Dances'.

Occasionally throughout April it was hard to keep up with the shifting landscape. Early in the month, there was a brief amount of concern as the BBC's *National Lottery* website stated that the 23 April edition would start halfway through the *Doctor Who* transmission of 'World War Three'. (This was later reported to be an error.) Viewers were unclear as to the final transmission time of 'The Unquiet Dead' because the funeral of Pope John Paul II had prompted rescheduling of the wedding of Prince Charles and Camilla Parker-Bowles, which in turn had moved the start time of the Grand National horse race. (Again, this turned out to be much ado about nothing, as the *Doctor Who* episode went out on schedule.) In fact, only once throughout the first series was there an alteration to the 7.00pm transmission time; 'The Empty Child' aired thirty-five minutes earlier due to the Eurovision Song Contest broadcast on 21 May. The same could not be said, however, for *Doctor Who*'s competition; the current run of *Ant & Dec's Saturday Night Takeaway* ended on 16 April, and the variety series had lost every outing against the BBC juggernaut. (On one occasion it won the overnight ratings, but later lost out as BARB released the final viewing figures.) ITV scrambled to find another programme that could face *Doctor Who* and believed they'd found it in *Celebrity Wrestling*, a show in which minor celebrities took on wresting *noms de guerre* and battled it out over a number of events. A kind of celebrity-based version of *Gladiators*, this took over the time slot on 23 April, but quickly failed to live up to expectations – or even come close to the previously-recorded *Ant & Dec* ratings – and was eventually relegated to an early Sunday broadcast time in mid-May.

The BBC continued running trailers – nowhere near the level of hype as seen in the weeks prior to the broadcast of 'Rose' in late March, but still keeping the series in the public eye. A six-second trailer of an alien spacecraft striking the Westminster clock tower ('Aliens of London') was shown in mid-April, while on 25 April television and radio trailers began to promote the much-lauded return of the Daleks. Newspapers such as the *Observer*, the *Mirror*, the *Sun* and *The Times* continued to feature previews and early reviews of each episode, piquing viewer interest. Websites continued to keep *Doctor Who* fans up to date; the BBC's official *Doctor Who* site was complemented with several specially-themed sites such as: www.whoisdoctorwho.co.uk based on Clive's website as seen in 'Rose', then 'taken over' by Mickey as the series progressed; www.unit.org.uk, a UNIT-themed site with a special password (initially 'bison', then 'buffalo' and later 'badwolf') taking the reader to secret areas; www.geocomtex.net, a 'corporate' website for Van Statten's firm as seen in 'Dalek'; and, debuting late in the broadcast season around the first week of June, www.badwolf.org.uk, inspired by the season's continuing 'Bad Wolf' hints and themes. The BBC South East Wales website opened up a *Doctor Who* 'locations guide', updated each week after the episode's first transmission with details of Welsh locations used on the programme, while BBC Radio Wales, BBC Wiltshire and other official channels featured their own specially themed *Doctor Who* areas. Fan websites also reaped the benefits, with many long-time sites putting special focus on continuing updates to the new series. Among the most prominent existing sites were the *Doctor Who* Appreciation Society's site, the *Doctor Who Cuttings Archive*, *Outpost Gallifrey*, *Planet Who*, *TachyonTV* (with a comic spin on the new series), the *Tragical History Tour*, the *Image Archive*, the *Doctor Who Reference Guide*, *A Brief History of Time Travel* and *Nitro Nine*. Newer sites also cropped up on a regular basis.

While coming nowhere near the level of hyperbole that had marked the latter half of March, April 2005 featured a huge amount of press coverage from newspapers, magazines, online journals and even local press. 1 April's *Canterbury Adscene* revealed that the management of Marks & Spencer retailers had removed window dummies from storefronts: 'More than 50 worried parents contacted the city centre store this week after their children said they were terrified of going inside. They claimed the opening episode of the new Time Lord's adventures, which showed plastic mannequins coming to life and attacking humans, had given their children nightmares.' *Spiked Online* said on 3 April about the first two episode of the series, that the TARDIS: '... has been knocked off course by fanwankery ... I like it when programme makers have the good grace to take material like *Doctor Who* seriously in its own terms, regardless of how ridiculous those terms are.' *Media Guardian* on 4 April alluded to Eccleston's departure and Tennant's purported casting as being: '... an example of tactical cunning worthy of Davros himself. The BBC has known for three months that Christopher Eccleston wouldn't do a second series of *Doctor Who*, but played dumb for fear the star's imminent departure would puncture the hype around the show's return ... Christopher Eccleston says he quit *Doctor Who* because he was worried about being typecast. You shouldn't have worried about that, Chris – you'll always be DCI Bilborough to us.' *Manchester Online* discussed co-owner Bob Horsefield's plans to develop the Web Film Studios in Salford: 'Our aim is to get the new series of *Doctor Who* filmed here.' The *Daily Express* on 4 April reviewed episode two under the heading 'Forget the laughs, Doc, give us fear' and noted that

Cassandra reminded the reviewer of someone when she announced she'd had 708 operations: 'Yes, of course. Anne Robinson.' (This was a reference to recent news reports about popular quiz master Robinson (*The Weakest Link*) having had cosmetic surgery.) The Sci-Fi Channel's *Science Fiction Weekly* said that the most astonishing change to *Doctor Who* was that 'instead of casting an actor who is basically playing a version of himself, the ninth Doctor is a serious, intense character actor.'

Simon Pegg's role in the series was covered by many news services including *SkyNews,* the *Daily Record* and the *Western Mail* on 5 April, noting that he 'makes a cameo appearance in episode seven of the sci-fi show, as controller of the 500th floor of a mysterious building from which time travellers do not return.' *The Times* on the same day posted a convincing argument for the next Doctor to be played by a black actor: 'Positive role models in society may improve kids' results at school. They offer a sense of belonging and being part of the mainstream. They give you something to aim for.' On 6 April, *This Is Gwent* focused on the recording done in Monmouth late the previous year, which it said 'looked like a scene from Dickensian times,' while the *Western Mail* talked about Cardiff Theatrical Services, the Welsh set-building company working on the show. 'It was a really satisfying contract to win,' Simon Cornish, CTS construction manager, told the paper, 'even though we had been sworn to secrecy about the design.' The *Western Mail* also said that 'it's just a shame that every glamorous shot of Cardiff has to masquerade as London with the addition of a strategically-placed Underground sign,' while the *Leicester Mercury* opined that Eccleston was 'currently playing the Doctor as a grinning and occasionally bad-tempered nincompoop.' *ITV Teletext* on 8 April interviewed Mike Tucker of the special effects team: 'You do spend a lot of time making models and setting them up only to destroy them in a matter of seconds, but it's part of the job. And I got to work on the new Dalek – what a bonus!' The *Metro* reported that the BBC would no longer be putting up posters for the new series as they kept getting stolen; said a BBC source to the *Metro's* 'Green Room' column, 'They are just getting steamed off and collectors are selling them on the Net.' On the subject of his departure, the *Mirror* said Eccleston was: '... some doctor! Isn't that what NHS dentists do?' *Express Newsline* noted that the lack of period architecture in Cardiff 'drove the BBC team to Swansea, which has far more Victorian buildings.' The *Daily Star* asked its readers to meet the new Prime Minister: '... and he's full of hot air! It's an 8ft slimy green alien called a Slitheen. And it just can't stop breaking wind!'

MID-APRIL: 'THE UNQUIET DEAD,' 'ALIENS OF LONDON' AND 'WORLD WAR THREE'

Perhaps no single British mainstream news publication was more dedicated to the new series than *Radio Times*. The stalwart of television news and information, and Britain's highest-selling magazine of any description, it featured weekly episode synopses, interviews and feature articles, and released a gorgeous *Doctor Who* special for the week of 26 March-1 April, with a fold-out front cover revealing the Doctor and Rose standing in front of the gold-and-green TARDIS console. *Radio Times* occasionally made it impossible to keep secrets from the general audience, with cover tag-lines such as '*Doctor Who* Meets Dickens' on the 9-15 April edition (which interviewed writer Mark Gatiss and called that week's story, 'The Unquiet Dead', the Pick of the Day). The following week's edition featured a photo of Rose and a Slitheen ('After an alien spaceship crash-lands, the Doctor must save the world – but not before facing the wrath of Rose's mum ...') The 23-29 April edition boasted an exclusive on 'Doctor Who Monsters in the Making: meet the Slitheen!' on the front cover (but by then, one could naturally assume viewers had seen 'Aliens of London'; this was the week of the second half of the Slitheen story, 'World War Three'). The same week, Radio Times discussed the departure of Christopher Eccleston, noting: 'Audiences can be very proprietorial about their TV heroes, and Doctor Who devotees are probably the most committed of all ... If there's one thing to be learnt about the extreme reaction to Eccleston's decision, it's that audiences' affections are not to be trifled with.' At the end of April, Radio Times gave special treatment to another landmark: another foldout cover and lead story, celebrating the return of the Daleks, all in a week that also saw Britain going to the polls for the General Election – a usual subject for the Radio Times to feature on the cover. 'One of the television's greatest icons is back on the box – and it's not very happy. But we are, just to see a Dalek head to head with the Doc once more.'

There was a surprise in the Guardian's 'Guide' section on 9 April, when the normally vituperative Charlie Brooker offered his own praise: 'I simply can't stand by and let this week's episode, "The Unquiet Dead", pass by without comment, for the following reason: I think it may be the single best piece of family-oriented entertainment BBC has broadcast in its entire history ... TV really doesn't get better than this, ever.' The paper also summed up advertising in the modern era, pointing to Doctor Who as a perfect example: 'The bloggers blog, the journalists scrawl, the campaign has started. Then comes the illicit "leak" of the first episode on the Internet. Given that every hardcore Whoey is bound to be a techy and certain to have broadband Internet, it is an absolutely perfect move. Too perfect, maybe, although the BBC denies responsibility.' The Western Mail noted that Davies 'may be causing a stir with his scripts for Doctor Who but Russell T Davies has admitted that his last TV series [Mine All Mine] proved to be a flop simply because it wasn't good enough.' Davies himself told the icNetwork he wouldn't let a woman become the next Time Lord: 'Imagine having to explain that one to your kids – that Doctor Who has lost his willy!' The Guardian asked, 'What was that dreadful smell at just after seven o'clock on Saturday night? Why, it was the nation's under-12s reacting as under-12s will to the opening scene of Doctor Who.' Digital Spy lamented the weekend's failure of the Sky+ planner (the automated box used to record television onto a digital video recorder), causing grief to some Doctor Who viewers. The Metro was largely positive on 'The Unquiet Dead': 'This is the classic stuff today's little 'uns will look back on with childhood nostalgia. And Saturday's episode was another absolute cracker.' The Sunday Mirror wondered: 'When did Chris Eccleston install a spray-tanning booth in the TARDIS? And did the weapons inspectors in Iraq find more evidence of chemistry than we're witnessing between Eccleston and Billie Piper? And if the Doctor is such an expert on time, how come he hasn't told the producers these new episodes are 15 minutes too long?' And Media Week covered the massive phone kiosk ad campaign that was planned to take place shortly for the new series DVDs: said Matthew Parkes of 2Entertain, 'Telephone kiosk advertising is the perfect medium for advertising a brand so closely tied with the iconic TARDIS police call box.'

'Who better to put Swansea on TV screens around the world than city-born writer Russell T Davies?' asked the South Evening Post on 11 April. The Northern Echo, on the other hand, commented that 'the Doctor's sense of direction hasn't improved,' referring to the Doctor's landing in Cardiff instead of Naples in episode three. The paper also commented on the developing relationship between the Doctor and Rose: 'There's a look here, a remark there. I wouldn't be surprised if, so to speak, she finds herself under the doctor.' Former series star Richard Franklin (who played Captain Yates in the seventies) sent a terse letter to the *Brighton Evening Argus* commenting on Eccleston's departure from the series, lamenting what he felt was the actor's consideration of the role as: '... no more than a stepping stone. I find this insulting and ungrateful to the fans, who would have taken him to their hearts, and to the BBC, who have given him the accolade of a unique television role ... His departure is not much thanks for a leg-up most actors would have given their right arm for and a glaring example of the greed, selfishness and cult of celebrity which blights modern Britain.' In America, MSNBC reporter Michael Okwu called the series a 'science fiction spoof' in a report on the nightly *Countdown with Keith Olbermann* series; anchor Olbermann replied that, given a choice between the series and watching the Charles-Camilla wedding, 'I'd watch *Doctor Who* every time.'

As of 13 April, a new controversy surrounding the series emerged. After the episode had broadcast, the BBC posted word that 'The Unquiet Dead' was 'not for the under-eights', targeted instead for older children and adults, mostly due to the horror of dead bodies. Responding to complaints after broadcast, BBC Television apparently issued a statement that said, in part: 'The programme sets out to balance the right amount of humour, drama and suspense in each episode. In "The Unquiet Dead" ... the comic character of the Welsh undertaker and a larger than life Charles Dickens together with the laughter and bravery shown by the Doctor and Rose in the face of danger were, we believe, vital elements in putting this "ghost story" into the right context for a family audience.' This was followed by a story the next day that the BBC had rescinded its own warning: 'A statement on the BBC's complaints website on Wednesday saying the show was not for children under eight had been "a mistake" [said a BBC spokesperson]. Monsters in the early evening show "may be scary" but content was carefully considered for all of the pre-watershed audience ... We leave it to parents' discretion to ultimately decide.' *The Times* noted that there was a BBC investigation into future episodes to see how scary they were, while writer Mark Gatiss appeared on Radio Four and Radio Five Live to address comments, saying he was 'Quietly thrilled' by the reaction, observing that *Doctor Who* is about healthy scares. 'Children can be too cosseted these days.' The *Daily Express* claimed that the BBC had been 'forced to slap an age warning' on the series, while *Manchester Online* interviewed Tory MP Tim Collins who said that the series was perfectly suitable for children as young as six: 'I was watching it and thoroughly enjoying being scared out of my wits when I was six or seven.' Finally, the *Daily Record* on 21 April opined that the series had always been a thriller: 'Millions of us were scared witless in the '60s, '70s and '80s and were, at times, hiding behind the sofa. As far as I know, it didn't do any of us damage. The real problem is the adults who complained. If they really have an issue about the show why didn't they just switch off immediately?'

The transmission of the two-part serial 'Aliens of London' and 'World War Three' beginning on 16 April prompted its own minor controversy, when by chance it coincided with the lead up to the scheduled British elections. 'In a recent interview,' said the BBC internal magazine *Ariel*, 'Davies admitted that programme makers had to check with Editorial Policy before screening the episode.' An edition of the *Northern Echo* the following week said that Prime Minister Tony Blair should have gone on *Doctor Who*, referring to the Prime Minister's appearance on *Ant & Dec* the week before, 'because that programme [*Doctor Who*] gets a bigger audience' . 'But any publicity is good publicity,' the reporter noted, as the Doctor said during the two-part story, 'If you want aliens, you've got them – they're in Downing Street.'

The Times later asked, 'So what has Russell T Davies, chief writer and executive producer of *Doctor Who*, got against Tony Blair?' claiming that the Slitheen 'only reveal their true selves when they lie.' The rumour about the 'lying' revelations was later debunked by Davies.

SFX released a new issue, positively gushing about the forthcoming 'Dalek' episode, which would air at the end of the month: 'This is hard-as-nails *Who*. This is the *Who* the fans were clamouring for ... It's hard to conceive that *Doctor Who* can get much better than this ...'

The *Evening Standard* commented on 'another hit from *Doctor Who*' as it talked about the scenes of the alien spacecraft crashing into the Big Ben clock tower in 'Aliens of London': 'Special effects convincing enough to send adults as well as children scurrying behind the sofa.' The *Guardian* on 18 April called 'Aliens of London': 'The best episode yet ... Now that's what I call entertainment.' *The Times* made the story its Pick of the Day, but with a small caveat: 'Davies's cartoonish sense of humour is one of the main obstacles standing in the way of the current series improving on the Pertwee and Baker eras. His reliance on noisy bodily functions (the burping bin in the first episode, the farting lizards here) might appeal to the eight-year-old in him that he aims the new show at.' Channel 4's Teletext service featured Christopher Eccleston's astrological chart: 'Such a heavy Aquarian presence ensures he will never allow himself to be typecast in any way ... Expect the unexpected.' The trade magazine *Variety* interviewed Davies as part of a larger news story on 'Why I live outside London' and said that the new series: '... proves that there is life, and entertainment, outside London. It also reflects a wider psychological and constitutional shift that started when Prime Minister Tony Blair took office eight years ago, with a promise to give a greater voice to the nations and regions that make up the United Kingdom.' The *Stage* noted: 'If ITV had the ability, with hindsight, to cherry-pick dream acquisitions to graft onto its triumphant soaps, I'd say it would be *Jamie's School Dinners* and *Doctor Who*, which are both examples of bravery being rewarded and going against received wisdom – revivals rarely work or can be sustained. A pointer to the future?' *Prospect* magazine on 19 April said that *Doctor Who's* return has had the most impact of any of the current retro-television fare, saying, 'Over the past weeks you could not escape the Dalek jokes, Ron Grainer's haunting music, the forty-something nostalgia,' and doubting the future of the series: 'As [networks] haemorrhage viewers, they keep looking back to a lost, golden age when everyone knew what the big networks were there for. Wheeling out the Daleks is just a symptom of a loss of nerve.'

LATE APRIL: 'DALEK'

The transmission of 'Dalek' prompted its own share of comments. ITV Teletext made the episode its pick of the week: 'Peppered with in-jokes, hilariously hum-drum details and Russell T Davies's trademark dialogue, this is pacy, satisfying television, which remains just the right side of kitsch.' Teletext also ran an interview with writer Rob Shearman, who said: 'It takes a skilful writer to make you afraid of a giant pepper pot with a sink plunger stuck to the front of it.' Nicholas Briggs appeared on BBC Radio Berkshire on 28 April with a demonstration of how he does the Dalek voices, while Davies commented that the Daleks have *always* been able to fly. The *Guardian* put the series at the top of its 'Must' list: 'It's the moment several generations have been waiting for: the return of *Doctor Who's* most terrifying enemies.' *Newsquest Media Group* profiled Oliver Hopkins, an extra in 'Dalek', who: '... gets exterminated on his first-ever television appearance – and he couldn't be more delighted.' Said Hopkins, 'I'm pretty realistic about the fact it could be edited out, or you might only get to see my arm. But even so, I've had a brilliant experience and it won't look bad on my CV.' Billie Piper 'got her revenge on estranged husband Chris Evans by setting the Daleks on him,' said the *Daily Star*. 'She got one of the telly baddies to shout: Exterminate! Exterminate! down the phone at him.' As Nicholas Briggs told the paper, 'Billie came up to me on set with her mobile and she'd tell the person on the other end, "There's someone to speak to you." Then she'd hand over the phone and I'd go, "Exterminate! Exterminate! You are an enemy of the Daleks!" She did it with all her friends.' However, not everyone was enamoured with the return of the Daleks: MediaWatch (formerly the NVLA, founded by the infamous Mary Whitehouse) on 25 April condemned the episode, on the basis that: '[it] depicts an evil character telling one of his henchmen to "canoodle and spoon" with the Doctor's assistant, Rose. Van Statten also tortures the Doctor by binding him to a crucifix with metal shackles.' MediaWatch branded the BBC 'irresponsible' for including 'such inappropriate imagery and language: this is not a programme designed for children.' And ex-*Doctor Who* script editor Christopher Bidmead told the 28 April *Daily Telegraph* that the series was 'quality television' but that it 'just isn't *Doctor Who*.'

As April drew to a close, some of the press became even more offbeat. Billie Piper suggested in *Cult Times* magazine, out the last week of April, that she wanted to do a musical episode: 'I love *Buffy*. And I love *Buffy* the Musical [a musical episode of the series, called 'Once More With Feeling']. That's a really great show. I'm trying to convince Russell to write one, and I think he will as long as he can star in it.' The *Daily Mirror* reported on 29 April that Eccleston had come under fire from former Doctor, Peter Davison: 'He is letting down the programme. His commitment should have been for at least a couple, maybe three, series. I hate to see, after all the effort that went into getting the programme back on TV, *Doctor Who* scuppered by an actor saying "I don't want to do this anymore."' The *Mirror* also covered Piper's appearance on the XFM radio breakfast show, in which she told host Christian O'Connell that she didn't have a clue who Davros was. 'I'm usually out socialising,' she said, asked whether or not she watched the series. 'I'm going to wait and watch the whole box set [of DVDs] in one go.'

A reader of the *South Wales Echo* corrected an earlier report that 'The Unquiet Dead' had been recorded entirely in Swansea (and Monmouth): 'A great deal of the internal and some external scenes were actually filmed at the Headlands National Children's Home in Penarth,' wrote school principal Dave Haswell. 'The principal actors Christopher Eccleston, Billie Piper and Simon Callow were only too happy to sign autographs and chat with our children between [recording].' The *Sunday Times* reported that Eccleston had refused to campaign for Labour in the elections. Davies spoke to *Gay Times*, and told them he was flabbergasted by the ratings: 'No-one ever expected those viewing figures. No-one in even the most drunken meeting ever thought that.' And Davies also noted that the character Captain Jack would: '... quite obviously ... sleep with anyone. One of my favourite bits is where Jack thinks he's going to his death, and he does a big "goodbye" speech to Rose and gives her a kiss, then does a big speech to the Doctor and gives him a kiss. Just a little kiss. His character's from the 51st Century, so I thought, "If we're not like that in the 51st Century, when will we be?"'

RENEWAL

The premature announcement in late March and early April of Eccleston's departure had overshadowed the *other* important *Doctor Who* story. *Media Guardian* and the *Stage* had simultaneously broken the news on 30 March that a second series of *Doctor Who* had been commissioned, with an extra bonus episode to be shot in 2005 and shown as a Christmas special. 'The BBC has wasted no time in commissioning a Christmas special and second series of its *Doctor Who* revival, less than a week after the time traveller returned to BBC1 after an absence of 16 years with nearly 10 million viewers,' said the reports, noting that Eccleston's future in the role was still unconfirmed (as the BBC Press Office had yet to issue its announcement in this regard.) Tranter had, in fact, commissioned the Christmas special and the second series on 29 March, only three days after the series had begun and had beaten *Ant & Dec* soundly in the ratings. Speaking at the Broadcasting Press Guild luncheon, Tranter noted that Eccleston's and Piper's contracts included options for more series but it was not yet certain if they would return (which, of course, would be revealed the following day).

'It's fantastic news,' said Davies on the BBC's *Doctor Who* website, which had announced that he would pen the script for the Christmas episode. 'It's been a tense and jittery time because the production team has been working on plans for Series Two – scripts are being written already! – without knowing if it would ever get made. We could all have ended up unemployed. But now we can put all those plans into action and get going. It's particularly good for BBC Wales. This is a major flagship show for the region, and their staff and crews are the best you could find. It's a tribute to them that *Doctor Who* is returning. *Cymru am byth*!' Of course, *Doctor Who* was at this point lacking a leading man.

Eyes turned toward Billie Piper, as the *Popbitch* gossip site reported the actress might leave at some stage in the next season, following in Eccleston's footsteps. Noel Clarke (Mickey) told GMTV on 25 April that he would be returning for the following year. The *Sun* led with a 21 April story that the stars of the top British comedy series *Little Britain*, actors David Walliams and Matt Lucas, would have cameo roles in the second series of *Doctor Who*. Walliams was, at one point, also suggested by some media outlets as penning a script for the second series, a report rapidly quashed by producer Phil Collinson.

Another writer's name did leak out in mid-April: Toby Whithouse, whose credits included creating and writing Channel 4's *No Angels* (2004-), writing for *Attachments* (2000), *Outlaws* and *Where The Heart Is* (1997), and writing the stage the play *Jump, Mr Malinoff, Jump* (2004, winner of the Verity Bargate Award). Other series for which he was penning episodes in the spring of 2005 were *Other People*, *Scarlet and Guy* and *Hotel Babylon*. Whithouse's participation was confirmed at the end of April by *Doctor Who Magazine*, which announced that he would be joined by returning writers Mark Gatiss ('The Unquiet Dead') and Steven Moffat ('The Empty Child' / 'The Doctor Dances'), and by two new names, Matt Jones and Tom MacRae. MacRae, writer of the pilot episode of Sky One's *Mile High* (2003), the BAFTA-nominated drama *School's Out* (2002), *Money Can Buy You Love* and *UgetMe* (2003), and script editor on *Nine Lives* (2002) and *As If* (2001), was currently writing for both Channel 4 (*No Angels*) and an original series for the BBC. Whithouse was unknown to many *Doctor Who* fans. Jones, however, was a different story. In addition to script editing *Linda Green* (2001), *Clocking Off* (2000) and Davies's own *Queer as Folk* (1999-2000), Jones had written both the *Doctor Who* novel *Bad Therapy* (1996) for Virgin Publishing and a novel called *Beyond the Sun* (1997) in their New Adventures series featuring the character Bernice Summerfield. His first ever professional *Doctor Who* commission had come in 1995, for the *Decalog 2* short story anthology, also from Virgin Publishing; his contribution, *The Nine-Day Queen*, had been described by the anthology's co-editor Stephen James Walker as: 'Possibly the finest *Doctor Who* short story I have ever read.' Jones had also been a regular columnist for *Doctor Who Magazine* from 1995 until 1998.

Doctor Who Magazine revealed that Davies himself would pen five scripts for the second season, with seven shared amongst the other five writers, and one additional script yet to be assigned; there would be seven one-off adventures and three two-part stories. Jones's script, with the working title 'The Satan Pit', would, according to Davies, be 'as scary as possible'. 'Julie, Russell, and I have chosen a mixture of old and new, all with bold, wild imaginations, to launch Series Two with wit, flair, energy, and, no doubt, plenty of scares along the way,' said producer Phil Collinson. 'Russell has drawn up an overall plan for the whole series, with synopses of the tone and setting for each episode, although the writers have then had the absolute freedom to create what they want.' He also mentioned that the Christmas special, written by Davies, would be shot as part of the second series filming block ... avoiding the sensitive topic of which Doctor it would feature, as at the time it was still unclear that Eccleston was done with the role and Tennant was now the man at the helm of the TARDIS. Collinson was looking toward the future: 'The adventures cover the full range – trips to the future, the past, and yes, we'll be setting foot on alien worlds! We're planning lots of weird and wonderful new creations, as well as the return of a familiar face or two.'

While the first year was still only half over, series two would soon be a reality.

CHAPTER TWELVE:
COMING OF AGE

What a difference eighteen months can make. In mid-September 2003, *Doctor Who* was part of the past, a fading icon of a vanishing era in British television. Eighteen months later, *Doctor Who* was not only back, but back with a vengeance: it was now a powerful force for BBC Television on Saturday night, and Christopher Eccleston and Billie Piper were recognised faces all over Britain. Not a bad way to end that interregnum period. It seemed that nothing would stop the *Doctor Who* juggernaut.

Of course, there are always pitfalls along the way ... Eccleston's departure had been a stumbling block early on, and there were still obstacles on the way: the joyous welcome in the press had begun to fade, and now *Doctor Who* would be forced to show its true colours. The series continued on UK and Canadian television, with Australian broadcasts soon to begin. But as April ended and May began, it seemed there was only one story on the minds of the press: the return of the Daleks.

A MOMENT SHARED

Until now, interested parties outside the UK had been able to watch the drama unfold only through the eyes of the press and the Internet. That wasn't the case with the sixth episode, 'Dalek', which, through a fortuitous error on the part of the BBC, was to be the first – and so far, only – episode transmitted across the Internet at the same time as it was broadcast.

'When plans of a secret BBC test to stream its UK channels over the internet leaked out,' wrote Paul Hayes in the *Stage*, in an article published on 17 May, 'overseas users logged on. Many said they would be prepared to pay to do so again.' Indeed, the BBC's research and development arm, based in Kingswood Warren, had been conducting a test somewhat akin to the 'Listen Again' archive that would allow BBC Radio listeners to hear their favourite programmes again for up to a week after transmission. The 'Listen Again' feature had become quite popular, both for radio dramas – including the recent Radio 4 broadcasts of the newest adaptations of Douglas Adams's popular novel series, *The Hitchhikers' Guide to the Galaxy* – and for news and information programmes, and the BBC now sought to test the possibility of streaming video to UK-based broadband customers. Of course, such a move wouldn't likely be available to overseas customers; there would be complicated rights issues and potential complaints from UK viewers, who would protest the availability of programmes for free when residents were forced to pay the licence fee. Said Liz Mitchell of the BBC press office, the event was 'an internal demonstration stream ... intended for an internal audience.'

However, whether via a deliberate (and still undetermined) leak, or simply through being stumbled upon, the website addresses being used for the four channels under test (BBC1, BBC2, BBC4 and BBC News 24) were released into the *Doctor Who* fan community, spreading out across Internet forums and newsgroups. By the luck of the draw, this had happened on the morning of 30 April, the day of the transmission of 'Dalek'. 'The sudden revelation that if they had a broadband internet connection they could watch the episode completely free of charge at exactly the same time as their fellow fans in the UK,' wrote Hayes, 'was greeted with considerable surprise and delight by those posting on the message board(s).' Fans who had caught the information in time were overjoyed – and many expressed their interest in a pay-per-view scheme, not unlike recent developments in the online music industry, where such key players as Apple (using their iTunes product), Yahoo (MusicMatch) and the reconstituted Napster had entered the fray with downloadable songs keyed to specific computers through subscriptions, and micropayment plans had become the norm. 'I would pay an arm and a leg for live UK television,' wrote one fan as quoted in the *Stage*. 'If I could only have the five UK terrestrial stations ... I could probably afford $50/month just for that.' Of course, there would be technical problems to overcome, not the least of which would be how to sell the service to countries like Canada and Australia, whose broadcasters had already bought the series. 'It is unlikely that [they] ... would be particularly thrilled to know that a substantial chunk of the fan audience in their countries has had the opportunity to see such an eagerly-awaited episode already, for no charge and no profit to them,' wrote Hayes.

Meanwhile, by the following evening, Sunday 1 May, the feed had been cut. According to Mitchell, the BBC had become aware of the situation because of the publicity it had gained online. 'While this was not an ideal situation as the URL was not intended for a public audience,' Mitchell said, 'it was a simple technical error made while investigating technologies for encoding and transmission protocols, which was fixed as soon as possible.' The immediate popularity of the feed, however, did not go unnoticed. Despite the end of the test, for one brief moment in time, *Doctor Who* fans around the world could all participate in the same event, as 'Dalek' unfolded live on the Internet for everyone to enjoy.

DALEK RENAISSANCE

In late April, previews of and commentary about 'Dalek' continued to pour in. Calling the series 'Watercooler TV', the *Sun* at the very end of April admonished readers not to miss the 'truly explosive ending' and featured a photograph on its cover. The *Mirror* also featured a Dalek on its cover while the *Daily Star* gave away a free 'Sci-Fi Sounds' CD, which contained an arrangement of the *Doctor Who* theme. The *Scotsman* told viewers that the BBC was 'hoping the dreaded Daleks will exterminate the opposition in the ratings war when they make their return to the nation's TV screens', while quoting writer Rob Shearman as saying, 'People want to see the Dalek again, in all its glory, being taken seriously and killing rather brutally.' *The Times* said that the episode did not have the humour associated with the episodes written by Davies, but that the script was: '... strangely moving ... Tonight's episode manages to sneak in a message about the redemptive power of human kindness and the way in which victims can turn into oppressors. This new *Doctor Who* is an unqualified triumph.' Television coverage was extensive, including appearances by cast members and producers on BBC News, the BBC *Breakfast* programme and others, while Shearman appeared on BBC Radio 5's *Weekend Breakfast* in a recorded interview.

And 'Dalek' was a triumph in the reviews. The *Guardian*: 'Robert Shearman's script bamboozles expectations, offering a fresh take on the famous metal drama queens, here both more formidable and sympathetic than we've ever seen them in the past. Claustrophobic and suitably melodramatic, this should hopefully show 2005's kids what was always so wonderful about the iconic tin-rotters.' The *London Evening Standard*: 'It's heady, surprising, spiky and occasionally pretentious stuff, but I'll take this over ITV's spandex celeb-grappling any Saturday night.' The *Independent*: 'Robert Shearman, who scripted this episode, had some fun with the robot's famous limitations as a killing machine. "What are you going to do, sucker me to death?"' *The Times*: 'We got a surprisingly poignant story. And Eccleston's combination of blokeyness and otherworldly intensity came into its own here, but I can still see why he's already decided to leave the show. Just look at the Daleks; you don't see them in any other line of work.' The *People*: 'The episode worked in a way most of the previous ones didn't. It was well-written, not pointlessly camp, with a decent story.' The *Daily Express*: 'A splendidly scary but rather sad (and politically laboured) story ended with the Dalek exterminating itself because it had taken on human characteristics and was no longer motivated to kill everything that moved. As usual, the script fizzed with good jokes ...' The *Western Daily Press*: 'The stories are good, too, and Saturday's drama held my attention from start to finish as the Doctor took on the Daleks deep below Utah.' The *Sentinel*: ' Hang on, this isn't an episode of *Doctor Who*, it's an advert for the Welsh Tourist Board. In the end, overcome by the futility of its existence alone, it topped itself. I wasn't crying. I'd just poked myself in my eye.' The *London Evening Standard*: 'By turns dramatic, imaginative, ironic, allegorical – and touching – the storyline never faltered from first to last ... For once the BBC haven't put a foot wrong, and have even improved on the original.' *BBC Ceefax*: 'By the end of the show, you'll no longer think that Daleks are silly and that's quite an achievement.' And in the *Mirror*: 'For 30 pant sh*ttingly wonderful minutes BBC1's new *Doctor Who* was the best thing on telly. Ever.' Garry Bushell was a lone sniping voice in the *People*, writing, 'Why don't people being "chased" by Daleks simply run away? You see faster milk floats.'

Even children were having fun with the story. 'That's a nice Dalek. He's Rose's best friend,' wrote Amy, one of the four 'fear forecasters' engaged by the official BBC *Doctor Who* website. Beginning with the broadcast of 'World War Three', the site managers previewed each episode in front of four children – Amy, 4; Harry, 6; Samuel, 8; and Adam, 12 – in order to forecast the level of danger and scariness in each story. As the Dalek in this particular episode had started to 'kick bottom,' as the children said, Harry's reaction pretty much summed up their opinions: 'Woah. Woah! WOAH!' The 'Fear Forecast' segment continued on the website throughout the remainder of the first series.

The situation surrounding the episode, and its lead nasty, broke boundaries into the mainstream media as well. The *Observer* on 1 May noted that the BBC had been: '... braced for viewer complaints last night after screening possibly the most terrifying *Doctor Who* episode ever ... Four viewers complained to Ofcom after an earlier episode, claiming it was too scary for children, but the media watchdog chose not to investigate.' The *Sunday Express* lampooned the forthcoming election by tapping into the topicality of the Daleks, including a cartoon of the three main party leaders as Daleks chasing a terrified Britannia-type figure to a polling station. The *Sunday Sport* featured a centre-spread with a topless model draped over a Dalek in various poses ... And of course, there was some reaction to the episode: on 14 May the *Guardian* complained that it was: '... an infernal liberty on the part of the scriptwriter Russell T Davies to have the last Dalek liquidate itself a fortnight ago.' (To which Davies replied in a letter to the *Guardian* on 28 May, 'I surrender. You win. My neighbours have stuck your campaign message in their car windows and keep driving past me, shaking an angry fist in my direction. All right, all right, all right, the Daleks will be back. Hundreds of 'em. No more girly consciences either, they're back to being mean metal bastards. What d'you fancy next year? Cybermen?')

The initial overnight ratings for 'Dalek' matched expectations, peaking at nearly 9 million viewers. ITV1's new competitor for the time slot, *Celebrity Wrestling*, failed to come anywhere near the highs of its predecessor, *Ant & Dec's Saturday Night Takeaway*, winning only 3.05 million viewers. Several newspapers called the event a 'ratings disaster' for ITV; said the *Daily*

Record on 2 May, 'More than 800,000 deserted *Celebrity Wrestling* as ratings slumped to three million after just two weeks.' The *Daily Record* quoted an 'insider' as saying 'Saturday nights have turned into a total disaster and there's pressure for big changes to be made,' although an ITV spokesman said: 'There are no plans to reschedule Saturday nights. It just isn't happening.' *Broadcast* magazine called it: '... very bad news for ITV1. How long can they keep it in that slot? They would do better with a movie ... *Doctor Who* is absolutely trouncing them.' A week later, on 10 May, ITV moved *Celebrity Wrestling* off Saturday night; said BBC News, 'The show, which saw twelve personalities train and fight each other, was part of ITV's primetime schedule but failed to compete with the relaunched *Doctor Who*.' *Broadcast Now* reported that after the coming weekend, the time slot would be filled on ITV by films, including repeats of the *Star Wars* movies. A week later, the 8 May *Guardian* discussed ITV's turn to nostalgia 'in the face of Dalek threat': 'At a time when ITV is battling falling ratings and increased competition, it is hoping to regain the affection of viewers by broadcasting more than 30 hours of nostalgia-fuelled peak-time programming to celebrate its 50th birthday.'

Alongside the broadcast of 'Dalek' was another change, to the documentary series accompanying the show. *Doctor Who Confidential Cut Down* was the title of a fifteen-minute version of the half-hour series, which would for several weeks take the place of the half-hour format in the BBC3 Sunday night repeat. The quarter-hour version would remove all material from the 'classic' *Doctor Who* series in order to fit the tight timeslot necessary for BBC3's Sunday night schedule.

ECCLESTON MOVES ON

Even while the series was being broadcast, Christopher Eccleston was maintaining a certain distance, although some comments about his departure from the role were attributed to him in the press. On 1 May, the *Sunday Mirror* revived the debate about Eccleston's departure. 'He quit *Doctor Who* to head for Hollywood – but is Christopher Eccleston too miserable to be famous? Chris is rumoured to have rejected huge cash offers – a large advance on his £1 million salary – but his decision to leave may have been a smart move after all ... He could simply be being honest, or maybe he's just being awkward. Christopher did once admit, "I am not known for my charm ... I think I'm seen as a grumpy old sod." ... As for how the star will cope with the gaze of the world on his Salford retreat, only time will tell.' *The Times* observed that 'According to a mole within BBC Wales ... Eccleston quit after being presented with a fait accompli: the unappetising choice of starring in only half the next series (not enough) or another two full series (far too big a commitment). Who knows what really happened?' Camille Coduri, who had completed her first season work on the series as Jackie, told the *People* that Eccleston was: '... superb. Sometimes I'd have to look away because he'd make me laugh so much. It's a shame he's not doing the second series but people forget he'd been working on it for practically a year. I don't blame him for wanting to move on.' But Coduri did add: 'David Tennant will bring a different dimension to it, and he and Billie Piper will work brilliantly together.'

Also that day, the *Daily Star Sunday* commented on Christopher Eccleston's now-trademark leather jacket, claiming that 'he is too scared to wear it in the street in case a show-worshipping geek attacks him for it.' Said Eccleston, 'It could be in the cupboard for a while yet.' A few days later, Eccleston made waves on the football front, with it being reported that he'd donated £10,000 to help stop Manchester United being taken over by American businessman Malcolm Glazer. 'Christopher couldn't bear the thought of his beloved team falling into the hands of Glazer so dug deep to put an end to the team being take over,' said a report on *Sky News*. The *News of the World* couldn't help but mention that Eccleston and actress Siwan Morris were an item. Even the *Dead Ringers* comedy sketch series got into the act in mid-May, featuring a sketch about the 'real' reason Eccleston had left *Doctor Who*... supposedly that his very Northern family were, in fact, all *Star Trek* fans (explaining his ears as being a gift from his Ferengi father). According to *Dead Ringers*, Eccleston was now off to take a role in *Blake's 7: The Movie* ...

Later in the month, the new issue of *SFX* magazine raised the issue again, quoting Eccleston as saying that in the role: 'You can't have a life. You can't socialise. It's like having a TARDIS in your skull and every time you open your mouth you see a TARDIS. There were days when I got psoriasis, I got eczema. My face blew up in the Dalek episode. I looked literally disfigured with tiredness and poor skin.' He admitted that playing the Doctor was still a lot easier than the labouring jobs he took while he was a struggling actor in his twenties, but he pointed out that the hours were a grind. 'It is actually hard graft. With TV, you do a 14-hour day and then you're doing your line-learning.' But despite all this, 'I loved being part of that amazing team. By and large, it was a joy.' He even left open the possibility of returning to the role, but not on TV. 'If there was a radio version I would definitely look at that as it won't take up so much time.' By 16 May, it was announced that Eccleston was signed to star in the film *Double Life* from Cougar Films, a 'high concept sci-fi genre piece' written and directed by first season *Doctor Who* director Joe Ahearne. *SFX* reported that Ahearne would not be returning for the second series of the show: '... but not because of this ... I'm not involved with the second series because I've just done five episodes of the current series and spent seven months living in Cardiff since September last year, and as wonderful and fantastic and amazing as it is, it does take you over. I just want to get back to London really ...' On 20 May, several newspapers reported that Eccleston would be featured as Silas in the film version of the novel *The Da Vinci Code*. This wasn't to be, however, and the role instead went to Paul Bettany (*Master and Commander*).

There was much speculation as to when, exactly, Eccleston had taken the decision to leave. Davies insisted that it was always part of the plan; however, Eccleston's comments following the end of the recording of the first series indicated – rather cautiously – that he was done with the role, suggesting that the mutual parting wasn't quite what it appeared to be. Eccleston did attend the press launch in March, and did make public appearances throughout the transmission period, including a 1 June appearance at a local school in Surrey; said the *Surrey Comet* a day later: 'School leavers at Grey Court School felt honoured to meet the latest incarnation of *Doctor Who*.' Yet on 12 June, on the Eamonn Holmes-hosted Radio 5 Live chat show, Eccleston was asked if he had enjoyed working on the series. 'Mixed,' Eccleston replied, 'but that's a long story' – and he left it at that. Later, speaking to *Newsbeat*, Eccleston said that finishing the series was a relief after dealing with the BBC, but he'd still got something special out of it: 'The best thing about *Doctor Who* for me has been the response I've had from children, both in the street and the number of letters and drawings of me and Daleks, which are all over my wall at home. In all the twenty years I've been acting, I've never enjoyed a response so much as the one I've had from children, and I'm carrying that in my heart forever.' Meanwhile, the official *Doctor Who* site confirmed on 20 May that Eccleston's final appearance would be in the forthcoming thirteenth episode of the series, 'The Parting of the Ways'.

EARLY MAY: 'THE LONG GAME' AND 'FATHER'S DAY'

After the excitement of 'Dalek', attention turned to the following weekend's episode, 'The Long Game'. *Radio Times* gave the episode a fair amount of promotion in its 3 May edition, describing it as, 'A lively, if haphazard, outing for the Time Lord (and a shifty new "companion", Adam)', which 'takes a gruesome peek at the future of journalism.' In fact, much of *Radio Times*'s coverage had shifted to looking back at what had already been seen, including interviews with stunt performers and looks inside the Dalek from the previous instalment; only a quarter of the preview was given over to guest star Simon Pegg and the trouble he'd had saying one of his lines (involving the full name of the Jagrafess). Actress Tamsin Greig was briefly profiled for her work in 'The Long Game', though *Radio Times* had a mixed view of the story: '... a slavering nightmare of which Gerald Scarfe would be proud (send tots to bed though). But despite bubbling with great ideas, the story doesn't quite hang together, and with a dateline that far away, you'd expect a greater leap of imagination from the design department.' Other press sources covered the episode: *Zoo* magazine (3-9 May) featured an interview with Simon Pegg, along with a photo of the actor in his role as the Editor captioned with: 'He wasn't sure if the Rutger Hauer look was really working.' *ITV Teletext* made it their 'pick of the day': 'In this episode the camera is turned on the media – albeit in the year 200,000 ... Tonight's alien is truly the stuff of nightmares, so it might be best to get the kids behind the sofa straight away.' *BBC Ceefax* also made it their TV choice, even though: '... it's the first ho-hum episode of the new series ... Tonight Simon Pegg stars as the Editor in a not-even-thinly-veiled mockery of extreme journalism.' On 10 May, the *Daily Express* said that with this episode, *Doctor Who*: '... is still the best fun on the box. The joy of the series is that it does all the things sci-fi is meant to do – using imagined worlds to look askance at our own, questioning the present by thinking about the future – while also taking the mick out of the genre.' The *Guardian* noted that the episode: '... seemed comforting and reassuring ... Anything that satirises the profession of journalism is all right with me, but this did it with style.'

The *Sunday Mirror* called Piper 'Thrillie Piper' in a 2 May article about her role as Beatrice in the forthcoming adaptation of *Much Ado About Nothing*, which she was then filming on the south coast of Britain for the BBC, while new Doctor David Tennant was the focus of many news reports concerning his participation in a Radio 4 revival of the fondly-remembered BBC police series *Dixon of Dock Green*, in which he would play sidekick Andy Crawford. On 3 May, Tennant joined the mix of celebrities promoting Labour in the forthcoming election. He told the *Mirror*: 'I will be voting Labour this time because the alternative is a disaster area. Voting will take you thirty seconds and will last five years.' He also spoke to *Film Focus* at the European premiere of the film *Kingdom of Heaven*, when he said that taking over the title role of *Doctor Who* was: '... very exciting and very daunting, in equal measures. Just the amount of attention it gets is quite overwhelming. But there's no better show in the world.' He mentioned that the series would start shooting in July. Meanwhile, it was reported by the *Guardian* on 5 May that Tennant would play Brendan Block, a man with disturbing psychotic tendencies, in *Secret Smile* for ITV. Former Doctor Colin Baker praised Tennant in the *Belfast Telegraph* on 12 May and said he wasn't surprised that Eccleston gave up the role: 'Really, one is enough for any actor ... Christopher was so believable as Who, but David will be special too, as he is an absolute Doctor buff, which makes him perfect for the role.'

In Canada, meanwhile, the series saw ratings success as 'World War Three' pulled in

936,000 viewers on 3 May, the second highest number of viewers in that country (behind the debut episode, 'Rose'). The CBC network also debuted a six-part documentary series produced especially for the web, *Planet of the Doctor*, featuring interviews with former *Doctor Who* celebrities such as Verity Lambert, Elisabeth Sladen, Katy Manning and Terrance Dicks, as well as science fiction writer Robert J Sawyer and members of the *Doctor Who* Information Network, Canada's national fan organisation. The documentary also featured behind-the-scenes shots from various conventions and interviews with scientists about the nature of time travel and the influence of *Doctor Who* on science fiction and television.

As the week continued, the *Dead Ringers Election Special* was promoted with a trailer spoofing Eccleston's 'Trip of a Lifetime' trailer from March. *The Times Literary Supplement* on 5 May reviewed the first DVD release, saying that 'the first three episodes are at once enjoyable in themselves and a celebration of the show's past – the trip to the far future and the terrifying Victorian ghost story are both plots the show repeated time and again; a repetition known, when viewed favourably, as playing to your strengths rather than a mere obsession.' The *Independent* on the same day noted that recent efforts to use the Daleks to urge science fiction fans to vote Labour had backfired: Labour HQ had allegedly received a stern letter jointly sent from the BBC and the Terry Nation estate asking them to withdraw the villain from their campaign. 'The BBC takes very seriously the unauthorised use of its brands.' *The Times* reviewed the BBC4 production *Russell T Davies: Unscripted*, a one-hour biography of the series's executive producer, which said it was 'a short romp through his career to date, featuring lots of hand-waving and self deprecation from the man himself, as well as insightful asides from various former bosses.' The *Wessex Scene* said of the series, 'It is really quite good. Writer Russell T Davies ... ensured that the general tone of the show contained drama, character development and good-natured, self-mocking cheesiness in equal measure.'

'The Long Game' pulled in decent ratings on 7 May that nearly matched those of 'Dalek' the weekend before. However, by now the series had become more commonplace, and only a handful of headline reviews were noteworthy, including one in the *Sun*: 'This is one of the few shows the whole family can watch which doesn't have Heart in the title and a sickly sweet storyline. It is scary, intelligent and funny and has raised the bar for Saturday night TV. It's just a shame the powers that be ignored pleas from sci-fi fans to bring it back for so bloody long.' The *Daily Star* gave away a free CD titled *Doctor Who and Friends*, containing a mix of the classic series's theme tune by Mark Ayres originally created for the double-CD 'The Cult Files' in the early 1990's; the accompanying TV magazine picked *Doctor Who* as its five-star selection for the day, making much of Bruno Langley's appearance in the episode. The *Citizen* interviewed both Simon Pegg and Colin Prockter from the cast of the episode: 'I think it's going to be spectacular,' said Pegg. 'To be a *Doctor Who* villain was a bit of a dream come true, so I was very happy to do that.' And the *Mail on Sunday* noted that Piper would soon appear as the nemesis of the foul-mouthed teenager Vicky Pollard on the BBC3 comedy series *Little Britain*. '[Series creators Matt Lucas and David Walliams] knew an arch-enemy for Vicky would bring a new dimension to the chav sketches, and they told Billie she would be perfect ... She's now looking at her schedule to make sure she can fit it in.'

Attention turned to the next episode, 'Father's Day'. On 10 May, *Heat* magazine gave the episode five stars out of five: 'An extraordinary story told in ordinary surroundings, this one resembles a sci-fi *EastEnders*, with a hint of *Only Fools and Horses* ... Brilliantly emotional, *Doctor Who* has to be the most ingenious primetime drama in years.' *Reveal Magazine* called it an 'unmissable instalment'. *Radio Times* made the episode its top pick once again, with a double-spread behind-the-scenes feature dominated by a large photograph of one of the Reapers and an interview with writer Paul Cornell: 'Initially I thought of cloaked figures ... but then went for animals. I was thinking about snatching claws, like those piggy banks where the hand flashes out and grabs the coin – a scary predator-like motion.' *BBC Ceefax* also made 'Father's Day' its TV choice: 'No kidding: this is the best episode of the series so far. And it manages to be that despite having exasperating plot holes and convenient solutions. But what's so great is that while we get the usual monsters, this is really about Rose and her dad.' The *Sunday Telegraph* said: 'Piper is perfect, as ever, Eccleston is near his best ... and Shaun Dingwall is superb as Rose's ne'er-do-well dad. Was *Doctor Who* ever this dependably good before?'

The BBC Press Office was already looking a week ahead, on 12 May releasing its weekly *Features* document previewing 'The Empty Child' and its co-star John Barrowman, as well as the new *Doctor Who* exhibition soon to open in Brighton. In an accompanying press pack released on 18 May, the BBC interviewed Steven Moffat, writer of the forthcoming two-parter: 'I heard I'd got the job on the way to the Comedy Awards, where we won for my BBC2 series *Coupling*, and I got to meet (former Doctor Who) Peter Davison ... I remember me and (fellow *Doctor Who* writer) Mark Gatiss drunkenly pitching the return of the show to the BBC's Head of Comedy at a party once and him saying "It sounds very interesting, but I'm comedy".' Co-star Richard Wilson said he thought the writing of the two-part Moffat script was of high quality: 'I think that is one of the strengths of the new series of *Doctor Who*.' Barrowman noted that his character would be 'an intergalactic conman, and he starts off by trying to con the Doctor and Rose.' The Press Office also revealed that, for the first time, *Doctor Who* would temporarily shift from its normal time slot: 'The Empty Child' would air a half-hour earlier than usual in order to accommodate the 21 May live broadcast of the *Eurovision Song Contest*. *BBC News*, meanwhile, reported that 'The Empty Child' would be cut because of tone issues, stating that, 'The next episode of *Doctor Who* has been toned down after producers decided one scene was 'a bit too horrible'. The episode ... turns former *One Foot in the Grave* actor Richard Wilson's face into a gas mask – but producers have cut out the sound of his skull cracking.' Said Collinson, 'It's a little thing involving the scene with Richard Wilson's character and the gas mask,' although later reports revealed this to have been a simple tweak of the soundtrack of the episode, and a decision made entirely by the production team; as Collinson would later explain, there was no request from any BBC executives to make the change. The story also briefly mentioned 'some ruminations of bisexuality,' which, such as they were, would involve John Barrowman's character, Jack Harkness; however, these remained unchanged in the episodes.

Early May also saw repeated mentions of other, tangential *Doctor Who* subjects. Matthew Norman's Media Diary in the *Independent* on 10 May discussed possible censored material in 'World War Three': 'A shot of a newspaper headline including the term "sexing up" was thought too inflammatory during an election campaign, and was duly excised.' *Constantine* actress Rachel Weisz spoke to the London *Metro* newspaper, saying that she was upset that she'd never been asked to become a *Doctor Who* girl: 'I always dreamed I might play the role on stage or radio as I never thought they would bring it back.' *BBC News* suggested that a *Doctor Who* film might not yet be dead: 'BBC Films boss David Thompson confirmed that BBC Films is pushing ahead with its plans for a *Doctor Who* feature, the progress of which is dependent on how the new *Doctor Who* TV series is received in the US.' (Of course, there were no signs at that point of an American screening of the series.) The *Sun* said on 12 May that the BBC Model Unit was being shut down due to cost-cutting exercises, laying off a number of series crewmembers including Mike Tucker, who had worked on the series. *Private Eye* said that the BBC had informed Tucker and the Model Unit that their team 'would be made redundant – though they were welcome to reapply for freelance work.' But, said a BBC spokesperson, 'We'd work with Mike again on a freelance basis if there are projects requiring his expertise.' The *Methodist Recorder* on 14 May said the series had indeed been suitable for younger viewers, but 'one recent episode featured two scenes of torture that were certainly not appropriate for a children's programme.' On 16 May, many BBC and other news outlets turned their attention toward Brighton for the opening of the *Doctor Who* exhibition, while Davies joined the ITV Sunday night arts programme *The South Bank Show* to talk about his friend and contemporary Paul Abbott. Abbott discussed Davies's persuasion of him to leave writing *Coronation Street* for a producer's job on *Cracker* in 1993, as it meant a huge pay cut. 'It'll make you look taller!' Davies said he'd replied.

Davies also did several interviews regarding the rating given the series's impending DVD releases. The British Board of Film Classification (BBFC) announced in mid-May that the initial two discs, containing the first six episodes, would both be given a '12' rating – not to be sold to children under twelve years of age – because of violence in 'The Unquiet Dead' and 'Dalek', even though both episodes had aired in an early evening family slot on television. *BBC Ceefax* said it was because of 'violence and cruelty as a way of dealing with problems' while *The Times* remarked that the censors' claims had noted the series 'implies that the only way to resolve disputes is through force allied with cruelty.' The *Irish Independent* on 18 May said that 'the whole fun of *Doctor Who* is hiding behind the sofa at the scary bits.' Throwing cold water on the idea that children would take the ideas to the playground, the *Irish Independent* condemned the BBFC's actions: 'Where do these idiots come from? Gallifrey? We particularly liked their fear that kids might take it into the playground. Yeah, because kids really need inspiration to be beastly to each other during recess.' *The Times* felt largely the same: 'It's good to know that the BBFC are concerned that any Daleks who find their way through space and time into the nation's playgrounds should not be unmercifully bullied. But leaving aside the important issue of just how the nation's children should react to the arrival of a Dalek during lunch break (make sure it doesn't feel excluded by picking it first for the football team?) another ticklish question of space travel arises. Just what planet are these censors on?'

THE SHAPE OF SEASON TWO

Throughout May and June, clues continued to pour in regarding a second series of *Doctor Who* ... and a lot of rumours. One of the big rumours was that David Walliams of *Little Britain* fame – and a *Doctor Who* fan to boot – would be contributing a script. According to the *Mirror*, 'He was approached after BBC bosses decided his surreal sense of humour would be ideal for the revived show's wacky new storylines.' However, Phil Collinson was quick to point out that there was 'no truth in the tabloid rumours' in late May's edition of *Doctor Who Magazine*.

While it was still uncertain at the time whether or not Eccleston was completely done with the role – there were reports that he would be appearing in the Christmas special, although in truth he had recorded his last scenes in March and would be regenerating at the end of 'The Parting of the Ways' – the rumour mills began flying about Piper's ongoing participation. *Dreamwatch* magazine, in what was touted as an exclusive (yet posted in various online discussion forums by its editor prior to the press date, as a news item), stated that Piper would be leaving the series during its second season. 'She's not doing the full season,' Piper's agent apparently told *Dreamwatch*, indicating that Piper would likely appear in somewhere between three and seven episodes. Immediately, the UK press went ballistic, within a week picking up the story, in some cases (for instance the *Daily Star*) placing it on the front page ... in effect, setting the tone of the series as that of a show in crisis. With coverage in such papers as the *Sun*, the *Daily Mirror* and the *Evening Standard*, the BBC was forced to issue a new press release on 28 May: 'The BBC today confirmed that Billie Piper – who plays *Doctor Who*'s companion Rose – will return for the second series on BBC1.' According to a BBC spokesperson, quoted in the press release, 'Billie Piper will return for the second series of *Doctor Who*. It has not been confirmed how many episodes she will be in. We are awaiting storylines and scripts.' Newspapers were quick to point out that this wasn't exactly a denial, and in fact some speculated that if she wasn't appearing in all the episodes (whereas she had done in the first season), it was obvious she was being written out.

As was the case in 2003, the floodgates were now open for ample speculation on who the Doctor's next companion would be. The *Daily Mirror* called up a list of 'likely' replacements. Some of the more prominent names reported were Michelle Ryan (who played Zoe Slater in *EastEnders)* and Jennifer Ellison (formerly part of Channel 4's *Brookside*, but most recently seen in various 'celebrity' reality TV series; she had been equally hotly tipped as the next Bond girl in the same papers). The *Mirror* said in their report that auditions were now underway, 'and TV bosses are keen to sign a dark-haired girl with a posh accent.' Meanwhile, the *News of the World* on 29 May suggested that Piper wouldn't be leaving the series after all ... which, of course, could be explained by a slightly different reading of the BBC press release. The *People*, on the other hand, reported that Piper would earn an extra £120,000 after agreeing to star in four additional episodes of the series (possibly the source of the three- to seven-episode jump in various reports). 'It's great news she's on board for more,' the *People* quoted an 'insider' as saying. By late June, a mere month prior to the start of production, there was still no concrete word as to whether or not Piper would be staying for the whole year, or if there'd be another actress (or actor) joining the fray.

With a new Doctor and possibly a new companion along the way, would there be any familiar faces in store for series two? As a matter of fact, there would be ... in the form of some classic villains who would be making a return visit: the Cybermen, the emotionless cyborgs first introduced in 'The Tenth Planet' (1966) – the final story to star the original title actor, William Hartnell – who made appearances in the series alongside the first seven Doctors. *Doctor Who Magazine* confirmed the rumours that the Cybermen would appear, but meanwhile, Davies, in an 8 June interview with the UK *Press Association*, said that another favourite monster was probably not going to be seen. 'Oh no, we've done them,' Davies said of the popular Daleks. 'Because of what happens ... I'm not sure we can take the Daleks anywhere else after that.' The series would, however, feature some alien planets in the next year. 'I've been cautious about that in the first series because we want to get it right. It's one of those science fiction things that can go horribly wrong if it doesn't actually look like an alien planet. But I'm very confident we can do that now.'

Davies was rather circumspect in his discussions of the second series with *Press Association*, noting that the first season had been: '... everything I wanted it to be – the music is brilliant, the effects are brilliant. A lot of series don't reach a climax ... We just have to get on with it. And because we've got a new Doctor coming up it makes us worried all over again. But I think it's very healthy in that we don't rest on our laurels.' Davies confirmed that David Tennant would be in the Christmas special, to be aired some time in December; the special would be made as part of the season two block and would be Tennant's first full trip in the TARDIS. 'Having changes in the cast so early on is always a worry,' Davies said. 'But at the same time it's one of the things that keeps us on our toes. Just by casting David we're not becoming complacent because it's his face on screen and we've got to make it every bit as good, if not better, for his sake.'

THE NEW FANDOM

One of the expected by-products of a new *Doctor Who* series was a new generation of fans, devoted either solely to this new series or to a hybrid of the new and the 'classic' show. *Doctor Who* fandom had come a long way from local group meetings and mimeographed newsletters distributed via the post; the Internet had brought an immediacy to fan communities worldwide, and now, more than ever, aficionados of a particular television series, film or other genre could gather electronically. *Doctor Who* fandom began changing in the early 1990s, after the original series had gone off the air; early adopters migrated to listservers and other forms of mailing lists as the Internet began entering homes and workspaces. Communities on the GEnie, CompuServe and America Online paid communities slowly built up, then were pulled into the free-for-all of the World Wide Web. Now anyone could participate online from the privacy of their own home in the full range of fan activity: websites, mailing lists, Yahoo! Groups communities, LiveJournals (a particular system of personal 'blogging', or weblogging), newsgroups and discussion forums.

Yet the new series perhaps challenged expectations as its fan community developed. *Doctor Who* had always been about the archetypal hero and his trusty sidekick – never had it truly entered the realm of the romantic. While nothing was overtly expressed in the first season of the series – that is, besides the deep, personal relationship between the Doctor and Rose – the series was adopted into what has become known as 'shipper' fandom ... 'shipper' being a general term for emotional, intellectual and romantic relationships between well-drawn characters. There is a large community of 'shipper' fans, among whose many interests had previously been characters from *Buffy the Vampire Slayer, Stargate SG-1, Xena: Warrior Princess, Angel, The X-Files, Star Trek* and other popular genre series; sometimes derided by other fans for their lack of attention to the technical aspects of a particular show, be it continuity or plot logic, 'shipper' fans often find their interest lies in the actors and the characters they play, whether the Daleks invade Earth or not.

The key for this new and growing fandom was the intense personal bond shared between the Doctor and Rose Tyler. 'The relationship between the Doctor and Rose, for me, is just the icing on the cake,' said Lara Pascoe, who runs a popular LiveJournal community called *Time and Chips* devoted to the series and its 'shipper' fans. 'The chemistry and the scenes between them really drew me in and made me think this was a Doctor/companion relationship that could be deeper than the ones we had seen before.' Many of the site's users agreed: 'I think the idea was that these two were supposed to be close,' wrote Paul Guest. 'I initially started watching not only due to the fact I remembered the show as a child,' said Helen Jones, 'but also because I'd seen some of the promo interviews that had been done and was really interested in the idea of the relationship between Doctor/Rose, especially upon hearing Chris say it was a love story.' 'It was pure entertainment at its best,' wrote Claire Thompson. 'What first got me hooked was the imaginative plots and fun storylines. What keeps me hooked is the unfolding relationship between the Doctor and Rose. Seeing how these two very different beings can find common ground and how the Doctor has changed now he is the last of his kind and alone in the universe. It's just fascinating.' 'It was definitely Chris Eccleston,' wrote Amber Sinclair. 'I had seen him in *The Second Coming* about a month before the show aired, and after I saw him in the previews for *Doctor Who* I had to watch. I'm a girly girl, so the sci fi doesn't really get me going.' As Sarah Crauder wrote: 'There's something about the banter and ease that the Rose and Doctor have together that, for some reason, makes me shout "Kiss already!" at the screen.' Others see the relationship just a bit differently. 'I see the Doctor as being more of a surrogate father/friend/mentor to Rose rather than a romantic interest,' said Shelley Smarz. 'Adding romance to that mix would just heighten the squick factor ... That being said, I'd like to see the Doctor's sexuality explored (something which, I understand, some of fans of the old series are dead set against), just not with Rose. This doesn't mean that I'm not going to read shipper fic ... I just don't want to see it on the show.'

It was obvious that these new fans weren't simply regroupings of past collectives; there was new blood coming in, attracted not only to Eccleston and Piper, but also to the writing and production. 'The first thing that made me want to watch this show was the writers behind it,' said Tracy Payne on the *Time and Chips* website. 'I've never really watched the original (apart from the 1996 Paul McGann version) and I didn't think I'd be interested in this one, but once I started watching, I was very impressed with everything about it.' Rebecca Hampson agreed: 'It's obviously been made with a lot of passion and dedication and that comes across on screen. The Doctor/Rose relationship is one of my favourite elements, though.' Said Rachael Bundock, 'My attention was caught before the show even started, because of the general buzz going around about it – even the "old" fans seemed genuinely excited, and the younger people were excited to have a *Doctor Who* in their time.' It was also the sense of community these new fan collectives created among their users: 'The LiveJournal element is new to me,' wrote Katie Williams, 'but I'd never have become so embroiled in the fandom had I not been accompanied by so many other obsessive yet wonderful people!' Manuela Kusch agreed: 'I think that's LJ's appeal, to be less anonymous than on a mailing list. It's more a big room where you meet your friends whom you know from their personal blogs or other communities.' But of course, some of the fans came in for the same tried and true reasons, sharing their love of the characters with an interest in some old favourites: 'The Dalek attracted me to watch episode six (and then I went on to buy and watch the first ones),' said Emma Hardy. 'I'm a massive Dalek fan!' Tricia Stewart perhaps summed it up best: 'It *is* Doctor Who. It's *Doctor Who* all grown up.'

One of the major by-products of the Doctor/Rose relationship was the resurgence of women active in *Doctor Who* fandom. Much of British fandom had been dominated for years by male fans, though in other countries (the United States and Canada in particular), female fans had long been part of the political organisation of local fan clubs and conventions. While online discussion communities such as the Yahoo! groups and the USENet newsgroups and forums continued to be dominated by men as the new series debuted, the LiveJournal communities, various Internet fanfiction archives and other locales brought more women into the fold. 'Women have had virtually no impact on fandom ever since the *New Adventures* started coming out and the heart of fandom swung back from the female-dominated American fandom to its original UK, mostly male fandom home,' said Jennifer Adams Kelley, programme director of the *ChicagoTARDIS* convention. 'Although the TV movie brought an influx of active female fans into the fold, the vast majority of those women have been far more interested in Paul McGann as an actor than *Doctor Who* as a series. Even with the explosion of the Internet, and the now-easy ability to connect with other fans, it's still fairly uncommon to find a woman running a website, or owning a discussion board, or even writing much fanfic.' With the advent of the new series, however, a flood of women had begun participating in *Doctor Who* fandom, starting discussion lists and websites, and dominating much of the creative fan output. *Doctor Who* was certainly not just a show for men ...

LATE MAY: 'THE EMPTY CHILD' AND 'THE DOCTOR DANCES'

By 19 May there were indications of other countries to which *Doctor Who* would be sold: South Korean network KBS 2, a public broadcasting channel, would start transmitting the series as of 5 June under the name *Dacter Who* – the first BBC drama series to be sold to that country. Said Jungwon Lee, executive director of KBS media, 'We are very excited to launch *Doctor Who* on the network. We anticipate a great reaction from all age groups.' Davies noted: 'The Doctor has travelled far and wide and knows no boundary, and now the programme is doing much the same.' Finland's *TV2* Network acquired the series for transmission with subtitles, becoming the third European country (after the UK and the Netherlands) to acquire it. Even airlines were part of the mix – the Thomsonfly Airlines carrier had acquired the first episode as part of its in-flight video features, and now the *Telegraph* said on 28 May that the series had also been sold to such carriers as British Airways, Virgin Atlantic, Singapore Airlines and Air New Zealand, all of whom would be showing it within the next month. Over in Canada, the CBC network, which had transmitted the show beginning only ten days after its BBC1 premiere, announced it would begin repeating the series in mid-June on Sunday evenings. The worldwide appeal of the series wasn't lost on BBC Board Chairman, and one time staunch *Doctor Who* adversary, Michael Grade. Asked about it by BBC Radio Leeds on 19 May, he said he was 'enjoying the new series of *Doctor Who*' and called it 'a production for the 21st Century,' though he also remarked that his six-year old son was a fan of the show, so 'maybe I should ask for a blood test!' The international success was commented on by the Associated Press, which ran a syndicated article, circulated to America and Canada and many other nations, that said the series 'has become one of the biggest hits of Britain's television present'. Doctor Who Appreciation Society spokesman Antony Wainer told the Associated Press, 'All the *Doctor Who* furniture is there. That is the formula. And it still survives.'

Meanwhile, attention focused on 'The Empty Child', the first half of Steven Moffat's two-part story. The *Sun* offered an early picture preview (on 12 May) with a photo of Rose and Jack Harkness in front of the Big Ben clock face, while the *Daily Star* said: 'It's the green-eyed monster facing *Doctor Who* when he becomes jealous of sidekick Rose's new hunk.' *Radio Times* broke its streak of calling *Doctor Who* its pick of the day for Saturday with 'The Empty Child' – ironic considering how well it was received elsewhere – but still included coverage of the episode, calling it 'an enticing mystery set in a Blitz-ravaged London.' Also recommended was the ninth instalment of *Doctor Who Confidential*: 'This zesty little series is a goldmine for those who like their special effects with a little bit of elucidation.' *Heat* magazine said on 18 May, 'There's something about the sight of a bunch of zombie-like mutants with gas masks for faces that really gives us the willies. Add to the mix a hunky new love interest for Billie Piper's Rose and a wonderful cameo from Richard Wilson, and you have yet another triumphant episode.' *Closer* magazine on the same day said: 'This series just gets better and better.' The *AfterElton* website profiled John Barrowman, and specifically addressed the rumours that his character would be bisexual: 'With *Doctor Who*, Barrowman has a good chance to broaden his fame internationally, while also representing a bisexual man on TV.' Shortly after the airing of the episode, the *Daily Express* on 22 May called it 'a brilliantly crafted episode.' However, the *Huddersfield Examiner* asked on 2 June: 'Why did they get such basic details of the Blitz wrong? ... During the war, no light could be shown in case it acted as a guide to attacking bombers. Every window was covered with a blackout curtain and front doors were not opened until interior lights had been turned off. But not in *Doctor Who*. At the height of a bombing raid, RAF pilots stand on a balcony in the heart of London enjoying a drink with the curtains wide open and the lights blazing out behind them.'

The ratings for 'The Empty Child' were noticeably lower than for any other episode that had been seen so far. The instalment had been shifted to an earlier timeslot, 6.30 pm, to make way for the *Eurovision Song Contest*, and was also up against a rerun of the original *Star Wars* film on ITV1. Its audience share also dipped slightly – though, perhaps surprisingly, not below the previous low shareholder, 'Aliens of London'. However, the Sunday night repeat scored the highest viewer totals of the season to date, perhaps implying that more people had intended to watch the Saturday broadcast and had missed out due to the rescheduling.

The second half of the two-parter, 'The Doctor Dances', saw *Radio Times* again selecting the episode as its Saturday pick of the day: '... an enjoyable, even uplifting adventure ... The Doctor's way of dealing with the advancing hordes [of zombies] is as sweet as it is unexpected. It's the first of many pleasing surprises in tonight's episode ... If any watching grown-ups still can't remember why they fell in love with the show originally, this story ought to do the trick. Full of wonder and wit, it's also Christopher Eccleston's finest hour.' Steven Moffat told *Radio Times* he loved the whole notion of cliff-hangers: 'It is wonderful to build it up to that screaming pitch, and the series does – and this is a matter of absolute fact – have the best cliff-hanger music ever in the world.' John Barrowman was interviewed by the *Rainbow Network*: 'It's been great, but it's about to get much better! The thing is that I know what's going to happen, so I'm not watching it with the same baited breath that everybody else is. I know all the little secrets and storylines, but I am enjoying it; I think it's one of the better things on Saturday evening television.' 29 May's *Guardian* explored the episode and even called *Doctor Who* one of the two best series of 2005; its reviewer said that the episode: '... elevated an already great series into the realms of art ... You just don't get this sort of thing in British TV any more.' The overnight ratings for 'The Doctor Dances', released that same day, showed a further drop as the country enjoyed a bank holiday weekend and the approach of summer, although it was tempered by a rising audience share – and word that 'The Doctor Dances' was, in fact, the most watched programme of that entire Saturday, day or evening.

It was great news to cap a busy month for *Doctor Who*, but the hype was still in full swing. The week's edition of the *Stage* saw a pledge by Jane Tranter to open up early weekend evenings and bank holidays to family orientated drama following the success of *Doctor Who*. As Tranter told the magazine, the series: '... has shown there is a real appetite for part of the week being set aside for family drama ... It is clear that certain genres, such as fantasy or some real life situations, have the potential to get lots of people interested, but if you are going to appeal to an 11-year-old and a 41-year-old there has to be something in its presentation that is universal.' In the same issue, however, former Doctor Peter Davison said that his young children found the show 'too scary' and that he himself felt sorry for *Doctor Who* fans in the wake of Eccleston's departure: 'What it really needed, after all the effort and dedication of the fans over the years to get the show back on air, would be to have someone committed enough to stay with the role for two or three years. As it is, the fans must be disappointed and left feeling up in the air a bit.' The official *Doctor Who* website's Dalek game was scoring huge successes; the *Brand Republic* reported on 29 May that the game, 'The Last Dalek', had amassed 500,000 separate plays in just three weeks, with its popularity spreading around the globe. Andrew Marr, who had appeared in 'Aliens of London' and 'World War Three', was meanwhile said by *Dead Ringers* to have resigned as the BBC's political editor because he'd evolved into an uber-correspondent, and would from now on exist as a being of pure energy, reporting news from throughout the universe. And back in Canada, 809,000 viewers had seen 'Father's Day', slightly down because of the season finale of the *American Idol* programme it had gone up against, but still number two on Canadian networks and within the top four programmes for the evening on Canadian TV.

DOCTOR WHO DOWN UNDER

In anticipation of the 21 May debut of *Doctor Who* in Australia on the ABC Network, that country's press ramped up for a publicity barrage that, while nowhere near the levels of that of the UK, codified the popularity of the series there. News reports were followed by full-length promos for the series, stating '*Doctor Who* is coming to you!' with clips from the first batch of episodes.

The weekend prior to the debut, the Sunday papers were abuzz with previews of the series. The *Sydney Morning Herald* reported on 15 May that it had sent a reporter to the set while 'Dalek' was being recorded, and noted: 'Getting here, on the set to witness the much-discussed first reappearance of the Daleks, was an epic in itself, involving scores of telephone calls, e-mails and, finally, a signed confidentiality agreement.' Mark Gatiss told the *Herald*: 'For all of us who kept the torch burning all these years, including Russell, the best parlour game a *Doctor Who* fan can play is: wouldn't it be great if it came back. And suddenly it is, but you're dealing with a world of TV realities – ratings count, and it's a very different environment.' The *Herald's* television section, *The Guide*, would call the debut their 'show of the week,' noting that Davies 'overrides the cash-strapped production values of the past to make his new Doctor competitive in a high-tech market, but keeps his soul alive with such jokes as bicycle-pumped gadgetry in the TARDIS,' and announced that Tom Baker, the erstwhile fourth Doctor who had been so popular overseas, 'never had a TARDIS like this.' The *Melbourne Herald Sun* called the first episode 'OK – but the outlandish plot suffers a bit from the need to set up the initial meeting between the Doctor and Rose. But the second episode – where the Doctor takes Rose a billion years ahead in time to witness the death of Earth (to the jukebox accompaniment of the Britney Spears hit 'Toxic') – is a delight, filled with a fabulous array of weird aliens and neat techno-effects.' The Sydney *Sunday Telegraph* said that the Doctor: '... is back and he's making house calls. While a revival of the classic sci-fi series could easily have had Tom Baker choking on his scarf, it turns out that Christopher Eccleston, as the new Doctor, and Billie Piper, as his sidekick Rose, are more than adequate replacements.' The *Advertiser* ran a list of former Doctors and companions, and said: 'Gone are the creaky cardboard sets and comical special effects.' The *Sunday Age* also gave the show top marks: 'Fear not, dear viewer, there really is something more than *Desperate Housewives* on the horizon. The Doctor is back with a vengeance, a triumph of television in his ninth incarnation thanks to tight scripting, clever editing, dazzling effects and a gloriously full-blooded performance by actor Christopher Eccleston.' But it wasn't all smiles: the *Daily Telegraph*, instead of focusing on the new series, chose to criticise the *Doctor Who* Club of Australia for announcing Louise Jameson as a guest of their next Whovention convention.

By mid-week, the series was being promoted widely on radio and television as well. The *Eoin Cameron* breakfast show on 18 May ran a competition asking *Doctor Who* trivia questions on air, the prize being admittance to an advance screening of 'Rose' at the ABC studios. Phil Collinson and former *Doctor Who* companion Katy Manning were interviewed on the programme, complete with Dalek impersonators. The ABC's programme *How The Quest Was Won*, a news and lifestyle series, sent one of their reporters to visit the *Doctor Who* fan club in the western city of Perth. The radio station 612 ABC Brisbane also hosted a preview screening in conjunction with the Sir Thomas Brisbane Planetarian at Mt Coot-tha, including a discussion of the series afterward. According to the Australian Associated Press, the ABC was: '... so confident about new episodes of *Doctor Who* they have scheduled them for prime time Saturday night. The national broadcaster has bumped off the quirky machinations and breathtaking scenery of *Monarch of the Glen* and replaced it with a show best remembered for decidedly dodgy special effects. But it was a calculated decision.' The ABC's deputy programmer, Ian Taylor, told the AAP that he would be disappointed with anything less than a million viewers. 'Admittedly we're certainly a different territory with different tastes and opinions' than the UK, Taylor said, 'but I do think that [there are] enough people who are familiar with the original series and remember it fondly to at least take a peek at this. And I think too that younger viewers, be they anything from sort of 15 up, will be intrigued enough by what they read about this to have a look at one episode. Once you see one you'll be hooked and you'll be back for the rest of them.'

As the debut weekend approached, the press weighed in with its opinion of the show. 'Definitely an improvement on the old cardboard episodes of yore,' said the *Sydney Morning Herald* on 21 May. The *Courier Mail* said the series was *Doctor Who*: '... but not as we've known it ... The stories retain their inventiveness, and touches of whimsical English humour save the show from the earnestness which weighs down the better American sci-fis.' The Sydney *Daily Telegraph* said: 'Hiding behind the couch won't work any more. This is a darker, scarier *Who* that knows our old safety drills.' The *Age* called it a: '... new series that's light years ahead of its predecessors. It looks and feels great, like an intergalactic Cool Britannia cross-pollination between the cult classic of old, *Bridget Jones* and *The Goodies*.'

'Rose' debuted on Saturday 21 May and was among the weekend's top-rating shows, with 1.11 million reported viewers. Sydney's *Daily Telegraph* noted that the series: '... was first in its 7.30 pm timeslot for the ABC. It won in four of the five major capital cities, only just edged out by Channel 7's *Inspector Lynley* in Brisbane.' The second episode made a similar splash the following weekend, again making it into the nation's Top 50 programmes with 1.05 million viewers but placing higher on the weekly charts; in fact, it was ABC Television's fourth highest rated programme. The series was off to a good start in Australia, and with high ratings in Canada as well, *Doctor Who* was making an international impact.

THE BAD WOLF SCENARIO

One of the most fascinating themes seen in the first season was a continuing 'story arc' that played out through the episodes. Story arcs were nothing new to continuing drama; many American television series, like their British counterparts, had included them, and shows like *Buffy the Vampire Slayer*, *24*, and *Alias* capitalised on this approach.

'Bad Wolf' was clearly on the mind of faithful *Doctor Who* watchers as the first series moved toward its completion. What had been a minor throwaway line first heard from the Moxx of Balhoon in the second episode, was soon realised to be something underpinning the series. Later episodes showed: Rose confronted with the phrase by Gwyneth in 'The Unquiet Dead'; 'Bad Wolf' graffiti scrawled on the side of the TARDIS; and even a 'BadWolfTV' segment seen in the far future ('The Long Game'). The significance of this was confirmed when the season's penultimate episode was revealed to have the title 'Bad Wolf'.

The *Daily Star* on 16 May asked, 'Who's crying wolf? *Doctor Who* fans think they have found a hidden clue on the show about how the Time Lord will meet a nasty end.' Some of the more obvious speculation focused on whether the Daleks would be the 'bad wolf', or perhaps whether one of the adversaries from earlier in the season would return. Adam, the character played by Bruno Langley who was rather unceremoniously dumped from the TARDIS crew at the end of 'The Long Game', was rumoured to be returning toward the end of the season. (The rumours were further exacerbated when the official *Doctor Who* website editors 'accidentally' posted a web page that shouldn't have been there – the placeholder page for the season's twelfth episode – which clearly noted that Adam was returning: the page disappeared a day later, but not before fans had found it.) Another popular rumour was that the Face of Boe, a non-speaking alien character from the second episode, was the culprit; much of this had come from material contained in the BBC Books reference guide *Monsters and Villains*, in which it was noted that the Face of Boe had a secret that could be shared only with a 'homeless wandering traveller'.

Speculation on the episode was also at an all-time high, with questions ranging from how it would play out to how it might relate to a possible regeneration sequence. There were even concerns that *Doctor Who* viewers had been dealt a double-bluff, and that David Tennant would *not* appear as the tenth Doctor, that Eccleston was really staying all along. Confusing matters still further, incorrect casting information appeared on such websites as the Internet Movie Database (IMdB), a central database of television and film information submitted by members of the public. *Red Dwarf* actor Norman Lovett was said to be playing the Daleks' leader, Davros, and a fictional actor, James Melody, was apparently playing 'The Watcher', a character that had appeared in the 1981 story 'Logopolis' as a spectral image prior to the regeneration of Tom Baker's Doctor into Peter Davison's. There were even those who championed offbeat concepts – suggesting that maybe young Adam might be Dalek creator Davros himself – or that the Doctor really wasn't the Doctor ... that he was a false image, a *doppelganger*, the Bad Wolf, leaving the 'real' Doctor, the actor-in-waiting David Tennant, to take over the reins of the TARDIS from him.

But the truth stayed hidden. The official *Doctor Who* website noted that Davies had been keeping an eye on the various theories about the Bad Wolf, and no-one had yet got the right answer: 'Judging from the reactions I've had, a lot of people seem to think the Bad Wolf has already been revealed. Oh, it's the TV station. Oh, it's half a million Daleks ... I don't want to give anything away yet, but there is another revelation to come in Saturday's episode. We haven't discovered the true Bad Wolf yet.' Whether or not the average British television viewer had been paying attention was irrelevant; it was a bit of fun that loyal *Doctor Who* viewers could enjoy throughout the first year.

EARLY JUNE: 'BOOM TOWN' AND 'BAD WOLF'

As *Doctor Who* entered its final month of transmission, coverage began for the next episode, 'Boom Town'. *Radio Times* described this as 'frenetic fun' and said: 'The smile count is high and there's plenty of dramatic meat on the bones. But there's no time to develop it ... That said, it's slick, busy and, above all, great fun.' *Heat* magazine previewed the episode with a spoiler piece: 'Watch in wonder as the Doctor takes the Slitheen lady to dinner.' The *Star TV Mag* listed it as '5-star HOT': 'It's common for alarm bells to ring when plans are announced to build a nuclear power station. But the Doctor finds out this week that the proposal to build one in Cardiff is a little more controversial than most. Since it's hiding an alien plot to destroy Planet Earth, the local residents are going to be really cross.' BBC1 previewed the episode with a ten-second trailer – as had been done for the previous three episodes. This featured the Doctor and Rose and showed Margaret removing her Slitheen guise. By 4 June, the date of transmission, the *Western Mail* celebrated its success in being a part of the series: 'Tonight, Wales's national newspaper will feature in the latest instalment ... the Doctor is seen reading the paper ... [the] front-page coverage by the newspaper which tells the Doctor an alien is in town. Writer Russell T Davies said he wanted to include a copy of the newspaper in the show to prove the modern version of the cult classic is made in Wales.' Davies told the *Western Mail* that he read the paper: '... and I used it to make the show as Welsh as possible. We have had hundreds of people from Cardiff working on the programme, hosting venues, feeding the crew and appearing on camera, and when a city works that hard, I like it to try and feature as much of it as I can.' After the episode aired, the overnight ratings figures on 5 June showed a marked improvement on those for the previous couple of episodes, with 7.13 million viewers tuning in on first estimate and, as usual, *Doctor Who* first in its time slot.

There were also ruminations that weekend regarding the following episode, 'Bad Wolf' ... an adventure that, rumour had it, would see guest appearances from Trinny Woodall and Susannah Constantine of *What Not To Wear*, Anne Robinson of *The Weakest Link* and Davina McCall of *Big Brother*. The *Sun* and the *Star* both showed images of Trinny and Susannah in robot guise along with John Barrowman, an early leak of press photos from the episode. The *Sun* on 3 June covered Robinson's appearance, revealing her character name, 'Anne Droid', and including a photo of a contestant being zapped by her robot character. The same day, the *Mirror* and the *Daily Record* discussed Robinson's appearance, while *Hello!* magazine profiled the television presenter with a brief mention of her *Doctor Who* gig. The official *Doctor Who* website opened up its badwolf.org.uk spin-off site to promote the episode as well. *Radio Times* on 7 June said that the episode had 'plenty of fun poked at TV, including Jack getting a *What Not to Wear* makeover' and noted that the series: '... has a pretty good record in guest names ... Not one C-lister among them.' Said Davies to *Radio Times*, 'There is something about *Doctor Who* that opens doors.' And about Anne Robinson's star turn: 'The fact that she is killing off the contestants is a bit of a comment.'

Early the following week, on 8 June, *Heat* magazine said the episode provided: '... conclusive evidence that *Doctor Who* fan, chief writer and exec producer Russell T Davies is quite rightly behaving like a sweet-toothed kid in the world's best candy shop ... If you have hairs on the back of your neck, prepare for them to stand erect.' The *Daily Telegraph* called the episode 'proof that the writers of *Doctor Who* have really thought about what they are doing; have worked to give a real, satisfying and complex shape to Saturday-night schlock.' *Media Guardian* commented about the references to 'bad wolf' and said: 'One theory – spoiler alert! – is that the Doctor has been the unwitting star of a *Big Brother*-style reality show. Is nothing sacred? No word yet, though, on whether the climactic episode features the scariest *Doctor Who* monster yet – the Bazalgette.' (This was a reference to the name of the man whose company, Endemol, made the *Big Brother* series.) The *Daily Star* on 12 June praised 'the increasingly edible Chris Eccleston' and the idea of introducing death for losing reality TV contestants, and felt that it could liven up current schedules. 'As I'm in mourning over the end of *Doctor Who* next week, I'm taking a week off to cry over my Chris Eccleston posters ...' *Digital Spy* the same day called it an 'ace episode.' The show made the Critics' Choice in the *Financial Times*: 'It turns out that they are all to become the victims of sadistic future game shows that bear eerie similarities to contemporary shows, complete with replicant versions of Anne Robinson, Davina McCall, and Trinny and Susannah. Some will applaud this foursome for lending their voices to attacks on what they and their shows represent. Others will not.' Wrote Garry Bushell in the *People*, '*Big Brother* perked up last night ... A nice idea, but it didn't reflect the way telly is going. It was far too tame. The real *Big Brother* becomes dumber, coarser and nastier by the year.' *ITV Teletext* named it their TV Pick, while *BBC Ceefax* said: 'It's definitely bold, and you have to acknowledge that – this penultimate episode sees the Doctor trapped in the *Big Brother* house. Could go either way, couldn't it? ... Weird to think that we'll only see Eccleston one more time.' The *Guardian* opined: 'It's an interesting vision of TV in the future. You can see what Russell T Davies did to get there. He just observed what's been happening in the last few years – a huge increase in the number of channels, nastier programmes, more sinister powers behind the scenes – and he just took it a bit further.' The *Northern Echo* said that what was great about the show was: '... the way Davies and the other writers have taken the elements fans expect to see – slimy villains, incomprehensible technological talk, dodgy special effects and a sonic screwdriver – and coupled them with a crisper, cooler, more modern approach. The results have been unmissable. Rarely has a series so successfully been brought back from the dead ...' And Charlie Brooker in the *Guardian* wrote, 'Best. BBC. Family. Drama. Series. Ever.' Even though ratings for 'Bad Wolf' were ultimately down again, it still ranked highest in its time slot for the evening.

The genre magazines were full of *Doctor Who* coverage from previous weeks as well as targeted material on the forthcoming first series finale. *SFX* magazine featured an online treat in the form of a visualisation of the TARDIS interior, viewable with Quicktime, which was loaned to them by series visual consultant Bryan Hitch, who recalled: 'The simple, up front determination was that it needed to be big. Huge. From the earliest sketch I did, before I was even offered a job on the series, I was going for the big dome shape. The central section changed as we went and adapted to comments and requirements, and we were constantly reworking it in the finish.' Davies told *SFX*: 'I can't yet see us doing a hard sci-fi episode. The essence of [an early Saturday slot] is to keep it simple. Which doesn't mean dumb ... We've got to keep it strong and clean, emphasise the drama above the sci-fi.' He told the magazine that there would be a mix of traditional stories, some darker, some lighter. And speaking of the new Doctor: '[David Tennant] can do anything! And he will! This is the wonderful legacy of Chris Eccleston, he's made the part available for and desirable to our finest actors....the clothes will be different, because it'll be David's preferences.' *Doctor Who Magazine* also continued its own official coverage of the series, including continuing interviews with series actors and behind-the-scenes set reports from Benjamin Cook, who had been granted unprecedented access to the series as it developed.

In other press circles, BBC Worldwide issued notice on 2 June that it would promote the series at an upcoming Licensing International meeting in New York, possibly an effort to sell the series to America. *ITV Teletext* on 3 June asked, 'Is it time to Dai for *Doctor Who?*' in covering the day's episode set in Cardiff. The *Daily Star* the same day revealed the Daleks' return to the series in the final two episodes, while *Have I Got News For You?* on BBC1 closed its final episode of the series with a culmination of the running gag of Ian Hislop being the new Doctor as his face was morphed over a picture of Eccleston and Piper.

Radio 4's *Armando Iannucci's Charm Offensive* discussed the influence of television on teenage behaviour on 1 June, with one participant noting: 'There's no doubting that teenagers do copy what they see on TV ... There's a kid on my street ... all last week he was time-travelling and gurning!' Papers reported material from Davies's Production Notes column in *Doctor Who Magazine*, recounting that one member of the public, while trapped in his car after a crash, asked a paramedic for a mobile phone to ring his wife and get her to videotape 'Boom Town' for him. BBC1's *Points of View* on 4 June saw viewers complaining about the level of scariness in the recent two-part Steven Moffat tale, while Julie Gardner defended the series, stressing that the BBC was always careful not to show gratuitous violence or too much blood. Overseas, the *JoonAng Daily* of South Korea noted that the recent celebration of Queen Elizabeth II's birthday at the Grand Hyatt Hotel in Seoul had featured a TARDIS, which served as an entrance to the ballroom, a six-foot-tall Dalek and black-and-white footage of the series; Sue Hollands, the president of the British Association of Seoul, said in her opening address that *Doctor Who* was not only 'quintessentially British' but also 'familiar to expatriates.' The organisers of Germany's TV & Film Festival in Cologne announced that they would screen the first two episodes as part of this year's festivities in late June.

If there was any doubt that *Doctor Who* had achieved its goals to become part of the British mainstream, the *Guardian* on 8 June made it clear: 'Extraordinary at this stage of one's life to be rushing back from the coast on Saturday evening so as not to miss even the opening credits of *Doctor Who*. Not only because Russell T Davies's reinvention with Christopher Eccleston and Billie Piper is such an exhilarating (if sometimes baffling) ride, but because, while it lasts, *Doctor Who* is once again one of the rituals which make Saturday.'

ONE MORE SURPRISE...

As a season's-worth of episodes and the resultant press coverage headed for one last hurrah – the long-awaited season finale, 'The Parting of the Ways' – the production team had one final surprise up their sleeves. On 15 June, at a screening of the final episode at BAFTA, Davies and Jane Tranter surprised everyone by announcing that a *third* season of *Doctor Who* had been commissioned, along with a second Christmas special in late 2006. *The Stage* on 1 June had already noted that drama commissioning at the BBC would undergo a 'significant overhaul, with executives able to commission two or three series of popular shows at a time, in a bid to retain talent for future productions,' and it seemed appropriate that *Doctor Who* would receive the nod at such a time. The first Christmas special, meanwhile, now had a title: 'The Christmas Invasion'. And that wasn't all: Billie Piper, Tranter now said, was appearing in the entirety of the second season, quashing any doubt that she was returning to the series full time. It was also stated that John Barrowman (Jack) would be back, though not in the first block of episodes, and according to a report from *CBBC News* (later confirmed in *Doctor Who Magazine*), so would Noel Clarke (Mickey) and Camille Coduri (Jackie). Word also came through that the second series would be transmitted in 'early' 2006, and that there would be more episodes of *Doctor Who Confidential* for fans to enjoy. Davies was also said to be penning the one previously unassigned script. Davies was obviously pleased in a brief interview with *CBBC News*: 'What is most pleasing is that people have been watching this series as a family. I think a children's show should have a full range of emotions including grief and comedy.'

This followed a report earlier in the day on the BBC's official *Doctor Who* site that three directors had been assigned to the second series. Not only would James Hawes ('The Empty Child', 'The Doctor Dances') and Euros Lyn ('The End of the World', 'The Unquiet Dead') return for the second series, directing the first and second blocks of episodes respectively, but Graeme Harper would direct the third block of episodes, four in total. Harper was well known to *Doctor Who* fans as the director of the 1984 Peter Davison serial 'The Caves of Androzani', considered by many to be one of the best – if not *the* best – stories of the 'classic' series, and the 1985 Colin Baker adventure 'Revelation of the Daleks', widely considered to be the best of his tenure.

Reaction to a day of considerable good news was swift. 'To say I'm pleased by this fantastic news would be an incredible understatement,' wrote Richard Ormrod on the *Outpost Gallifrey* forum, which reported the news almost immediately after the BAFTA screening had finished. 'I'm now daring to hope *Doctor Who* will be on our screens for many years to come, but even three years of our favourite TV series is beyond my wildest expectations.' Paul Masters pointed out that the BBC 'must have an awful lot of confidence in both the show and the team.' Paul Dawson summed up the real bonus this would provide: 'On reflection, the best thing for me is that now my kids get the chance to grow up with *Doctor Who*, as I did back in the last century. That means a lot.'

Brian Robb, editor of *Dreamwatch* Magazine, explained on *Outpost Gallifrey* how the magazine's scoop about Billie Piper's career plans had been superseded in recent weeks: 'The *Dreamwatch* story was accurate: things change and she's back. I was there tonight at BAFTA and welcome the announcement that she's confirmed, along with everyone else ... We were congratulated by the *Mirror* on our "genuine, old fashioned scoop."' *Dreamwatch's* report was apparently based on information given to them directly by Piper's agent, and as Robb pointed out, negotiations behind the scenes can often change overnight.

Either way, Piper was now back for the full year, Barrowman was coming back at some point, Clarke and Coduri would return, and the series was confirmed for the foreseeable future. *Doctor Who* fans could not have asked for a better late-season gift.

IT ALL COMES DOWN TO THIS: 'THE PARTING OF THE WAYS'

As transmission of the final episode approached, the interest in *Doctor Who* – and the legacy of its heralded return to television – was unmatched since the hype of the week prior to transmission of 'Rose'. The day after the broadcast of 'Bad Wolf', the *Guardian* said that *Doctor Who* had: '... created a must-view Saturday night slot ... At a time when creative leadership in television is ... fragile and elusive ... Davies and his editors at the BBC have demonstrated that a passion for the medium, intelligently and uncynically deployed, can deliver what the contrived and compromised cannot – a big Saturday early evening audience of family viewers.' The *Guardian* opined that 'appointment viewing' was no longer an alien concept for children. 'It is a shame Christopher Eccleston signed up for only one series as it is unlikely he will encounter this quality of material to interpret many times in his career – and his audience will certainly never be more gripped and grateful, if a little scared.' *Broadcast*

Now also called the series a 'must view Saturday-night slot' that had achieved 'leading broadcast television back onto the path of righteousness.' The G8 Finance Ministers' meeting in London that weekend even had three Daleks on hand, while elsewhere, the 'kidnapping' of a Dalek – complete with ransom note – from Somerset was being reported. (The Dalek, taken from near Wookey Hole Caves, where a *Doctor Who* convention was about to take place, was later returned.)

Radio Times previewed the final episode in its weekly coverage, praising it as a: '... fantastic ending to a fantastic series ... As the Earth is plunged into a bloody war, the Doctor is forced to take drastic action. Will Rose lose her friend forever?' *Heat* magazine called it a: '... suitably stunning climax, and probably the most awesomely epic *Doctor Who* ever. BAFTAs must rain down.' *Star* magazine awarded the episode five stars, noting: 'All too soon, it's the end of the series, and Rose Tyler's friendship with the Doctor is tested when Earth plunges into all-out war ... Yikes on a bike.' *Closer* magazine said: 'As we all know, Christopher Eccleston is hanging up his TARDIS key (to be replaced by *Casanova*'s David Tennant), so prepare for a real cliff-hanger ending.' The official *Doctor Who* site posted daily trailers for the episode, short twenty-second clips counting down the days until the finale would appear, which were then screened on BBC television each weekday evening at 8pm; the site also revealed that the production team of *Doctor Who Confidential* had created a documentary called *The Ultimate Guide*, which would air prior to the season finale on 18 June. 'From a council estate to a battle in space, *Doctor Who: The Ultimate Guide*, will take us behind the scenes of the new series,' said the press release, 'to talk to cast and crew and celebrate all the triumphs and tears, smiles and trials shared between the Doctor, Rose and millions of fans, who have turned on to see a new *Who* at his alien best. *The Ultimate Guide* is just what the Doctor ordered.'

Doctor Who coverage and related press accounts this week were overwhelming. *TV & Satellite Week* ran promos for the episode in its 11-17 June edition. *Starburst* magazine featured interviews with cast members and producers, while *Cult Times* focused on the writers. The *Daily Mirror* TV magazine on 11 June featured the series on its cover, with a picture combining Anne Robinson's head with a Cyberman's body. The *Daily Star Sunday* on 12 June asked 'Who's afraid of the big bad wolf?' and said: 'There's not just one Dalek back – there's millions. And it's brilliant. But it's also the last of the series. Sniff.' The *Sunday Mail* reported that incoming Doctor David Tennant had been given an 'intergalactic seal of approval' by Tom Baker, the former *Doctor Who* star: 'I have caught a glimpse of Tennant and he has a kind of mercurial quality. I suppose it's star quality. You can believe he has secrets. I'm looking forward to David being hugely successful.' The *Big Brother* website recommended *Doctor Who*, for not-too-surprising reasons.

Christopher Eccleston continued his public role as humanitarian in voicing a new TV advert for the fight against some of the world's most deadly diseases, and even visited the television series *Top Gear* as he became their weekly 'Star in a Reasonably Priced Car', an appearance that secured nearly four million viewers, around half a million more than the series's usual performance. The car materialised on the race track starting line complete with TARDIS sound effect, and the actor completed a lap of 1'52". His recent success was rewarded with a photo cover on the University of Salford Alumni magazine; he'd completed a Foundation Degree in Drama and Theatre at the University in 1983 and been awarded an Honorary MA in 2001. Georgia Moffett, the daughter of former Doctor actor Peter Davison, spoke to the *Daily Express* on 15 June, explaining that she'd auditioned for the role of Rose and that, if the BBC needed a new companion actress now, 'I'd love to do it!' Anneke Wills, who had appeared in the series as the Doctor's companion Polly in the 1960s, was quoted by the *Mirror* on 15 June as saying that when she'd first seen Billie Piper, it had been like seeing her younger self through a time warp. John Barrowman was interviewed on GMTV on 17 June, noting that he had enjoyed his time in *Doctor Who*, especially being able to kiss both Piper *and* Eccleston. Across the pond, CBC Canada reported that the broadcasting figures for 'Boom Town' had spiked again, with three quarters of a million viewers recorded for the Tuesday night airing.

Davies wrote a piece for the *Guardian* on 12 June in which he reflected on the series to date: 'It seems to have worked, although you will not find me celebrating until after the last episode – sorry, season finale. And even then, I am not going to think too much about what worked. Beware the analysis. I went into the first series on instinct, and that's how it should stay. But I love this show as much as ever. It has not diminished as I feared it would. I can still catch a Jon Pertwee repeat on UK Gold and be happy as a Zygon. And as a writer, I have had a ball.' And Michael Grade, BBC Chairman, who had recently made public comments expressing a grudging respect for the series, now celebrated the success of the show in a speech at the Institute of Welsh Affairs in Cardiff: 'We will not dwell on the fact that I – in an earlier incarnation – took *Doctor Who* off the air. You live. You learn ... especially in Wales, you learn.' At around the same time, Davies made comments to the UK Press Association about the forthcoming Christmas special to be made as part of the next series block: 'We've got a Christmas special. Just wait until you see what we do with Santa!' Davies's comments and the success of the first series were revisited in the *Western Mail* on 15 June, when the paper asked: 'What has the new *Doctor Who* series really done for Welsh TV?' Noting that the production was the biggest network project ever to come out of BBC Wales, the paper said: 'Now, when the world of television takes a look at the pool of talent here in Wales, they will find that – like the TARDIS – it is much, much bigger than it looks from the outside.'

While the *Sun*, the *Mirror*, the *Guardian* and *The Times* all began to print photos from the episode, including images of vast Dalek armies, the BBC Press Office released its final press pack on 16 June, promoting the end of the first series and noting the confirmation of a third. 'The honest to God truth is I was shocked,' Davies said in the press statement about reactions to the first season. 'It's everything we hoped for. In January we were all sitting there hoping millions of people would watch; hoping that people would love it ... No-one's made anything like this in this country and we've pulled it off.' Davies said he thought adding David Tennant to the show: '... is like a whole new lease of life. I think one of dangers of success sometimes is that one can get too complacent. Putting David at the helm means we're all reinvigorated because we have got to be just as good, if not better, just for him. So it's actually very exciting, but at the same time scary. It's back to square one for us, so that's always a good place to be.' The next day, Davies appeared on BBC1 *Breakfast*, describing the major obstacles the series had been faced with: bringing back an old show, putting science-fiction in primetime, and the reputation of the series. 'Three big obstacles and we beat them all!' he told the hosts. 'Families are enjoying watching it together. People who think they don't like science-fiction seem to be enjoying it ... because it's funny as well. A lot of science-fiction is very sombre and military and self-possessed and self-aware, and you can have a good time watching *Doctor Who*.' Davies told *BBC News* on 17 June that Eccleston had turned around the reputation of the series. 'You have to admit that the name of the programme had become a joke and its reputation had become a cheap joke at that,' he said. 'And Chris, as one of the country's leading actors, by being willing to step up to the line and take on that part, has proved himself to be magnificent and has turned it around. So now you get actors like David Tennant who ... says he wouldn't have touched this part if Chris hadn't done it, because the part had become a joke. But Chris has salvaged it and made it new, and now we get to do one of the most famous parts of *Doctor Who* folklore – the moment when the Doctor regenerates and becomes a new person and yet stays exactly the same man.'

'And so it ends,' said the *Telegraph* on 19 June, the day after transmission. 'Another Doctor down the vortex, another Dalek invasion foiled and a mystery at least partially solved. The first series of the revived and revitalised *Doctor Who* ended last night amid Wagnerian choruses and swarms of airborne Daleks hell bent on reducing mankind to a giant, fleshy puddle. I can't imagine anyone of any age coming away feeling short-changed. For thirteen weeks, *Doctor Who* has breathed new life into that most mouldy of broadcasting concepts: family viewing.' The *Sunday Mirror* said: 'Fair's fair – that *Doctor Who* finale was flawless. But it didn't make up for the six or so ropey episodes (yes you, Slitheens) we've had to endure.' The *People* said, 'The BBC held a back-slapping BAFTA screening for last night's *Doctor Who*. Are they sure? The hit series has been fun, but it's also been flawed by feeble aliens (the Slitheen), childish fart jokes and the constant gurning of Chris Eccleston.' The *Herald* said the series: '... has had a satirical edge to it, a theme with a moral that, as with most half-decent science-fiction, has an application in the here and now. For Saturday's episode, the lesson involved a mechanical, in this case literally so, devotion to religion ... It was all done with great style, not a little wit and some authentic pathos.' The *Guardian* made the episode its Pick of the Day and said: 'In 1989, *Doctor Who* came to a close with Sylvester McCoy stumbling towards some bushes muttering about tea getting cold. In contrast, the triumphant new series's finale is nothing short of a Dalek-flavoured *Götterdämmerung* with the ultimate fate of humanity up for grabs ... Russell T Davies – thank you. Bye Chris. David Tennant – please don't screw it up.' The *Telegraph* opined that the time was right for *Doctor Who* to enter the film market, while the *Daily Star* warned that the BBC was bracing itself for 'a backlash from moral crusaders' over the kiss between the Doctor and Jack: 'This is totally inappropriate, considering *Doctor Who* goes out in the early evening and is meant to be for family viewing.' But the *Washington Blade* said of Jack, 'We should expect little less from Russell T Davies ... He's a 51st Century guy. He's just a little more flexible about who he dances with.' Saturday's episode was also promoted on radio, with appearances by *Doctor Who* Appreciation Society members on Radio 4's *Today* programme, and on BBC Radio Wales on Nicola Heyward Thomas's show and on *Good Morning Wales*.

The Sunday Times on 19 June asked: 'Why is *Doctor Who* such a success? Before it went on air, research suggested that no-one would want to watch it and that the BBC was heading for a £10 million disaster. The sci-fi series has confounded predictions by attracting seven million viewers.' The *Western Mail* quoted Davies as saying: 'At the outset, we were told by many people within the business that we were making an impossible programme. Demographic experts told us that a show designed for family viewing was unrealistic in the current TV climate. They said, "Don't aim for that." But we forged ahead, and we proved them wrong.' The *Daily Star* said that the end of the series was: 'One of the saddest moments for anyone watching telly. ... I'm sooooo glad it's ending. I can't take any more. It's simply too good. It's spoiling the rest of my telly viewing by making it rubbish in comparison. And professionally, I am running out of phrases to describe its magnificence.' The 19 June *Independent on Sunday* said that the series now being over for the year was: '... a shame, because the return of the eccentric time traveller has been a triumph for BBC Television and given many of us a much-needed "appointment to view" programme to watch on a Saturday night ... The reason *Doctor Who* was a triumph is that, for the first time for some years, we had a new (at least, it felt new) early-evening drama that could be watched by the whole family, something that many in television thought was close to impossible to achieve in the multi-channel age.' Matthew Norman's Media Diary in the *Independent* the same day said: 'The loss of Christopher Eccleston is a blow, of course (especially to those who have had the fabled pleasure of working with him), but we look forward to David Tennant in the next series.' Canada's *Globe and Mail* remarked that the country's fans would receive a second taste of the show: the series would go into reruns immediately. 'We are very happy with the numbers we got the first time when we telecast it as a hockey replacement,' CBC's programming director Slawko Klymkiw, said. 'They show how popular *Doctor Who* is and we wanted to give audiences another chance to see this fabulous, innovative series.'

'The Parting of the Ways' saw overnight ratings figures at approximately 6.1 million, which, while again down from earlier weeks, represented a massive audience share of nearly 42% and ranked first for the night. *Doctor Who*'s audience appreciation levels throughout the season had remained high, showing it as one of the most appreciated series on British television for the year, with the final episode scoring 89 (in the initial overnight appreciation index reports), against a television drama average of 78.

There was no mistaking the extraordinary popularity of the show as it ended its first series run. An annual poll conducted by Cult TV, the group running the annual Cult Television convention in the UK, revealed that *Doctor Who* had beaten *Star Trek* as the most popular cult series in the UK, ending *Star Trek*'s nine year reign at number one. *Doctor Who* wasn't just a popular series with the public; it was embraced by science fiction and television fans, and even those who had abandoned it years ago. As Ian Levine, who, as a former fan consultant to 1980s producer John Nathan-Turner, had been a detractor of the later years of the programme, remarked, 'We are phenomenally fortunate to have a series like this. British television has had nothing like this for sixteen years... [and there will be] nothing quite as good as this for a lot, lot longer.'

HERE'S TO THE FUTURE

'The Parting of the Ways' signified the end, and a new beginning, for *Doctor Who*. As Eccleston said goodbye and the smiling face of David Tennant was there to replace him, a single year became an era unto itself, and a memory, all at the same time. For many viewers and countless fans, Eccleston was the heart and soul of this new era; almost irreplaceable to some, he had brought in new viewers and had helped rejuvenate a television icon with unusual flair and humanity. Critics almost universally cheered him; fans welcomed him. *Doctor Who* would go on to a second series – or its twenty-eighth, depending on how you count – but with a change of lead actor.

The times had changed. On 20 June, Michael Grade offered his congratulations to BBC Director General Mark Thompson: 'To whoever commissioned it, those who executed it, the writers, the cast, the publicity folk that promoted it, the schedulers and of course the late Sydney Newman who invented the whole thing. I truly enjoyed it and watched it every week with my six and half year old son who is now a fan.' Elsewhere, the countdown to the next *Doctor Who* that would be televised, 'The Christmas Invasion', began with the BBC running trailers over several days immediately following the airing of 'The Parting of the Ways' ...

proof positive that the show would be back this winter for the special, so viewers should expect it (and a far cry from the events of 1989 when promises of the show's return were vague and insubstantial). To no-one's surprise, the second of the series's DVD releases debuted in a high position at number 5 on the weekly national DVD charts. New Zealanders got their wishes confirmed; the series would start for them on 7 July. 'The show promises to deliver all the excitement of good drama,' said PrimeTV in a statement, 'with a hero who never carries a gun. Fans should brace themselves for some exhilarating experiences and deadly confrontations.' Yet American fans were still in the dark. While many had seen at least part of the series due to a combination of 21st Century Internet networking and 20th Century videotape trading, most of the general US public remained blissfully unaware of the show, and so far, every report that suggested a possible sale might be imminent had turned out to be groundless. Still, there were always possibilities for the future.

As for the near future, it appeared that the show would be embracing more of its past. Reports surfaced in the *Sun* that the BBC had approached Elisabeth Sladen to reprise her *Doctor Who* role as Sarah Jane Smith, along with the robot dog K-9, for an episode in the second series. *Doctor Who Magazine* meanwhile announced a change in the script editor's office, as Simon Winstone – who had been part of Virgin's editorial team in the nineties and worked in that capacity on the acclaimed New Adventures novels – joined the production to replace the departing Elwen Rowlands. Rumours again abounded, many of them centring on David Tennant and suggesting that he might have signed on for only one season (later revealed to be a non-story, with confirmation that the BBC had in fact signed him for three years), and others surrounding the reasons (some of them financial) for the earlier uncertainty over the number of episodes Billie Piper might do for series two ... But all this was completely incidental, because the fact was, the *Doctor Who* production team was now committed to both a second and third year. New titles of second series episodes were revealed, including the peculiar 'School Reunion' and the eerie 'Army of Ghosts'. Noted thespian Stephen Fry was revealed to be possibly considering taking part in the second series, but as a writer instead of an actor. And attention turned toward true public recognition as the series, Eccleston and Piper were all nominated for the 2005 National Television Awards, with results to be announced later in the year.

It had been a spectacular year for *Doctor Who*. Once consigned to memory, a relic of a different age, it had left its wilderness years behind and was now the anchor of a new Saturday night of British television. The BBC, and the world, had taken notice of the blue police box and the enigmatic stranger that travelled within it, fighting alien nasties and setting the universe to rights, and at least two more years of his adventures were now guaranteed. And a fifteen-year interregnum was now simply one broken stone on a long path ... a science fiction series back on television – where it belonged.

Doctor Who was back.

And, hopefully, this time for good.

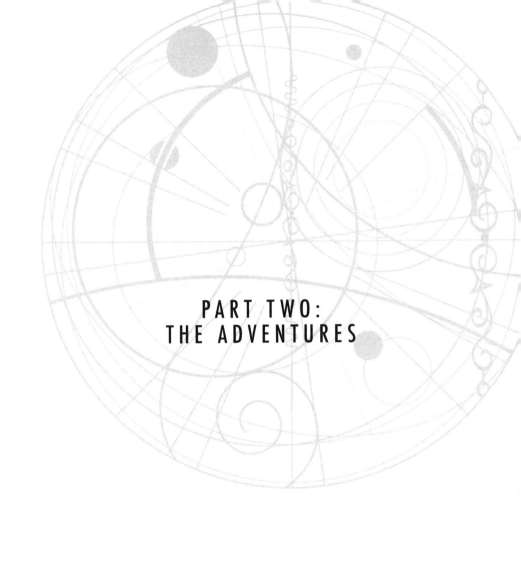

PART TWO:
THE ADVENTURES

EPISODE BY EPISODE

The following section covers the first season of the new *Doctor Who* series in depth by story, with both technical analysis and review, covering each of the thirteen episodes:

Rose	Episode 1	26 March 2005
The End of the World	Episode 2	2 April 2005
The Unquiet Dead	Episode 3	9 April 2005
Aliens of London	Episode 4	16 April 2005
World War Three	Episode 5	23 April 2005
Dalek	Episode 6	30 April 2005
The Long Game	Episode 7	7 May 2005
Father's Day	Episode 8	14 May 2005
The Empty Child	Episode 9	21 May 2005
The Doctor Dances	Episode 10	28 May 2005
Boom Town	Episode 11	4 June 2005
Bad Wolf	Episode 12	11 June 2005
The Parting of the Ways	Episode 13	18 June 2005

For the episode numbering, we have adopted the notation of 'series number' – ie '1' followed by the episode number. So 'Rose' is episode 101 and 'The Parting of the Ways' is episode 113.

Each episode is broken down into basic facts before being further explored in specific sections. Some or all of the following subsections may be used for each story:

WHERE AND WHEN: The date and fictional locations that each story is set in.

THE STORY UNFOLDS: Major plot elements and story threads revealed during the course of the episode.

THE DOCTOR AND ROSE TYLER: Information about, and developments concerning, the two main characters.

CHARACTER BUILDING: Significant information about other major characters.

BAD WOLF: The unfolding of the story arc(s), both in story as well as theme.

FANTASTIC!: The ninth Doctor's catchphrase, including where it shows up and when.

BODY COUNT: Who dies and where (a morbid curiosity, but unavoidable!)

THE DOCTOR'S MAGICAL SONIC SCREWDRIVER: Places where the Time Lord's trusty tool comes into play.

REALITY BITES: References to and connections between *Doctor Who* and the 'real' world.

LINKING THEMES: Links between the episodes.

SCENE MISSING: Unexplained events and unanswered questions, including pieces of the puzzle that the viewer must put together on his/her own.

ALTERED STATES: Items that changed at any point prior to transmission.

BEHIND THE SCENES: Clues about where each story was filmed, important factual information or developments in the production.

DULCET TONES: Details about popular music heard.

OFF THE SCREEN: Where to look out for some of the actors, directors and other important persons in other projects.

TECHNICAL GOOFS: The usual, unavoidable *faux pas* and errors made along the way.

CONTROVERSIES: Subjects of concern and debate.

INTERNAL CONSISTENCY: An analysis (contributed by Robert Franks with Matt Dale) of each episode's internal timing, as extrapolated from visual and verbal clues in the episode.

THEME ANALYSES: Our contributors' impressions of how each story rates on or against a particular theme or interest:

> *As Doctor Who for a Modern Audience* – Simon Catlow
> *As Television Drama* – Paul Hayes
> *As A Piece of Writing* – Sarah Hadley
> *The Doctor as a Mystery Figure* – Keith Topping
> *Special Themes, Genres and Modes* – Graeme Burk
> *In Style and Structure* – Cameron Mason
> *As Doctor Who Continuity* – Jon Preddle
> *From a Special Effects Viewpoint* – Scott Alan Woodard

These pieces were written shortly after each episode was first transmitted – the aim being to record contemporary reactions to the series as the drama unfolded – and so in some instances feature the writer's speculation about what might come up in later episodes (meaning that we now know, with hindsight, whether they were right or wrong!)

PANEL REVIEWS: Our nine panellists' short takes on each story. These were also written shortly after each episode was transmitted, rather than after the whole season had gone out.

EDITOR'S REVIEW: A final thought on each story.

101: ROSE

London shop girl Rose Tyler accidentally stumbles upon a deadly plot by an alien consciousness to animate plastic mannequins in an effort to take over the Earth ... and in the process, encounters a stranger with a very mysterious past who calls himself the Doctor.

FIRST TRANSMISSION: UK – 26 March 2005. Canada – 5 April 2005. Australia – 21 May 2005. New Zealand – 7 July 2005.
DURATION: 44'11"
WRITER: Russell T Davies
DIRECTOR: Keith Boak
CREDITED CAST: Christopher Eccleston (Doctor Who), Billie Piper (Rose Tyler), Camille Coduri (Jackie Tyler), Noel Clarke (Mickey Smith), Mark Benton (Clive), Elli Garnett (Caroline), Adam McCoy (Clive's Son), Alan Ruscoe (Auton), Paul Kasey (Auton), David Sant (Auton), Elizabeth Fost (Auton), Helen Otway (Auton), Nicholas Briggs (Nestene Voice)
   Autons originally created by Robert Holmes.

WHERE AND WHEN: London, present day (early 21st Century). The story takes place over two days including at Rose and Jackie Tyler's flat (in South East London), at Henrik's Department Store, at the home of Clive and his family, at Queens Arcade (a shopping centre), Tizano's Pizza, in Trafalgar Square, on the Embankment and both at, and below, the London Eye.

THE STORY UNFOLDS: The Nestene Consciousness is on Earth, attempting to take control of the planet. By using the London Eye it can transmit a signal to activate plastic mannequins, the Autons. The Nestene Consciousness needs Earth because of the toxins and dioxins in the atmosphere. Its food stock was destroyed in a war (revealed in later episodes to be the last of the Time Wars), and all its protein planets rotted, so Earth is now fair game. It can only be stopped by something the Doctor refers to as 'anti-plastic'. To help keep an Auton duplicate of Mickey stable, it keeps the human Mickey alive.
   Approaching the Consciousness to offer it the chance to leave Earth, the Doctor invokes Convention 15 of the Shadow Proclamation. The Doctor tried to save the Nestene in the war as well as many others, he claims. The Nestene discovers the existence of the TARDIS and the vial of anti-plastic that the Doctor is carrying and turns against him.
   Rose's flat appears to be in South East London. The long zoom in at the start of the episode (from orbit) is into the South East, and the Brandon Estate (where the exteriors were filmed) has an SE17 postcode; this is confirmed in 'Father's Day' which takes place nearby and is located in SE15.
   Rose eventually finds Clive's website. She doesn't believe Clive after meeting him, convinced he's a 'nutter'. Clive shows Rose photographs of the Doctor standing in the crowd at the Kennedy assassination in Dallas on 22 November 1963; of the Daniels family of Southampton 'and friend', in April 1912, the day before they were to set sail on the *Titanic* (they didn't go; Clive states 'reasons unknown' but perhaps the 'friend' in the photograph encouraged them not to take the trip); and a drawing of the Doctor that washed up on the coast of Sumatra in 1883 after the eruption of Krakatoa. When talking to Rose, Clive refers to

the Doctor as being 'your Doctor', perhaps suggesting that he believes there may be more of them.

Due to her association with the Doctor, the disembodied Auton arm latches onto Rose; Mickey throws it into the rubbish bin, but it returns to her flat through the cat-flap. (The Doctor traces the signal from the arm, arriving before it can do any damage.)

THE DOCTOR: The ninth Doctor has a Northern accent (specifically, from Salford) and wears a leather jacket. He has a new sonic screwdriver, which looks quite different from the ones used by previous incarnations. He may have recently regenerated; the implication as he looks into the mirror in the Tyler flat is that he hasn't seen his own reflection. He still travels in the TARDIS, shaped like a '1950s telephone box … it's a disguise' (or so he tells Rose). He avoids questions about where he comes from. He is also extremely alien to Rose (using her reference), forgetting at least twice that Mickey is supposedly dead. He has an odd sense of humour, drinks coffee (with milk) and reads a book in Rose's flat (or at least appears to) almost instantaneously. He fends off the amorous advances of Jackie Tyler ('There's a strange man in my bedroom!' '… No!') and talks to himself while he's alone: 'That'll never work, he's gay and she's an alien.' He tries his hand at shuffling cards, failing miserably. Although he does not make it clear to Rose, he presumably remembers the Autons from his earlier encounters with them.

ROSE TYLER: Rose is nineteen years old and lives with her mother, Jackie, in a London flat (on the Powell Estate, as we discover later in 'Aliens of London'). Her father died when she was a baby (see 'Father's Day'). She works for Henrik's Department Store in West London, and takes the bus to and from work. While at Jericho Street Junior School, she won the bronze in the under-sevens Gymnastics team. She has no A-levels. She left school to run off with someone named Jimmy Stones, and is now dating Mickey Smith. Rose's mother obviously feels she needs direction in her life (perhaps because of memories of Rose's father – though she isn't very encouraging), and wants her to claim for compensation after she is 'nearly killed' during the Henrik's explosion, even though Rose tells her she was nowhere near the blast. (Jackie claims that Rose is suffering from 'genuine shock and trauma'.) Rose is naturally incredulous at the inner size of the TARDIS but deals well with the culture shock, immediately recognising that the Doctor is an alien and that his ship is alien. She chastises the Doctor for forgetting about Mickey on two occasions. Later, she realises Mickey isn't what she needs in her life and she leaves him for the Doctor.

CHARACTER BUILDING: *Jackie Tyler* – Jackie is a single mother (who apparently works, though we don't know where) and has one daughter, Rose; the two live together in a flat in a London council estate. Jackie has a compensation-based mindset and is easily distracted by a pretty face (in this case, the Doctor's). She's easily startled and doesn't trust quickly, but obviously cares about her daughter. She is later attacked by Autons after she goes out for a late-night shopping excursion, narrowly escaping being killed at the hands of bridal mannequins.

Mickey Smith – Rose Tyler's boyfriend, a Londoner of mixed descent. He cares about her, but not enough to miss seeing a sports match on TV down at the pub. Possibly a smoker (as he wears a T-shirt with the logo of Gudang Garam, an international clove cigarette manufacturer) although we don't view it. The Autons kidnap Mickey and he's terrified, so much so that he reverts to an almost pre-adolescent state toward the end of the story. His duplicate has what appears to be slicked-down, box-trimmed hair and stutters.

BAD WOLF: There is no clear reference to 'Bad Wolf' in this episode, although Rose wears a red hooded sweat shirt which perhaps references Little Red Riding Hood? It has been suggested that the Nestene Consciousness mouths the words 'bad wolf' at one point.

FANTASTIC!: The original appearance of the phrase... the Doctor shouts 'Fantastic!' as Rose points out the London Eye and he recognises it as the Auton transmitter.

BODY COUNT: Clive is killed at the shopping mall as the Autons begin their rampage. Mickey is believed dead for a while, but he is still alive in the Nestene lair. It is not known how many people are killed in the Auton attack.

THE DOCTOR'S MAGICAL SONIC SCREWDRIVER: The Doctor uses it to short out the elevator controls at Henrik's and tracks the Auton signal to Rose's flat. He disconnects the Nestene's link to the arm in Rose's flat with it and locks the back door of Tizano's Pizza. The screwdriver is also used in the TARDIS as the Doctor connects Auton Mickey's head to the console.

REALITY BITES: Due to a technical problem during the original transmission on BBC1 there was a sound glitch, allowing a few seconds of crowd sounds and the voice of presenter Graham Norton to briefly intercede. (See Chapter 11.)

While it exists on the real Internet, *Search-wise.net* is not a real search engine website. Says the site's privacy information, 'Owned and operated by Compuhire (Eccentric Trading Company Ltd), this website has been set up for clearance purposes so that it can be used in film and TV productions when scripts require that a search engine is shown in vision.' Rose uses this website to search for the Doctor's identity; after several tries, the search words 'Doctor Blue Box' come up with Clive's website: '... do you know this man?'

The buses seen crossing the Thames in the sequence with the Doctor and Rose are night buses, which replace the regular daytime services from around midnight until six or seven in the morning. According to director Keith Boak, interviewed on *Doctor Who Confidential*, there were almost no buses coming through at the time of evening the crew was filming the sequence, obviously done at a very late hour. The production team waited until a bus came along, ready to shoot at a moment's notice. 'I'm sick of red London buses, kept getting in the back of my shot,' Eccleston noted with a smile.

The BBC's official *Doctor Who* website featured a spin-off site, 'Who Is Doctor Who?' It was inferred (and later stated outright) on there that Mickey took over the ownership of the site from Clive, who had maintained it as an online presence to find others who had encountered the Doctor. The Doctor will later ask Mickey to shut it down (by giving him a CD containing a virus; see 'World War Three').

This story is the only one of the first season not to have a pre-credits sequence. The opening descent and line 'Run for your life!' were used for the very first trailer broadcast on BBC1 in January 2005.

LINKING THEMES: The Nestene Consciousness and the Autons were created by Robert

Holmes and were first featured in the 1970 *Doctor Who* serial 'Spearhead from Space'. They returned once again in 1971 for 'Terror of the Autons'. In 'Rose', the Autons are never referred to by name, except in the closing credits.

Rose's encounter with the Autons is foreshadowed in the opening moments of the episode, as she runs into the store and the storefront is briefly seen, where several sinister-looking mannequins reside.

When Rose calls Jackie on her mobile phone at the end of the episode yet doesn't speak, her mother doesn't know she's safe. Rose's chat with Jackie as the latter was about to go out late-night shopping is likely to be the last communication between the two for an entire year, as her phone call in the next episode (from Jackie's perspective) is unlikely to have taken place after this episode occurs. (See 'The End of the World' and 'Aliens of London'.)

After Rose leaves the department store, she runs past a familiar police public call box, the first glimpse in this new series of the TARDIS. Later, she has much the same reaction as prior companions, specifically that the ship is bigger on the inside ...

The Doctor and Rose's exchange on the bank of the Thames has some very clever dialogue: 'How come you sounds like you're from the North?' countered with 'Lots of planets have a North!' and Rose's bewilderment about what a police box is ('It's a disguise!' the Doctor says cheerily).

The Doctor is credited as 'Doctor Who' in the closing credits to all the episodes of this season. This was the case on *Doctor Who* from 1963 until 1981. From the nineteenth season in 1982 until the twenty sixth season in 1989, the character was credited as 'The Doctor'. The 1996 television movie starring Paul McGann had no on-screen credit featuring the character name.

SCENE MISSING: In Rose's flat, the Doctor looks into a mirror and comments on his appearance. Is this a suggestion that perhaps he is looking upon himself for the very first time in this incarnation? As we discover later, Clive's thorough research shows this same Doctor in various other time zones. It is perhaps unlikely the Doctor would not have seen his own reflection and been amused by it if he'd been around for a while. Clive's pictures *could* be images from actions taken by the Doctor in his own future, though considering how short-lived this particular incarnation would be, these are either from gaps in between stories or simply that he's just looking in the mirror. Another possibility: the images are from a future altered in some way by the Time War, negating their existence but leaving traces behind.

When the news report states that there are no fatalities in the fire, have they not discovered the body of Wilson, the electrician, whom the Doctor states earlier has already died? (Perhaps he, too, had been replaced by an Auton body double?) Incidentally, his identity as noted on the placard is H P Wilson, CEO; possibly a coincidence, but the Prime Minister during the transmission of the first Auton story was Harold Wilson.

Why was the person in the flat across the street from Clive's house putting out a nearly-empty wheelie bin on the street in the middle of the day? There are a number of theories. Could it be that the Nestene has eaten the protein waste and recycled anything plastic, leaving the bits of cardboard seen at the bottom of the bin? Was the bin equipped with the same 'warp shunt' technology mentioned later in the episode so it could teleport items back to the Nestene base? This would address how Auton Mickey was created and sat in the car so quickly and also where the real Mickey went ... if the rubbish was 'shunted' out to leave room for it to swallow Mickey, then perhaps the sound the bin makes is that of a warp shunt as it teleports Mickey back to base and exchanges him with the copy.

Other unanswered questions: Why is Jackie Tyler blow-drying her hair when it is already dry? (Perhaps to style it, but still ...) Why does the light shining on the TARDIS in the Nestene lair magically go out as the TARDIS dematerialises? Why does the Auton's arm hover in mid air as it's reanimated in Rose's flat? And how did the Autons get the TARDIS down into the pit so quickly? How and why were the Autons in the department store at the start activated when the Nestene had not started sending its signal as yet?

ALTERED STATES: The original recording of 'Rose' included a sequence where a burning couch blew out through Henrik's windows and fell onto the street, narrowly missing Rose, but the sequence was missing from the final version.

In the pre-airing publicity, Clive and his wife were referred to as having the surname Finch. There is no evidence of this in the transmitted story. However, there is a reference to a 'Finch's' store during the brief exchange between Rose and her mother in their kitchen, suggesting the surname was either dropped from the script prior to transmission or wires had been crossed and the surname was never intended.

The copy of 'Rose' sent to prospective buyers (and leaked over the Internet three weeks before transmission) largely followed the final transmitted version, though the music used over the opening and closing credits was different; the theme in the leaked version was a spec sample by musician Mark Ayres used only until the final version was created. A segment of music played over the Doctor's and Rose's walk to the TARDIS was removed from the final version; it was, however, restored to the print for the May 2005 DVD release. (There are also minor sound effects differences in a couple of instances, and the picture cropping is slightly different on the leaked print.) Several changes were made between the two versions to the credits list; in the leaked version, Ian Grutchfield, BBC Brand Manager, receives a credit, but does not on final transmission; Noel Clarke is credited as 'Mickey' in the leaked episode, and not 'Mickey Smith' as in the final version. The following people were credited only in the final broadcast: Ron Grainer (original theme music); Holly Lumsden and Paul Kulik (Stunt Performers); Gwenllian Llwyd (Art Department Co-ordinator); Phill Shellard and Adrian Anscombe (Standby Props); Jenny Bowers (Graphic Artist); and Mike Tucker (Model Unit Supervisor). In the leaked version, Yolanda Peart-Smith (Wardrobe Supervisor) is credited as 'Assistant Costume Supervisor' (and part of her surname is spelled 'Pearl'); Lowri Thomas (Location Manager) is credited as 'Unit Manager'; there is a slight title change for Debi Griffiths and Kath Blackman ('A/Production Accountant' instead of the more explanatory 'Assistant Production Accountant'); and Andrew Smith (Construction Manager) is credited as Andy Smith. There were also two corrections made to the credits for the final transmitted version, Paul Perrott (3D VFX Artist) is changed from 'Porl Perrot' (though this credit would revert to 'Porl' for later episodes and for the DVD release of 'Rose') and Alberto Montanes (2D VFX Artist) instead of 'Alberta Montanes'. The leaked version did not feature a 'Next time ...' preview, although the broadcast version and the DVD release did.

Throughout the season, the Canadian broadcasts of each episode featured a special introduction by Christopher Eccleston following scenes from the previous episode. Canadian viewers (except those receiving HD broadcasts) saw the credits differently, as the broadcaster chose to display them as a split-screen with previews of other series on the screen at the same time.

BEHIND THE SCENES: 'Rose' was recorded in a variety of locations around Cardiff and

London. The Henrik's department store is really Howells, a large department store in Cardiff city centre, while the Henrik's basement scenes were filmed nearby in the basement of the University Hospital of Wales. Queens Arcade is a Cardiff shopping mall used in the episode. The doorway of the police station is the back door of the Toad at the Exhibition pub on Working Street, while a shoe shop near the Arcade was converted into 'Classic Brides' for the sequence with the bridal Autons. The alley where the Doctor leaves Rose and Mickey, and returns for Rose, is actually St David's Market, just behind St David's Hall in the centre of Cardiff. Clive's street is located in Grangetown, a suburb of Cardiff, and a paper mill in the same area was used for the interior scenes of the Nestene lair. The sequences in Tizano's Pizza were recorded in a real restaurant called La Fosse in The Hayes in Cardiff, while the scenes outside the restaurant were shot at the Cardiff Royal Infirmary. Although the stairwell sequences outside the Tyler flat were recorded in a council estate in Cardiff near the Gabalfa Interchange, the Brandon Estate in Southwark, London was used for most of the external recording near Rose's home. Other recording done in London included night work on the Embankment, across the Thames from the London Eye. The brief shots of Piper and Noel Clarke in the plaza at the beginning were recorded in Trafalgar Square. The TARDIS interiors, as well as the Tyler flat, were recorded in a warehouse, the Paper Mill, in Newport in Wales. Two sequences were shot well after the rest of the episode when it was determined that it was running short; these included extending the Doctor and Rose's walk to the TARDIS, and the scenes in Jackie's bedroom.

The main battle of the episode, outside Queens Arcade, was recorded overnight and ended at approximately five o'clock in the morning! The bridal Autons (used to film the breakout from Classic Brides, the final filmed sequence on the night) were played by Elizabeth Fost, Helen Otway and Holly Lumsden, while David Sant, Paul Kasey, Paul Kulik and Alan Ruscoe play primary Autons in both the street battle sequence as well as in the attack on Rose in the Henrik's basement. Lumsden and Kulik are credited as stunt performers while the others are listed in the cast.

Several types of leather jackets were considered when trying to find the Doctor's costume. Costume designer Lucinda Wright said she did not want people to wonder 'Which costume this week?' so they settled on a final version (one Eccleston says he would not have picked himself) which gave the Doctor the appearance of an 'action man'.

DULCET TONES: The incidental music for this and all subsequent episodes of the first series is composed and conducted by Murray Gold. Some of the themes in this episode (especially the cues first heard at the beginning of the story, in the montage of Rose's day at work) are heard again in later episodes. Gold rearranged the classic *Doctor Who* theme as originally composed by Ron Grainer for the series.

OFF THE SCREEN: Camille Coduri made her stage debut at a young age like her *Doctor Who* TV 'daughter' Billie Piper. After attending Kingsway Princeton College, participating in the Lyric Youth Theatre in London's West End and doing improvisational theatre, she featured in roles in *Boon* (1987 and 1991), *Campaign* (1988), *A Prayer for the Dying* (1987), *Nuns on the Run* (1990), *King Ralph* (1991), *Rumpole of the Bailey* (1992) and *Mrs Caldicot's Cabbage War* (2000) (in which she coincidentally also played the role of 'Jackie'). Coduri met her husband, Christopher Fulford, while filming *A Prayer for the Dying*. Noel Clarke is best known as Wyman Ian Norris in the BBC drama series *Auf Wiedersehen, Pet* (2002-2004); his credits include *Metrosexuality* (1999), *Judge John Deed* (2001), *Waking the Dead* (2000), *Casualty* (2001), *The Last Angel* (2002), *Doctors* (2003) and *Holby City* (2004) as well as co-writing the short film *Licks* (2002) with Geoff Carino and penning the screenplay for the 2005 film *Kidulthood*. Clarke had previously won a Laurence Olivier Award for Most Promising Newcomer for his performance in the Royal Court Theatre production of *Where Do We Live* (2002). Mark Benton has been seen in *Murphy's Law* (2001) (in the recurring role of Father McBride), *The Second Coming* (2003), *Clocking Off* (2002-3), *Micawber* (2001), *See You Friday* (1997), *Early Doors* (2003), *Breeze Block* (2002), *Swiss Tony* (2003) and in guest roles in a number of other television series; he is also probably best known in the UK for a series of adverts for the Nationwide Building Society. Nicholas Briggs has worked as a director, composer, writer and actor. On television he has appeared in *The League of Gentlemen* (2002) and *Coupling* (2004) as a Dalek Voice. He has written and acted in numerous *Doctor Who* audio drama and spin-off projects including many for Big Finish (notably their *Dalek Empire* ranges, which he wrote and directed, and their *Judge Dredd* range), BBV and Reeltime Pictures. He is the presenter and interviewer for Reeltime Pictures's *Myth Makers* series of interview productions. Elli Garnett was in *Casualty* (2003) and *Doctors* (2001) and the TV-movie *A Likeness in Stone* (2000). Adam McCoy played Josh McLoughlin in *Brookside* (2000-1) and appeared in *Holby City* (2004). Alan Ruscoe played roles in *Star Wars: Episode I – The Phantom Menace* (1999) and *Star Wars: Episode II – Attack of the Clones* (2002) and also appeared in *The Fifth Element* (1997). Director Keith Boak previously directed on *Holby City* (2004), *Mersey Beat* (2001), *Harbour Lights* (1999), *The Knock* (2000), *Sunburn* (1999), *Wokenwell* (1997), *NY-LON* (2004), *Out of the Blue* (1995), *The Royal* (2003) and *City Central* (1998); Russell T Davies later told *Doctor Who Magazine* that Boak: '... directed one of my first ever paid scripts, a 5-minute piece for the BBC's *Def 2* slot.'

TECHNICAL GOOFS: The opening pan heads from space toward Britain from over the coast of North America, down into Rose's flat, at which time it is 7.30am; this is impossible as it would not be light over the Atlantic at this time. Though the department store is called 'Henrik's', the BBC news report seen in the episode refers to it as 'Henricks'. The BBC News clock says 20.45 when beginning the report, then several minutes later in the story, it reads the same time. While Jackie is being attacked by the bridal Autons, we see all three Autons' hands dropping, revealing their guns. A later shot of Jackie being threatened shows only two hands have dropped; the third Auton hand drops at that point as well. A microphone can be seen in the shot after the Nestene identifies the TARDIS. The clock on the mantle in the Tyler flat changes time from the evening of the first day (when it is clearly 8.45) to the next morning (when it reads 9.05), however the second hand never appears to move, suggesting that the clock is broken. The plastic tentacles that capture Mickey seem to switch hands; he turns around so that the bin is behind him, but nothing's tangled. The telephone number on the 'For Sale' sign near Clive's home is 0207 946000, one fewer digit than required for a London phone number. There's a clear shot of estate agents Fletcher Morgan's telephone number – a Cardiff number – when Rose watches the explosion at the department store. The final Auton attack supposedly takes place on a busy London street, but the location used was a pedestrianised area, and this is clearly visible in some shots – there are no road markings and a bus stop sign appears to sit in the middle of the 'road'.

CONTROVERSIES: The wheelie bin's mysterious burp, a moment apparently aimed at the younger audience, caused concern among some fans upon transmission, as did the minor parallels between Clive the conspiracy theorist webmaster and online *Doctor Who* fans.

INTERNAL CONSISTENCY: *The Date:* A definitive date for this episode is given in episode four, 'Aliens of London', which notes that Rose disappeared on 6 March 2005; the Doctor's arrival and subsequent solution to the Auton problem at Henrik's (and his first meeting with Rose) takes place the night before, 5 March 2005. (The date is noted on the missing persons notices posted at Rose's flat.)

However ... even though this definitive date is seen on screen, there is an alternative view. There is enough evidence in the episode to identify a different day, starting with the fact that 5 March 2005 was not a Wednesday (it was a Saturday); the next episode, 'The End of the World', shows us that the first day must be a Wednesday (since when Rose calls her, Jackie is wearing the same clothing and is seen obviously prior to her encounter with the Autons; also, the second day cannot be Sunday because of her late-night shopping excursion).

The presence of the London Eye means that the episode must be set at some point after January 2000, while Mickey's tax disc suggests a time period between April 2004 and March 2005. The presence of a 2004/5 Transport for London logo on a black cab also suggests either of these years. The lottery money, which the security guard seems to have collected from the staff at Henrik's Department Store for a syndicate before passing to Rose, suggests either a Wednesday or a Saturday setting for day one of the episode. A sports match starts late in the day that Mickey wants to watch at 7.30 pm (at 8.45, he hopes to catch the last 10 minutes). This could be any type of match, however. Clive mentions spending 'Summer money in winter months', suggesting a non-summer setting ... unless, of course, they're budgeting ahead. But it's most likely autumn or spring. Sale signs at Henrik's that are definitely *not* for pre- or post-Christmas sales suggest a non-winter setting, as does the lack of a Christmas tree in Trafalgar Square. Sunshine combined with Mickey's jacket also suggests spring or autumn. (It's bright but breezy throughout all daytime scenes.) Clive's son is off school, suggesting the possibility of a school holiday, which would support either an August or Easter setting. All this does not fit in with the 6 March date.

On the other hand, Henrik's Department Store's opening hours are most likely around 9 am to 7 pm, as would be normal for West End London. Assuming day one is not a Sunday, which would have shorter hours, we know the sun sets shortly after closing; it's dusk when Rose tries to leave, and pitch black when Henrik's explodes. Due to the oddities of British Summer time, there's only a 7.05 pm sunset in late summer. Rose and Mickey go to a restaurant in the early evening and it's pitch black outside, suggesting a non-summer setting. In the scenes that follow, Rose and the Doctor *do* end up at Big Ben at 10.30 pm, but this is after a TARDIS trip controlled (or at least guided) by a melting Auton head, which could have jolted them forward a few hours.

Taking place prior to March 2005 due to the tax disc, an Autumn assumption because of the sunset, suggests that 2004 is a better option. This is a distinct possibility: London's 2012 Olympic bid banners were put up in 2004, and the Search-Wise website is copyrighted 2004. (The copy of *The Lovely Bones* seen in Rose's flat was published earlier.)

Day two *might* be a weekend ... but has late night shopping available, which is usually mid-week in the UK. It also has a rubbish collection, as noted by the fact that Clive's neighbour wheels out the rubbish bin; this also rarely occurs on the weekend. The Routemaster buses seen, meanwhile, were mostly decommissioned in August 2004, although some seem to have been kept on the streets and may still be in use.

Given that the rubbish collection guides one toward a weekday and the lottery money collection toward Wednesday in particular, the nearest Wednesday that year to a 7.05 pm sunset is 18 August 2004, with a 7.12 pm sunset. It's likely Rose doesn't try leaving until a few minutes after the shop closing time, anyway (normally staff would leave later than this). Additionally, as we discover in 'The End of the World', the phone call Rose makes to her mother takes place on Wednesday from Jackie's point of view, and this is clearly a Jackie who hasn't yet experienced the encounter with the Autons; she still hasn't spoken to her daughter after she was attacked (Rose phones her, then hangs up and goes with the Doctor) and she mentions lottery money, which leads us to believe that this is actually during the same day and Rose is still technically at work before her first brush with the Doctor.

Therefore, day one of this episode, the day the Doctor meets Rose for the first time in Henrik's Department Store, must actually be Wednesday 18 August 2004, and not Saturday 5 March 2005 as the fourth episode suggests.

For the sake of completeness, it should be noted that Clive's website – the version fans can visit online via the official *Doctor Who* website, that is – features mocked-up security camera photos dating day two to 26 May 2005.

Timing: It's easy to pinpoint when the latest *Doctor Who* adventure begins – at 7.30 am on a Wednesday (see 'The Date', above). Rose is up and off to work at Henrik's department store, along with meeting her boyfriend for lunch. Most department stores like this would close around 7 pm; which is backed up by the fact that it is close to sunset when Rose almost leaves, and very dark when she eventually does leave the building some ten minutes later. After her brief encounter with the Doctor, Rose is at home watching a news report at 8.45 pm (there is some doubt over this as the time doesn't update on the television, but this might have been some technical fault at the broadcasters). Mickey leaves the apartment by 9 pm and let's hope Rose is off to sleep soon as she's going to need a good rest, as we'll see. Day two of 'Rose' starts off at 7.30 am again, and by the time the Doctor arrives at Rose and Jackie's flat it is 9.05 am. This is immediately followed by the walk/chat about aliens and the Earth spinning, which means that Rose probably arrives at Mickey's apartment no later than 10 am to use his computer. If we assume that she immediately e-mails Clive and that the two of them exchange e-mails throughout the day then we can guess that she and Mickey drive to Clive's house at about 6 to 6.30 pm that evening. This scene shows a lot of long shadows (so either early morning or early evening), and as we will see it will be dark again within an hour and a half. Rose spends no more than half an hour with Clive, and then she and Auton Mickey are off to dinner by 7 pm. Although the restaurant is very empty for this time of night, it is unlikely that Auton Mickey would delay long before trying to get information from Rose. Again, it is dark outside when the Doctor and Rose enter the TARDIS. There seems to be some time lost when the TARDIS moves, so perhaps it moves slightly through time on this trip as well. The Doctor and Rose arrive at the Thames/London Eye at approximately 10.30 that evening (as seen on the Westminster Tower clock), although some night buses appear to be running early. If the shops in this area stay open till 11 pm on a Thursday night then everything fits, and after the Nestene Consciousness is defeated, Rose runs into the TARDIS no later than 11 pm.

Note that while Russell Davies's 'Production Notes' column in *Doctor Who Magazine* gives his tongue-in-cheek theory that an 'invasion of the time-altering Zagbots' was the cause for missing time between the restaurant scenes and the confrontation with the Nestene, there is no on-screen evidence for this and no reason to believe that the TARDIS didn't simply jump in time when it moved.

THEME ANALYSES

As Doctor Who For A Modern Audience: Russell T Davies has always been upfront about his intent to produce 'a full-blooded drama which embraces the *Doctor Who* heritage, at the same time as introducing the character to a modern audience,' and 'Rose' is certainly a very positive start. The fundamental concept of the Doctor as a mysterious adventurer in space and time is retained, but introduced gradually, reinforcing his status as an enigma but also letting the revelation resonate when Rose's very ordinary life takes an unexpected turn because of him. The presentation is key to the modernisation, as the contemporary alien invasion plot is very traditional (something the choice of monster accentuates) but the way it's shown through Rose is much more intriguing. The original series preferred strong plotting above characterisation, whereas the reverse is true for 'Rose'. The frenetic pace of the episode is the biggest concession to the demands of modern television, which leaves little room for depth in the plot. Davies's script compensates with a blend of humour and action (with time even for an archetypal corridor chase!) which when combined with the glossy production values makes the episode an energetic and entertaining ride. In terms of substance, 'Rose' treads familiar ground with the essential contemporising coming through the way the drama is presented. As 'Rose' is, effectively, a pilot episode, this approach works – this time – but to create a *Doctor Who* series that the modern audience will appreciate consistently, the stories will need to develop a little more weight whilst building upon the strong character foundations secured here.

As Television Drama: 'Rose' is a fascinating clash of the familiar and the different. The comedy-drama depiction of council estate life could almost come straight from the pen of Davies's great friend and contemporary Paul Abbott and his *Shameless* series on Channel 4, and Murray Gold's score – particularly in the early scenes – contains echoes of his own work on that show. London is there in all its familiar glory, although this is perhaps a more self-aware, deliberately iconic depiction of the city than in other shows, one that's all the more impressive for having been shot mostly in Cardiff with only a few days on location in London. Another link to contemporary drama is the presence of the seemingly ubiquitous Mark Benton – does British television drama have a 'Benton quota' the channels are required to fulfil these days? He's as excellent as ever, albeit playing the stock 'Mark Benton character' that he seems to portray in just about every role he does. If that's the familiar, however, then the different is very different – a home-grown fantasy-based series in BBC1 family prime-time for the first time since the flawed *Randall & Hopkirk (Deceased)* revival ended in 2001. Christopher Eccleston is a delightful surprise as he shakes off the perceived image that he can do only 'miserable Northerner' roles, a reputation built up with a decade of work in acclaimed series such as *Cracker* and *Our Friends in the North*, although this weighty dramatic background does bring kudos to his casting. All in all, it's a blast of fresh air amongst the rest of the BBC's drama output, and an extremely welcome one.

As A Piece of Writing: 'Rose' is so quick-fire, and so full of wonderful, quotable dialogue, it takes a couple of viewings to realise the plot is nearly non-existent. *Doctor Who* has never, and should never be about technical explanations, but that doesn't excuse the Nestene Consciousness's scheme being so thin. Why does it take Mickey hostage, and why only him?

Why does plastic Mickey act the way he does? And how does the Consciousness learn to speak English in time for one line? The obvious goal is to familiarise us with the Doctor and Rose above all else, and for the first episode, that's enough – but things are going to have to improve quickly. More immediately, two clever writing tactics are already starting to emerge. First off, Davies is sharp enough to understand that living dummies, hungry trash bins and a headless plastic boyfriend are going to be scary to kids, but won't hold adults for long; by covering these moments with humour, he gives grown-ups their entertainment and some kids, at least, a bit of reassurance. Secondly, the use of partial backstory is notable (and explains the Nestene language barrier). Davies is clearly setting us up for a plot arc, and a long mystery to boot. What is this War, and how did it so affect the Doctor? My brain has just one answer: Daleks. But we'll just have to wait and see ...

The Doctor As A Mystery Figure: 'The Doctor is never cruel or cowardly,' writer Terrance Dicks famously noted, concluding that the Doctor is always a hero. 'That much hasn't changed and it never will.' Yet the Doctor also remains a figure of mystery. This central paradox is one of the main reasons why such an enigmatic creation continues to exert a powerful influence across the generations. In Christopher Eccleston's first few moments as the Doctor, we see all the required elements; energy, wisdom and pithy humour. To say that 'Rose' is 'just like *Doctor Who*' might be stating the obvious, but that was my immediate impression.

Themes, Genres and Modes: 'Rose' has something previous revamps of the series (on TV and online) have not had: humour. I don't think in the wildest dream of many fanboys or fangirls would there be a scene in a *Doctor Who* revival like the one where the Doctor has to fend off an Auton arm while Rose blithely makes coffee. That's not to say there aren't strong elements of horror and drama in 'Rose' as well. In some respects, the script bears a strong resemblance to season sixteen stories like 'The Stones of Blood' in how it deftly moves between the comedic and the scary. But, at the end of the day Davies has remembered something many fans have forgotten over the years: *Doctor Who* is, at heart, a comedy where everything is treated with utter seriousness and yet nothing is taken truly seriously. And with that masterstroke, *Doctor Who* has become a force to be reckoned with once more.

In Style and Structure: In order to reintroduce *Doctor Who* to an audience, Davies has gone back to how the series first introduced the Doctor, and that is through the eyes of other characters. However, in 'Rose', Davies has kept the story focused entirely around Rose and her ordinary life. The Doctor's role becomes larger only as Rose consciously chooses to become more involved with the Doctor; he offers her the excitement and unpredictability her own life currently doesn't have. This pushes the Nestene invasion aspect of the plot into the background until Rose's story intersects, but there are enough clues spread throughout the episode for viewers to construct a basic plot line of the events leading up the Doctor meeting Rose, and his actions when Rose isn't around. Apart from the opening montage sequence highlighting aspects of Rose's life, there's a higher level of energy and pacing in scenes involving the Doctor, which is a deliberate contrast to scenes that focus on Rose's life. While the story is very much self contained, there are many hints and references throughout to an ongoing story line involving many alien species in a war, a war so big that humanity doesn't even see it take place. As the series progresses, future episodes will most likely expand on this point, possibly even showing part of this war. In terms of story style and structure, 'Rose' does everything right to gain the initial attention of an audience, and then to keep them interested until the conclusion of the episode.

As Doctor Who Continuity: Unlike in the earlier 'reimagining' of *Doctor Who* in the 1996 TV movie, there were only a few winks to the past in 'Rose'. In fact, I had to think hard afterwards as to what continuity elements there were! The Autons (although not named as such in dialogue) had previously appeared in 'Spearhead from Space' (1970) and 'Terror of the Autons' (1971). Davies wisely avoided addressing the UNIT years' dating issues by not even mentioning the fact that the Doctor had encountered them before, let alone in which decade. During Clive's exposition scene, we see references to past – or future? – adventures with the ninth Doctor in Dallas 1963 (a lovely in-joke referring to the transmission date of the series's first episode), on Krakatoa in 1883 (mentioned also in 'Inferno,' 1970) and in England when the *Titanic* set out on its maiden voyage in 1912. (And was the cat-flap joke a reference to 'Survival' (1989), perhaps?) As for the TARDIS, gone are the white walls and static set of the old days, and in comes the impressive high-tech but now organic look of the 1996 TV movie. We even get the acronym Time And Relative Dimension In Space, with 'Dimension' once again in the singular, as in the 'classic' series's earliest seasons. The sonic screwdriver has also been given an upgrade. The Doctor's origins as an alien and a Time Lord are only alluded to; I suspect more will be revealed over the next twelve weeks – there is certainly no need to alienate new viewers by dumping it all in our laps on the first night.

From A Special Effects Viewpoint: When we first met the Nestene Consciousness back in 1970, it appeared as little more than a bin bag smeared with petroleum jelly, thrashing about behind a pane of glass. In that story, 'Spearhead from Space', we had a new face in the TARDIS, homicidal showroom dummies and a new female companion ... Hmm, sound familiar? Thirty-five years on and the Nestene Consciousness has returned, only this time, the high-tech world of CGI (thanks to the Oscar-winning team from The Mill) has brought forth an impressive amorphous, fiery blob of frenetic, animated goo. And as for the Nestene's servants (the Autons), while the originals were genuinely creepy in their own way, the technical limitations of the time (and that dreaded thing called 'budget') reduced animated showroom dummies to stuntmen donning fairly simple rubber masks and boiler suits. In 'Rose', the latest make-up techniques have allowed for full torso sculpted suits and superbly detailed masks. These are mobile, living mannequins, and these are the mindless, synthetic threats that the late Robert Holmes surely must have envisioned when he penned his original script back in 1969. As our first glimpse into the new, higher-budget world of *Doctor Who*, the Autons and the Nestene Consciousness are impressive indeed!

PANEL REVIEWS

Doctor Who is back! Rather like the title sequence for the series, 'Rose' evokes and freely accesses the old while at the same time it does something new. The result is just good, old fashioned fun. That Davies has been able to distil everything that's needed to introduce the *Doctor Who* concept and the character of the Doctor into the first six minutes is, frankly, a staggering feat. And it's these six minutes that drive the rest of the story, which makes it even more impressive. Like 1963's opening episode, 'An Unearthly Child', 'Rose' is about an ordinary person who gets caught up in a mystery and finds something extraordinary. While all Barbara Wright discovered was the TARDIS, Rose Tyler gets a primer on *Doctor Who* itself:

monsters, danger, death and a scary, mad, eccentric hero. This focus on Rose pushes the whys and wherefores of the Doctor into backstory, which maddens some fans but makes the mythology just that much more intriguing. Likewise while there are old monsters in 'Rose', the story isn't about them. They're used more as shorthand for what an iconic *Doctor Who* monster should be like. And with things already going to hell in a handcart, the Doctor is in the thick of things, a fully-fledged hero from the first second we see him. That's a brilliant piece of writing that gets the audience on side immediately. The pairing of Eccleston and Piper is the best thing about the story. Christopher Eccleston has the same childlike charm yet alien gravitas that made Tom Baker so well loved. But Billie Piper is the biggest revelation of 'Rose'. Her portrayal seems down-to-earth and honest. 'Rose' is not about how the Doctor takes Rose Tyler away from her dull life but rather how she realises that there is more to life than what she has. By the end of 'Rose' we have no doubt of that. Rose is confident without being arrogant, and vulnerable without being weak. While Keith Boak's direction seems indifferent at best, sloppy at worst, Davies's script features sparkling, witty dialogue and some really funny jokes. In the end, what we have is *Doctor Who* that the general viewing public might love. And surprise, surprise, they do! – *Graeme Burk*

'Rose' is both a good introduction and re-introduction to the world of *Doctor Who* as Davies wisely opts for a basic approach, focusing on a girl whose life is about to be transformed through an encounter with the mysterious and whirlwind-like Doctor, who will sweep her up into a maelstrom of adventure and danger. Davies's script deliberately underplays the menace of the Auton invasion, as establishing Rose and the Doctor is more important than the threat itself, and by presenting the consequences from her perspective it gives the drama a more personal and involving feel. This episode succeeds brilliantly in establishing an exhilarating mixture of wit and thrills, which is so much fun to watch. Although Christopher Eccleston's Doctor lurks in the background early on, he is a commanding presence, with his ability to flip between jovial and serious in a heartbeat making him tremendously endearing. Billie Piper is equally impressive, her compassionate performance as Rose contrasting with Eccleston's purposeful Doctor, demonstrating the qualities these two characters can offer each other. The stunning chemistry between the two leads is one of the reasons why the drama is so engaging and compulsive. Although the insubstantial plot could have been better, which is something also true of one or two of the special effects, in the context of 'Rose' these concerns matter little as ultimately the episode's intrinsic charm wins out. It's truly wonderful to see *Doctor Who* revived and redefined in such vivacious style. – *Simon Catlow*

My Time Lord sense is tingling ... or is that just the chills running up and down my spine? After nine years it is refreshing to know that down inside I can still be this excited about *Doctor Who*. The first episode doesn't disappoint in that respect as there are plenty of moments for us to point to in the years to come and say, 'See why this is one of the best series around'. However, there are plenty of drawbacks, too. 'Rose' in many ways is a very typical pilot episode for contemporary television. It accomplishes its main task of introducing the two main characters and the overall concepts of the series. After that the plot sort of falls off – what exactly is 'anti-plastic' anyway? It feels like we've been dropped in mid-way through Episode 3 of a classic series story. Everything moves so quickly that hopefully the audience won't notice that the other two and a half episodes are missing, and with them the Nestene's plan, the Doctor's involvement and exactly why a plastic creature needs to kill all the humans and take over the world. The one other thing to distract the viewer is the two new stars of the series. Christopher Eccleston is a seasoned actor, but Billie Piper is a huge surprise. We are lucky to have her first major acting job be *Doctor Who* as she seemingly effortlessly brings the character of Rose to life. We were warned that there might be more than just friendship between this Doctor/companion team and this whole episode just feels like their first date. It'll be interesting to see this 'romance' blossom. – *Robert Franks*

It's back – and this time, I think it's going to succeed. 'Rose' is good in many ways: two wonderful lead actors, memorable dialogue, a better budget than ever before. It's great, however, because it barely resembles the old show at all. Previous eras of the show denoted themselves by changing the style of *Doctor Who* without altering its traditional format. The McCoy years, for instance, might seem like a totally different show to a Pertwee fan, but both eras boil down to the same base framework. 'Rose' takes the opposite approach; the format is new, and the dramatic emphasis has shifted, but the style of the thing – the fun and adventure, the unique sense of humour – is completely familiar, straight out of the early Graham Williams-produced era, or even a lighter Philip Hinchcliffe-produced story. Similarly, Christopher Eccleston's Doctor is a wonderful, familiar creation, blending the best of what's come before, but the surprise treat is Billie Piper's Rose, who actually feels like a real human being caught up in the Doctor's world. Davies definitely seems to know what he's doing in almost every regard – although I am disappointed he killed Clive, a far more interesting guy than Mickey. And that brings up a good point: there are a few things I don't like about 'Rose', certainly, but most of them can be explained by the fact that first episodes are always a bit shaky. There is marvellous potential here, and I can't wait for next week. – *Sarah Hadley*

It's hard to describe just what a delight 'Rose' is to watch – funny, very quotable but exciting and very different all at the same time. The whole thing is a real joy for me. Yes, there are problems – the plot is neither the greatest nor the most complex the series has ever come up with, but to criticise that would be to miss the point. In this establishing episode, the Nestene threat exists merely as a framework to hang the meeting of the Doctor and Rose upon, and it achieves this admirably. The Doctor is charismatic, funny, intelligent, heroic and mysterious all at the same time – one minute messing up an attempt to shuffle a pack of cards, then later dropping dark hints about 'the War' in his confrontation with the Nestene. One of the original ideas suggested for the character's origins way back in 1963 was that he was a shell-shocked survivor of a 'Galactic War' tens of thousands of years in the future, and although this idea was never developed on screen, it's a nice piece of symmetry. Billie Piper is terrific too as Rose, although perhaps her 'mockney' accent takes a little getting used to. Altogether though this is great fun, terrifically involving and a fantastic kick-start to the new series. – *Paul Hayes*

Sixteen years is a long time to wait for a new series of *Doctor Who*, and Davies has gone for the right elements in order to attract an audience. We get an immediate alien threat to modern day Earth, and most importantly, the threat can turn the ordinary into the deadly. Bringing back the Nestenes was an inspired choice as monster, and the sequences involving Autons on the attack are exciting and memorable. Billie Piper makes an impressive debut as Rose, giving an engaging performance. Christopher Eccleston is brilliant, his Doctor is energetic and witty, yet displays a serious side. Rose is at the centre of the story, and her journey from her ordinary life to choosing a life of excitement with the Doctor is the main focal point. Camille Coduri puts in a lively performance as Rose's mother, Jackie, making the character rather self-centred. Noel Clarke is interesting as Mickey, showing the character's comic potential while offering clues as to how the character could become more serious. Mark Benton is very serious and likeable as Clive, a role that was potentially open to being played up outrageously. 'Rose' is a superb start to 'the trip of a lifetime', establishing an exciting new era of the series. – *Cameron Mason*

'Fantastic!' We've waited fifteen years for new *Doctor Who*, and the BBC has delivered the goods! 'Rose' was an excellent reintroduction to the series. Though by no means perfect (more on this later), we got what was promised – *Doctor Who* for the new millennium. Christopher Eccleston made an indelible impression as the ninth Doctor. I still can't get out of my head his 'What?' / 'What is it?' / 'Fantastic!' confusion surrounding the London Eye, or his singular response of 'No' to Jackie Tyler's 'advances'. Many other Eccle-isms (to coin a phrase) spring to mind. Eccleston said at the start that he saw the Doctor as someone who cares about people and loves life. And this showed in his performance. I was a bit unsure about him when he was cast, but I had faith in Davies and the BBC to get it right, and from this one episode alone I knew they were on the ball. Billie Piper was also a delightful surprise, making Rose instantly likeable, gutsy and not afraid to speak her mind. The producers spoke of the chemistry between Eccleston and Piper, and this was readily apparent from their performances. This relationship is something I shall enjoy watching develop over the next twelve weeks. A couple of things grated however. The burping wheelie bin was a bit OTT. And at times the incidental music was too intrusive and swamped out the dialogue, especially in the first scenes with the Doctor and Rose in Henrik's, and again during the final confrontation between the Doctor and the Consciousness. And why kill off Clive? He was such an interesting character; I would rather have seen more of him than the bland Mickey Smith. It's been a long wait, but *Doctor Who* is back! – *Jon Preddle*

'Rose' is a fine episode, full of Davies's trademark strengths of humour and characterisation. The opening moments are 'London' and 'now', exactly as the beginnings of '100,000 BC' and 'Spearhead from Space' were. When Eccleston states 'Lots of planets have a North', and 'That won't last – he's gay and she's an alien', you're hearing lines that today's eight-year olds will be quoting out loud in twenty years time, just as my generation casually remembers dialogue from 'Pyramids of Mars' or 'Inferno'. The effects are smart, the Autons are scary and Billie is terrific. (I think they were clever not turning her into an outright Buffy-clone, but giving her a sweet vulnerability alongside the martial arts moves.) Some minor aesthetics aside – a couple of the supporting cast seem not to have read the brochure – 'Rose' is, frankly, a huge relief. He's back, and it really is about time. – *Keith Topping*

Take a dash of '100,000 BC' (a story told, almost exclusively, from outside the Doctor's world, looking in), a pinch of 'Spearhead From Space' (the Nestene Consciousness and the marauding Autons) and a splash of the 1996 TV movie (quite a few similarities, actually). Bake for forty-five minutes, and *voila*, you get 'Rose'. This is not to say that there isn't plenty of original and truly magical material here, but there are definite links to these stories that cannot be denied. 'Rose' is a well-produced re-introduction to *Doctor Who* that succeeds in numerous ways. All the elements are there: the Doctor himself, the TARDIS, monsters and the threat of alien conquest, and all this is presented to us through the eyes of a fresh-faced, nineteen year old Earth girl. Unlike any previous story in the series's long history, however, we (and Rose) blunder into the Doctor's world in the midst of one of his adventures. There's no set-up, there's no hint of what is to come, in fact the monsters (the Autons) actually reveal themselves less than five minutes into the story! And this makes it clear that we're in for quite an exciting ride! As Davies has himself stated about the new series: 'We want it to be everything the old series was with a big wad of 2005 shoved into it ...' I couldn't have put it better myself. Bring on episode two! – *Scott Alan Woodard*

EDITOR'S REVIEW: The single most important problem I had when facing writing *Back To The Vortex* was in knowing that *Doctor Who* for 2005 – a tried and tested formula in the hands of an untried and untested production crew – could turn out to be a disaster. Consequently, 26 March 2005 could fly by, and I could hate it ... It would be a nightmare continuing writing about something I didn't enjoy. You can therefore imagine my excitement and relief when I fell in love with 'Rose' ... my worries now a thing of the past, here was the *Doctor Who* I wanted and remembered and cherished.

It didn't happen straight away, of course ... I wasn't sure what to make of 'Rose' on my first viewing. Perhaps it was the pacing I wasn't used to; this was like no *Doctor Who* ever seen or produced before, a drama series with Hollywood charisma and British sensibilities. There was a mayhem apparent in its opening moments, with a blast of synth-pop running roughshod over sped-up film as Rose Tyler jumps off a bus. The creepiness afforded a few minutes later, in Rose's first, terrifying glimpse of the Autons, moved the episode away from the flash-bang toward the sublime, and for once, it began to feel like what one might expect of the legacy that this would represent. Yet perhaps it was on my second viewing that it felt more familiar, more like it always had been ... and therein lay the defining moment for me, which was after Christopher Eccleston's cry of 'Fantastic' followed by the two heroes joining hands as they ran over Westminster Bridge toward their destiny. It was at that moment that this *Doctor Who* fan, so far unaffected by this new incarnation, fell in love with the series all over again ... that moment of fearlessness, of fun and the spirit of adventure, racing toward danger without regret, all the while understanding the risks involved.

Eccleston makes a definitive first impression in his opening scenes, taking charge of the situation immediately (in fact *being* in charge of the situation before we even see him) and leading Rose out of Henrik's. He is strangely enigmatic, alternating between his vacuous, almost childlike nature when he and Rose go on their walk to the TARDIS (the look on his face after he waves and says 'Hello!' is priceless), and the grim, serious, almost angry expression seen as he turns and leaves Rose behind, bidding her to forget him. In this first episode, I found Eccleston's performance to be up to par, but it now seems almost muted compared to later appearances ...

Billie Piper, on the other hand, is no doubt this series's greatest surprise. From the scepticism and general concern that arose when she was first cast, Piper has transcended any thoughts that she might have been cast for stunt value: Rose is realistic and genuine, expressing a pathos matched by her worldly innocence and her cunning street smarts. After only one episode, I can say unequivocally that Billie Piper is my favourite thing about the new *Doctor Who*, and I'm delighted that she will be returning for its second year.

'Rose' is by no means perfect, but it is almost impossibly strong as both a pilot and a restoration, told completely from the angle of the supporting character. There are secrets everywhere and plot threads left dangling intentionally – what is this horrible war we've heard of? Where are the rest of the Doctor's people? They're never irritating, but rather they captivate us into wanting to know more of the story. Meanwhile, as far as adventures go, this brief and largely inconsequential encounter, pitting the Doctor against an old adversary who can be defeated by nothing more than Rose's gymnastics moves, is nothing but harmless fun. We have no doubt in our minds that the Doctor will save the day, but at the same time, we aren't quite sure that everything is what it seems by the end of the episode.

There are many ways that Davies could have reinvented *Doctor Who* for a modern audience: with a time-honoured link to the past (as Philip Segal did, mostly successfully, in the 1996 *Doctor Who* movie – which also drew on 'Spearhead from Space', albeit different bits of it, for inspiration, making that surely one of the most influential 'classic' stories of all), with a complete break with established continuity, or with any of a myriad forms of storytelling. 'Rose' doesn't choose the grandiose; it aims to tell a simple story to reintroduce us to an old friend we may not know as well as we'd like, meet a new friend who offers something special, and thrust forward boldly in the spirit of high adventure. What a glorious way to start a new era. – *Shaun Lyon*

102: THE END OF THE WORLD

The Doctor takes Rose to see the end of the Earth, five billion years in her future on the orbital observation station Platform One. But what is supposed to be a tranquil and artistic affair soon turns deadly, as a swarm of mechanical spiders overtakes the station ... and one of its honoured guests plans a lethal surprise.

FIRST TRANSMISSION: UK – 2 April 2005. Canada – 12 April 2005. Australia – 28 May 2005. New Zealand – 14 July 2005.
DURATION: 44'45"
WRITER: Russell T Davies
DIRECTOR: Euros Lyn
CREDITED CAST: Christopher Eccleston (Doctor Who), Billie Piper (Rose Tyler), Simon Day (Steward), Yasmin Bannerman (Jabe), Jimmy Vee (Moxx of Balhoon), Zoë Wanamaker (Cassandra), Camille Coduri (Jackie Tyler), Beccy Armory (Raffalo), Sara Stewart (Computer Voice), Silas Carson (Alien Voices)

WHERE AND WHEN: Platform One, orbiting Earth in the year 5.5/apple/26, approximately the year Five Billion AD, the day the sun expands, an event that heralds the end of the world. There is a sequence in Jackie Tyler's flat in London, at around the time Rose left her in 'Rose'. Also, there's a final sequence set in London at some point around the time Rose left.

The Doctor's first trip forward lands them in the early 22nd Century, 100 years in Rose's future ('That's a bit boring, though,' the Doctor says). The TARDIS then arrives ten thousand years in the future, 12,005, in the New Roman Empire, but they don't stay. The Doctor finally transports them to Platform One in the far future. Neither of these earlier arrival points is seen in the episode.

THE STORY UNFOLDS: The orbital Platform One automated observatory, the 'height of the Alpha Class', is owned by the Corporation, which moves it from one system to another to observe artistic events. It functions as an observation platform and hospitality centre for the wealthy. The station forbids the use of weapons, teleportation and religion. (Teleportation is specifically forbidden under Peace Treaty 5.4/cup/16, which may also be a date.) Its main hall is called the Manchester Suite and the station is a 'maximum hospitality zone'. The Doctor notes that the claims about it sound like it's 'unsinkable', a half-hearted reference to the *Titanic*. It is protected by gravity shields and sun shields that keep out the harsh light, heat and stresses, and can repair itself automatically.

Earth has been protected from destruction by the National Trust, including shifting its continents back into their 'classic' positions (in other words, the way 21st Century humans knew them). Earth is currently uninhabited. Gravity satellites orbit the planet. 'Earthdeath' will take place at the announced time of 15.39, thirty minutes after the start of the welcoming party in the Manchester Suite (see 'Internal Consistency and Timing' below).

Among the guests at the Earthdeath event are: Trees, tree-people from the Forest of Cheem, notably Jabe, Lute and Coffa; the Moxx of Balhoon; the Adherents of the Repeated Meme from Financial Family Seven; the brothers Hop Pyleen who invented hyposlip travel systems;

227

Cal 'Spark Plug'; Mr and Mrs Pakoo; and the ambassadors from the City-State of Binding Light. The sponsor of the main event is the Face of Boe, an alien head in a large transparent container, from the Silver Devastation; and the special guest is the last human, the Lady Cassandra O'Brien Dot Delta Seventeen.

Jabe says she's at the event out of 'respect for the Earth'; also it's a case of having to be seen at the right occasions. The Trees have roots everywhere and there's always money in land, but Jabe's people respect the Earth as her ancestors were transplanted from Earth's tropical rainforests.

Gifts are exchanged between guests; Jabe offers a gift to the Doctor of a cutting from her grandfather, a small tree-plant. The Doctor, not anticipating the exchange, offers her 'air from my lungs'. He does the same for the Moxx of Balhoon, who offers as his gift his bodily fluids (spitting on Rose), and to the Adherents, who in return offer 'a gift of peace in all good faith', small silver orbs. Cassandra's gifts include the last ostrich egg (she confuses the ostrich with the legend of the dragons, and possibly with her third husband) and a large classic 1950s Wurlitzer jukebox (which she believes to be an Apple iPod).

The TARDIS is parked in private gallery 15, where the Doctor receives a valet ticket that says 'Have a nice day'. The ship has a telepathic field that gets inside one's brain and translates for the occupant (not all of the aliens speak English, as he tells Rose) – and perhaps alters their consciousness to adjust visual communication as well (as all the writing, including the valet ticket, is in English). The TARDIS shakes violently while in flight.

Platform One is invaded by spiders, four-legged metallic creatures with a central red-laser eye and claw-like appendages, measuring not more than a foot across. They emerge from the metal orbs given as gifts by the Adherents. The Doctor recognises the Adherents as remote-controlled androids and shuts them down, revealing Cassandra as the real culprit; she had hoped to create a hostage situation, including herself, as the compensation would have been enormous. ('Five billion years and it still comes down to money,' comments the Doctor.) She has shares in her fellow observers' rival companies and has a secret teleporter to get away. The Doctor brings her back by reversing the teleportation unit (which was hidden in the ostrich egg).

THE DOCTOR: The Doctor is the last of his kind; we discover in this episode that he is the only Time Lord left after some great calamity. The Trees know of his people; Jabe is startled to discover he is alive when she scans him, believing his existence impossible. Jabe is sympathetic to him, telling him that she has discovered his secret; she knows where he is from and she's sorry (in response to which, he sheds a tear). He uses a wallet containing a paper that is 'slightly psychic', which enables him to get whoever he shows it to, to see whatever he wants them to see; he uses this to save time with the Steward by presenting his and Rose's credentials. He claims that he doesn't generally carry any money. He allows Cassandra to die after returning her to Platform One and accusing her of murdering others; Rose asks him to help her but he refuses. Later, when returning Rose to the present day, he admits the truth about his people's destruction to her. His home planet (Gallifrey, though not named in the story) was involved in a war that resulted in his people's destruction. He is now the last of the Time Lords, the only survivor.

ROSE TYLER: Rose's initially positive reaction toward going forward in time in the TARDIS eventually gives way to culture shock as she is confronted by so many aliens and the destruction of her homeworld. Noting how alien the aliens are, the Doctor says he's glad he didn't take her to the deep South (presumably in America). She loves chips and would rather die than undergo plastic surgery, especially the number of operations Cassandra has had. The Doctor makes adjustments to her mobile phone so that she can make calls through time, which she then does to call her mother and thus assuage her feelings of alienation and homesickness. She mourns the fact that no-one was looking as the Earth died; they were busy dealing with the catastrophe on the station. But she feels somewhat better when the Doctor returns her to her own time.

CHARACTER BUILDING: *Jabe* – As she is a creature in tune with nature, the 'sound of metal' makes no sense to her. She asks if Rose is the Doctor's wife, partner, concubine and/or prostitute. (Rose tells the Doctor and Jabe to 'go pollinate'.) Identifying the Doctor by use of an organic, hand-held device, she discovers the truth about his origins and his current predicament, and empathises with his pain. She can use liana as whips, keeping them concealed and using them only when necessary. Jabe is accompanied by Lute and Coffa, who mourn her when she dies saving the Doctor's life.

Cassandra – Has endured 708 operations (number 709 is scheduled for the following week; she's having her blood bleached) and has become a disembodied sheath of skin with a face, suspended in a metal frame with her brain contained in a jar of liquid below. Cassandra used to be male; as a boy she lived with her family in a house on one side of the Los Angeles crevasse. She doesn't look 'a day over two-thousand', which means she could be that old or considerably more. She believes herself to be the last 'pure' human; as humanity has colonised the universe, touching every star in the sky (or so people say), it has 'mingled' with other races, and the 'new humans' and 'proto-humans' and 'digi-humans' and 'humanish' she calls mongrels. Her father was a Texan, her mother was from the Arctic Desert; they were born on Earth and were the last to be buried in its soil. She says she is here to honour them and to say goodbye, but her true motivations are somewhat different. She is accompanied by two surgeon-like attendants in white who moisturise her with spray wands. Rose compares her to Michael Jackson and calls her a 'bitchy trampoline'.

The Steward – A large, blue-skinned humanoid who is the caretaker of Platform One; only he and his staff are on board, the rest is controlled by the computer (or the 'metalmind', as Jabe calls it). He has previously worked on Platforms One, Three, Six and Fifteen, all without incident. His servitors are also blue skinned but all of diminutive size. The Steward's servants need permission to speak. He dies as a result of Cassandra's sabotage.

Raffalo – A 'plumber' who dies ignominiously when she enters a maintenance duct at junction 19 to fix the hot water in the Face of Boe's suite and happens upon the spiders. Raffalo and, presumably, her colleagues, are from Crispallion, part of the Jagget Brocade, affiliated to the Scarlet Junction, complex 56.

The Moxx of Balhoon – A diminutive, pudgy blue alien from the solicitors Jolco and Jolco, the Moxx sits in his own mobile travel disc. He dies when one of the sunbeams hits him after the Platform's shields fail.

BAD WOLF: During the reception in the Manchester Suite, after the Steward's death, the Moxx of Balhoon mentions to the Face of Boe that this is the 'Bad Wolf scenario'. Also, following up on the 'Little Red Riding Hood' theory from 'Rose', Jackie is doing the laundry when Rose phones her, and makes a comment that Rose's red top is falling apart.

FANTASTIC!: Jabe tells the Doctor that Platform One is fully automated, and if they get into trouble then there's no one around to help them. The Doctor comments, 'Fantastic,' rather dejectedly. Jabe wonders why that's so fantastic ...

BODY COUNT: Jabe sacrifices her life for the Doctor to allow him to stop the station from being destroyed. The Steward and Raffalo are both killed by the spiders, who deactivate the sun filters in the Steward's office and pull Raffalo into the ducting (although we don't know what they do to her there). The Moxx of Balhoon is vaporised by a sunbeam cracking through the outer hull. Cassandra is killed when the heat causes her to dry out ... her stretched face exploding under the increased tension. However maybe she didn't die, as her brain was in the glass container beneath her flawless face ...

THE DOCTOR'S MAGICAL SONIC SCREWDRIVER: It allows the Doctor to access Platform One's systems to open and close viewing panels, unlock doors and connect to the computer on five occasions. It also opens an access panel in the Engine Room and fails at various settings to deactivate a spider (which Jabe then captures for the Doctor).

REALITY BITES: The National Trust is presumably a far-future version of the same organisation that exists today: the National Trust for Places of Historic Interest or Natural Beauty in England, Wales and Northern Ireland. Founded in 1895 by three Victorian philanthropists, the Trust is a guardian for the nation in the acquisition and protection of threatened coastline, countryside and buildings. More information is available at www.nationaltrust.org.uk.

In the street at the end of the episode, a vendor is selling copies of *The Big Issue*, a 'news and current events magazine written by professional journalists and sold on the streets by vendors looking to overcome the crises surrounding homelessness.'

The Doctor asks Rose to stay in the room where the sun shields are failing. 'Where am I going to go?' she asks, 'Ipswich?' – a reference to the English town ... and more specifically, to Davies's series *Dark Season*, in which the same line was uttered by Kate Winslet's character Veet.

Although not seen closely in the story (though images were available on the BBC website), the rendering of Jabe's scanning device by designer Matthew Savage features a DNA sampler that detects nine separate DNA strands in its analysis of the Doctor, one for each of his nine incarnations. The Manchester Suite also features display cases that include Earth artefacts such as the Magna Carta and a first edition of *Harry Potter and the Philosopher's Stone*. Again, these were not seen in the episode and their presence was revealed by the presenters of BBC's *Blue Peter* who were reporting from the set.

LINKING THEMES: The Doctor mentions the war that destroyed his home planet. This is possibly the same war that destroyed the Nestene Consciousness's homeworld (see 'Rose').

While this episode features the final annihilation of the planet Earth, it is not the first *Doctor Who* story to do so; see 'As *Doctor Who* Continuity' below.

Rose's phone call home obviously takes place – from Jackie's perspective – on the first day of 'Rose'; Jackie says it's Wednesday during the call.

The Doctor notes that he 'came first in jiggery-pokery', a comment which is very reminiscent of his boasts in earlier incarnations that he is a master of everything.

SCENE MISSING: Is the Doctor aware of Cassandra's complicity all the time? The Doctor's face, when Cassandra starts presenting her gifts, suddenly switches to a 'something's wrong' look. From that moment on, the Doctor might suspect that Cassandra is up to something, he just doesn't know what that something is until the engine trouble begins and he discovers the spider sabotage; it's therefore really no surprise when he identifies Cassandra as the culprit once there's an action of which to accuse her. His ease of discovering what's inside the ostrich egg goes along with this theory.

Cassandra notes that her father was a Texan; however, given that it's five billion years from now, would Texas still exist? Or a classic jukebox? Also, Cassandra's plot to hold her fellow passengers hostage – when she is also on the doomed space platform – is never made completely clear. To whom was Cassandra speaking as she was teleported back to Platform One?

Why does no-one hear the spiders' constant clacking as they walk? Their infiltration of Platform One's systems notwithstanding, it seems very improbable that the touch of one button in the Steward's office would allow the sunfilter to come down and kill him, especially since it is of vital importance to the well-being of the station's passengers. And why did the Steward look directly into the sunlight as he was about to die? (Rose does the same thing later.) Why did the crackling exoglass not immediately shatter outward under the pressure of the station's atmosphere?

BEHIND THE SCENES: Much of this episode was recorded inside the Welsh National Temple of Peace and Health in Cathays Park, Cardiff. Opened in 1938, the Temple of Peace was a gift from Lord David Davies of Llandinam (Montgomeryshire) to the Welsh people; he wanted the Temple to be a 'memorial to those gallant men from all nations who gave their lives in the war that was to end war.' The Temple's marble-faced Main Hall was used as the audience chamber on Platform One; the production team built the 'window' in one end of the Main Hall, draping green screen for CGI work on one side. The interior design was duplicated in-studio for the smaller observation room where the Doctor and Rose talk, and where Rose is later trapped. The corridor ducts that the Doctor and Jabe use to access the station's systems are really the ducts at BBC Wales Broadcasting House in Cardiff; location manager Clive Evans found them while scouting for sets. The ventilation chamber was created only partially in-studio, with the doorway, the opposing wall segment and the catwalk that connects them being the only real sets; CGI was used to recreate the large chamber and fans (with a wind machine used to simulate the ventilation). The closing scenes were recorded in November in downtown Cardiff on Queen Street; there is a Welsh dragon visible (albeit only slightly) in the background.

Various aspects of this story are fleshed out in Justin Richards's factual book *Monsters and Villains* (BBC, 2005), to which Davies contributed several pieces of background information. According to that text, the ostrich became extinct in 2051. Cassandra is said to have been born as Brian Edward Cobbs, and the book gives her a back-story; it also does the same for the Moxx of Balhoon and the Face of Boe, including noting that legend says that the Face of Boe holds one final secret, and that he will speak this secret, with his final breath, to one person and one person alone. (The person is not named but the implication is that this is the Doctor.) Jabe's full name is given as the Treeform Jabe Ceth Ceth Jafe. Some of the honorifics spoken by the Steward (which were cut from the transmission) would have given the full name of Cal 'Spark Plug' MacNannovich and his entourage, the Brothers Hop Pyleen from the exalted clifftops of Rex Vox Jax, and the previously-unidentified chosen scholars of Class Fifty-Five from the University of Rago Rago Five Six Rago.

Cassandra's dialogue was performed during recording by actress Clare Cage; Wanamaker later recorded her dialogue separately and it was dubbed onto the final episode. Cassandra was a digital creation by The Mill, superimposing the face (and sometimes the rest of the skin) onto a metal frame in the shot.

The episode originally ran short on time, so the sequences with Rose and Raffalo were written and recorded much later on, in February 2005, and edited into the story. At the time the bulk of the episode had been recorded and Beccy Armory was not in the cast. The sequence featuring Jackie Tyler was shot separately, several weeks prior to the rest of the episode during the recording of 'Rose'; Camille Coduri wears the same clothing as in her first appearance in that episode. *Doctor Who Magazine* confirmed that the sequence was directed by Euros Lyn and the similarities are due to detailed continuity observation.

Original sketches for Jabe included bark-like skin, possibly based on an oak or an ash, but she was eventually modelled on a silver birch, which is why she has smooth and shiny skin. The Moxx of Balhoon was originally to be a CGI creation, possibly 'a bowl of blue fat' hovering around the room, but this was changed; he was played by a dwarf actor, Jimmy Vee, in a prosthetic mask/body suit. His travel cart was pulled across the floor on wires.

Doctor Who Confidential revealed that the sequence with the Doctor stepping through the fan blades was reshot, perhaps to give it a more ethereal or mystical air than in the original sequence.

There were rumours that this story suffered from a lack of dwarf actors to take the roles of the Steward's subordinates; these rumours made the news circuit some months after recording on the story was complete. The dwarf aliens are predominantly children in this episode, and were all uncredited; they included Elliott Truman, Brian Conway, Dan Allen, Billy Mcleary, James Price, Thomas Drewson, Jake Rees, Darius Huntley, Alex Francis, Stefan Stone, Jack Thomas and Matthew Rawcliffe.

DULCET TONES: 'Tainted Love' by Soft Cell – The band's first commercial single (following an EP and a limited edition 7"), backed with 'Where Did Our Love Go', was released in the UK on 7" vinyl in July 1981 and reached number 1 in August (with a 12" version coming out shortly after), later becoming that year's best-selling single. It featured on Soft Cell's first album 'Non Stop Erotic Cabaret' (LP/Cassette) in December 1981, which reached number 5 in the UK charts, and the track has appeared on almost every Soft Cell reissue and compilation album ever since. 'Tainted Love' was released in Australia in 1981, backed with 'Where Did Our Love Go' as in the UK, and similarly in the USA in May 1982, reaching number 8 in the US charts. Cassandra plays this to demonstrate her 'iPod'. (Heard at 9.58-11.01)

'Toxic' by Britney Spears – Her fifteenth single, and the second from the 'In The Zone' album, was released in January 2004 and reached number 1 in twenty-two countries. The album itself had been released in November 2003, and had already reached number 13 in the UK charts, number 1 in America and number 10 in Australia. Cassandra plays this track as the world ends. The opening three instances of the main riff have been edited out. (Heard at 28.19-29.06)

Cassandra's 'iPod' – the jukebox – carries 7" vinyl disc copies of these 'classic ballads'. 'Toxic' is in fact not currently available on general release as a 7" vinyl (just as DJ-only white-label promos), only as a 12". Of course, it is feasible that at some point in the future it will be released on this format. Cassandra quotes the song lyrics 'Burn, Baby, Burn', referring to the song 'Disco Inferno' by the Trammps (or possibly a recent-ish single by Ash).

OFF THE SCREEN: Zoë Wanamaker has an extensive resume on stage, in film and on television, but is perhaps best known to genre fans for her portrayal of Quidditch coach Madame Hooch in the film *Harry Potter and the Philosopher's Stone* (2001) (aka *Harry Potter and the Sorcerer's Stone* in North America), as Clarice Groan in the adaptation of Mervyn Peake's *Gormenghast* (2000), and as Clemmy in the acclaimed BBC ecological thriller *Edge of Darkness* (1985). She's also been seen in *My Family* (2000-5), *Prime Suspect* (1995), *Love Hurts* (1992-4), *Memento Mori* (1992), *The Tragedy of Richard III* (1983), *David Copperfield* (1999), *Othello* (1990) and *Marple: A Murder Is Announced* (2005). Simon Day – who is not the Simon Day of *The Fast Show*, with whom he is often confused – was in *Churchill: The Hollywood Years* (2004) and played first officer Randy Navarro in the *Red Dwarf* episode 'Holoship' (1992). Yasmin Bannerman played Blue McCormack in *Mersey Beat* (2002) and also appeared in *Red Dwarf* (as the ground controller in 'Back In The Red: Part 3,' 1999), as Jessica in *Cold Feet* (2000), in the series *Holby City* (2002) and *In Deep* (2002), and in the films *Maybe Baby* (2000) and *Killing Me Softly* (2002). Sara Stewart, here only in voiceover, has appeared in the series *NCS Manhunt* (2001), *Rebus* (2000-1), *Monarch of the Glen* (2003), *Supply and Demand* (1998) and *Drop the Dead Donkey* (1990), and in the films *The Winslow Boy* (1999), *London Voodoo* (2004) and *Batman Begins* (2005). Beccy Armory appeared as Martine in *Family* (2003) and as Lara in *Harry and Cosh* (1999). Silas Carson has been seen in all three recent *Star Wars* prequels as Jedi master Ki-Adi-Mundi and Trade Federation Viceroy Nute Gunray, and has been seen on television in *Jeremiah* (1998), *Metrosexuality* (1999), *Waking the Dead* (2004), *The Bill* (1999), *Lie With Me* (2004), *The Grid* (2004) and *Always and Everyone* (1999). Native Welsh director Euros Lyn's previous directing credits include *Pam Fi Duw?* (1997), *Sunday Stories* (1997), *Belonging Ill* (2002), *Cutting It* (2004) and *Casualty*.

TECHNICAL GOOFS: The placement of the control switch to restore Platform One's shields is incredibly inopportune; why is it on the far end of a long catwalk suspended directly under ventilation fans? More importantly, why is the catwalk placed so close to the top of the ventilation shaft so that passage is practically impassable when the fans are running? Why does the Doctor take his time getting across, especially when Jabe later burns to her death?

Although the temperature in the air shaft is supposed to be high enough for Jabe to burn, and that in the Manchester Suite sufficiently high for Cassandra to dry out quickly, the Doctor and Rose never sweat, and none of the other guests seems to be bothered by the heat. (Fans of the original *Doctor Who* novels will no doubt point out that it is established there that Time Lords, unlike humans, do not sweat.) Rose's hairstyle changes during the sequence where she discusses being the last human with Cassandra; long-shots are in one style, close-ups in another.

Jackie's flat appears to have shrubs outside her kitchen window, however, being up at least four storeys, it's very unlikely that the trees would have grown that high.

As the room Rose is trapped in is scorched, the level of the burning is above her head in close-up shots but at shoulder level in wide shots.

CONTROVERSIES: The Doctor's stone-hearted steadfastness in allowing Cassandra to die is quite unlike how he might be expected to react. Also of concern to some fans has been the apparently new explanation for the Earth's destruction, contradicting earlier stories (see 'As *Doctor Who* Continuity' below).

INTERNAL CONSISTENCY: This episode takes place immediately after 'Rose,' so for Rose it is very late evening (as the other adventure ended at about 11pm her time). The Doctor and Rose are onboard Platform One for approximately ten minutes before the Steward announces that it is thirty minutes to Earthdeath. The other computer announcements are as follows:

- Earthdeath in 25 minutes; this is 4'46" after the Steward's announcement: timing is off.
- Earthdeath in 20 minutes; this is 2'32" after the last announcement, and they both occur during the same scene (leading up to Rose's phone call): timing is way off.
- Earthdeath in 15 minutes; this is 4'38" after the last announcement: timing is off.
- Earthdeath in 10 minutes; this is 5'53" after the last announcement: timing is off.
- Earthdeath in 5 minutes; this is 2'33" after the last announcement: timing is off.
- Earthdeath in 2 minutes; this is 3'33" after the last announcement: timing is off.
- Earthdeath countdown ends; this is 26'54" since the Steward announced 30" until Earthdeath, so overall the timings are pretty close, but not perfect.

Since Earthdeath is a partially natural phenomenon, it is possible that Platform One's computer is updating to allow for new information, hence the time anomalies. Accounting for 16 seconds close to Earthdeath, where time slows down, Rose spends just over 40 minutes in the year 5.5/apple/26, making this possibly one of the shortest complete adventures (individual episodes and sequences within 'The Keys of Marinus' (1964), 'The Chase' (1965) and 'The Daleks' Master Plan' (1965/6) notwithstanding) of *Doctor Who*, and one of the very few stories shown almost in real time.

THEME ANALYSES

As *Doctor Who* For A Modern Audience: 'The End Of The World' provides another variation on a time-honoured *Doctor Who* plot, this time isolating a group of strangers in a confined environment with the threat coming from the machinations of one within. This idea is cultivated into a script with wide appeal through again using Rose as the viewer's way into the drama, with her perspective of seeing a gaggle of bizarre alien beings perhaps reflecting that of the modern mainstream audience. But it's the considered moments of introspection that make the episode most memorable, such as the Doctor's shedding of a single tear for his lost race or Rose's overwhelmed reaction to the aliens as the sound of Soft Cell's 'Tainted Love' plays in the background. That is typical of Davies's script, which is awash with pop culture references that help make the science fiction scenario of the destruction of Earth more accessible by taking wry digs at contemporary issues; and because of the context they are delivered in, they work very successfully. The way Davies handles Rose's reaction to time travel, considering her actions in leaving her life behind for an uncertain future with a total stranger, also helps to define her as not your typical companion. She seems much more believable, and these foundations make scenes like the closing one here as effective as it is. It is perhaps surprising that Rose slips so easily into the 'damsel in distress' routine at one point here, needing the Doctor to save her from the sunburn of death, when much effort has been put into moving away from the generic idea of a companion's role. At least the situation allows for some suitably ironic dialogue from the Doctor in recognising this.

As Television Drama: Plainly and simply, there is absolutely nothing else even remotely like this being made for British television, nor has there been for some time. Jed Mercurio's *Invasion: Earth* (1998) was the last drama series to present a prime time BBC1 audience with out-and-out alien creatures, but even that was rather more in the *Quatermass* 'they come to us' tradition. For a drama with aliens in outer space on the BBC, you pretty much have to go all the way back to the original run of *Doctor Who* itself. Thus 'The End of the World' is quite a culture shock for a generation of television viewers unused to seeing anything like this performed with British accents, with the contrast to regular UK drama perhaps heightened by the inclusion in the cast of such a familiar voice – if not face, on this occasion! – as that of Zoë Wanamaker. It's certainly brave of the BBC to have put this up as a flagship Saturday evening show, given that similar sci-fi of American origin has been effectively banished to minority slots ever since Jonathan Powell decided that *Star Trek: The Next Generation* wasn't good enough for BBC1 in the late 1980s. Whatever misgivings there might be about presenting the general audience with something so ... well ... alien so early in the new series's run, it's a joy to see something so very different being made by the BBC, and almost certainly something no other broadcaster in the UK would have even considered making in the current television climate.

As A Piece of Writing: The writing is 'for real' this week, instead of a bunch of funny one-liners without a plot, but it seems clunky all the same. Many elements seem borrowed from other sources, such as *The Hitchhiker's Guide to the Galaxy, Dune, Star Wars* and the *Indiana Jones* series. Even the Moxx and Cassandra are reminiscent of an earlier *Who* villain, Sil. Nods of this kind can be fun, sure, but nothing feels cohesive; the story only really gels during a few set-pieces between the Doctor and Rose at the beginning and end, and between the Doctor and Jabe toward the middle. More worryingly, Davies makes some points about intolerance that are about as subtle as a sledgehammer (an unfortunate trait of some of his other work), indicating it is something humans are unusually capable of: first Rose, and then Lady Cassandra, discriminate against others. He suggests that the other races may have grown beyond such petty concerns. Why, then, does he allow the Doctor to be so callous? The death of Cassandra is disturbing enough, but the Doctor's refusal to save her is worse. More damning still is his earlier quip to the alien delegates, some of whom are about to fry alive: 'You lot – just chill!' Yes, Davies is trying to tell us the Doctor has been hardened by death, but without an earlier point of reference to his compassion, I'm not sure the new audience will grasp this. His attitude toward Mickey last week was snarky and alien; now he just seems needlessly cruel.

The Doctor As A Mystery Figure: Ah, *Doctor Who and the Spiders from Mars*! 'Imagine the impossible', the Doctor tells Rose near the start of this exhilarating ride into the future. Your actual *proper Doctor Who*, this is – an enclosed environment with a sense of danger and excitement, mystery and wonder. I *love* 'The End of the World' – once it hit stride, after a strangely low-key TARDIS sequence, it *sang*. There's a classic menagerie of weird and outrageous alien species. Rose's pointed discussion with the Doctor on his lack of humanity is given a breathtaking context when the Doctor and Jabe reveal Gallifrey's demise. Then, in a self-sacrifice moment worthy of the Doctor himself, a life is given for the greater good. A tree dies to bring you this salvation, ladies and gentlemen.

Themes, Genres and Modes: 'The End of the World' enters mostly untested ground in *Doctor Who* and gives us a good-old fashioned romance. While there isn't any kissing – God forbid that happen in *Doctor Who!* – many of the conventions are adhered to nonetheless. Romances are often about people finding themselves, or finding a missing piece of themselves, through someone else, and then facing adversity that leads either to bitter or to sweet ends. 'The End of the World' gives us both. The Doctor's relationship with Jabe is flirtatious in ways we've never seen our hero engage in before, and in that one scene where she says she knows who he is and how sorry she is, the Doctor regains a part of his identity he was avoiding. It's beautiful but ultimately doomed. On the other hand, we have Rose, who has a total crush on the Doctor – watch the way she looks at him as they walk for chips at the end of the episode if you don't believe me – and who is overwhelmed by the danger life with the Doctor brings, and yet finds something awesome in it. And the Doctor finds something in Rose he is missing, which makes his admission of being a Time Lord at the end of the episode all the more powerful.

In Style and Structure: The story of 'The End of The World' unfolds virtually in real time, with the major aspect of the plot playing out over a period of thirty minutes for the characters. Telling a murder mystery style story in this format exposes how simple and straightforward the genre can be. The mystery is set up very quickly and leads into a greater threat of Platform One facing destruction, before a simple tweak with the sonic screwdriver leads the Doctor straight to the villain of the piece. The villain escapes, only to be brought to justice by the Doctor after Platform One is made safe once more. There's much character development and exploration of Rose and the Doctor throughout the episode; Rose's dealing with culture shock (culminating with a phone call home to her mother), the Doctor's interactions with Jabe, and the heart to heart between the Doctor and Rose in the final scene. As with 'Rose', the pace of the episode is fast, but the character scenes give the story some breathing space and allow for the audience to connect with the characters. The 'Time War' plot is touched upon once more, as how it has affected the Doctor is revealed. 'The End of the World' takes the opportunity to add depth to the Doctor and Rose without too much sacrifice of the driving plot of the story.

As Doctor Who Continuity: Oh boy, where do I start? Davies is a fan of the series, and yet this one episode alone contradicts (deliberately?) much of what the series previously established about Earth's fate millions of years in the future. For starters, Earth was (supposedly) engulfed by the sun in 'The Ark' (1966) some 10 million years hence, and this was confirmed in 'Frontios' (1984), and yet here we have the Earth still existing several billion years later. The reference to the New Roman Empire of the year 12,005 is greatly at odds with the devastated world as depicted in 'The Sontaran Experiment' (1974) from supposedly the same era (although the 'empires' spoken of by the humans in that story could be reinterpreted as the New Roman Empire). Yes, continuity cops are going to have a field-day trying to make all this work! Is there any relevance to the two references to the *Titanic* in as many stories? Will there be others in later stories? Bringing things up to date, we get further hints of the Doctor's involvement in the Nestene war, during which – shock! – Gallifrey is destroyed! Is this an acknowledgement of the ongoing saga of the BBC novels, or is Davies going to drop on us a double-whammy double-bluff at the end of the season? I'll put my money on there being something huuuuuge in episodes 12 and 13 that will bring startling closure to this attention-grabbing arc ... Despite the continuity anomalies, I'm going to give bonus points to Davies for confirming once and for all that the TARDIS is responsible for translating alien languages into English!

From A Special Effects Viewpoint: While 'Rose' showed us a contemporary Earth where the aliens are the outsiders, 'The End of the World' completely reverses that perspective. Aboard a massive space platform in orbit around a dying Earth (truly impressive CGI creations that rival most anything we've seen in big-budget American science fiction television), The Doctor and Rose find themselves surrounded by numerous aliens of varying size and shape. From the massive, animatronic Face of Boe, to the diminutive, mostly foam-latex Moxx of Balhoon, we are witness to a veritable tour-de-force of creature effects, and for the most part, the quality of all creations present is impressive indeed! It's quite clear to see where a large chunk of this episode's budget went. I was surprised by a few technical issues with said make-ups, though. The Steward is featured heavily, yet his make-up is little more than liberally applied blue crËme and contact lenses. The Moxx of Balhoon, while a great little creation, suffered from a light-weight body that shifted whenever actor Jimmy Vee turned his head (which could have been resolved with a little Velcro between the foam body and his gliding base). And finally, while Jabe stands out as my personal favourite, I can't help but wonder why the effects crew insisted on a make-up appliance that covered her entire upper chest area. In her final scenes, the appliance wrinkled quite badly to the point of distraction. Overall, this episode clearly illustrates the technical differences between old and new *Doctor Who*

PANEL REVIEWS

This is everything I thought Davies's *Doctor Who* would be: *Doctor Who* with real emotion, funny dialogue, heartbreaking moments, a couple of earnest preachy bits, and a pop soundtrack. All this is to say, essentially, wow. 'The End of the World' is what *Doctor Who* was meant to come back for. There are so many great moments here. When the Doctor started grooving to the sounds of Soft Cell on an 'iPod' I knew we were in for something good. When I saw him shedding a tear for his lost race, I knew we were in for something special. The fantastically tense set pieces that bridge all this just made it all the more worthwhile. And the presence of Cassandra O'Brien, who surely must be the winner of the much fought-after title of Campest *Doctor Who* Villain Ever, pushes the whole thing into the territory of the utterly sublime. Eccleston and Piper are nothing short of astonishing. Their performances in the final five minutes just floored me, not because of what the revelations mean to the storyline or continuity but because this scene was about a character opening up his deepest inner pain. Eccleston and Piper deliver these lines with such utter conviction and real heartfelt emotion that we get past the ephemera of Gallifrey being gone and get to the real essence of what's happening here, which is the Doctor allowing himself to trust someone for the first time in ages. That's absolutely wonderful.– *Graeme Burk*

This episode might easily have been simply an excuse to parade the talents of the various design departments, swathed as it is in fine CGI and exotic alien creatures, but Davies's continued focus on the characters of the Doctor and Rose turns an engaging little mystery plot into something much more intriguing. He dwells on her decision to board the TARDIS, showing Rose come around to the possibilities of time travel after being initially overwhelmed by the sheer number of aliens surrounding her, but also her awareness of what she's left behind to achieve this fantastic voyage. The Doctor's progression shifts towards his own background, with his flirty relationship with the Tree Jabe (played with great subtlety by Yasmin Bannerman) suggesting he buries his depths beneath a boisterous exterior deliberately to hide his innate sadness. Christopher Eccleston is particularly emotive in these small, moving revelatory scenes, and by hinting further about the mysterious War, there's a real sense of tantalisingly laying the foundation of a backstory to explore at a later date. Despite these more serious parts, 'The End Of The World' is still light and fun with its humour keeping it entertaining, despite there being a number of plot elements – such as the potential suspects – that would have benefited from greater development. – *Simon Catlow*

For years we've been able to hold our heads high when our *Star Trek* cousins have pointed out wobbly sets or crude special effects – *Doctor Who* had better, more well-rounded scripts. Until now. *The End of the World* finally puts our series up there with the best of them when it comes to CGI and effects, but we suffer the indignity of a very one-dimensional story. That's not to say that the second episode doesn't have some good points to recommend it (aside from the aforementioned effects). Davies is best at writing for characters, and it shows here again. One of the most likeable characters we've met in the series so far, Ruffalo, has a good exchange with Rose before being dragged to her untimely death (one assumes). Billie Piper just keeps on impressing whether she's realising that she went off with a strange old man, or just repeating lines from old Russell T Davies dramas. Eccleston is also proving that he was worth every penny as this season's arc unfolds. One moment he seems to be the happy-go-lucky traveller we've come to know, and the next he's the sad remnant of a dead planet. The main problems with the script are poorly thought-out ideas. Cassandra just isn't bothered that her main plot has been foiled, and I'm sure that her backup plan didn't make a lot of sense to the younger audience (run behind the sofa, the Last Human has got shares in rival companies!) The biggest flaw though is those damn fans. No engineer in his right mind would design something like that. There appears to be nothing under the walkway, so why not just lower it by three metres, or raise the fans up higher. That's just sloppy writing. But, I have to admit, the whole thing looks pretty! – *Robert Franks*

Compared to 'Rose', this is both better and worse. The first fifteen minutes are a sheer delight – I love the way the TARDIS runs like an irritable old car, not to mention the alien delegates, Rose's realistic fear and indecision, and the Doctor's great speech about death. I never thought I'd say it, but even seeing him rock out to Soft Cell is quite fun. Things start sticking around the halfway point, though, and don't recover until the lovely coda on Earth; the scenes with Jabe and the Doctor are wonderful, true, but the story feels disjointed and even preachy. Some of the pop culture references, reminiscent of *Buffy*-style dialogue, date the episode in a way that's going to be more irritating than the old series's special effects ever were. The real deterrent, however, is the climax of the episode, one of the most callous I've ever seen in televised *Doctor Who*; I'm still staggered that Davies thought this a good idea for only the second episode. Regardless, the two leads remain wonderful, with special praise for Billie Piper, who is well on her way to being the companion we can all empathise with. I have the feeling I might like this episode better when I can examine it in the context of the whole season, but as it stands right now, 'The End of the World' seems deeply flawed. – *Sarah Hadley*

There's no denying that 'The End of the World' has its faults. The *Galaxy Quest*-style sequence of the Doctor having to run through the blades to the ludicrously-placed reset switch; Rose having nothing to do other than be trapped in a room for the last quarter of the episode; the ease with which the Doctor is able to bring Cassandra back to the Platform. But it's carried off with such style and wit that it's incredibly hard to dislike. The dialogue sparkles, there are some superb throwaway gags, and best of all, Davies creates some wonderful supporting characters, who are marvellously performed. Rose's encounter with Raffalo is perfectly done, although Davies misses a trick in not having Rose later learn of the plumber's death. In Jabe, we get a very early candidate for best supporting character of the season, and the scene in which she confronts the Doctor with her knowledge of who – or rather, what – he is really stands out. Aside from Cassandra's animation appearing a little too cartoonish when she speaks, the episode looks wonderful, and the design departments and The Mill should all be praised. By all accounts a lot of effort was put into the look of this episode, and it shows. Style over content? Perhaps. But when the style is this engaging and entertaining, it's hard not to be swept along with it. – *Paul Hayes*

The stars of 'The End of the World' would have to be The Mill. They've created a believable space station, the destruction of the Earth, mechanoid 'spiders' and the last human, Cassandra (voiced by a superb Zoë Wanamaker). There's a stunning performance from Yasmin Bannerman as the regal Jabe. Bannerman and Christopher Eccleston have a real chemistry that makes their scenes together just shine. Eccleston gives a very emotional performance as the Doctor, visibly showing grief, emotional pain and anger. There are some flaws to the story, though. For about a third of it, Rose is menaced by sunlight in a locked room, and the sequence where the Doctor needs to reach a reset switch seems to be out of a computer game. The murder mystery aspect, while well constructed, is very simple and obvious; a casualty of the series's forty-five minute episode structure. Many of the alien representatives featured seem to be there just as window dressing, with only Cassandra, Jabe and the Moxx of Balhoon getting any real screen time and development. Overall, 'The End of the World' does a good job of illustrating that *Doctor Who* can still do stories set in the future with a realistic setting and aliens.– *Cameron Mason*

If 'Rose' was 'Spearhead from Space' with CGI, then 'The End of the World' has to be 'The Curse of Peladon' with CGI – and a bit of 'The Ark in Space' chucked in for good measure. (The collection of bizarre alien delegates also recalls 'Mission to the Unknown'.) It's obvious where the budget went this week: the creature designs and special effects (and music) were superb; the designers and artists should be very proud of what they've achieved here, and it would be criminal if they didn't get a BAFTA. A much lighter episode than 'Rose', with many laugh-out-loud moments; the grinning Doctor eagerly pumping away at the TARDIS console springs instantly to mind. Other favourite bits were Rose realising she's talking to a twig and the touching moment with Jabe in the service tunnel (the Doctor's silence and pained expression spoke volumes); and I loved the idea that – as Rose pointed out – no-one on the platform actually saw the Earth die ... Indeed the only ones who did see 'the end of the world' were we, the TV audience. Think about it. I particularly liked the way in which the script was coordinated so from the TARDIS's arrival on the Platform the story played out in virtually real time, counting down the thirty minutes to Earthdeath, which did indeed occur half an hour later. And I even didn't mind Britney Spears! As with 'Rose', we are left with many unanswered questions and tantalising hints of something much bigger looming on the horizon, specifically the 'Bad Wolf scenario' mentioned by the Moxx of Balhoon, which must tie in somehow with those images of the same words that we've seen in location photos and the trailers of later episodes. A top notch effort by all involved. – *Jon Preddle*

Atom-bombs of caustic wit are passed between the characters like breath from each other's lungs. It starts *funny* – with 'He's blue' 'Yeah' 'Okay' – and doesn't stop being funny until it becomes thrilling and sad. There's an amusing deconstruction of the mental processes behind cosmetic surgery, and the smile on Eccleston's face when he grooves to Soft Cell is justification for the episode's existence alone. Big concepts, little victories, moral ambiguity and a hint of mature and passionate romance – it's all here. There are some minor imperfections, but any episode of *any* show that ends with a universal truism – that a packet of chips makes *everything* all right again – is hitting a seam of pure gold. *Magnificent.* – *Keith Topping*

Honestly, what's not to like about 'The End Of The World'? It's exciting, visually stunning, fun, emotional and did I mention exciting? This is the *Doctor Who* that they've been hyping for months! This is *Doctor Who* for the 21st Century! This is the episode that truly has something for everyone! From my perspective, I really have only one problem with this particular story, and that's the rather silly placement of the system-restore switch (*Galaxy Quest* anyone?). To coin a phrase from the fifth Doctor's own lips: 'There should have been another way.' That aside, from the moment Rose rushes into the TARDIS (a nice, direct continuation from the preceding episode) to their quest for chips on a busy pavement, you really are on the trip of a lifetime. While 'Rose' certainly entertained, 'The End Of The World' positively thrilled. I'm finding myself quoting lines (and really terrific lines to boot) and occasionally revisiting those same emotions I felt when a tear left the Doctor's eye or when he revealed to Rose that Gallifrey was no more. This was a great adventure and one that clearly showed us what is to come in this incredible new series. So good is this episode that they actually managed to make a Britney Spears song (albeit a song penned by UK artist Cathy Dennis) 'work'! – *Scott Alan Woodard*

EDITOR'S REVIEW: I'm not exactly certain what it is that I love so much about 'The End of the World'. I'm a sentimentalist at heart, and deep, moving character pieces grounded in reality do it for me far more often than wham-bang action sequences or bone-chilling horror. To me, the nature of *Doctor Who* has always been a character study framed by the stories rather than the other way around; that sort of thing, moving a bunch of one-dimensional cardboard characters around through a series of convoluted set pieces, is better suited for the *Star Wars* prequels than *Doctor Who*. That essence has always been the heart of *Doctor Who*, when Tom Baker used his wits and charm to get himself out of a situation, when Jon Pertwee went from science to suave at the drop of a hat.

'The End of the World' is, at its heart, a very simple runaround with a plot that doesn't exactly hold together, the ultimate villain of the piece having not only one but two simultaneous – and overwhelmingly contradictory – endgames (a hostage situation *and* a mass murder – aren't they mutually exclusive?) Much of the action is spent running up and down corridors; Rose is trapped in a room facing almost certain death; and characters are ultimately sacrificed for trivial reasons. I still cannot figure out why Jabe had to die … The Doctor certainly took his sweet time to get across that bridge. Robbing us of the Moxx of

Balhoon with a stray sun bolt also felt like a needless waste.

So why, I ask myself, does none of this matter? Plot complications have always been at the heart of *Doctor Who* stories, and corridor-runs part of its charm. For me, it goes back to the characters, their motivations and personalities. In only its second outing, the new *Doctor Who* manages to create a worthwhile character (other than the regulars) about whom I actually care and wish we could see again; Yasmin Bannerman is an absolute delight in her portrayal of Jabe, creating a sage, wizened yet delicate being showing true empathy for the Doctor's plight. While kudos must be given to the special effects wizards for such a marvellous (and obviously expensive) job creating Cassandra, Zoë Wanamaker's portrayal adds so much to the role on screen. Simon Day is terrific as the authentic, unflappable bureaucrat – his switching between panic mode and his level-headed reassurance of the guests over the loudspeaker in one quick flash is very well done.

But most of all, and perhaps the best example in the entire first series, Christopher Eccleston and Billie Piper show what extraordinary actors they are. For all his grinning nonsense, it comes down to one moment for Eccleston, alone with Jabe in the ductway, shedding a tear for his fallen homeworld. Meanwhile, Piper carries the entire story, proving 'Rose' was no accident and that she really does have that gift of star quality blended with pathos to demonstrate the rare art of fully realising a character from the start. The two scenes that start in the Manchester Suite at the end, Rose mourning the loss of Earth while no-one was looking, and then joining the Doctor on a busy London street, realising that time is only an illusion, comprise what is arguably one of the most powerful and emotionally resonant sequences in *Doctor Who* history. Compare that to the silliness of this series as Britney Spears's 'Toxic' plays on the jukebox (something that would be over the top anywhere else, but works absolutely perfectly here), and you begin to understand the great dichotomy: *Doctor Who* is not about alien invasions or monsters or hidden agendas, but instead about the Doctor, his friends, and their travels and adventures and the bond they share.

That's why 'The End of the World' works so well – it deepens that friendship between the Doctor and Rose without going overboard, and doesn't just talk about important subjects, in this case why we should care about mother Earth instead of abusing it. While most of the first season is well above average, 'The End of the World' remains my favourite story to date – the cast more than make up for any plot inconsistencies, it's nicely shot, beautifully realised, and I dare you not to shed a tear at the end. Exquisite. – *Shaun Lyon*

103: THE UNQUIET DEAD

Having shown Rose the future, the Doctor now decides to take her on a trip into the past ... but a visit to 1869 Cardiff brings the two into dangerous territory as they face the walking dead, spectral alien images in the gas lines, and an important figure from Earth's literary history.

FIRST TRANSMISSION: UK – 9 April 2005. Canada – 19 April 2005. Australia – 4 June 2005. New Zealand – 21 July 2005.
DURATION: 44'49"
WRITER: Mark Gatiss
DIRECTOR: Euros Lyn
CREDITED CAST: Christopher Eccleston (Doctor Who), Billie Piper (Rose Tyler), Simon Callow (Charles Dickens), Alan David (Gabriel Sneed), Eve Myles (Gwyneth), Huw Rhys (Redpath), Jennifer Hill (Mrs Peace), Wayne Cater (Stage Manager), Meic Povey (Driver), Zoe Thorne (The Gelth)

WHERE AND WHEN: Cardiff and Llandaff, 24 December 1869. The Doctor originally aimed for Naples on Christmas Eve 1860, but somehow got thrown off course. Dickens's reading takes place at the Taliesin Lodge.

THE STORY UNFOLDS: The Gelth are gaseous alien beings, apparently the last of their kind, from the other side of the universe. They are trapped inside an interspatial rift, a weak point in time and space (the cause of some ghost stories, as the Doctor says) which is slowly getting wider. They once had physical form until they lost it during the Time War, when 'the whole universe convulsed'. They can enter and animate the bodies of dead human beings, as the dead decompose and produce the requisite gas they need; however, they cannot maintain the human forms for long, as Earth's normal atmosphere is hostile to them. They travel through the gas ducts of Cardiff, the gas bringing them out of their bodies and into their spectral state. The Doctor holds a séance with Rose, Dickens, the undertaker Sneed and Sneed's assistant, the telepathic Gwyneth ('I love a happy medium') to contact the Gelth. While the creatures initially appear and claim to be benevolent, in reality they are hostile, and their claimed 'few' in number actually means 'a few billion', all looking for new host bodies.

Sneed's house, he says, always had a reputation for being haunted, but the dead started getting restless three months earlier; now they are walking in droves, though they do keep fragments of their former lives in memory. The Doctor identifies the house's morgue as the weak point of the rift.

Charles Dickens will be reading from his 'many and sundry works' on Christmas Eve in a free performance to honour the Children's Hospital; at the event he reads from *A Christmas Carol* and probably other of his writings as well (see 'Internal Consistency'). Noted on the display poster (barely visible in the episode, but clearer in behind-the-scenes photos) is the fact that the 'doors open at seven, performance commences at half past', and that C&J Shaw, Printer, High Street, Cardiff, printed the bill. The reading is interrupted by Mrs Peace.

THE DOCTOR: Holding the spirit of adventure, the Doctor smiles when he first hears the screams from the Taliesin Lodge, and immediately heads there. While Rose changes her outfit for something more suited to the period, he stays in his leather jacket (though he changes his shirt), assuming he will blend in, though Dickens gives him a hard time about it. He's Charles Dickens's 'number one fan' and thinks 'The Signalman' is the best short story ever written ... although he believes the American section in *Martin Chuzzlewit* is rubbish. He is hostile when dealing with Rose's inability to come to terms with a different morality. Rose tells him that it's no wonder that he never stays still, considering he can see days that are dead and gone, 'a hundred thousand sunsets ago' (a life 'better with two' rather than with the Doctor on his own, as she says). The Doctor witnessed the fall of Troy (in 'The Myth Makers') and World War Five, and pushed boxes at the Boston Tea Party (and now he laments he's going to die in a dungeon in Cardiff).

ROSE TYLER: Period costuming excites her; as the Doctor notes, going out in the 21st Century clothes she has on would start a riot (he refers to her as *Barbarella*, referencing the comic strip and Jane Fonda film of the same name). Her first step outside the TARDIS into the snow, into history, overwhelms her. She hated every second of school, as did Gwyneth. She used to go around the shops with her mate Shirin to look at boys. Gwyneth tells her that her father is probably waiting for her in heaven and that she's been thinking about him more than ever recently (which clues in Rose to her clairvoyance and foreshadows 'Father's Day'). She believes it's wrong to sacrifice dead bodies so that the Gelth may survive, and she becomes protective of Gwyneth; the Doctor asks if she carries a donor card, which to him is precisely the same thing. In the midst of a desperate situation, she doesn't seem to understand that it isn't impossible for her to die in her own past, and mourns the death of Gwyneth because no-one will know she gave her life to save the world.

CHARACTER BUILDING: *Charles Dickens* – The great English novelist is in Cardiff for the benefit for the Children's Hospital, and misses his family ... even though he has had problems with them. He isn't impressed with the Doctor until his ego is flattered. He doesn't understand the term 'fan', except as a means of keeping oneself cool. Only the ladies call him 'Charlie', though the Doctor knows all about it and calls him 'Charlie-Boy'. He doesn't believe in anything but what his eyes show him, that is until meeting the Doctor, when his world is now suddenly one of 'spectres and jack-o-lanterns'. He later shakes his apprehension when he rescues the Doctor and Rose from the Gelth zombies by turning on all the gas valves in Sneed's home to draw them out of their host bodies. After the Gelth are defeated, he wants to take the mail coach to London and make amends with his family. To his satisfaction, the Doctor tells him his books will live forever. He plans to incorporate recent events into his latest novel, but alas, history will take its course and Dickens will die within six months.

Gabriel Sneed – Proprietor of Sneed & Company Undertakers, 7 Temperance Court, Llandaff. He's known that something is afoot for some time, with all the bodies rising from the dead ('The stiffs are getting lively again!') He is apparently good at his job; he once did a favour for the bishop, making his nephew look like a cherub even though he'd been a fortnight in the weir. Sneed kidnaps Rose, knocking her out with chloroform after she sees Mrs Peace's dead body in the back of the hearse.

Gwyneth – Mr Sneed's servant, she is obsequious and knows her place. She lost her parents to the 'flu when she was 12. She went to school every Sunday, where they 'did sums and everything', but one time she didn't go and she ran down to Heath all on her own. She currently has her eye on the butcher's boy, who has a lovely smile, but won't tell him about her feelings. Sneed pays her eight pounds a year (although she would have been happy with six). Gwyneth has special powers ('the sight', Sneed calls them) which amount to telepathy and clairvoyance; she can detect the presence of the Gelth, including the body of Mrs Peace, which she tracks to Taliesin Lodge. She is terrified of the recent deaths and believes something terrible is happening in Sneed's home. She can read Rose's mind, including her memories of her father's death, the 'half-naked' people running about London, the metal boxes (cars) racing past, and metal birds in the skies (aeroplanes). The Doctor realises she is the key to solving the situation, as she grew up on the rift. Gwyneth ultimately gives her life to close it.

Redpath and *Mrs Peace* – Mrs Peace has recently died; Redpath is her grandson. Both are taken over by the Gelth (Peace kills Redpath while possessed). Peace holds knowledge of her former life when she goes to see Charles Dickens, which she'd planned to do when she was still alive.

BAD WOLF: When Gwyneth reads Rose's mind in the cellar, she sees the things Rose has seen, 'The darkness ... the big bad wolf!' It terrifies her.

FANTASTIC!: The Doctor says 'Fantastic!' as he enters the Taliesin lodge and sees the shimmering, floating Gelth being for the first time. The Doctor also thanks Dickens with, 'Nice to meet you – Fantastic!' as they say goodbye outside the TARDIS.

BODY COUNT: Mrs Peace is dead at the outset, and her grandson Redpath soon joins her. Sneed is killed by one of the corpses and is immediately possessed by a Gelth being. Gwyneth gives her life to close the rift, blowing up the Sneed and Company building in the process.

THE DOCTOR'S MAGICAL SONIC SCREWDRIVER: The Doctor uses it as a tool when working under the TARDIS console.

REALITY BITES: One of the most celebrated novelists in the history of English literature, Charles John Huffam Dickens (1812-1870) is the author of many well-remembered texts including *Oliver Twist, A Christmas Carol, Nicholas Nickleby, David Copperfield, Bleak House, Little Dorrit, Great Expectations* and *A Tale of Two Cities*. Dickens's final, unfinished piece, *The Mystery of Edwin Drood,* as this episode posits, was originally to feature a killer that wasn't of this Earth. *The Mystery of Edwin Drood and the Blue Elementals* would have been his revised title, he notes. However, Dickens died in June 1870 before he could complete his manuscript, and this adventure with the Gelth was apparently lost to history. (In reality, Dickens finished exactly half the story before his death, and his friends indicated that Edwin's uncle would have been revealed as the murderer – just as Charles states was his original intention here.)

Sneed's reference to the fact that 'One fellow, used to be a Sexton, tumbled into his own funeral' could be a reference to Dickens's short story 'The Story of the Goblins Who Stole a Sexton'. Also, the final line, 'God bless us, every one,' is from *A Christmas Carol*.

Dickens uses William Shakespeare's name as an expletive ('What the Shakespeare is going on?') This seems to be an ironic play on the phrase 'What the Dickens?', which was originally invented by Shakespeare for the play *The Merry Wives of Windsor*, probably written in 1597-8.

LINKING THEMES: The TARDIS, as always, is wildly uncontrollable in the vortex; even with Rose's help the Doctor cannot keep it steady, although that fact amuses both of them no end. The Doctor gives Rose directions to the wardrobe ('First left, second right, third on the left, go straight ahead, under the stairs, past the bins, fifth door on your left').

As the undead Mrs Peace stands in the audience at the Lodge and the Gelth are released, Dickens asks, 'What ... phantasmagoria is this?' *Phantasmagoria* was, not too coincidentally, the title of writer Gatiss's first *Doctor Who* audio play for Big Finish Productions (1999).

The Gelth rift will be mentioned again in a later episode, 'Boom Town', in which it is noted to have shifted slightly (or at least to exist as a linear tear in space-time).

SCENE MISSING: The Gelth note that the Time War was invisible to lower species (such as humans from Earth) but devastating to higher forms, obviously the Doctor's people inclusive. Contrary to perceptions in the 'classic' series, time can and will be rewritten instantaneously and any change the Doctor or Rose makes can alter the future. This goes against much of the 'laws of Time' the Doctor has previously espoused; however, with his people now gone, these laws are presumably no longer in effect. It also is directly contradicted later in the season (see 'Father's Day').

While the Doctor previously told Rose that he carried no money (in 'The End of the World'), he has enough from this period to buy a newspaper (which, incidentally, is the *Cardiff and Merthyr Guardian*, subtitled the *Glamorgan, Monmouth and Brecon Gazette*, visible only in production photos). It's also odd that he has the correct currency, given that he was expecting to be in Naples. (Perhaps he now has psychic money as well as psychic paper?)

An industrial city like Cardiff in the 1860s would have been powered by town gas – a deadly mixture rich in carbon monoxide. There's no way the human characters could have stayed in a room full of this gas without more difficulty breathing.

Other unanswered questions: Why does Sneed have chloroform on him to knock Rose unconscious? (Perhaps he expected to use it on Mrs. Peace ... but that begs the question, why would he think chloroform would stop the undead?) Why does Dickens feel the need to hire a mail coach at the end, when he clearly has his own coach and driver? (Is this a local driver only, perhaps?) Why does the Doctor presume that Gwyneth was dead from the moment she stepped under the archway, as she clearly acts of her own volition after this point? (Was he being figurative instead of literal: doomed from the start?) And does the explosion at the end destroy the non-corporeal Gelth? (It does seal the rift and stop them from coming through, but there are flickers in the gas lines which suggest that maybe a few survived on Earth and live on to plot another day.)

BEHIND THE SCENES: The exterior sequences for 'The Unquiet Dead' were recorded on location in Monmouth and Swansea, both of which doubled for Victorian Cardiff during production. The location of the TARDIS's arrival was shot in White Swan Court, while the exterior of Sneed's parlour was shot at Beaufort Arms Court, both in Monmouth. Cambrian Place in Swansea was transformed into a wintry Cardiff, complete with pedestrian traffic and carollers, while the exterior of the Exchange building in Cambrian Place became the entrance to Taliesin Lodge. Interiors at Sneed's home were recorded in the Headlands National Children's Home in Penarth, the basement doubling for the morgue. The interiors at the Lodge were recorded inside Cardiff's New Theatre.

The special effects people working on this series are paying attention to even the most exquisite detail: when the TARDIS demateralises at the end, the snow that has gathered on the window sills remains behind, twisting in the breeze as it falls down to the ground.

According to Gatiss, Gwyneth was originally to die midway through the episode; a subsequent polish of the script expanded her role and added some of the darker humour to what had otherwise been a rather grim story.

Over seventy extras were employed during 'The Unquiet Dead', working in a difficult environment – the snow was actually made of paper and blew everywhere. Actress Zoe Thorne, playing the Gelth, was recorded bathed in blue, red and green lights against a black background, with the light source manipulated to create a 3D effect. Many make-up tricks (rather than prosthetics) were used to create the undead zombies that the Gelth inhabit.

Behind the scenes, the amount of visual effects work required kept increasing, as the ethereal Gelth solid forms (such as those seen during the séance) became more difficult to realise. The glowing Gelth forms were achieved by a team of 3D artists led by Chris Tucker.

OFF THE SCREEN: Esteemed character actor Simon Callow CBE is an award winning thespian and director first prompted to take to the stage by Sir Laurence Olivier himself; his many credits include such films as *Four Weddings and a Funeral* (1994) and *A Room With a View* (1985) – which both saw him being nominated for a BAFTA award for Best Supporting Actor – as well as *Amadeus* (1984), *Shakespeare in Love* (1998), *Postcards from the Edge* (1990), The *Phantom of the Opera* (2004), *Jefferson in Paris* (1995) and *James and the Giant Peach* (1996). On television, he has appeared in the HBO miniseries *Angels in America* (2003) and playing Tom Chance in the comedy series *Chance in a Million* (1984). He has played Dickens on stage and in several TV productions apart from *Doctor Who*, including *The Mystery of Charles Dickens* (2000) and *Hans Christian Andersen: My Life as a Fairy Tale* (2001). Prior to appearing in the film version of *Amadeus*, he played the title role on stage. Alan David has an extensive television resume with appearances on *Casualty* (1990/1999), *Goodnight Sweetheart* (1999), *The Royal* (2005), *Hetty Wainthropp Investigates* (1996), *Heartbeat* (1994/2002), *Cracker* (1993), *Lovejoy* (1993), *Peak Practice* (1994), *Juliet Bravo* (1984), *Remington Steele* (1986), *The Twilight Zone* (1986) and *The Brittas Empire* (1996). His films include *The Great Indoors* (2000), *The Man Who Cried* (2000), *Wimbledon* (2004) and the television miniseries *Empire* (2005). Eve Myles has played Ceri Lewis in the BBC Wales television series *Belonging* since 1999 and has also appeared in *EastEnders* (2003), *Score* (2001), *Colditz* (2005) and *These Foolish Things* (2005). Huw Rhys has been seen in *Life Begins* (2004) and *Spooks* (2004). Jennifer Hill appeared on *Z Cars* (1975/1977), *Tenko* (1981), *Hunter's Walk* (1974) and *Mine All Mine* (2004). Her films include *Carry On Jack* (1963) and *Human Traffic* (1999). Wayne Cater appeared in *Topsy-Turvy* (1999) and *The Dance of Shiva* (1998). Meic Povey (full name: Michael Povey) appeared in the long running Welsh soap opera *Pobol y Cwm*, and in *Minder* (1982-89) as Detective Jones. Zoe Thorne has appeared in *Holby City* (2004), *Doctors* (2003), *The Vice* (2002) and *Casualty* (2001). Her other credits include *New Year's Day* (2001), *Procter* (2002) and *Marple: The Body in the Library* (2004).

TECHNICAL GOOFS: As Sneed and Gwyneth approach the Taliesin Lodge in their hearse, a modern road sign can clearly be seen in the background. There is a modern light switch in Sneed's parlour. In the scene in the pantry, the Doctor's jacket is in shot before he appears, but it's clearly in the wrong place. Redpath's eyes move when Dickens opens his coffin.

CONTROVERSIES: There is a considerable subtext of a romantic attraction in the Doctor-Rose relationship in this episode, perhaps more so than in the previous two, especially when the Doctor says he is glad to have met her. Also, a possible bias against Cardiff is demonstrated in the writing on two occasions – both early on when the Doctor and Rose are together on the street, and later in the cellar – and the Doctor says the city name with some slight disdain. Rose reacts much the same way (although this could simply be her realising she's in a place she's familiar with, rather than any negative reaction).

INTERNAL CONSISTENCY: The first clock we see in this serial is in Sneed's sitting room, and it says 10.50 pm. The séance begins at 11.00 pm. The next scene is set at 11.30 pm, so Gwyneth has been unconscious for approximately thirty minutes after the séance. From here the evening runs pretty much as seen: the group encounter the Gelth in the morgue at about 11.40 pm and the house blows up at approximately 11.45 pm. If Dickens's carriage has been waiting for him then it is conceivable that he, the Doctor and Rose are returned to the city in a few minutes, or if they walk, it would take them approximately 40 minutes. This puts the final scenes set outside the TARDIS early on Christmas Day, 1869. Working backwards, if Rose is rescued at approximately 10.45 pm, then the Doctor and Dickens must have left the theatre no more than 10 minutes before that. (The distance from mid-town Cardiff to Llandaff is approximately 2.7 miles, and with an average speed of a horse and carriage being 25 mph the journey should take no more than 7-10 minutes.) This would have the Gelth erupting from Mrs Peace at around 10.25 to 10.30 pm. Dickens is up to the point in his reading of *A Christmas Carol* where he is describing Marley's face in the knocker – this is approximately 10 minutes into the story, which would put the beginning of the reading at approximately 10.15 pm. He is a few minutes late to the start of his performance, which obviously must have been scheduled to begin at 10 pm, and after some warm-up with the audience got into the bulk of his 90 minute reading. The poster in Dickens's dressing room states that the 'Doors open at seven, performance commences at half past', but it also confirms 'Extension of time, by special license' which would indicate that the theatre had special consideration for serving alcohol after the generally recognised 10 pm licence cut-off time of the late 19th Century. As there is no way to account for such a large amount of missing time, Dickens's performance must have consisted of two parts – the first starting at 7.30 and the second at 10 pm. This puts the TARDIS's arrival sometime between 9.30 and 10 pm. The pre-credits private viewing would have been closer to 9 pm, and Mr Sneed must have been unconscious for approximately 30 minutes (to give Mrs Peace time to walk to town – approximately 40 minutes – and be at the theatre before Sneed and Gwyneth can pursue her in the hearse).

THEME ANALYSES

As Doctor Who For A Modern Audience: Mark Gatiss's 'The Unquiet Dead' is easily the most 'traditional' episode of the new *Doctor Who* so far, utilising a whole host of techniques very common to the original series such as a pseudo-historical plot, an encounter with a famous historical figure, and aliens pretending to be something they aren't in order to take advantage of humanity. Nevertheless, this is not a backwards-looking exercise in nostalgia, for the script is laced with black humour and horror combined with the pace, energy and strong character moments that have come to typify the modern approach this production team has achieved, meaning that its effectiveness as *Doctor Who* for today's audience again comes down to its presentation. One of the most significant changes in the landscape of television in recent years, both within genre programming and more mainstream fare, has been the increased popularity of story 'arcs' where individual stories build up into a whole greater than its parts. It's clear with repeated emphasis on the 'Time War' and another mention of the 'Bad Wolf' that there's much more to this Doctor's back-story than we've learned so far. With the Gelth convincingly depicted, their situation allows Gatiss to re-emphasise the Doctor's alien-ness by contrasting his morality with Rose's, as he seems to help whomever and whatever he can, irrespective of what it means to others.

As Television Drama: It's a terrible cliché to say it, but were the BBC's obituary ever to be written then one of the first things that would go down on the list of accolades would be how good they were at making costume dramas, particularly those set in the frilly world of 19th Century Britain. It's a cliché though because it's true, and the sight of Andrew Davies-scripted adaptations of classic novels of the 1800s has become a very familiar one on BBC television over the past decade or so. Indeed, one of BBC Wales's last major BBC1 network dramas before *Doctor Who* was just such a serial, a four-part dramatisation of Anthony Trollope's *He Knew He Was Right*, starring the likes of Bill Nighy and David Tennant. The BBC's experience of and skill at pulling off convincing period settings really pays off here, as 'The Unquiet Dead' utterly convinces in its setting of 19th Century Cardiff, never falling into the common telefantasy trap of making the past look very obviously like a backlot with a few hired costumes and old-world words thrown in. However, it's not simply other costume drama that springs to mind – perhaps simply because of the association with writer Mark Gatiss, the snowy, threatening winter landscape of the 2000 *The League of Gentlemen* Christmas Special also comes to mind, with its mixture of the macabre and the humorous. This heady mixture is quite striking, particularly on an early Saturday evening, and once again goes to show how unlike anything else of its type or in its timeslot the new series of *Doctor Who* is.

As A Piece of Writing: Whenever I disliked something in the writing over the past two episodes, I'd think, 'Well, before long, we'll see what a different writer can do.' Right I was to wait, too. Mark Gatiss's episode has a much firmer grasp on both the plotting and pacing of a forty-five-minute adventure than either of Davies's scripts so far, and the emphasis is genuinely on story, with funny lines and character moments still present, but more of a secondary concern. To be honest, I like it better that way. It still seems as if there are a few kinks to be worked out – Gwyneth's and Rose's mid-episode conversation is so long it just stops the story dead, and two or three of those minutes could've been put to better use at the climax – but by and large, the episode manages its time very well. It also has subtlety, which I appreciate; there's an ethical debate between the Doctor and Rose that makes sense, and doesn't talk down to the viewer. Most stunningly, Gatiss manages to have a shocking and violent ending that could've been just as bad as last week's, except he understands how to make it effective for the audience without discarding the Doctor's integrity. Gwyneth's sacrifice is firmly in the mould of the old show, and we're even given one of those silly-but-needed *Who* explanations – she was already dead, see! – that somehow makes it all okay. Well done, Mr Gatiss. Are you free again this time, next year?

The Doctor As A Mystery Figure: A mysterious figure, with a beautiful companion, arrives at a marginally insignificant moment in history and manages to help save the world from horrible aliens. Whilst last week's episode was 'base under siege', this one mines another of

Doctor Who's more traditional dramatic avenues, the pseudo-historical. Mark Gatiss's folly of Gothic Victoriana is so cunningly constructed that, for the first time this season, the pace and fury drops and we actually have a chance to marvel at the sheer cleverness of the script. Take, for instance, Rose's sense of wonder at the concept of being able to visit a once-in-forever moment for a second time. It's impossible, she notes, before looking at the Doctor and adding 'except for you.'

Themes, Genres and Modes: The Doctor praises Dickens's 'The Signalman' as one of the best short stories ever written. Dickens's 1866 tale – about a traveller who encounters a lonely railway signalman haunted by spectres that are rationally discounted by the traveller until it transpires that they were in fact predicting the signalman's own death – is the key to understanding Mark Gatiss's inspirations for this story. Gatiss plays with all the conventions of the Victorian ghost story, particularly the tension between the rational and the supernatural, with Dickens himself being a rationalist rather like the traveller in 'The Signalman'. This being *Doctor Who*, of course, there aren't really phantasms, just aliens, and so for once the forces of rational thought win, albeit with an expanded purview of what fits into 'rational thought' …

In Style and Structure: Stylistically, 'The Unquiet Dead' draws on a number of aspects of the Victorian era. The audience is introduced to Charles Dickens as he prepares to give a recital in a theatre or music hall, a major form of public entertainment in Victorian Britain. Class structure and class divisions of the Victorian era are explored when Rose assists Gwyneth with some kitchen duties, with Rose being surprised at Gwyneth's level of education and rate of pay. The Victorian obsession with the occult and mysticism is also looked at in Gatiss's script, with Gwyneth's 'gift' of the 'second sight' being a major plot point as a séance is conducted (with the tricks of frauds discussed), and as Gwyneth is used as a conduit point to open up a rift in time. It's through this rift that the story touches upon the Time War plot line, with the Gelth having been directly affected by the War. Structurally, 'The Unquiet Dead' is very straightforward, with the main story playing out smoothly throughout the episode. The minor plot points are focused on characters and develop out of the main storyline. Overall, 'The Unquiet Dead' is well paced, perfectly fitting the forty-five minute format.

As Doctor Who Continuity: Goodness! What the Dickens is going on? The Time War! The Big Bad Wolf! Ah, so this is Davies's master plan; boy, this season is going to be soooo cool! A few nods to the past this time around; the idea that ghosts were manifestations caused by local time fissures was first proposed in 'Image of the Fendahl' (1977); the Doctor mentions the fall of Troy (he was there, as seen in 'The Myth Makers' in 1965), while the Boston Tea Party and World War Five are further 'unseen' adventures. (And World War Three is literally just two episodes away!) And that's about it; not much to discuss here, so let's look at the Big Bad Wolf arc. The Bad Wolf was mentioned in passing in the previous episode, and so far 'the War' has cropped up in all three. Who or what is the BBW? *Doctor Who*'s afraid of the Big Bad Wolf? It's interesting to note that so far everyone that Rose has had a lengthy conversation with has died (Clive, Raffalo, Cassandra, Sneed, and Gwyneth). Is she cursed in some way? A lot to take in and absorb after just three weeks, but this is going to be a one hell of a fun ride. We know the Bad Wolf pops up again in 'Aliens of London' (the words are painted on the TARDIS) – so roll on episode four!

From A Special Effects Viewpoint: 'The Unquiet Dead' marks a welcome return to the 'gothic horror' stories of producer Philip Hinchcliffe's era (in particular, 'The Talons Of Weng-Chiang'), and along with this setting come fanciful monsters, here in the shape of the walking dead and wispy blue phantoms. Focusing first on the zombies, we see skilfully applied make-ups (complete with iris-free contacts) thanks to make-up designer Davy Jones, but when one compares these with the work presented in the behind-the-scenes documentaries and photos, it's sadly apparent that a lot of the exquisite detail was somehow lost once the video cameras captured them (and perhaps once the post-production film-look treatment was applied, as well). The Gelth in their spectral form are really the visual stars of the show, though, looking like an updated, though wholly digital, version of the spirits from the famous climax of *Raiders Of The Lost Ark*. The marriage of the live-action, though digitally processed, actress Zoe Thorne with the computer-generated ghostly forms is close to perfect and extremely effective. The other effects elements in this episode that should be commented on include some nice manipulation of live gas flames (usually to indicate imminent appearances of the Gelth) and the dramatic destruction of the building belonging to Sneed & Co (possibly a mixture of models and CGI as I'm sure the production company was not given permission to destroy an actual building!)

PANEL REVIEWS

'The Unquiet Dead' is the first real misstep of the new series. It is all veneer. On the surface, it seems to offer the sort of television *Who* we've all waited for, in particular the idealised Victoriana of 'The Talons of Weng-Chiang' with ghosts and gaslight and night shooting. And yet get past the veneer and 'The Unquiet Dead' is small-scaled and unambitious. There was something inspired in the idea of the Gelth needing human corpses to survive, and the particular moral debate that opened up was interesting, but, ho hum, let's just make them evil and then have the Doctor do absolutely nothing except fret, and leave it to the high-profile guest star to come up with a bizarre idea to save everyone. It's a great shame, as it's beautifully directed, there's a delightful *The League of Gentlemen*-esque pre-credit sequence, and there are some lovely moments (Rose stepping out of the TARDIS into the snow-covered past; Gwyneth asserting she can make decisions of her own; Dickens meeting a fanboy Doctor; 'What the Shakespeare?'). The performances are all superb, particularly those of Eve Miles and Simon Callow. But none of this helps to create a cohesive whole. – *Graeme Burk*

'The Unquiet Dead' is the best episode of the new series to date, as Mark Gatiss draws us into the highly evocative atmosphere of Victorian Cardiff, where the dead are rising. The idea is not particularly innovative but Gatiss uses it as a foundation for an entertaining and engaging story that embraces this series's goals to be simultaneously funny and scary. The more substantial plot when mixed with the superb character moments, such as Rose's girl talk with Gwyneth and the Doctor's admission of being 'so glad' at meeting his companion, gives the episode a more rounded dramatic feel than its predecessors. Despite some predictable development – like the twist about the Gelth's true intentions – the story proves engaging thanks to the use of horror, and Gatiss's dark sense of humour that keeps it from getting too nasty. Charles Dickens's inclusion could have been an indulgence, but Simon Callow brings great charm to the part, making the character's Scrooge-like journey believable and inspiring. While Eccleston and Piper continue to impress, credit must also go to Alan David and Eve Myles as Sneed and Gwyneth. The former gets all the best lines and makes the undertaker trying to cope with his clients returning from the dead all the more memorable, while Myles plays his servant with such an endearing vulnerability that it's impossible not to be moved by her. – *Simon Catlow*

The future and the past – throw in a 'sideways' story and it would be the first production team's vision all over again. 'The Unquiet Dead' is in many ways traditional *Doctor Who*, however I can't help feeling that the whole thing is rushed again. It's not a matter of the current format of the series, but that the Doctor and Rose visit the past for a few fleeting hours – managing to stop an alien invasion decades in the making. For all their stealth in convincing the Doctor to help them, the Gelth are defeated pitifully quickly. Sneed and Gwyneth are reminiscent of many 'Holmesian duos', particularly Lightfoot and Jago (from 'The Talons of Weng-Chiang'). Without a lot of screen time, we come to learn Gwyneth's life story and actually feel sorry for old Sneed when his neck snaps. It's again the main characters that impress the most. The Doctor looks at Rose as if realising for the very first time what a lovely young woman he's travelling with. And, Rose's reaction to stepping into the past – literally – makes one pause to think what it would actually be like to do the same thing. I think that's one of the wonders Davies wants to bring to the series – how we would actually feel visiting the past or the future through Rose's eyes – and so far he's succeeding. – *Robert Franks*

Finally! An episode to be thoroughly enjoyed. Hopefully, it's a sign that the new series is really starting to find its feet, because everything's firing on all cylinders this week – even the title is fantastic! Mark Gatiss understands the qualities that really give the show that special something, and he's put together a great blend of scares, moody moments, a little technobabble, and a few laughs. Intriguingly, splendid though they are, Eccleston and Piper are overshadowed this time by two guest performers – and I found I didn't mind at all. Simon Callow brings Charles Dickens to life, investing him with a full-bodied spirit you wouldn't think possible in less than forty minutes of screen time; he is, thankfully, no 'stock' historical figure. And although she's a little more of a traditional supporting character, Eve Myles's Gwyneth steals many of the scenes she's in. Special mention, too, for the effects; the Gelth impressed me tremendously, never once looking anything but convincing and scary – you'd never guess they came from the same team as the cheap, Z-movie matte shots of 'Rose'. 'The Unquiet Dead' isn't perfect, of course, but it's damn close – possibly the best we old-schoolers can expect from the new, faster format. This is proper *Doctor Who*, and no mistake. – *Sarah Hadley*

Doctor Who always seems to work well when it sends some alien threat into a 19th Century setting, which makes it hardly surprising that Davies chose to use the Victorian era for the ninth Doctor's and Rose's first trip into the past. Getting Mark Gatiss to write this episode was his second masterstroke, Gatiss being on top form with a superbly pitched mix of the wicked and the witty. The guest cast keep up the uniformly high standard, with Simon Callow being, as widely expected, superb as Charles Dickens, a role he had already made his own long before 'The Unquiet Dead' came along. Eccleston and Piper are likewise excellent, my only criticism of the Doctor's role in proceedings being that he rather seems to give up when the real threat of the Gelth is revealed, with Dickens being the one left to save the day. His misjudgement of the creatures didn't bother me as much, however – he is clearly scarred by this 'Time War' about which we are learning a little more each episode, and naively eager to help those

similarly affected by the conflict. Euros Lyn's direction is well-paced and keeps the script moving along, but never too fast despite the restriction of the forty-five-minute format. In short, another very strong and highly entertaining episode – can it really get better than this?
– *Paul Hayes*

The TARDIS skips Naples, going for 1869 Cardiff, where not all the dead rest in peace. Mark Gatiss has written a script full of witty and memorable lines that draws upon many aspects of the Victorian era in order to tell a superb story. Simon Callow is Charles Dickens, weary and a bit cynical; the highlight of the episode would have to be the scene with the Doctor doing a 'fan boy' routine with Dickens – praising many of his works to high heaven, then criticising the one story he didn't like. Billie Piper is superb as Rose, and is paired up with Eve Myles's tragic Gwyneth. The concept of the Gelth is very interesting, and the story touches upon a few moral issues, quickly dealing with them as the true nature of the Gelth is revealed. The Mill's work on creating the visual appearance of the Gelth is nothing short of spectacular, with Zoe Thorne as the 'voice' and 'face' of the Gelth putting in a performance both sympathetic and menacing. It's through the Gelth that the scarier moments are played out to great effect. What ties all this together is the realistic and convincing design work in creating the look of Victorian Cardiff, which is utterly believable. Unmissable. – *Cameron Mason*

Mark Gatiss is a writer whose work I have admired ever since I read his *Doctor Who* novel *Nightshade* back in 1992. And with his first TV *Doctor Who* script (discounting spoofs!) he doesn't disappoint one iota. It is full of the sort of trademark innuendo, clever one-liners and chilling horror that make *The League of Gentlemen* so engagingly grotesque. 'The Unquiet Dead' kicks off with a truly creepy pre-credits teaser, and ends with a wonderful farewell scene. If the walking dead don't send the under-tens scurrying behind their sofas then I'll eat my Dapol Mel figure for breakfast. Simon Callow makes a charming Dickens; and his reaction to the Doctor's 'fan' enthusiasm was priceless. Favourite moments: Rose's 'One small step for a woman' as she steps into the past; the Doctor's 'That's more like it' when someone screams; and the Doctor's tortured look when contemplating his impending 'death' in a Cardiff dungeon! (But I'm going to tempt fate and take a point off for the gratuitous name-dropping of Gatiss's Big Finish play, *Phantasmagoria*!) Once again the BBC has excelled in costume and production design. Compare these sets with those in 'Ghost Light'. The computer-wizardry of The Mill reaches new heights of excellence, though the 'spirits' were a bit too reminiscent of those from *Raiders of the Lost Ark*. I'm sure 'The Unquiet Dead' is going to be a 'giant maggot' – one that the general public will remember in years to come. – *Jon Preddle*

There are a trio of lovely performances in 'The Unquiet Dead' besides Eccleston's and Piper's. Alan David and Eve Myles put in precise cameos amid the rising corpses of 19th Century Cardiff (cue a couple of amusing examples of Swansea-based bigotry against the Welsh capital in the script). Then there's Simon Callow – one of the great actors of his generation – wonderful as a confused, weary and slightly vain Charles Dickens. Chuckle at his incredulity when the Doctor asks him about perceived padding in *Martin Chuzzlewit*. 'I thought you said you were my fan?' asks a bemused Dickens. 'Ah, well, if you can't take criticism,' replies the Doctor in an incisive sideways glance at *Doctor Who* fandom's constant need to pick everything apart. If truth be told, Dickens was often a bit of a hack, although this author shares the Doctor's admiration of 'The Signalman'. 'The Unquiet Dead' is yet another reminder of the vast potential of *Doctor Who* to tell stories that other series simply cannot. And, in its touching coda, Gatiss provides another moment to go along with last week's 'last of the Time Lords' scene that will inspire the next generation of fans. Three down, and all's well ... – *Keith Topping*

Zombies and ghosts galore! No, this isn't an episode of *Buffy*, this is *Doctor Who* direct from the twisted pen of *The League Of Gentlemen*'s own Mark Gatiss. And this isn't Sunnydale, California, it's Cardiff, Christmas Eve, 1869. Welcome to 'The Unquiet Dead', an adventure that marks the end of a trilogy of sorts, where part one was set in the present day, part two in the distant future and part three in the past. There's so much to this story that I liked and yet, in some ways, it managed to fall just short of the mark as a wholly successful *Doctor Who* tale. The setting is superb, the costuming top-notch, the acting (particularly that of Simon Callow) is impressive, but the story just seems a tad 'average'. I gather the intent was to show that while the Doctor typically embraces all that is alien, always reaching out with a sympathetic hand, alliances are never guaranteed; but unfortunately, this actually goes against one of the long-standing messages of the series. We come away from 'The Unquiet Dead' believing that it's actually best to look at strangers with suspicion and distrust. It seems that this could have (and should have) been explored a bit more, but the restrictions of the forty-five minute episode format meant that we went from curiosity to sympathy to anger and the need for revenge within a few short moments. This was a 'good' episode of *Doctor Who*, and I definitely welcomed a voice that wasn't exclusively Davies's, but it's a shame that this wasn't a *great* episode. – *Scott Alan Woodard*

EDITOR'S REVIEW: I've never been what you would call a fan of 'historical' adventures in *Doctor Who*; history interests me, but far too often, *Doctor Who*'s voyages into the past (at least the ones that I've seen) have been little more than corridor runarounds in period costume. That's recently changed as I've come to appreciate such classics as 'The Aztecs' and 'The Romans', but I must confess that 'The Unquiet Dead' was probably at the bottom of my list of expectations prior to transmission ... even with the gorgeous location photographs that had been revealed as the episode was recorded.

How delightful, then, that 'The Unquiet Dead' turned out to be a spirited adventure full of twists and turns, with some great characters and real heart. Simon Callow – without a doubt one of the finest guest stars in *Doctor Who* history – excels at the role of Charles Dickens (but then, he *would*, considering how good an actor he is and how often he's played the role before) and turns what could have been a futile attempt at historical tie-in into something really special. (The scene at the end with Dickens, the Doctor and Rose at the TARDIS, especially when Dickens discovers his books live on forever, is one of the highlights of the first season – a beautiful statement about the classy timelessness of *Doctor Who* and more emotionally resonant given that, beyond the context of the story, it is Dickens we know to be real.) The rest of the cast is excellent, with Eve Myles striking a particularly positive note as the servant girl Gwyneth, demonstrating a blend of humour and steadfastness as she toils for Sneed but helping the Doctor and Rose without hesitation. I must also give kudos to Alan David's wickedly bumbling Sneed, the apparent master of his own domain who has no idea how truly blind he is.

The production values are certainly one of the most satisfying things about this episode. The particular importance placed upon location photography in 'The Unquiet Dead' paid off with resounding success, with Monmouth and Swansea appearing exactly as one would expect a wintry Cardiff of the Victorian era to look. The attention to detail – such as in the theatre bills – evidences the unusual amount of care shown by the production team of this series; often one can successfully compare that sort of devotion to the overall product once it reaches the screens. The period costumes and accoutrements add that extra touch of class (even more so given the Doctor's refusal to change *his* outfit!)

If I have one small complaint, it is that the story is wrapped up a bit quickly and perhaps too neatly for such an important event as an extra-dimensional alien invasion. Sadly, the forty-five-minute format that *Doctor Who* has taken in this recent incarnation tends to lend itself to quick and tidy resolution of story elements. However, a good writer can make this work to advantage, and here Mark Gatiss has presented us the dichotomy of a major happening wrapped up with an easy resolution as one person giving her life without any hesitation ... and he does it beautifully. With Gwyneth he paints the picture of selflessness from her first moment, and by the end, we completely believe in what she's done, even if she didn't quite understand it herself.

This also marks the first time that many fans really started paying attention to the 'Bad Wolf' story arc that would run through the first series. While its appearance in the previous episode was a throwaway line, in this episode it becomes obvious that the producers are in this for the long haul. Bravo; it's about time *Doctor Who* joined other great science fiction and fantasy drama series with this sort of approach to storytelling, and I'm looking forward to similar experiences in future years.

'The Unquiet Dead' is a triumph of style and substance in equal measure, one of the best of the first season, and an exciting romp in time worthy of the *Doctor Who* name. Beautiful set pieces, clever direction, great acting, fun dialogue, a lovely ending, a satisfying resolution to the story, and then it's topped off with the magnificence of Simon Callow. This is certainly one to use to hook your friends on the new *Doctor Who*. – *Shaun Lyon*

104: ALIENS OF LONDON

The Doctor brings Rose back home – a year late, but just in time for the crash-landing of a spacecraft. Is it Earth's first contact with alien life? Or simply an elaborate hoax? As the Doctor soon discovers, the truth is far more sinister ... the Slitheen have come to Earth, and their conspiracy rises all the way to the top of the British government.

FIRST TRANSMISSION: UK – 16 April 2005. Canada – 26 April 2005. Australia – 11 June 2005. New Zealand – 28 July 2005.
DURATION: 45'02"
WRITER: Russell T Davies
DIRECTOR: Keith Boak
CREDITED CAST: Christopher Eccleston (Doctor Who), Billie Piper (Rose Tyler), Camille Coduri (Jackie Tyler), Noel Clarke (Mickey Smith), Penelope Wilton (Harriet Jones), Annette Badland (Margaret Blaine), David Verrey (Joseph Green), Rupert Vansittart (General Asquith), Navin Chowdhry (Indra Ganesh), Naoko Mori (Doctor Sato), Eric Potts (Oliver Charles), Steve Speirs (Strickland), Ceris Jones (Policeman), Jack Tarlton (Reporter), Lachele Carl (Reporter), Fiesta Mei Ling (Ru), Basil Chung (Bau), Jimmy Vee (Alien), Corey Doabe (Spray Painter), Elizabeth Fost (Slitheen), Paul Kasey (Slitheen), Alan Ruscoe (Slitheen), Matt Baker (As Himself), Andrew Marr (As Himself)

WHERE AND WHEN: London, March 2006, including at Rose and Jackie's flat in South East London, at Albion Hospital, and at 10 Downing Street, Central London. (See 'Rose' for an alternate take on the timeframe of the story.)

THE STORY UNFOLDS: A spaceship belonging to the Slitheen crash-lands in Central London. While humanity deals with the ramifications of contact with outer space, the Prime Minister has mysteriously vanished, leading to a takeover by MP Joseph Green ... in actuality an alien Slitheen whose intentions, while obviously hostile, are unknown. The spaceship was detected being launched from Earth, from somewhere in the North Sea (where something had been detected by a satellite at a depth of 100 fathoms), three days beforehand; the ship followed a slingshot trajectory around the planet before it crashed. (The TARDIS seems to be able to scan events that took place in the recent past, such as detecting the trajectory two days after it happened.) The Prime Minister's car seems to have vanished without a trace, although it transpires that another Slitheen, posing as Margaret Blaine MP, killed him. The entire attack is an elaborate setup, designed to lure Earth's alien experts into one location; the ID cards they are given to wear are part of the trap, activated by alien technology to electrocute the humans.

When a body of 'non-terrestrial origin' is found in the wreckage of the crashed spacecraft by army divers, it is brought to the secure facility at Albion Hospital and tended to by Dr Sato. The 'alien' turns out to be a terrestrial pig, its brain adapted and enhanced with Slitheen technology.

The Slitheen are large, yellow/green alien beings with round black eyes (protected by lateral eyelids). They occupy the bodies of humans by apparently plasticising their epidermis, disposing of the insides, then compressing themselves to fit inside their hosts' skin. Due to the equipment needed to compress their large frames, they are naturally flatulent (which they explain away in a variety of manners, including as nervous stomachs), though they haven't quite perfected the resultant gas exchange; as the Slitheen posing as Margaret notes, 'it's getting ridiculous'. They occupy large-figured humans because they cannot compact into any smaller size.

The Doctor and Rose have been gone a year, and the Doctor first discovers his error in timing when he sees a missing persons appeal poster stuck to a pillar in the courtyard outside Rose's flat. According to the poster, Rose has been missing from her home since 6 March 2005 and she is described as 19 years old, 5'4" in height, slim build with shoulder-length blonde hair. Among the various types of flyers posted is a 'Missing' poster (most likely printed immediately after her disappearance), a 'Where is Rose?' flyer (which says 'It is now six months since Rose Tyler went missing from her home') and a police appeal for assistance.

THE DOCTOR: He tells Jackie and the policeman that he 'sort of employed Rose as my companion' (the policeman asks if it's some sort of sexual relationship, the implication being obvious). Jackie slaps him across the face when he tells her he really *is* a Doctor; in over nine hundred years, he says, he's never been slapped by someone's mother. (Rose is incredulous at his immense age – 'one hell of an age gap'). He doesn't 'do families' (another way of saying that he won't let Jackie travel with them). He doesn't recognise the ship that crashes; as he tells Rose, this is why he travels, to see history unfold right in front of him. He takes the TARDIS to Albion Hospital and, naturally, runs right into the soldiers ... but manages to give them orders anyway (using the code 'Defence Plan Delta') including ordering a lock down of the Hospital when the 'alien' escapes. His name, the words 'blue box' and the name 'TARDIS' all set off a Code Nine alert; the emergency protocols activate an automatic search on the phone lines, alerting the authorities to the presence of the Earth's 'ultimate alien expert'. He's located after Jackie calls the police, and escorted to 10 Downing Street to aid in investigating the (fake) alien invasion.

ROSE TYLER: She's been gone an entire year, but initially believes she's been away only twelve hours. She first tells her mother she's been at her friend Shirin's, but then amends this to explaining that she's been travelling – but her passport is still in the drawer. She's used to watching major events on television, which is what everyone else does in times of crisis. She's not certain if the Doctor will leave her behind, but feels better when he gives her a spare TARDIS key. She thinks the inside of the car that takes her to 10 Downing Street is 'a bit posh' and that if she'd known this, she should have had herself arrested before. (The Doctor explains that they are being escorted, not arrested.) She chides the Doctor (rather than flatter him as he wants) by telling him that the world's biggest expert on alien knowledge is Patrick Moore.

CHARACTER BUILDING: *Jackie Tyler* – Has spent the past year searching for her daughter, who disappeared with the Doctor during the Auton attack ('Rose'). She thought Rose was dead and doesn't deal well with her answer of having been 'travelling'. She's been asked out by someone named Billy Croony. She is a little too human for the Doctor, who is astounded that she pays more attention to herself than the alien landing; she later throws a house party, toasting 'the Martians'. Her neighbour Ru says she owes Mickey an apology. Jackie turns the Doctor in to the military, worried that he is acting untoward with her daughter and freaked out by seeing the inside of the TARDIS, but is visited by Strickland, a police commissioner ... who is also a Slitheen and attempts to kill her.

Mickey Smith – His girlfriend having vanished, Mickey was the prime suspect in the police investigation of her disappearance until the Doctor returned, taken in five times for questioning. He's waited twelve months for Rose and the Doctor to return; he looked every day for her for an entire year. He hasn't seen anyone else (romantically). The Doctor antagonises him and calls him 'Ricky'. Mickey thinks it's a strange way to invade the Earth, with the aliens putting the world on red alert with a crash landing. He knows that the Doctor used to work for UNIT (he's spent the last twelve months reading up on the Doctor and other unidentified research).

Harriet Jones – MP for Flydale North (a fictional constituency, although you wouldn't believe it judging by the prevalence of mentions it received on message boards on genuine political websites following the broadcast and leading up to the 2005 General Election). She's at 10 Downing Street because of a prior appointment at 3.15 pm on the day of the spaceship crash. She makes an overture of bringing coffee to Indra, a junior secretary, though he sees through her 'cunning plan' to gain access to the acting Prime Minister. She considers herself a 'faithful back bencher' who doesn't get to Number 10 very often. She's prepared a paper on cottage hospitals; she's worked out a system whereby they don't have to be excluded from Centres of Excellence status, mostly because her mother is in Flydale Infirmary. She tries to slip her paper into the acting Prime Minister's briefcase, stumbles upon the emergency procedures for alien invasion, and hides in a closet to avoid detection when Green enters the office. She, Rose and Indra face off against the Slitheen masquerading as Margaret Blaine.

Joseph Green – MP for Hartley Dale (another fictional constituency), and Chairman of the Parliamentary Commission on the Monitoring of Sugar Standards in Exported Confectionary. His body has been occupied by a Slitheen.

General Asquith – Military leader in the British Army. He thinks of this as the 'greatest crisis in modern history,' supervises Dr Sato's research at Albion, and believes Joseph Green's leadership has been abysmal. He is killed and occupied by one of the Slitheen who had previously pretended to be Oliver Charles.

Margaret Blaine – A representative of MI5, she has been replaced by one of the Slitheen. The alien said she personally escorted the Prime Minister to his car, but was actually responsible for his death. Releasing excess gases causes her to 'shake her booty'.

Oliver Charles – A transport liaison, and another Slitheen, who later discards this body to take over General Asquith. He has enjoyed a wife, a mistress and a young farmer ... This Slitheen has obviously been very busy.

Indra Ganesh – Junior Secretary with the Ministry of Defence (MoD), he is oblivious to the Slitheen plot, interested only in the crisis at hand. He is killed by the Slitheen posing as Margaret Blaine.

The Reporters – The male reporter for BBC News is named Tom. He reports live from the banks of the Thames and Albion Hospital. His female American counterpart states that as a result of the crashed spaceship, all flights over North America have been grounded and the Secretary General (presumably of the United Nations) has asked that people 'watch the skies'.

BAD WOLF: A young boy spray paints the words BAD WOLF on the side of the TARDIS. There is also, of course, the matter of a little pig running through Albion Hospital ...

FANTASTIC!: The Doctor tells Rose, 'This is fantastic,' when they get stuck in the gridlock of Central London after the alien ship crashes.

BODY COUNT: Quite high – the Prime Minister has been murdered, and the Slitheen have killed everyone whose bodies they've taken over. Those we know of are Joseph Green, Margaret Blaine, Strickland, Oliver Charles and General Asquith (the latter witnessed by Harriet). Indra Ganesh is killed by the Slitheen posing as Margaret, and the attendant alien experts from UNIT are all killed by the Slitheen pretending to be Green.

THE DOCTOR'S MAGICAL SONIC SCREWDRIVER: It unlocks the Albion Hospital supply closet that the TARDIS materialises in. The Doctor uses it to make repairs to the underside of the controls of his 'frankly magnificent time ship'.

REALITY BITES: Former BBC Political Editor Andrew Marr plays himself, in an appearance widely covered by the British press; Marr is stationed outside 10 Downing Street (or, rather, the alternate location serving as its entrance) reporting on the events at the residence and the comings and goings of dignitaries. BBC News 24 plays on the television seen at points during the episode, although the telephone numbers displayed on screen are fake. Also, *Blue Peter* host Matt Baker plays himself in another piece seen on television during the episode, decorating an edible spaceship cake on the programme during the alien landing.

The Doctor says that Lloyd George used to drink him under the table. David Lloyd George (1863-1945) was born in Manchester, though was brought up in Wales and considered himself to be a Welshman. He was Prime Minister from 1916 to 1922. He visited Hitler in 1936 in an unsuccessful attempt to dissuade the dictator from his fascist expansion across Europe, and later became an opponent of appeasement before his death. (Coincidentally, his Liberal nemesis in Parliament prior to his installation as Prime Minister was Herbert Asquith, namesake of General Asquith in this story.)

Sir Patrick Moore CBE (1923-) is a well-known British astronomer, novelist and television personality.

While it's a colloquialism in common usage, Big Ben is actually the name of the clock bell of St Stephen's Tower (but since Big Ben is used as a generic term for tower, bell and clock, the Doctor and BBC News can be forgiven). The Doctor likens the 'alien' pig to a mermaid; he compares it to what Victorian showmen used to draw crowds, glueing the skull of a cat to the skeleton of a fish and then displaying the result. St Thomas' Hospital is the nearest hospital to the part of the Thames where the alien ship crashes.

One of the telephone numbers seen in this episode works; the phone number on one of the doors of the army vehicle that blocks the Doctor and Rose from seeing the crash site belongs to the freephone Army Driving Line.

The BBC's official *Doctor Who* website added a subsidiary site after the transmission of this episode. Called unit.org.uk, this was a fictional information site about UNIT.

The American news channel seen in this episode is called AMNN, perhaps after the CNN network (possibly AMerican News Network?)

LINKING THEMES: Invited to 10 Downing Street during the alien emergency are several representatives from UNIT, the United Nations Intelligence Taskforce. UNIT was a major component of the original *Doctor Who* series, the Doctor having served as their unpaid scientific advisor (mostly during the Doctor's third incarnation).

The TARDIS isn't at its best anymore (possibly because the Time Lords no longer exist), and among the Doctor's remedies for when it malfunctions is a mallet he uses to strike the console. The TARDIS key glows when the TARDIS is about to materialise; this idea is later developed in 'Father's Day'. The Doctor says that the TARDIS scanner gets all the 'basic packages', including the football (probably referring to satellite television).

A dark-haired female at the briefing has a name badge that reads FROST. This is visible on page 77 of the BBC's *Monsters and Villains* book. While not implicit, this could be a reference to Muriel Frost, a UNIT character who appeared in several instalments of the *Doctor Who Magazine* comic strip and later in the audio play *The Fires of Vulcan*.

SCENE MISSING: Why do the Slitheen glow from the inside when they open up their forehead zippers? And why can't the zipper be seen, for that matter? (See 'Technical Goofs'.) They seem to exude some form of electric energy, possibly from the compression equipment, and this also seems to affect the lights in the rooms, as they go off as the zippers are unzipped.

How can the clock tower still continue running considering it's been struck by a spaceship? The Big Ben clock reads 9.58am (or, rather, 2.02pm, considering the film is being played in reverse; see 'Technical Goofs') when the alien ship strikes it, but the clock shows 6.12pm when it's shown on television later in the day.

Why is the Doctor continuing to deny his age? The television series states his age as 953 in 'Time and the Rani' (and if you include non-televised adventures later on, he ages at least 150 years in his seventh and eighth incarnations; of course, that's a matter for debate).

Other questions: Why is Joseph Green promoted to acting Prime Minister? For an MP with such a dubious distinction, he seems to take over with ease (of course, that's assuming that he doesn't have a more secret official role in the government). There are, however, a number of Slitheen that appear later that could have assisted his rise to power. How does Jackie Tyler suddenly know that the Doctor's ship is called the TARDIS? (Unless she's heard it off camera, we don't see her being told the name.) How does the Doctor immediately know that Rose has been gone a year? (He doesn't have enough time to go back into the TARDIS, and all he sees is the date on the poster; unless, of course, he knows he's landed on that date and just plain forgot what year it had been before, or realises he has misread twelve months as twelve hours on the TARDIS equipment.)

ALTERED STATES: *Radio Times* credited Fiesta Mei Ling and Basil Chung as 'Chinese Woman' and 'Chinese Man', which was also the way they had been credited in early press for the episode. Plans to call this episode 'Aliens of London, Part One' were dropped.

BEHIND THE SCENES: The Cardiff Royal Infirmary was used as Albion Hospital. The semi-circular Infirmary sign over the entrance was blacked out with fabric and the words 'Albion Hospital' transposed upon it. An empty room inside the Infirmary was blacked out using blue fabric sheets on the window exteriors, turning it into Dr Sato's mortuary; the sequence with Dr Sato and General Asquith together was the first scene recorded for this season. Brought on location were a genuine Saxon APC (Armoured Personnel Carrier) of the British army and military police vehicles. The sequence where the Doctor and Rose are stopped by traffic was recorded on the street outside the Infirmary. (There was also a Mini Cooper photographed by fans on the first day of recording ... but instead of a prop, it turned out to be executive producer Julie Gardner's car.)

The sequence where the Doctor chases the pig – Christopher Eccleston's first work on *Doctor Who* – was also recorded inside the building. A building façade on John Adam Street in Central London was redressed to become 10 Downing Street (although with a slightly different typestyle for the number for the fictional version) for the arrivals, Marr's reports and Green's press conference, while the seventeenth-century Hensol Castle in the Vale of Glamorgan was used to record the 10 Downing Street interiors, including the hallways and the Cabinet office. The Brandon Estate in Kennington was again used for the Powell Estate courtyard where the TARDIS lands, as well as the exteriors of Rose's flat, the rooftop and the balcony where revellers gather to celebrate the aliens' arrival. Interiors of the Tyler flat, the TARDIS and the American TV newsroom were recorded in studio.

In the scene in the sedan, both Eccleston and Piper are actually seated in the same seat; rather than remounting the camera on the right side to film the Doctor on the left, Eccleston sat in the same seat and the video was reversed (noticeable in that the mole on Eccleston's right cheek is on the wrong side). The same can be seen when the Doctor speed-reads the UNIT documents in the briefing room; again, the mole is on the 'wrong' side.

For the alien crash landing, video footage of the Thames was used by the computer animation team to recreate the surface of the water as a model spacecraft hit it. Various splashes of water and sand were incorporated into the final image, as well as a CGI crest of water that hits and blocks out the camera.

DULCET TONES: 'Starman' by David Bowie – Bowie's second single, released July 1969, backed with 'The Wild Eyed Boy From Freecloud', reached number 5 in the UK charts and number 15 in the US. It later attained the UK number 1 spot on its 1975 re-release. It featured on his second album, 'David Bowie/Space Oddity' (November 1969), which was an instant success and has been reissued many times around the world. This is playing at one of the alien welcome house parties, very quietly, as the Doctor is giving Rose her own TARDIS key. (Heard 14.31-15.34)

OFF THE SCREEN: Esteemed actress Penelope Wilton OBE is a recipient of the London Critics' Circle Theatre Award and the London *Evening Standard* Theatre Award for performances in such plays as *Much Ado About Nothing, The Deep Blue Sea, The Little Foxes* and *Man and Superman*, and has been seen in such films as *The French Lieutenant's Woman* (1981), *Cry Freedom* (1987), *Blame it on the Bellboy* (1992), *Clockwise* (1986), *Calendar Girls* (2003), *Pride and Prejudice* (2005), *Shaun of the Dead* (2004) and *Alice Through the Looking Glass* (1998), and the television series *Ever Decreasing Circles* (1984-1989), *Bob & Rose* (2001, *Falling* (2005) and *Screaming* (1992). She was made an Officer of the Order of the British Empire in 2004. Annette Badland is best known to fans for playing Griselda Fishfinger in *Jabberwocky* (1977) and has been seen in *Beyond Bedlam* (1993), *The Queen's Nose* (1995), *Gulliver's Travels* (1996), *Little Voice* (1998), *Mrs Caldicot's Cabbage War* (2000), *Club Le Monde* (2002) and the television production of *Casanova* (2005); she is also a regular on the BBC1 series *Cutting It* (2002-) and has made appearances on *Bergerac* (1981-1984), *Making Out* (1989-1991), *Holding On* (1997), *Coronation Street* (2005), *Jackanory* (1995), *2point4 Children* (1991/1993), *Born and Bred* (2002), *Holby City* (1999), *Judge John Deed* (2005) and *The Worst Witch* (1998/1999), among countless other television roles. David Verrey was seen in *Bridget Jones: The Edge of Reason* (2004), on the series *Family Affairs* (1999) and *Knightmare* (1989) and the *Red Dwarf* episode 'Only The Good' (1999). Rupert Vansittart was a regular on *Harry Enfield's Brand Spanking New Show* (2000), plays the role of Lord Ashfordly on ITV's popular drama *Heartbeat* (1992-), and has featured in the films *Cutthroat*

Island (1995), *Braveheart* (1995), *Four Weddings and a Funeral* (1994), *The Remains of the Day* (1993) and *Half Moon Street* (1986) and in the series *Mr Bean* (1994/5), *Randall and Hopkirk (Deceased)* (2001) and *The Bill* (2000). Navin Chowdhry played Kurt McKenna on *Teachers* (2001-2003) and Ralph in *NY-LON* (2004), as well as the recurring role of Sanjay Singh in episodes of *Dalziel and Pascoe* (1997). Naoko Mori was in *Topsy-Turvy* (1999), *Hackers* (1995) and *Spiceworld: The Movie* (1997) and in the series *Casualty* (1993/4), but is perhaps best known as the daffy Sarah (*aka* Titicaca) on *Absolutely Fabulous* (1992-2003). Eric Potts played Mr Moore in *Brookside* (1998-2000) and has guested on *Coronation Street* (1996/1998). Steve Speirs was seen in *The Musketeer* (2001) and in *Cor Blimey!* (2000) and voiced Captain Tarpals in *Star Wars: Episode I – The Phantom Menace* (1999). Ceris Jones appeared in *House!* (2000) and *Sex Lives of the Potato Men* (2004). Jack Tarlton starred as the title character in the miniseries *The Genius of Mozart* (2004). Lachele Carl was in *My Beautiful Son* (2001). Fiesta Mei Ling has appeared in episodes of *Terry and June* (1983) and *The Professionals* (1980). Basil Chung was seen in *Gangs of New York* (2002). Young actor Corey Doabe made his television debut in this story.

Award-winning journalist Andrew Marr served as the BBC's Political Editor from 2000 to 2005. Having joined the *Scotsman* as a junior business reporter in 1981, he went on to become a Parliamentary correspondent in 1984, and a political correspondent in 1986. He has written for the *Daily Express,* the *Observer,* the *Economist* and the *Independent,* the latter of which he also edited until 1998. Marr hosts the BBC Radio 4 programme *Start The Week* and took over the BBC1 Sunday morning series *Breakfast* from Sir David Frost in the summer of 2005.

Durham-born Matt Baker has been a presenter on the long-running children's series *Blue Peter* since 1999. His dog Meg frequently appears alongside him on the series. Prior to *Blue Peter*, Baker was an accomplished gymnast. He has also been seen acting in *Compere* (2002) and *Right Love, Wrong Time* (2005).

TECHNICAL GOOFS: When the alien ship crashes into the clock tower, the video is transposed so that the numbers on the clock are reversed.

The BBC News 24 channel loses its clock in early parts of the episode, though it's back on screen when Jackie telephones the emergency services. The police commissioner that attacks Jackie has a visible zipper on his forehead but none of the others does. Harriet and Rose appear to walk through the very door Ganesh forbids them earlier to enter (though this could simply be misleading camera work; the door could in fact be off to the right, not the actual doorway they pass through). The doorway into the Cabinet room is closed when Harriet Jones walks in, but is then ajar when the Slitheen and General Asquith arrive.

CONTROVERSIES: In response to being told that having his face slapped hurt, Rose chides the Doctor with the friendly insult: 'You're so gay!' While this was obviously meant as a mild quip, some fans took serious offence at the line. The 'space pig' produced some consternation, especially when photos were first seen; of course, it works well once explained in the context of the story (assuming that the viewer hasn't switched channels by that point). Then, of course, the most controversial part of the episode: the flatulence, which – despite being given a logical explanation in the episode – turned off some viewers and media alike.

The BBC's decision to run the 'Next Week' preview straight after the cliff-hanger raised howls of protests and complaints to the BBC's Duty Office. As a result, the conclusion of the first episode of the next two-part story, 'The Empty Child', had the 'Next Week' section moved to the *end* of the episode, after the closing credits, and the continuity announcer warned people to look away if they didn't want to know what happened next. Unfortunately this positive achievement was not carried through to the final two-parter, when 'Bad Wolf' ended with the preview back crashing the cliff-hanger ending once more.

INTERNAL CONSISTENCY: The Doctor thinks it's been twelve hours since he and Rose left present-day London, but it has actually been twelve months. The poster the Doctor sees confirms that 'Rose Tyler has been missing from her home on the Powell Estate since 6th March 2005'. This places 'Aliens of London' in March 2006, most likely the last week of the month. (6 March 2005 was a Sunday, but the events of 'Rose' definitely make it seem as though the two days involved for that earlier story are a Wednesday and Thursday. However there is an argument that dates in the *Doctor Who* universe do not fall on the same days of the week as those in the 'real world'. For example, Monday 16 July 1966 is mentioned in 'The War Machines' and this is off by two days – 16 July 1966 was actually a Saturday.

The spaceship crashes into Big Ben at 9.58 am. This is after Rose, Jackie and the Doctor have had time to talk and call the police – putting the TARDIS's arrival at close to 8 or 9 am. As the Doctor watches the news reports later, the clock now says 6.12 pm (although this is probably wildly inaccurate as two sides of the clock have been blown away, which can't have been healthy for the timing mechanism). At one point the channel is flipped to CBBC, and *Blue Peter* is being broadcast; it airs on that network from 6 pm to 6.30 pm, tying in with the 6.12 time seen on the clock. (The American news programme is called AMNN – with a six hour difference between London and New York during the last week of March, this further points to that time of the month.)

Later that same evening the Doctor visits Albion Hospital and encounters Dr Sato and the alien pig at 10.47 pm. He then returns to the Powell Estate where Jackie, confused and scared, calls the emergency line at 11.08 pm. By approximately 11.30 pm the Doctor and Rose are picked up by the authorities and taken to 10 Downing Street. The end of the episode brings us close to midnight as the Slitheen unleash their trap ...

THEME ANALYSES

As Doctor Who For A Modern Audience: *Doctor Who* companions almost never return home, and if they do, it's to leave, not pop in for a quick chat with their family. But that's precisely what Rose does in 'Aliens Of London'. By making Rose's homecoming a year after she left, Davies seizes the opportunity to tackle 'domestic' matters head on and do something totally new for the series. Rose's emotional depth is strengthened as she's forced to confront the consequences her decision to board the TARDIS has had on those she loves. Bringing back Jackie and Mickey as recurring characters is another innovation as it gives the show the feel of having an ensemble cast, which is highly unusual for *Doctor Who*, with the only comparable time in the series's past being the UNIT seasons of the early 1970s. Their presence shows the increased focus on characterisation and demonstrates the importance of the human angle. The presentation of the episode plays its part in generating mass viewer appeal, in particular in the way the invasion is reported through the media coverage in a plausible attempt to show how everyday people would view such extraordinary events. As a two-part story, this episode revives the traditional cliff-hanger so integral to the original *Who*, but it seems very out of place here. The job of enticing the viewer back for next week's instalment has passed to the 'next time' preview, and as the latter gives away much about how the cliff-hanger is resolved, it shows that they cannot function together, certainly in situations dealing with the archetypal Doctor/companion in peril moment.

As Television Drama: With its central London setting and threat of an incursion by stealth, the closest comparator to 'Aliens of London' currently running on British television would be the spy drama *Spooks*, produced independently for BBC1 by Kudos Film & Television since 2002. This is the first time in the current run, though, where *Doctor Who* suffers slightly by the comparison – no matter how good the filmised digibeta video format looks, it can never compete in basic picture quality with the slickness and glossiness of a Super 16mm film production such as *Spooks*. The effects are certainly more ambitious, however, with the shot of St Stephen's Tower taking a sideswipe from the spaceship being probably one of the most impressive model effects seen on British television for many a year. Mention has been made of the 'soap opera' elements of this episode, although the scenes in Jackie's flat never feel particularly like any British soap – indeed, with the gaggle of friends and family gathered in the flat to watch the television coverage, it feels once again like something the characters of *Shameless* might do were an alien spacecraft to crash land on the Chatsworth Estate. Overall, though, it's not as impressive as the previous three episodes – there was possibly an argument for saying that each of the three was the best piece of drama transmitted by the BBC in its respective week, but with the likes of episode three of Davies's own *Casanova* showing on BBC1 two days after this, it can't be said here.

As A Piece of Writing: I think this episode is best viewed as not just an attempt to return to the mid-70s stories, where the Doctor rushed about every week saving the military from its own stupidity, but as a rather self-knowing spoof of them. That works better than it should, actually; the Doctor's plotline runs along at a fair clip, and the ridiculousness of the pig is funny when we learn it was, indeed, just a pig. The self-referential humour in general is quite amusing – the *Blue Peter* clip, Harriet Jones playing the role of the old-style companion, Rose being returned to the wrong date – but the rest of the jokes don't fare nearly as well. Mickey's the chief culprit, as neither his pratfalls, nor his boasting, nor his machismo are especially funny, but the 'gas exchange' goes a bit too far as well. Whether Davies's plotting ability has improved will be revealed next week, but for now, the somewhat more relaxed pace is a welcome change, and allows many of the secondary characters to make a bigger impact than normal. Jackie, in particular, has benefited from an evolution beyond the stock 'clueless mum' character. What puzzles me, though, is the appearance of that old chestnut UNIT. Maybe they will have a larger role in the next episode, but as it stands they seem to have been included as little more than a fan in-joke. I guess we'll just have to wait and see ...

The Doctor As A Mystery Figure: Using familiar contemporary geographical landmarks in a science fiction setting to provide the audience with a kick of realpolitik is one of the oldest tricks in the book, and it's genuinely comforting to see *Doctor Who* destroying Big Ben early in this episode. From there the Doctor, for once, finds himself on the outside of an alien invasion of London – watching events unfold on television and through distant glimpses of earth-shattering revelations. A bystander rather than a player, one might say. That, in itself, is an interesting dramatic avenue, but it's quickly forgotten as his not-so-mysterious past comes back to propel him, fully, into the centre of the action just in time for the episode's climax.

Themes, Genres and Modes: With a good lot of action set at 10 Downing Street, 'Aliens of

London' opts for the political thriller. *Doctor Who* hasn't done one of these before, where characters are in the corridors of power witnessing sinister things going on, all leading up to the unveiling of a mystery to reveal a serious threat. In grand *Doctor Who* tradition, what we get is a send up of the political thriller: while Tom Clancy would give us tactical experts and analysts, Davies gives us Harriet Jones, MP for Flydale North, who is far funnier and more delightful than all the Jack Ryans in the world. And the Doctor solves the mystery in about ninety seconds after arriving at Downing Street.

In Style and Structure: Stylistically, and structurally, Davies uses the media, and specifically television, for three main purposes throughout the episode. First, efficiently to get across exposition to the audience showing and telling how the military and government react to the UFO crash-landing. Secondly, to show how this event has affected the United Kingdom and the wider world politically, culturally and religiously. Finally, to get the Doctor and Rose into the heart of the story at 10 Downing Street. There's an interesting balance between humour and horror in 'Aliens of London'. Davies uses the humour of the disguised aliens passing wind as a counterpoint to later scenes dealing with the horrific nature of the aliens and how they create their disguises. The issue of class structure is touched upon once more, through the interactions of politician Harriet Jones with public servant Indra Ganesh; in all the chaos going on at Number 10, she's the only one to show a moment of human kindness to him. Davies builds the story up to a triple cliff-hanger, which, while each is a variation on the same theme, ends the episode effectively. This will no doubt do its job and entice audiences back next week to see how it will be resolved.

As Doctor Who Continuity: Big Ben gets smashed, and yet it's still standing in the 22nd century at the time of 'The Dalek Invasion of Earth' (1964). Obviously the landmark gets rebuilt (for the second time in the ninth Doctor's lifespan – it was fairly damaged in the novel *The Clockwise Man* as well). The ninth Doctor claims to be 900 years old, but the seventh Doctor was 953 in 'Time and the Rani' (1987). It's open to interpretation, with the ninth Doctor saying he's been travelling for 900 years (well, at least that's how I'm going to interpret it!) Good old UNIT gets a name-check. I'm relieved the producers resisted the obvious by not bringing back previous characters such as the Brigadier for cameos in the 10 Downing Street scenes. The Tylers' home is in the Powell Estate, which is probably a nod to Jonathan Powell, who was Head of Series and Serials when *Doctor Who* was rested in 1989. There's lots of continuity with 'Rose', of course: we now know the years in which the 'present' day segments are set: 2005 and 2006. Interestingly, *Doctor Who* is now starting to catch up with its own past continuity, in that the early 21st Century is the period in which Salamander rose to power ('The Enemy of the World', 1967), and from which the Doctor's companion Zoe Heriot comes, a time when there were deep space rockets and space stations. In terms of the on-going 'Big Bad Wolf' saga, the TARDIS gets spray-painted with the words BAD WOLF. And I'm sure we've all got our own pet theories as to the implications this will have in later episodes. So, we've got the Big Bad Wolf, Rose is clearly Red Riding Hood, and this episode gives us a wee little pig. I'm dying to know what it all means!

From A Special Effects Viewpoint: Our second contemporary Earth invasion for the new series ('Rose' being the first) ... and an episode that gives us some technically impressive sequences alongside some relatively mediocre (and even poor) special effects and creature suits. The scene depicting the crash-landing of the spaceship in the Thames is handled extremely well with some fabulous model work by *Doctor Who* effects veteran Mike Tucker and his crew, but once the 'aliens' begin to grace our screens, it all starts to go a bit pear-shaped. The 'realistic' pig-man comes across as just a tad too cartoonish to me (less anatomically correct and more 'Pigs In Space'). And then there are the Slitheen. These are, in my opinion, unsuccessful creations. Their bodies are a decent design, but the wobbly, phallic necks and comical baby faces are just this side of unacceptable. As for the CGI versions, they are simply too dissimilar to the live-action costumes to make the action believable; even the colour scheme is visibly different. I certainly appreciate the attempt to bring eight-foot-tall beasties to life on a TV budget, but something simply didn't click here and it may well have its origins at the design phase. And here I thought the days of rubbery *Doctor Who* monsters were long over.

PANEL REVIEWS

Doctor Who fans love talking about what is 'traditional' *Doctor Who*. And yet, in spite of the previous story being set in Philip Hinchcliffe's Victoriana, probably the most 'traditional' *Doctor Who* story this season is 'Aliens of London'. It certainly is the closest Davies is going to get to pure Robert Holmes pastiche. The best thing about this story are the 'Holmesian' touches: the broad, even grotesque, characters; the satirical flourishes; the bizarre aliens; the use of esoteric historical facts; and the subversion of the alien invasion. Frankly, the farting Slitheen is just the sort of thing that Robert Holmes would have done had he thought he could get away with it. (Look at what he put into his 1980s stories when he realised he could get away with it!) Admittedly the domestic stuff obscures this truth a little, but it's so fabulous we have to forgive it: the pre-credits sequence is brilliant and the implications of the Doctor taking Rose away accidentally for twelve months are really well thought through. And who could have guessed from his performance in 'Rose' that Noel Clarke can act? Mickey was one of the best things about this episode, and the Doctor's antagonistic relationship with him worth viewing alone. 'Aliens of London' isn't going to blow down the doors the way 'The End of the World' did, but it's funny and smart just like *Doctor Who* should be. – *Graeme Burk*

'Aliens Of London' returns the series to Davies's more whimsical stylings, with aliens zipping themselves up in human bodies and taking over 10 Downing Street. And farting. A lot. This descent into crudity is distracting but not overly so, although it does make it difficult to take the Slitheen threat seriously. Perhaps that's the point though. This is also the first two-part storyline, which gives the episode a much more relaxed pace that feels very appropriate given the emphasis on Rose's return home. The scenes of Rose facing Jackie and Mickey after being away for a whole year are by far the most gratifying bits of the episode as they do something innovative with the role of the companion, ensuring that Rose is already well on her way to becoming one of the most rounded of that elite group. It is perhaps difficult to judge it individually as only half its story has been told, but it's an ok beginning with some good moments – the Doctor's discovery of the soldiers, his sadness over the pigman's execution, Harriet Jones's persistence – and more lightweight fun. I do feel that we're getting to the point when we need something more serious and dramatic though, to give the series greater variety and balance, which if 'World War Three' continues in the same manner, it won't be able to afford. – *Simon Catlow*

On the one hand, 'Aliens of London' is a mess. The plot is not all that great, some of the acting is mediocre at best, and the direction is just all over the place. However, I found myself liking this episode more than the previous three. I think this is because a lot is happening. In the other episodes so far, the Doctor and Rose show up, and within a matter of a couple of hours have foiled plots years in the making – it just seems too easy. Here the Doctor actually takes time to investigate and look at the clues to figure out what is going on. Of course it could be said that this is also a detriment to the story as there are too many subplots being explored. The most interesting has to be Rose's unique return home. Davies has put more thought into the consequences of time travel and brought that forward. That twist is probably the best thing about this pair of episodes. The fart jokes didn't bother me all that much and I'm sure it made the kids giggle. But at the end of the day, all these things add up and just leave a jumbled mess. – *Robert Franks*

You know, I was all set to really tear into this episode – and then I watched it again. I think it's one that deserves the re-evaluation of a second viewing, because without so many expectations – it is, by far, the episode we'd had the most hints about long before broadcast – it stops needing to be a big event and quietly settles into being a good, if very familiar, little runaround. Its major problem is that as the first episode of the first two-parter, it should have and even could have been great; what we have instead is a pleasant, traditional script, hampered slightly by overdone humour and far more by Keith Boak's uninspired direction. Out of every four times I winced, three of them were surely for directorial choices: the excessively colour-timed shots of the Doctor and Rose on the rooftop, and of the police escort, that look so artificial; the emerging Slitheen heads that are obviously CGI; and the excruciatingly drawn-out, never-ending cliff-hanger. Boak has an abrasive editing style, he arranges special effects shots poorly, and at certain moments, he even allows the actors to descend into camp. I don't like it, and it's unfortunate, because otherwise there's a lot to enjoy: the Doctor's enthusiasm ('Yesterday you were tiny and made of clay!'); his anger at seeing life needlessly killed; Penelope Wilton's endlessly cheery Harriet Jones; and most of all, those wonderful scenes of Rose dealing with her return home. All told, it's a mixed bag – but not nearly as bad as the first viewing implies. – *Sarah Hadley*

'Aliens of London' is the first episode of the new series that I felt wasn't superb. Of course it's probably unrealistic to expect every one of the episodes to be as good as the first three, but the problem that I had with this offering was how uneven it was. There was much to like – the basic plot idea of alien invaders faking an alien invasion; the Doctor's reaction to the death of the pig; Rose finding out she'd been gone for a year instead of just twelve hours. All this was very good stuff, well done, but for each such instance there was something that made me uneasy. Mickey's pratfalling; the Doctor's attitude towards him; and of course the Slitheen flatulence. I know it probably makes me sound like an uptight old fanboy who just doesn't 'get it', but the latter made me cringe. The episode was entertaining enough in its way, but I couldn't help thinking how much better it would have been if the invasion had been done dead straight, instead of as the vague send-up it seemed to be. Not bad *Doctor Who* perhaps in the context of everything that's ever gone before, but weak in comparison with the rest of the season so far. – *Paul Hayes*

Rarely are family members and loved ones of the Doctor's companions seen, and when they are, most of them meet a horrible fate. This makes the scenes showing Rose dealing with the fallout from her disappearance with her mother and Mickey poignant to watch, while they also slowly show the build-up of the main plot line of 'Aliens of London'. Noel Clarke as Mickey provides some effective humour, executing a well timed crash into a wall, and getting caught at the wrong end of an argument with the Doctor. The visual effects work is superb, with the highlight being the sequence showing the UFO crash-landing in the Thames, combining model work and CGI, and taking out a well known London icon along the way. The humorous element of the disguised aliens passing wind won't be to everyone's tastes; indeed, the only people to find it funny within the episode itself are the aliens, but it's not all laughs when it comes to this particular species. To top it off, there's a brilliant triple cliff-hanger, setting up events for the next episode. – *Cameron Mason*

Oh, dear. It was inevitable there would be a duff episode. Things were going quite nicely, starting with the emotionally charged reunion between Rose and her Mum (I didn't see that inspired twist coming!) and the impressive spaceship crash – but then the silly aliens in human guise appeared. With zips. (Yes, I got the joke; *Doctor Who* aliens always have visible zips.) It might have worked if it wasn't for the 'farting', and the giggling. What on Earth was Davies thinking? I thought this was *Doctor Who*, not *Red Dwarf*. The script, which had some interesting concepts and ideas, probably looked good on paper, but simply was poorly executed. Granted that this episode contained some of the first sequences recorded for the series, and the cast and crew were probably finding their feet, but some of the acting by the guest cast was cringe-worthy, and the direction flat, patchy and disjointed. I found the (serious) sub-plot at *cheü* Tyler far more engaging than the (supposedly humorous) alien invasion main plotline. As for the Slitheen, they were badly animated and not scary in the slightest, looking more like a cross between ET and the ridiculous mutant from *Alien Resurrection*. I don't want to appear totally brutal, as there were a number of nice moments, like the conversations between the Doctor and Rose (Billie Piper is superb in these), the Doctor's discomfort being around so many humans, and the clever *Blue Peter* 'cameo'. I hope part two is an improvement, but based on the trailers, I don't think it will be. – *Jon Preddle*

'Aliens of London' is, possibly, the first episode of the new era that isn't wholly successful. Davies's script is often brilliant – his take on military SF and his cheeky irreverence for a few sacred cows (farting aliens taking over the government, pigs in space) make him come across as someone who delights in playing with form. But, on this occasion, that seems to have been somewhat at the expense of substance, as a whole twenty minutes goes by in the middle of the episode where, basically, nothing happens. You could get away with those sort of conceits in a six-parter in the Jon Pertwee era, but it's a bit more difficult these days. Plus, one or two of the supporting cast didn't seem to know whether they were in something that was supposed to be horrific or *Teletubbies* with better production values. Nevertheless, it's hardly a disaster as, once again, the jokes are all fantastic, there's some very nice characterisation on offer, and Eccleston is superb – particularly when he barges into a meeting of the top brass like he owns the place. – *Keith Topping*

(singing) Ah-ooooo, 'Aliens of London' ... It began as an amusing romp (the scene where the Doctor realises he has brought Rose back to Earth twelve months later instead of twelve hours is grand), but then the disguised Slitheen began farting, giggling like children and farting some

more, but because it was only episode four of the new series, and because I've been watching it with a wide-open mind, I bit my tongue (and lips and cheeks) each time it occurred! Fortunately, we are given a nicely emotional side-story involving Rose, Mickey and Rose's mother, Jackie, as well as the delightful Harriet Jones, MP for Flydale North, wonderfully portrayed by Penelope Wilton. But apart from these characters and their own interesting and charming stories, there's not a lot here that stands out. We've already had our contemporary Earth invasion story in 'Rose', and so overall this one feels a bit samey, and the farting aliens make it slightly embarrassing. No question about it, this is my least favourite, thus far. – *Scott Alan Woodard*

EDITOR'S REVIEW: 'Aliens of London' is something of a low point in the first season. It's not that it's a bad story, per se; it just all seems rather lacklustre. The Doctor comes to Earth, fights with Rose's mum, runs around a hospital, finds out some swarthy aliens are trying to take over, and pontificates (albeit more so than usual). 'Aliens of London' was one of the first episodes recorded, and it shows; it bears some of the less successful directorial aspects of 'Rose' but none of its most precious touches (many of which would be relegated to the second half, 'World War Three'). Some might say it's impossible fully to review and appreciate the first half of a two-part story, but taken on its merits – even under the assumption that the Doctor will once more save the day and live to tell the tale – it still all seems a bit normal and boring, even for him.

Also, I can definitely appreciate juvenile humour with the best of them (I was once a preteen, after all), but the inclusion of flatulence in this episode was an example of overkill; Joseph Green's 'nervous stomach' was passable enough, and obviously Strickland's little issue toward the end was a plot revelation (the bad guy's after Jackie). There was no need, however, for the gross display of flatulence at 10 Downing Street, and I didn't need to know that Margaret Blaine was 'shaking her booty'. Enough is, frankly, enough.

What ultimately saves this episode is that the performances, and some of the characters, more than make up for the story. The single best thing about this episode is Noel Clarke; I thought his performance in 'Rose' lacked coherence, whereas 'Aliens of London' (and 'World War Three') demonstrates that, given the right material, he can excel. He has a natural chemistry with Eccleston and Piper, and an unusual way of pouting without actually doing it that's just charming. Likewise, after five minutes of Penelope Wilton's portrayal of Harriet Jones, you want to follow her home and eat cake; she's delightful, like someone's mother that everyone on the block adores. (Wilton goes on to prove in the next episode that this isn't a fluke; she's a marvellous actress, worthy of the role.) Camille Coduri turns what could have been a one-note, one-dimensional mother character into a real person, especially when she berates the Doctor and slaps him across the face; she annoyed me in 'Rose', and now I feel she's more fully realised and far more interesting. The other actors served their purposes, although I was a bit irritated that they killed off Indra Ganesh so quickly and that Dr Sato didn't have enough to do (I'm a fan of *Absolutely Fabulous* and I adore Naoko Mori.)

'Aliens of London' definitely improves upon second and subsequent viewings; the first time round, all I could focus on was the farting and those silly Slitheen outfits. And the Slitheen's plan to gather all the alien experts in one place ... had they not considered a convention? Probably far easier than infiltrating the British government. The Rose-Jackie interplay is very believable, and the Doctor-Mickey relationship is worth watching by itself. It's also marvellous to see the Doctor relegated to watching history on television, and even though I'm not as familiar with him as British viewers, it's obvious that Andrew Marr is good at his job. Given the dialogue he speaks, I'd be quite surprised if the man didn't have to do second and third takes from the laughter alone (the Minister for Sugar Exports in Confectionary, indeed!)

While it's at the bottom of my list on this season's roster of episodes, 'Aliens of London' is still a light-hearted diversion with some substantial themes (alien invasion, the slaughter of innocents – like the pig – and the bonds between its characters). There would be far better to recommend in *Doctor Who* series one ... but if this is represents the nadir of the first season, then I'm certainly satisfied with the outcome. – *Shaun Lyon*

105: WORLD WAR THREE

The Slitheen plot is underway. As the Doctor, Rose and Harriet Jones race against time to prevent the Earth from being turned into a scrap heap, Mickey and Jackie find new strength both to fend off their Slitheen pursuer and to help save the world before it's destroyed by nuclear Armageddon.

FIRST TRANSMISSION: UK – 23 April 2005. Canada – 3 May 2005. Australia – 18 June 2005. New Zealand – 4 August 2005.
DURATION: 42'56"
WRITER: Russell T Davies
DIRECTOR: Keith Boak
CREDITED CAST: Christopher Eccleston (Doctor Who), Billie Piper (Rose Tyler), Camille Coduri (Jackie Tyler), Noel Clarke (Mickey Smith), Penelope Wilton (Harriet Jones), Annette Badland (Margaret Blaine), David Verrey (Joseph Green), Rupert Vansittart (General Asquith), Morgan Hopkins (Sergeant Price), Steve Speirs (Strickland), Jack Tarlton (Reporter), Lachele Carl (Reporter), Corey Doabe (Spray Painter), Elizabeth Fost (Slitheen), Paul Kasey (Slitheen), Alan Ruscoe (Slitheen), Andrew Marr (As Himself)

WHERE AND WHEN: London, March 2006, immediately after 'Aliens of London', including at Rose's and Jackie's flat in South East London, and 10 Downing Street. (See 'Rose' for an alternate take on the timeframe of the story.)

THE STORY UNFOLDS: The Slitheen are here on Earth to reduce it to molten slag, and then sell it off piecemeal as radioactive fuel for massive profits during a galactic recession. The Doctor knows that one of their spaceships is submerged in the North Sea and that they've murdered their way to the top of government. They didn't use the Prime Minister's body, because they couldn't compress down to his size. They crashed their ship in Central London to cause an international spectacle, so that later calls for nuclear strikes would be more easily answered; they would then turn the missiles upon other countries, prompting retaliation until the world is obliterated. They are believed destroyed by a warhead aimed at 10 Downing Street.

Slitheen is not their species name, but a family surname; the Slitheen on Earth are part of a family business, far from their homeworld. Judging by their shape, their ritualistic hunting tendencies, their yellow/green colour, sense of smell, the pig-enhancing technology, their slipstream engine, the scent of their gas emissions (a bad breath smell that can be likened to calcium decay) and their hyphenated surnames, the Doctor realises where the Slitheen are from, the planet Raxacoricofallapatorius, narrowing the choice down from over 5,000 worlds. They are made of living calcium, which is weakened by their compression field; they are therefore susceptible to acetic acid, which makes them explode on contact. The device around the Slitheen's necks is a compression field generator, which shrinks them down a bit; the gas produced by the creatures is a by-product of the reduction. They can move quickly when they want to, despite their large feet and clawed hands. They enjoy the thrill of a hunt as it 'purifies the blood', according to one of their number. They can smell human sweat and fear, as well as hormones and adrenaline. The emission from a standard fire extinguisher repels them.

The identification cards given to the Doctor and the UNIT officers can be activated to electrocute their wearers, but the Doctor is able to withstand the assault.

The UNIT secure website is accessible on the public internet with only a single password, which the Doctor knows is 'buffalo' (though this might possibly be a back-door entry into the system that only the Doctor knows about). The site is tracking the Slitheen spaceship in the North Sea and intercepting a transmission it is beaming into space. Mickey, with the Doctor's assistance on the telephone, uses the site to load and launch a non-nuclear missile (a subharpoon UGM-84A missile), and stops counter-defence 556 aimed at stopping the missile when it's on radar. While the missile destroys Number 10, the Cabinet room bunker ('made in Britain', explains Harriet) is safe. The Doctor uses the TARDIS to stop the Slitheen transmission.

Among the new arrivals at 10 Downing Street – the gathering of the rest of the Slitheen family – are Group Captain Tennant James of the RAF; Ewan McAllister, the deputy secretary for the Scottish Parliament; and, most unusually, Sylvia Dillane, chairman of the North Sea Boating Club.

THE DOCTOR: He's not able to persuade the military soldiers that Green and Asquith are Slitheen, and becomes a fugitive. He claims to feel very strongly that if someone wishes to execute a prisoner, they shouldn't stand said prisoner against a set of lift doors. He is very impressed by Harriet Jones, but can't shake the sense that he's heard of her. (Only late in the story does he remember why.) He's forced to swallow his pride when he admits he needs Mickey, and changes his mind about the boy after he helps stop the Slitheen. He 'doesn't do families' and refuses to join Jackie for dinner, saying he wants to ride a plasma storm in the Horsehead Nebula instead. After admitting that Mickey's not the idiot he once believed the boy to be, the Doctor gives him a CD containing a virus to remove any and all trace of himself from the Internet; in essence, the Doctor will cease to exist on Earth's computers.

ROSE TYLER: She wishes she had a Slitheen compression field so she'd be a size smaller. Harriet thinks she's a very violent young woman (as she wants to launch a nuclear bomb at the Slitheen). Without knowing what the Doctor's plans are for her, she accepts them blindly because she trusts him. She knows that one can survive an earthquake by standing under a doorway, and reasons that the cupboard in the Cabinet room can probably keep them alive when the missile strikes. Her mobile phone displays 'Tardis Calling' and shows a police box icon when the Doctor phones her from the telephone within the TARDIS.

CHARACTER BUILDING: *Harriet Jones* – While fearful of the Slitheen, Harriet is calm and collected under pressure, and doesn't like jokes during serious situations. She commands the Doctor to implement his dangerous final plan to use the warhead; as she says, she's the only elected representative in the Cabinet room. She voted against military strike options in recent British history. She considers herself a life-long back-bencher in Parliament, but after the Slitheen are destroyed she takes charge of the situation. As the Doctor finally recalls, Harriet Jones becomes a three-term Prime Minister and the 'architect of Britain's Golden Age'.

Jackie Tyler – Mickey has seen her when she's had a few drinks. She thinks it's embarrassing that Mickey saved her life (since he says she hates him so much). After everything she feels the Doctor has put her through, she just wants to know if Rose will be safe (and he cannot answer her). Jackie calls the aliens Slikeen. She's not happy that Harriet takes all the credit on television after the plot has been foiled instead of Rose. She's distrustful of the Doctor, even after Rose's life is safe, but she invites him to dinner; she wonders if the Doctor eats grass and safety pins and things and whether he drinks. She doesn't want Rose to leave again.

Mickey Smith – He saves Jackie from almost certain death at the hands of the Slitheen, then stops fleeing momentarily to take a photograph of the one that attacked her on his mobile camera phone, which he later sends to Rose on her 'super' mobile. He thinks that the Doctor has brought the death and destruction upon them. He has several drawings of police boxes in his bedroom, including a small sketch attached to his computer monitor. He's incredulous that everyone is calling the Slitheen attack a hoax. The Doctor offers him a place in the TARDIS; he refuses, but conspires with the Doctor to make Rose think that it's the Doctor who doesn't want him to travel with them, thus making Mickey seem better in Rose's eyes.

Joseph Green – The true name of the creature inhabiting his body is Jocrassa Fel Fotch Pasameer-Day Slitheen. He says he's being poisoned by the gas exchange and needs to be naked (that is, to be without the plasticised human body suit). Asquith comments that his body is 'magnificent'. He addresses the nations of the world and calls upon the UN for a pre-emptive nuclear strike against the aliens.

Margaret Blaine – The Slitheen inside her body has a childlike sense of humour, giggling and finding the gas emissions very funny. She is delighted that the phone in the Prime Minister's office is really red.

Sergeant Price – Military soldier who follows orders to the letter, including Joseph Green's and General Asquith's command that the Doctor be shot on sight, even though it obviously doesn't sit well with him. He evacuates 10 Downing Street before it's destroyed.

Strickland – Mickey ambushes him and rescues Jackie from his clutches. The real name of the creature inside is Slip Fel Fotch Pasameer-Day Slitheen. He is killed by Mickey and Jackie after being doused with vinegar; Jocrassa Fel Fotch says he can feel his brother's death.

The Reporters – While not referenced in the episode, further footage of the news broadcasts about the alien 'invasion' could be found on the BBC-run whoisdoctorwho.co.uk website (the site that, in fictional terms, was originally set up by Clive and is now being maintained by Mickey); in this, the male reporter is given the surname Hutchison, and the female reporter is called Mal Loup (French for 'bad wolf'). The footage is expanded from what is seen on screen in this episode.

BAD WOLF: The 'Bad Wolf' graffiti on the TARDIS is being removed by the spray-painting boy at the end of the story.

FANTASTIC!: The Doctor doesn't say 'fantastic' in this episode!

BODY COUNT: The Slitheen are believed destroyed in the blast at Number 10 Downing Street. As far as can be ascertained there are nine of the creatures there. (However, one escapes; see 'Boom Town'.)

THE DOCTOR'S MAGICAL SONIC SCREWDRIVER: The Doctor uses it to close the lift door when confronted by both soldiers and a Slitheen. He later threatens to explode a flask of spirits by 'triplicating the flammability of the alcohol' with the device (even though he actually just makes that up). It's used by the Doctor to scan the sides of the impenetrable shutters in the Cabinet room.

REALITY BITES: In this story, Harriet Jones reveals that nuclear weapons require release codes that are kept secret by the United Nations, saying that Britain cannot access them without a special resolution from the UN. This is not the case in the 'real' world: the United Kingdom owns its own warheads and does not need additional information from other nations to launch them. However it does not own the missiles on which the warheads are mounted; the British government leases the missiles from the United States.

Hannibal crossed the Alps by dissolving boulders with vinegar, says Harriet, a clue for Mickey and Jackie as to how to defeat the Slitheen attacking them. Harriet later mentions Hannibal again as the bunker is about to be struck by the missile.

According to the Doctor, 10 Downing Street was marshland two thousand years ago; in 1730 it was occupied by a 'nice man' named Mr Chicken (implying he's met him); and in 1796 the 'Cabinet room' would have been the safest place in the building. Three-inch thick steel walls were installed in 1991. The Cabinet room has no terminals and no outside access. The emergency protocols in the Cabinet room include a list of people who can help in an alien invasion; all of them are, unfortunately, dead. 'Mr Chicken' was the last private resident of 10 Downing Street; little is known about him except that he moved out of the residence in the early 1730s, to be replaced by Sir Robert Walpole, First Lord of the Treasury and considered to be the first Prime Minister.

Joseph Green mentions 'massive weapons of destruction' in his impassioned speech to the UN, an obvious riff on the term 'weapons of mass destruction' used by government officials in the US and UK during the 2003 war with Iraq.

The BBC-run unit.org.uk website featured a secure area that functioned much in the same way as the site Mickey accesses on screen. whoisdoctorwho.co.uk also exists in the real world, and reveals that Mickey did not use the CD as he was instructed to at the end of this episode.

On original transmission, the Canadian broadcast omitted the pre-credits teaser. A different pre-credits montage was put together by the CBC, consisting only of clips from 'Aliens of London'; the new material included in the original teaser was not featured, and so not seen by Canadian viewers.

LINKING THEMES: 'But he's got a Northern accent!' Harriet exclaims; Rose replies that 'Lots of planets have a North,' repeating the Doctor's explanation from 'Rose'.

The phone inside the TARDIS is a corded, 1970's-type handset.

The Doctor claims that the UNIT officials 'would have gathered for a weather balloon'. This could possibly be a reference to the weather balloon in 'The Three Doctors' (1972), or to the supposed UFO crash at Roswell in 1947, which was explained away as being a weather balloon.

On at least one previous occasion ('Robot', 1974), the UK had been the custodian of the UN's secret nuclear weapons codes. Perhaps different UN countries take it in turns to hold the codes?

SCENE MISSING: Rose knows that the Slitheen ship has slipstream technology, but the Doctor does not tell her this (at least not on screen). And she has never been around when gas was expelled from a Slitheen, so how does she know about this? Harriet seems to know about the 'alien' pig, but was not present when it was dissected. It's possible that the Doctor and

Harriet exchanged this information off screen.

The harpoon missile used in the episode was discontinued on British ships in 2005, so should not be around if this story takes place in March 2006 (see 'Rose' for an alternate take on the timing); however, this must be a different type of UGM-84A with a longer range, as it's nearly 200 nautical miles from the launch point (near Plymouth) to Central London, which is further than the weapon could normally reach.

With access to a spaceship, why do the Slitheen rely upon a convoluted plot to get humanity to destroy itself? (Perhaps they don't have the capability, but they do seem to possess some fairly advanced technology.) Why, for that matter, would they not take over a more hostile country instead of one of the world's stable democracies? When out of their human 'skins' the Slitheen still speak with the voice of the person they were impersonating. Perhaps this is part of the function of the device around their necks ... but at the same time, why is their voice then tinged with electronics?

There are nine Slitheen in the room at the end of the episode; given that we've seen a total of only seven, and one (Strickland) is dead, where did the others come from?

Other unanswered questions: How does the Doctor know the Slitheen have hyphenated surnames (given that he says so, and it's the last piece of the puzzle pointing him toward Raxacoricofallapatorius)? Why do UNIT and the Royal Navy allow access to British defence through the use of a common password on a website, even via a back-door? Why are both the crashed alien ship and Big Ben still billowing smoke nearly a day after the crash? Why does the United Nations go with British information about a mothership in orbit around the Earth, when in actuality no ship exists and no-one has any concrete proof? How does the Doctor locate the kid who spray-painted his TARDIS, to get him to remove the graffiti? And why, when the Doctor removes his electrified ID badge and jams it onto one of the Slitheen's compression field generators, do all the Slitheen become electrified at the same time? (Yes, they're linked ... but are they really transmitting electricity between them?)

ALTERED STATES: The working title for this episode was '10 Downing Street'.

BEHIND THE SCENES: Much of the story was recorded in the same locales as 'Aliens of London'; the one new location is the exterior of a ruined building in Newport, which is redressed with a metal wall to become the remains of the Cabinet room bunker.

Indra Ganesh is seen in this episode as a dead body but is uncredited (though *Radio Times* did list him).

OFF THE SCREEN: Morgan Hopkins has appeared in episodes of *Chosen* (2004) and *Murphy's Law* (2004) and in the film *The Testimony of Taliesin Jones* (2000). (See 'Aliens of London' for other members of the cast.)

TECHNICAL GOOFS: Steve Speirs' surname was misspelled in the end credits as 'Spiers'. As the Doctor opens the TARDIS door, right before he tells the spray-painting kid to finish up and leave, the interior of the prop (specifically, one of the side windows) can be clearly seen. The reporter (Tom) says that the streets of London are deserted; however, there still appears to be plenty of traffic and things look normal in the city in other shots. The Slitheens' shadows can be seen during the electrocution sequences, albeit briefly. (They are the ones illuminating the rooms, so how can they cast shadows?) The zipper on the Slitheen

Strickland's head from the previous episode has now magically disappeared. Technically, Mickey never actually sets the course for the missile ...

CONTROVERSIES: The fact that a missile is launched by Mickey using a website from his bedroom, hits 10 Downing Street, manages to destroy the building utterly and *doesn't* appear to even injure the Doctor, Rose or Harriet Jones, or indeed anyone else, was considered by many to be implausible. The flatulence, while reduced from part one was still a subject of considerable debate.

INTERNAL CONSISTENCY: Picking up from the previous episode, it is approximately midnight at 10 Downing Street. From here events run smoothly and no large chunks of time are missing. At one point Jackie comments that it is 3.00 am, but she is probably exaggerating from the shock. (Maybe she saw the time on Mickey's computer, but it's likely well after that when she makes her remark.) Sunrise the following day is close to 6.30 am (definitely setting the events in the last week of March). There is another American news programme, which claims 'It's midnight here in New York'; with the six hour time difference only during this one week each year, it must actually be closer to 12.30 am. There are no more definite time references in this episode. The entire sequence of events seems to be wrapped up fairly quickly, though. It is night time when the Doctor decides to leave and calls Rose, and sunset is at about 7.30 pm during this time of the year.

THEME ANALYSES

As Doctor Who For A Modern Audience: 'World War Three' takes a typical *Doctor Who* plot of alien infiltration and gives it a contemporary twist. Out goes the traditional motivation of conquest and in comes the far more modern one of greed, as the Slitheens want to sell the irradiated carcass of the Earth to feed their business profits. Of course, the setting of one of the most distinctive political addresses in Britain demands satire, and Davies duly obliges with Joseph Green's speech about the 'massive weapons of destruction capable of being deployed within forty-five seconds'. It's perhaps an obvious target, but in the context of an invasion whose ultimate purpose is the pursuit of fuel, it's very funny. Davies also puts a lot of nods to modern life in his script, with Mickey taking a snapshot of the Slitheen with his mobile phone, as well as his use of the Internet to hack into top secret international organisations and fire missiles at the heart of government. What impresses the most about this episode in terms of appealing to today's audience is the emotional depth, as characters respond to the events they witness and evolve their relationships as a result– as demonstrated by Jackie's and Mickey's reluctant acceptance of Rose's dangerous life with the Doctor. Ultimately, this series is all about the relationship between the Doctor and Rose and Davies demonstrates how strong their bond is when the Doctor hesitates over his radical plan to end the Slitheen threat because of his affection for his companion, even when many more lives are at stake.

As Television Drama: With the world poised on the brink of Armageddon and the countdown being seen through the medium of anxious TV news reporters, the television drama of recent memory that most quickly springs to mind in comparison to 'World War Three' is Davies's own *The Second Coming*, screened in February 2003. That two-parter had a bigger budget look and a more epic feel to it, but for an Earth-shattering event, the Slitheen's attempted invasion still feels very small-scale and confined. Not normally a bad thing for

Doctor Who, but when the story is being played on this level, it does make it feel as if there is an extra layer missing, not necessarily spectacle but a wider picture of what's going on – even a few panicked crowd shots would do it. Nonetheless, the foiling of the Slitheen plot provides a far more satisfying conclusion than did the last out-and-out alien invasion depicted on British television, *Invasion: Earth* in 1998. This big-budget BBC/Sci-Fi Channel co-production had the edge in glossiness and production values, but more than loses out to new *Doctor Who* in terms of script and story. With the use of mock news footage and the scenes of destruction being wrought right in the heart of London, the episode also evokes the 'What If?' style drama-documentaries pondering possible terrorist attacks, natural disasters or outbreaks of disease that the BBC have become so fond of in recent years, and it also more than stands up in comparison with those.

As A Piece of Writing: Unfortunately, the plot never does start to make sense. It's a dreadful hash of every teens-investigate-conspiracy show ever made, with a generous helping of *Scooby Doo* to make it even more ridiculous. I found myself constantly questioning why Davies had bothered to include educational references – the history of 10 Downing Street, the anecdote about Hannibal, what to do in an earthquake – in an episode that claims all of Britain's armed forces can be accessed via a single Internet password, and that a massive, televised news event could be covered up mere days later. Even more than last week, the episode feels like it was supposed to be an outright comedy, but someone forgot to take the memo. The Slitheen are bumbling, oafish, and conflicted as to what their actual goal is – are they trying to sell this 'godforsaken rock' for profit, or are they just out for a joy ride? Their characterisation is dreadfully inconsistent. What makes it all doubly sad, however, is that when the script clicks, it really clicks: when the Doctor offers a drink to Harriet Jones, when Mickey and Jackie have to work together, and in the final scenes that lead up to Rose and the Doctor's departure. Davies makes the Doctor's offer both exciting and a little bit creepy, and we're left, along with Jackie, wondering whether or not Rose made the right choice. Davies has ably demonstrated, again, that his great strength is in characterisation and dialogue; I just wish he could get someone to help him with the actual storylines.

The Doctor As A Mystery Figure: 'You want aliens, you've got them,' the Doctor tells the security forces with considerable glee early in this episode. 'They're inside Downing Street.' That's just one of a number of sly, knowing examples of pointed political – and social – comment slipped by Davies into this witty and involving script. (Alien weapon of mass destruction that can be launched 'in forty-five seconds', for example.) And, at the end, the Doctor – with a bit of help from Mickey and a secret UNIT website – gets to blow up the government. Well, it's every schoolboy's dream, isn't it?

Themes, Genres and Modes: While 'Aliens of London' was more a parody of a political thriller, 'World War Three' shows the other side of the coin and gives us outright political satire. As many have commented, it's amazing this episode went out during the lead up to a UK General Election. With Slitheen-turned-Acting Prime Minister Joseph Green talking about 'Massive Weapons of Destruction' that can destroy the earth in forty-five seconds as a cover for a plot to destroy the Earth to sell it off as a fuel source, it's hard not to see what Davies was commenting on. But then, it wasn't hard to see what lay behind Robert Holmes's 'The Sun Makers' back in 1977. Indeed, it can be argued that such political satire dates back to the very first *Doctor Who* story, with the struggle to control fire in the final three episodes of '100,000 BC' being a sly commentary on nuclear weapons in a post-Cuban Missile Crisis world. In which case, Davies is taking part in one of the grandest and oldest traditions in *Doctor Who*.

In Style and Structure: In some respects, 'World War Three' is stylistically and structurally similar to 'Aliens of London', yet it develops these aspects rather than just retreading them. The media are once more used to deliver exposition quite effectively, building up to a dramatic climax. Davies has constructed the main action of the episode around two locations: 10 Downing Street and Mickey's flat. The tension and drama is evidenced through character grouping and interaction. In one thread, the Doctor, Rose and Harriet are trapped in the Cabinet room in Downing Street; their only contact with the outside world is through Rose's mobile phone. The other features Jackie and Mickey, the Doctor's only hope of defeating the Slitheen's scheme. In both, one character develops beyond their previously established role in the story, while the relationships with the other characters grow deeper. These elements develop in parallel as the episode progresses, and the events in one thread influence the other. A minor plotline also exists, that of the Slitheen, with more information revealed about them either through their actions or by a process of deduction based on prior knowledge. Rather than falling flat, 'World War Three' effectively picks up where 'Aliens of London' left off, in developing the story and characters.

As Doctor Who Continuity: Nothing dates science fiction more than off-the-mark predictions as to what the near future will be like. Davies offers the vision that Harriet Jones will be Prime Minister of Britain for three successive terms, which would make her final period in office around the year 2017. It's a casual throwaway line, but it's an important one as it tells us that Britain will have peace and prosperity for some twelve or so years leading up to that date. But by creating this image of the future, Davies has shot himself in the foot, as it means there can't be any threats or invasions of Britain (one of the core ingredients of *Doctor Who*) between 2006 and 2017! According to already 'established' *Doctor Who* future history, this era was when the allied zones of the world were collapsing under the dictatorship of the evil Salamander, as seen in the 1967/68 serial 'The Enemy of the World'. Obviously one of the great challenges of writing for this modern series of *Doctor Who* is knowing just how much of the series's rich past should be acknowledged and how much can be safely jettisoned and ignored! It seems clear which of these approaches Davies prefers.

From A Special Effects Viewpoint: The rubbery Slitheen are still lumbering about (both in suit and CGI form) and, once again, they fail to impress, coming across as a bit silly instead of threatening (regardless of the size of their claws). I did find the one Slitheen's reaction to the vinegar thrown in its face to be very convincing (thanks to the suit performer and some nice facial puppeteering), but overall, I still couldn't help but see the odd gap around the mid-section where the abdomen floated over the legs, or cringe when the mouths operated, showing us a range of motion limited to open and closed. And as in 'Aliens of London', the attempts at generating the Slitheen by computer were ambitious, but the visible differences between the suits and the computer-generated creations were very noticeable. The missile effects were quite nice (in particular, the shot of the missile moving horizontally across the London skyline was very good) and, once again, a round of applause should be given to Mike Tucker and his model crew, this time for the impressive destruction of 10 Downing Street.

PANEL REVIEWS

Such a great lead-up, such a huge let-down. The Slitheen are awesome (I love that it's their last name and not the name of their race), and Camille Coduri and Noel Clarke are superb. But most of the episode sees the Doctor, Rose and Harriet stuck in one room where the action consists mainly of the bane of modern drama: talking on a cell phone. The scenes where the Doctor remotely helps Jackie and Mickey defeat a Slitheen are great, but the rest of it is one guy talking while another guy types on a computer. Both 'Aliens of London' and 'World War Three' are book ended by superb sequences in Rose's estate. The Doctor offering Mickey a chance to travel with him and Rose (and then covering for him with Rose when he declines) almost makes the disappointment of the rest of the episode worthwhile. And we get to see the genius of Davies's take on *Doctor Who*: while many saw the lack of any evidence of the Doctor's domestic life in the original TV series as suggesting that it was something that happened off-screen – an idea explored in some of the original *Doctor Who* novels – Davies makes it a basic trait of the character: the Doctor does not enjoy domestic situations at all. That's a truly clever innovation that is surprisingly faithful to the character we grew up with. – *Graeme Burk*

A shift into a slightly darker area makes 'World War Three' more interesting than its predecessor by focusing upon the true intent of the Slitheen, and whether or not Rose will elect to remain in London at the conclusion. With the toilet humour toned down, but still present, the Slitheen are much more effective as greedy profiteers, out to destroy the Earth and sell it off piece by piece. But, as seems to be the case with Davies's scripts, it's the human angle centred around Rose that proves most appealing. There's no doubt that she'll choose the Doctor over her home, but Davies makes us think about what it's like for those she leaves behind in a way that's never been done before, which leads to the fantastic bittersweet ending when Mickey and Jackie are left waiting. Unfortunately, the episode suffers from some too-convenient plotting; Mickey's hacking of suspiciously susceptible computers borders on the ridiculous. The confrontation between the Doctor and the Slitheen inside Margaret Blaine is particularly well played by Eccleston and Badland, with her dawning realisation of doubt being absolutely superb in breaking her confident exterior. While this two part adventure has succeeded in giving the lead and supporting characters greater depth, it's a shame that the storyline itself wasn't a bit stronger. Ironically, this might have worked better as a single episode. – *Simon Catlow*

Things don't get better here. All the bits of 'Aliens of London' get thrown in, plus a few new ones, and again not all of it works well together. On the plus side, the Slitheen family aren't interested in the same old alien invasion scheme. But they seem to have gone to a lot of trouble to create a war. Wouldn't it have been easier just to have fired some nuclear warheads from their own spacecraft? (If they have spaceships, surely they have or can use some form of nuclear technology?) If their spaceship can take off from Earth without being noticed and crash back down without anyone but the Doctor working out where it came from, then they certainly could have easily caused a war this way. Jackie and Mickey get a lot more to do in this episode, and for once Mickey comes across as almost a good character. Jackie, on the other hand, seems more like a companion from the classic series – screaming and running away from the aliens but quick on her feet when it comes to finding the ingredients to destroy the Slitheen – she'd have given Sarah Jane a good run for her money. The whole thing really falls apart for me when the Doctor instructs Mickey to launch a missile via UNIT's web site (would such access really be available online?) and then not only do the Doctor, Rose and Harriet survive the blast, but they are completely unscathed! Both this and the previous episode seem to be more about returning Rose home and the consequences of this than telling a good alien invasion story. – *Robert Franks*

My, those Slitheen are pretty rubbish after all, aren't they. After a good, if not great, beginning, things completely fall apart this week, and I finally realise what it is that's bothered me about all of Davies's episodes so far: he seems to have confused writing for children with writing down to them. Although some humorous moments in past weeks have pointed in that direction, this time it's glaringly obvious: the plot is so thin, so badly constructed, it's practically a cartoon. All this mumbo-jumbo about needing the UN's permission is little more than a contrived plot device, complete with nonsense logic (so, can we all fire missiles from our home computer?) and a weak jab at modern-day politics ('massive weapons of destruction' indeed). Maybe I wouldn't care so much if the villains weren't so pitiful; you can spot the difference between the costumed and computer-generated Slitheen from so far away, it's actually funny, and why they need to constantly get in and out of their human suits is beyond me. Thankfully – mercifully, even – Davies is proving that strong characters manage to rise above bad material, a little like the early seasons of *Buffy*, where even a stupid episode had fun moments and witty dialogue. Mickey and Jackie are both used to great advantage, and Christopher Eccleston has a wonderful repartee with Penelope Wilton. It's just a shame about the other ninety percent! Do us a favour: don't bring back the Slitheen, okay? They really stink. – *Sarah Hadley*

What a difference a week makes. 'World War Three' is an altogether tighter, pacier affair than the opening instalment of this two-parter, helped no doubt by the need to rattle through the story quickly enough to leave enough room for the coda with Rose leaving her mother properly at the end. While the actual plot is not the strongest Davies has ever served up, the performances and the dialogue are just about enough to paper over any cracks. It is nice to see the Slitheen going against some of the alien race clichés of the series and being just a family rather than an entire species, adding to the already impressive work previous episodes have done in improving the show's track record in the creation of new and strange cultures. Of the humans, Mickey is particularly well written and played in this episode, with Noel Clarke being able to add some bravery and seriousness to the character, and it's good to see the Doctor finally being nice towards him at the end. An improvement on the last episode then, and a solid effort overall, but it's the trailer for episode six tacked onto the end that really gets the heart racing. – *Paul Hayes*

'World War Three' is a fine conclusion to the story started in 'Aliens of London', resolving most plot threads quite neatly, while glossing over others. There is also room for aspects of character development. The decision to frame certain scenes of CGI rendered Slitheen in static shots made some chase sequences seem a bit dull and lifeless. However, the disappointment of these scenes is more than made up for by the superb sequence showing the flight of the missile and its detonation, which takes out another famous London icon. One of the biggest moments in the episode is when Rose shows how much she trusts the Doctor, illustrating how far their relationship has developed in such a short space of time. Mickey really comes into the fore, developing out of the comic relief mould and showing how calm and capable the character can be, a transformation that Noel Clarke carries off admirably. Similarly, Harriet Jones matures as a character, making some hard decisions and showing why she will become the important figure in history the Doctor remembers. – *Cameron Mason*

I want to like 'World War Three'. Honestly, I really do ... but ... Farting, giggling 'human' aliens in part one were bad enough, but in part two, I thought the walls were supposed to wobble, not the monsters. If the Slitheen had been treated seriously and with some degree of actual threat or realism, 'World War Three' might just have worked. Instead it's an embarrassing mess. While the Slitheen's motives were reminiscent of the Dominators' from the 1968 serial (turning a planet into radioactive fuel), there were original concepts and clever ideas in Davies's script that were just struggling to get out but were hindered by poor design and sloppy direction. For instance, the mismatched cutting from fast and sleek CGI Slitheen to bouncing 'Mr Blobbys' was unforgivable. And those locked-off wide-shots of empty corridors just screamed 'Here come the monsters!' One need only take a look at the Vogons in the recent *Hitchhikers' Guide to the Galaxy* movie, or the aliens from Peter Jackson's 1987 masterpiece, *Bad Taste*, for good examples of how effective the Slitheen could have been if handled in a menacing way. – *Jon Preddle*

The incredible pace of the first thirty minutes or so (and Keith Boak's highly assured direction) conspire to hide a few basic flaws – both dramatic and aesthetic. But, the performances by the cast are mostly good (Annette Badland, Penelope Wilton, Andrew Marr and, especially, Noel Clarke) and there are odd quiet moments of introspection and class, like the Doctor's sad apology to a corpse for having been unable to prevent his death. The somewhat odd decision to include a lengthy coda works magnificently well. 'If you saw it out there, you'd never stay home,' Rose tells Jackie, whilst the best scene of the episode sees the Doctor and Mickey reconciled in understanding before a somewhat sad and regretful climax. Much more than 'Aliens of London', the second part shows that multi-episode stories can work within the new forty-five minute formula, but also that *Doctor Who* has changed with the times and, as a result, many of the old 'rules' no longer apply. – *Keith Topping*

Quite a strange animal, this. A two-part story (essentially one ninety minute adventure with a 'brief' week-long intermission) penned by Davies, but for whatever reasons, the second part was infinitely superior to the first! From the moment the cliff-hanger from episode one was resolved (with the Doctor somehow simultaneously shocking all the Slitheen), things moved at a terrific pace with moments of tension, sweetness and humour (and not the 'breaking-wind' sort). While it was somewhat disappointing that the elimination of the Slitheen was handled via something as crude as a missile (the Brigadier would have been proud), this was a solid and entertaining adventure. Still, some of the best material in this episode was the stuff featuring Jackie and Mickey, who make a terrific duo. (I adored the somewhat detached hug Mickey gave Jackie to comfort her in the kitchen.) Fun, and significantly higher on my list than its predecessor. – *Scott Alan Woodard*

EDITOR'S REVIEW: As with its predecessor, 'Aliens of London', there is a lot here to enjoy and admire; Noel Clarke is wonderful, and the interplay between him and the Doctor at the end (and, later, the Doctor's insistence that Mickey cannot join them) is marvellous. Penelope Wilton is remarkable, one of the best guest stars I can ever remember in *Doctor*

Who, and Camille Coduri's Jackie is completely believable ... she'd rather do something, anything, than risk her daughter's death. The fact that 'Slitheen' is a surname and not the name of the alien race is terrific. 'World War Three' simply has more of these scenes and nuances than 'Aliens of London', and consequently I find it to be the better of the two.

But something seems to be missing that I just can't put my finger on. I didn't like the farting aliens, and thankfully it's toned down here. Perhaps it's simply that the entire thing just seems so contrived. The characters move from scene to scene with abandon, the plot jumps from hole to hole. Why on Earth would Jackie answer the door at 3 am when there's a monster chasing her? (Yes, Mickey told her to. Same thing.) How could the Doctor not know where the Slitheen are from if he could pick a planet of living calcium out of five thousand names? (And for that matter, how could he narrow it down in such a short time?) Why would the United Nations give up missile codes for a nuclear attack, sight unseen? And how could Mickey take command of a missile through an Internet website?

And am I the only person who shook his head when the Doctor was asked if there was anyone outside that could help him, and he said 'No'? There's this silver-haired retired Brigadier out there that I'm sure no *Doctor Who* fan, and certainly no *Doctor Who* producer, has forgotten.

I think that it's a question of scale. *Doctor Who* works best when it deals with the small and tangible: alien nasties and bad guys and vicious plots. It seldom works when dealing with the large-scale politics of real-world Earth. We can believe the existence of a secret paramilitary organisation governed by the United Nations; we have trouble, however, in dealing with the dichotomy between what we know about real-world government and the way these people behave. It's hard to represent the real world in *Doctor Who*, and a lone reporter on an empty set filling in for the 24-hour news cycle of CNN or Fox News doesn't fit into that. A United Nations that would unilaterally accept nuclear warheads being shot into space doesn't quite work for me. I know better. One would perhaps cry 'suspension of disbelief' at this point, and I'm certainly not above doing that. It's just that when you're critically reviewing something, these sorts of things niggle.

But even with the general sense that large portions of the story are missing that would make this more well-rounded and enjoyable, there's still so much to enjoy. Even with the flaws present, these two episodes never truly *fail* in the sense that some of the original series episodes did: there is too much to enjoy in the individual character moments for this to be a waste. I love Harriet Jones; Mickey and Jackie are utilised well; and some of the dialogue is sharp and crisp. 'Aliens of London' and 'World War Three' create a very light-hearted, if flawed, story that works as a diversion, but doesn't stand up to more detailed scrutiny. But they still have a lot of heart and some great dialogue and acting, so I can't say I didn't enjoy them. Please, though, a plea to the producers: no more farting aliens, ever. – *Shaun Lyon*

106: DALEK

After tracking an alien SOS call to an underground facility of the Geocomtex Corporation in 21st Century Utah, the Doctor and Rose meet the company's CEO, Henry van Statten, a collector of alien antiquities who has a very unique specimen in his collection ... something that according to the Doctor should not exist...

FIRST TRANSMISSION: UK – 30 April 2005. Canada – 10 May 2005. Australia – 25 June 2005. New Zealand – 11 August 2005.
DURATION: 45'20"
WRITER: Robert Shearman
DIRECTOR: Joe Ahearne
CREDITED CAST: Christopher Eccleston (Doctor Who), Billie Piper (Rose Tyler), Bruno Langley (Adam), Corey Johnson (Henry van Statten), Anna-Louise Plowman (Goddard), Nigel Whitmey (Simmons), John Schwab (Bywater), Jana Carpenter (De Maggio), Steven Beckingham (Polkowski), Joe Montana (Commander), Nicholas Briggs (Dalek Voice), Barnaby Edwards (Dalek Operator)
Daleks originally created by Terry Nation.

WHERE AND WHEN: An underground Geocomtex facility, Utah, North America, 2012. The nearest major town is Salt Lake City.

THE STORY UNFOLDS: Fifty years ago, a lone Dalek fell to Earth on the Ascension Islands like a meteorite. The Dalek spent three days in the crater, burning, in terrible pain; it possibly went insane. It was later sold at private auction, moving from one collection to another. Henry van Statten of Geocomtex bought it as the only living specimen in his private collection, calling it a 'Metaltron'.

The TARDIS arrives fifty-three floors below the Utah desert in a Geocomtex facility near Salt Lake City, which includes laboratories and an alien artefact museum, following receipt of a distress call (seemingly sent by the Dalek). The museum has many sorts of extraterrestrial artefacts including chunks of meteorite, moon dust, the milometer from the Roswell spaceship, a stuffed Slitheen arm, what appear to be busts of several alien heads, and a Cyberman head (although it is never identified as such). Touching the glass cases sets off the alarms.

Geocomtex has made many advances using alien technology; broadband (high-speed Internet access) comes from Roswell, for example. The cure for the common cold was cultured from bacteria found in a Russian crater (but has been kept in the laboratory to keep palliatives in business). An alien musical device, operated by touch, was recently purchased for $800,000; van Statten thinks it's less than impressive.

After the incident with the Dalek, the base is to be closed and filled with cement, Diana Goddard having usurped his position.

THE DOCTOR: The Doctor is at once terrified of and astonished by the Dalek, which exists when it shouldn't. He calls the Dalek a 'great space dustbin'. He is put in restraints by van Statten when his own identity as an alien is discovered. He has two hearts, as van Statten discovers by scanning him. He would make a good Dalek, his nemesis says after he tries to talk it into killing itself. He is forced to close the bulkheads to van Statten's facility, even at the cost of Rose's life (as he believes), to stop the Dalek from getting out.

ROSE TYLER: She threatens to smack van Statten after he refers to her as the Doctor's 'little cat-burglar accomplice' and keeps calling her 'she'. She is not afraid of the Dalek (at first), which respects her for that fact; this changes later as she is trapped with the creature. She tells the Doctor that she wouldn't have missed this trip for the world. Later, she questions the Doctor himself over his violent actions toward the Dalek.

CHARACTER BUILDING: *The Dalek* – The last of its kind (or so we are led to believe), it has been in terrible pain, inflicted by the employees at Geocomtex. It hasn't spoken before seeing the Doctor, who it calls an enemy of the Daleks. It is able to renew itself using Rose's DNA (extrapolating the biomatter of a time traveller enabled it to regenerate), and recharges using the power reserves of the base, draining the power from the entire western US; it also absorbs the Internet through the Geocomtex hub. It can stop bullets in mid-flight using defensive screens and can levitate up stairs. The Doctor says it can calculate a thousand billion combinations in one second. The Dalek absorbs some of Rose's humanity and this contaminates it. The creature does not kill her; instead, the Dalek uses her as a bargaining chip. Later, it begins to question its own purpose and wants freedom; the creature inside the Dalek casing reveals itself to the open air in order to feel sunlight on itself. Unable to come to terms with itself, it pleads with Rose to order it to kill itself, and when she does, it creates a contained explosion.

Henry van Statten – A powerful man, owner of Geocomtex. He claims to own the Internet (but lets the world think otherwise). He commands the respect of the US President, even though it's a respect that isn't shared (when the President is 10 points down in the polls, van Statten says he wants him replaced). He fires subordinates by having their memories wiped and leaving them along the side of a road. He believes that employees are expendable and the Dalek isn't. He's a computer genius. He's later taken into custody to have his memory wiped and to be left alongside a road somewhere.

Adam – A Geocomtex research assistant who catalogues the company's alien artefacts, Adam would give anything to see the alien beings and far-off places he's dreamed about. He's a genius scouted by one of van Statten's men; he logged onto the US defence system aged 8 and almost caused World War Three. He recently bought ten artefacts for van Statten at auction. Van Statten variously calls him 'Little Lord Fauntleroy' and 'English' (the irony here being that Fauntleroy was an American character) and tells him and Rose to go 'canoodle' or 'spoon' or do 'whatever it is [the] English do'. The Doctor thinks that Adam's 'a bit pretty' for Rose. Adam has kept some of the alien artefacts ('uncatalogued ones') for himself. Having nowhere to go once Goddard takes over the facility after the Dalek has been defeated, he follows the Doctor and Rose into the TARDIS.

Diana Goddard – Likely a high-ranking official of this particular Geocomtex facility (although van Statten doesn't know her personally). She impresses him with a joke about Democrats ('They're just so funny, sir?') She later takes over Geocomtex from van Statten.

Simmons – A technician, or rather a torturer, who works on the Dalek to get it to speak. The Dalek uses its sucker arm to kill him.

BAD WOLF: As van Statten's helicopter descends to the Geocomtex site, a voice is heard on the loudspeaker: 'Attention all personnel, Bad Wolf One descending, Bad Wolf One descending ...'

FANTASTIC!: The Doctor says 'fantastic' (twice) as he laughs with relief that the Dalek's weapon does not function. (Adam also says it, in his laboratory, causing Rose to make a comparison between the two.)

BODY COUNT: The Dalek torturer Simmons, Bywater and De Maggio and the entire company of soldiers die in various battles with the escaped Dalek (including by electrocution in a water-soaked warehouse); Goddard notes that two hundred people have died during the battles. The Dalek kills itself. Also, although both van Statten and his former aide Polkowski are not killed, both have been sentenced to memory wipes and will be left to fend for themselves by the roadside.

REALITY BITES: The original concepts for 'Dalek' can be found in *Jubilee*, a *Doctor Who* audio adventure from Big Finish written by Shearman and starring Colin Baker. Shearman was asked to take this basic story and rework it as a new series episode; in the audio, the Doctor is confronted with a lone Dalek, survivor of a terrible battle, although it is set in an alternate-reality United Kingdom. One of the characters, Lamb, tortures the Dalek; the role was played in that story by Kai Simmons, and Simmons here is the name of the Dalek torturer. In both stories, the voice of the Dalek was performed by Nicholas Briggs. One of the props created as set dressing for the television episode, seen in photos on the BBC official website, was a pizza box from 'Jubilee Pizza'; a tribute to the audio story.

Diana Goddard is named after Jane Goddard, Shearman's wife and an actress who has appeared in many *Doctor Who* audios.

For the Dalek to drain the world of information is almost impossible; given the entire structure and backbone of the Internet, even in the near future, it would likely take much longer than is shown here. (On the other hand, it is possible, given van Statten's secrecy surrounding his 'ownership' of the internet, that he keeps a constant backup of the entire web on his own servers.) In addition, draining the entire Western United States of electrical power would be impossible in so short a time, given the limited power transmission capabilities of the electrical grid (unless there have been some major developments since 2005).

Van Statten is said to be in charge of the American political system, replacing US Presidents at will. In doing so, he would have to have full charge of all voting mechanisms, leading to the possibility that by 2012, all US polling places are equipped with electronic voting. This episode takes place during the primaries leading up to the US elections, so this is likely to be in the first half of that year.

The official BBC website featured a Dalek-themed web game based on this episode (which included, among other things, a reference to International Electromatics, a company from the original series story 'The Invasion', 1968). Also available to visit was an officially-sanctioned spin-off site, geocomtex.net, which was supposedly the 'official' website of the company – this included several 'Bad Wolf' references (along with another mention of International Electromatics), such as a product 'Node Stabilised (Lupus and Nocens variants)' and a Morse code spelling of B-A-D-W-O-L-F that was apparently the pin setting for the RH-390 S12. (This replaced a brief, much ruder, Morse sequence that stayed online for less than a day.) The website also debunked fan theories that a flashing light in 'Aliens of London' sequenced 'M-E-D-B-I-L-E-T-O-V' (a political message in reverse). Another of the promotional sites, whoisdoctorwho.co.uk, featured an 'interview' with van Statten, and a competition to win a trip to the Geocomtex HQ – a competition won by a young Adam Mitchell.

This was the first (and so far, only) episode simulcast over the Internet during transmission; see Chapter 12.

LINKING THEMES: The Daleks are a race of mutated life forms placed in battle-armoured metal; they were genetically-engineered to remove every emotion except hate. The Doctor refers to the creator of the Daleks as a genius who was 'king of his own little world', referring to (but not naming) the scientist Davros introduced in the 1975 story 'Genesis of the Daleks'.

The Time War was fought between the Time Lords (the Doctor's people) and the Dalek race. The Daleks were wiped out in one second – and the Doctor made it happen – while the Time Lords burned with the Daleks at the end of the war.

In both the episode and in the press that accompanied it, much attention was focused upon the Dalek levitating. This is actually not the first time we have seen a Dalek levitate on camera; the same feat was achieved in the classic series stories 'Revelation of the Daleks' (1985) and 'Remembrance of the Daleks' (1988), and as far back as 'The Chase' (1965) Daleks were seen to have been able to get up and down flights of stairs, although this was not actually depicted on camera.

Adam mentions that the United Nations have been keeping alien landings quiet; this is a reference to UNIT, seen in the previous two episodes and in the original series.

Among the items the Doctor and Rose see in the exhibit hall is a Cyberman head. The Cybermen, a race of beings who adapted their bodies with technology and eventually lost their humanity, were seen in many episodes of the original series. The head is similar to the design seen in the story 'Revenge of the Cybermen' (1975). On its display case (seen in photos), the text reads: 'Extraterrestrial Cyborg Specimen incomplete; Recovered from underground sewer; Location London, United Kingdom; Date 1975'. (This implies it is from the story 'The Invasion' (1968), which was set at this time and which featured the Cybermen in the sewers of London.) Coincidentally, the TARDIS lands 53 floors below ground; the same number of floors featured in the classic series story 'The Deadly Assassin'.

SCENE MISSING: Why, if the last person to touch the Dalek burst into flames, does that not happen to Rose? Does this mean that Rose would have died the same way, had she not travelled through time? And what, genetically, on a cellular level, and so forth, has happened to Rose, if she has been so altered by simply travelling through time ?

The Cyberman head is of a type as seen in 'Revenge of the Cybermen'. That story took place in the 29th Century, far later than this story.

Pain features prominently in this story. Why does the Dalek feel pain when Simmons attempts to cut into its battle armour, yet not feel the sunlight on its 'face'? Why does the Doctor wince in pain when being scanned by van Statten? (And why does this scan only show his hearts and ribs?)

The lift goes up as far as the first sub-level. Why doesn't it go all the way up to the surface? This implies that there is no above-ground structure for the Geocomtex facility.

What does Goddard hope to achieve by getting rid of van Statten in such a manner? Surely his empire has all sorts of security checks in place that require passwords, access codes, signatures, etc, that only he would have.

Has something happened to America, geographically, by 2012? On the electronic map used by the Doctor, van Statten and Goddard in the executive office, half of Michigan (the upper peninsula) has vanished, and the states of Massachusetts, Connecticut, Rhode Island, Vermont and New Hampshire are all identified as one state.

Other questions: Why is the base's helipad the only escape route? (Can't they start running across the desert, if need be?) Why has Adam never been to the Dalek's cage before, even though he's so interested in alien life and easily accesses it when he goes there with Rose? Why would Rose identify the Doctor as an alien when they're surrounded by guards? Why does no one take any notice of the TARDIS in the museum? It's obviously an alien artefact that doesn't belong there. Why does the Doctor believe that the Dalek can be stopped by closing the bulkhead, when the creature obviously has enough power to take out the roof? Why does the Dalek take control of the communications system but not the security system (to open the bulkhead)? And how does the Doctor know that the next flight to Heathrow leaves at 15.00? (Yes, this is obviously tongue-in-cheek.)

BEHIND THE SCENES: Much of this episode was recorded on location at the Millennium Stadium in Cardiff, with corridors, storage spaces and stairwells redressed by the *Doctor Who* production staff to become the Geocomtex bunker. The alien museum was a seldom-used room within the National Museum of Wales in Cardiff. The executive office was recorded at the studio in Newport. The visual display on van Statten's computer was a sheet of Lucite; effects were added later.

'Return of the Daleks' was an early possible title for the episode, which went through a number of changes before finally settling on the simple 'Dalek'.

DULCET TONES: Composer Murray Gold used a choral arrangement for this episode, creating an almost operatic score that emphasised the climactic breakout of the Daleks from its chains.

OFF THE SCREEN: Bruno Langley is best known for playing Todd Grimshaw, the first on-screen openly gay character in the long-running ITV soap *Coronation Street* (2001-2004); he also appeared in the first series of *Linda Green* (2001). Corey Johnson has been seen in the films *A Sound of Thunder* (2005), *Endgame* (2001), *Harrison's Flowers* (2000), *The Mummy* (1999) and *Saving Private Ryan* (1998), and in the TV miniseries *Band of Brothers* (2001). Anna-Louise Plowman is best known as Osiris (formerly Dr Sarah Gardner), a recurring villain in *Stargate SG-1* (2000/2002/2004); she also appeared in *FairyTale: A True Story* (1997), *Shanghai Knights* (2003) and the miniseries *He Knew He Was Right* (2004). Nigel Whitmey played the recurring role of Dan Wilder in *Casualty* (2003-4) and as Odysseus in the miniseries *Helen of Troy* (2003), and has been seen in *The 51st State* (2001), *Saving Private Ryan* (1998), *Jefferson in Paris* (1995) and *Shining Through* (1992). John Schwab was seen in *The Order* (2003), *Nothing to Declare* (2001) and director Joe Ahearne's docu-drama *Space Odyssey: Voyage to the Planets* (2004), and is also a videogame voice-over artist. Jana Carpenter has been seen in *The Criminal* (1999) and *Marple: The Murder at the Vicarage* (2004). Steven Beckingham is in director Roberto Benigni's *La Tigre e la Neve* (2005). Joe Montana (not to be confused with the American football legend) played Achilles in *Helen of*

Troy (2003) and has been seen in *The Bourne Identity* (2002) and *Down* (2001) and in the series *Keen Eddie* (2003), *Lovejoy* (1993) and *Randall and Hopkirk (Deceased)* (2001). Barnaby Edwards has featured in and directed many *Doctor Who* audio adventures for Big Finish Productions and also appeared as a Dalek in the BBC documentary *Doctor Who: Thirty Years in the TARDIS* (1993). Director Joe Ahearne's directing credits include episodes of the TV series *This Life* (1996-1997), *Trance* (2001), *Strange* (2002-2003) and the aforementioned *Space Odyssey: Voyage to the Planets* (2004) which he also wrote, as well as the miniseries *Ultraviolet* (1998) and the recent production *Double Life* (2006) with Christopher Eccleston.

TECHNICAL GOOFS: Adam enters the TARDIS at the end of the episode despite the fact that it has already begun to dematerialise. In the lift with the Dalek, Billie Piper's mouth moves, silently, perhaps counting moments until her next line, or mouthing the Dalek's lines, although more likely this is just Rose's jaw trembling slightly with nerves. Goddard's mention of 'the Ascension Islands' is a mistake; there's only one island (although given the state of the US map – see above – maybe there are more than one by this time).

CONTROVERSIES: Though 'Dalek' was a popular story, the fact that the new series's first Dalek tale featured just a lone Dalek with emotional issues did hit a particular nerve with some viewers. This story was also noted for being unusually violent, with a bloody aftermath. A particular line uttered by the Dalek, 'What use are emotions if you will not save the woman you love?' provoked strong reactions from some fans (although the story's writer claims not to have been responsible for this line of dialogue).

INTERNAL CONSISTENCY: While it is not possible to pinpoint an exact time for this story, the action takes place very swiftly, with little time passing off-screen. The pre-credits sequence in the museum may have been minutes or hours before the arrival of van Statten in his helicopter. His arrival is during daylight but impossible to place other than that. The action from this point takes place for the most part in real time, and the Dalek reaches the surface a little over an hour later. There is also some time lapse before the final scene as Goddard has had time to consider filling in the bunker with concrete, but this amounts to probably no more than a few hours.

THEME ANALYSES

As *Doctor Who* For A Modern Audience: This may not be the first new series revival of an old enemy, but unlike the Autons in 'Rose', the Dalek and its nature are very much the focus here, the aim being both to show why they have become so iconic and to challenge the audience's expectations. Shearman's audio play that provided the inspiration for 'Dalek' was, in part, about the idea that these evil killers had had their status diminished through merchandising – how can anyone be scared of something that once advertised Kit-Kat chocolate bars? So the early part of this episode is about the restoration of fear, showing the Dalek as a malevolent, calculating entity capable of wiping out van Statten's security forces with little trouble. But it's the Doctor's fear of what these creatures can do that is most effective in invigorating their menace, because it leads to revelations about the backdrop to the series with the Time War, heightening the tension and emotional intensity. The Dalek itself has had some innovative reinvention in its design that makes it far more functional, with the CGI helping it do things that it never did before. But while the spectacular battle sequences impress, it's how 'Dalek' makes us *feel* for this metal mutant that has the biggest impact. While the 'absorption of a time-traveller's DNA' justification for the transformation is rather dubious, the way in which Nicholas Briggs's vocal performance invokes sorrow is convincing, and it's because of this that the Doctor's quest for vengeance becomes so disturbing. By questioning the Doctor's actions and motivations, the script revises the audience's perspectives on the lead character, making for a far more complex characterisation due to the moral ambiguity.

As Television Drama: British television drama series do not often set episodes in the United States. There are very obvious budgetary and cultural reasons for this, but also there's the fact that there are so many American imports readily available to watch that it's rather pointless. Nonetheless, it does happen from time to time – 2002's first revival season *of Auf Wiedersehen, Pet* took place partly in Arizona, and Channel 4's 2004 series *NY-LON* was set partly in New York and partly in London. In both those cases, however, the shows' production crews actually went to the locations in which they were set, whereas in this case the furthest West the *Doctor Who* team got was, as usual, Cardiff. However, the story being located in an underground base in a confined setting, it never seems too fake an environment, and indeed the apocalyptic overtones make it feel, once again, more like a docu-drama. With the American guest cast, it also runs close to seeming like an imported fantasy series, given that US shows have been just about the only sci-fi seen on UK screens for the decade and a half prior to this new series of *Doctor Who*, but somehow it still manages to feel like something separate from that tradition.

As A Piece of Writing: Hooray! Finally, an episode rolls around that simply nails the forty-five-minute format. There's enough time for a proper set-up, an action-packed middle, and both a structurally- and emotionally-satisfying ending that *means* something. 'Dalek' is also a testament to *Doctor Who*'s flexibility; although we see the same germ of an idea from Shearman's *Jubilee*, that concept has been taken in entirely new and surprising directions. For the record, I enjoyed both versions, and I enjoyed them as individual entities – which proves the strength of the writing. The classic moments of 'Dalek' however – the ones that, I think, people will be watching and re-watching for years, putting into clip shows, wearing out their DVD players by fast reversing back to again and again – are original both to 'Dalek' and to *Doctor Who* as a whole. The Doctor's verbal showdown with the Dalek creature is a tour-de-force totally unlike anything seen in the old show, and similarly, the Dalek's suicide is the sort of emotional development we've never really seen before (notwithstanding the Doctor having effectively talked a Dalek into committing suicide by convincing it that it was the last of its kind at the end of 'Remembrance of the Daleks,' 1988). Are these elements so good by virtue of their very originality, or on the strength of their own merits? Some of both, and that's okay. That's how the writing of 'Dalek' feels overall: slightly based around the idea of novelty, of showmanship (Look! Its midsection can swivel ... now!), but so tight and refined it doesn't matter; even when the episode loses its novelty, it will still remain highly enjoyable, and almost certainly be regarded a classic.

The Doctor As A Mystery Figure: Two sequences particularly deserve highlighting – a quite beautifully underplayed moment when the Doctor finds the head of a Cyberman as a museum exhibit and reflects, wistfully, on the fact that he is getting old, and then the initial Doctor/Dalek confrontation. The latter is one of the great moments in *Doctor Who*'s history

– effortlessly menacing and sinister and including, in apparently throwaway lines, the entire story of the fate of the Daleks and the Time Lords.

Themes, Genres and Modes: While 'Dalek' is a standout action adventure story – in fact it's probably the first story this season to get the action quotient right – it's more than just '*Die Hard* of the Daleks'. It is also a dark psychological drama like *Silence of the Lambs*, in which Doctor and Dalek are pitted in a struggle where both parties define themselves by what they most abhor, and in so doing become that which they hate. The Doctor is transformed so much by blind hate that the Dalek tells him that he would make a good Dalek, while the Dalek becomes more human, to its utter disgust. The final confrontation between the two is stunning as both realise this and do the thing that restores them: the Doctor drops the gun and the Dalek asks for orders to self-destruct. This is the sort of psychological struggle that elevates a piece of drama well above a simple romp, and that gives 'Dalek' a dark edge that the series desperately needed at this point.

In Style and Structure: There are a lot of basic story elements used in 'Dalek' – the prison containing only one mysterious prisoner, a breakout, and perhaps the most iconic *Doctor Who* story element of them all; the isolated base under siege. Yet for Shearman's script these provide merely the backdrop against which another story takes place, a story developed from the complex web of relationships between Rose, the Doctor and the Dalek. Rose has a close bond with both the Doctor and the Dalek, and can see the positives and negatives in both; indeed, at the episode's climax, the Dalek and the Doctor briefly swap roles, highlighting how close in nature to each other they really are. Shearman also explores the nature and character of both the Doctor and the Dalek through parallel story lines; both are physically and emotionally tortured, both are dealing with 'survivor guilt', but ultimately the Doctor survives all; he can adapt and change whereas the Daleks are unable to function beyond their set pattern of behaviour.

As Doctor Who Continuity: In 'Genesis of the Daleks' (1975), the Doctor was there when the first ever Dalek was unveiled. And now, in 'Dalek', we get a nice symmetry in that the Doctor is a witness to the death of the last ever Dalek. Van Statten's monster museum was a continuity-spotter's paradise. I particularly liked the moment with the Cyberman head (and especially Ahearne's clever shot in which the reflection of the helmet was framed 'over' the Doctor's head, giving the illusion he was wearing it). But goodness only knows how van Statten came to possess such an item, since the events of 'Revenge of the Cybermen' (1975) took place hundreds of years in the future. There is also a glimpse of the head of an Alien (presumably a prop from *Alien vs Predator* (2005), on which several of the *Doctor Who* effects team worked) and possibly an Alien egg in the background. In fact this is not the first time there has been an on-screen connection between *Doctor Who* and the *Alien* series of films: in the 'Mindwarp' segment of 'The Trial of a Time Lord' (1986), a chest-burster is one of the specimens in Crozier's laboratory. With yet another victim of the last great Time War making an appearance, the Doctor must be getting absolutely paranoid by now! The Nestenes, the Moxx, the Gelth, and now a Dalek. Whatever next?

From A Special Effects Viewpoint: It looks like a Dalek, but it has a few new tricks inside its shell this time around. The respect for the original design by Raymond P Cusick is apparent, but the new series design team has come up with a few clever additions and modifications never before seen. The moment the central section of the new Dalek rotated to fire on soldiers attacking from behind, I actually cheered aloud! It's one of those upgrades that makes perfect sense. Same thing for the now multi-functional plunger that sucked the life out of Simmons and manipulated a security keypad. As for the CGI versions of the Dalek, while a few shots showed their computer origins, I actually wonder how many I missed. I get the feeling that there were several more shots in the mix that, while I believed them to be the full-scale working Dalek prop, were most likely CGI models. Finally, there's the Dalek mutant revealed at the end of the story. While previous versions of the creature have been little more than undulating blobs of latex or silicone, the new creature is fully articulated and sculpted in such a way as to make it appear rather pathetic. It's a sign of a successful animatronic puppet when the audience actually feels something for it!

PANEL REVIEWS

Like any *Doctor Who* fan, I have longed in my heart for the Daleks to be cooler than they actually are. I know I'm not alone, because back in the 1980s the Dalek story always shot to the top of the *Doctor Who Magazine* Season Survey ('The Caves of Androzani' was *not* the winner for Season 21!), just because in each of those stories the Daleks always did something really cool-looking – blow up in a visceral way, look good in white, climb stairs – that they'd not been seen to do previously. On that principle alone, 'Dalek' has an edge that is almost exponentially greater than its predecessors. Because the eponymous Mark III Travel Machine from Skaro is cooler than any other Dalek *ever*. It doesn't look like a guy in a fibreglass suit on ball casters anymore. Never mind the flying and the 360-degree extermination action, the Dalek here *feels* alien and dangerous in a way I've never seen before – the close-ups of the eyestalk are really eerie. It was a *brilliant* idea to add little servo noises to everything it does as well – the sort of thing I wish they had thought of in the sixties. The result is a Dalek that is a credible threat, not a joke. There's more to 'Dalek' than mere pepperpot spectacle. Shearman has written a script that effortlessly moves from dark psychological drama to action adventure. Christopher Eccleston makes the most of what's given to him here, and it's refreshing to see him performing a good script with an excellent director in Joe Ahearne. And I'm becoming convinced that Billie Piper is incapable of giving a bad performance. Rose spends much of the episode with the Dalek and yet you feel that she actually has a rapport with something that's being manipulated off-stage by radio control. But the real surprise of this story is the Dalek itself – not just because it does cool things, but because it is a fascinating *character*: manipulative, scary and yet – against its will – frightened. Credit must also go to Nick Briggs's superb voice performance in this. The moment where it opens itself up to reveal the actual creature inside is perfect for the story by showing us how truly vulnerable the Dalek is. And by doing something never before done on TV, this also gives a sign that we really have ramped up to the next level of *Doctor Who*. As my 12 year-old goddaughter said upon seeing this scene, that's awesome. – *Graeme Burk*

Shearman's *Doctor Who* audio pedigree is arguably second to none, and it's easy to see why it was decided to draw inspiration from the premise of *Jubilee*, with its lone Dalek held captive, driven insane through isolation and torture. The script's intent is twofold in making the Daleks frightening once more but also in making us think about the Doctor's relationship with them, which proves even more pertinent given the revelations contained within 'Dalek' about the Time War. The former is achieved predominantly through some stunning action sequences that demonstrate how viciously inventive this Dalek is at killing, with some intelligent updates to the design accentuating this, but also at how manipulative it can be as it lures Rose into feeling sympathy for it, which it then exploits to engineer its escape. However, this encounter also changes the creature within, leading to some extremely provocative drama as we see the boundaries between the Daleks and the Doctor being drawn closer together to question who the real monster is. Eccleston's intensity is brought to bear magnificently in his best performance so far as the Doctor faces his greatest fear, while Nicholas Briggs's vocal performance as the Dalek turns the best villain seen in the series into, surprisingly, the most sympathetic one. But 'Dalek' suffers from some problems with distracting, extraneous scenes – the Dalek elevation exists purely to exterminate the myth that they can't climb stairs – and the excellent Anna-Louise Plowman is criminally underused. But these minor concerns cannot undermine the power and pathos of the drama of 'Dalek'. – *Simon Catlow*

A fan's dream come true – a new series of *Doctor Who* and then we find out the Daleks are returning to battle the ninth Doctor as well. And the opening moments don't disappoint, with their presentation of a collection of alien artefacts and even a Cyberman head. . It seems as if the production team are finally starting to get a grip on how to make these forty-five-minute episodes. This one is full of action from beginning to end and the pace never lets up. For once, the Dalek is much more than a cipher for evil, but would we really expect less from a Shearman script? With *Jubilee*, Shearman had more time to expand on the madness of the creature. Here this is simplified with genetic input from Rose, and in many ways this works better. It makes more sense that the Dalek is slowly absorbing Rose's emotions and changing. The end is left vague enough to be interpreted a couple of ways (does the Dalek want freedom from its Dalek side, or from the new human emotions?) and both work just as powerfully. When was the last time a Dalek story made us think so much? – *Robert Franks*

I think this is not only the best episode of the new series, by far, but also the best example of televised *Doctor Who* since Peter Davison left the role over twenty years ago. Admittedly, I'm a tiny bit biased; I've known Shearman casually for a few years, and though I haven't really talked to him since he got this commission, I knew – just knew! – that the end result would be stunning. It's a rare thing to have such high expectations met, but there you are; the script, combined with Ahearne's masterful direction, makes for some damn fine *Doctor Who*. Admittedly, the plot device of Rose's DNA is slightly glossed over (how does that work, exactly?), and I go back and forth on Murray Gold's music – the quieter, subtle themes are wonderful, and I even like the moments where he takes a page from Danny Elfman, but then there are the overbearing, sweeping choral movements that seem to be preparing us for the second coming of Christ! Still, that doesn't take away from the story being as great as it is: moving, affecting, scary, grim, and sad. Christopher Eccleston is now well and truly the Doctor, and something fundamental has clicked into place – we're no longer watching the *Doctor Who* of the past, but a new and fantastic *Doctor Who* for today. Oh, to be twelve again! – *Sarah Hadley*

It's very easy to pick holes in this episode – Rose being monumentally thick in the pre-titles sequence, pointing out that the Doctor is an alien when they're surrounded by armed guards and stuffed, mounted and encased bits of alien; Adam never having been down to see the

Dalek before despite being so interested in alien life, but getting there easily enough when Rose demands it; and the Dalek uttering 'What use are emotions if you will not save the woman you love?', a line so bad it sounds like the tagline to a third-rate Hollywood movie, and without doubt the worst piece of dialogue to be heard in the new series so far. However, there is also much to like – the Dalek going on the rampage and killing hundreds, and using guile and cunning for probably the first time in the television series since way back in 'The Power of the Daleks' (1966). Van Statten is a great villain, and the episode is excellently played all round. On the visual side everything looks superb, especially the Dalek, and Ahearne's direction may well be the best seen in the new series so far – the framing of the Doctor's head in the reflection of the Cyberman's helmet was probably my favourite touch of his. I'm not convinced about the ending, but at least the Dalek killed itself rather than suffer the 'infection' it had picked up, and on the whole this was a very entertaining and well-executed slice of *Doctor Who*, 2005 style. – *Paul Hayes*

Shearman's script doesn't waste a word and is full of many quotable lines. There are also many memorable set pieces scattered throughout the episode, including the shocking scene where the Dalek exterminates a hoarde of soldiers, scientists and lawyers with only three shots. Ahearne does an excellent job with direction, using some unusual camera angles to pull off some superb shots. Gold's incidental music is superb, enhancing the tension and emotions of the story. The true star of 'Dalek' would have to be the Dalek itself – the team operating it and Nicholas Briggs, whose performance brings the Dalek to life and imbues it with a real sense of character. Piper is wonderful in her scenes with the Dalek, showing a real bond with it. Eccleston gives his most powerful and emotional performance so far in the series, showing the emotional impact the Daleks have had on the Doctor. The fear factor has been put back into the Daleks in a big way, but just as important, pity and empathy can also be felt for the lone Dalek, given all that it has been through. – *Cameron Mason*

I've never been a great fan of the Daleks (Dalekmania never reached New Zealand when I was a lad) but having said that, I was very much looking forward to 'Dalek'. After the Slitheen debacle, it's a relief to have *Doctor Who* back on form with probably the most eagerly anticipated instalment of the new series. With modern special effects and CGI technology, Daleks can now do pretty much anything; and they do! Watching this gave me (a 40-something) icy chills down my spine, so goodness only knows how today's 8 year olds are going to react! Shearman's superb script had it all; torture scenes; gun battles; a Bond-esque villain; and the highest death count so far. Eccleston delivered his most extreme performance to date. I can't imagine any of the other Doctors delivering the 'Why don't you just die!' line with quite the same level of venomous intensity. This Doctor is certainly carrying a lot of baggage and, after all she's experienced, Rose (as well as the viewer) must be beginning to realise there's far more to him than she first thought. With clever use of point of view, colour and shadow, Ahearne has effectively demonstrated just how alien the Daleks can be, which – if the rumours are true – bodes well for episodes 12 and 13. If the rights issues hadn't been resolved I doubt the story would have been as effective or memorable had it featured whatever the replacement monster was to be. 'Dalek' is certainly one of my favourites so far. – *Jon Preddle*

The first episode of the new series to fully engage me on an emotional as well as a visceral and intellectual level, Shearman's lyrical hymn to humanity's strengths includes, in its opening sequence, a critical summation of much of *Doctor Who*'s past (indeed, you could say, the entire Troughton era). Here we find the Doctor and his companion stumbling into an efficiently-run quasi-militaristic base, which has the effect of throwing a lighted match into a box of fireworks. Explosions, inevitably, follow. Somewhat *Stargate*-like in some of its conceits (an underground facility, the collection of alien artefacts, Anna-Louise Plowman's delicious performance), the episode also follows the recent trend of featuring further political comment – in this case an implicit critique on the 2004 Iraqi prisoner-torture scandal. Eccleston gives a stunning, extremely sardonic performance as a vaguely sadistic and clearly somewhat unbalanced Doctor. When he's told 'You would make a good Dalek', it's actually hard not to agree. Some elements don't work so well – Adam casually informing Rose that van Statten 'owns' the Internet, for example – and, whilst Langley puts in an energetic performance, the decision to take him off in the TARDIS at the end comes completely out of left-field. Nevertheless, the plus-points of 'Dalek' massively outweigh these minor quibbles. A dark, nefarious howl of rage with a poetic core ('This is not life, this is sickness'), amazing effects and Billie Piper melting the hardest hearts to slush. For once, it's difficult not to echo the Doctor's latest catchphrase. 'Fantastic!' – *Keith Topping*

They're back (well, one of them is, anyway)! After seventeen years, the Daleks have returned to where they belong – in a truly superb episode of *Doctor Who*. Shearman has crafted an exciting and emotionally-charged tale that stands out (at least for me) as the best of the series thus far. Rose, once again, takes centre stage, being the unintentional cause of all that transpires in the story, and Billie Piper continues to impress. As for the rest of the cast, Eccleston gives us considerable range from his highly charged *mano a plunger* exchange with the 'Metaltron' to his heartfelt sadness when believing Rose has been killed. Henry van Statten is a fun and believable 'villain' and Adam Mitchell is a genuinely likeable boy-genius. And lastly, there's the Dalek itself. While many fans have reacted negatively to the humanisation of the Dalek creature, I had no problem buying this. The creature has been isolated, tortured and altogether emasculated (in regards to the removal of its weapon). On top of that, I assume that it absorbed more than just DNA from Rose, thus its desperation and desire for freedom. A really remarkable story and an excellent forty-five minutes of television, regardless which side of the Atlantic you're standing on. – *Scott Alan Woodard*

EDITOR'S REVIEW: By and large, I really enjoyed 'Dalek'. It was definitely a different kind of episode, of the type not seen often in *Doctor Who*, where the Doctor ends up being on the wrong side of an argument. At least that's the point made here; the Doctor has become so blindly worked up by his hatred for this awful thing that is responsible for the death of his world, that he can't see the opportunities presented by its metamorphosis. Not that Rose was going to succeed in turning this Dalek into Uncle Fluffy with toys for children every Christmas ... This was a Dalek conflicted by itself, its programming to kill and destroy tempered solely by the fact that Rose Tyler is just far too nice a person for her own good. The very idea that the Doctor would have to be stopped from doing something terrible – cold blooded murder – is an idea largely avoided by *Doctor Who* of yesteryear, and it takes a brave storyteller to make points like that, when the only thing standing between an enraged Doctor, brandishing a Big Gigantic Gun, and his mortal enemy, a Dalek that's just murdered two hundred people, is the only person in the world who understands them both.

The problem I had with 'Dalek' on first viewing was not in the subject matter or its characterisation of the Doctor or Rose, but rather in the underlying situation that brings them into this conflict. It's not that the idea of a multi-billion dollar corporation with a paramilitary force at its beck and call and its fingers firmly in the American political pie isn't realistic (because some would argue that that's already the case), but that this corporation would happen to have caught the last remaining Dalek, strung it up in a private laboratory, tortured it beyond belief and yet would then allow the Doctor – a complete stranger – to intercede so quickly. Much akin to the end of 'World War Three', when everything seemed to be wrapped up in such a neat little package as Mickey was able to launch a missile using an Internet website, it almost felt as though the Doctor's entire journey through this episode had been scripted ... not in the traditional sense, but that he was being guided to do it. Shearman's script was subject to over a dozen rewrites – a common factor in many scripts this year – but maybe with the sudden change to a new enemy and then back again, it started to feel a bit forced.

Still, there is so much that's good to be found in 'Dalek' that a contrived framework isn't a deal-breaker, and an examination of its many layers demonstrates something more. It's so beautifully put together, utilising the Millennium Stadium in Cardiff for some wonderful cinematography that almost feels like it's been shot in a genuine underground bunker in the Utah desert. Murray Gold's music is fantastic, perfectly setting the scene for what transpires; I gained even more respect for him (even though I've been enjoying his scoring since the first episode!) when I watched *Doctor Who Confidential* and saw exactly what went into creating the music. (That haunting choral score is wonderful.) The cast give quite good performances, the American accents very well done by a mixed cast of American, British and New Zealand actors. (Anna-Louise Plowman tends to falter a bit here and there with her pronunciation, but I like her so much from her appearances in *Stargate SG-1* that I didn't pay that much attention.) Adam strikes me as a bit too eager for his own good, although Bruno Langley is a welcome addition to the crew. Nick Briggs is magnificent as always as the Dalek voice, and there were moments that I thought I heard the voice of the Daleks' creator, Davros, sneaking through. Bravo.

I'd humbly request that someone get Joe Ahearne to change his mind about not directing again next year. He's got a brilliant touch. (He's gone and booked himself to write and direct a film. Bah! Hopefully he'll be back to work on *Doctor Who* at some point, because I'll miss him!) And why isn't Shearman writing for the second series? What a disappointment that we don't get to enjoy more from this consistently inventive and original voice.

'Dalek' met with almost universal praise as the first true classic of the new *Doctor Who* series; it deserves it. I confess I was not as awestruck as others were about this episode at first, but I've since discovered that the more subtle nuances and themes – the gun-toting Doctor's moral dilemma, Rose's precious gift for empathy and the Dalek's quest to become more than itself – shine through on repeat viewings. This is perhaps Shearman's greatest gift: the ability to craft a story that becomes more complicated as we teach ourselves to understand it, much like we appreciate a wine after it ages in the cask. 'Dalek' is well scripted, nicely crafted, and full of important statements on the meaning of life and the terrible things we do when we're full of rage and anger. Definitely a winner. – *Shaun Lyon*

107: THE LONG GAME

In the far future, Satellite Five controls the news, which it packages and broadcasts across the Earth's massive Empire. But at the heart of this megalithic news conglomerate is something frightening ... and the Doctor, realising history has gone wildly off course, sets off for the mysterious Floor 500 to find it. But who is the Editor truly working for?

FIRST TRANSMISSION: UK – 7 May 2005. Canada – 17 May 2005. Australia – 2 July 2005. New Zealand – August 18.
DURATION: 44'25"
WRITER: Russell T Davies
DIRECTOR: Brian Grant
CREDITED CAST: Christopher Eccleston (Doctor Who), Billie Piper (Rose Tyler), Bruno Langley (Adam), Simon Pegg (the Editor), Tamsin Greig (Nurse), Christine Adams (Cathica), Anna Maxwell-Martin (Suki), Colin Prockter (Head Chef), Judy Holt (Adam's Mum)

WHERE AND WHEN: Satellite Five, an orbital space platform high above Earth in the year 200,000, during the Fourth Great and Bountiful Human Empire. Also at Adam's parents' home (likely circa 2012).

THE STORY UNFOLDS: The TARDIS has arrived on floor 139 of Satellite Five, a public space for the employees of the station that broadcasts six hundred channels to all corners of the universe. Satellite Five has been broadcasting for 91 years, and the Doctor believes it is responsible for holding humanity back. In fact, Satellite Five – and indeed all of humanity – are under the thrall of a massive alien being called the Mighty Jagrafess of the Holy Hadrojassic Maxarodenfoe, which occupies the space above floor 500. The Jagrafess has kept humanity in check through the selective editing of the news, creating a climate of fear and keeping the Earth's borders closed.

Employees of Satellite Five work, eat and sleep on the same floor. They are occasionally 'promoted' to floor 500, wherein lies the Jagrafess. Floor 500 is an icy tomb, all the heat channelled to the lower floors in order to keep the Jagrafess cool. The rumours on the station, however, are that the walls on floor 500 are made of gold. Once you're promoted there, you don't come back. Floor 16 is for medical non-emergency treatment. Suki says that the Freedom Foundation has been monitoring Satellite Five's transmissions and has proof that the facts have been manipulated by the Editor and his boss.

Earth at this time should be at its height, the Doctor notes. The planet is covered with megacities that extend upwards into the clouds and are visible from orbit. Earth now has a population of 96 billion, has five moons and is the hub of a massive empire covering a million planets with a million species of alien life. The era, says the Doctor, represents the human race at its most intelligent, with fine food, good manners, great culture. Unfortunately, Satellite Five represents none of this, which puzzles the Doctor and leads him to investigate further.

Compressed information streams into a 'journalist' through the use of an info-spike, an access port in the journalist's brain located on the front of the forehead. The journalist sifts through the data and uses a collective of other journalists with simpler chips implanted in their heads to process and transmit the data. The info-spikes can be programmed to open by a number of means, but the default setting is with the snap of one's fingers. The Doctor believes this technology is wrong for this era.

There are no aliens on Satellite Five, even though Cathica believes there's no reason why there shouldn't be; immigration's tightened up, the price of spacewarp has doubled and the government of Chavic Five has collapsed.

Cathica's news brief for the Doctor includes mentioning 200 dead in sandstorms on the New Venus Archipelago (called NVA 27 on screen); Glasgow water riots being into their third day (though the screen says 'Water riots on Caledonia Prime'); spacelane 77 closed by sunspot activity (on screen, 'Solar flares rage at 5.9'); and the Face of Boe having announced that he's pregnant. (Another news broadcast reports that solar activity has increased on spacelane 556; all commercial flights have been diverted.) Company policy (and the law) is that news must be open, honest and unbiased.

In the future, television channels are a mixed bag, such as the interestingly titled 'Channel Happyface+1' (signified with a symbol), Channel McB, and Bad Wolf TV. Credit Five is the local cash machine system. Much of the writing on the food containers is in some sort of eastern script, possibly Chinese. The head chef serves kronkburgers for two credits twenty, and zaffic is a beef flavoured ice. A vomitomatic involves having nanotermites implanted in the lining of one's throat; in the event of sickness they freeze the waste so it can be ejected cleanly.

THE DOCTOR: He feels that time travellers must throw themselves into the period, not just read about it or get warned about what's to come. He represents himself as testing Cathica and Suki in company promotion in order to get information out of them, and later watches as Cathica performs her duties under the guise of a 'management inspection'. He'll hug anyone. A full security scan doesn't pick him up (it says he's 'no-one'). He suspects that Satellite Five is being controlled by something, keeping back the progress of humanity. He uses override 215.9976/31 to access Floor 500, though he realises that he is being led there by the Editor.

ROSE TYLER: The Doctor lets Rose impress Adam by passing her information about where they've arrived, just so she can show off for their new friend. The Doctor believes she asks the right sort of questions. She is also 'no-one' according to the Satellite Five computers. She lends Adam her mobile phone (equipped with the time device) to call his family. While Adam isn't good enough to be the Doctor's companion, she is, the Time Lord says.

CHARACTER BUILDING: *Adam Mitchell* – We learn Adam's surname in this episode. After Rose and the Doctor tell him where they are, he faints from overexcitement. He thinks he's time-sick. He misleads Rose into thinking he's having major culture shock, when he really wants to get away to take advantage of this technology and whatever information he can glean. The Doctor gives him a credit bar with unlimited credit. He tells the Nurse he's a student from the University of Mars, and uses the credit bar to pay for an info-spike. (The nurse arranges for a vomitomatic to be installed in him, as well, as a special offer.) His parents' names are Sandra and Jeff. Adam uses Rose's mobile phone to transmit information to his parents' answering machine, which the Doctor later destroys. The Doctor leaves Adam at his parents' home, saying he's not good enough to travel in the TARDIS.

The Editor – Servitor of the Jagrafess (whom he calls Max) on floor 500. He has somehow adapted to the intense cold. He represents a consortium of banks that has long-term investments in Satellite Five; the Jagrafess is his client. He discovers the identity of the Doctor and Rose through Adam's connection to the computer network. He tries to 'resign' when the Jagrafess is defeated, but is trapped and apparently dies when the creature explodes.

Cathica – Her full name is Cathica Santini Khadeni. She's been applying for promotion to floor 500 for three years. She aids the Doctor and Rose by helping them break into the computer system, and later follows them up to floor 500. After hearing that the Editor and the Jagrafess now have the power to rewrite history, she uses the antiquated info-spike machine on floor 500 to access the computer, thereby to terminating the cooling system and disabling Satellite Five. The Doctor leaves her to tell the truth about Satellite Five in the news broadcasts and to change the course of history to the way it should be.

Suki –Her full name (or rather, her cover story) is Suki Macrae Cantrell, she was born in 199'89 in the Independent Republic of Morocco, and her hobbies include reading and archaeology; she says she wanted to work for Satellite Five to raise money for her sister's schooling. She asks Cathica to say goodbye to someone named Steve for her when she is 'promoted'. However, her real identity is Eva St Julienne, the last surviving member of the Freedom 15, a group of self-declared anarchists; this true identity was hidden behind a genetic graft. On uncovering her deception, the Editor 'promotes' her to Floor 500, where she is killed (though the chip in her head keeps working and allows the Editor to use her to run the monitoring systems).

The Nurse – She offers Adam either a head chip (for 100 credits) or a full info-spike (for 10,000 credits) and tells him that unlimited credit can buy a skilled picosurgeon and rapid installation.

The Mighty Jagrafess of the Holy Hadrojassic Maxarodenfoe – An immense being with a single gaping, toothy mouth, it lives above the Editor's control room on the 500th floor of Satellite Five, which acts as its life-support system. It needs the cold to survive. Cathica's interference turns the tables on the Jagrafess, heating up its lair, and it explodes.

BAD WOLF: The note about the Face of Boe 'expecting Baby Boemina' is broadcast on the Bad Wolf TV channel.

FANTASTIC!: There are no instances in this episode.

BODY COUNT: Suki is killed by the Jagrafess (though her body is still used through her implanted chip). The Jagrafess is destroyed by Cathica. It is presumed that the Editor dies in the explosion of the Jagrafess.

THE DOCTOR'S MAGICAL SONIC SCREWDRIVER: The Doctor gives himself (and Adam) unlimited credit on a credit bar by interfacing it with the cash machine. Rose uses it to break the Doctor out of his manacles in the Editor's control room. The Doctor uses it to destroy the answering machine.

REALITY BITES: The news set-up on Satellite Five parodies the global news channels of the 21st Century (specifically FOX News, which Davies mentioned in an article in the *Guardian*, and Sky News) and their ability to manipulate the information they are sworn to report. As the Editor says at one point, 'Create a climate of fear, and it's easy to keep the borders closed. It's just a matter of emphasis. The right word in the right broadcast repeated often enough can destabilise an economy, invent an enemy, change a vote.'

In the far future, people still dress as in the early 21st Century. Plastic water bottles and styrofoam tableware are also still in use.

According to Adam's research on the Satellite's computer system, the computer microprocessor became redundant in 2019, replaced by a system called Single Molecule Transcription.

LINKING THEMES: The Face of Boe, who was previously seen in 'The End of the World', is briefly seen on the television screen during the news report about his pregnancy. Kronkburgers were first referred to in the comic strip 'The Iron Legion,' originally published in *Doctor Who Magazine.*

Rose gives her mobile phone to Adam to use to call his family. This was altered by the Doctor in 'The End of the World' to allow her to transmit a signal through time; it allows Adam to do the same. It is unknown how it functions, but Adam calls his parents in 2012, given that he is supposed to be away at the Geocomtex facility in Utah ('Dalek').

Adam's parents appear to live on the same street as Clive did in 'Rose'.

The Doctor leaves Cathica and the people of Satellite Five to their own devisings, so history can sort itself out. As is usually the case, things are bound to go wrong. (See 'Bad Wolf'.)

SCENE MISSING: Why is there an unused info-spike station, and several frozen dead bodies, on floor 500? Why does no-one arriving on floor 500 demonstrate their intolerance for the extreme cold? Even Suki, wearing only a light blouse, barely registers the chill. Also, why does Suki's true personality not come out until she's confronted? (Is her alternative personality hidden in her subconscious and brought out only when the Editor reveals her identity?)

Why does Cathica's info-spike never open when the Editor clicks his fingers while questioning the Doctor and Rose? (Perhaps hers is tuned solely to her own clicking?)

The future dating conventions have become very confusing. Suki was born in 199'89 (the ' pronounced fully as 'apostrophe'). If this means the year 199,089 then she's 911 years of age; if it's 199,890, she's 110 years old; and if it's 199,989, that would make her age eleven. This suggests that at some point the numbering of years has been changed from the system understood in the 21st Century.

Why are there no alien species aboard Satellite Five? This plot point is mentioned during the episode, and it is inferred that the news manipulates humanity's impressions of other species. However, this point is not returned to, and there is no clear indication in the episode as to why this is the case.

How old is the Face of Boe? This episode takes place 200,000 years in the future; 'The End of the World', where he was also seen, takes place over five billion years in the future. Is it the same creature or a descendant? Or maybe he can travel in time?

Why would the Doctor, who abhors changing time (especially since we are shown in the next episode that doing so can have disastrous consequences), leave Adam in his own time with the advanced alien technology of the info-spike still inside him? Regardless of whether or not he wanted to teach Adam a lesson, it is certainly possible that an unscrupulous lad like Adam would take advantage of the situation. If Adam was capable of getting the future information onto an answering machine – considering that the link was between the computer and himself and not with the mobile phone – then would he not be capable of figuring out how to take advantage of his implant to change history for his benefit? (Also, earlier in the episode, why does the Doctor immediately presume Adam is to blame? Even though he is, could the Doctor not believe that it was done to him on purpose?)

Other unanswered questions: Why does Adam's info-spike open when someone else clicks their fingers? Why does the Editor not realise that Rose and the Doctor don't belong in the info-spike room, especially since he figures out Suki's identity so quickly? Why does Cathica instantly start helping the Doctor, even though she has worked for Satellite Five for years? And why didn't the Jagrafess simply expel the excess heat into space?

ALTERED STATES: While she's not named on screen, *Doctor Who Magazine* first identified Adam's Mum (played by Judy Holt) as being called 'Sandra'. Also, Christine Adams was first noted as playing 'Cath' rather than Cathica.

BEHIND THE SCENES: The Satellite Five complex was created entirely within the studio, in both the regular *Doctor Who* studios in Newport and elsewhere in Wales.

An early title considered for this episode was 'The Companion Who Couldn't', based upon Adam's sudden departure. In early drafts of the script, Adam was given another motivation for his underhand behaviour: to discover information that might be used to cure his very ill father back in 2012. This subplot was removed from the final version, making him seem more straightforwardly treacherous.

Guest star Simon Pegg was approached to play Rose's father in 'Father's Day' but was unavailable for the relevant recording dates. This episode was directed by Brian Grant, his sole contribution to the series, and was recorded after the block of 'Dalek'/'Father's Day' and before the two-parter 'The Empty Child'/'The Doctor Dances'. Davies noted in the episode preview in *Doctor Who Magazine* that he first came up with the plot of this story twenty years earlier.

OFF THE SCREEN: Simon Pegg is a well-known writer and comedian, having created the television series *Spaced* (1999) and the film *Shaun of the Dead* (2004) and appeared in *24 Hour Party People* (2002), *The League of Gentlemen's Apocalypse* (2005), *The Reckoning* (2003), *Band of Brothers* (2001), *Faith in the Future* (1995) and *Big Train* (1998). He also made an appearance in the *Doctor Who* audio play 'Invaders from Mars' (2002) produced by Big Finish. Tamsin Greig is best known as Fran Katzenjammer in the surrealist Channel 4 sitcom *Black Books* (2000-2004) and as the voice of Debbie Aldridge in Radio 4's long running soap opera *The Archers*, as well as for roles in *Neverwhere* (1996) and *Green Wing* (2004); she also appeared, with Simon Pegg, in *Shaun of the Dead*. Christine Adams played Katherine Williams Osgood in *NY-LON* (2004) and has appeared in *Submerged* (2005) and *Batman Begins* (2005), as well as playing a rogue female Jaffa warrior in the *Stargate SG-1* episode 'Birthright' (2003). Anna Maxwell-Martin has appeared in *North & South* (2004) and *Bleak House* (2005). Colin Prockter wrote for the TV series *Luna* (1983) and has appeared in *Coronation Street* (1995), *The Infinite Worlds of HG Wells* (2001) and episodes of *Z Cars* (1969), *The Famous Five* (1997), *Casualty* (2003) and *The Bill* (2002). Judy Holt has had recurring roles in *The Bill* (2002), *Hollyoaks* (2004), *At Home with the Braithwaites* (2000) and *Seeing Red* (2000) and has appeared in *Springhill* (1996), *Children's Ward* (1988) and *Queer As Folk 2* (2000). Director Brian Grant's credits include *Clocking Off* (2000-2003), *Bugs* (1997), *Hex* (2004), *As If* (2001-2002), *Love Bytes* (2004), *Highlander: The Raven* (1999) and *She-Wolf of London* (1990-1991).

TECHNICAL GOOFS: Cathica talks about there being a flood in Glasgow but the screen clearly shows another planet, Caledonia Prime. (However, Caledonia is another name for Scotland, so this could imply that there is a settlement called Glasgow on another planet.) When Suki exits the lift onto Floor 500 her arms are in different positions depending on whether the camera shot is from the front or the back. In Adam's home, the parting in his hair is on his left side, but when he turns to face his mother, it's on his right. The briefly-seen shot of the exterior of Adam's parents' home is stock footage from 'Rose', seen on the same road as Clive lived; there is even the same 'For Sale' sign visible.

CONTROVERSIES: The notion that in the year 200,000, fashion styles and other details of daily life aboard Satellite Five look very much as they do in 2005. The sudden abandonment of Adam. Many fans speculated that Adam would turn out to have some sort of relationship to the Daleks, considering that the info-spike on his forehead made him look vaguely like their creator, Davros.

INTERNAL CONSISTENCY: There is little in the episode to pinpoint a specific time, but events seem to happen in real time for the most part. The TARDIS crew appears to arrive during a shift break (possibly lunch). As Cathica takes the Doctor and his friends to the 'newsroom' she is worried about her twenty minute break being over, so has probably been with them for most of her break. There are also a few minutes missing during Adam's 'ten minute' surgery. Overall, another short adventure in real time, as it takes just over an hour for the Doctor to defeat the Jagrafess and return control of Satellite Five to the humans.

THEME ANALYSES

As Doctor Who For A Modern Audience: Davies's 'The Long Game' is a slice of old school *Doctor Who* with its plot involving a closed society, unknowingly enslaved by a malign influence, where the Doctor's arrival serves as the catalyst to break the status quo. The driving force behind this episode is the concept that the media can manipulate a population into believing whatever it wants it to believe, and that it's been done in a very subtle manner with the Great and Bountiful Human Empire's growth stunted and its people completely oblivious. The role of the Editor is perhaps symptomatic of the approach of this series, as rather than being a one note power-hungry megalomaniac, he's a businessman performing a role for his employer. Although why the Mighty Jagrafess of the Holy Hadrojassic Maxarodenfoe is actually doing what it is doing is left unanswered. 'The Long Game' also examines the companion's role by questioning whether everyone who travels with the Doctor would just fall into line – as all the Doctor's past companions seem to have done, perhaps with the exception of Turlough – and resist the temptation to use time travel to benefit themselves. Despite his actions being unsavoury, Adam's somewhat egregious reaction is probably truer to how most people would behave than Rose's more enlightened outlook, but by highlighting the difference between the characters, Davies shows just how good a companion Rose is.

As Television Drama: The presence in the cast of Simon Pegg, best known to television audiences for his groundbreaking sitcom *Spaced*, and Tamsin Greig, again known for comedy through her appearances in *Black Books* and *Green Wing*, immediately makes the viewer associate 'The Long Game' more with British sitcoms than other television drama programmes. Both Pegg and Greig also appeared, albeit very briefly in the latter's case, in the hit 2004 movie *Shaun of the Dead*, which with its blend of comedy and seriously-treated horror is actually probably rather closer in tone to this season of *Doctor Who* than most other film or television productions of recent years, although *Doctor Who*'s humour is somewhat less overt! Nonetheless, as with 'The End of the World', in terms of look, feel and setting there's absolutely nothing else home-made on British television that you can compare this with, which is perhaps why *Doctor Who* stands out so much and attracted such a good audience on Saturday nights – it's not simply more of the same, and you won't see anything like it anywhere else. Even the subtext, the satirising of television news coverage, is an area usually dealt with more frequently by comedy programmes, such as Chris Morris's legendary 1994 series *The Day Today*, which pastiched the approach that most news programmes took to the material they presented. It's not as gritty or as heavyweight as other dramas shown the same week, such as BBC2's acclaimed police series *Conviction*, but it's a lot more colourful and a lot more fun!

As A Piece of Writing: If the previous episode showed how to write awesome new *Doctor Who*, this one is a crash course in moderately entertaining, very traditional mediocrity. The entire episode echoes stories from the original series's much-criticised seasons 23 and 24, in particular tweaking certain memories of 'Paradise Towers' and 'Dragonfire', and giving much screen time to a somewhat unlikeable new companion. This story was allegedly submitted to the *Doctor Who* production office around 1980, and though it's been very much developed since then, you can still see vestiges of the old characters: the Doctor and Rose talk almost as equals, rather like the fourth Doctor and Romana, and Adam is very much in the Adric mould of the smug, self-assured genius. I do wonder if the original story didn't expand its horizons more than the finished episode, though. 'The Long Game' feels like the first half of a four-part story, with an ending quickly tacked on; as a result, the supporting characters suffer (the Editor never achieves any real depth), no motivations are given, and there are no explanations as to why the Jagrafess is there, how it turns people into zombies, or even how the Editor can stand the cold. Possibly, over a twenty-year period, Davies just couldn't stand back and view the material with an impartial eye. Unfortunately the end result simply doesn't make sense; it all feels unusually rooted in the past, with a lot of unrealised potential.

The Doctor As A Mystery Figure: The episode's main flaw – and it's something that has become a little recurring riff this season – is the ninth Doctor's often reactive, rather than proactive, relationship to the plot. Things tend to happen around him rather than because he's there. Even the episode's denouement arrives due to the actions of another character whilst the Doctor is chained up. Still, that's a very minor quibble about an episode that can rail so successfully against corporate and tabloid sleaze and very literal mind control. The mystery, in this instance, comes from the situation in which the Doctor finds himself rather than the Doctor's presence within a (previously non-mysterious) setting.

Themes, Genres and Modes: Once upon a time, science fiction was about telling tales of the future that were really tales of the present and that refracted a particular generation's hopes, aspirations and fears. We can see this in *Doctor Who*: back in the early seventies, we had stories like 'Colony In Space', full of ambitions about space travel and technology and yet fearful of what will happen to the Earth to necessitate such colonisation in the first place. 'The Long Game' fits comfortably within this tradition of future-as-commentary-on-present, especially as Davies's pot-shots at current trends aren't particularly subtle. The idea of a future where the media is a key apparatus of keeping people enslaved isn't particularly new – George Orwell did it back in 1949 as part of a small book called *Nineteen Eighty-Four* – but Davies adds some new and interesting spins with the idea of 'journalists' becoming nothing more than extra processing RAM for a media packaging system that has filtered out the need to ask questions. If future generations of kids learn to ask questions of our news gathering and presentation services as a result of this, then that's no bad thing.

In Style and Structure: The opening scenes of the Doctor showing his new companion the future of humanity might seem a little familiar, but they are used to show the contrast between Rose and Adam. Rose, after being overwhelmed by culture shock, just needs to touch base with her home in order to relax, whereas Adam decides to learn of future developments in order to gain from them himself when he returns home. There are 'A' and 'B' plotlines played out over the course of the episode; the 'A' story being the Doctor and Rose looking into the mystery of Floor 500, while the 'B' story revolves around Adam's exploration of the future. Both plotlines come together quite neatly at the climax. The Doctor is used as a catalyst in 'The Long Game'; without his curiosity and interference, the Jagrafess and Editor's plans would have gone on to their conclusion (whatever that was intended to be), at humanity's cost. Davies makes use of English folklore, specifically Dick Whittington, in setting up the attainment of floor 500 as an aspirational aim, where 'the walls are made of gold'. There are other cultural echoes scattered throughout the story, including a reference to the ballad 'Danny Boy'. Davies taps into current issues through his use of the media, showing how far the media can go in controlling people's lives, right down to not just influencing, but directing how people think; a relevant issue for modern society.

As Doctor Who Continuity: Davies has again served up a glimpse of his own (very warped!) vision for Earth in the distant future; this time some 200,000 years away. It's the Fourth Great and Bountiful Human Empire: the First was probably that seen in 'The Mutants' (1972) and 'Frontier in Space' (1973), and the Second Roman Empire was name-checked in 'The End of the World'. The Third might be that which arose once the humans on Pluto had returned to Earth at the conclusion of 'The Sun Makers' (1977), in which mankind was again held in perpetual slavery by an alien consortium. Will the gullible human race never learn?! And speaking of 'The Sun Makers', in that story, the Collector dismissed Gallifrey – and its oligarchic rulers the Time Lords – as being totally unsuitable for exploitation by the Usurians. But if Gallifrey still existed tens of thousands of years in the future, it makes my head hurt just trying to contemplate how this can be, considering that Gallifrey was destroyed in the great Time War. Of course, we don't know *when* this great battle between the Daleks and the Time Lords occurred – was it in the 1800s, when the Gelth were affected ('The Unquiet Dead'), or did it happen in the present day, when the Nestene world was destroyed ('Rose'), or the future? Oh dear, I think I need a lie down ...

From A Special Effects Viewpoint: CGI is king in this particular story, giving us everything from the exterior shots of Satellite Five to the brain access panels in both Cathica's and Adam's foreheads to the massive Mighty Jagrafess itself. All these effects are handled well, but the smallest impressed me the most. We've seen a similar space station model in 'The End of the World' (and it actually looked a bit more impressive in that story), and gooey-looking computer-generated monsters are nothing new, but the little 'brain doors' are something special. When Adam is touching the thin, metal shutters in his forehead with his fingers and the metal shifts and snaps (a nice accompanying audio effect, by the way), you believe it. It would be one thing to have it simply open and shut, but having the actor interact with it makes it seem solid and altogether real. This is an episode that no doubt had The Mill's computer render-farm working at full capacity.

PANEL REVIEWS

There's a series of advertisements in Britain for a wood preserver where the person pitching the product says 'It does exactly what it says on the tin.' 'The Long Game' is like that. It's not the standout story of the season, but it does what it says on the tin, so to speak: giving an effective, entertaining, and often surprising *Doctor Who* story. Brian Grant's direction is confident, the art direction is gorgeous in its use of colour, and it has some great moments of horror and drama. Simon Pegg in particular is unbelievably creepy – he acts like he's the smartest, most stylish and funniest guy alive, even though he's an accountant working with desiccated corpses taking orders from a piece of meat hanging from the ceiling. It's the story of Adam though that really captures the imagination. As the Doctor said to another wayward companion back in the 1980s, enlightenment is the choice. Bruno Langley does a superb job conveying the hubris involved in consistently making bad choices that jeopardise more than the lives of the Doctor. His comeuppance at the end is delightful. It's a story that suffers in some ways from the forty-five minute format – there's a lot that gets crammed in – but wanting more isn't necessarily a bad thing. – *Graeme Burk*

'The Long Game' is an odd beast that shouldn't work, but surprisingly does. Lacking anything special to distinguish it, this is the first 'regular' adventure of the new series and everything feels a bit off-kilter. For once, the focus isn't on the Doctor and Rose, who are disappointingly sidelined a little, but on seeing their affect on others. The journalism satire is underdeveloped, with no real answers about the ultimate purpose of the scheme, and the episode's core message that individuality will ultimately triumph over conformity is a thematic area that's been well-mined before. What's more interesting is the concept of a society that has become enslaved without anyone noticing anything is wrong, thanks to the instigator gaining control of how information is disseminated; but without knowing the reasons why this has been done, it makes everything seem a bit vague. The Adam plotline, showing a companion who abuses the privilege of time travel to enrich himself, is an obvious idea that surprisingly has never been done before but creates the episode's most memorable moments with his encounter with Tamsin Greig's seductive Nurse and his eventual return home to face his Mum. Despite looking rather old-fashioned, 'The Long Game' is redeemed by the casting that lets Simon Pegg deliver an energetic turn as the smarmy Editor and Christine Adams and Anna Maxwell-Martin provide effective and believable supporting performances. This episode must go down as an average one, but it's certainly agreeable that even weaker stories like this can still entertain. – *Simon Catlow*

An old fashioned *Doctor Who* story of sorts, this one starts out simply enough but throws in new companion Adam Mitchell to mix things up. Adam seems like a cross between Adric and Turlough. (I was half expecting him to pull out his *Blue Peter* badge for mathematical excellence.) As in 'Aliens of London', the Doctor has to investigate what's going on, but this time all the subplots work better and push the main story ahead. There are a lot of unexplained items (mostly about the Editor) but that doesn't change the fact this is a good, solid adventure. Eccleston's Doctor is beginning to show more and more depth as the season progresses. There is a small scene here when the Doctor and Rose arrive on Floor 500 and the former becomes concerned for the latter's safety. As Rose heads off to investigate, the next scene shows that the Doctor has taken the lead – a subtle but keen move on the part of the production team. This Doctor may seem flippant and always smiling, but he's acutely aware of what's going on around him and ready to be serious when it's called for. – *Robert Franks*

It's 'The End of the World' all over again – or is it? 'The Long Game' tries to mirror certain key points of that earlier episode, mostly to contrast the experiences and choices of Rose against those of the new kid, Adam. As a result, it sometimes feels like a diluted version of the earlier work, although this one comes off as having a better pace, more interesting characters, and a more traditional storyline – despite the fact it never quite gels. Even the set design is a throwback to the old series, a strange mid-'80s 'futuristic' look that seems both abrasive and cheap, indicating that the production team may have seen it as something of a filler episode. Really, it's not that bad – it's Davies's best-paced script yet, there are lots of funny moments, and we get just enough of Adam to understand both his point of view and why the Doctor throws him out. The main problem is that not much actually seems to happen, and when it does, there's no resolution. Simon Pegg spends most of the episode talking to himself, the Doctor and Rose don't make much of an impact, and we never learn anything about the Jagrafess beyond 'it's there, it's scary, we can blow it up'. For the first time in the series, I found myself neither pleased nor displeased with the episode, but largely apathetic. It just felt like there should have been more. – *Sarah Hadley*

I enjoyed 'The Long Game' – although oddly not so much on first viewing. I think that, perhaps more so than the other episodes so far this season, it's a story that really benefits from repeated viewing, although this is perhaps not such good news for the general audience who'll only want to see it once. First time around I felt there were problems with the pace, but this didn't bother me at all on second viewing. I also initially felt it was far too similar to 'The End of the World', but again I came to realise that this actually serves a purpose, highlighting the differences between Rose's and Adam's reactions to their first trips in the TARDIS, with the phone call home this time forming an important plot point. The production, direction and supporting cast – particularly Simon Pegg – are excellent. The Jagrafess is one of the greatest CGI creations The Mill have come up with so far in the series, a really disturbing monster that I hope has burned its image onto the memories of all the children who watched the episode. If I have one complaint it's the fact that once again the Doctor doesn't get to be particularly proactive or heroic in the resolution to the storyline. This is something I hope that upcoming episodes start to redress. – *Paul Hayes*

The highlight of 'The Long Game' would have to be the guest characters. Simon Pegg is brilliant as the Editor, charming yet utterly ruthless. Tamsin Greig makes the Nurse an efficient, yet slightly disturbing character. Bruno Langley shows Adam's darker side, his initial curiosity turning into deception for personal gain; however, he doesn't play Adam as being evil, just selfish. An interesting element is that the Doctor treats Adam as Rose's companion, rather than his own. Christopher Eccleston plays up this aspect beautifully with some well timed and executed lines and put-downs, with Billie Piper bouncing off these moments just as well; this adds a lighter side to their relationship. The design work of Satellite Five is reminiscent of Platform One, but in such a way that the latter looks like a development from the former. The CGI rendition of the Jagrafess is suitably glutinous and grotesque, all flesh and teeth. The whole story revolves around the media, and makes some important and relevant statements about the extent to which the media influences modern society. 'The Long Game' is an enjoyable contrast to the previous story, with similarly important themes at its heart. – *Cameron Mason*

I can't shake off this feeling of *déjà vu*. A satellite in orbit above Earth, thousands of years in the future; the Doctor accessing the main computer using unconventional means; the Face of Boe; a mobile phone call back through time; a CGI creation exploding in a shower of goop; a 'return to Earth' coda. Didn't we see all that in 'The End of the World'? Despite these similarities, there was certainly much to enjoy in this entertaining romp: some nicely timed moments of black humour, including Adam's faint and everything with Tamsin Greig; and the fact that the Mitchells' dog was just so ... jumpy. Simon Pegg sensibly downplayed the potentially OTT Editor, one of the more chilling (geddit?!) characters we've had to date. I also enjoyed the solid B-plot concerning Adam's dangerous venture. (And please, just because he's travelled in the TARDIS and appeared in two consecutive stories, this does not make him a companion! Besides, the Doctor doesn't even like him.) There was some beautiful camerawork: the pan when Suki pulls her gun, and the cutting between shots at the TARDIS in one smooth movement. The CGI for the gruesome Jagfress-who-fling-whatsit (why does Davies have this obsession with ridiculously long and hard-to-pronounce names?!) was a vast improvement on that for the Nestene in 'Rose'. In the accompanying *Doctor Who Confidential* episode, Davies claimed that all would be revealed at a later date as to how the Jassa-whatsit-thingumy got to Satellite Five. But shouldn't such a vital plot point have been highlighted within the episode itself? And isn't the title just a little too obscure? There can't be that many savvy viewers (e.g. children) who would understand a slang expression for long term financial risk! – *Jon Preddle*

A virulent, if somewhat heavy-handed, parody of crass media manipulation, the basic message of 'The Long Game' appears to be 'Don't believe anything you read/see and always think for yourself.' Which, you know, is something well worth saying frankly, and it's certainly in the grand traditions of the series's past. The satire is, for the most part, far less specific than might have been expected (though there's a spitefully funny dig at Max Hastings, the former editor of the *Daily Telegraph* and the *Evening Standard*), but lines like 'We are the news' clearly show exactly the targets at which Davies was aiming when he wrote this. 'The Long Game' is, actually, something of a curio. It's clever and has good jokes and some great performances (Simon Pegg, with able support from Christine Adams and Anna Maxwell-Martin). I did wonder if it might not be a bit 'talky' for the younger audience but then, it's also got a great scary moment with a skeleton and a blobby alien menace with big teeth. Adam proved to be a short-lived addition to the TARDIS crew, and you did somewhat sense that he was there purely to show, by comparison, just how far Rose has come in such a short space of time. Ultimately, as the nurse notes when presented with Adam's credits, 'That'll do nicely'. – *Keith Topping*

To me, 'The Long Game' has all the trappings of a classic *Doctor Who* story: a space station in the far future, a mystery to be solved, a villainous figure hiding in the shadows, and above it all (literally, in this case), an alien menace pulling all the strings. It's an enjoyable adventure, but it all comes off feeling only half there, presenting the audience with some unanswered questions, including one enormous one: why is The Mighty Jagrafess interfering with humanity in the first place? The supporting cast is very good, with Simon Pegg gnawing at the scenery a bit, Tamsin Greig playing a rather odd (and strangely seductive) member of the medical staff, Bruno Langley taking charge as Adam Mitchell, the lovely Christine Adams as Cathica and the adorable Anna Maxwell Martin as Suki. The big star of the show, though, is the Jagrafess itself, depicted as an undulating, brown, slimy mass with a maw of nasty-looking sharp teeth. We're told that it is somehow behind all the lies and propaganda dominating the news coming out of Satellite Five, yet its appearance doesn't suggest any intelligence at all. Is there something pulling the Jagrafess's strings? There's a thought! Overall, a decent story, but I'm definitely looking forward to seeing how it ends. – *Scott Alan Woodard*

EDITOR'S REVIEW: All the advance word that had leaked out about 'The Long Game' inspired less than confidence: rushed, ridiculous, cheesy, and probably a few other choice adjectives muttered in Internet chat rooms. Taken down to its base elements, 'The Long Game' isn't the most in-depth examination of the manipulation of the masses by the popular media, and it certainly doesn't do more than touch briefly on the whole tangle before it returns to the Doctor, who's basically standing around waiting to get a few choice quips in before the Mighty Jagrafess of the Exceedingly Overcomplicated Genus-name explodes. (Once again we find the Doctor being merely part of the action instead of directing or influencing it, but this wouldn't be the first, or last, time.)

Doctor Who, you see, has never needed to be the end-all, be-all of satire. The original might have had a few choice words to say about tolerance and acceptance, but down to its bare elements the episodes really were less about the message and more about the spirit of adventure (and running up and down corridors ... don't forget those corridors!) 'The Long Game' might *appear* at first glance to be a satire on FOX News or Sky News, but it's not ... it's about an alien being that's doing something very nasty. We lose the enjoyment value of something when we overanalyse it, even when it's our job to do so.

'The Long Game' had a lot going for it. There's Adam, whose story has all the merit of being witness to a car crash ... you know it's ugly, but you can't stop watching it. (I'd like to think of myself as being like the Adam of 'Dalek,' all wide-eyed and full of wanderlust; here he follows his natural course from eternal optimist to greedy nitwit, and I can't help but wonder if I'd even *consider* the same thing. I hope not.) There's Cathica, who – glory be! – presents a strong woman of colour who finds strength within herself to save the day and take on the consequences. Christine Adams does a wonderful job with the role, and had she not been here as a guest shot already, she'd be a prime candidate for a *Doctor Who* companion (a companion of colour being something that, to its detriment, this otherwise progressive series has yet to feature on television).

And there's Simon Pegg. I confess I'm not familiar with Mr Pegg's other roles, apart from his brief turn in a *Big Finish* audio (no, I've never seen *Shaun of the Dead*, namesake or not.) I wouldn't have been able to tell you what all the fuss was about ... but, here I am, about to add to it. He's magnificent, with just the right touch of humour and cowardice and false bravado and everything mixed into a little white-frosted package. I'm actually disturbed that the character appears to have been killed off, because he would have made an interesting villain ... a corporate lackey, possessing all the knowledge of the Time Lords. He could have built himself one of those dandy little TARDIS consoles and, whoosh! Off he goes to corner the stock market. Or something.

Where I'm not comfortable with 'The Long Game' is in its dreadful realisation of the future. Styrofoam cups? Burger joints? If this had been the year 2100, maybe, just maybe I could have appreciated it more. But 200,000? One would think they'd be serving meals by direct transmat, zipping the food from the grill right into your stomach, bypassing all that needless chewing and swallowing. I was quite disappointed in the series finale of *Star Trek: Enterprise* when I found out that six years had passed and none of the characters had developed ... but, 197,900 years and we're still drinking flavoured ice and eating out of styrofoam tins? If that's not stagnation, I don't know what is.

While 'The Long Game' may have its logic flaws, Eccleston and Piper and company obviously had fun with it, Simon Pegg is marvellously slimy, and there are a few interesting themes toyed with (if not well developed). It also turns out to be something of a set up for events to come later in the season, explaining its title after the fact. In fact, it's a very light-hearted diversion ... where the real moral of the story is, don't irritate the Doctor or he'll leave you trapped in your overbearing mother's home with no hope of rescue. And who wants that?
– *Shaun Lyon*

108: FATHER'S DAY

The Doctor takes Rose back to see the father she barely knew, Pete Tyler, on the day of his death, but Rose changes the course of history by saving him. Soon, the world has gone wrong, the three are trapped inside a church with the last survivors of humanity, and the Reapers wait outside to devour the damaged parts of time before it's set back on its proper course ...

FIRST TRANSMISSION: UK – 14 May 2005. Canada – 24 May 2005. Australia – 9 July 2005. New Zealand – 25 August 2005.
DURATION: 42'51"
WRITER: Paul Cornell
DIRECTOR: Joe Ahearne
CREDITED CAST: Christopher Eccleston (Doctor Who), Billie Piper (Rose Tyler), Camille Coduri (Jackie Tyler), Shaun Dingwall (Pete Tyler), Robert Barton (Registrar), Julia Joyce (Young Rose), Christopher Llewellyn (Stuart), Frank Rozelaar-Green (Sonny), Natalie Jones (Sarah), Eirlys Bellin (Bev), Rhian James (Suzie), Casey Dyer (Young Mickey).

WHERE AND WHEN: South East London, 7 November 1987, including on several streets, at the Tyler flat and at the Parish church of St Christopher; also, in Jackie's bedroom, at some point later when Rose is beyond toddler-hood (possibly early 1990s), and in a registry office when Pete and Jackie Tyler marry (likely mid-1980s). Pete Tyler dies (or is meant to die) on Georgian Road. The TARDIS arrives on Walterley Street, SE15, in the London Borough of Southwark.

THE STORY UNFOLDS: The Reapers are creatures of the web of time, sterilising its wounds by consuming everything affected in altered timelines. The alteration of time – specifically, Rose saving her father's life – calls them into existence. The Reapers begin removing individuals from reality, then moving on to entire groups of people, including a playground full of families. The weather turns cold as their influence is felt. They cannot penetrate the church; the older something is, the stronger it is against them. As time goes on, they start to consume everything on Earth; smoke rises from London with no sirens heard.

Having already witnessed Pete's death once, the Doctor agrees to take Rose to the same period one more time, and the two watch their earlier selves from around a corner. The second time, however, proves too much for Rose, who saves her father's life; the earlier versions that had watched the accident the first time immediately disappear from existence. Almost instantly, the Reapers arrive, spying on the events (which we see as telescopic red-coloured visuals). The TARDIS is thrown out of this timeline, its shell becoming an ordinary police box ... but it later signals that it still exists by making the Doctor's TARDIS key glow. The car that was meant to hit Pete Tyler is stuck in a time loop, appearing on roads (and disappearing again) near where Pete is currently located. Rose recognises a piece of music on the radio as something that hasn't come out yet, and instead of calling the TARDIS, her mobile phone picks up an electronic message from 1876.

Among the posters seen on the buildings are a Socialist Worker's Party advert ('No third term for Thatcher'), an 'Energise' poster (dated 20.11.87 with a happy face) and an advert for an independent band called Amphibians. The car that kills Pete is a beige Peugeot, licence number NEH 793 W. The numbers 23-6-801, posited by fans as important (as they were featured in photographs on the official *Doctor Who* website), appear on one of the bus stop signs created for this episode; at one point they also appear on a hymn board. The official *Doctor Who* website later revealed that it wasn't an intentional story point; it had 'started as a mistake on the Psalm board in episode 8, and became a bit of misleading fun.'

THE DOCTOR: After Rose saves her father's life, the Doctor believes that he's 'done it again' and has picked up 'another stupid ape'. While his entire world and his family died, he hasn't been able to go back and save them because of the damage it could cause to time. When he realises the TARDIS has been affected, he understands the trouble and rescues the few people he can (including Rose) by corralling them into the church. He delights in finally having the final say in an argument with Jackie. For once, he says he doesn't have a plan. Stuart and Sarah's story affects him, as he's never had a life like they've had. The Reapers consume him, but later, Pete's sacrifice restores him to reality.

ROSE TYLER: She decides she wants to see her father, so she and the Doctor visit her parents' wedding and then the day her dad died. She gives the Doctor back the TARDIS key after telling him that for once he's not the most important man in her life. Even the notion that her father thinks of her as a woman (since he doesn't know who she is at first) repulses her. Rose never knew her parents were having marital issues or that her father was somewhat different in character from the way Jackie told her he was. When she touches Jackie's baby (that is, herself) and creates a paradox, she allows the Reapers into the church. After Pete realises what he must do, she gets the opportunity to be there with him when he dies. She describes him as the most wonderful man in the world.

CHARACTER BUILDING: *Pete Tyler* – Rose's father was born on 15 September 1954, and died on 7 November 1987. Peter Alan Tyler forgot his wife's full name during their wedding ceremony. He'd gone to get a wedding present (a vase) for the Hoskins-Clark wedding and was accidentally struck by a hit-and-run driver while getting out of his car; he died alone, before the ambulance arrived. He drove a green Mark 3 Ford Escort, licence D 602 PKW. Rose was told that he was very clever; but in fact, he was not a businessman but a bit of a 'Del Boy' (see 'Linking Themes'), making money selling 'tonic water' and Betamax videotapes, and was apparently cheating on Jackie with several women including a cloakroom attendant. He believes strongly that he's met Rose before, which is confirmed when she calls him 'Dad' in his car as he swerves to avoid the oncoming car outside the church; later, he gives his car keys to her, trusting her implicitly, and finally works out the truth about her. Rose tells him he was a good father, always telling her bedtime stories and taking his family for picnics ... He knows then that she's lying, and that he is supposed to be dead. Pete gives his life by stepping in front of the car that was always meant to kill him, in order to set time right again. In the new timeline created by Pete's sacrifice, the driver gets out and waits for the police, while an unidentified girl (Rose) sits with Pete as he dies, holding his hand.

Jackie Tyler – Before Pete died, Jackie and he were having issues; she believed he was useless and an 'accident waiting to happen', and never knew where the next meal was coming from. (At one point, she threatens him with divorce.) She always wished someone had been there for Pete when he was struck. Her full maiden name is Jacqueline Andrea Suzette Prentice. She had longer, curlier hair (much like an Olivia Newton-John style) in the 1980s. She eventually comes to believe that Rose is her grown up daughter, and gets the chance to say goodbye to Pete before he dies.

Mickey Smith – A young boy at the time of the wedding, he's being pushed on the swings at a nearby park when his mother and everyone else in the area is harvested by the Reapers, and he runs to the church for safety. He immediately runs to Rose for a hug; Jackie comments that he grabs hold of what's passing and holds on for dear life.

Stuart Hoskins & Sarah Clark – Friends of the Tyler family, they were to be married on the day Pete died. After the time damage, many expected visitors (such as Uncle Stephen and Aunt Lillian and all the Baxters) do not arrive for the wedding. Stuart's father is Sonny, who believes his son is marrying Sarah because he's 'knocked her up'. Sarah's friends are Bev and Suzie; Jackie brings Sarah to the wedding. Stuart and Sarah first met outside the Beat Box Club at two in the morning; she'd lost her purse and he took her home, writing her number on the back of his hand.

BAD WOLF: Scrawled on one of the 'Energise' posters at the corner where the Doctor and Rose witness Pete's death are these words.

FANTASTIC!: The Doctor exclaims 'Fantastic!' after Stuart gives him Sonny's mobile phone, which contains the battery he needs.

BODY COUNT: Pete Tyler, who has to die to set history right again. The Reapers kill Sonny (Stuart's father), the vicar (named Reverend Simon Holmes on the church noticeboard, as seen in behind-the-scenes photographs), a housewife, a gardener, everyone (except Mickey) in a local playground, passers-by outside the church, and even the Doctor; in fact, they appear to destroy everyone on Earth except the occupants of the church. However, everyone who was killed by the Reapers after the time anomaly in the revised timeline is restored when the timeline is fixed, so really only Pete dies in the story.

THE DOCTOR'S MAGICAL SONIC SCREWDRIVER: The Doctor uses it in an effort to bring the TARDIS back by way of the battery in Sonny's phone.

REALITY BITES: The message both Rose and the Doctor hear via the mobile phones is comprised of the first-ever electronic transmission of speech, on 10 March 1876. They were of Alexander Graham Bell saying: 'Watson, come here, I need you'. However, there is still some debate on the exact wording (which could have been 'I want you').

The Doctor's statement that 'The past is another country' is an allusion to the opening line of the novel *The Go-Between* by L P Hartley (1895-1972): 'The past is a foreign country. Things go differently there.' (The Doctor also notes the similarity between 1987 and Rose's time, noting that while the past is indeed another country, 'This is just the Isle of Wight.')

The Reapers are based somewhat of the concept of Grim Reapers, agents of Death that appear throughout classic literature.

LINKING THEMES: The Doctor warns Rose against touching herself as a baby, and also fails to stop Rose from changing time by saving her dad. This flies against most of established *Doctor Who* lore that suggests that there are laws of time that cannot be broken (although they can be bent slightly). Even without the Time Lords, the Doctor still has issues breaking these laws (as he indicates to Rose, commenting that being in the same place a second time is almost too much, even for him).

Before their destruction, says the Doctor, the Time Lords would have stopped this situation from happening and the Reapers from coming, but that's no longer possible.

Rose calls her father a 'Del Boy'. This is in reference both to the character of Derek Trotter played by David Jason in the long-running BBC sitcom *Only Fools and Horses* and to the type of character he is – a street-wise seller of dodgy goods.

The whoisdoctorwho.co.uk website painted Mickey as being resentful of the fact that the Doctor 'made' Rose watch her father die. Also, according to behind the scenes photographs on the official site, one of the church notice boards featured a photograph also seen in Clive's shed, although this isn't seen clearly in the episode (and is likely one of many reused set pieces).

ALTERED STATES: In pre-airing press material, Casey Dyer was credited as 'Boy' in order to keep his identity as the young Mickey Smith a surprise.

The working title for this episode was 'Wounded Time'.

SCENE MISSING: Rose is apparently nineteen years old in March 2005, meaning that she had to have been born prior to March 1986; however, in 'Father's Day', which takes place in November 1987, Rose is still a baby instead of being nearly two years of age.

How does the Doctor know where the church is? The TARDIS is located near Pete's flat. Pete and Rose then drive to the church, so it must be some distance away since the phantom car follows them for most of the way. The Doctor then runs to the church on foot!

Why, if the Reapers have more trouble with something as it gets older, do they go for the oldest person in the group first (Sonny), and seem to have no trouble consuming the Doctor?

Why does Alexander Graham Bell's phone message continually repeat on Rose's mobile phone and the portable phone belonging to Stuart's father? For that matter, why does the music on the radio in Pete's car suddenly change to something in his own future?

How does time restore itself so that Pete *did* in fact die outside the church, but Jackie doesn't remember who Rose was or what happened with the Reapers? Why does Jackie not recognise the Doctor when she sees him later?

What does the Doctor need the battery for? He adjusts it with his sonic screwdriver, but later simply sticks the key into a lock (seemingly in thin air) and waits for the TARDIS to reappear. Why, for that matter, does the TARDIS key glow and the TARDIS come back for them? And why does the Doctor not realise that there is an object burning inside his coat?

Other unanswered questions: What exactly attracts the Reapers? Why do they devour no-one but the Doctor inside the church? Why does one of the Reapers not eat either Sarah Clark or Jackie Tyler when it has the opportunity? And why does the car continually follow Pete, especially rounding the corner outside the church where it has no other reason to be?

BEHIND THE SCENES: Recording for this episode was done primarily at the Parish church of St Paul's in Grangetown, Cardiff, redressed as St Christopher's, and on streets nearby including Llanmaes Street. A boardroom at the offices of ITV Wales in Cardiff served as the registry office where Pete and Jackie got married.

The Reapers were another creation realised entirely by CGI; the sounds they made were created by manipulating the sounds made by vultures, with reverberation and other noises layered on top.

DULCET TONES: 'Never Can Say Goodbye' by the Communards – Their seventh UK single, a cover version of an old Jackson 5 hit, it reached number 4 in November 1987, and appeared on their second album 'Red' that year. Lead singer Jimmy Somerville (previously of Bronski Beat) would later find arguably more success as a solo artist. This can be heard playing as Rose first steps out of the TARDIS into 1987. (Heard 3:08-3:36.)

'Never Gonna Give You Up' by Rick Astley – His first single, released in the UK in July 1987, reached number 1 in 16 countries and became the best selling single of 1987 in the UK. It headlined his first album, 'Whenever You Need Somebody', released in November 1987 in the UK (reaching number 1) and in June 1998 in the US (reaching number 10 and going double platinum). Pete Tyler has this playing on his car stereo on the way to the wedding. (Heard 12:31-13:06.)

'Don't Mug Yourself' by the Streets – This was Mike Skinner's fourth UK single, from the album 'Original Pirate Material', which reached number 21 in November 2002 in the UK. Pete Tyler's car stereo starts playing this as a result of the interferences with time. (Heard 13:10-13:35.)

OFF THE SCREEN: Shaun Dingwall portrayed DC Mark Rivers in the series *Touching Evil* (1997) and has been seen in such productions as *Lloyd & Hill* (2001), *Underground* (1999), *The Phoenix and the Carpet* (1997) and *Soldier Soldier* (1991). Frank Rozelaar-Green has appeared in *Micawber* (2001), *Slayers Try* (1997), *Restoration* (1995) and *Lucifer* (1987). Christopher Llewellyn was in *The Black Dog* (1999). Eirlys Bellin was in *The Magic Paintbrush: A Story From China* (2000) and has appeared in mostly Welsh theatre productions. Julia Joyce was seen in *Prime Suspect 6* (2003) and *Life Isn't All Ha Ha Hee Hee* (2005). Rhian James appeared in *The Englishman Who Went Up A Hill But Came Down a Mountain* (1995) and the series *Pobol y Cwm* and *Mostyn Fflint* (2004). Natalie Jones appeared in episodes of *Casualty* (1998) and *Cadfael* (1998). Robert Barton also appeared in *Casualty* (2004) and in the film *ET the Extra-Terrestrial* (1982).

TECHNICAL GOOFS: While the geography is accurate (SE15 is correctly identified as Southwark) the buses aren't numbered correctly. After the accidents, both at the beginning and at the end of the episode, Pete Tyler has no visible wounds or bleeding. Some of the cars seen in the background are more modern than 1987, or have number plates with a typeface used after 2001.

CONTROVERSIES: Much of the controversy provoked by this episode surrounds the impracticality of the time paradox, and the fact that the Doctor allows Rose to come to this time knowing what it will do to her *and* how it could damage the timeline.

INTERNAL CONSISTENCY: The TARDIS first makes a quick trip to the day of Jackie's and Pete's wedding. There are no clues to pick a time for this short visit. The next journey drops the Doctor and Rose off at SE15, Walterley Street, in late afternoon on Saturday 7 November 1987. Although, again, there are no clues to a direct time of day, sunset on this date was at 4.46 pm in London. It is an overcast Autumn day, but obviously at least mid-afternoon.

Pete's original death was on Georgian Road, which would presumably be near the Powell Estate (as he is parking to drop by the flat; perhaps this was in front of it?). It is late afternoon by the time of Pete's new death and he comments that he has had 'extra hours', meaning at least a couple of hours have passed since they took shelter in the church.

THEME ANALYSES

As Doctor Who For A Modern Audience: This episode, in its intense, emotional focus, demonstrates the production team's confidence in evolving the concept of *Doctor Who* for today's viewers. The placing of 'Father's Day' within the season is spot on, coming at a moment when the audience's rapport with Rose has grown sufficiently to be able to take such a demanding storyline and to appreciate Rose's reactions to the opportunity time travel gives her to save the father she never knew. To have it following 'The Long Game' also allows an interesting contrast between Rose's justification for abusing the privilege the Doctor has afforded her and Adam's, but while both have inherently selfish motivations, Rose cannot be blamed for wanting to save a life that was taken prematurely. Despite the drama being pitched more emotionally than usual, Cornell's script remains recognisably *Doctor Who* by providing a science fiction element in the form of the Reapers, who arrive to take advantage of the situation, thus ensuring that the episode never strays towards sensationalist melodrama. This episode demonstrates the importance of character evolution, as the Doctor has learnt enough compassion from Rose to allow her the indulgence of revisiting her own past but is still naÔve enough to misjudge her when it comes to restraining her natural instincts to help where she can. While he's angry with Rose, the Doctor cares enough for her to risk the lives of the whole of humanity to find a way to keep Pete alive for her, rather than take the easier option of restoring order to the flow of time by ensuring his death.

As Television Drama: It's usually seen as a criticism – particularly in *Doctor Who* fan circles – to compare something to a soap opera, but I don't at all mean to criticise when I say that 'Father's Day' evokes the spirit of the BBC's flagship popular drama of the past twenty years, *EastEnders*. Not *EastEnders* as it is now, so much as when it was at its height in the 1980s, very much around the time this episode is set. Strong, recognisable characters and rather more passion and care in the writing are what seem to have marked it out in those days, and of course the London setting and doomed wedding seen here do help the comparison along a little! This grounding in the traditions of regular prime time drama is nicely subverted by the whole science-fiction/time paradox element to the episode, which in its depiction and execution cannot help but invite comparison more to *Sapphire & Steel*, the much-admired ITV science-fiction series of the late 1970s and early 1980s, than to most *Doctor Who* that we have seen in the past. The plot doesn't hang together quite as tightly as in most *Sapphire & Steel* stories, but the creepy and the poignant come together very nicely here, just as they so often did in the earlier series. 'Father's Day' does, however, have the advantage of being rather better produced, and with this slick production and affecting writing and performances, can hold its head up high with the best of contemporary British television drama.

As A Piece of Writing: This episode has most of the things you need for good drama – a set of strong characters, some good conflict, a nice bit of danger to drive the plot, a solid pace, and several touching, interpersonal moments. The dialogue is good, and we're starting to see an increased amount of lines that seem tailor-made for Christopher Eccleston's and Billie Piper's individual strengths. On the surface, then, it glides along really well – if you saw this episode in a foreign language, you would probably be able to figure out roughly what was going on, and that's admirable indeed. Unfortunately, most of the specific mechanics of time travel/time paradox either don't make sense or aren't explained at all. Although the Doctor offers a few, minimal explanations, we never do learn how it all works – my natural inclination would be to think that any change to the timeline, no matter how small, could have terrible consequences, but that seems not to be the case. We're never told quite how much of everyone's memory is erased; does Rose remember meeting her father, for instance? Where does Jackie's memory change from the old timeline to the new? Does the Doctor, the one possibly 'exempt' character, remember having died? There are other problems, too – how exactly does the key and a charged battery bring back the TARDIS? Why do the Reapers attack the vicar instead of the bride? If you can gloss over all this, you're probably going to have a good time – but that's a lot to ask of any literate adult, especially one who's come upon this kind of story before.

The Doctor As A Mystery Figure: 'You're not related to my wife, by any chance?' There's something very Tom Baker about the Doctor in this episode – the eccentric but brilliant figure of mystery from the future who bulldozes his way into the chaos of the past and takes charge. (See, for instance, Eccleston's wide-eyed joy at finally getting to tell Jackie to shut up.) Yet that's the only point to which comparisons to the previous series can comfortably stretch because, quite frankly, there has never been a *Doctor Who* story remotely like it.

Themes, Genres and Modes: *Doctor Who* has not often delved into stories that explored the mechanics of time travel: 'The Space Museum' (1964), 'Day of the Daleks' (1972) and 'Mawdryn Undead' (1983) are probably the three main contenders. There's a reason for that: time travel is a device in *Doctor Who*, a method of getting from one temporal place to another. The show is not about time travel. If it was, it would become *Star Trek* (under the most recent administration). Even this story, which sets up some nifty and elaborate time paradoxes (that it then proceeds to break!), and its moral lesson about not changing history for one's own ends, are not *really* about time travel. They're elaborate camouflage for a drama centred around family, itself relatively unknown territory in *Doctor Who*; indeed, the Doctor has asserted all season, 'I don't do domestics' – watch how he gets up from the pew beside Rose the moment Jackie and Pete start rowing! 'Father's Day' greatly resembles dramas like *Field of Dreams* or *Frequency*, where a child learns about his or her deceased father in a whole new light thanks to supernatural circumstances. But while these stories end with the promise of a renewed relationship with Dad, 'Father's Day' takes it away, because people need to be accountable for mistakes they've made, no matter what the personal cost may be. That's a harsh but true lesson for 7 pm on a Saturday night, or any night for that matter.

In Style and Structure: 'Father's Day' is arguably most influenced by the style and structure of the series *Sapphire & Steel*: a crack in time is made, which is then taken advantage of, leading to terrifying events for those caught up in the action. This is resolved by something revealed as background at the start of the story, be it a simple object or details about a character, and time returns to normal. This structure allows Rose to get to know her father, and through that, the concept of Pete Tyler as hero figure is examined, deconstructed and redefined. In parallel to this, the relationship between the Doctor and Rose undergoes a similar cycle of examination, deconstruction and redefinition, ending up stronger for all the trials it has gone through. The menace of the Reapers develops as the story progresses. First, events are shown from the Reapers' point of view, then the aftershock of a Reaper attack is shown, before at last we see the terrifying Reapers themselves. As the action moves inside the church, the threat of the Reapers is all around the building as they try to find a way to get at the remaining humans. The episode is bookended by scenes of Jackie telling a young Rose about her father and his death; the first scene tells things as Rose knew them, the second tells things as they were left following Rose's interference, and the rewriting of history as a result. This brings the episode to a satisfying conclusion.

As Doctor Who Continuity: Depending on your grasp of paradox mechanics, paradoxes can be engaging and fun to decipher (especially if you work them out with a diagram!), but sometimes they just induce headaches. Ironically, for a series dealing with time travel, *Doctor Who* has rarely broached the subject of temporal paradoxes, probably because it is too hard to get it right! 'Day of the Daleks' explored them back in 1972. And it did made perfect sense, so well done to the writer! Two unintentional paradoxes appeared in the series and in both cases they were side-effects of poor scripting, direction and/or editing. In 'Mawdryn Undead' (1983) the Brigadier's TARDIS homing device travels from 1983 to 1977 to 1983 to 1977, ad infinitum; while in 'The Trial of a Time Lord' (1986) the sixth Doctor and Mel never actually meet for the 'first' time. In 'Father's Day' we witness another infinitum loop. Events are changed in 'Father's Day' with the result that Pete Tyler is not alone when he dies. When Rose travels with the Doctor she would no longer nurse the 'original' desire to be with her father when he died, so she (presumably) wouldn't ask the Doctor to take her to 1987, so the events of 'Father's Day' never take place. And so Tyler is killed by a hit and run driver and dies alone – and the paradox loop continues in that ever-repeating cycle. I'd welcome an explanation as to how this one works!

From A Special Effects Viewpoint: Make way for the Reapers, another new batch of *Doctor Who* monsters (along with the Slitheen and the Gelth), this time completely computer generated. While the creatures look pretty spectacular, some of the best moments in the episode are when we see only hints of the beasts (the eerie silhouettes beyond the stained glass windows, for example), but there are some fine composited scenes of the creatures interacting with human actors (the attack on the father-in-law is particularly good, with the creature's body glowing as the victim is 'absorbed'). Another terrific scene is when one of the Reapers is clinging to the exterior of the church and its clawed wing scrapes at the wall, knocking bits of mortar and stone to the ground. They look organic (mottled, reptilian skin, glowing red eyes, leathery wings and scythe-like tail) and are genuinely frightening. Yet another impressive creation from The Mill.

PANEL REVIEWS

Ten Things To Love About 'Father's Day': 1. The way the car that killed Pete does a ghostly lap around the church again and again, which is one of the most eerie sights in *Doctor Who*, ever. 2. Murray Gold's music, particularly how his main theme is a cunning riff on 'Someday My Prince Will Come'. 3. Shaun Dingwall and Billie Piper, whose scenes together are stunning in their honesty. Piper even manages the impressive feat of eclipsing Christopher Eccleston. 4. The 1987 setting, which just feels absolutely right, down to the Rick Astley playing on the car radio. 5. The scene where the Doctor opens the TARDIS and discovers it to be empty. 6. Joe Ahearne's direction, which makes a virtue of the small scale of the story and sets it in a creepy, empty world that has an incredible nightmare-like quality to it. 7. The brilliant pre-credits sequence, which feels like nothing *Doctor Who* has ever done before. 8. The Reapers, which add to the overall off-kilter nightmarish feel of the story. 9. The moment where the Doctor tells Stuart and Sarah that their first meeting at a pub makes them utterly unique, one of dozens of amazing moments in Cornell's sublime script. 10. The ending, which is one of the most profoundly moving moments this season. People who get bogged down in the miry details of the time travel plot or the story logic are philistines: emotions are what matters in any television story, and 'Father's Day' is creepy, sad, haunting and gloriously redemptive. It's great television. – *Graeme Burk*

'Father's Day' is quite unlike any televised *Doctor Who* previously attempted because of its meaningful focus on emotion and drama, with much of this success down to strong capitalisation upon the tremendous existing characterisation of Rose. Paul Cornell was the defining voice of an entire era of non-television *Doctor Who*, specifically in the original novels, and so his promotion to the series proper was always going to be a bit special, but he has excelled himself with a beautiful script that's moving and poignant whilst maintaining the intoxicating fusion of danger and excitement that has made this series work. Although the ending, with Pete's self-sacrifice to save the world, is inevitable, the magnificence of Cornell's story lies in how we reach that conclusion as Rose learns about her dad and he learns about himself in the process. The explanations behind some of the plot developments are a little vague and unsatisfying but these concerns prove irrelevant when compared with the power and emotion of the drama. The exceptional performances of Shaun Dingwall and Billie Piper as father and daughter make this episode so extraordinary, as they are so raw and intense that it's impossible not to be moved by the unfolding story around them. This is not only an incredible piece of *Doctor Who*, but it is also an astonishing piece of television. – *Simon Catlow*

Wow! Has another episode of *Doctor Who* ever been as dramatic? Sure, we've had plenty of adventures, but here there are so many little touching moments that bring a lump to the throat. That doesn't alter the fact that the Doctor clearly states in 'The Unquiet Dead' that history can be easily changed, but here it causes all sorts of problems. But that one glaring inconsistency aside, there is little else to find wrong with this episode. Just when you think the Doctor is going to tell Sarah and Stuart how insignificant they are, he completely astounds you by making them feel like the most important people in the world. 'Why does everyone always think we're a couple?' Rose asks. Yet the writers do appear to treat them as a couple; they are very dear friends that care deeply for each other. The Doctor tries desperately to find some other way out of the situation without having to break Rose's heart – even to the point of sacrificing himself. In the end, the big hero here is Pete. He figures out what is happening and doesn't shy away from it. He may never have been there reading bedtime stories or taking Rose on picnics, but when she needs him most, he doesn't let her down. – *Robert Franks*

I really worked myself into a quandary over this one. For the past seven weeks, whenever I sat down to watch the new *Doctor Who*, I've tried to remember that it is first and foremost meant for kids. That's a little bit tough – after all, I was strictly a *Star Trek: The Next Generation* girl until I was eleven years old – but it's given me an interesting counterbalance to my own, grown-up point of view. When it came to 'Father's Day', though, I completely forgot. I really disliked it, right from the start. A lot of that comes from having not expected much out of this episode anyway, but I've also never liked convoluted time paradox stories – and that, I think, is where I really trapped myself. By getting so caught up in the bad, even non-existent logic of the time paradox device, I forgot to really consider the emotional aspects of the story. Watching it again, I realised that, as a child, I wouldn't have cared about how the Doctor's key can reconstruct the TARDIS, or if Rose retains two sets of memories. I'd have been caught up in the story of a girl who sees her father as a hero – something I surely would have identified with – and a father who finally gets to be that hero for his little girl. So the cynical, 21-year-old fan didn't care for it much. Fair enough. I think the 8-year-old girl would have liked it a lot, probably cried, certainly clung to her dad's arm a little harder that night. And, when it's all said and done, guess which is more important? – *Sarah Hadley*

'Father's Day' is without a doubt one of the real gems of the season so far. It's in many ways a brave piece of television to stick on at seven o'clock on a Saturday evening, being rather slower-paced and more thoughtful than almost anything else you'd see in such a slot, but I think the series can more than afford such contemplative moments based on its performance in the ratings and reviews so far. Cornell delivers an affecting script that pushes all the right emotional buttons and also has a suitable level of time travel creepiness – the ever-repeating Alexander Graham Bell line on the telephone being my favourite touch. The performances from the entire cast are terrific, particularly Dingwall and Piper, and even Camille Coduri manages to just about convince as a Jackie Tyler some eighteen years younger. Even the Doctor gets to be brave and heroic for a change this season, and he has a lovely moment with the bride and groom at the wedding – 'I've never had a life like that.' Perfect. Yes, there are some plot holes, and once again the Doctor doesn't actually save the day – even being killed off ten minutes before the end! – but this is on the whole a fantastic little episode. – *Paul Hayes*

Billie Piper puts in a standout performance in 'Father's Day', as Rose goes through a whole range of emotions as she gets to know her father personally, rather than through the stories told by Jackie. Guest star Shaun Dingwall puts in a powerful performance as Pete Tyler, making the character very well-rounded and real. The scenes he shares with Piper are a joy to watch, yet bitter-sweet given how the episode ends. The relationship between Pete and Jackie also comes across quite strongly, thanks to Cornell's script and the work of Camille Coduri and Dingwall. Christopher Eccleston gives a mesmerising performance as the Doctor, trying to save humanity, and coming to terms with Rose's actions. The concept of the Reapers is well realised by The Mill, who have given them a horrific appearance. Murray Gold's incidental music complements the action and once more picks up on the emotional undertones of the story. There are a couple of problems with the in-story logic, as the self-sacrificial actions of the Doctor contradict what he earlier told the wedding attendees about the Reapers. Nevertheless, an extremely powerful and emotional episode that once more explores the relationship between the Doctor and Rose. – *Cameron Mason*

'Father's Day' is either one of the best stories of the season ... or it's the worst. And which way it tilts depends on just one thing: was the nonsensical, incomprehensible and totally illogical time paradox/Reaper sub-plot *deliberately* written to be that way (to sign post something to happen later on in the season, perhaps?) ... or ... did it turn out this way due to sloppy execution? I'm a great fan of time paradox stories (*Terminator, Back to the Future, et al*) – especially when the makers demonstrate their absolute understanding of paradox mechanics and the viewer is treated with some degree of intelligence. Sadly, the attempt fails in both those regards. There is no exposition to explain the hows and whys; things just seem to happen without logical reason for them to do so – a particular failing of the 1996 *Doctor Who* movie. For instance, why does the hit and run vehicle appear in three different locations? Why do the 'first' Doctor and Rose vanish and where do they go? It makes my head spin just thinking about it! The temporal complexities will, however, probably be completely invisible to many viewers, who will no doubt focus upon the *other* plotline. 'Father's Day' is going to be remembered for being the emotional tear-jerker about Rose and her father, an acting *tour de force* from Billie Piper and Shaun Dingwall. I desperately want to give full marks because of the wonderful Rose and Pete scenes, but the production must be judged as a whole, and because of the paradox dilemma I can't. – *Jon Preddle*

In using a keynote saying like 'be careful what you wish for, it might just come true', Paul Cornell drags *Doctor Who* kicking and screaming into the Joss Whedon school of allegorical, post-modern TV deconstruction. In previous eras, the main focus of a story such as this may have been on the mind-boggling temporal mechanics entailed in crossing time streams. Here, it's ordinariness and emotion to the fore. It's the time-travel story that Muriel Spark might've written if *Doctor Who* had ever been bold enough to ask her. 'Father's Day' is brilliant in its conceits and its execution. Too often in the past, *Doctor Who* has existed in some kind of emotional vacuum – full of bright and gaudy surface that, when scratched, reveals a paucity of thought and honesty beneath. No poetry. No soul. The imagery in 'Father's Day' is fundamentally iconic (the ominously repeating car, the Reapers, the empty TARDIS) but the heart of the story lies in its little details of everyday life – particularly the Doctor's conversation with the soon-to-be-married couple about how no-one is 'no-one' in an interconnected universe. One can pick at a few holes here and there. (Why, exactly, does the Doctor allow Rose to place the universe in jeopardy not once but twice?) But to do so is cheap and wrong in the context of a story about magnificence in unexpected places. This is especially true of Pete Tyler's self-sacrifice (one of this year's recurring themes) and in the tender and true portrayals of lost love rediscovered and self-worth regained by Billie Piper and Shaun Dingwall. About fifteen years ago I sat in a coffee shop in Covent Garden talking to my friend Paul Cornell on the day that his first novel had been commissioned. Who would have predicted it would come to this? Eleven out of ten. – *Keith Topping*

'Father's Day' is a very good time travel story, but only a fair *Doctor Who* adventure. There's really little here to link it to the vast universe of everyone's favourite Time Lord, and it actually feels a tad out-of-place among the other episodes of the series. Most *Doctor Who* adventures keep the audience guessing right up until the end, when the Doctor comes up with some clever solution to the problem. 'Father's Day' tosses paradoxes into our faces at the outset and then rather blatantly offers up the means to the end in the form of the reappearing car. As a fan of time travel stories, I foresaw the inevitable self-sacrifice of Rose's father the moment the car popped into existence in a different location. Ultimately, though, 'Father's Day' actually works as an excellent piece of television when the story is set aside and the focus is on the relationship between Rose and the father she never knew. There is some really touching stuff here and the actors handle it all superbly. It provides yet another example of Billie Piper's impressive acting ability. – *Scott Alan Woodard*

EDITOR'S REVIEW: 'Father's Day' is probably not only the most unusual episode this season, but the most atypical *Doctor Who* ever produced for television. It's not the usual alien-monsters-invade-Earth tale or far-future-intrigue soap plot, but instead tells a genuine and personal story about the characters we've come to know. In that, it's quite archetypal; it resolves some issues set up in the very first episode, in which we find single-mother Jackie caring for her daughter. It also addresses something only touched upon briefly in the original series: the idea of going back to see someone you've lost. *Doctor Who* always avoided that with its cheeky 'laws of time' rules, and it's nice to see the format become so flexible in this new series (with the absence of the holier-than-thou Time Lords) that the Doctor now feels he can take Rose back to see her late father. It's also interesting to see how utterly fallible the Doctor is, blindly trusting that she won't attempt to rescue the father she never knew.

'Father's Day' also attempts something rarely seen in *Doctor Who*: a lyrical plot, held together not only by the story and the dialogue, but also by sheer poetic structure. This is evident from the moment it starts, narrated by Rose almost as a tribute to her dad, with subsequent scenes peeling away layers until we're ultimately presented with one act of kindness that goes horribly awry. Paul Cornell has always had a gift for this sort of sentimentalism; if you've read any of his novels, you know how he uses language to paint a picture instead of simply capturing the story scene by scene. Here, he does it very satisfactorily, and it works because it's matched by what is perhaps Billie Piper's finest acting this season. Piper is magnificent at carrying the emotional weight of the character and this story. Her performance is matched by an utterly delightful one from Shaun Dingwall, who presents the viewer with sympathy even when we discover he's not the man we (or Rose) thought he would be.

If there is any real failure in this episode, it is to satisfactorily present the world outside the personal story of Rose and her father. Perhaps that is for the best; forty-five minutes is hardly enough time to capture the bigger picture ... and yet we're left wondering about this mysterious gathering of Reapers (never quite satisfactorily explained, even if we're supposed to think of them as nothing but leeches feeding off the discarded tissues of time) and what they have done to the rest of the Earth. Sure, we are told that London is burning and we see them pick off residents of the area one by one, but while damage is being done, it never escalates to more than just a few people stuck in a church until the Doctor is consumed. *That* is where 'Father's Day' breaks the mould completely; the Doctor is actually dead. While we know he'll eventually be back, that's one of those moments where you know, you just know, that nobody has any idea of how to get out of this situation. Killing the Doctor was probably the biggest surprise of the episode, and I'm glad they took that route instead of simply having the Doctor save the day (which, let's face it, he really hasn't done much of this year). Of course, one could argue that he deserved it, just this once, considering how utterly stupid he probably was in bringing Rose here in the first place.

One other quibble, and I don't believe it's a minor one: I did not like the fact that the Doctor called Rose a 'stupid ape' *at all*, regardless of the situation or his anger. This is our hero, after all, a 900-plus-year-old time traveller who has spent much of his life dealing with all sorts of human beings from Earth. He invited *her* into the TARDIS – not once but twice, returning to see if she'd change her mind. The Doctor has shown many sides of himself over the years, but *never* has he displayed the utter contempt for humanity he's shown on rare occasions this season. Less of that next year, please.

Regardless of the issues with the Reapers and their existence, the laws of time, what in the world Alexander Graham Bell had to do with it or otherwise (let's be honest here, does it really matter?), 'Father's Day' is a bridge between the first and last batch of episodes, a momentary pause to reflect and examine, and perhaps bury some personal demons before setting off once again. It's also as close as *Doctor Who* has ever come to poetry, and as such it was a refreshing change, even if it is probably the most inconsequential adventure of the year – as far as we're concerned, anyway; I'm sure Rose would disagree. It's a collection of moments, not unlike our own lives, and we get to see them through Rose's eyes. I'm thankful that we have characters in this series who are worthy of that attention. – *Shaun Lyon*

109: THE EMPTY CHILD

The TARDIS follows an extraterrestrial cylinder back in time to London, 1941, at the height of the Blitz. While Rose enjoys the amorous advances of Jack Harkness, another time traveller from the far future, the Doctor investigates a strange illness plaguing the city, which he soon learns is centred on a frightened young boy searching for his mummy ...

FIRST TRANSMISSION: UK – 21 May 2005. Canada – 31 May 2005. Australia – 16 July 2005. New Zealand – 6 September 2005.
DURATION: 41'54"
WRITER: Steven Moffat
DIRECTOR: James Hawes
CREDITED CAST: Christopher Eccleston (Doctor Who), Billie Piper (Rose Tyler), Kate Harvey (Nightclub Singer), Albert Valentine (The Child), Florence Hoath (Nancy), Cheryl Fergison (Mrs Lloyd), Damian Samuels (Mr Lloyd), John Barrowman (Jack Harkness), Robert Hands (Algy), Joseph Tremain (Jim), Jordan Murphy (Ernie), Brandon Miller (Alf), Richard Wilson (Dr Constantine), Noah Johnson (Voice of The Empty Child), Dian Perry (Computer Voice).

WHERE AND WHEN: London, 1941, at the height of the Blitz (probably spring), including in and around a nightclub, the Lloyd residence, Limehouse Green Station and Albion Hospital.

THE STORY UNFOLDS: One night, a cylindrical capsule crash lands at Limehouse Green Station near Albion Hospital in London. Whatever was inside is a mystery, but soon people nearby are affected by a virus that manifests physical injury as plague by rewriting human DNA. A young boy who had died due to massive head trauma, partial collapse of his right chest cavity and scarring to the back of his hand, was present in the hospital at the time the plague first began and was wearing a gas-mask. Within a week, everyone in the hospital had developed the same injuries, and developed a gas-mask like apparatus on their faces, extending and extruding from their very skin. The boy disappeared from room 802 and is now wandering the streets. Dr Constantine, a physician at Albion, says the plague victims are not dead.

Captain Jack's ship is a Chula vessel equipped with a tractor beam; it catches Rose in a light field as she falls from a barrage balloon through the London sky. The air in his ship is full of nanogenes; subatomic robots that repair three layers of Rose's skin. The ship is invisible (but can be made visible again) and is moored off the top of the Big Ben clock tower. Jack can reactivate the lights and bells of the clock with a small device from the ship. He explains that the crashed capsule is a Chula warship and will be destroyed in two hours by a German bomb.

The Doctor compares Nancy's actions feeding the local homeless children to Marxism in action (or perhaps a West End musical; a flippant reference to *Oliver!*) The Limehouse Green Station crash site has been surrounded by a fence and covered with an awning.

The capsule turns out not to be a warship at all, but an 'ambulance', apparently the last one in existence. It jumped several time tracks on its way to Earth, meaning that by the time the TARDIS arrives, it has been there for several weeks. It bore the colour mauve, which the

Doctor says is the universally recognised colour for danger.

THE DOCTOR: He is baffled by humans' fixation on red as a colour signifying danger (while to other species, he claims, it is camp); by milk coming from cows; and by the tendency of his companions, even Rose, to wander off. Not realising he's arrived during the Blitz, he's initially puzzled by the amused reactions of the nightclub patrons when he asks if anything's fallen from the sky. He says he knows what it's like being the only one left out in the cold. Nancy thinks he has a big nose and big ears (and wonders if they have special powers, since nobody else seems to be able to follow her). He 'has his moments', he remarks when Constantine asks if he's a doctor. Jack considers that the Doctor is dressed like a U-boat captain.

ROSE TYLER: She's fascinated by alien technology ('alien tech', she calls it, or 'Spock', a reference to the character from *Star Trek*). She says she's taking her T-shirt, which bears a large Union Jack design, 'out for a spin'. Jack's computer describes her as a 'non-contemporaneous life form'. She faints after being rescued and later is quite smitten with Jack. The psychic paper she hands Jack says she has a boyfriend named Mickey Smith, but she considers herself to be foot-loose and fancy-free (and 'very available').

CHARACTER BUILDING: *Jack Harkness* – A former agent for a mysterious organisation called the Time Agency, he is now a freelancer (though he likes to think of himself as a criminal/con man). He saw the Chula ambulance and used it to trick the TARDIS into following it, hoping that he could sell the capsule to the Doctor and Rose before they found out it was junk. He likes the retro look of the TARDIS exterior ('Nice panels!'). His first rule of camouflage is, park somewhere you remember. He is taken with Rose but still plans to con her and the Doctor. His official identification is as a Captain in the Royal Air Force, 133 Squadron, American volunteer. Like the Doctor, he uses psychic paper for identification purposes (though what Rose actually sees on the psychic paper is that he's single and that he works out). He thinks Rose has an 'excellent bottom' (though his fellow Air Force officer Algy thinks he's referring to him) and knows she's not from this time period because of her mobile phone, her watch and the fabrics she's wearing.

Nancy – A young woman, homeless herself but driven to feed the hungry and abandoned children of London. She enters houses during air raids, either scavenging for food or, in the case of the Lloyds' house, inviting local children inside to eat. She believes very strongly in good table manners. Nancy warns the Doctor about the 'empty child' and later sends him to see Dr Constantine about the mysterious cylinder that fell from the sky. She stores food inside a container in a disused train car.

Dr Constantine – A doctor at Albion Hospital, who has lost his children and grandchildren in the war. He has been involved in studying the mysterious plague, and is now infected by it. It transforms him into a gas-masked zombie before the Doctor's eyes.

The Empty Child – Nancy claims that the child is her little brother, Jamie, who followed her out while she was looking for food on the night of the crash and ended up as he is today. She says he is now 'empty'. He can make his voice heard through phone lines, including a telephone mounted within the external door of the TARDIS. He can also activate radios and toys, making them all channel his voice, asking for his mummy.

Mr Lloyd – His first name is Arthur. He and his wife and family take refuge in their air raid shelter, which allows Nancy and the homeless children to partake of their newly cooked meal. The children wonder how he could have got such plentiful food on wartime rations, thinking it's probably black-market. The house next door to his has 'Danger – Keep Out' signs, and 'We are still living in this blasted …' written on boards covering the front window (the rest of the phrase is unseen).

The Children – One boy, Alf, was evacuated to a farm, but there was a man there (a comment made with much gravitas, suggesting that this man abused him, either physically or sexually); much the same happened to another, Ernie. They follow Nancy to various houses to eat.

BAD WOLF: No actual references this time, but a more subtle (and dubious) one: Nancy refers to the Doctor as having a big nose and big ears, a possible allusion to the line, 'What big ears you have!' from the Little Red Riding Hood story.

FANTASTIC!: No mention in this episode.

BODY COUNT: There are no deaths in the episode (other than the casualties of war from the air raid, which are unseen). However, there are plenty of gas-masked zombies at Albion Hospital and the child roaming the streets. Dr Constantine is already affected but develops the final symptoms of the plague during the episode.

THE DOCTOR'S MAGICAL SONIC SCREWDRIVER: The Doctor uses it to scan the bodies at Albion Hospital. And, as usual, to get through various doors and gates, including into Albion Hospital.

REALITY BITES: The Doctor's reference, 'I don't know what you do to Hitler, but you scare the hell out of me!' is a paraphrase of the Duke of Wellington's famous remark about his soldiers that 'I don't know what effect these men will have on the enemy but, by God, they frighten me.'

Rose refers several times to Spock, one of the most famous characters from *Star Trek*. (However Jack Harkness has no idea who Spock is.)

The episode takes place during the Blitz of London, carried out by the German Luftwaffe between 7 September 1940 and 16 May 1941. Barrage balloons, large inflatables used as an anti-aircraft device during World War II, are positioned over London, clouding the skies to prevent bombers flying low enough to drop payloads. At the height of deployment, there were hundreds of balloons in the skies over London. Barrage balloons had metal hawsers and not rope, and were secured to the ground to prevent planes flying under them … so the bombing raid seen on screen is inaccurate.

Jack refers to himself as being part of the 133 Squadron. This squadron was populated with American volunteers prior to the United States's entry into World War II; these volunteers did not qualify for service in the US Air Force for several reasons (medical, academic grounds, and so on). However, the 133 Squadron was actually founded in August 1941, possibly after this episode is set (see 'Internal Consistency').

The Chula name came from an Indian/Bangladeshi fusion restaurant in London where several of the series's writers met after being assigned their episodes.

EPISODE 109

LINKING THEMES: The Doctor uses the cover of being Dr John Smith from the Ministry of Asteroids, as displayed on his psychic paper. This pseudonym was first taken by the Doctor in 'The Wheel in Space' (1968) and subsequently reappeared throughout the original *Doctor Who* series. He also reacts to Dr Constantine's comment about having lost his descendents, possibly a reference to the Doctor's own granddaughter Susan, although this could equally be a reaction to his people being destroyed in the Time War.

Time Agents were first mentioned in the story 'The Talons of Weng-Chiang' (1977).

Albion Hospital was the setting of part of 'Aliens of London'.

SCENE MISSING: London seems to be lit very brightly considering that it's being attacked during the Blitz. Neighbourhoods still seem to have some street light (outside the Lloyd home, for example) while Albion Hospital hasn't covered all its windows with blackout material. There also seems to be a lot of excess light in the neighbourhoods visited by the Doctor and Rose.

In the middle of the narrative, Jack suddenly confesses to being a con artist. Why? He might have suddenly realised the Doctor and Rose weren't the people he thought they were, but wouldn't he have merely thought of a different (and still workable) plan instead of confessing all? Also, how exactly is Jack's con supposed to work? Why tell Rose that the 'warship' will be blown up in two hours time when a true Time Agent would be able to get to the crash site before the explosion, or even to travel back in time to check Jack's claims that it was a warship at all.

Why does the TARDIS console explode when all the Doctor's doing is pursuing a capsule through the time vortex?

Why does Rose grab the rope and not look up into the sky to see the barrage balloon floating above her? (For that matter, why does the empty child suddenly say 'balloon!' when he's supposed to be a zombie?)

Why does the Doctor look at his watch before announcing that it's 1941? (Perhaps his watch tells the year as well as the time? But then, how would he explain not knowing that a year had passed at the start of 'Aliens of London'?) And how, during a time of great food shortage, is there a rather well-fed cat wandering the streets?

ALTERED STATES: During the broadcast of the accompanying *Doctor Who Confidential*, it was noticed that during the sequence when Jack saves Rose in the light beam, Jack refers to her 'mobile phone' instead of her 'cell phone' as heard in the episode. This was changed to the American 'cell phone' because the character has an American accent and one assumes therefore that Jack has immersed himself in that culture in order to best pull off his cons.

According to news reports, there was a minor edit made to this episode to remove the sound of a skull cracking. (Later, it was reported that this was not a change made by BBC executives and had nothing to do with the 6.30 pm timeslot as claimed by the press.) Said series producer Phil Collinson at a BBC screening, reported by BBC News, 'It's a little thing involving the scene with Richard Wilson's character and the gas mask. The whole sound effect that went with that was a lot more visceral. We watched it for the first time and said that was crossing over the line because it was a bit too horrible.'

The explanation of the nanogenes being the method of curing Rose's rope burns was omitted from the original Canadian broadcast. This episode also featured the first (and only) time Canada's CBC put together their *own* trailer for the following week's episode, as opposed to relying on the BBC's version; the CBC version doesn't divulge so many plot details, but unfortunately does reveal the solution to the cliff-hanger!

BEHIND THE SCENES: Following complaints after the transmission of 'Aliens of London', the cliff-hanger ending did not lead immediately into a preview of the following week's story; the preview followed the end credits. This was billed as the 'scariest episode yet' by several sources.

This episode was recorded partially at two locations that had previously been used by the production: the Cardiff Royal Infirmary, which once again doubled for Albion Hospital (both the exterior as well as inside where the Doctor, Rose and Jack are confronted by the zombies), and the Headlands National Children's Home in Penarth (used as the funeral parlour in 'The Unquiet Dead'), which now served as the interior of the nightclub. The Barry Island railway station was used for exterior shots, including the Doctor confronting Nancy at the railway station as well as the crash site. A home in Grangetown, Cardiff, was used for the settings around the Lloyd home, including the garden where the air raid shelter was located, while a nearby alley was the location of the TARDIS's arrival. An aircraft hanger on RAF St Athan in the Vale of Glamorgan was used for some elements of the sequence where Rose hangs by rope from the barrage balloon, the other elements being shot in the series's studio in Newport, where additional interior segments for other scenes were also recorded.

DULCET TONES: 'It Had To Be You' by Isham Jones and Gus Kahn – This classic song was written in 1924, music by Jones and lyrics by Kahn, and was first performed by singer Marion Harris. It gained popularity and was later recorded by Ruth Etting in 1936 for the film *Melody in May*, then appeared in the musical *Show Business* in 1944. The song has been recorded by numerous artists over the years including Frank Sinatra, Bing Crosby, Count Basie, Billie Holiday and Harry Connick Jr. The song is being sung as the Doctor walks into the nightclub. (Heard from approximately 2:51 on ...)

'Moonlight Serenade' by Glenn Miller – A jazz classic predating the UK singles charts, although it was rereleased posthumously by Miller's orchestra in March 1954 (when it reached number 12 in the UK) and again in January 1976 (reaching number 13). Jack plays this music while attempting to woo Rose. (Heard 25:48-27:15)

OFF THE SCREEN: Born in Scotland but raised in America, John Barrowman is a well known theatre performer who has starred in a multitude of large-scale stage productions including *Beauty and the Beast* (1999), *Miss Saigon, The Phantom of the Opera, Sunset Boulevard* (1994-97), *Aspects of Love, Evita, Hair* (1993), *Grease, Chicago, Anything Goes* (1989/2002) and *A Few Good Men* (2005). He also starred in two American television series, the short-lived NBC soap *Titans* (2000) and the flashy CBS drama *Central Park West* (1995); presented the UK children's programme *Live and Kicking* (1993); and appeared in films such as *DeLovely* (2004) and *The Producers* (2005). Legendary character actor Richard Wilson is best known as Victor Meldrew in the BBC comedy *One Foot in the Grave* (1990-2000), and has also been seen in the television series *Born and Bred* (2004), *Life As We Know It* (2001), *High Stakes* (2001), *Life Support* (1999), *Under the Hammer* (1993), *High and Dry* (1987) and *Only When I Laugh* (1979), as well as the films *A Passage to India* (1984), *How to Get Ahead in Advertising* (1989), *A Dry White Season* (1989) and *The Other Side of Paradise* (1992). Florence Hoath played Paul McGann's daughter in *FairyTale: A True Story* (1997) and was also seen in *Back to the Secret Garden* (2001) and *Marple: The Body in the Library* (2004) as well as the series *The Demon Headmaster* (1996). Cheryl Fergison was in *Genghis Cohn* (1993), *Eskimo Day* (1996) and *Cold Enough for Snow* (1997). Damian Samuels was seen in the American series *Keen Eddie* (2003). Dian Perry was seen in *Nelly Nut Live!* (2004). Robert Hands was in *Anna and the King* (1999) and *Killing Hitler* (2003) and in episodes of *Heartbeat* (1993, 2003) and *Peak Practice* (1997). Joseph Tremain was in *Oliver Twist* (2005) and the series *Morris 2274* (2003). Jordan Murphy was in episodes of *The Bill* (2005) and *Casualty* (2004). Brandon Miller was in *The Debt* (2003) and *Menace* (2002). Kate Harvey is an accomplished singer who has appeared in the *Riverdance* musical. Director James Hawes's previous work includes *Sea of Souls* (2004), *Holby City* (1999), *The Mrs Bradley Mysteries* (1999), *The Bill* (1998) and *Lawrence of Arabia: The Battle for the Arab World* (2003).

TECHNICAL GOOFS: The table in the Lloyd house seems to have exactly enough place settings for all the street children, Nancy and the Doctor. Algy should not understand Jack's use of the term 'excellent bottom', since no one referred to the backside in that way at this time. The Big Ben clock hands seem to be stuck permanently at 9.30 pm (and the clock was not shut down during air raids). Nancy manages to whistle with her fingers, even though her fingers are gloved. Jack's ship scanner shows a side-on view of Rose inside the tractor beam, when it should show a front view looking upwards from the ship. The inside of the police box door of the TARDIS is painted white (including the area around the phone), but the phone panel is blue. When the Doctor takes to the nightclub stage to ask about anything falling from the sky, he has his right arm and hand raised and gesticulating, but in several shots of him from behind, it's his left arm that's up and moving.

CONTROVERSIES: The anachronisms, such as Jack's rifle possibly being out of period, the TARDIS phone being reminiscent of early twentieth-century models when the box itself is from the 1950's, and the nightclub singer performing in a style reminiscent of later years; and possible inconsistency over the Doctor's age, which is stated as 953 in 'Time and the Rani' (1987), yet here the Doctor claims that he's been travelling for 900 years.

INTERNAL CONSISTENCY: *The Date* – The Doctor notes that it is 1941. During the period of intense bombing from November 1940 to May 1941, London was a major target of the barrage. The absence of snow or other winter weather suggests the spring of 1941. Since it is obvious this adventure takes place during the Blitz, it is likely set some time in April or May (especially since everyone is dressed for warmer weather). However, considering that the 133 Squadron that Jack is supposed to be part of wasn't formed until August of that year, it could take place months later, during a more quiet period in the skies over London (but on a really busy night!)

Timing – It is 9.30 pm as Jack treats Rose to a dance on top of his spaceship. As most scenes take place in close to real time, the TARDIS must have arrived no sooner than 9 pm in the alley. We know from 'Aliens of London' that Albion Hospital is close to the Thames and Westminster (less than five miles, given its identification as being at Limehouse), so it wouldn't have taken long for Rose and Jack to get to the hospital to meet the Doctor. The child appears to menace Nancy at the Lloyd household at about 10.12 pm, although the hall clock appears to display a slightly different time. This means there is approximately thirty minutes missing in the latter part of the episode for the characters to get from location to location.

THEME ANALYSES

As Doctor Who For A Modern Audience: This is another story that uses elements that would not have been out of place within the original series of *Doctor Who* such as the historical setting, the presence of an intergalactic rogue, and some kind of malign influence at work where it should not be. But to make it work for today's audience, these familiar aspects are all approached with a modern twist such as the wartime location established through the Doctor's impromptu (and totally unintentional) stand-up routine at the club and the incredible CGI effects of Rose's barrage balloon jaunt. More pop culture references feature with Rose's urging of the Doctor to give her some 'Spock', which taps into the idea that the methods of the Doctor aren't what she's been imagining based on her expectations of how futuristic heroes have been portrayed before. This then neatly ties into her brush with Captain Jack Harkness, whose flashy gadgets and winning smile are more than enough to sweep her off her feet. Their relationship is much more flirty and overt than those that companions traditionally develop. With the friendship between the Doctor and Rose portrayed more ambiguously, the obvious attraction between Jack and Rose gives the show the start of a different dynamic.

As Television Drama: If 'Father's Day' was the new *Doctor Who* series echoing *Sapphire & Steel*, then 'The Empty Child' does very much the same with another venerable institution of British television science-fiction, Nigel Kneale's *Quatermass* serials of the 1950s. That said, Kneale created so many standards of the genre that it's hard to know whether such allusions are deliberate or merely subconscious. Nevertheless, a crashed spaceship in the heart of London having a devastating effect upon those who come into contact with it does contain echoes of both *The Quatermass Experiment* and *Quatermass and the Pit*; not the first time in the show's long history that a *Doctor Who* story has owed some sort of debt to those productions. The Second World War setting also evokes the similarly-placed flashback sections of *Invasion: Earth*, which were far and away the best parts of that 1998 BBC1 effort, and also similarly *Quatermass*-tinged. The time period also provides, as with 'The Unquiet Dead', a reminder of just how well the BBC does period drama. BBC Wales in particular have recent experience of such war dramas involving children, with a 2003 Christmas adaptation of *Carrie's War*, script edited by the new series's Elwen Rowlands, although that story takes place in a somewhat less chilling world than the one depicted by 'The Empty Child'.

As A Piece of Writing: There's something basically unsettling about the sound of a child calling out, pleadingly and repetitively, for someone who isn't there. In this episode, Steven Moffat has tapped into a vein of fear everyone understands, and it works to tremendous effect. Although there are numerous comic lines (especially from the Doctor), the tone of the whole episode is dark and grim, helped by, but not focused upon, the night time setting. The scene where the various objects come alive in the house – the mechanical toy, the radio, the telephone – is as disturbing as any horror film, and a situation where something unpleasant wants to get in always elicits a few good chills. They're known quantities, however; to some degree, we expect those scenes from the nature of the story. Moffat really turns up the heat toward the end of the episode, when the scene with Dr Constantine becomes both horrific and very sad. All these scary elements are unusual for *Doctor Who*, but Moffat has ordered them into an extremely traditional framework that is the closest we've had to a 1960s episode. Unlike 'The Unquiet Dead', though, it's less a remake of old stories and more a modern update based on the old framework: the Doctor and companion are immediately split up; the Doctor is in search of something or someone and keeps getting sent somewhere new; the companion finds a romantic interest and a plot point that dovetails into the main storyline. It's a great, tried-and-true approach, and it should be no surprise to anyone that this is a big hit with the fans. The real question is whether the second part will be able to live up to our expectations.

The Doctor As A Mystery Figure: 1941 – a time of suspicion and paranoia in a country on the verge of invasion and losing its identity forever. The mystery of the Doctor in this episode is, as on many previous occasions, his uncanny ability to blend seamlessly into the period aesthetic – air raids, Anderson shelters, rationing and black market profiteering. This is a Doctor equally at home in a swanky nightclub asking hilarious unanswered questions or getting some proper information whilst sharing an illegal meal with a group of hungry street urchins. And, in that short scene with the cat or his magical (and historically accurate) 'damp little island' speech, we witness a Doctor completely at ease with his place in the era and the universe. 'I'm not sure if it's Marxism in action or a West End musical,' he notes, concerning Nancy's scheme for feeding the stray children of London. It's also a perfect metaphor for the Doctor's adventures.

Themes, Genres and Modes: It's been said over and over that *Doctor Who*'s purpose is to scare kids. And yet, until 'The Empty Child', the series (both classic and current) had only *hinted* at terrifying children without actually *doing* it. Well, nuts to that. 'The Empty Child' is *scary*. In fact this episode (and 'The Doctor Dances') may well be one of the best uses of full-out horror in *Doctor Who* ever. The use of the child is sublime: that all this fear and human destruction is the result of something in the body of a faceless four year-old is a frightening concept. The revelation that the patients *aren't* wearing gas masks is deeply unsettling, but it's the logical extension of a favourite theme in British genre television, namely body horror, that stems back all the way to *The Quatermass Experiment*. 'The Empty Child' holds to the tradition of that, and to Steven Moffat's self-professed favourite story 'The Ark In Space', and yet it adds a new nuance: while these stories featured people becoming something alien, here, the horror is in becoming something alien even though it looks commonplace (though unnerving). Furthermore, writer Moffat and director Hawes recognise the cardinal rule of horror: don't show as much as you think you should, but when you do, go for the jugular. Put this all together and *that's* why Dr Constantine's transformation is so scary.

In Style and Structure: The style of 'The Empty Child' is somewhat dictated by its World War II setting, with the main elements used being a smoke-filled club, an air raid and the armed forces. Steven Moffat makes use of these elements to help establish the setting of the story, with the club neatly leading into the air raid and to the armed forces. There's a link back to 'Aliens of London' in the use of Albion Hospital as a setting, and it plays a similar role here as it did then in progressing the story. The stylistic use of darkness and shadows suggests that director James Hawes has been influenced by the archetypal look of film noir, which works well with the story style and setting. There are two plot lines set up, the A plot being the Doctor and Nancy, with the B plot being Rose and Jack. The link between both plot lines is the empty child, who leads the regular characters to the main character they are going to interact with in the episode. Each plot line develops in parallel in terms of story revelations, before Nancy carries on her own story and Rose and Jack's story links up with the Doctor's. As for the child, it is kept as a mystery figure for much of the episode, with information emerging gradually as the action progresses. The most important information about the child is revealed in order to set up a chilling cliff-hanger.

As Doctor Who Continuity: The mysterious Captain Jack Harkness is a Time Agent; but these pseudo Time Lords from the 51st Century are not a new concept; they were first mentioned way back in 1977 in a throwaway line from Robert Holmes's 'The Talons of Weng-Chiang'! With the Time Lords now out of the picture, will the Time Agents appear later in the season? Much is made of the fact that Harkness is an (albeit freelance) operative, so it would seem most peculiar to reintroduce the Agency to the series but then do nothing further with them. I shall watch keenly to see if/how this develops. Moffat throws in another old concept – that of time tracks, a temporal fixture first introduced (and causing bother) in 'The Space Museum' (1965) – but never spoken of again (until now). Meanwhile, the Doctor's old 'alias' Dr John Smith is used for the first time since 'The Time Warrior' (1973). With such a long gap, it remains somewhat odd that the ninth Doctor would still be using it. These sorts of verbal references to the past were rampant in the eighties, and have so far been conspicuous by their absence from the new series. In 2005, continuity references are like buses – you wait nine weeks for one, and then three of them show up in one episode!

From A Special Effects Viewpoint: It seems as though I'm frequently bandying about terms like 'tour de force' when describing the effects in the new series. Up to this point, we've had crashing spaceships, lumbering Slitheen, wispy Gelth and realistic missile strikes (along with a number of other fantastic creations). Here, again, we're served a platter brimming with impressive sequences ranging from the busy skies over London thick with bombers, explosions and barrage balloons, to Captain Jack's space/time ship, to one of the creepiest on-screen physical transformations I have ever seen! Make-ups in this story consist solely of simple scars on the backs of hands (that occasionally look to be little more than grease-paint) and the inherently spooky gasmasks (man, I hate those things) apparently 'fused' to the faces of the numerous victims. In regards to that aforementioned 'transformation', it is extremely convincing. Whether or not it would have been even more convincing had we been allowed the cracking skull sound effect to accompany the visuals is unknown, but it is a genuinely terrifying sequence all the same. Marvellous (and scary) stuff!

PANEL REVIEWS

The English language is such a complex and highly nuanced system of expression and yet all I find myself saying over and over again is ... *wow*. Never mind the stunning flight by barrage balloon, the Doctor's exchanges with Nancy and the kids, the charming first appearance of Jack or the creepy first appearance of the child ... Steven Moffat had me at 'hello' with the Doctor and Rose bantering about the need to come to Earth for milk and Rose's frustration that the Doctor won't give her any Spock. Steven Moffat and James Hawes show everyone how *Doctor Who* really ought to be done. Hawes's direction is cinematic and exciting, and Moffat packs his script with brilliantly funny dialogue to throw us off balance from the really dark and scary moments. Jack's admission that the Chula warship is a con comes a titch easy, but come on, after watching Richard Wilson get turned into an empty child, do you really care? – *Graeme Burk*

'The Empty Child' is a fantastic beginning to this two-part story, with Moffat's script using its wartime setting brilliantly to create the second horror story of the series. What makes this so appealing is the presentation of the mystery, with a mad chase after a dangerous alien artefact taking the Doctor and Rose deep into the heart of London during the Blitz, but then raising more and more questions about what's really happening. Moffat is mostly known for comedy series rather than drama these days, but he uses his humour subtly to offset and underplay the horror that is at the heart of the episode. A child in a gasmask is not, in itself, frightening, but when it becomes clear that its constant cries for its mummy are something more sinister, then it becomes incredibly disturbing. Despite some suspect reasoning to get her to climb the rope, Rose's barrage balloon trip leads to a spectacular sequence of a bombing raid above the capital, which is one of the most praiseworthy CGI scenes, although Dr Constantine's horrific transformation is also tremendously effective. The regulars are both on great form, and in Florence Hoath's Nancy we have the latest in a long line of very likeable and believable supporting characters that have become one of the trademarks of this series. With stunning direction and inventive production design, this is certainly the most cinematic (and best overall) episode to date, marred only by a rather unoriginal cliff-hanger.– *Simon Catlow*

I started watching *Doctor Who* in my teens and have never once been scared by it – until now! I actually found myself thinking, 'This is too frightening for children.' Moffat proves he is as good with drama as he is with comedy. The script is simply sparkling with style and wit – just look at Nancy's comment about the Doctor's ears. The only drawback is the overuse of technology. The tractor beam that saves Rose is a bit too convenient. John Barrowman seems a good actor, but he isn't given much to do in this episode. Let's hope future episodes make better use of his character. Too bad they didn't also ask Florence Hoath to join the regular cast, as she's brilliant. For someone as young as Nancy to stand up to the haughtiness of the ninth Doctor is impressive. I don't know how anything else this season is going to top this. – *Robert Franks*

This is one of the episodes I've most anticipated all season, and once again, I'm not disappointed. It's dark, eerie, has a few good scares for both kids and adults, and – oh yes – it feels like the perfect first half of a two-parter. Though the pacing is possibly the most laconic yet – the actors have to get through pages and pages of dialogue – it all seems to work to the episode's benefit; allowing us time to get into the mystery while increasing the atmosphere and suspense. The direction is excellent, with James Hawes offering us an unflinchingly dark episode that would rarely have been attempted in the past. There are scenes where you can just barely see the characters' outlines in the night, and it works wonderfully. Christopher Eccleston gets the bulk of the great moments here, but he's joined by the best guest cast all year – John Barrowman is appropriately charming and sly (despite some awkward Americanisms-that-aren't), the wonderful Florence Hoath is a great surrogate companion, and Richard Wilson steals his one scene. The most memorable sequence for me was the changing face of Dr Constantine. I'd heard the BBC were worried about a special effect, but I shrugged it off, thinking it would be nothing compared with scenes in American television. When I actually came to the scene, however, I found it genuinely disturbing; it's sold by both a vividly persuasive special effect and the performances of Wilson and Eccleston. For me, it's one of the few truly frightening moments in all of *Doctor Who*, at the climax of one of the few really spooky episodes. The show that looked too cheap to scare me at twelve has certainly grown up; this is wonderful on every front. – *Sarah Hadley*

Dark and spooky and set in the past with a malign alien influence at work, 'The Empty Child' ticks all the boxes for making classic *Doctor Who*. It's not simply a case of assembling all the right ingredients and hoping something good comes out, however – Moffat's script has been written with care, and its well-structured, well-paced plot contains some fantastic lines, and even an appearance of the 'Doctor who?' joke that for once doesn't make you want to cringe. Anybody who's followed any of Moffat's previous work on such shows as *Coupling* will know that cleverly interconnecting, well-thought-out plot threads are a speciality of his, and he works together the various disparate elements of 'The Empty Child' with his usual skill. The Doctor gets to be proactive and more traditionally Doctorish for a change, and Rose finds herself unusually helpless and then swept off her feet by a handsome stranger – it's probably the most like classic series *Doctor Who* we've seen so far this season. James Hawes's direction is wonderful, and quite noir-ish at times, and he is well supported by good production values and impressive effects that do an excellent job of convincing us we're in Blitz-torn London. I can't wait to see how this one turns out! – *Paul Hayes*

'The Empty Child' is fantastic and very well written. No scene is wasted and there is some excellent material for all the characters, including a lovely moment between Christopher Eccleston and a cat. Florence Hoath turns in a wonderful performance as Nancy, bringing out the character's mothering instinct when looking after the homeless children. Richard Wilson is dignified as Dr Constantine, a small, but important, role in the story. The best of the guest actors would have to be John Barrowman as Captain Jack Harkness, who brings the character to life with an enthusiastic flair. The empty child himself is wonderful, with the direction (including shots from the point of view of the child), haunting voice, costume and makeup design bringing to life a truly memorable figure. The Mill have done some excellent work in terms of creating the air raid going on around Rose, Jack's technology and the eerie morphing effect showing the infection of the child taking hold. The haunting images of those infected by the child add a sense of horror to the story, which is well used to create a memorable cliffhanger. – *Cameron Mason*

I'm going to say it up front – 'The Empty Child' is simply superb; my number one episode of the season so far. Moffat's script was the exact opposite of what I was expecting; my only exposure to his TV writing was through the outrageously camp *Doctor Who* spoof 'The Curse of Fatal Death'. 'The Empty Child' was anything but camp! While 'The Unquiet Dead' was spooky, 'The Empty Child' is downright CREEPY (and that's in bold capitals underlined!) I initially thought the gas-mask face was just a silly, low-budget effect, but then we witnessed Dr Constantine's grotesque transformation – a truly unforgettable image. Indeed, all the production values of this episode – the special effects, direction, and acting (particularly from Florence Hoath) – were outstanding. The attention to detail in the 1940s costumes and set dressing alone proves that the BBC cares enough to get the detail right (although I think they did slip up a bit with the lack of blackout during the Blitz scenes). 'The Empty Child' will also be remembered for introducing Captain Jack Harkness. There's certainly more to Jack than meets the eye. Davies clearly has a hidden agenda for Harkness, presumably with a pay-off towards the end of the season. Frustratingly, 'The Empty Child' ends with so many questions. I'll be extremely disappointed if 'The Doctor Dances' fails to deliver any answers. – *Jon Preddle*

'Human DNA is being rewritten. By an idiot.' Steven Moffat's noted ease with humorous dialogue produces possibly the funniest *Doctor Who* of the season. It's also the scariest. 'I want to find a blonde in a Union Jack. A specific one. I didn't just wake up this morning with a craving,' and 'Flag-girl was bad enough, but U-Boat captain?' Laugh-out-loud moments in an episode that also explores a deep and troubling subject matter. Moffat's script is neatly complemented by James Hawes's outstanding direction, which creates visual images that may scar the memories of a generation of viewers. The gas-mask wearing zombies, for instance, or the sequence in which Rose and Jack dance to 'Moonlight Serenade' on an invisible spaceship with Big Ben as a backdrop. Captain Jack – a square-jawed, bisexual, intergalactic conman – brings a necessary element of sexual tension to the show, which is long overdue, frankly. The effects recreate, chillingly, the wasteland of Blitz-torn London. The acting honours go to Florence Hoath and Richard Wilson, but also to Billie Piper and John Barrowman, whose flirtatious double-act promises great things for the future. But the best aspect of this episode, by far, is Christopher Eccleston wise-cracking his way across war-ravaged London like a cosmic joker in the finest traditions of Patrick Troughton and Tom Baker. With just a trace of Peter Davison's vulnerability, here we have a Doctor who is a perfect symbol for the 21st Century: knowing, pithy, dangerous ... but just a shade neurotic about his nose and ears. A hero. – *Keith Topping*

There were rumours that this episode was going to be scary, and those rumours were proved absolutely true. I had hoped that 'The Unquiet Dead' (thanks largely to its Victorian setting) was going to be the spookiest of the series, but while there were some eerie moments in that particular story, 'The Empty Child' really played up the fear to come out as the clear winner. The setting is a great one, the atmosphere is exquisite (damp, fog-laden streets and authentic-looking sets and costumes), and the cast of characters is exemplary. Florence Hoath really pulls out all the stops with a top-notch performance, and while watching, I found myself imagining the possibility of her joining the TARDIS crew. The gang of children also surprised with some genuine performances. As for the plot, it's absorbing, and it keeps the audience guessing and wondering what's behind the unpleasantness walking the streets of London in the form of a small, desperate boy. I should also mention one other delightful addition, that of Captain Jack Harkness. From the moment of his introduction, he is instantly likeable, and after we peel a few layers away and discover some of his secrets, his role in the story expands and becomes even more interesting. While it would still be a gripping and genuinely scary *Doctor Who* adventure *sans* Jack Harkness, he does bring some lighter moments into an otherwise grim tale, and he is a welcome addition. Easily my second favourite of the new series so far (just slightly behind 'Dalek'). – *Scott Alan Woodard*

EDITOR'S REVIEW: After what seems like an inconsequential side step and a slightly dubious (if well-told) trip to allow Rose to muck up the timelines, 'The Empty Child' sets *Doctor Who* back on course to be the adventure series we all know. Instead of an object lesson or an accidental by-product, here we have the Doctor clearly following a threat to its logical conclusion (or, at least, its logical cliff-hanger), including getting involved with the plot and actually helping shape it. Colourful characters abound here, with Florence Hoath spotlighted as a young woman devoted to a particular and noble (if not necessarily public) cause and doing an exceptional job with the role. I'm not familiar with Richard Wilson myself, but he also fits the part of the aged and slightly daffy Dr Constantine with ease.

However, 'The Empty Child' belongs to John Barrowman, and for one fleeting moment in this first series of the new *Doctor Who*, Christopher Eccleston and Billie Piper are outshined. Jack Harkness is headstrong, full of himself, swaggering in that Han Solo-ish way he only wishes he could master, and probably spends every night alone reading a book of quips to provide endless amusement to party guests ... but he's a wonderful addition to the mythos and a reminder that *Doctor Who can* work with a party of three in the TARDIS. I was delighted to discover that he'd be along for the ride (at least for the immediate future, if not necessarily in future years) and can only hope that the writing for Jack stays as strong as it is here.

That's not to say that Eccleston or Piper aren't brilliant in this episode; even some of the problems I've had in the past with Eccleston's delivery of certain lines aren't visible here, as his reaction in the nightclub is utterly superb and his rapport with the wayward children in the Lloyd home is priceless. The carefree way he manages to slip by the children (and Nancy) and seat himself at table without anyone noticing would be silly anywhere else, yet works here, and I think that's likely because we're so busy focusing on the plot that we'll take anything in our stride. Rose's sudden fixation on Spock and later on Jack are also perfectly believable; in the grand spirit of adventure, both the Doctor and Rose (who I sometimes felt had earlier been dragged, albeit mostly willingly, on a very long leash) finally display that they're *both* having fun at this. Still, even though Eccleston and Piper make a great pair, 'The Empty Child' truly becomes electric when the two are joined by Barrowman, putting Rose into the role of go-between for two competing, yet endearing, personalities.

Steven Moffat proves with this single foray into *Doctor Who* dramatic fiction that he is a master at creating rich and believable dialogue. Those of you who have experienced his work as writer of *Coupling* will know what I mean; creating and establishing good plot is one thing, but scripting can be an entirely different matter, and lines that look good on paper can sound forced and cringeworthy in the heat of the moment. Of course, Moffat's previous experience with *Doctor Who* – and that would be the Comic Relief charity special *The Curse of Fatal Death* – demonstrated some of this talent, but who knew that a man who truly authenticated the 'fart joke' in *Doctor Who* back in the 1990s would later be penning such brilliance as mauve being the universal symbol for danger because red's too camp ... Well, the mind boggles. I'm very much looking forward to the second half of this story, because if it's anywhere near the quality of 'The Empty Child,' we'll have ourselves a story worthy of being called a true classic. – *Shaun Lyon*

110: THE DOCTOR DANCES

Time is running out ... more and more people are being transformed into gas-masked zombies by the mysterious plague; the Doctor, Rose and Jack are trapped inside Albion Hospital; and the mysterious and haunting young boy is coming to find them. What *really* happened to him, and what does it have to do with the crashed Chula medical capsule?

FIRST TRANSMISSION: UK – 28 May 2005. Canada – 7 June 2005. Australia – 23 July 2005. New Zealand – 13 September 2005.
DURATION: 42'50"
WRITER: Steven Moffat
DIRECTOR: James Hawes
CREDITED CAST: Christopher Eccleston (Doctor Who), Billie Piper (Rose Tyler), Albert Valentine (The Child), Florence Hoath (Nancy), John Barrowman (Jack), Luke Perry (Timothy Lloyd), Damian Samuels (Mr Lloyd), Cheryl Fergison (Mrs Lloyd), Joseph Tremain (Jim), Jordan Murphy (Ernie), Robert Hands (Algy), Martin Hodgson (Jenkins), Richard Wilson (Dr Constantine), Vilma Hollingbery (Mrs Harcourt), Noah Johnson (Voice of The Empty Child), Dian Perry (Computer Voice).

WHERE AND WHEN: London, 1941, immediately after 'The Empty Child', including at Albion Hospital, in the Lloyd residence and at the Limehouse Green railway station. Also on board Jack's ship and the TARDIS.

THE STORY UNFOLDS: The Chula medical transport that crashed in London was actually a battlefield ambulance filled with enough nanogenes – microscopic robots that heal wounds and restructure DNA – to rebuild an entire species. The nanogenes escaped from the crashed container, and the first being they came upon was a dead child, Jamie. Using Jamie as a template, they restored him to life, and then started restructuring humanity using the information from the boy – and assuming that his injuries and the gas mask he wore were normal anatomical features for this species.

Emergency protocols protect the Chula ambulance; these delay the Doctor from opening the vessel and also recall the altered humans in its defence. The capsule is designed to aid battle troops, and is using the gas-masked humans as warriors, with the child as their leader.

Jack mistakenly thought the ambulance was burned out and empty. He carries a 51st Century sonic blaster from the weapon factories at Villengard, which were destroyed when the main reactor went critical and vaporised the lot. The weapon has a square digital blast pattern and can not only vaporise metal but restore it as well (in what Jack describes as a 'digital rewind'). The Doctor switches his blaster with a banana (a 'good source of potassium!')

Apparently, most people notice when they've been teleported, but the Doctor and Rose don't; they're too engrossed in conversation about Jack and dancing.

Room 802 at Albion Hospital is where the Child was incarcerated. The room is decorated with his drawings. The zombies respond to what would otherwise scold a child, e.g. 'go to your room!'

Jack's ship is also a Chula craft. He 'borrowed' it from a woman. It's equipped with a personal teleporter keyed to his molecular structure (which Jack subsequently overrides to transport the Doctor and Rose there). Both the ship and the child can 'om-com' (take over any equipment with a speaker grille to create two-way communication). The ship is filled with millions of nanogenes. Emergency protocol 417 on Jack's ship is a martini with a little too much vermouth; the last time he was sentenced to death, he ordered four hypervodkas for breakfast and woke up in bed with both his executioners ... a 'lovely couple' he subsequently stayed in touch with.

THE DOCTOR: He likes bananas and he's been to the banana grove on the spot where the Villengard factory used to be (and indeed implies he might even have been responsible for the explosion that destroyed the factory). He argues with Jack over their respective sonic devices and escape tactics. Rose assumes he doesn't dance; he's been around for 900 years, he tells her, and she should assume that he's danced at some point – the world doesn't end because he dances. Rose thinks he's experiencing 'captain envy' with Jack. He is able to affect the nanogenes to reverse the damage and restore everyone's humanity. And it turns out that he can dance after all.

ROSE TYLER: She tells Jack he has a nice 'blast pattern' (when he uses his blaster) and describes his weapon as a 'squareness gun'. She saves the day when she uses the blaster to shoot through the floor and help Jack and the Doctor escape from the zombies. She thinks Jack is great-looking and trusts him because he saved her life ('Blokewise, that's up there with ... flossing') and because he's like the Doctor, except with dating and dancing. She then asks the Doctor to dance. She once got a red bicycle for Christmas when she was 12 (and the Doctor implies that he's the one who gave it to her!)

CHARACTER BUILDING: *Jack Harkness* – Jack left the Time Agency because they stole two years of his memories; he has no idea what he did during that time, and therefore he thinks the Doctor's right not to trust him. (He wasn't defrocked; as he says, 'Nobody takes my frock'.) He is from the 51st Century. He has a personal teleporter and chides the Doctor over the supposed inadequacy of his sonic screwdriver. He says he 'never had a chance' when he saw Rose and had to rescue her. He got to know Algy well during his time here; he's more the man's type than Rose is. Far from being a coward, as Rose thinks he is when he leaves them behind, he actually goes back to his ship to stop the German bomb from hitting the medical transport. He joins the Doctor and Rose in the TARDIS as its newest passenger.

Nancy – As a teenage single mother in 1941, she told everyone Jamie was her brother, but in fact he's really her son. The child nearly kills her but instead leaves because of the Doctor's actions. She blackmails Mr Lloyd with his guilty secret, obtaining from him a torch and some wire cutters, and more food. She tries to get into the bomb site using the wire cutters because, as she tells the children, the child is always after her. Nancy believes Rose when hearing that she's from the future, and is relieved to hear that the Germans don't win the war. She and the now-restored Jamie seek help from Dr Constantine.

Dr Constantine – The Doctor asks him not to make a big deal about being such a good physician after the effects of the nanogenes are reversed. When Mrs Harcourt queries the number of legs that she has – she had just one before the nanogenes 'repaired' her – he wonders if it's possible that she miscounted because there's a war on.

The Empty Child – Jamie died when the Chula craft crashed and was revived by the nanogenes it contained.

Mr Lloyd – He's been secretly messing around with Mr Haverstock, the local butcher, which is how he has managed to obtain so much food for his family.

The Children – Some thought that Nancy was dead or had run off, so they went back to her hideout. Ernie led them there because they need her 'for thinking'; Nancy tells Ernie to look after the children when she leaves. Jim tries to write a letter to his dad with a damaged typewriter, but he doesn't know where his dad is or even how to write. Later the typewriter mysteriously types all by itself.

BAD WOLF: The German bomb that Jack stops from hitting the Chula capsule is emblasoned with the words 'Schlechter Wolf'. (This translates roughly as 'more badly wolf' but the point is made.)

FANTASTIC!: The Doctor says 'Fantastic!' after returning to the TARDIS, where he's insufferably pleased with himself that everything's turned out well.

BODY COUNT: 'Everybody lives!'

THE DOCTOR'S MAGICAL SONIC SCREWDRIVER: He tries to use it (unsuccessfully) to stop the altered humans from approaching. He locks the door in Albion Hospital with it, trapping himself, Jack and Rose inside. He tries to loosen the bars on the windows on the seventh floor at Albion, unsuccessfully. Setting 2428D reattaches barbed wire.

REALITY BITES: Pompeii was a city in the Bay of Naples, a municipality of Rome destroyed by the eruption of Mount Vesuvius in AD 79. The eruption buried the city (along with its sister town of Herculaneum) in volcanic ash. It was rediscovered by an Italian architect in 1599, and excavations started in 1748. Jack prefers the Blitz to Pompeii as a time period to carry out his con.

Limehouse Green is obviously meant to be the railway station in the Limehouse Basin, on the north shore of the Thames and currently on the London, Tilbury and Southend Line and the Docklands Light Railway. (The phrase 'Limehouse Green' is also the name of a techno CD single by Ant & Mark Verso.)

LINKING THEMES: Very few links to the past, although the Doctor is familiar with both the time period and the Chula, including their technology.

The Doctor experiences Pompeii first hand in an audio story, *The Fires of Vulcan* by Steve Lyons, released by Big Finish.

Jack's origin in the 51st Century ties in well to the future established in the story 'The Talons of Weng-Chiang' (1977).

SCENE MISSING: What, exactly, is the child's method of communication? He can take advantage of om-com technology (anything with a speaker grille) but also a typewriter and a toy (as seen in 'The Empty Child'). Why does the child 'break character' (his constant pursuit for his mummy) with a taunt for the Doctor when he and Jack are communicating over the radio? (He also does this in 'The Empty Child' in noting the balloon above him.) And how, for that matter, does Jack hear the Doctor if there's no microphone to pick his voice up? Clearly this is a benefit of the om-com technology … whatever that is!

Why does Jack take the bomb out into space where he's suddenly confronted by possible death, instead of, for example, dropping it into the English Channel? Or, if he can't drop it, maybe get back to Earth and leave the ship before it explodes? (His ship can hover, so why can't he jump out and swim! We're talking life and death here, after all!)

Why does Nancy attempt to escape the Lloyd home through the back door – and risk coming into contact with the Lloyds, who she knows are out there – instead of leaving through the front door?

When did Rose – a girl from a housing estate in 2005 – learn how to dance in a style popularised in the 1940s? (Would it *really* be likely that she'd taken lessons?) And how in the world, even given all its many uses, can the sonic screwdriver repair barbed wire!?

BEHIND THE SCENES: For a list of locations used in the episode, see 'The Empty Child'.

Steven Moffat mentioned during an interview that he'd been asked to write a scene at the last minute for this two-parter. The scene in question had to be two minutes long, shouldn't feature either of the regulars, was to be all on one set and no props would be used. The scene he eventually penned was the one with Nancy, the kids and the self-typing typewriter.

The official BBC *Doctor Who* spin-off website whoisdoctorwho suggested that 'Schlechter Wolf' was written on a variety of bombs dropped during the Blitz, found during recent archaeological digs and reported to UNIT (which, of course, would probably waste their time, but why quibble?)

DULCET TONES: 'Moonlight Serenade' and 'In The Mood' by Glenn Miller – Jack attempts to woo Rose with 'Moonlight Serenade' earlier in the story (see 'The Empty Child' for details) and then plays it to her to block the transmissions in this episode. Finally, the Doctor tries to dance to the track at the end of the story, before giving up and playing 'In The Mood'. ('Moonlight Serenade' heard at 16:09-16:21 and 16:56-18:26; 'In The Mood' heard at 39:44-41:26.)

OFF THE SCREEN: Vilma Hollingbery was in the series *The Management* (1988), *The River* (1989), *Sitting Pretty* (1992), *London Bridge* (1995) and *Grass* (2003). Martin Hodgson was also seen in *Pompeii: The Last Day* (2003). Luke Perry should not be confused with his *Beverly Hills: 90210* namesake (this was his first television role). (See 'The Empty Child' for other members of the cast.)

TECHNICAL GOOFS: The view outside Jack's ship doesn't look like space; it looks like a blue screen. The trains at the railway station have post-war livery on them. Nancy asks to use the bathroom (most homes during that period had outside toilets; at any rate, at the time they weren't referred to as bathrooms!)

CONTROVERSIES: For the first time, sexuality is addressed in *Doctor Who* through more than just one or two double entendres; Jack makes some very overt statements, backed up by the Doctor's claims, that bisexuality is a norm in the future. It's briefly touched on in 'The Empty Child' but is unavoidable here, including 'dancing' being used in several instances to signify more than just that.

INTERNAL CONSISTENCY: There is a much clearer view of the clock at the Lloyd household over Jamie's shoulder in this episode – it gives the time as10.12 pm. This is happening at the same time as the Doctor, Rose and Jack are being menaced at the hospital. Jamie is still walking to each location, so he has to have time to get to the hospital as the Doctor looks for his room. There appears to be a couple of minutes missing as the Doctor and Rose wait for Jack to teleport them, as Nancy has time to visit the other children and get to the crash site. However, as the Doctor notes that it takes only ten minutes for Jack to do this, it's reason enough to believe that, like the Lloyd household, the children's hideout must be close to Albion Hospital and Limehouse Green Station. Taking into account some of the missing minutes, approximately forty-five minutes to an hour passes, which means that the bomb almost falls on the Doctor at approximately 11-11.15 pm. This is about one hour and forty-five minutes after Jack approximated two hours to explosion; taking into account the fifteen or so minutes to clear the area and get back to the TARDIS to pick up Jack, this puts the explosion pretty much at 11.30 pm, when Jack predicted (although it was the Chula ship that blew up, and not a German bomb as Jack had assumed).

THEME ANALYSES

As Doctor Who For A Modern Audience: Much of this episode shows how evolution rather than revolution has been the prime consideration in bringing this series to life for today's viewers. The cliff-hanger resolution illustrates this brilliantly as it provides a fresh twist, with the Doctor's scolding of the advancing gas-masked zombies being unusual and unexpected. This scene demonstrates the Doctor's realisation of the relationship between these gas-masked figures and the child, advancing the plot in the process rather than providing just a convenient escape. The ending shows the optimism of the series well, with the horror of the initial situation giving way to the uplifting 'Everybody lives!' finale, which, as the Doctor remarks, is a very rare thing indeed. This subversion of expectation also extends to the reasoning for why the plague began in the first place, as there's no arch villain manipulating events to empower himself in the clichéd manner of old, but a simple misunderstanding at a genetic level – a misunderstanding that maternal love overcomes. With the stigma of a teen pregnancy being part of the plot, it shows how more socially relevant issues can be examined in a way that was very unlikely in the original series, and the inclusion of this reflects changes in what people want to see. This is also true of the more ambiguous characterisation demonstrated by Moffat through the different interpretations of Nancy's confrontation with the owner of the house she and the other homeless children raided.

As Television Drama: Richard Wilson seems to be playing a slightly less warm and fluffy version of the Dr Newman character he could be seen playing the same week in the latest series of BBC1's 1950s-set rural drama *Born and Bred*, as this story shares a certain nostalgic quality with that other series. 'The Doctor Dances' has the same kind of almost idealised, 'theme park Britain' feel to its depiction of history as *Born and Bred* and its precursor, ITV's perennially-popular gentle1960s police drama *Heartbeat*. While that element is strong, there's also a harder, grittier edge given by the revelation of Nancy's young, unmarried mother status. Combined with the Doctor's – admittedly tongue-in-cheek – rallying cry for the welfare state, it almost feels like the sort of social realist stuff the BBC would serve up in *Play for Today* during that strand's1970s heyday. However, it also has a humour, warmth, wit and imagination that mark it out in a way that is unique to *Doctor Who*. It's almost a sort of distillation of some of the very best elements of British television drama past and present, and remains highly impressive when compared with any other contemporary popular drama output.

As A Piece of Writing: It's got to be a hard job writing the second episode of a two-part story. At one level, you know you have to maintain or exceed the quality of the preceding instalment; on another, you have to offer up something fresh and new, so the audience doesn't get bored. Happily, Steven Moffat manages both with considerable aplomb. This is a scary episode, but less so than the last; instead, a greater emphasis has been put on humour, with many of the funniest lines we've heard all season. There's also much more focus on the relationship between the Doctor and Rose, understandably lessened in 'The Empty Child', where they spent most of the episode apart. Perhaps the biggest accomplishment is that together, both episodes feel like a complete and well-rounded story, going from a very dark beginning to a hopeful and positive climax. The nanogenes are something of a quick fix, like many of the solutions we've seen in previous weeks, but as they are established early in the first part of the two-parter, it doesn't feel like we've had the rug pulled out from under our feet. Everything feels deliberate, well-paced, and expertly designed. This could so easily have been 'just another World War Two science fiction story', but instead, we have what looks to be a new classic, a fan favourite, and – finally! – a smart, modern story we can use to convert ... er, clue our friends in on the fun of *Doctor Who*.

The Doctor As A Mystery Figure: The cosmic-sage element of the Doctor's personality hasn't been overplayed so far this season. It's there occasionally – in 'The End of the World' and 'Father's Day' most notably – but the ninth Doctor's more usual *modus operandi* is to get the best out of those around him by encouraging their untapped potential. In 'The Doctor Dances', for once it's the title character who works on hunches and universal truisms to provide a vital piece in the jigsaw-like solution. One in which, implausibly but magnificently, 'Just this once – everybody lives!' Yet, possibly because of this fact, the Doctor's usual 'mysterious stranger from the future' role is somewhat usurped by Jack, a dashing intergalactic conman with a heart of gold whose (almost) self-sacrifice towards the end of the episode provides the story's main element of redemption. Yet beyond the *Dr Strangelove* allusions and quiet introspection of gallows humour with a nice Martini lies a Doctor begging some unseen higher power to 'give me a day like this.' Someone, for once, listened.

Themes, Genres and Modes: I was tempted simply to copy and paste what I said before about horror – especially as the series, as it progresses, continues to prove that less is more with that genre – but as I've promised to address something new every episode, instead I'll focus on territory less familiar to *Doctor Who* but more in keeping with Steven Moffat's previous work: romantic comedy. 'The Doctor Dances' gives the Doctor a rival for Rose's affections in the form of Jack, and witty battles across and between the sexes ensue to see who gets noticed by the heroine. As Steven Moffat explained in *Doctor Who Confidential*, the whole argument about the sonic screwdriver (while also employing the writer's tendency to cheekily send up the series conventions) is about sex: about impressing Rose. But because it's *Doctor Who*, there's another whole level of nuance here. The episode poses the question: 'Does the Doctor "dance"?' (in all the subtextual glory that 'dancing' implies). It's a good question, because for a romantic comedy to truly work, the men need to be able to 'dance', and the Doctor is not known for his skills in this area. The story happily skates around this, even as the Doctor vies with Jack for Rose's attention, and in the end we learn that the Doctor can dance ... but does he 'dance'?

In Style and Structure: 'The Doctor Dances' maintains the style of 'The Empty Child' in terms of setting, with the action taking place mostly at the bomb site in the middle of an air raid. Period music is used well to create atmosphere, and as a subtle reminder of the setting. The story resolution comes through the Doctor acting as a catalyst for another character's actions, before he steps in to spread the solution so that it covers all infected by the child. The theme of 'dancing' permeates the story, and can be read as either directly referring to dancing or as a euphemism for something else. This threads through the interactions between the Doctor, Rose and Jack; allowing for some conflict between the Doctor and Jack, much to Rose's amusement. For the first half of the episode, there is still a definitive A and B plot structure to the story, before Nancy's story leads her to the Doctor, Rose and Jack. Overall, 'The Empty Child' and 'The Doctor Dances' are a spectacular two part story, the first episode establishing and developing the plot, the second adding in a twist and then resolving and concluding on a high.

As Doctor Who Continuity: It always struck me as odd that it took until the twenty-sixth season before *Doctor Who* ventured into the era of the Second World War. The BBC was more than capable of recreating that period; stock props and costumes from *Colditz, Secret Army, Goodnight Sweetheart,* and so on, probably fill numerous storage warehouses at Television Centre. But even then, 'The Curse of Fenric' was confined to British shores rather than being set on the European fronts. One might be forgiven for wondering whether or not the hostilities even took place in the *Doctor Who* universe, but in fact the Second World War does get a few casual mentions during the original series. The third Doctor used the curious description 'the Hitler War' in 'The Time Monster' (1972), and the parallel universe in 'Inferno' (1970) was a post-war Republic. Amelia Ducat was said once to have manned an ack-ack gun ('The Seeds of Doom', 1976), and Oscar Botcherby's father to have been killed in battle ('The Two Doctors', 1985). And on the subject of war, is the Chula ambulance a remnant of the Time War? The Doctor is certainly familiar with Chula technology. 'Everybody lives!' declares the Doctor; and it's true. Indeed, there have been only a handful of *Doctor Who* stories in which no-one dies: 'Inside the Spaceship' (1964), 'Snakedance' and 'Terminus' (both 1983) being the best-known examples.

From A Special Effects Viewpoint: The bombers are still flying overhead, the gas masks are still there, and we see a few glimpses of additional facial transformations (and they're still creepy as heck). One additional element that should be mentioned is Jack's Chula space/time ship; in particular, the scenes near the story's end of it moving through deep space. While we have seen giant space stations and the daylight 'crash' landing of the Slitheen ship in the Thames, this is the first time that we have seen something of this type and, once again, The Mill handle it very well. We've seen sequences like this in the various *Star Trek* series and in big Hollywood science fiction films, but it's a bit unusual for *Doctor Who*, so much so that it's almost jarring when it graces our screens. Although some effects sequences in the 'classic' series worked admirably, most notably the space station shots in 'The Trial of a Time Lord' (1986) and the space craft effects in 'Underworld' and 'The Invasion of Time' (both 1978), this new sequence gives yet another clear indication that this is *Doctor Who* for the 21st Century, and I for one am thrilled with it.

PANEL REVIEWS

One of my all-time favourite tunes is the Glenn Miller Orchestra's rendition of 'Moonlight Serenade'. It's a pretty melody, but the big band sound adds such lushness, such texture, that it at once evokes feelings of romance and visions of bygone places. The result is one of the most gorgeous pieces of music ever recorded. And yet, think about it, to create that very sound you have to have a full orchestra working in perfect harmony. Anything else would create a lesser song. 'The Doctor Dances' is just like that. Everything works together, from James Hawes's brilliant direction, to Steven Moffat's script that moves from a scary moment like Nancy being chained to a table being guarded by someone about to transform into a child-creature, to a funny moment like the Doctor egging on Rose about how people from the 51st Century 'dance', to an uplifting moment where Rose tells Nancy the British will win the war. And then there are the actual performances, particularly those from Florence Hoath and Christopher Eccleston. But all these things pale compared with the climax, which is one of the most uplifting things I've ever seen in *Doctor Who*. Watching the emotionally damaged Doctor exultant that everybody lives put tears in my eyes and it's one of Eccleston's greatest moments in the role. And then they top that by bringing all the romantic tension to a head with a charming dance number no less. To paraphrase the Doctor, we all need more days like this. – *Graeme Burk*

In many ways, 'The Doctor Dances' is the epitome of what a good second half should be. It continues the high quality of the preceding episode, accentuating the level of suspense through a heightening of the tension but also revealing fresh insights upon its main supporting characters, making this a very satisfying end to a wonderful adventure. Scenes such as the child making its presence known in room 802 and the emergence of the gas-mask zombies from the hospital are extremely effective, but it's really the way Moffat handles the characters that makes this episode special. The rivalry between Jack and the Doctor is great fun to watch, giving the story some of its best humour – particularly the Doctor's reluctance to admit that his own sonic device is just a screwdriver – and by the end, the latest addition to the TARDIS crew is revealed as someone who will nobly sacrifice himself to save others. John Barrowman is very likeable as Jack, although as ever when there is more than one companion, the focus on introducing him means that Rose is sidelined. Florence Hoath is even better as Nancy than she was the week before, showing her character's struggle to admit that Jamie is her son beautifully, while Eccleston's delight during the resolution is fantastically infectious and tops one of his most commanding performances as the Doctor. When style and substance combine as well as they do here, the result is the very best type of *Doctor Who*. – *Simon Catlow*

From a very clever resolution to the cliff-hanger, to the suave moves of the Doctor in the TARDIS, this episode sets out to resolve all the mysteries posed in the first instalment. In many ways this is a better episode – Jack gets a lot more time to fill us in on what type of a man he is, and Florence Hoath gets another chance to shine as a stand-out guest star. Rose spends time weighing up the relative merits of Jack and the Doctor, but proves she's a good choice for travelling companion when she jumps in to help with whatever the situation is. And, the Doctor – we see him all but say 'I'm interested in relationships' and be happier than I think we've ever seen any of the Doctors. On a less positive note, I'm not keen on having the resolution rely so heavily on the nanogenes. They're an over-used concept in science-fiction right now (but quickly becoming science fact) and it just seems too obvious a solution. That isn't enough though to dampen the spirits of this episode. Everybody lives (except, of course, those that died in the air raid earlier that evening). – *Robert Franks*

If 'The Empty Child' worked because it was scary, witty and sad all at once, 'The Doctor Dances' succeeds because it offers the exact same mixture, but in a very different dose. Like last week, there is an air of sadness about everyone – people mourning other people, wanting people they can't have, looking for help that just isn't coming. This time, though, there's a difference – everybody wins, maybe not forever, but certainly for today. It's a wonderful message that's been tried once or twice in *Doctor Who*, most notably in the 1996 TV movie (complete with a similar, 'magical' solution), but has never really succeeded before. This episode connected with me on an emotional level that 'Father's Day' simply didn't, going a long way toward glossing over the fluffy scientific explanations – although, really, the nanogenes aren't any worse than the 'anti-plastic' or 'DNA absorption' we saw earlier this year, simple *deus ex machinas* built to keep the story going without interrupting the audience high. And the time just flies by in this episode; it's the first week I've laughed out loud at most of the jokes, the first time I completely didn't mind the romantic subtext, the first time I was intrigued to see what a second companion might bring to the TARDIS crew dynamic. I will admit I found the many references to Jack's sexuality rather heavy-handed and overdone, especially for what is ostensibly a family show, but that's my only complaint. If 'Dalek' paved the way forward for snappy, taut, single forty-five-minute episodes, this two-parter shows old-school *Doctor Who* done right. It proves, without a doubt, that the good Doctor still has the moves – he just has to remember how to dance. – *Sarah Hadley*

It was sometimes the case in 'classic' *Doctor Who* that a brilliant opening episode would be let down by the subsequent resolution of a story. However, that's not the case here – indeed, if it's possible, 'The Doctor Dances' actually comes close to being even better than 'The Empty Child', and that's quite something. I have an extremely hard time finding anything to criticise in this episode – Steven Moffat's script is brilliantly plotted and filled with wonderful dialogue; James Hawes's direction continues to impress with its subtlety and style, and altogether the overriding impression is one of everybody involved on both sides of the camera pulling together and working as hard as they could to create the best piece of television they could possibly make. It's in a way an atypical *Doctor Who* episode in that it contains no real villain as such and has a happy ending, but it works superbly and is right up there with the very greatest examples ever made. It really is wonderful to watch, and if the other eleven episodes of the series had consisted of nothing but shots of the paint on the TARDIS prop drying, it would have been worth it for having this two-parter to treasure. As the Doctor himself says, 'I need more days like this!' – *Paul Hayes*

Steven Moffat smoothly resolves the story set up in 'The Empty Child' in 'The Doctor Dances', and provides many more great character moments. The character thread of the Doctor's jealousy towards Jack plays out throughout the episode, and it is resolved in a way that's not really expected, but suits the two characters. The empty child continues to be a haunting presence, as the eerie vocal performance plays a large part in building up the tense and scary atmosphere of many scenes. The resolution of the mystery ties neatly into Nancy's story, explaining some of the character's actions, with Florence Hoath again putting in a strong performance. Christopher Eccleston pulls out all stops in the climatic scenes at the bomb site, showing the Doctor's delight at how well the situation is resolved. John Barrowman again puts in an enthusiastic performance as Jack, with the character slowly building up a rapport with the Doctor and Rose. The Mill have again created some excellent effects, such as the nanogenes and the image of Albion Hospital seamlessly added to long shots of the bomb site. The charming final scene of the Doctor and Rose dancing perfectly brings the episode (and the story) to a close. – *Cameron Mason*

What an incredible piece of work. Following on from the cracking cliff-hanger, 'The Doctor Dances' races along at a breathless pace to a wholly satisfying conclusion that had me clapping in delight as everything that was left unresolved in part one fell neatly into place. The revelation about the true relationship between Nancy and Jamie was totally unexpected, and the truth behind the mutation was a complete surprise, despite being signposted in part one! In 'Dalek', Eccleston was at his most intense. For 'The Doctor Dances' he gives an outrageously humorous performance, proving once and for all to any nay-sayers that yes, he can be funny – one of the primary reasons why he took on the role of the Doctor in the first place. The banter between Jack and the Doctor is wonderfully mad in a Spike/Angel sort of way; long may this rivalry continue. A favourite moment for me is the Doctor and Rose dancing in the TARDIS, so surreal and yet it seems so normal – and my feet were tapping along with the jazz riff at the end of the episode. These are not only two of the best episodes this season, but of *Doctor Who*, period. Messrs Moffat and Hawes please come back for season two ... – *Jon Preddle*

'Lots to do. Beat the Germans ... Don't forget the Welfare State!' It may start with a relatively weak resolution to last week's cliff-hanger (although even here, there's a pithy comment to undercut any bathetic negativity) but that's a minor complaint. Elsewhere, 'The Doctor Dances' is a major (and when I say major, I mean, brigadier-general) achievement. The dialogue is the kind of material that makes your toes tingle ('I've got a banana and, at a pinch, you could put up some shelves'; 'Rose, I'm trying to resonate concrete'; 'I think you're experiencing captain-envy!'). In lesser hands than Steven Moffat's, the script's dependence on a central euphemistic metaphor ('dancing' as a simile for sex in all its forms) could have been disastrous. Here, it's drop-dead funny and, more importantly, informative. There are many wonderful moments, but perhaps the best of the lot is the Doctor's sheer joy when an accidental confluence of circumstances produces a happy ending. ('Twenty years to pop music! You're gonna love it!') And, just so that everyone gets the message, there's a life-affirming coda that extends the 'nobody dies' concept (something rare in *Doctor Who*) with the introduction of a new companion to boot. I love 'The Doctor Dances'. I think it's a story with heart, with soul. A thing of rare honesty and humanity in a compromised television landscape of hateful lowest-common-denominator ideas. I didn't think Paul Cornell's episode could possibly be bettered as the highlight of this quite remarkable television resurrection. I was wrong. – *Keith Topping*

At the conclusion of my review for 'The Empty Child', I stated that it was my second favourite episode of the new series. When the credits for 'The Doctor Dances' scrolled up my screen, I realised that, combined, 'The Empty Child' and 'The Doctor Dances' were now my favourite single story of this series. When viewed as a whole, the two-parter feels nothing short of a really terrific motion picture. The mystery deepens, Nancy continues to shine (particularly during scenes like her one-on-one confrontation with Mr Lloyd) and, of course, the Doctor gets to dance. This scene, in particular, stands out as a personal favourite. The playful relationship between Rose and the Doctor is exemplified here with Rose simply wanting to pass the time with a dance while the Doctor, still focused on the terrifying situation around them, allows himself just one brief moment of innocent pleasure with his best friend; but even when he takes up Rose's hands, he first examines them for injury before making a single dance move. Little scenes like this develop characters so much more than lengthy, fictionalised tales of their past histories. And let us not forget one more truly beautiful scene, that of the Doctor's realisation that 'Everybody lives'. The absolute joy expressed by the Doctor (thanks to Eccleston's performance) is truly touching. – *Scott Alan Woodard*

EDITOR'S REVIEW: And here we are. Second halves can build on the strengths of their first parts, or they can be abysmal failures, tying up all the loose ends in a neat little package without any thought as to the consequences. Thankfully, 'The Doctor Dances' manages to exhibit the former, bringing to a close the events set up so beautifully in 'The Empty Child' with flawless ease and significant payoff, both on a dramatic level as well as an emotional high.

One of the things that sets 'The Doctor Dances' apart from other episodes (even 'The Empty Child') is its sardonic yet captivating wit ... never bitter, always clever and impressive, where even the tiniest pun can go a long way. (Who would have thought that the Doctor could actually get away with the ol' banana/gun switcheroo, and not only have it work, but manage to pull off a handy comment about potassium without it falling flat?) The dialogue in this episode is never forced; it flows freely and genuinely, no matter who is speaking. Happily, it's a cavalcade of excellent actors – Eccleston, Piper, Barrowman, Hoath – who perform it beautifully. Barrowman, who already proved his acting credentials on his first outing, has now succeeded in becoming one of the brightest additions to the *Doctor Who* universe since ... well, since Billie Piper. The scenes between Barrowman, Eccleston and Piper flow well, with more stunning dialogue courtesy of Moffat that engenders a sense of trust between them. The moment he joins the TARDIS crew, Jack fits perfectly.

The other point that helps this episode excel is its breathtaking sense of style. I'm not talking about visual style – yes, 1941 London looks like 1941 London, the interior of Jack's ship is terrific; that's all par for the course now, given this outstanding crew of technical wizards and set designers, and having been done so well in 'The Empty Child'. Think back, if you're a *Doctor Who* fan, to the classic years, and see if you can find another instance where the Doctor dancing with his companion to the tune of 'In the Mood' would fit. I can't. There's a genuine feeling of class that evolves from the script; it's humanitarian and sensitive, from the Doctor's comments about the welfare state to Nancy's selflessness and Jack's conscience overriding his sense of adventure. Whether we're watching him pull the banana switch or pondering how in the world the sonic screwdriver can repair barbed wire, we're still captivated by this unfolding story. Which, shock of all shocks, manages to make complete sense at the conclusion, with all the loose ends tied up well, and Jack's selfless act rewarded with an open door into the Doctor's world – a door we know by now he doesn't open for just anyone.

This is what *Doctor Who* should be, what it *needs* to be: adventure for the sake of adventure, without all that needless mucking about with grand, sweeping moral messages or concepts. The Doctor arrives with his companions, he investigates and he saves the day. Most of us look forward to watching *Doctor Who* precisely *because* of that fun; we delighted in the past at Tom Baker's cornball jokes, because that was the Doctor. Here, Eccleston demonstrates that same wit and wonder that captivated many of us the first time around, and uses it to his advantage. When he dances at the end, safe in the knowledge that 'Everybody lives!', we're celebrating with him ... the zombies are all back to normal, Nancy has her son back, and in a few years' time, the Allies will win the war. And good old Dr Constantine can therefore get away with his deadpan questioning of Mrs Harcourt, wondering (but not really) if she could have miscounted her legs.

It's a rare instance when a story like this can be so powerful and so silly at the same time, in a way that is unique to *Doctor Who*. While I've said that 'The End of the World' is my personal favourite, and it remains so mostly for its unparalleled sentimentality, I recognise the triumph of style and substance Moffat has crafted in this and its first half. Judging the two halves side by side, the first chapter is excellent, but this one's unmatched. 'The Doctor Dances' is, without a doubt, the best episode of this season. – *Shaun Lyon*

111: BOOM TOWN

The TARDIS returns to the present day, as a brief trip to Cardiff reunites the TARDIS crew with an old friend ... and an old adversary they thought was dead. While Rose struggles to put the past behind her, Mickey longs for something that will never be, Jack finds his place among the crew, and the Doctor has an important decision to make.

FIRST TRANSMISSION: UK – 4 June 2005. Canada – 14 June 2005. Australia – 30 July 2005. New Zealand – 20 September 2005.
DURATION: 43'18"
WRITER: Russell T Davies
DIRECTOR: Joe Ahearne
CREDITED CAST: Christopher Eccleston (Doctor Who), Billie Piper (Rose Tyler), William Thomas (Mr Cleaver), Annette Badland (Margaret), John Barrowman (Captain Jack), Noel Clarke (Mickey), Mali Harries (Cathy), Aled Pedrick (Idris Hopper), Alan Ruscoe (Slitheen)

WHERE AND WHEN: Cardiff, early 21st Century (likely September 2006), including the City Hall and along the waterfront. The story is captioned 'six months later' than the events seen in 'World War Three'.

THE STORY UNFOLDS: The Blaidd Drwg Project (known in Welsh as the *Prosiect Y Blaidd Drwg*) is a large nuclear power development in the centre of Cardiff, a 'monument to Welsh industry', spearheaded by its new mayor, Margaret Blaine, a Slitheen in disguise.

Cardiff has a rift running through the middle of the city, like an invisible earthquake fault between different dimensions. Using energy leeched from the scar created by the closing of the rift in 1869 ('The Unquiet Dead'), the TARDIS is parked over it to allow it to absorb the temporal radiation and to 'refuel' over a period of several days. Meanwhile, when Blaidd Drwg reaches capacity, it is designed to go into meltdown, which will open the rift and cause an enormous explosion that will destroy the planet.

Reporter Cathy Salt tracks deaths connected with the Blaidd Drwg project: a team of European safety inspectors (who misunderstood a danger warning in Welsh because they were French), the Cardiff Heritage Committee (electrocution in a swimming pool), the architect ('accidentally' hit by Margaret with her car) and Mr Cleaver ('Slipped on an icy patch'), who found design flaws in the project that could create a disaster a thousand times worse than at Chernobyl. Margaret says that the entire south coast of Wales could fall into the sea and no-one in London would notice.

A tribophysical waveform macro-kinetic extrapolator is a kind of pan-dimensional surfboard that fell into Margaret's hands (at a discount sale) – it can convert an explosion to project an energy bubble to protect the rider, which Margaret will use to escape. Jack uses the power in it to partially refuel the TARDIS, which will take twelve hours. Jack tells his fellow crewmembers to execute a '5756 strategy' to capture Margaret, which covers all exits from a building, and which the Doctor eventually says is a nice plan. Their groups are 'armed' with mobile phones.

The planet Raxacoricofallapatorius has the death penalty; the Slitheen family was tried in absentia and found guilty, and Margaret must be executed on return. Public executions there are slow, involving lowering the condemned into boiling acetic acid. Raxacoricofallapatorian females can project a poison dart from their fingers, or exhale poison through their lungs, while under duress. During their dinner 'date', both the Doctor and Margaret wear bracelets that confine them to a space of up to ten feet apart; if they separate further, Margaret will be electrocuted by 10,000 volts.

The TARDIS's recent trips have included journeys to the planet Justicia, the Glass Pyramids of San Kaloon and a cold world called Woman Wept (which has a continent that, seen from above, looks like a woman lamenting) with a thousand-mile-long beach and a frozen sea with hundred-foot waves.

THE DOCTOR: He jokingly tells Jack to buy him a drink if he wants a hug like the one Mickey gives Rose. Mickey calls him 'big ears'. His holiday in Cardiff is interrupted by seeing Margaret's face in the paper. He is challenged by her requests, especially to go to dinner with someone he has condemned to death on her homeworld. He believes she spared Cathy's life but knows Margaret is still a killer, which is confirmed to him later when she shows her true colours. Margaret tells him that he is also a killer or has a god complex, walking in and out of situations on a whim.

ROSE TYLER: Mickey brings Rose her passport from London (a ruse she created in order to see him). She heads off with him, planning to have a pizza and spend the night in a hotel; but she won't tell the Doctor because it's none of his business. She feels guilt (finally) for abandoning Mickey at the end, and goes back to look for him, but he makes sure she doesn't find him.

CHARACTER BUILDING: *Jack Harkness* – Mickey calls him 'Jumpin' Jack Flash' and wonders if he's the 'captain of the innuendo squad'. He doesn't quite understand early 21st Century slang (he still thinks 'bad' means good and 'cheesy' is good). He tells the Doctor, Rose and Mickey that he was once on an expedition with fifteen others (naked!) and ran up against something with large tusks, but Rose doesn't believe him.

Margaret Blaine – The last survivor of the Slitheen family on Earth, Blon Fel Fotch Pasameer-Day Slitheen escaped the destruction of 10 Downing Street ('World War Three') with a personal teleporter embedded in her jewellery (which sent her to a rubbish skip on the Isle of Dogs). She has been careful to prevent any photographs being taken of her. She went after her first kill at age thirteen, prompted by her father, who would have killed her if she hadn't. She's impressed by the TARDIS and feels guilty that she couldn't rescue her family. She had a penthouse flat in Cardiff with two bedrooms and a bayside view. The Doctor reminds her that she killed the owner of the body she's now wearing. Idris Hopper is her assistant. After admitting that all she wanted was to be given a second chance, she is regressed back to an egg, when she looks into the heart of the TARDIS. The Doctor says he will return the egg to a hatchery on Raxacoricofallapatorius so she has a second chance to grow up.

Mickey Smith – He comes to Cardiff to give Rose her passport, arriving at Cardiff Central station. The Doctor still calls him Ricky. Jack has not met him before. He thinks Margaret deserved to die. He's now (or so he claims) dating a woman named Trisha Delaney (someone from a local shop, who has a brother named Rob and used to be 'a bit big'); he says he is seeing her because Rose walked out on him. He's jealous because Rose runs from him to help the

Doctor stop the rift opening.

Cathy Salt – A reporter for the *Cardiff Gazette*. She originally runs up against Margaret Blaine while investigating the Blaidd Drwg project. She's marrying her boyfriend Jeffrey next month (on the 19th); she's also three months pregnant with a baby but doesn't show (and it was a 'nice' accident). This information makes Margaret change her mind about killing her.

Mr Cleaver – The government's nuclear advisor. He has been worried about the Blaidd Drwg project for some time, having checked the designs repeatedly. He is later killed by Margaret, revealing her true nature, and decapitated. Before he died, he posted some of his findings on Blaidd Drwg online.

BAD WOLF: 'Blaidd Drwg' means Bad Wolf in Welsh. The Doctor and Rose finally start taking notice of the words 'Bad Wolf' appearing around them, although the Doctor puts it down to coincidence.

FANTASTIC!: The Doctor says 'fantastic' when he discovers Margaret's 'surfboard'. (Honourable mention: Mickey tells Rose she looks fantastic.)

BODY COUNT: Only one actually seen during the episode – Mr Cleaver. However, it can be inferred that when the rift opens, given that so many people are injured, there might have been a few deaths as well.

THE DOCTOR'S MAGICAL SONIC SCREWDRIVER: The Doctor uses it to take control of Margaret's personal teleporter.

REALITY BITES: The *Western Mail* newspaper is real, and the paper ran an article on 4 June 2005 noting its use in the episode, saying that Davies had wanted to include a copy of the newspaper in the show to prove it was made in Wales.

The Doctor explains that real police boxes were features on street corners in the 1950s and 60s, used to provide telephones to those who needed to call for help and also to provide temporary incarceration to criminals until transport arrived. Rose compares Margaret's incarceration in the TARDIS to this use.

The Doctor and Margaret eat at Bistro 10, a real restaurant serving 'universal cuisine' on Mermaid Quay in Cardiff Bay. Mickey's nickname for Jack refers to the song 'Jumpin' Jack Flash' by the Rolling Stones. Jack makes a 'W' gesture with his fingers, a street gesture (largely associated with the 'Valley Girl' stereotype of the 1980s) used to signify 'Whatever!'

Cleaver refers to the disaster at Chernobyl, a city in northern Ukraine (within the former Soviet Union) and site of a disastrous nuclear power plant accident on 26 April 1986.

LINKING THEMES: This episode is a sequel to 'Aliens of London'/'World War Three', in that it deals with the fate of the last Slitheen on Earth and allows Rose to confront the issues between herself and Mickey that she left hanging at the conclusion of that two-parter. Scenes from those episodes are shown at the start, captioned simply 'Previously'.

The rift that threatens Cardiff is the one that was sealed in 'The Unquiet Dead'. Rose mentions the Gelth and Gwyneth's sacrifice in 1869. The Doctor refers to his conversation with Rose in 'The End of the World' about the TARDIS granting its passengers the ability to translate alien languages; Mickey refers to the Doctor's big ears and looking in a mirror, which he did in 'Rose'.

The Doctor mentions the TARDIS's chameleon circuit (its cloaking device, designed to disguise itself within its surroundings) getting stuck in the shape of a police box in the 1960s ... a reference to the explanation given by the Doctor in the very first *Doctor Who* serial in 1963. He says he hasn't fixed it because he likes it this way, and nobody seems to notice the box when it arrives. The TARDIS has a 'heart' and is telepathic, both facts mentioned before in the series. The opening scene after the main credits is of a train pulling into the train station, very reminiscent of 'Black Orchid' (1982). The term 'tribophysics' was first used in 'Pyramids of Mars' (1975). Idris asks his visitor, 'Doctor who?', which is an obvious reference to the series's title.

The reference to the planet Justicia ties in to the BBC Books novel *The Monsters Inside* (2005).

ALTERED STATES: Mali Harries's character was credited as Cathy 'Salt' in the pre-airing publicity, while Aled Pedrick was credited with the mis-spelled surname 'Pedick'.

SCENE MISSING: The title 'Lord Mayor' is an honorific, granted by the Queen, so how can Margaret Blaine – an MI5 officer or liaison who's almost certainly been pegged as a traitor (at the very least) by a sitting MP (Harriet Jones, 'World War Three') – have been elected to that office without any scandal breaking? Surely, Harriet Jones would have briefed the authorities as to the circumstances surrounding the death of the Prime Minister and several Cabinet members, including naming names as to who had been behind it?

How is Margaret able to get permission as Mayor to demolish Cardiff Castle in order to build a power plant? A 2000-year-old landmark would certainly be protected, and it would take far longer to go through planning and design procedures than six months. (See 'Behind the Scenes', below.)

Why did Margaret not teleport directly to her ship after ending up on the Isle of Dogs? Why do none of the attendees of the gathering in her office react to the title of the project? (Would *anyone* commission a project named 'Bad Wolf'?) It also seems she's not a popular mayor; when all hell breaks loose, no-one seems to show any concern for her safety.

Other questions: Why does the man in the café not react when the Doctor rips the newspaper from his hands? Why is Mickey surprised that police boxes are real? (He'd been researching the Doctor for at least a year; surely he would have come across a police box being linked to the Doctor in his investigations?)

BEHIND THE SCENES: This episode was intended by the production team to be a spotlight for the city of Cardiff, so all the exteriors were recorded there, mostly in the Plas Roald Dahl on Cardiff Bay outside the Wales Millennium Centre and the shopping district there, including the Bistro 10 (for the Doctor's and Margaret's dinner), the Bosphorus restaurant (the lunch scene) and the Terra Nova bar. The Glamorgan building at Cardiff University doubled as City Hall. On the Wales Millennium Centre are written the Welsh words 'Creu Gwir Fel Gwydr O Ffwrnais' as well as the English translation, 'In These Stones Horizons Sing'; the words are from a poem by Cardiff-born poet/sailor Gwyneth Lewis.

The image from the front of the *Western Mail* seen in this episode can be viewed on the official *Doctor Who* website. The text of the article 'New Mayor, new Cardiff' notes that the reason why plans to demolish Cardiff Castle are so easily obtained is that it is 'a symbol of

English oppression'. In addition, it indicates that protestors against the Blaidd Drwg project were also casualties, when a train carrying them was derailed by an aggressive sheep. The article mentions a newly established 'Independent Republic of Cornwall'.

Davies has admitted that at one point he considered using this episode's slot for a story about the volcanic destruction of Pompeii.

OFF THE SCREEN: William Thomas played Martin in the *Doctor Who* story 'Remembrance of the Daleks' (1988) and is here the first guest actor from the original series to play a role in the new. He has also played William James in *Belonging* (1999) and has been seen in *Catfish in Black Bean Sauce* (1999), *We Are Seven* (1989) and *Antony and Cleopatra* (1974). Mali Harries was seen in *Brief Encounters* (2005) and *The Inspector Lynley Mysteries: A Suitable Vengeance* (2003) and featured in several episodes of *Foyle's War* (2002-2003), as well as in the Radio 4 play *Running Away With The Hairdresser* (2005). Aled Pedrick is a young stage actor and musician and winner of Wales's Bryn Terfel Urdd Gobaith Cymru music scholarship in 2004.

TECHNICAL GOOFS: On the sign in the Mayor's office, Blaidd Drwg isn't translated into English while the rest of the sign is. (Yes, it's deliberate ... but still doesn't make much sense!) The Doctor removes Margaret's wrist band at one point but they still carry on holding hands. The digitally created cracks in the pavement don't displace anything; they're also not visible on street-level shots, whereas they are when shown from above, and Rose doesn't dodge any of them. The police car at the end should have the logo 'Heddlu' on it and the ambulance should have 'Ambwlance', both Welsh, but they don't.

CONTROVERSIES: Former BBC Director General Greg Dyke said on 25 June 2005 that using Cardiff as a setting was a 'flaw' and accused the BBC of trying to produce the series for peanuts. 'As a lifelong *Doctor Who* viewer, I don't believe the series was without flaws. Given that the Doctor is a time traveller, able to go anywhere at any time, he did end up on Earth a disappointing number of times during the thirteen episodes and, even worse, he kept turning up in Cardiff. I haven't got anything against the capital of Wales, but if I could land anywhere in the universe at any time, would I really go to Cardiff more than once?' Of course, the series is *made* in Wales!

INTERNAL CONSISTENCY: A setting approximately six months after 'World War Three' would place this story in late September or early October 2006. Mr Cleaver is murdered in the pre-credits sequence, but this is referred to by Cathy as having happened 'recently', probably no more than a few days before the main action of the story. There are very few clues to place exact times for this story, but it appears that Mickey arrives in Cardiff just before lunchtime. After he meets up with the TARDIS crew, they have a late lunch, while Margaret meets with Cathy in the ladies's room. It is tea time (late afternoon) when the Doctor calls on the Mayor. The story then skips to evening – if we assume this story is set in early autumn then sunset would be around 6.30 pm. This means the later events of the episode could have started any time after this. There seem to be a few slight jumps in time, but again the episode plays out pretty much in real time. The rift is closed some thirty to forty-five minutes later and the TARDIS is off to Raxacoricofallapatorius.

THEME ANALYSES

As Doctor Who For A Modern Audience: Not counting two-part adventures, 'Boom Town' is this series's first sequel, picking up on an escaped Slitheen six months after the rest of her family went boom in Downing Street. By taking advantage of the Cardiff rift created in 'The Unquiet Dead' and reviving the Rose/Mickey storyline, this episode is also entwined tightly with the overall internal series continuity already established. Rose's relationship with Mickey has been rather ambiguous since she left him to travel, but this episode highlights character growth, showing how both have developed and making them quite different from the people they were before, with doubt, anger and jealousy creeping in on both sides. Davies brings out his themes more overtly through the Doctor's and Margaret's dinnertime discussion of her situation, continuing the recurring ideas of drawing a fine line between the Doctor and the monster he fights and examining the consequences of his actions. This also marks the first on-screen acknowledgement by the Doctor of the Bad Wolf meme that has run covertly throughout the series, showing that there is more going on with these stories than it initially appears. While this isn't an out-and-out 'arc', ongoing storylines and concepts have become a major part of modern television drama, as they reward attentive long-term viewers with an additional bonus; and when done as subtly as Bad Wolf, shown here as the name of the proposed nuclear power plant, they are not intrusive or off-putting to the mainstream audience.

As Television Drama: When the Doctor, Rose, Jack and Mickey strode in line up the steps of the council building in this story, ready to confront Margaret, I couldn't help but be reminded of one of the features of the TV series *Spooks*, and, indeed, of *Buffy the Vampire Slayer*. It was that part of those shows' title sequences where you see the main group of leads striding purposefully in line down some gloomily-lit corridor, ready to go into action or confront the enemy. Of course, this similarity might have been purely accidental, but some of the other iconography of the episode was not – one of Davies's stated intentions here was to create a piece of drama that showed Cardiff off and made it look beautiful in the same way that ITV's hugely popular comedy-drama series *Cold Feet* had done for Manchester. *Cold Feet* isn't the only series to have been set in that other city of course – BBC1's hairdressing saga *Cutting It* also takes place there, and just as 'The Doctor Dances' saw Richard Wilson in *Doctor Who* and then in the first episode of the new season of his regular series a few days later, so here Annette Badland returned in *Cutting It* a few days after 'Boom Town' was shown. In a way, it's a shame *Doctor Who* wasn't included in the 'The ONE for drama' trail the channel was running around this time, as of all the new *Doctor Who* episodes so far, 'Boom Town' feels the most similar to, and fits most comfortably with, the BBC's other contemporary output. Whether or not that's a good thing in a series that normally thrives on its difference from such output, however, is a different matter.

As A Piece of Writing: This is a hard one to discuss, writing-wise, because the major characters have been introduced before, and most of the pivotal scenes are based around conversations. Perhaps the single most important aspect of the episode is its handling of both light and dark elements, and its managing – for once – to go off on a very moralistic tangent. Margaret Blaine, alternately a figure of humour and of menace, is the perfect messenger for Davies's ethical script, and though I doubt they'll really be resolved this season, some very good points are made about the Doctor's ethics. Unfortunately, the sub-plot with Mickey and

Rose, also (more limitedly) about morals, is much weaker, and this leads naturally into an area of concern. Over the past few weeks, we've seen an increase in sexually-related dialogue. Morally and ethically, this is very modern, but it's questionable whether it's simply too much for what is ostensibly a family programme. The nadir comes in this episode, when Rose agrees with Mickey to get a hotel room and spend the night. While this is certainly a real-life situation, it seems very odd coming from the role model for girls in the audience, particularly without any consequences (as an American show would insist upon). Is it the right decision to include such material? I'm not sure, but it seems like something that should be more carefully considered for future episodes. As it stands, this kind of dialogue often comes off as unpleasantly glib, and almost always unnecessary.

The Doctor As A Mystery Figure: There's a moment in 'Boom Town' that, in its own quiet way, sums up one of the reasons behind the success of the 2005 revival of *Doctor Who*. It comes in the middle of an, essentially, quite lightweight and fluffy episode with plenty of laughs – the Russell T Davies version of 'Carnival of Monsters', if you like. The Doctor and his Slitheen nemesis, Margaret, are busy charming each other between barbed threats over dinner – something of a first for the Doctor. And then, completely out of left-field, Eccleston delivers a stunning, angry thirty seconds of raw emotion as he describes the ways in which killers can find a spark of humanity within them once in a while to enable them to live with themselves and their dreadful deeds. Margaret replies, noting that only a killer himself would know this. Then, she adds a gruesome description of the method of public execution on Raxacoricofallapatorius. Jack's right, you know ... there really *aren't* enough excuses to say that word more often.

Themes, Genres and Modes: *Doctor Who* tends to rely on action, and doesn't get much opportunity to come down to give us the simpler joy of watching two people pretending to be someone else and talking about the things that are important to their situation. That's the core of drama, and at its best 'Boom Town' gives us these moments, from the 'kitchen sink' relational pain as Mickey expresses his anguish and heartbreak, to the loftier discussions between one who kills in the name of profit and another who kills in the name of peace and justice. Both discussions give compelling insights into the (purposely or accidentally) darker parts of our shared human soul and yet they come in an episode of a science fiction series for adults and children alike. How nifty is that?

In Style and Structure: The first few moments of 'Boom Town' come across like a highlights package: there are some wonderful shots of Cardiff, the regular and recurring cast have some great moments, and there's the return of the Slitheen. Even Murray Gold gets into the act, with his score revisiting past pieces of incidental music. There's a neat red herring set up, leading the audience to think that the nuclear power station will be the threat, but this just serves as a entrance point to Margaret's real scheme. Most of the action that follows is designed to move the story and characters to the major sequence of the episode, the dinner between the Doctor and Margaret, and their discussion on morality. The narrative splits into two main stories: the Doctor and Margaret, and Rose and Mickey. These two narrative strands run in parallel, exploring the same two themes of consequences and second chances. In one strand the character of Margaret 'Blon Slitheen' Blaine is the focus, while in the other the focus is on the relationship between Mickey and Rose. By the conclusion of 'Boom Town', one thread comes to a relatively positive conclusion, the other comes to an abrupt and negative end. What starts off looking like a relatively 'light' episode develops into an intriguing character and relationship study that provides no simple answers.

As Doctor Who Continuity: Someone's been doing their homework! It's nice to see some major continuity links between this season's stories (the return of the rift from 'The Unquiet Dead'), and it is also pleasing to have an indication of the passing of time for the TARDIS travellers – Rose tells Mickey of the alien planets she has been to off-screen. With this entire season set on or around Earth, it's still a great shame that we have been denied alien landscapes (something to be rectified in Series Two?). Some fans have criticised the notion of the TARDIS needing to refuel, but this is not at all at odds with the series' past: one only needs to consider 'Time-Flight' (1982) and 'Vengeance on Varos' (1985) to see that external sources can be used to power a TARDIS. (And besides, now that Gallifrey is gone, the TARDIS can no longer be linked to the Eye of Harmony.) The TARDIS energy source housed under the console is a concept introduced way back in 'Inside the Spaceship' (1964). I'd go so far as to say that 'Boom Town' has the highest quotient of continuity links so far this season. Now, I can't go without a mention of Bad Wolf. The tension and music builds up to a great moment in which the Doctor finally acknowledges Bad Wolf and senses that something is wrong – but then he shrugs it off with a curt dismissal. Come on! That had better not be all we're getting!

From A Special Effects Viewpoint: A member of the Slitheen family once again graces our screens with its sickly yellow/green, fleshy body and odd-looking baby face, but here, a bit more time is spent with its complicated CGI and animatronic facial features, giving us a lovely little scene where slowly shuttered eyes, delicately manipulated mouth servos and a couple of nicely performed head and neck moves convey sadness and loss. The biggest 'stars' of this particular show, though, are (once again) the visual effects provided by The Mill. The earthquake-generated fissures appearing in the concrete and the swirling rift above the TARDIS are both nice touches. Apart from that, there's really nothing new in this particular story, unless you count the plastic Raxacoricofallapatorian egg (complete with rubbery dreadlocks) that gets tossed about at the end of the story.

PANEL REVIEWS

'Boom Town' is the closest I ever want to see *Doctor Who* come to being like *Buffy The Vampire Slayer*. I spent years wincing at Buffy and her mates talking to each other with breezy, self-referential smugness, and the first five minutes of 'Boom Town' nearly had me in the foetal position in fear that Joss Whedon had taken over Russell Davies's brain. But then we had the sublime scene between the Doctor and the Mayor's assistant ('She's climbing out the window, isn't she?') and if everything wasn't forgiven, then an active truce was declared. I'm sure we also have Mr Whedon to thank for an episode where all that really happens is that the characters talk to each other about the consequences of their actions, but I don't mind that because the drama between Rose and Mickey and the Doctor and Margaret was so compelling. Rose and Mickey, because it was so gut wrenching to see the consequences of Rose's cavalier attitude on Mickey (Noel Clarke is superb); the Doctor and Margaret because it starts out funny and then becomes deeply pointed ('That's how you live with yourself. That's how you slaughter millions, because once in a while, on a whim, if the wind is in the right direction, you happen to be kind'). Overall, 'Boom Town' seems like the sparsely-populated, cheaply-made episode that usually comes before the big-budget blow-out of a season finale that it is. And yet there are moments like the one where Margaret, stripped out of her skin suit and fully revealed as a Slitheen, sits on a toilet and wistfully mourns the family she's lost, and you realise that there's something special even in this. – *Graeme Burk*

'Boom Town' stands out as something rather different from the rest of the series. It's a slow-paced character story with no real plot, shown by the quick and casual dismissal of the Blaidd Drwg project in favour of the dual examination of the Doctor's lifestyle and of how far apart Rose and Mickey have become. The moral issues the Doctor's dinner date with Margaret raises are probably the most interesting part of the episode as, much as in 'Dalek', it asks us to question his role and lifestyle whilst asking if monsters can change their nature. The disappointing *deus ex machina* ending provides a too convenient solution, which is typical of an episode that is surprisingly uneven. Another aspect that proves frustrating is the revelation that Rose has already visited alien worlds. This should have been an important moment for her – and one that the audience deserved to witness – in the same way as her first trips into the past and future were, and the experience is given up cheaply in an aside. The biggest victim of the script's emphasis is Jack, who feels superfluous here, something not helped by the smugness festering in both the writing and performance of the character. It also feels wrong that a companion who has only just joined should seem so *au fait* with the Doctor's time ship. There are some good elements here, but somehow it feels as if it doesn't add up to much in the end. – *Simon Catlow*

I'm finding it hard to hit upon good points in 'Boom Town'. The regulars are all up to par, and Annette Badland makes a pleasant and amusing return, but the episode just does nothing for me. It seems that Davies wanted the Doctor to think about the consequences his actions have. However, the only real trouble in the episode is caused by the Doctor and his companions, as they forgot to check for booby traps on Margaret's pan-dimensional surfboard. In the aftermath, the Doctor doesn't even leave the TARDIS to see how many people have been injured or killed by his ship opening the rift. And, speaking of the TARDIS, what is this light coming from the console? 'The heart of the TARDIS' the Doctor calls it, and it immediately stops the rift and fixes things up. If it could do that all along, why did it wait so long? And then there's Mickey's and Rose's interaction in the story. Rose has chosen to leave him, not once, but twice – she's not in love with Mickey – so why does she want to see him here? That bit makes no sense and just makes the whole episode feel like a waste of time. – *Robert Franks*

For a story that boasts a lot of humour, but never builds to much of a dramatic crescendo, 'Boom Town' works surprisingly well. The episode is truly a character piece, showing off Davies's very best skills as a writer, and with such great lines and strong performances it's okay, just this once, that nothing much actually *happens*. Davies finally manages to satisfy the story structure he's been using all season – starting off light and becoming darker as the story progresses – partly because the regular cast (even Noel Clarke!) finally seem completely comfortable, and partly because he doesn't have to introduce an entirely new villain. Although an appearance by the Master or Gwyneth, as was rumoured, might have been more exciting, the re-appearance of the Slitheen is completely justified; in fact, it's the only villain that logically satisfies the needs of the story. Joe Ahearne manages to get more out of two cursory transformation scenes here than all the earlier ones combined, and while I still don't want them back for season two, I didn't mind a few more minutes with the Raxacoricofallapatorians as much as I thought I would. While this episode isn't a full-blown classic – if nothing else, the 'heart of the TARDIS' solution seems to come entirely out of left field – I have the feeling it could turn into a 'comfort food' episode, one that becomes popular among fans because of the laidback feel and great chemistry among the regulars. I mean, hey – has Billie Piper *ever* been more adorable? – *Sarah Hadley*

'Boom Town' very much feels like the calm before the storm – even without having yet seen the final two episodes of the season, I had the distinct impression that this was a bit of a breather before all hell gets let loose next week. As such, it works well as a nice change of pace, with Davies crafting what is probably his best episode since way back with 'The End of the World'. The confrontations with Margaret are very nicely done, even if her plans do seem to be a lot of nonsense designed just to set up said confrontations in the script. Badland's character is far more interesting here than in 'Aliens of London' and 'World War Three', particularly in the well-executed moment when she doesn't, erm, execute the local journalist. Again, as with 'Father's Day', there's an issue as to how enthralling some of the younger audience will have found this one, but overall another enjoyable episode with some good performances – it's just a shame that, after such a promising debut story, Jack was so thoroughly sidelined this week, a casualty of having two companions in a forty-five minute episode, I suppose, particularly with Mickey to fit in as well. – *Paul Hayes*

Russell T Davies has written a very interesting episode here that begins in a rather light mood, and concludes on a serious note. Annette Badland is superb as Margaret Blaine, with the script exploring the nature of her character. The centrepiece is the dinner scene between Margaret and the Doctor, with the Doctor's morality explored. Eccleston gives an intense performance, especially in this scene. Piper is superb as Rose, while Noel Clarke makes a welcome return as Mickey, with the story making good use of the character. Only John Barrowman seems under used, but Jack has a strong role in most of the scenes in which he appears, especially the early sequences in the TARDIS and at Cardiff Town Hall. The resolution of the story makes use of the TARDIS in a rather unexpected way, but one that ties in well with the issues explored in the script. A rather enjoyable episode despite the suggestions of its initial scenes. – *Cameron Mason*

Sandwiched between two major two-parters, 'Boom Town' is the calm before the storm of the final two episodes. But does anyone else get the impression that this was written in a hurry? At its heart, 'Boom Town' is trying to be a morality play with the Doctor's motives under question, but it is undermined by a number of significant holes in the plot. The real Margaret Blaine (an MI5 agent) is dead, and yet 'Slitheen' Blaine gets elected as Mayor of Cardiff with relative ease? Why was the extrapolator device hidden in the model of the power station? Was the rift a tacked-on afterthought because the story required at least *something* exciting to happen in the forty-five minutes? With the Doctor/Margaret and Rose/Mickey paired off for their respective narratives, poor old Jack in only his second story (on screen, at least) gets sidelined to the TARDIS. A total waste of character potential. And the Slitheen weren't exactly the most successful of the new monsters, so it is a surprise to see them back – but thank you Joe Ahearne for sparing us from gratuitous farting and repetitive forehead unzippings this time round! Still, Davies gives us some wonderfully silly comedy moments in the first half: the delightful exchanges between the Doctor and Jack; the 'high-five' routine; and best of all, our fantastic foursome playing at *The Professionals* when they go to the council building, the latter enhanced by some inspired direction. Despite best intentions, 'Boom Town' is really just filler material. – *Jon Preddle*

'Dinner in bondage. Works for me.' One of the more 'talky' episodes of the season, 'Boom Town' for the most part works due to its cunning juxtaposition of heavy moral and intellectual themes in contrast to the episode's also deliberately *New Avengers*-style action and pacing. Not that there's necessarily anything wrong with this, though quite what the show's growing under-10 fan base made of it all, I'm not sure. In fact, they probably didn't even notice, they'd have found plenty to enjoy elsewhere. Firstly, there's the terrific wisecracking trio of Eccleston, Barrowman and Piper – who are fast on their way to becoming *the* definitive TARDIS team. The less successful elements are few – for once Murray Gold's music is a shade clumsy and intrusive, whilst any attempt to display Cardiff as anything other than a carbuncle on the behind of humanity is, sadly, doomed to failure. Elsewhere, there are many other good things on display – great performances by Noel Clarke and Annette Badland; some neat old-school continuity for us anoraks (references to the chameleon circuit and the TARDIS being telepathic) and, in a story that concerns the pain of consequences and second chances, a really clever deflection – for one week, at least – of the 'Bad Wolf' conundrum. – *Keith Topping*

The Slitheen of Raxacoricofallapatorius have returned (apparently Mr Davies didn't get my memo), but this time (thanks solely to Annette Badland's superb performance as Margaret), we're shown that there's more to these creatures than just farting and belching. While there is a lot of humour in this particular episode, there are also a number of emotional moments, including a very sweet scene between Blon/Margaret and a young journalist, as well as a fair number of bits of dialogue with the Doctor. Unfortunately, though, there are a lot of messy plot points and unanswered questions surrounding all these clever moments. Why on Earth (literally) did Blon/Margaret have the architectural model-maker incorporate the cosmic surfboard extrapolator thingy into the model of the reactor? Why, after all this time, did the TARDIS open up, mesmerise and regress an occupant for no particular reason? And most importantly, why, after fleshing out the character of Blon/Margaret for most of the episode, is there a need to suddenly make her truly 'bad'. I, for one, was really looking forward to a little redemption on her part (and a little forgiveness on the part of the Doctor). – *Scott Alan Woodard*

EDITOR'S REVIEW: What an odd little episode. What starts out as a drama and slowly turns into a madcap caper metamorphoses again into a statement on the death penalty and personal responsibility, and a character study of Rose's allegiance to the Doctor and her feelings for Mickey. If 'Father's Day' was atypical of *Doctor Who* in its style of storytelling, 'Boom Town' is atypical in a different way: it's a tightly-scripted breather after the high adventure of the 1940s and before the final two-parter that for once shows that evil isn't always what it's cracked up to be.

Kudos for much of this episode's success must go to Annette Badland. I confess I was not a huge fan of her character in her previous two-parter; here, we suddenly discover that a being that we thought was consumed with profit and unfettered by a conscience and a sense of humour (other than a taste for the morbid) suddenly has both in spades, whether she's reduced to guilt after considering killing Cathy or laughing alongside the Doctor at the hilarity of her predicament after she escaped death the last time. Badland gives this episode a very special touch, and it's full of moments where the actress has a chance to shine: the fiendish smile on her face as she remarks on her 'dinner in bondage' as if she has a cunning plan to seduce the Doctor, or the hilarity of her 'date' with the Time Lord as she attempts not once, but three times, to kill him. The rapport between Badland and Eccleston is wonderful on camera, as is the familiarity that exists by now between Piper and Clarke as two people who obviously enjoy being together but are separated by miles of uncertainty and personal choices.

The quality of the acting from the regular cast – and I include Barrowman and Clarke in this now, for both are as much a part of the *Doctor Who* mythos as any companion or recurring character could be – matches the story. If I have any complaint, it is that Eccleston and Piper are given so much to do, and that so much of the story has such ramifications for Mickey, that Barrowman's Jack is reduced to staying inside the TARDIS for much of the action. Not that he's simply idling as events pass him by; he's obviously hard at work. But in the second half of the episode he doesn't fare as well as in the lovely team shots in the first half, especially in the sequence that starts with the four climbing the stairs of City Hall (with that wonderfully resonant score first heard in the opening moments of 'Rose' back for a reprise) and ends up with a madcap and slapstick chase through the halls.

Indeed, while 'Boom Town' remains a basic find-the-villain, capture-the-villain, torment-the-villain and resolve-the-plot affair, it's what it says, not just how it says it, that resonates the most. 'Boom Town' attempts to place the Doctor into combat with his conscience: what do you do when the only solution to a problem is to destroy the problem's creator? The Doctor is obviously a man firmly opposed to the death penalty; we've seen time and time again that he believes in the sanctity of life and the freedom to choose one's destiny. Yet here he is presented with a conundrum: does he take a life to save lives, in this case ending Margaret's existence by taking her home and thereby saving Cardiff, and the planet, from certain doom? The problem could of course be solved by his taking her off Earth and to somewhere else entirely, but the quandary is needed in dramatic terms as it is a dilemma that the Doctor will face on a much grander scale by the end of the season. (The 'heart of the TARDIS' is a big part of it here, again setting the stage for what will become the end of the season's *deus ex machina*.)

On paper, I imagine that 'Boom Town' largely looked like an experiment, and possibly even a disaster waiting to happen; it has large amounts of dialogue, not as much running up and down corridors or solving problems, and presents its drama in metaphors and supposition. With an excellent director at its helm, and in the capable hands of actors able to present the material so convincingly, 'Boom Town' achieves its success – it's not the epitome of the season, mind, but a thoughtful piece examining some of *Doctor Who*'s fundamental themes, and underscoring the qualifications and enlightened 21st Century sensibilities Davies brings to this series. And besides, the Doctor goes on a date with a Slitheen and it doesn't end up being silly; that in itself is an accomplishment. – *Shaun Lyon*

112: BAD WOLF

The Doctor awakens in a futuristic version of the *Big Brother* house, where being voted out means disintegration. Rose fights for her life on *The Weakest Link* while squaring off against a robotic hostess and almost certain death. Jack finds himself facing a makeover on *What Not To Wear*, but not just a change in fashion. Why have they been brought into these deadly games? And who is behind it all?

FIRST TRANSMISSION: UK – 11 June 2005. Canada – 21 June 2005. Australia – 6 August 2005. New Zealand – 27 September 2005.
DURATION: 42'47"
WRITER: Russell T Davies
DIRECTOR: Joe Ahearne
CREDITED CAST: Christopher Eccleston (Doctor Who), Billie Piper (Rose Tyler), John Barrowman (Captain Jack), Jo Joyner (Lynda), Jamie Bradley (Strood), Abi Eniola (Crosbie), Davina McCall (Voice of Davinadroid), Paterson Joseph (Rodrick), Jenna Russell (Floor Manager), Anne Robinson (Voice of Anne Droid), Trinny Woodall (Voice of Trine-E), Susannah Constantine (Voice of Zu-Zana), Jo Stone Fewings (Male Programmer), Nisha Nayar (Female Programmer), Dominic Burgess (Agorax), Karren Winchester (Fitch), Kate Loustau (Colleen), Sebastian Armesto (Broff), Martha Cope (Controller), Sam Callis (Security Guard), Alan Ruscoe (Android), Paul Kasey (Android), Barnaby Edwards (Dalek Operator), Nicholas Pegg (Dalek Operator), David Hankinson (Dalek Operator), Nicholas Briggs (Dalek Voice)

Daleks originally created by Terry Nation.

The Weakest Link format created by Fintan Coyle and Cathy Dunning.

Big Brother is an original format by Endemol Netherlands BV, licensed by Endemol International BV.

Big Brother logo by kind permission of Channel Four.

WHERE AND WHEN: The Game Station, formerly Satellite 5, orbiting Earth, circa 200,100 (a hundred years after the events of 'The Long Game').

THE STORY UNFOLDS: In the century that has passed since he left it ('The Long Game'), the Fourth Great and Bountiful Human Empire has vanished and Satellite 5 (renamed the Game Station) has been taken over by the Bad Wolf Corporation. After the Doctor's interference, the news channels stopped broadcasting overnight, the government and economy collapsed, and Earth was led into 100 years of hell. The Game Station (and presumably its other counterparts) now broadcasts ten thousand channels and runs over a hundred different games with captive contestants chosen at random from Earth's population, whether they agree or not.

The Bad Wolf Corporation is being manipulated by the Daleks; they waited in dark space, guiding humanity for many years while they rebuilt themselves following the Time War. The energy blasts used to kill contestants in the games are actually transmat beams that teleport humans to the Dalek fleet without raising suspicion. Besides the games, the Game Station also broadcasts another signal that ensures the Dalek fleet, carrying nearly half a million Daleks, remains concealed, just outside the Solar System.

The Doctor is trapped in a futuristic version of the house from *Big Brother*, complete with a television screen, cameras and a diary room with a big red chair; the series is broadcast on Channel 44,000. Lynda says that the house has a deadlock seal, which every house has had since *Big Brother 504* when all the contestants walked out. The house has exoglass (first mentioned in 'The End of the World'), which would take a nuclear bomb to get through. Eviction leads to disintegration and players have ten seconds to leave.

Rose arrives via transmat on the set of *The Weakest Link* shortly before broadcast. Rodrick says that the word of the Anne Droid (modelled after the original presenter of the show, Anne Robinson) is law. Rose's name is already on her contestant podium. Contestants who are voted out are apparently disintegrated.

Jack is sent to a room where the makeover robots Trine-E and Zu-Zana (based on Trinny and Susannah from the original *What Not To Wear* show) intend to give him a new image. After his clothes are disintegrated by a defabricator, he is given new clothing (including a leather jacket with a 'pirate/buccaneer' quality and a tennis outfit), and finally, preparations are made for a facial (and possibly even head-replacing) makeover using chainsaws and drills.

After leaving Cardiff ('Boom Town') the TARDIS went to Raxacoricofallapatorius to return Margaret's egg, then to Kyoto, Japan in 1336; the Doctor, Rose and Jack had just escaped from there when they were snatched by transmat beams that were fifteen million times more powerful than normal and were thus able to penetrate the TARDIS.

Earth appears grey and dusty from orbit. The Great Atlantic Smog Storm has been going for twenty years, causing the air to be unbreathable outside. A President Schwarzenegger is mentioned, possibly Arnold Schwarzenegger who was elected Governor of California in 2003 (although at present only naturally born citizens are eligible for the Presidency of the United States, so perhaps this refers to a descendant of his). Lynda says no-one has a garden anymore and that no-one has called the Game Station 'Satellite 5' in a hundred years. Those who do not pay their TV licence are executed. Archive Six apparently contains all transmat records in and out of the station, and is currently out of bounds to employees; in fact, it contains the TARDIS.

Earlier contestants in the current *Big Brother* house, judging by the names on the finger-paintings on the wall, included Jenny, Cindy, Gary, Monaj and Pavitch, as well as Linda ('with an i') who was forcibly evicted because she damaged a camera. (The official *Doctor Who* website also listed other names: Darian, Skip and Leigh.)

Answers to questions in the *Weakest Link* game include the following: The month of Pandoff (not Clavadoe) comes after Hoob in the Pan Traffic Calendar. 'Default' is the social security payment option given to Martian drones. The Great Cobalt Pyramid is built on the remains of the Torchwood Institute. The Grexnik is married to Lord Drayvole in the holovid series *Jupiter Rising*. The Grand Central Ravine is named after the 'ancient' British city of Sheffield. The Face of Boe is the oldest inhabitant of the Isop Galaxy. The President of the Red Velvets was Hoshbin Frane. The food Gaffabeque originated on the planet Lucifer. A paab (not a goffle) is the distance between the Emperor Jate's nose and his fingertip. Stella Pok Baint is famous for hats. The Icelandic city Pola Ventura hosted Murder Spree Twenty.

THE DOCTOR: He has amnesia when he first arrives in the *Big Brother* house, and only later remembers what happened to him and his friends. He destroys the house camera to be forcibly evicted but isn't disintegrated, proving that whoever brought him here wants him alive. Lynda says he looks good for someone who was here a hundred years earlier. ('I moisturise,' he replies). He likes Lynda and says he wouldn't mind if she joined the TARDIS crew. After he thinks Rose has been killed, he is incarcerated (along with Jack and Lynda), photographed, and sentenced to the lunar penal colony to be held without trial or appeal. He carries a gun to Floor 500, but never intends to use it.

ROSE TYLER: She doesn't understand her predicament at first, laughing at the other contestants. Anne Droid tells her she's obviously unemployed but still has enough money to buy peroxide (for her hair). Rodrick thinks she's stupid (for not knowing the Princess Vosaheen's surname in the game). The Anne Droid 'disintegrates' her after she loses the final round of the game to Rodrick.

CHARACTER BUILDING: *Jack Harkness* – He has a classic lantern jaw, which his robot hosts say is 'so last year', and carries an 'Oklahoma farmboy' image. He got his denim at a little store in Cardiff called Top Shop. After the defabricator removes his clothes, he boasts that the show's viewing figures 'just went up'. He's hidden a compact laser deluxe in a place he doesn't want to talk about. He turns the defabricator into a weapon. He becomes violent after he thinks Rose is killed, and flirts with both Davitch and Lynda.

Lynda Moss – A contestant in the House, Lynda ('with a y, not an i') wonders if the outside world likes her; the Doctor tells her she's sweet. When she first arrived in the house, she was sick for days because of the transmat. The Doctor asks her to come with him, which she does.

The Controller – Operator of the Game Station, a blind human woman connected to an electro-sensory web – into which she was installed when she was five years old. She lets the Doctor wander without stopping him – in fact, she is the one who brought him to the Game Station. Her transmissions are blocked to the Daleks during solar flares, and she hid him and his friends in the games, which the Daleks don't monitor, so that she could warn him of the impending Dalek invasion while the flares were active. The Daleks discover her treachery and she is brought to their ship to be killed.

The Programmers – Administrators of the games on the Game Station. They're baffled by the appearance of the TARDIS crew, as if the game is running itself, and have heard rumours about this station for years. The male programmer, Davitch Pavale, fancies his female colleague. He also tells the Doctor that he's kept a record of all the unauthorised transmats and encrypted signals that have been occurring for years.

Strood and Crosbie – Contestants in the *Big Brother* house in which the Doctor is trapped. Strood has been there all nine weeks. Crosbie is the eighth contestant to be evicted by the viewers.

Weakest Link Contestants – Rose's co-contestants include Finch (an older woman), Broff (a teenaged boy), Colleen (a dark-haired woman), Agorax (a young man), and Rodrick, who is playing to win by keeping Rose around as long as possible.

BAD WOLF: The Bad Wolf Corporation runs the Game Station. Rose reacts, remembering this phrase in her recent past; brief clips are seen of Bad Wolf occurrences from 'The Unquiet Dead', 'Dalek', 'Boom Town', 'Aliens of London' and 'The Long Game'.

FANTASTIC!: No instances in this episode.

BODY COUNT: Finch, Colleen and Agorax are apparently disintegrated during the *Weakest Link* game, as is Broff when he tries to flee in terror, and Crosbie is evicted from the

Big Brother house. Although it is later revealed that all of them were merely transmatted to the Dalek fleet, it is unlikely they survived there for long. The Controller is killed on the Dalek ship. Rose is also believed dead by the Doctor and Jack.

THE DOCTOR'S MAGICAL SONIC SCREWDRIVER: The Doctor tries to use it to open the house doorway (unsuccessfully), to examine various areas of the house, to damage the camera, and finally to escape from the eviction hallway. The security officer tries to find out what it is from the Doctor, who refuses to tell him.

REALITY BITES: Trappings from the real-life television series are seen in this episode. The *Big Brother* house to which the Doctor is brought features the series's theme music and its trademark eye logo (redesigned and enhanced by the *Big Brother* team themselves), while the set designs from *The Weakest Link* matches the televised version. Also heard is Anne Robinson's infamous catchphrase, 'You are the weakest link ... goodbye!') Robot versions of Robinson, Trinny Woodall and Susannah Constantine are used as their counterparts in the games, along with a heard-but-not-seen counterpart of Davina McCall from *Big Brother*.

The Game Station's games are mostly versions of past and current British game and reality series: ten floors (sixty concurrent versions) of *Big Brother*, plus *Call My Bluff* (with real guns), *Countdown* (thirty seconds to stop a bomb from exploding), *Ground Force* (losers are turned into compost), *Wipe Out* (which 'speaks for itself'), *Stars In Their Eyes* (those who don't sing are blinded). There's also one mentioned by the Doctor that doesn't exist in the 'real' world: *Bear With Me* (three people have to live with a bear).

The reference to 'Channel 44,000' is perhaps a reference to Channel 4, whereas the entire episode parodies the genre of reality television. The *Weakest Link* segment refers to popular novelist Jackie Collins and her book 'Lucky'.

The official BBC *Doctor Who* website said that Lynda Moss was a 30-year-old account technician from New Kingswood; Strood is 28, from Torchwood, and works in a telephone salon; and Crosbie is a 35-year-old tram chef from Liverpool Sponge.

Interestingly, 'Torchwood,' mentioned in the *Weakest Link* game, is an anagram for *Doctor Who* ... coincidence?

LINKING THEMES: As noted in the flashbacks in the opening moments, this episode follows on from the events of 'The Long Game'. The Doctor later describes what is happening on the station as a 'long game', with the Jagrafess being installed by the true architects, the Daleks.

Jack knows that the Doctor has two hearts, which fact he uses to locate him on the station. There is a comment about a 'lunar penal colony', which could be the one seen in 'Frontier in Space' (1973) (but since the Earth now has five moons, it may refer to something different).

The matter transportation procedure used here is called a transmat, which was first developed on Earth around the 21st Century ('The Seeds of Death', 1969). The Face of Boe, subject of one of the questions in Rose's game, was seen in 'The End of the World' and briefly in 'The Long Game'; in this episode he is stated to be from the Isop Galaxy, where the planet Vortis is located as noted in 'The Web Planet' (1965). The Daleks' use of a human controller has been seen before, notably in 'Remembrance of the Daleks' (1988) where they used a young girl. A planet called Lucifer was the setting of *Lucifer Rising* by Jim Mortimore, a novel in Virgin's *Doctor Who* New Adventures range.

EPISODE 112

SCENE MISSING: Why do human beings nearly two hundred thousand years in the future recreate game shows from the 20th Century? (Surely this is even more unbelievable than the use of styrofoam takeaway containers in 'The Long Game'?) Lynda also speaks of the games as if the way they're played (including the deaths) is unusual; does she have knowledge of their 20th Century counterparts?

Why do the Daleks not simply kill Rose when the Doctor threatens to rescue her? Also, why is Rose transmatted to a command centre on the Dalek ship? It is inferred that the Daleks know that she is an associate of the Doctor before she is brought here, so why not transport her to a holding cell? (These questions are partly answered in 'The Parting of the Ways'.)

Why does the Doctor assume these are post-Time War Daleks instead of time travellers from prior to the War? (Did the Time War eradicate them from existence altogether? If so, is the Doctor unable to go back into a place in his own past that he fought them, like when he brings Rose to a point in *her* own past? And does this also apply for Gallifrey as well?)

How does Jack know so quickly that the areas other than the one he was in are running games? (*What Not To Wear* isn't a game show, after all.)

Other unanswered questions: Why does Jack keep his gun in an 'unusual' place (not to mention, how?) Does he expect to be fully undressed often (his previous 'naked' excursion mentioned in 'Boom Town' notwithstanding)? Where are the images of the Dalek fleet coming from (especially the image that pulls back to show the entire Dalek fleet)? Why does Lynda assume the Doctor knows who she is, considering there are sixty simultaneous *Big Brother* broadcasts going on? And why, if the contestants are being sent to the Daleks, are they *really* killed on some of the game shows like *Call My Bluff* and *Ground Force*? Or perhaps these deaths are also faked.

BEHIND THE SCENES: This episode was recorded entirely on the *Doctor Who* set in Newport, except for the interiors of the *Big Brother* house, which were recorded inside a flat in Canton, Cardiff.

The only cut to the first series requested by BBC executives was to this episode: John Barrowman's naked backside, after the defabricator had removed his clothing.

The trailer for this episode at the conclusion of 'Boom Town' completely gave away the ending, revealing the presence of the Daleks. Also, on its first broadcast, the BBC1 announcer mistakenly referred to the series as 'Doctor Woo'.

As early as 29 June 2004, the *Daily Star* had reported that the series would feature a *Big Brother*-style house, but had claimed that this episode would 'feature historic figures including Shakespeare, Henry VIII and Einstein – who are locked up together.' It's unclear as to whether this was an early draft of the storyline or if it was from Davies's original outline. (At one point it was also rumoured to be from 'Dalek', which was said to include a Dalek among the 'historic figures'). Rumours also persisted for a time that this story would feature the Master.

DULCET TONES: The recognisable theme music from *Big Brother*, and various stings from *The Weakest Link*, are used in their respective games.

OFF THE SCREEN: Jo Joyner starred as Beth in *No Angels* (2004) and has been seen in *North & South* (2004) and *Serious and Organised* (2003). Paterson Joseph played the Marquis de Carabas in Neil Gaiman's *Neverwhere* (1996), voiced the role of Nigel Townsend in the BBC Cult webcast adaptations of Amber Benson and Christopher Golden's *The Ghosts of*

Albion, and has been seen in recurring roles in *Casualty* (1997), *William and Mary* (2003) and *Green Wing* (2004). Jamie Bradley hosted the Canadian teen series *Street Cents* (1989-2005), played several roles in *Lexx* (1997, 2001) and appeared in *Perfect Strangers* (2001) and *Mrs Caldicot's Cabbage War* (2000). Nicholas Pegg has acted extensively in *Doctor Who* audios for Big Finish, as well as writing and directing the Colin Baker audio *The Spectre of Lanyon Moor*, and directing the audios *The Holy Terror*, *Bang-Bang-a-Boom!*, *Loups-Garoux* and *Shada*. He was also on-screen in the BBV direct-to-video drama *The Terror Game* (1994). Abi Eniola was in *Elidor* (2004) and *Extremely Dangerous* (1999). Jenna Russell played Deborah Gilder on *Born and Bred* (2002-) and has been seen in *Peak Practice* (2000), *Picking up the Pieces* (1998) and *On the Up* (1990); she also was the singer of the theme song for *Red Dwarf* (1988-1999). Jo Stone Fewings played Danny in *Mine All Mine* (2004) and was seen in *Best of Both Worlds* (2000), *Soldier Soldier* (1991) and *Medics* (1990). Nisha Nayar appeared in the original *Doctor Who* series as a Red Kang (but was uncredited) in the story 'Paradise Towers' (1987); she also appeared in *Rose and Maloney* (2004), *Sirens* (2002), *In America* (2002) and *Big Bad World* (1999). Martha Cope was in the film *Alfie* (2004) and on television in *Family Affairs* (2002), *Ultraviolet* (1998) and *The Bill* (1997). Sam Callis played the recurring role of Karl Radford on *The Bill* (2004) and appeared in *Kidulthood* (2005). Dominic Burgess was in *Batman Begins* (2005). Kate Loustau was in *Lara Croft Tomb Raider: The Cradle of Life* (2003), *The Dave Saint Show* (2000) and *Elizabeth* (1998). Sebastian Armesto was seen in *The Bill* (2005). David Hankinson was in *A Little Rain Must Fall* (1997).

Anne Robinson is the internationally recognised host of the game show *The Weakest Link*, both the original created in the UK for BBC Television (2000-) and the American version aired on the NBC network (2001-2003). She started as a journalist, working on the *Daily Mail*, *Sunday Times* and *Daily Mirror*, eventually becoming Assistant Editor of the *Daily Mirror* throughout the 1980s and early 1990s, the first woman to regularly edit a national newspaper. She also presented the BBC1 consumer affairs show *Watchdog* (1993-2001) and hosts the irregular televised quiz *Test the Nation*.

Davina McCall is the presenter of the UK version of the Dutch-originated game show *Big Brother* (2000-). She has also presented *Love on a Saturday Night* (2004), *Reborn in the USA* (2003), *Popstars: the Rivals* (2002), *The Vault* (2002), *Oblivious* (2001) and *Don't Try This At Home* (2001), all for ITV; *Streetmate* (1998) for Channel 4; and various programmes for MTV Networks. She also appeared in the series *Sam's Game* (2001).

Trinny Woodall and Susannah Constantine are the presenters of the BBC fashion series *What Not To Wear* (2001-), aired internationally on BBC-owned networks.

TECHNICAL GOOFS: The Doctor says that the Jagrafess was installed on the station a hundred years earlier, but it had already been there ninety-one years prior to 'The Long Game'. At one point, the *What Not To Wear* robots have exposed their carving equipment, but the next scene shows them reverted back to their normal arms. The Controller can walk correctly even though she apparently hasn't moved since she was five. The Dalek fleet has been masked from sonar ... but sonar cannot be used in space as sound cannot travel in a vacuum. Lynda says that the contestants in *Big Brother* 504 walked out but later says that she thinks she and the Doctor are the first to get outside their house. (Perhaps all of 504's contestants were eliminated?)

CONTROVERSIES: Use of the trappings of three familiar television shows – nearly two hundred thousand years in the future, natch – caused some consternation among viewers, as did the Doctor once again carrying a gun (even though he never intended to use it). Jack's continued flirtations were also the subject of some controversy (though his flirtation with the programmer is subtle; as the Doctor notes, for Jack, just saying 'Hello' is flirting). The placing of the trailer for the next week's episode again upset some, coming right at the start of the closing credits and containing significant 'spoilers'.

INTERNAL CONSISTENCY: Events occur pretty much at the same time for the Doctor, Rose and Jack. It takes approximately twenty to thirty minutes for the Doctor to break out of the *Big Brother* house, Jack to escape his make-over and Rose to complete a game of *The Weakest Link*. At one point the floor manager of that gameshow announces they have 'ten to solar flares', but she does not indicate ten what. At various times the Controller announces the same solar flares in Delta point 7, Delta point 1 and Delta point 03, but this does not seem to correspond to any known timeframe. The arrest of the Doctor, Jack and Lynda could have taken up anywhere from ten to twenty minutes, but not much time has passed as Rose has only just arrived on the Dalek ship. Overall this story takes place in little over an hour from when the travellers first arrive.

THEME ANALYSES

As Doctor Who For A Modern Audience: The two main aims of 'Bad Wolf' are to poke fun at the ubiquitous fad of reality television gameshows by mocking their cruelty and to set up an epic season finale. It's a very postmodern idea to feature the Doctor, Rose and Jack in satires of existing series such as *Big Brother* and *The Weakest Link*, which the viewers will either have seen or at least be familiar with. This is only emphasised further by the incorporation of the voices of the real-life presenters, music, logos and similar sets. The structure of past *Doctor Who* series meant that there was a climax every four weeks or so as individual stories ended, but it's much more common now for series to build to a big event episode to conclude the series. 'Bad Wolf' begins that process by drawing upon the rich tapestry of backstory weaved into the episodes that went before it. Davies's creation of the Time War, the effects of which have underpinned the Doctor's evolving characterisation throughout the series, really pays off as the suspense of who is behind the malevolent plans for humanity builds brilliantly to the unmasking of the Daleks. There's no sense that this is just another encounter with them, as there sometimes was in the 'classic' series, only the feeling that these creatures are truly worthy of being the Doctor's greatest enemy. Thanks to the impressive use of CGI, this is matched onscreen as we witness the might and massive scale of the Dalek horde, waiting to pounce upon the unsuspecting Earth.

As Television Drama: We're back in Nigel Kneale territory again here, with 'Bad Wolf' covering much of the same ground as Kneale's *The Year of the Sex Olympics*, an acclaimed 1968 entry into BBC2's *Theatre 625* plays anthology strand. However, the treatments of the reality-television obsessed future are very different – whereas Kneale's piece was a biting satire on what he feared television might become in an age where 'Big Brother' was a character in a George Orwell novel, Davies is writing in an age wherein much of what Kneale predicted has already come to pass, and his treatment of the programmes concerned is more affectionate mocking than barbed allegory. Given Davies's known obsession with television in all its forms, it's perhaps not surprising that he treats the reality genre this way, and although it's hard not to argue that Kneale's approach was the more effective of the two, Davies's still works in the context of *Doctor Who*. Elsewhere, there's another familiar face popping up from one of Davies's previous productions, as Jo Stone-Fewings basically plays his part in exactly the same way he played Danny, the 'Englishman abroad' in Swansea, in *Mine All Mine*. This isn't a criticism, more of an observation – doubtless a similar type of performance was required and Davies called upon somebody he knew could deliver that type of characterisation very well.

As A Piece of Writing: It's interesting to realise that, more or less, last week's trailer told us this entire episode in a nutshell – and yet, 'Bad Wolf' still manages to be incredibly entertaining. Davies has abandoned his earlier, lighter authorial touch for something still quite funny, but darker by leaps and bounds, as befits the sense of impending doom. He's kept his focus on characters, but the plot's growing importance carries the episode all the way from its beginning 'in media res' to the cliff-hanger we've all waited for, cleverly covering the fact that many of the characters – in fact, nearly all of them besides the Doctor and Jack – are there just as gears to keep the story going. It's a smart technique. Rose takes probably the least active role she's had in the series to date, but her importance to the others keeps her very much in mind; characters like Rodrick, the Controller, and even Lynda don't really have unique personalities or identities, but their brief roles in the drama as catalysts make them seem more important than they are. All of this serves to deepen the characters of the Doctor and of Jack, to contrast them with each other, and to allow us to feel their anxiety. It seems unlikely that any viewer of this episode could walk away without their adrenaline pumping and their excitement for next week increased. It's the perfect way to write the first half of a season finale – always, always leave the audience wanting more.

The Doctor As A Mystery Figure: Mystery comes in various shapes and sizes but here, for once, the Doctor is as much in the dark as everyone else as to why he's ended up in the middle of another outrageous situation. Partly, it's all his fault. (This is, after all, a world – at least in part – owing its existence to the Doctor's actions in 'The Long Game'.) And, partly, it's the result of a sly Dalek master plan. (Stealth-guiding humanity into becoming a race of brain-dead sheep who do nothing but watch television.) The idea of reality television voyeurism as a replacement for reality itself isn't new in drama, and therein lies the episode's main flaw. The mean-spirited nature of much reality TV means that the genre can't really stand up to much parodying without becoming a little too like the real thing. And, ironically, *Doctor Who*'s very success *in competition with* the kind of reality shows that ITV have been putting up against it makes some of this episode seem a little arch. A bit like kicking a dog when it's down. We fought that war, already. And we won. Of course, when the script was written, nobody could have predicted that.

Themes, Genres and Modes: We have television series like *The X-Files* to thank for what is now known as 'the MythArc episode'. These are episodes of an ongoing series that bring to the forefront the ongoing mythos that 'arcs' throughout a season (and indeed the series). *Doctor Who* doesn't have an elaborate government conspiracy or a Cigarette Smoking Man or even a Deep Throat, but this episode marks the first time the series has presented a MythArc episode, as Bad Wolf and the Time War – the backstory and mythology to which have been in the background all season – finally come front and centre. Naturally, the episode doesn't actually resolve any of it: not only is there a season finale next week to do that, but the

MythArc episode is often not about *resolving* any ongoing mysteries, so much as throwing more nuances of them in viewers' faces. Which, to its credit, 'Bad Wolf' does marvellously.

In Style and Structure: Davies has really taken to the opportunities presented by 'Bad Wolf' in subverting well known reality TV shows with a lethal twist; if you lose the game, you lose your life. This is set up by presenting the shows as they are known, then gradually introducing the new elements. This unfolds the same way for each show, so that the audience discovers the nature of the show as the TARDIS crew do. What helps all this is that not only have the respective styles of the featured shows been used, but also the presenters have contributed by voicing their futuristic counterparts. There are a number of layers of control within the episode: the games are run by programmers who are led by the Controller who in turn is a pawn of the Daleks. The TARDIS crew learn various pieces of information about where they are and Earth's recent history. These two elements run in parallel, allowing the episode to develop fairly evenly; only when it is required for dramatic purposes is a large revelation unveiled in one element without the equivalent taking place for the other shortly afterwards. Bad Wolf raises its head in a big way after the double bluff in 'Boom Town', with Rose's reflection on when she's seen or heard references to the term appearing as a piece of foreshadowing for the next episode.

As Doctor Who Continuity: 'Bad Wolf' is a sequel to 'The Long Game'. Or is 'The Long Game' the prequel to 'Bad Wolf'? This connection between the two means that a re-evaluation of 'The Long Game' is due. The absurd *Weakest Link* questions immediately reminded me of a similar set up in Big Finish's *The One Doctor* in which the sixth Doctor was confronted with a number of equally outlandish game-show questions. One *Weakest Link* round offered what would have to be the most unlikely continuity references ever: the Face of Boe (in his/her/its third appearance this season) comes from the Isop Galaxy – which was visited by the first Doctor in 1965's 'The Web Planet'. (While I think of it, there was also a mention of venom grubs, from the same story, in 'Boom Town'.) If the Face of Boe is Davies's signature name (like Robert Holmes's Tellurians, and Eric Saward's speelsnapes) can we perhaps expect further appearances in the next series? And sticking with references to the 1960s, the design of the Dalek saucers evokes that of their ships in the *TV Century 21* comic strips, and adapted for the updated miniature effects on the DVD release of 'The Dalek Invasion of Earth' (1964). The Dalek control room also has the same 'heartbeat' sound effect as in numerous earlier Dalek stories. Nice touches.

From A Special Effects Viewpoint: Oh, there's some grand stuff here ... the oh-so-amusing Anne Droid, the two *What Not To Wear* robots, all the CGI stuff (the exteriors of Satellite 5/Game Station and the *massive* fleet of Dalek ships) and, lastly, the Daleks themselves. The robot costumes are beautifully fabricated and the performances by the artists inside them deserve a lot of praise. The fluid motions of Trine-E and Zu-Zana are worthy of note in that they really do come across as eerily robotic. Then there's the Dalek fleet, which looks positively menacing (and kudos to the production team for giving the Daleks 'flying saucers' – a really nice, retro touch). As for the Daleks, while we were all thrilled to see one trundling about back in episode six, there's something really special about setting eyes on a few more. My understanding is that only three complete Dalek props were manufactured for the series, but through the magic of television, that number was increased. The Dalek menace has truly returned to our screens, and the final episode of the series is certain to dramatically inflate that menace.

PANEL REVIEWS

'Bad Wolf' starts as a *Max Headroom*-esque parody of reality TV and then just as its world of contemporary television-as-gladiatorial-entertainment (not a new theme, even by *Who* standards) wears out its welcome, it pulls back to reveal something even more exciting. While many have claimed that 'Father's Day' has its roots in the *Doctor Who* New Adventures novels of the 1990s, I would argue that the story most like these books is, in fact, 'Bad Wolf'. Elements across the series are being gathered together to reveal something bigger and grander while the effectiveness of the Doctor's work is questioned. There's even a companion who carries a gun and gets a nude scene! Speaking of which, John Barrowman steals the show – his scenes with the *What Not To Wear* androids are delightful and give him some great moments before the Rose-heavy finale. My main quibble with the episode is to do with the Daleks themselves: namely, what the heck was up with the Dalek that wobbled as it talked? It's as though the production crew wanted to over-compensate for the great design work on 'Dalek', and yet they didn't need to. We know it's talking. It has voice lights. The twitching and shuffling may have been the way they did it in the original series, but it makes them look amateurish and cheap now. Thank goodness I had Eccleston delivering his brilliant closing speech to distract me from that or I would have become *really* irritated! – *Graeme Burk*

Surprisingly, 'Bad Wolf' doesn't go anywhere near revealing the true meaning of the words that have plagued the Doctor and Rose throughout the course of this series, but what it does do is set up a tantalisingly spectacular endgame with the Daleks, achieved in a highly satisfying manner. The homicidal gameshows that start the episode could have been deeply clichéd, but the use of actual formats gives the idea a spark of novelty and allows Davies to accord equal weight to the three leads' subplots. The reality-TV satire doesn't last long enough to irritate as it soon gives way to the greater mystery of who instigated the Game Station with its vicious brand of programming that has enslaved the human race, much like the Jagrafess did one hundred years previously. This change of tone is handled well through a gradual heightening of tension that lets the Daleks' eventual appearance have real impact. The Doctor's stunned silence on witnessing Rose's 'death' is just brilliant, Eccleston conveying so much desolation without uttering a single word. However, even this is overshadowed by the stunning climax that encompasses so many great moments, from the 'Like I was ever going to shoot' line to Jack's and the Doctor's delight that Rose is still alive to the Doctor's determination to 'wipe every last stinking Dalek out of the sky.' The last ten minutes of 'Bad Wolf' is some of the best *Doctor Who* Davies has written so far, and leaves the viewer desperate for what happens next ... – *Simon Catlow*

The season is coming to an end and the pieces are finally starting to come together as Davies pulls out all the stops and proves why he's the man trusted with the revival of *Doctor Who*. A lot of his other episodes this year have seemed rushed and not as polished as those from the other writers, but this one has all the hallmarks I've come to expect from him. The story is a very tongue-in-cheek take on popular reality and game shows, with just the right mix of humour and terror. Anyone else might have got that balance wrong, but here it's pulled off so well you really believe that some 200,000 years hence Anne Robinson will still be remembered for cutting barbs and annihilating people. Along the way we are dropped more and more clues

– some of them even more obvious to us long-time fans. The final few moments of this episode are brilliant and some of the best bits from the whole season for me. I've always enjoyed Davies's writing most when he relies on his actors and directors to carry a scene with their skills and let the audience be taken along through just their expressions. When the Doctor tells the Dalek 'No,' Rose's face shows a look of desperation – she can't believe this is happening. And then, a moment later, when against an entire Dalek army he tells Rose he is coming for her, just the look on Piper's face tells us that she never doubted him, that she believes in him, and that she knows he can work miracles. It takes a brilliant actor and director to pull this off, but it takes a great writer to trust that they can. – *Robert Franks*

The series is really firing on all cylinders now. It took a significant upward swing with 'Dalek', but only since 'The Empty Child' has every episode really been a positive experience. Imagine my added delight, then, to find that the somewhat corny concept of killer game shows was only a tiny part of such an entertaining episode. As is proper, we see both the Doctor and his companions in their element, fighting to reach each other and escape danger. The humour is very well balanced by the more dramatic elements, some of which are quite scary for this kind of show. The Controller is especially effective, inspiring some great direction from Joe Ahearne (note the shots that both introduce her and see her demise), and the villains have a great reveal, undermined only by last week's trailer. And the regulars, too, are fantastic: the Doctor's despair over Rose's apparent fate is a great contrast to Jack's anger, and we have yet another classic confrontation between the Doctor and his worst enemies. It's all a big lead-up to next week, sure, but I don't think it could have been a more exciting one. And as if that's not enough, there's that voice in the trailer ... that voice! I have to admit: in the closing moments of 'Bad Wolf', I was punching my fist in the air – and I just couldn't make myself stop. – *Sarah Hadley*

I was one of those fans who heard rumours of the content of 'Bad Wolf' and therefore approached the episode with some trepidation. Anne Robinson? *Big Brother*? Trinny and Susannah? I hoped for the best but feared the worst. In the end it turned out that my hopes were right and my fears groundless, as Davies turned in without a shadow of a doubt his best script of the season to date. The various television formats are well-portrayed and incorporated brilliantly into the plot, and the episode really cranks up the tension as the world of the Game Station takes on an increasingly sinister aspect. All the regulars are on fine form, particularly Barrowman, who excels both in his comic material with the *What Not to Wear* robots, and in his angry, fraught emotion after Rose's apparent death, wonderfully delivering the 'Don't you touch him!' line as the guards arrest the Doctor. The guest cast are also well-selected, particularly Jo Joyner as the endearing Lynda, although I fear that given how likeable she is, she may not be long for this world once the Daleks turn up. Speaking of said pepperpots, they're wonderful here – Davies and Ahearne create a believable, menacing and intimidating invading army, and I cannot wait to see how this all wraps up next week. One thing's for sure – I can't see very many people getting out of this one alive. – *Paul Hayes*

'Bad Wolf' is an episode of two halves. The first half is focused on the reality TV shows, and how each member of the TARDIS crew reacts to their particular situation, which gives insight into each of them. Rose finds it amusing, until the deadly nature of the game emerges; Jack takes it all in his stride, quietly waiting for the time to make a move; and the Doctor immediately wants to escape and take on those who put him there in the first place. The second half of the episode revolves around the TARDIS crew discovering where they are, and who is behind it all. Jo Joyner gives a very likeable performance as Lynda, and plays very well off Eccleston; while Paterson Joseph portrays Rodrick as a very selfish person, a good contrast to Rose. Jo Stone-Fewings and Nisha Nayar have a real rapport as male and female programmers, fleshing out their characters well. There are visual clues subtly appearing in the background of a number of early scenes, giving alert viewers an opportunity to guess ahead as to where the TARDIS crew have been taken, and who their real enemy is. The final fifteen minutes of the episode really picks up the pace and energy, leading into an exciting cliff-hanger. – *Cameron Mason*

TV game and reality shows bore me to tears, so I was rather dubious about this aspect of the episode. And as I have only a passing familiarity with the named shows, I was concerned I wouldn't get the 'joke'. But thankfully my fears were allayed when the three games made sense in context (with plenty of groan-worthy innuendo on the *What Not to Wear* set). 'Bad Wolf' is really three stories in one – the games, the mystery behind the Game Station and Bad Wolf itself, and of course the Daleks. And Davies pulls it off magnificently, interweaving all three into the same narrative. And just as things fire off on all cylinders, the episode comes to an end, leaving me shouting 'No, not yet!' as the credits roll. This is without doubt Davies's strongest script, which is a sure sign that his carefully constructed master plan is at last making sense, and about to reach its fan-theory-shattering climax. Rose's apparent demise deals exactly what it was set up for – immediate shock value – while the Doctor's reaction when he sees the Bad Wolf Corporation logo and later realises he was directly responsible for this whole mess leaves a lasting impression. And the talented Joe Ahearne uses claustrophobia and dark sets to heighten the air of impending doom. I even found the design of the albino controller particularly disturbing, and for a foolish moment I was convinced the BBC had deceived us all and brought back the Cybermen! Wonderful stuff! – *Jon Preddle*

'Ladies, your viewing figures just went up.' This isn't just a game, the Doctor tells Lynda-with-a-y as they escape from a wonderfully *faux Big Brother* house and into the heart of the Game Station. 'There's something else going on.' How right he is. What that something is seems, largely, to be a forty-five minute exercise in cracking one-liners. 'Bad Wolf' works almost entirely because of its dialogue. (The plot, such as it is, can be reduced to a, very literal, Troughtonesque *escape-capture-escape* run-around for all bar the final ten minutes.) So, we must look to the aesthetics (Jack's leather-boy West Hollywood attire) and to witty throwaway conceits (be honest, if contestants in *Countdown* had thirty seconds to defuse a bomb, *you'd* watch it, wouldn't you?) for the best moments. Then, we get to the last act, with the Controller's pathetic attempts at rebellion against her 'masters', the Doctor giving his gun to the hostages that he's holding and, best of all, his brazenly informing the Daleks that he intends to rescue Rose, save the world and *then*, with no regrets, wipe them all out. The latter is a 'punch the air' moment that beats just about anything we've ever seen from this show. Cue thirty seconds of panic-stricken Dalek shrieking. 'Bad Wolf' adds to the age-old 'Doctor-as-hero' strand of *Doctor Who* writing. Its construction may not be wholly successful, but its ultimate execution is as good as it gets. – *Keith Topping*

I am not (nor have I ever been) a fan of reality television and thus, the first half of 'Bad Wolf' didn't do very much for me. The scenes set outside the games were far more interesting, and the moment the Doctor managed to escape from the 'Big Brother' house, everything took a turn for the better in my opinion (even if I will admit to finding the 'Anne Droid' rather amusing). Beyond that, a lot of interesting stuff is tossed at us in this episode: reality television gone wild, a mysterious female Controller suspended in a web of glowing cables, the Bad Wolf Corporation, the return of Satellite 5, and, of course, a smattering of Daleks. We're meant to believe that all the questions from the series will be answered in this or the next episode, but oddly, even more questions are posed before the credits roll. Perhaps I missed something, but I'm still a tad confused about the Controller and her predecessors, which presumably include the Mighty Jagrafess of the Holy Hadrojassic Maxarodenfoe, and what their actual purpose was (in the grand Dalek scheme of things). The action does rise beautifully in this episode, though, and the scene of the Doctor telling Rose (who has been captured by the Daleks) that he will be coming for her made me cheer with glee. It's sad knowing that the end (for Mr Eccleston) is truly nigh, but I can't wait to see it! – *Scott Alan Woodard*

EDITOR'S REVIEW: There are things on television you'd never expect to see. I would never, for example, expect to see the *Gilligan's Island* cast turn out to occupy the same island as the characters from *Lost*, nor would I expect *Buffy* to face off against the prince of darkness himself, Dracula. (Oops, my mistake ... that one did happen.) That's why you'd never expect to see a *Doctor Who* story in which the Doctor gets trapped in the *Big Brother* house, or that Rose would find herself facing off against the television equivalent of Dracula's bride, Anne Robinson. Yet Davies has done it, and Eccleston's been a housemate, and Robinson's quipped about the bleach job on Piper's hair. Who knew?

There is something to be said when pop culture becomes so trendy, it transcends that barrier and becomes the norm. Five years ago, if someone had said that the Doctor being trapped inside a reality television series would be the perfect basis for a future episode, they'd probably have attracted raised eyebrows. Now, as Davies's script for the penultimate episode of the season has proven, even what many consider passé can be made serious and even deadly given the right circumstances. Robots in the guise of the *What Not To Wear* ladies, replete with chain saws, goes from hilariously camp to terrifyingly serious – and given direct conflict with the swagger of Barrowman's postmodern man, both at the same time. Likewise, 'housemates' and 'eviction' and 'the diary room' aren't what you'd first expect to show up in a *Doctor Who* story, but the dichotomy of Eccleston's serious attitude and carefree demeanour at the same moment can carry him through a scene that looks ridiculous, but is obviously horrifyingly deadly.

That is the beauty of 'Bad Wolf', as Davies proves he is a master at conjoining images of fun and fear in one setting. Very few writers could get away with the Daleks ultimately being behind a revival of *The Weakest Link*. Of course, they're not *really*, and we understand that in the context of the story; it's the human weakness for spectacle that ultimately revives some rather crummy 21st Century reality pap. (How this story can get away with such a revival nearly *two hundred thousand years* in the future is easy: the subject is never brought up. So much for a consistent universe.)

When all is said and done, everything that's happening can be blamed on the Doctor, after all; 'Bad Wolf' becomes more than just a standard, run-of-the-mill *Doctor Who* episode, graduating to being a reckoning for the Doctor himself. As we realise during the story, his ally in 'The Long Game', Cathica, probably grew to hate him as the world she herself was part of suddenly collapsed around her; the people the Doctor thought he was helping were condemned to an existence of selective extermination and pitiful excuses for entertainment. And now, it's time for the Doctor, as the old saying goes, to pay the piper. (No pun intended.)

A quality script is nothing without quality actors, and as in previous instalments the regulars shine; Eccleston doesn't even look silly in that big red chair (well, okay, just a bit, but not *too* much), while Piper's maniacal laughter fades to a very convincing desperation as her fellow contestants get reduced to their respective atoms all around her, and Barrowman ... well, how many people besides John Barrowman can pull off the line, 'Ladies, your viewing figures just went up' and get away with it? Add to that the 'sweet' Lynda Moss (wonderfully played by Jo Joyner) and the slimy Rodrick (Paterson Joseph, emoting as always with his piercing eyes) and the ingredients are all there for a winner.

'Bad Wolf' probably looked amazingly silly on paper. It probably *felt* amazingly silly in production, too, and after about five minutes of watching it, it's still that: just absolutely amazingly silly and terribly fun. For a while. Then it turns deadly serious. The unveiling of the Daleks is probably not surprising to anyone who has kept up with the show (after all, the BBC itself spoiled the surprise in its own trailer the week before), but somehow, the juxtaposition of Dalek evil and *Big Brother* isn't as hard to swallow as one would believe. From start to finish, 'Bad Wolf' is a study in contrasts between the absurd and the sinister, and a silly story is enhanced by some wonderful dialogue, great acting and terrific production values, and in the process becomes one of the absolute highlights of the first series. Brilliant. – *Shaun Lyon*

113: THE PARTING OF THE WAYS

The Dalek war machine, reborn from the ashes of the Time War, is poised to launch an all-out attack against Earth. The Doctor, Jack Harkness and a handful of powerless allies defend themselves aboard the Game Station from a Dalek Emperor with a god complex, while Rose Tyler faces returning to a life she no longer wants. But all is not yet lost. The Bad Wolf is coming ...

FIRST TRANSMISSION: UK – 18 June 2005. Canada – 28 June 2005. Australia – 13 August 2005. New Zealand – 4 October 2005.
DURATION: 45'30"
WRITER: Russell T Davies
DIRECTOR: Joe Ahearne
CREDITED CAST: Christopher Eccleston (Doctor Who), Billie Piper (Rose Tyler), John Barrowman (Captain Jack), Jo Stone Fewings (Male Programmer), Jo Joyner (Lynda), Paterson Joseph (Rodrick), Nisha Nayar (Female Programmer), Noel Clarke (Mickey), Camille Coduri (Jackie), Anne Robinson (Voice of Anne Droid), Nicholas Briggs (Dalek Voice), Paul Kasey (Android), Barnaby Edwards (Dalek Operator), Nicholas Pegg (Dalek Operator), David Hankinson (Dalek Operator), and introducing David Tennant as Doctor Who
Daleks originally created by Terry Nation.
The Weakest Link format created by Fintan Coyle and Cathy Dunning.
Big Brother is an original format by Endemol Netherlands BV, licensed by Endemol International BV.
Big Brother logo by kind permission of Channel Four. (The *Big Brother* theme and logo are used only in the episode recap.)

WHERE AND WHEN: The Dalek command ship and the Game Station, formerly Satellite 5, in the year 200,100. Also, near Rose's home in London, some time after 'Boom Town' (likely after September 2006).

THE STORY UNFOLDS: The Time War – a massive conflict between the Time Lords and the Daleks – was once waged for control of the universe. The Time Lords lost and were destroyed, but were able to take the Daleks with them; both races vanished out of time and space. The only three survivors of the Time War (that we know of) were the Doctor, who escaped in his TARDIS; the lone Dalek that crash landed on Earth ('Dalek'); and the Emperor Dalek, whose ship fell through time. The Emperor was crippled but rebuilt its race quietly in dark space, slowly infiltrating Earth and harvesting prisoners, refugees and the dispossessed (and, presumably, those transmatted from the Games Station, though this is never overtly stated) for genetic material, using only one cell in a billion to create new Daleks. The Emperor considers the truth about the mutants' human origins to be blasphemy; it now believes itself to be the god of the Daleks – and wants Earth to be its new temple, a new Dalek paradise.

The Doctor intends to recalibrate the transmitters on the Game Station to create a delta wave of Van Cassadyne energy to destroy the Daleks. However, the wave destroys brain activity and will kill everything organic – human and Dalek – within its range, leaving the Doctor with something of a dilemma.

The Daleks fire missiles at the TARDIS, which is protected by a force field created using the extrapolator device obtained from Blon Slitheen ('Boom Town'). It also protects the TARDIS crew from the Daleks on their ship, and later the top six levels of the Game Station from direct assault by the Dalek fleet. Jack uses the gun he created from the defabricator ('Bad Wolf') on a Dalek, but the one shot completely drains it of power. Jack says that Dalek force fields can be penetrated with bastic bullets, which the station's guards have, but in fact they seem to work only with concentrated fire on the eye stalks. The Daleks break into the station on floor 494, below the bubble created by the extrapolator. The doors on the station are made of hydrocombination, which will temporarily keep the invaders out. The Daleks meanwhile attack the Earth and bombard whole continents including Europa, Pacifica, the New American Alliance and Australasia.

About a hundred people remain on the station, including Rodrick, who doesn't believe in the Daleks and refuses to fight. Only the two programmers, the floor manager from the *Weakest Link* game, a few of the guards and a small handful of others join Jack and Lynda for the fight.

The Doctor has previously recorded Emergency Program One, a hologram, to activate on the TARDIS in case of fatal danger; the TARDIS will take Rose back home and then deactivate itself to prevent an enemy from getting hold of it. (There is the implication that the hologram is self-aware, as it turns toward Rose to address her; it might be a standard emergency program that the TARDIS customises to its occupant.)

The Doctor mentions the planet Barcelona, where he says there are dogs with no noses. Mickey discusses a pizza place on Midnight Row (presumably in London) which, to Jackie's surprise, actually sells pizza.

THE DOCTOR: The ancient legends of the Dalek homeworld call the Doctor 'the Oncoming Storm'. The Daleks fear him. He sends Rose back in time to save her, and asks her to let the TARDIS die. The Emperor Dalek says it wants to see the Doctor become like it, a 'great exterminator', and calls him a coward (as the lone Dalek did before, in 'Dalek') when he cannot bring himself to destroy humanity on Earth to stop the Daleks. To save Rose's life, he takes the energy of the time vortex into himself through a kiss and releases it back in the TARDIS, but the process overwhelms him and forces him to regenerate.

THE (NEW) DOCTOR: He has longer hair and sideburns, and a bright smile. Having new teeth, he claims, feels 'weird'.

ROSE TYLER: The Daleks keep her alive because she knows the Doctor and may be able to predict his actions. She's slightly jealous of Lynda's connection with the Doctor. The Doctor has shown her a better way of living life, and she refuses to let go. She enlists Mickey and, later, her mother to help open the heart of the TARDIS, which releases the time vortex to possess her. She uses this power to destroy the Daleks, possibly throughout the entirety of space and time, to reanimate Jack, and is saved by the Doctor when he kisses her, though she doesn't remember any of it.

CHARACTER BUILDING: *Jack Harkness* – He thought the Time War was just a legend. He attempts to incite the Game Station's remaining inhabitants to join the fight against the Daleks. He trusts the Doctor, and vice versa, when faced with the possibility of certain death.

He says goodbye to the Doctor and Rose, thinking they'll all die, and kisses both of them. The Daleks kill him. However, when he's later revived by the time vortex-affected Rose, he narrowly misses returning to the TARDIS which, with the Doctor and Rose unaware he's survived the assault, leaves him behind.

Mickey Smith – As soon as he hears the TARDIS materialise, he runs from Clifton Parade to find it. Rose tells him there's nothing left for her at home, so he decides to help her get back to the Doctor and won't let her quit. He now drives a Mini Cooper instead of a Volkswagen bug.

Jackie Tyler – She and Mickey take Rose out for food when her daughter returns. She's hated the Doctor in the past, although now realises he protected Rose. She wants her daughter to stop trying to get back to the Doctor, but when she's told that Rose got to see her father before he died – and that Pete would have wanted her to try – she borrows a rescue recovery vehicle from her friend Rodrigo to help Rose break into the heart of the TARDIS.

Lynda Moss – She obviously likes the Doctor, and he reciprocates, a fact that earns her some jealous glances from Rose. She would like to continue to travel with the Doctor when all this is over. She refuses to leave the Game Station when it is evacuated and volunteers to help Jack defend the station by monitoring the Daleks. She dies when the Daleks break into an observation room on the Games Station and she's blown out into space through the broken viewing portal.

The Programmers – The female programmer tells the male programmer (Davitch) that, if they survive, she'll go out for a drink with him. However, they don't survive.

BAD WOLF: The truth is finally told: Rose *herself* is the Bad Wolf. Consumed by the time vortex, Rose scatters the words from the wall of the Games Station through time and space as a message to herself in the past, to the effect that she should return to save the Doctor. When Rose sees the words written on the ground and brick walls of a playground on Earth after she's been returned there by the TARDIS, she realises the message is directed specifically at her, but believes it's from the Doctor; later, she realises that she herself sent the message. (There is a further instance of 'Bad Wolf' in the episode ; it is written on a poster on the wall of the chip shop she goes to with Mickey and Jackie.) It is implied (but not specifically stated) that she scatters the words 'Bad Wolf' from the sign of the owners of the Game Station, the Bad Wolf Corporation, and that this is therefore the source of the phrase.

FANTASTIC!: The Doctor (or rather, his hologram) tells Rose to have herself a fantastic life as he sends her away. Later, he says it while talking about Barcelona. Immediately before he regenerates, he tells Rose she was: '... fantastic, absolutely fantastic ... and you know what? So was I.'

BODY COUNT: In their assault on the Game Station, the Daleks kill everyone remaining there: Jack (who is later brought back to life by Rose), Lynda Moss, the programmers, Rodrick, the floor manager, the guards ... everyone else sheltering on floor 000 ... The Anne Droid is also destroyed (but not before transmatting three Daleks to who–knows–where). And, of course, the ninth Doctor 'dies' ...

THE DOCTOR'S MAGICAL SONIC SCREWDRIVER: He uses it to remote-activate the TARDIS to take Rose home.

REALITY BITES: This was the only episode not screened for the press prior to broadcast, and no preview tapes were made available. (However, the story was screened for ticket holders at the British Academy of Film and Television Arts on 15 June.) The official *Doctor Who* website carried a warning from the producers for fans to 'avoid the internet' and spoilers in magazines and newspapers, in order not to ruin the episode for themselves. (Of course, many didn't take the advice!)

Rose's experience looking into the heart of the TARDIS alludes to Friedrich Nietzche's *Beyond Good and Evil*: 'And if you gaze for long into an abyss, the abyss gazes also into you.' Rose looks into the TARDIS, and says that it looked into her as well.

The series's opening credits sequence makes use of the quantum physics theory of Doppler Shift – light from moving objects will appear to have different wavelengths depending on the relative motion of the source and the observer. Objects moving farther away have a red shift and objects approaching have a blue shift. While this does not correlate directly to time travel, the series's producers have made consistent use of this throughout the season. Whenever the TARDIS is seen in the time vortex moving into the future a red vortex is used ('The End of the World') and when travelling into the past a blue vortex is used ('The Unquiet Dead', 'The Empty Child'). In this episode both are featured – a blue vortex when the Doctor sends Rose home and a red vortex when she returns to rescue him.

David Tennant was one of the stars of the 2004 BBC1 musical drama series *Blackpool*, a performance that, according to Steven Moffat in an interview in *SFX*, led Moffat to e-mail Davies and say, 'There's Doctor Ten.' Davies's reply was apparently, 'You're not the first person to say that. In fact, you're the fourth.'

LINKING THEMES: The Doctor says that the reason he can't go back a week and warn anyone about the Daleks is that he has become part of events and is stuck in the timeline ... very much akin to the 'laws of time' noted throughout the history of the 'classic' series. He also discusses the Time Lords' way of 'cheating death' through regenerating; this will be the ninth time he's done it.

The idea of the Doctor being referred to as 'the Oncoming Storm' by the Daleks (and by other races including the Draconians, as seen on TV in story 'Frontier in Space,' 1973), originated in Virgin Publishing's New Adventures range of *Doctor Who* novels: it was first coined in *Love and War* by Paul Cornell. The closing line, to the effect that the Doctor will take Rose to Barcelona, is an in-joke reference to a moment in *Doctor Who* history at the end of 'Revelation of the Daleks' (1985) when the Doctor's announcement that he would take his companion to Blackpool (reduced to just the first letter of the word on transmission) was forestalled by BBC executives who had put the series on hiatus.

The opening of the 'heart of the TARDIS' to stop Blon Slitheen from 'Boom Town' is glimpsed briefly. Rose tells Jackie about her trip to see her father ('Father's Day'), confessing that she was the girl who stayed with Pete as he died. It is not explicitly confirmed whether or not Jackie remembers Pete having had someone with him when he died, thus leaving open the question as to whether Jackie's memories are of the 'original' time line or the 'new' one created by the actions of the Doctor and Rose.

The TARDIS was said in the 'classic' series to be nearly indestructible, yet here it is protected from the Dalek weapons only by virtue of the extrapolator's force field. (This may not be an inconsistency, however; given that the Daleks have previously fought a Time War against the Time Lords, it can perhaps be surmised that they know how to overcome a

TARDIS's usual invulnerability.) Likewise, the TARDIS no longer seems to enjoy its 'state of grace' in which weapons cannot fire inside; the Dalek and Jack both fire weapons. (However, the 'state of grace' had already stopped working by the end of the 'classic' series, so again this is not really an inconsistency.) The Doctor can land the TARDIS around someone (or something, like a Dalek), hence Rose suddenly being inside the ship. This was previously seen in 'The Time Monster' (1972) and 'Logopolis' (1981).

Bastic bullets were first mentioned in 'Revelation of the Daleks' (1985). Delta waves were first mentioned in 'Kinda' (1982), where the Doctor augments them to induce Nyssa into a restorative sleep.

SCENE MISSING: What, exactly, was 'Bad Wolf' all about? It was obviously a message Rose sent back in time to herself (we are told this by her) but it seems to do nothing other than tell her to go back to the Doctor (for which, a simple 'Rose, go back to the Doctor' would have sufficed!) Also, while the viewer saw numerous occurrences of 'Bad Wolf' as Rose travelled, she obviously didn't – it's unlikely she overheard the Moxx of Balhoon ('The End of the World'); she might have heard the announcement of the landing helicopter ('Dalek') but it's not clear; she possibly missed the writing on the poster ('Father's Day'); and unless she speaks German, she probably doesn't know what 'Schlechter Wolf' means ('The Doctor Dances') even if she saw the bomb itself. It is also possible, given their travels to other worlds only mentioned in the stories, that there were other, unseen 'Bad Wolf' occurrences.

Since the TARDIS has always been, and still appears to be, indestructible (the Doctor notes in 'Rose' that the combined hordes of Genghis Khan couldn't get through the door), why is it in danger from Dalek missiles? Or is this simply a ruse to get them to fire, hence activating the extrapolator to create the force field in the first place? (See also the speculation above.)

Why does the Doctor have to regenerate after exposure to the time vortex? Rose experiences it full strength and recovers immediately. (Though he says it's only flowing through her, she seems to be able to harness its energy, enough to send the 'Bad Wolf' message *and* give life back to Jack.) The Doctor, on the other hand, takes it in, gets rid of it a lot faster, and then needs to regenerate. Also, how does the Doctor retrieve the energy of the time vortex out of Rose using a kiss, and then blow it back into the TARDIS?

Why are both the Doctor and the Daleks certain that human kind will be nearly destroyed except for a few scattered colonies, as the Doctor says? *Doctor Who* has demonstrated for decades that humanity escaped Earth and settled across the stars, creating a massive stellar empire (indeed, at the time of this story, it's *supposed* to be the Fourth Great and Bountiful Human Empire), so it's very likely that Earth bears only a small percentage of the period's humankind. Also, why does the Doctor hesitate to stop the Daleks with the delta wave because of the unbelievable loss of life it will create, yet allow countless billions to die when the Daleks attack and decimate four continents?

And are the Daleks truly gone? Rose says she can see all of them throughout time and space and destroy them ... But that's a question for the next season, and beyond.

BEHIND THE SCENES: 'The Parting of the Ways' was recorded primarily on the *Doctor Who* set in Newport, except for the exterior sequences at the café and in the playground, which were both recorded at Loudon Square, Butetown, Cardiff.

Replacing the standard preview for the following week's episode was the *Doctor Who* logo amended with the words 'will return in The Christmas Invasion'; the announcer also noted that the series would be back at Christmas.

Jenna Russell returns as the floor manager from 'Bad Wolf' to help in the fight against the Daleks, but is uncredited – even though she does have a line late in the episode ('You lied to me! The bullets don't work!').

The episode did not feature any new material in its pre-credits sequence. The recap from the previous week led straight into the opening titles.

TECHNICAL GOOFS: The Doctor alternately refers to the Daleks as having had all their emotions removed, and to their feeling hatred. The glass that protects Lynda from the cold of space – very likely the same exoglass used in the *Big Brother* house and also on Platform One in 'The End of the World' where the term was first used – shatters easily from a Dalek gun, even though it's supposed to be resistant to meteors. (However, she alludes to the poor quality of Earth workmanship, so this *could* be deliberate.) The Dalek inside the TARDIS, captured by the Doctor at the beginning, disappears part-way through the episode. The weapons Jack and the defenders use are 20th Century rifles. The Dalek whose eye malfunctions from a weapons blast is never seen to be hit by a bullet. When Mickey is trying to open the TARDIS console by using his car to haul on it via a metal chain, the car doesn't suddenly lurch forward when the chain breaks, as one would expect, but is immediately at a standstill. Later, the same thing happens with the rescue recovery truck. (Plus, there are no tyre marks on the road.)

CONTROVERSIES: Not just one kiss, but two ... At any other time, a kiss by John Barrowman on the lips of Christopher Eccleston would have been considered big news. However, the Doctor saves his companion Rose with a kiss as well, provoking considerable discussion about the nature of the Doctor's relationship with his associates. Jack being left behind (even though the Doctor and Rose didn't know he was still alive) caused much consternation, as did the death of Lynda Moss.

INTERNAL CONSISTENCY: This episode picks up directly after the previous one, with the Doctor rescuing Rose only moments after he promised to save her. The Doctor spends less than ten minutes talking with the Daleks before he heads back to the Game Station. At one point, Davitch says that the Dalek fleet will take twenty-two minutes to reach Earth, but they arrive in half that time, so we are missing a few minutes of the preparation for the fight (even though the Daleks seem to have accelerated during the journey). Rose seems to spend a few hours back home and has time to eat lunch with Mickey and Jackie as well as to try to open the TARDIS with first Mickey's car and then Jackie's borrowed truck. This all apparently happens in one afternoon. The battle for the Game Station takes place seemingly in real time, with just a few small gaps – twenty-five to thirty minutes at most. Rose arrives back with the TARDIS in time to save the day before she and the Doctor leave some five minutes later ... and just a few minutes after that, David Tennant makes his entrance as the new Doctor.

THEME ANALYSES

As Doctor Who For A Modern Audience: Davies has written a big event episode to mark the end of the series and conclude the Eccleston era. The end is foreshadowed by the atmosphere of hopelessness the script engenders as everything is at stake for our heroes. This series has already given us a Dalek episode where their fear of the unlike was a major theme, and 'The Parting Of The Ways' adds a modern twist to their existence by pitching the Daleks as religious zealots, worshipping their Emperor as God. This is a very relevant change of perspective, making them a scarier force, as now their desire to exterminate humanity is not just through hate for the unlike but to fulfil the Emperor's dream of creating 'heaven on Earth' for his followers. The Doctor's confrontation with the Emperor also leads into a philosophical debate about whether it's better to be the killer or to be the coward, which is explored through the Doctor's choice between destroying two races to save the rest of the universe or standing back and letting the Daleks triumph. With many aspects of the production, the presentation is key to tailoring this *Doctor Who* for today's audience and the regeneration sequence is no different. There are similarities between the ninth Doctor's sacrifice to save Rose and the fifth Doctor's sacrifice to save Peri, but whereas the latter was played for tragedy, the former retains the heady blend of emotion and adventure that has made this series so memorable. As the ninth Doctor tries to make light of what he's done and the change that's coming, it provokes sadness for his death but also joy for all he has achieved and the arrival of a new, tenth incarnation.

As Television Drama: The concept of the dramatic, plot-thread-resolving 'season finale' episode seemed to go out of fashion in British television drama for a few years around the turn of the century. *Casualty* always used to do them, upping the ante each year with increasingly bigger lorry, train or plane crashes, or having the hospital staff threatened by mad gunmen and the like. But once that show switched to a year-round format, the finale idea was lost. In recent years however, *Spooks* has brought back the season-ending event episode to BBC1, finishing its first two runs with tense cliff-hangers and killing off one of the original team of regulars at the end of the third. 'The Parting of the Ways' picks up that ball and runs with it, delivering an epic, emotional resolution to everything that has been built up not just in the previous episode, but the rest of the series as well. To top it all, it ends with the re-casting of the leading character. This is something almost never seen on British television outside of soap operas and occasionally sitcoms; and even there, it's usually a case of bringing in a similar actor to play the same part rather than changing the whole appearance and personality of the character. It will be very interesting to see how the audience takes to David Tennant as the tenth Doctor, but given what a fine season we've had and what a good actor he is, all the signs are promising for a fantastic future for new *Doctor Who*.

As A Piece of Writing: 'The Parting of the Ways' follows an unfortunate pattern that has plagued nearly all of Davies's episodes: it starts strong, well-rounded, funny, even tense, but around the halfway mark things become corny, overwrought and overstated. Jack and the Doctor, the stars of last week's episode, gradually fade away to make room for Rose's subplot, and while the Doctor makes a strong return to form, it seems too little, too late. Even the regeneration is rushed, with a lot of dramatic potential lost because the Doctor never seems truly weak nor in pain; it's hard to see Eccleston go because he's been short-changed as a character, not because he's saved the day. The worst aspect of the writing, though, is the resolution of the Bad Wolf mystery. With so much emphasis put on Rose and her story throughout the season, to offer such an implausible, overly-complicated explanation is unforgivable. At the end of the day, the season's writing is typical of TV writing in general – a few great scripts, a few clunkers, most somewhere in between. The most successful episodes have been those not written by Davies, however, which is unfortunate as he's also the individual guiding the show – a show that, ultimately, doesn't quite hang together because of the emphasis placed on two little words.

The Doctor As A Mystery Figure: It's not often that we learn something significant about the Doctor's mysterious past, so any such moments of revelation need to be commented upon. The discovery that, in the ancient legends of the Dalek homeworld, the Doctor is known as 'the Oncoming Storm' shouldn't really surprise anyone. After all, 'that ruddy Time Lord who keeps ruining our plans for universal domination' probably loses a lot in translation. 'The Parting of the Ways' asks some searching questions about the Doctor's lifestyle, such as whether or not his view that passive cowardice is preferable to heroic genocide is a valid one. Despite his numerous attempts to leave the past lost in the dark, fate catches up with him here, and there's almost relief in the Doctor's voice when he tells the Emperor that, just maybe it's time he *was* exterminated. The episode also includes one massive MacGuffin, and it's the key enigma of the whole season – the identity of Bad Wolf. And it does so amid much quasi-biblical dialogue, Nietzschean allusion and a thinly-veiled comment on religious fanaticism. Not bad for forty-five minutes' work, frankly.

Themes, Genres and Modes: Over the past thirteen episodes, we have seen how *Doctor Who* dabbles in all sorts of different areas of storytelling. Really, when it comes down to it, it's all in aid of creating a genre of its own: a *Doctor Who* story. As 'The Parting of the Ways' demonstrates, *Doctor Who* uses elements of comedy ('I like floor 495'), horror (Lynda seeing the Daleks outside), romance (it climaxes in a kiss!), family drama (Rose and Jackie), psychological drama ('Coward, always'), political satire (Daleks-as-religious-extremists), MythArc (Bad Wolf explained, perhaps) even Rom-Com (watch Rose's reactions to Lynda!) *Doctor Who* draws from not just one of these aspects each episode, but from a whole multitude, and it throws in heroic melodrama and mixes them all together. That's what's made *Doctor Who* so great for forty-plus years, and what made *Doctor Who* such a fantastic viewing experience in 2005.

In Style and Structure: 'The Parting of the Ways' is built around the battle to save the Earth from the Daleks; all the action, all the character moments revolve around this. The Doctor does what he does best in improvising a solution, Jack fulfils the action role and Rose plays the most important part of all. The battle sequences show not only how strong the Daleks are, but also the resilient nature of humanity, fighting until the end. Ultimately, this is the Doctor and Rose's story, and the strength of their relationship is really brought out here, through the Doctor's motivation for sending Rose home, and her reasons for returning to the battle. By sending Rose back to Earth, Davies can not only show the audience how her time with the Doctor has changed her, by putting her back into the ordinary, but also how Mickey and Jackie initially react to and ultimately respect Rose's decision to return to the Doctor, and even help her to achieve this. The mystery of the recurring Bad Wolf references is finally solved, and in a way that plays against all the assumptions made by the Doctor and Rose – and no doubt by most of the audience – prior to this episode. It makes sense as presented here, but re-watching previous episodes will no doubt determine whether or not the red herrings and wrong assumptions have made it seem too weak. Overall, 'The Parting of the Ways' provides a wonderful conclusion to a story that started not just in the previous episode, but right back at the start of 'Rose'.

As Doctor Who Continuity: As the season finale, 'The Parting of the Ways' has two vital functions to perform: provide a satisfactory conclusion to the ninth Doctor's era, and tie up any loose ends from the previous twelve weeks. And it succeeded in both quite admirably. We get back-references to 'Father's Day' and 'Boom Town', as well as the long-awaited resolution to the mystery of the Bad Wolf. Fan online forums were rife with extravagant theories about this, some of them rather extreme (it's the Master! the Rani! the Kandyman! Pralix from 'The Pirate Planet'!), so I was somewhat relieved that the solution was simple rather than convoluted. Davies is a clever writer, able to twist something straightforward and create a storm in a tea cup. A regeneration for the Doctor is a key event in *Doctor Who* lore, and it's important that each is handled with the right level of emotion. Although the planned element of surprise was spoiled, it was still a tearful moment to see Doc Chris become Doc Dave. For the fourth time (at least on screen) the Doctor regenerated inside the TARDIS, but now we know that Time Lords can do it standing up!

From A Special Effects Viewpoint: Daleks, Daleks everywhere! Welcome to the epic conclusion of the new series of *Doctor Who*! While the kitchen sink was sadly absent, everything else that could possibly feature in a Dalek story was present: hundreds, nay *thousands* of Daleks (some gliding about, some zooming through the vacuum of space and a few blowing apart), a colossal and gloriously redesigned Emperor Dalek, numerous spaceships, glowing disintegrations (thanks to the mystical power of the time vortex) and a couple of skeletal exterminations (a nice throwback to an effect that first appeared in 1988's 'Remembrance Of The Daleks'). On top of that, we were also given a really nice fusion of special effects techniques. The Emperor Dalek, for example, was a wonderful hybrid of model and CGI, and the results were superb. It's one of those incredibly complicated shots that becomes even more impressive when one breaks it down into its component parts: skilfully crafted Emperor Dalek model (thanks to Mike Tucker and his team), CGI background (and foreground Daleks), live actors (and 'live' Daleks) shot in front of a green screen, and the whole mess brilliantly composited into something unseen in the series until now. A fabulous technical triumph and a thrilling conclusion to the series.

PANEL REVIEWS

When I saw 'The Parting of the Ways' for the first time, I really enjoyed it. I felt it had a lot in common with the last episodes in most of Davies's work, in that it was a great ending not only to a single two-part story but also to the whole season. (It referenced practically every other story, too – for example, Rose's line, 'Everything must die', echoed the Doctor's own comments about Cassandra on Platform One). While I thought the climax was a bit contrived, it was at least set up three episodes before (and the scenes with Mickey, Jackie and Rose were worth it). Overall, I had some minor qualms – particularly over the Daleks being depicted as religious extremists and made subservient to a Davros-like figure in the Emperor (surely unnecessary after they had been shown to be quite capable of speaking for themselves as in 'Dalek') – but found it otherwise to be a fun, exciting ride with some lovely scenes and incredible spectacle, capped by the heart-rending departure of Christopher Eccleston. Then I watched it with my 12 year-old goddaughter and everything changed. She's been watching *Doctor Who* with me for years, and she loves the new series, but she responded to 'The Parting of the Ways' like no other episode ever. She snapped upright when she saw the Daleks advance out into space toward the Game Station. She high-fived me when Jackie arrived with the tow truck. She was seriously freaked out by Lynda's death. She was similarly saddened by Jack's demise. (Jack was already declared to be 'hot', by the way.). And as she absently chewed her pinky finger, eyes wide, she was transfixed by Rose's climactic actions, though, bless her, she thought the kiss was gross. She was pained at the Eccleston Doctor's departure and then said, 'He's quirky' in response to David Tennant's first line. We walked home, and all the way she was talking about Tennant's 'triangular' face ('He needs a haircut') and quoting Rose as she casts Bad Wolf into time and space. And that's when it hit me: this is more than just a fun, exciting ride. This is great television that captivates, excites, scares and moves grown-ups and kids alike. Watching with my goddaughter gave me a renewed appreciation of how brilliant this show really is. I know neither of us can wait for 'The Christmas Invasion'. – *Graeme Burk*

Sombre and downbeat, 'The Parting Of The Ways' isn't what we've come to expect from Davies, but this impressive, doom-laden finale is all the better for the contrast. After the initial confrontation with the Daleks, some momentum is lost as the focus shifts towards examining how the supporting characters cope with facing the menace of the invaders. The downside of this is that the Doctor spends much of this episode alone, but his decision to send Rose home leads to some of the best drama. Only Davies could get away with cutting from the advancing Dalek army to a discussion about the quality of a London chip shop's coleslaw, but it demonstrates so well how this series has gone about grounding the fantastical in down-to-earth reality. Characterisation is again the most important thing here, with the Doctor influencing and inspiring all those around him. The most important aspect of this is his effect on Rose, who won't give up on him now that he has opened her eyes to extraordinary possibilities. While it's touching to see the extent of the sacrifice Rose is prepared to make to save her Doctor, it is disappointing to discover that she is the Bad Wolf, with the power to conveniently wipe out the Daleks, providing an easy way out. What redeems the story is the Doctor's surrender of his own life to save Rose, as that and the incredibly moving (yet strangely fun) regeneration prove a wonderful end to a brilliant series. Eccleston and Piper were both fantastic, and with a lively first impression from David Tennant, there is an incredibly strong foundation for the second series to build upon. – *Simon Catlow*

After 'Bad Wolf', almost anything other than a full scale battle was going to seem anti-climactic. And we certainly get one of the best realised Dalek armies ever. It's too bad that these new Daleks are overshadowed for most of the episode by their 'God'. It would have been interesting to see what other changes had been implanted in these new Daleks. The Daleks appear to have enough fire power to destroy everything on Earth, and indeed they appear to melt three continents just after their arrival. It hardly seems likely that some ten minutes later there could be any surviving humans on the planet, yet the Doctor is unwilling to wipe the Daleks out with the delta wave. Is this shades of 'Genesis of the Daleks' (1975), or does the Doctor actually believe there could be some humans left alive? Also, I have yet to figure out how pulling down on the TARDIS console will pop open one of the panels or how exactly Rose works out that Bad Wolf means she can get back to the Doctor – minor quibbles surely. The climax however seems more at home in *Buffy* than in *Doctor Who*. A previously unknown source of godlike power existing in the TARDIS that can be harnessed at any time, and that can fix anything, including by restoring life. (Did someone mention the TV movie?) Why wouldn't the Doctor have used this in the past? Of course, we know it cost him his ninth life, but surely giving up one of his lives would have been worth it to stop the entire fleet before they even reached Earth. Still, it was breathtaking. All of it was breathtaking – it really was the trip of a lifetime! – *Robert Franks*

The momentum I felt last week is gone. It's sad, really, because while this isn't a great episode, it's not terrible, either – it's an acceptable episode that happens to be a very, very weak season finale. Things are going fine until Rose gets sent away in the TARDIS, when it suddenly becomes apparent that, yet again, we're getting a story that is supposed to connect 'emotionally' without actually making sense. We spend way too much time on Earth; the Dalek invasion is quickly sidelined; and disappointingly, the whole Bad Wolf concept – the element the whole season has hung on! – turns out to be little more than gobbledygook. Worst of all, the Doctor isn't even allowed to shine before his own death. Eccleston has some good speeches, true, but he's otherwise wasted sitting amongst a mess of cables for forty-five minutes. How am I supposed to feel the loss of a hero who hasn't done anything heroic? I like this new *Doctor Who*; I enjoy watching it each week, and I recognise that this is only the first season and it's very much a work in progress. However, I can't help but admit I'm pleased that we have more variety in writers next year, and I would hope, in turn, that the focus of the show shifts slightly to live up to its name. No more gimmicks. No more companions-who-aren't. Even though Rose is a fantastic character, this show isn't called *Rose Who*; it's *Doctor Who*, and I want, more than anything, to see more of the Doctor. You're doing so much of it right, Mr Davies – please don't cry wolf on us again next year. – *Sarah Hadley*

'The Parting of the Ways' has a lot to do in just forty-five minutes – resolve the 'Bad Wolf' arc, show a massive Dalek invasion, kill off the ninth Doctor and of course attempt to tell a good story at the same time. Fortunately, it achieves all this, and not only that but delivers drama and emotion in spades. The epic feel of the Dalek attack is wonderfully realised, with the desperate last stand of Jack and the station staff, their deaths – particularly poor Lynda's – and the massacre of the innocents down on floor zero all packing a weighty emotional punch. The Doctor's return of Rose to London does the same, and the ensuing Mickey and Jackie scenes even manage not to feel too forced into the plot. Davies finally delivers on all the Bad Wolf hints without it seeming like a disappointment or an anti-climax, and overall the whole thing comes together to form a wonderfully memorable and dramatic episode of *Doctor Who*. If I have one complaint it's that the Daleks become little more than henchmen to their Emperor, as they always used to do with Davros, but aside from that, there's little to be faulted here. A wonderful end to what has been, the occasional weakness aside, a wonderful season. It's very sad to lose Christopher Eccleston, though – he was superb in the part, and you feel that had he done more, he could have been remembered as one of the truly great Doctors, if not the greatest. – *Paul Hayes*

'The Parting of the Ways' is an extraordinary final episode, in which the stakes are high. There are three brilliant character moments that really get to the heart of the TARDIS crew: Rose realising why she can't stay home, Jack leading the battle right to the end, and the Doctor realising he can't cause mutual destruction again. Eccleston puts all his energy into a standout performance, showing why his Doctor is so easy to like, and why he will be missed. Piper also gives a powerful performance as Rose. Their scenes together light up the screen, and there is a subtle sadness running through all of them. The Daleks are well used, with many sequences displaying their power, alien nature, and utter ruthlessness. The Dalek spacecraft exterior and interior are well designed. The iconic Dalek Emperor also looks spectacular, and Nicholas Briggs's vocal performance gives it a sense of immense power and extreme insanity. How the battle ends will no doubt raise many eyebrows, but it is something that has been foreshadowed to some degree in previous episodes. Joe Ahearne's direction is dynamic and energetic, suiting the episode. Murray Gold's score is wonderful, and is superbly used to highlight the mood and movement of each scene it features in. Just when it looks like the story has wrapped up, there's the heartbreaking final scene in the TARDIS, and things won't be the same again. – *Cameron Mason*

'The Parting of the Ways' delivered something no-one would ever have dreamt was possible on a *Doctor Who* budget. A Dalek army. Compare the awesome CGI swarm of thousands to the pathetic image of three rather battered Daleks trundling across the lawn in 'Day of the Daleks' to see just how things have progressed since 1972! I watched 'Rose' all those weeks ago with a group of friends. For a celebratory farewell to the Eccleston era, most of us reconvened for episode thirteen. In stunned silence we watched Jack's (apparent) death, Billie Piper's terrific performance as Rose, Lynda's sad demise and the Doctor's farewells. The series needed to end on an apocalyptic note – it was the ninth Doctor's last gasp, after all. Although the Daleks had branded him a coward, we knew he was not a killer. And in just that brief scene alone, we learned exactly what it was that made the ninth Doctor tick, and why Eccleston portrayed him the way he did. It's sad but nevertheless appropriate that this character revelation was made in his ultimate adventure. And what an adventure! As for THAT ending, any shock value the regeneration built itself up for had been lost when news of Eccleston's departure leaked back in March, but there must be some lucky viewers out there who were oblivious to this and for whom the change was a complete surprise – I am so envious of them! Davies and Ahearne delivered a heart-racing, exciting and dare I say it virtually flawless piece of television drama, the perfect end to thirteen weeks of fun and adventure. Everything and more a fan could have asked for. – *Jon Preddle*

If 'The Parting of the Ways' has a message, it's actually quite a downbeat one. 'Everybody dies,' as Rose/Wolf notes, shortly before she/it destroys the greatest Dalek force in history with a few waves of her hand. And, for an encore, she raises the dead. I, actually, had remarkably few problems with the *deus ex machina* aspects of the resolution – I enjoyed the, seemingly deliberate, *Buffy* and *Angel* riffs especially. I've little time for the school of thought that believes that magic (in all its forms) has no place in *Doctor Who*. It's a TV show about time travel, and if that isn't magic, then what is? The episode's reliance on a slab of pseudo-science (force fields, delta waves and the passing of mystical powers through a kiss) likewise didn't raise any hackles. My chief complaint concerning 'The Parting of the Ways', in fact, was that there was a shade too much faffing around in contemporary London with Rose, Mickey and Jackie, when what we all really wanted to focus on was what was going on back in the future. Jack's resurrection wasn't really 'earned' either, although I like the character a great deal and I'm glad he's returning next year. And his parting kiss to the Doctor was worth the licence fee on its own. 'You were fantastic, Rose Tyler ... And, you know what? So was I,' notes the Doctor in Eccleston's final, manic moments in the role. And he was. Two lines of amusing dialogue and a cheeky grin on David Tennant's face as the tenth Doctor's era begins reminds us why *Doctor Who* remains unique in television. The Doctor *will* return, and I couldn't be happier. – *Keith Topping*

The promise of a final solution to the elaborate mystery of the Bad Wolf references (and Davies's revelation that no-one was even close with their theories prior to broadcast) was reason enough for fans and non-fans alike to tune in, but while Rose being behind the whole thing makes a certain sense, I can't help but feel a tad disappointed. Perhaps a lot of that had to do with the many clever and elaborate theories dismissed by Mr Davies (everything from a well-preserved Adam to a future incarnation of the Doctor!) that so many of us paid close attention to. It also didn't help that the Face Of Boe's role was played up with two televised appearances and an intriguing little comment in the *Doctor Who: Monsters And Villains* book. There's a lot of other wonderful stuff in this episode, though; so much so that 'The Parting Of The Ways' comes in at number four in my overall new series rankings! Billie Piper delivers an outstanding performance (possibly the best of the series), with the emotionally charged scene in the café with Mickey and Jackie being most impressive. Lots of other little things thrilled me in this episode, such as the little detail of the Dalek's dome lights flashing as it said 'Exterminate' before shattering the glass on the observation deck, resulting in Lynda's demise, and the chance to once again hear a Dalek utter the words: 'My vision is impaired, I cannot see!' Priceless. All in all, a spectacular conclusion to a spectacular first series! Mr Eccleston, we hardly knew ye. – *Scott Alan Woodard*

EDITOR'S REVIEW: I was somewhat disappointed with 'The Parting of the Ways'. Season finales often don't live up to our expectations, and with so many plot threads to be resolved, it was only natural that something might be lost in translation. I must clarify this, however, with the point that I believe this to have been one of *Doctor Who's* most consistently good seasons; it's been, to use the vernacular, one hell of a ride. The acting has been fantastic (to borrow Eccleston's oft-used catchphrase, and yes I'm including him in on that), the writing has been almost uniformly superb, the visuals and design extraordinary, and the adventure square on the mark.

There are often times when we set ourselves up for something so wonderful, so truly groundbreaking, that anything that deviates from that perfect vision is a disappointment. This is, I think, what happened to me. The resolution of the 'Bad Wolf' storyline made sense, to a degree, but was somehow invalidated by how trite it ultimately was. The Daleks getting religion was a brilliant idea in principle – and the Dalek Emperor's ravings that it had now become God were perhaps a logical extension of these familiar villains of the past – but the sudden revelation that to stop them would mean destroying the Earth in the process was just a bit too obvious and shallow. There was an awful lot of flash-bang that reminded me of the old Shakespeare line about 'sound and fury, signifying nothing'. The resolution of the cliff-hanger was too quick, even in comparison with others this year. They seemed to skip out on a lot of previously established *Doctor Who* continuity ... Not that I'm a continuity cop or anything (break a rule for a good story and I can live with it), but since when can a Dalek destroy the TARDIS? And, since when does the Doctor kiss the time vortex out of his companion?

Yes, that's quibbling with a resolution that probably had no chance of living up to the set-up, but herein lies a niggling problem I've had now with several episodes: the easy, giveaway ending. On some television series I could mention, the writers purposely paint themselves into a corner, relishing the challenge of writing their way out of it; I guess that's one way to look at things, but works only when there's enough material there to sort out a logical conclusion and keep the plot threads from unravelling (not to mention a certain amount of luck that it will all work out in the end). Far too often, it's a mess; one doesn't set out to make a quilt without a pattern, and a story is often like a quilt, its set pieces representative of panels stitched together by the plot. With 'The Parting of the Ways', there were a number of plot threads that needed to be resolved: the Bad Wolf scenario, the return of the Daleks and their Emperor, resolution of the Doctor/Rose relationship, and the regeneration. Easy enough when you look at it from that angle, but much harder in execution, as there are several instances when the story seems suddenly to switch gears. Take, for instance, the Doctor's hard work for most of the episode attempting to finish a device that he ends up not using; didn't he once think about the consequences of what it would be to hit that switch and decimate all life on Earth?

This does not mean that 'The Parting of the Ways' isn't worthwhile; there is still plenty to enjoy. While I didn't like seeing Lynda Moss die – part of me thought briefly that they really *were* going to replace Rose, like the recent rumours had suggested (well, okay, that took about three seconds to work out, but I digress; stranger things *have* happened in this show) – her death was perhaps one of the most chilling moments of the episode. The sequence between Billie Piper, Noel Clarke and Camille Coduri is a lovely bookend to their performances in 'Rose', most especially in Jackie's sudden turnaround when she realises the Doctor did exactly what she asked him to: keep her daughter safe. (Looking back over the full season, the contributions Clarke and Coduri have made cannot be understated; they <u>feel</u> familial to us, exactly like Davies set out to do.) Piper pulls off quite a stunning performance in turning the time vortex-afflicted Rose into an almost totally unrecognisable new character, complete with different vocal inflections and a worldliness Rose never demonstrated during the course of the year. And the kiss between her and the Doctor just *works* here, to an extent that it never has before in the context of the show.

But I absolutely *loathed* the idea that Jack, one of my favourite *Doctor Who* characters (in just five episodes), would die. Thankfully he got a reprieve at the end, even though there was always doubt (as this was widely reported to be his last episode). A plea to the production team, however: *please* bring Jack back sooner rather than later. He's proof that, contrary to the conventional wisdom, *Doctor Who* works perfectly well with a TARDIS crew of three; and the rapport he showed with Piper and Eccleston – underlined perhaps by a wonderful piece of dialogue, 'Never doubted him, never will' – demonstrated that John Barrowman deserves to be a regular on this show.

Which brings us to the end. I don't like regenerations; I find them equally overdramatic and sentimental, and they represent a change that isn't necessarily for the better. There wasn't enough time, I'm afraid, for us to get to know Eccleston's Doctor, despite thirteen weeks of quality performances, and I confess that I'm not this incarnation's greatest fan. (Eccleston is certainly a very good actor, very talented and capable, but often times he's irritated me beyond reason; although I admit that some of that is the fault of the script, especially the 'stupid ape' comments, which I'm afraid I just couldn't get past.) Nevertheless, for a transition that came far before its time, it was handled with dignity and style, explained easily with the flair for dialogue Davies has repeatedly demonstrated he possesses over the course of this year. For a Doctor who didn't get the chance to show us a beginning, he gets a remarkable ending, a proper send-off that never becomes too mushy but allows him to say his piece. Meanwhile, I couldn't help but smile the moment I saw David Tennant's grin on screen; matter-of-fact, down to business, it's off to the next adventure faster than you can say 'Barcelona!' I can't wait to see 'The Christmas Invasion', entirely because I can't wait to see *his* portrayal of the next incarnation of the Doctor.

EPISODE 113

Thirteen episodes ago, if you had asked me if lightning could strike twice – if this series would amount to 'proper' *Doctor Who* – I would have hesitated. My faith in the people behind it was unshaken, but capturing the essence of something as timeless and innovative as *Doctor Who* isn't easy. It's not science fiction, exactly; it's not a children's series, either. *Doctor Who* is a blend of imagination and wonder, a serious drama screened through a novelty filter. It emphasises that, beneath the trappings of a solitary alien travelling through time and space in a police box, it's really about the human condition: the uniqueness we possess, the frailties we struggle through, and the darkness we live with each day. It's not just about telling stories, it's about telling them a certain way, with certain sensibilities. Davies's track record showed he had the credentials to pull it off, but it would take the right ingredients to make it a winner. How marvellous, then, to see that a talented cast and crew have come together to create something more than the sum of its parts: thirteen weeks of wit and wonder, stories that stress that timeless quality *Doctor Who* has always shown. It's had its flaws and occasional missteps, but taken as a whole, it's been a very worthwhile experience, a stunning and welcome return, and a terrific first season.

Fantastic, you might say. – *Shaun Lyon*

AFTERWORD

Where were you when you heard *Doctor Who* was coming back? I know where I was. Right here in this office. Sitting on this chair. Looking at this computer screen. Reading the news on *Outpost Gallifrey*.

I never thought it would happen. I wasn't even sure if I wanted it to, really. The best we could hope for, with television nowadays being what it is, would be some compromised movie-length edition, or something that would run for half a dozen episodes on some specialist satellite channel. The idea that it would be *big*, a mainstream hit that seemed to be celebrated on the front cover of every magazine in Britain, a programme that would be openly discussed in pubs and playgrounds – hey, something that my *wife* would watch ... That was just an impossible dream. Surely.

I'm often asked what it was like when I found out I would be writing an episode of the new *Doctor Who* series. (And I was climbing the walls with excitement, of course.) Or how I felt walking on to the set of my very own story and meeting my very own Dalek. (Ditto.) But, you know, actually nothing has been as gobsmackingly wonderful as loading up the Internet that September morning and finding out that the show was being revived in the first place. Russell didn't need to give me a dream job to make me happy. I was already ecstatic!

And over the course of the last eighteen months, so faithfully chronicled by Shaun here, it's been looking at his website that has kept my excitement up. Whenever it threatened to get a bit too much like hard work, or I began to get tired of typing the word 'exterminate', all I'd need do was look at the best site on the web and get my batteries recharged. And I know I wasn't the only one.

I hope you had a trip of a lifetime. I did.

Rob Shearman
June 2005

APPENDICES

APPENDIX A:
DOCTOR WHO CONFIDENTIAL

In conjunction with the production of *Doctor Who*, BBC Wales commissioned a special thirteen-part documentary series, *Doctor Who Confidential*, which gained unparalleled access to the production of the series. A half-hour programme would be transmitted after the conclusion of each *Doctor Who* episode, on the digital channel BBC3. The series was produced by Gillane Seaborne under executive producer Mark Cossey for BBC Wales, and was narrated by Simon Pegg, who would guest star in episode 7, 'The Long Game'.

Additionally, the production team of *Doctor Who Confidential* was responsible for two separate documentary specials: *Doctor Who: A New Dimension,* transmitted on BBC1 on the series's debut date, 26 March, at 5.25 pm, and narrated by David Tennant; and *The Ultimate Guide,* transmitted on BBC1 on the date of the final episode, 18 June, at 6.15 pm, narrated by Pegg. The episodes of *Confidential* were also webcast on the BBC official *Doctor Who* website.

During the run of the series, dozens of interviews were conducted and used in the series, along with clips from *Doctor Who* spanning its entire forty-two year history. Among the many personalities interviewed for comments were executive producers Russell T Davies and Julie Gardner; producer Phil Collinson; BBC1 Controller Lorraine Heggessey; stars Christopher Eccleston and Billie Piper; writers Paul Cornell, Robert Shearman, Mark Gatiss and Steven Moffat; cast members Noel Clarke, Camille Coduri, Simon Pegg, John Barrowman, Shaun Dingwall, Corey Johnson, Richard Wilson, Bruno Langley, Alan Ruscoe, Nicholas Briggs, Annette Badland, Elizabeth Fost and Barnaby Edwards; costume designer Lucinda Wright; visual effects producer Will Cohen; script editor Helen Raynor; directors Keith Boak, Euros Lyn, James Hawes and Joe Ahearne; *Doctor Who Magazine* editor Clayton Hickman; production designer Edward Thomas; director of photography Ernie Vincze; prosthetics designer Neill Gorton; *Big Finish* producer Gary Russell; compositor David Bowman; critic Andrew Collins; Doctor Who movie actor Eric Roberts; presenter John Humphreys; and original series stars Tom Baker, Peter Davison, Colin Baker, Sylvester McCoy, Elisabeth Sladen, Nicola Bryant, Katy Manning, Louise Jameson, Sarah Sutton, Sophie Aldred, Richard Franklin and Nicholas Courtney.

The following is a brief guide to each episode of the thirteen-instalment documentary series and its two specials.

ND-DOCTOR WHO: A NEW DIMENSION
Transmission: 26 March 2005, 5.25 pm, BBC1
Preceding the transmission on premiere day in the UK, this special half-hour preview documentary examined the long-term success of *Doctor Who*, exploring the eras of the series marked by their lead actors, as well as providing a preview of what could be expected in the upcoming thirteen-part *Doctor Who* series. It was bookended by trailers for the new series. The special was narrated by David Tennant, whose identity at the time as Christopher Eccleston's successor had not been announced.

1-BRINGING BACK THE DOCTOR
Transmission: 26 March 2005, 7.45 pm, BBC3
The first regular episode covered the first night's recording and the start of the series, and

recapped all eight previous Doctors and the legacy of *Doctor Who* fandom, through its fans, the audios, the books, and so forth. Among the material featured was the first 'proper' night's recording in London after five days of Cardiff photography for 'Rose', including sequences shot at the Embankment, and the first scene with Eccleston and Piper together.

2 - THE GOOD, THE BAD AND THE UGLY

Transmission: 2 April 2005, 7.45 pm, BBC3

This episode featured both a look at the production of 'The End of the World' and an analysis of the aliens and monsters of the series, new and 'classic'. Costuming, make-up and prosthetics for aliens were explored, as well as the staggering number of effects shots employed from The Mill for the episode, including the realisation of Platform One, the scorching sun and the spiders, and the wizardry involved in bringing Cassandra to life.

3 - TARDIS TALES

Transmission: 9 April 2005, 7.45 pm, BBC3

An exploration of the TARDIS: its origins in *Doctor Who*, its mythology and its status as a cultural icon, and how the new series production team updated it for a new generation. Also included was a look behind the scenes at the recording of 'The Unquiet Dead' on location in Swansea and Monmouth, creating the Gelth ghosts and special make-up effects used for the undead.

4 - I GET A SIDE-KICK OUT OF YOU

Transmission: 16 April 2005, 7.45 pm, BBC3

Focused on the *Doctor Who* assistants of yesteryear – mostly on the females, of course – including their costumes, their propensity to scream and their relationship to the Doctor. Also discussed the kiss between the Doctor and Grace in the 1996 *Doctor Who* movie. A montage of clips of companions over the years from the original series was also included.

5 - WHY ON EARTH?

Transmission: 23 April 2005, 7.45 pm, BBC3

A discussion of the Doctor's fascination with Earth, including material about the United Nations Intelligence Taskforce (UNIT). Also featured a look behind the scenes at the production of the two-part story 'Aliens of London' and 'World War Three', including interviewing the people behind and inside the Slitheen, creating the Slitheen ship crash, the pig pilot and the destruction of 10 Downing Street.

6 - DALEK

Transmission: 30 April 2005, 7.45 pm, BBC3

Doctor Who's famous Daleks return, and this episode looked at their history and popularity, and their contribution toward the series's longevity. Scenes from the recording of 'Dalek' were shown, as well as Nicholas Briggs's experiences voicing the Daleks. Murray Gold was interviewed about his music, including the scoring for this particular episode.

7 - THE DARK SIDE

Transmission: 7 May 2005, 7.45 pm, BBC3

Villains in *Doctor Who*, specifically evil geniuses, were explored, as the production went behind the scenes of recording 'The Long Game' with Simon Pegg. The episode looked back at villains of the past in the series, with special focus on the Master and Davros, and also the creation of the Mighty Jagrafess.

8-TIME TROUBLE
Transmission: 14 May 2005, 7.45 pm, BBC3
Emotional drama in *Doctor Who* was explored through interviews and clips of the recording of 'Father's Day', as well as clips from the original series examining the emotional impact of the Doctor's actions and his relationships with his companions. Also seen was the period costuming involved in creating the 'look' of the 1980s, and the digital creation of the Reapers.

9-SPECIAL EFFECTS
Transmission: 21 May 2005, 7.10 pm, BBC3
An examination of the show's visual effects, with emphasis on some of the difficult accomplishments on 'The Empty Child', such as Rose's flight over London and Jack's spacecraft. Design elements and colours were explored, as well as the task of recreating the 1940s and the thought put into how the TARDIS would appear and disappear. A story breakdown session with the director and producers was also glimpsed. This episode, like the story it accompanied, was transmitted early due to the *Eurovision Song Contest*.

10-WEIRD SCIENCE
Transmission: 28 May 2005, 7.45 pm, BBC3
Technology – and how indistinguishable it can sometimes be from magic – was examined, with clips showcasing the Cybermen, the TARDIS, and new items such as psychic paper, nanoprobes, the info-spikes and the sonic screwdriver. Also discussed was how the Doctor uses science to solve problems. More behind-the-scenes production footage was presented from 'The Empty Child' and 'The Doctor Dances'.

11-UNSUNG HEROES AND VIOLENT DEATH
Transmission: 4 June 2005, 7.45 pm, BBC3
The violence in *Doctor Who* was explored, set amongst scenes from the recording of 'Boom Town'. Clips were shown of some of the series's more violent episodes, and there was a discussion of self-appointed TV 'watchdog' Mary Whitehouse's campaign in the 70s against violence in the show. Also explored was the nature of heroism and risk in the new series, from Mickey Smith and Gwyneth to Cathica and Raffalo.

12-THE WORLD OF WHO
Transmission: 11 June 2005, 7.45 pm, BBC3
The success of *Doctor Who* as more than a series was explored, as well as its global following, including scenes from various conventions over the years and interviews from the recent Dimensions 2004 convention in the UK and Gallifrey 2005 in Los Angeles, an exploration of *Big Finish's* production of audio adventures, and footage from the opening of the new exhibition in Brighton. Also seen were clips from the production of 'Bad Wolf'.

13-THE LAST BATTLE

Transmission: 18 June 2005, 7.45 pm, BBC3

One last mission ... *Doctor Who Confidential* concluded with a look at 'The Parting of the Ways' and Christopher Eccleston's last battle with the Daleks. Eccleston's tenure was focused on, as well as the experiences of Billie Piper and John Barrowman. The final moments of 'The Parting of the Ways' were explored, including the moments leading to the regeneration, followed by a retrospective of moments from series one.

UG-THE ULTIMATE GUIDE

Transmission: 18 June 2005, 6.15 pm, BBC1

Produced to air prior to the transmission of the final episode, this special featured a compilation of interviews and clips from this season's *Doctor Who Confidential* programmes as well as a brief hint of what could be expected from that night's story. Simon Pegg narrated.

CREDITS

Artist Contracts: Lesley Longhurst (1, 13, UG)

Assistant Producer: Zoë Rushton (4); Geoff Evans (12)

Camera: Eric Huyton (1-13, ND, UG); Andy Smith (1-7, 9-13, UG); Mat Bryant (1, 3, 4, 8-13, UG); Nick Jardine (1, 2, 4, 8, 10, 11, ND, UG); Aled Jenkins (4, 8, 12, 13, UG); Chris Pain (6, 7, ND); Danny Dimitroff (10, 11); Jon Podpadec (2-5, UG); Johnny Rogers (5, UG); Paul Cox (10, 11, UG)

Colourists: Jon Everett (2-4, 7-13); Richard Doel (1, 5); Simon Meek (4); Gareth Owens (6); Chris Packman (ND, UG)

Copyright Contracts: Robert Bruce (1, 13, UG)

Countdown Graphics: Lee Binding (ND)

Cyfle Trainee: Bethan Evans (7)

Dubbing: Peter Jeffreys (1-3, 6-12); Mark Ferda (4, 5, 13); Steve Hudson (ND)

Dubbing Mixer: Steve Hudson (UG)

Editor: Sven Brooks (1, ND); Ian Hunt (2, 3, 5, 6, ND); Rob Mansell (2-6, 8, ND); Ian Pitch (2, 3, 6, ND); Tim Dawson (2, 3, 6); Stewart Barlow (4); Caroline Lynch-Blosse (4, 9); Sara Jones (7, 10); Tom Appleby (10, 11, 13, ND); Lee Buers (12, ND)

Executive Producer: Mark Cossey (1-13, ND, UG)

Executive Producers for Dr Who: Russell T Davies (1-13, ND, UG); Julie Gardner (1-13, ND, UG); Mal Young (1-13, ND, UG)

Insert Directors: Tony Lee (UG); Adam Page (UG); Griff Rowland (UG); Rebecca Sanderson (UG)

Insert Editors: Ian Hunt (UG); Sven Brooks(UG); Caroline Lynch-Blosse (UG); Tim Dawson (UG); Rob Mansell (UG); Sara Jones (UG)

Junior Researcher: Alexander Gratton (1-13, UG)

Narrator: Simon Pegg (1-13, UG); David Tennant (ND)

Produced and Directed By: Gillane Seaborne (1, 13, ND, UG); Adam Page (2-6, 8, 12, ND); Tony Lee (4, 9, 11); Griff Rowland (7, 10)

Production Co-ordinators: Caroline Harris (1-7, ND); Hannah Simpson (8-13, ND, UG)

Production Managers: Catherine Gosling (1-13, ND); Zoë Scott (7-13, ND, UG)

Production Secretary: Hannah Simpson (1-7)

Programme Editor: Tom Appleby (UG)
Researchers: Geoff Evans (1-11, 13, ND, UG); Stephen Thomas (1-13, UG); Zoë Rushton (1-3, 5-13, ND, UG)
Runners: Maxine Hughes (1-13, ND, UG); Hannah Williams (1-11, 13, ND, UG); Lucy Lutman (7-13, UG); Nic Britz (7-13, UG); Bethan Evans (10-13, UG)
Series Producer: Gillane Seaborne (2-12)
Sound: Kevin Meredith (1-13, ND, UG); Les Mowbray (2-7, 10-13, UG); Phil Turner (1, 3, 4, 8-13, UG); Roger Van Koningsveld (1, 3, 6-8, 10-13, ND, UG, credited as "Roger van K" on all but 1, ND, UG); Steve Hoy (1, 4, 9-11, 13, UG); Graham Ross (1, 2, UG); Richard Maxwell (1, 2, ND, UG); Paul Baker (2-4, UG); Maz Tajiki (4, UG); Simon Cole (5); Peter Eason (8, 10, 11, UG); Ryan Windley (8, 9, UG)
Thanks To: Andrew Pixley (1, 13); Clayton Hickman (1, 13)
Titles: Liquid (1); Rheea Aranha (ND, UG)
Title Music Arrangement: Murray Gold (ND); Andy Coles (ND)
Title Music: Mike Westergaard (1)

APPENDIX B:
THE NOVELS AND COMICS

BBC Books and Panini Comics (in *Doctor Who Magazine*) currently publish *Doctor Who* fiction featuring the further adventures of the ninth Doctor and Rose. The following is a guide to those adventures that have so far been published.

NOVELS

THE CLOCKWISE MAN

WRITER: Justin Richards
PUBLICATION DATE: 19 May 2005 (originally scheduled for April 2005)
COVER: Landscape photos by Alamy/Charles Bowman, Design by Henry Steadman
COMMISSIONING EDITORS: Shirley Patton and Stuart Cooper
CREATIVE DIRECTOR: Justin Richards
EDITOR: Stephen Cole

WHERE AND WHEN: London, October 1924; it begins on a Tuesday and takes place across three days. The book is set between 'The Unquiet Dead' and 'The Empty Child' (the Doctor and Rose are travelling alone) and is probably set just before 'Dalek' as there are no references to Adam.

SYNOPSIS: Arriving in 1924 to see the British Empire Exhibition, Rose and the Doctor rescue a man who is being attacked. The man is in the service of Sir George Harding, one of a group who intend to return Freddie, the young heir to the Tsar of Russia, to his rightful place. Two of their cohorts, Repel and Aske, are a mysterious pair – everyone having a different variation of their life stories – and another, Melissa Heart, remains very secretive as to her appearance, hiding behind a mask. Heart, who has mistaken the Doctor for the war criminal Shade Vassily, is later revealed to be a disfigured alien using clockwork robots. A final confrontation takes place at the Big Ben clock tower. Freddie dies in the battle.

THE STORY UNFOLDS: The Doctor uses the sonic screwdriver for lock-picking and it can be used to cauterise wounds. Rose is reminded of Gwyneth ('The Unquiet Dead') at one point. The Doctor says he has 'been in wars ... far too many' and jokingly calls Rose 'Taylor'. Vassily was the dictator of Katuria. There are numerous adjustments and successful sabotage attempts made on the Big Ben clock, which presumably are later sorted out ... ready for it to be demolished in 'Aliens of London' eighty-two years later.

PUBLISHING NOTES: With Justin Richards unable to edit his own work, Stephen Cole (writer of *The Monsters Inside* and Richards's predecessor at BBC Books, as well as being the editor of Richards's *Invisible Detective* range of novels from Simon and Schuster) stepped in to do this. The cover depicts the silhouette of Portcullis House which was not built until the late 20th Century.

BAD WOLF: Melissa Heart accuses the Doctor of turning up 'like a bad wolf'. Rose corrects her – the phrase is 'a bad penny'. (p120)

THE MONSTERS INSIDE

WRITER: Stephen Cole
PUBLICATION DATE: 19 May 2005 (originally scheduled for April 2005)
COVER: Landscape photos by Corbis, Design by Henry Steadman
COMMISSIONING EDITORS: Shirley Patton and Stuart Cooper
CREATIVE DIRECTOR AND EDITOR: Justin Richards

WHERE AND WHEN: The Justicia System, 2501. The story takes place over a few days (on several planets, with different orbits, making it hard to pin down precisely). The book is set between 'The End of the World' and 'The Empty Child' (as the Doctor and Rose are travelling alone), and probably before 'Dalek' as, again, there are no references to Adam. Also, this is set prior to *Winner Takes All*, as this novel features Rose's first trip to an alien world.

SYNOPSIS: The Doctor takes Rose to her first alien world, Justice Alpha, but they are ambushed and separated as it transpires they have unwittingly broken into a planet on the prison solar system of Justicia. The Doctor is recruited into the SCAT project on Justice Prime by Lazlee Flowers to work on a gravity wave experiment, and thrown in a cell with two Slitheen prisoners – Ecktosca Fel Fotch Happen-Bar and Dram Fel Fotch. Rose has meanwhile been taken to Justice Beta to be kept in a juvenile detention centre. The Doctor cons his warder into arranging a transfer for Rose to help him with the SCAT project, but does not realise that his warder's boss is also from the Slitheen planet – she is Ermernshrew, from the rival family Blathereen. The SCAT project turns out to be a front for research into creating planetary portal generators, as part of a Blathereen plot to shift the system around the galaxy to aid the destruction of suns for nuclear fission. The Doctor, Rose and their friends defeat the Blathereen patriarch, Don Arco, and Ermenshrew. They leave, but do not realise that the Slitheen prisoners now have plans to pick up where the Blathereen left off ...

THE STORY UNFOLDS: The SCAT project, run on Justice Prime, stands for Species-Led Creative and Advanced Technologies; it appears to be a way of putting brilliant criminal minds to good use, set up by EarthGov, but turns out to be a Slitheen plan. SCAT allows prisoners to walk freely as there is an automated defence system against any type of antisocial behaviour. Justice Alpha is primarily for historical-style punishments, such as building pyramids similar to those in Egypt. Trespassing into Justicia is punishable by an automatic twenty-five-year sentence. Justice Beta is for juvenile criminals, and juveniles related to criminals who are carrying out sentences on other worlds. Justice Gamma is reserved mainly for drug addicts. There are plantations on Justice Epsilon. The Justicia system is nineteen light years away from the New Washington system. Justicia is referenced in 'Boom Town'.

The Doctor makes a reference to 20th Century entertainer Bob Hope. The Slitheen have photos of their family disguised as Meeps (*Doctor Who Magazine*) and Kraals ('The Android Invasion', 1975). The Slitheen (and presumably other members of their race) have superior digestive systems to humans and do not need to eat as often. Jackie's phone number ends 7398. Rose made the Doctor spend a day watching *EastEnders* at the flat a while back (likely just prior to *The Monsters Inside*). Flowers uses the sonic screwdriver as a mini light.

BAD WOLF: The Blathereen pilot, trying to get through a locked door, is described as being like 'the big bad wolf ... ready to blow our house down'. (p136)

WINNER TAKES ALL

WRITER: Jacqueline Rayner
PUBLICATION DATE: 19 May 2005 (originally scheduled for April 2005)
COVER: Landscape photos by Corbis, Design by Henry Steadman
COMMISSIONING EDITORS: Shirley Patton and Stuart Cooper
CREATIVE DIRECTOR AND EDITOR: Justin Richards

WHERE AND WHEN: London, 2006, and the planet Toop. The story takes place during one day. The book is set between 'World War Three' and 'The Empty Child' (as the Doctor and Rose are traveling alone, and they have already been back to see Jackie and Mickey at least once). Once again, it is probably set before 'Dalek', as there are no references to Adam.

SYNOPSIS: The Doctor and Rose return to London to find a local lottery is being run by people in hedgehog costumes, in which the prize is a video game (*Death to Mantodeans*), or a holiday from which no-one seems to return. Along with Mickey they investigate, and discover that the hedgehog people are actually the Quevvils, who are using the holidaymakers as remote-control warriors, controlled by the game players. Rose ends up on the planet Toop, being controlled by the Doctor (with help from a young boy, Robert) in a subversive attempt to end the games and rescue the players. They are successful, return Robert to 2006, and then leave for further adventures ...

THE STORY UNFOLDS: The TARDIS lands in the Powell Estate, near a Chinese takeaway, where it has landed before. Jackie lives at 48 Bucknall House. Darren Pye was a childhood nemesis of Rose's, and also of Johnny Dean's and most of the Powell Estate, and seems to be two years older than her. Rose has a teddy bear called Mr Tedopoulos. She refers to the Nestene Consciousness and the Slitheen.

The bulk of the book is set on the planet Toop, location of the Mantodean stronghold. Robert is a fan of a work of fiction that seems strikingly similar to the *Harry Potter...* novels, another that sounds similar to *Buffy the Vampire Slayer*, and also the *Star Wars* films. Monstrithology is the study of Monster Spotting (possibly). The Cookie Monster is apparently an alien. Mickey has GCSEs.

The ninth Doctor is over 6 feet tall. Rose went to Hampton Court on a school trip in 1998 – the Doctor visited in the 1700s. The Quevvils can shoot spikes from their bodies, and have the technology to remote-control humans. Despite being roughly twenty-five, Mickey sometimes socialises at the local youth club with Jason Jones, Anil Rawat and Kevin. The Doctor often cries, and he uses the phrase 'Mickey the idiot' from 'World War Three'.

PUBLISHING NOTES: Originally announced as *Death Players*. The design in the background of the front and back covers, and on the spines of each of the novels, matches up with a sequence of designs used above the chapter headings throughout the books. This was confirmed in a BBC press release to accompany the books as a Gallifreyan numbering system, and as a result the books should be read in the following order: *The Clockwise Man*, *The Monsters Inside*, *Winner Takes All*.

BAD WOLF: Mickey has a pile of computer games on his floor, including *Gran Turismo*, *Resident Evil*, *Bad Wolf* and *TimeSplitters 2* (p22).

COMING SOON
To be published in September 2005:
The Deviant Strain by Justin Richards
Only Human by Gareth Roberts
The Stealers of Dreams by Steve Lyons

COMICS

THE LOVE INVASION

WRITERS: Gareth Roberts (script), Gareth Roberts/Clayton Hickman (story)
ILLUSTRATORS: Mike Collins (pencil art), David A Roach (inks), Dylan Teague/James Offredi (part 2) (colours), Roger Landridge (lettering)
EDITORIAL: Clayton Hickman (editor), Scott Gray (consultant)
PUBLICATION: *Doctor Who Magazine* issues 355-7; 31 March 2005, 28 April 2005, 26 May 2005

WHERE AND WHEN: London, 1966, including Carnaby Street, the future Powell Estate, St Merrion's Uni Hospital on Cottingham Street, and the Post Office Tower. The story takes place during one day and is most likely set between 'World War Three' and 'Dalek'.

SYNOPSIS: *Part One* – The Doctor and Rose are concerned about the 'Lend-a-Hand' industry taking off in London, and the Brandon Mews estate appearing where the Powell Estate should be – they discover a dead alien in the toilets of a pub, and the Doctor chases the killer to a hospital where she attacks him. Meanwhile Rose joins 'Lend-a-Hand' and, discovering an alien there, escapes.
Part Two – The Doctor survives the attack and discovers that the killer, Charlotte Cobb, is after the 'Lend-a-Hand' girls. They meet up with Rose, and her new friend Shirley, and Charlotte explains her story – she suspects the 'Lend-a-Hand' girls of killing her husband Peter, a researcher. The four go to investigate 'Lend-a-Hand' and discover the alien there is a Kustollian, who are not due to invade Earth until 3046 – this one intends to destroy the Moon.
Part Three – The alien, Igrax, explains that he regretted the devastating war in 3046 so came back in time to alter human history so their paths never crossed with that of the Kustollians. To aid him in this, he has been manipulating the women of London to spread peace through 'Lend-a-Hand'. They use Peter Cobb's research to turn these girls back to normal, and then head to the Post Office Tower to stop Igrax from launching his missiles at the Moon.

THE STORY UNFOLDS: This is an early adventure for Rose – she still hasn't adjusted to travelling too far into the past, although she *has* changed her hoodie. The Doctor steals a horse and cart belonging to Brambell Merchants, Trotters Lane (a treble homage: to Wilfred Brambell who played the old rag and bone man Steptoe in the BBC's sitcom *Steptoe and Son*; to the first episode of *Doctor Who* where the junkyard is in Totter's Lane; and possibly a third allusion to Del and Rodney Trotter from the BBC sitcom *Only Fools and Horses*). Rose got a D in GSCE Science. The Doctor claims that there are lots of time travellers at the grassy knoll in Texas, 1963, all trying to stop Kennedy's assassination (possibly a reference to events in the Virgin Publishing *Doctor Who* novel *Who Killed Kennedy*). The Doctor watches *Space: 1999*. Ben Jackson and Polly, companions to the first Doctor, seem to be at the Post Office Tower, as the former can be seen proposing to the latter. (This places the story after July, when the story 'The Faceless Ones' (1967), their final regular appearance on TV, was set). The Doctor uses his sonic screwdriver not only to light up a train carriage, but also seemingly to cause a pair of JCBs to destroy the Brandon Mews Estate.

BAD WOLF: On a poster in the pub (Part Two, page six of the comic).

PUBLISHING NOTES: Originally the first ninth Doctor comic strip was set to be written by Russell T Davies, but this fell through as he was too busy. Following the postponement of the TV series's debut by a couple of weeks, *Doctor Who Magazine* 354 went without a strip (instead of the planned appearance of Part One), and the remaining parts to this story were all delayed by a month.

ART ATTACK

WRITER: Mike Collins
ILLUSTRATORS: Mike Collins (pencil art), Kris Justice (inks), Dylan Teague (colours), Roger Langridge (lettering)
EDITORIAL: Clayton Hickman (editor), Scott Gray (consultant)
PUBLICATION: *Doctor Who Magazine* issue 358; 23 June 2005

WHERE AND WHEN: The Oriel Gallery, 37th Century, and Cazkelf's homeworld.

SYNOPSIS: The Doctor and Rose visit the opening of a trans-dimension gallery to see the Mona Lisa, and are confronted by extravagant artist Cazkelf the Transcendent. Cazkelf plans to use the gallery to transmit a homing message back to his home planet, but the Doctor takes him there to show him his race is now dead.

THE STORY UNFOLDS: The sonic screwdriver is used to feedback Cazkelf's signal. Rose travels to an alien world, placing this story after *The Monsters Inside*. Alpha Centauri (or one of its race) is present at the opening of the Oriel, as is a Meep, a Draconian, a Dominator, Professor Asimoff (from prior comic strips) and some Gastropods. The Doctor knew Damien Hurst and was present for the painting of the Mona Lisa. Rose went to Parc Asterix with her friend Shareen when they were on a school trip to the Louvre. Oriel is actually Welsh for 'gallery'. World War Five happened prior to this story.

BAD WOLF: None. Outside her visit to her parents' wedding, this is the only of Rose's trips that we witness that does *not* feature these words. It may, of course, have been a part of one of the many works of art that we do not see during the adventure.

APPENDIX C:
THE RATINGS WAR

One of the most crucial aspects of *Doctor Who* for the BBC and the new series production team was how well it would do in the ratings, the all important information that would govern whether the series would continue on into a second year and beyond. The following is a detailed breakdown and analysis of *Doctor Who*'s UK ratings for its 2005 season.

INTRODUCTION

One in five people in the UK watched the first broadcast of 'Rose'. The BBC's barrage of publicity successfully drew a huge (in 2005 terms) audience to the opening episode. This effectively established the maximum potentially interested audience, although two million seem not to have wanted to watch the new series again after its debut. But, more importantly, the majority stayed with the series once the hype had started to die down – *Doctor Who* consistently had a 'reach' (proportion of the population watching the show at any point) of about 15%.

It also had a steady audience share (i.e. its proportion of all those watching any television during its timeslot) of about 40%. This compares with an average BBC1 peaktime share of about 25%. At the start of its run, *Doctor Who*'s share in its timeslot was fairly evenly matched by that of *Ant & Dec's Saturday Night Takeaway*, although generally a little ahead. Once the latter had concluded its run, ITV1 briefly substituted *Celebrity Wrestling*. The disastrous performance of that show, with ratings of only two or three million and a share well below 20%, led to its swift removal from that timeslot. A selection of movies in the slot from then on failed to make any improvement in ITV1's Saturday evening performance, precipitating a round of press comment and speculation that ITV was now 'in crisis'. On a couple of occasions, it was actually a channel other than ITV1 that gave *Doctor Who* its closest competition.

In fact, only one factor had any serious impact on *Doctor Who*'s ratings for this series: the weather. Hot, sunny days could lose the show around a million BBC1 viewers, although, with the television audience down generally when the weather was good, the series always maintained its chart position relative to other programmes (see below). More importantly, the figures for timeshifted (video) recordings and BBC3 repeats for *Doctor Who* tended to rise quite dramatically – and at a rate notably higher than for other shows – when the headline Saturday evening figure declined.

CONSOLIDATED FINAL RATINGS

The following is a detailed breakdown of the final, consolidated ratings for the series, including time-shifted video recordings, featuring the final reported viewer count in millions for the initial Saturday night broadcast, the audience share (percentage of viewers who tuned into the broadcast versus other programmes), the Audience Appreciation Index (or AI, an index based upon a rating of 0 to 100 from a demographic sample of viewers) and the audience reach (percentage of total televisions tuned into the broadcast), as well as the final ratings of the top competitor for the time slot.

Note that the Audience Appreciation figures are not supplied by BARB. The information listed here includes the *final* index, reported many weeks after the initial broadcast (hence later figures not being available at press time) as well as the overnight AI indexes which were released much earlier, usually within 24 hours after broadcast. The final AI sampling involves considerably more research and review.

Episode	Viewing Figure	Share	AI*	Reach	Competitor Figure
Rose	10.81m	44.84%	76 (81)	20	7.47m ITV1 (a)
The End of the World	7.97m	37.84%	76 (79)	14	6.23m ITV1
The Unquiet Dead	8.86m	37.78%	80 (80)	16	7.26m ITV1
Aliens of London	7.63m	35.67%	82 (81)	14	7.37m ITV1
World War Three	7.98m	40.15%	81 (82)	14	3.92m ITV1 (b)
Dalek	8.63m	44.89%	84 (84)	16	3.06m ITV1
The Long Game	8.01m	40.39%	** (81)	14	2.64m BBC2 (c)
Father's Day	8.06m	44.38%	** (83)	15	2.44m C4 (d)
The Empty Child	7.11m	36.59%	** (84)	13	4.09m ITV1 (e)
The Doctor Dances	6.86m	38.53%	** (85)	12	3.31m ITV1
Boom Town	7.69m	38.55%	** (82)	14	3.41m ITV1
Bad Wolf	6.81m	37.92%	** (85)	12	3.65m ITV1
The Parting of the Ways	6.91m	43.96%	** (89)	13	2.49m ITV1
Series Average	7.95m	40.11%	80 (83)	14	

Source for viewing figures: Broadcasters Audience Research Board Ltd (BARB)
m: Millions of viewers

* Final AI figure (if known), with initial reported AI figure in parentheses (AI figures not sourced from BARB)
** unavailable at press time
(a) ITV1 competition Ant & Dec's Saturday Night Takeaway
(b) ITV1 schedules Celebrity Wrestling after end of Ant & Dec series
(c) Porridge repeat
(d) Screening of The Dam Busters on Channel 4
(e) ITV1 schedules blockbuster movies after moving Celebrity Wrestling

This notes the relative solidity of *Doctor Who*'s performance: a series low of just under seven million and a high of a little under nine million (plus, of course, the 'event' television of 'Rose' which should be considered separately simply for the novelty value of it being the first episode in fifteen years). The performances of other series during this time varied widely, such as *Coronation Street* (a high in this period of 13.11m, a low of 7.55m) and *EastEnders* (high 11.5m, low 8.45m) – including a steady drift downwards, thanks to seasonal changes that depress viewing figures across all channels and all programmes.

At least as important as a measure of *Doctor Who*'s 2005 success are the ratings attained by other high-profile, prime-time dramas: while serial dramas like *Casualty* consistently matched *Doctor Who* throughout this period, series like *Murphy's Law* were judged successes with ratings of around five million. Audience figures of three or four million are generally enough to get a BBC1 or ITV1 show into its channel's top twenty for the week.

The final averaged figures should be treated with some caution, however. 'The Unquiet Dead' made headlines not only for its 'scary' content, but also for apparently having better figures than those for both the Grand National and a royal wedding. This is not quite true – the horse race itself had much higher audiences than *Doctor Who*, but the lengthy 'pre-race' and 'post-race' analysis that was broadcast attracted significantly lower interest, hence the lower overall average; similarly, the actual televised wedding achieved a higher peak than its average would suggest, although not quite high enough to beat the Gelth. Of course the same in some ways applies to most episodes of the new series, as can be seen in the table of overnight figures below.

Another point of interest: *Doctor Who* seemed to perform even better in multichannel households (termed 'MH', these are households with access to digital, cable or satellite services). 'Dalek', the fourteenth most watched programme of the week of its broadcast across the five main channels, actually managed tenth place in the MH chart by proving more popular than most episodes of *Emmerdale*.

BBC audience research in late June revealed that the series officially averaged 8.2 million viewers, with a 40% average audience share. 'Rose' achieved the highest viewer rating for a new Doctor, and was the second highest-rated launch of a new series of *Doctor Who*, behind the seventeenth season in 1979.

CHART POSITIONS

The following is a breakdown of each episode and its position on British television: as compared with other BBC1 series on Saturday; as compared with other BBC1 series during the week; in its particular time slot; in comparison with other terrestrial (non-satellite/digital) channels on Saturday; and in comparison with terrestrial channels for the week:

Episode	BBC1 Saturday	BBC1 Week	Timeslot	Terrestrial Saturday	Terrestrial Week
Rose	1	3	1	1	7
The End of the World	1	6	1	1	19
The Unquiet Dead	1	5	1	1	15
Aliens of London	2	6	1	2	18
World War Three	2	6	1	2	20
Dalek	1	5	1	1	14
The Long Game	2	6	1	2	17
Father's Day	1	5	1	1	17
The Empty Child	3	8	1	3	21
The Doctor Dances	1	7	1	1	18
Boom Town	2	7	1	2	18
Bad Wolf	2	8	1	2	19
The Parting of the Ways	1	7	1	1	17

Source: Broadcasters Audience Research Board Ltd (BARB)

The chart domination by the main three television soaps (*EastEnders*, *Coronation Street* and *Emmerdale*) remained unaffected during this period, and the composition of the various weekly 'top ten' lists also remained fairly consistent.

THE OVERNIGHTS

While official viewing figures from BARB took time before being reported (usually around ten days to two weeks after broadcast), initial audience ratings were normally available on the Sunday following a Saturday evening broadcast. While *Doctor Who* performed strongly and consistently against *Ant & Dec's Saturday Night Takeaway*, ITV1's replacement for that show when it ended its run lost the channel between three and five million Saturday evening viewers. However, there was no appreciable rise in *Doctor Who*'s figures when its competition changed. ITV1's missing millions seemingly had no interest in watching *Doctor Who*. So it seems likely that the figures for *Rose* represented the absolute summit of *Doctor Who*'s pulling power. With a peak of 10.6m people watching on broadcast, no other episode could come close – apparently, a couple of million people watched at least some of that first episode and never came back for more.

At least 1.5m people were turning to BBC1 every Saturday at 7 pm specifically for *Doctor Who*, and the show consistently gained viewers throughout each episode's duration. Strangely (or perhaps not), these viewers do not appear to have been drawn from other channels – the number of people watching television went up for *Doctor Who*. To take one example, in the week 'The Long Game' was broadcast, the preceding BBC1 show (*Strictly Dance Fever*) had 4.22m viewers, a 27.2% share, the total viewing audience at that time being 15.51m. 'The Long Game' received an overnight average of 7.51m, representing a 38.9% share of an average total audience of 19.31m in its timeslot. This means that the total *television* audience increased by 3.8m, while BBC1's audience rose by 3.29m just for *Doctor Who*. It is not, of course, possible (without examining a detailed breakdown of every television channel's ratings) to say for sure that *Doctor Who* took over 85% of that incoming audience – but BBC1 promptly lost 3.1m of its audience, a million or so of them children going to bed, when 'The Long Game' finished, and that pattern is quite convincingly repeated across the thirteen weeks of the show's run.

The results for later episodes need some perspective. Episode 9 was in an earlier timeslot than the rest of the series (thanks to the annual *Eurovision Song Contest*) and had the misfortune to be broadcast on an evening when the television schedules experienced major disruptions (caused by extensive extra time in the FA Cup Final football that afternoon). In that timeslot, it maintained a 35% audience share, against a BBC1 average of 23%, and attracted about two million more viewers than the usual occupant of the slot, *Strictly Dance Fever*. It also managed almost twice the audience attracted for *Star Wars: The Phantom Menace* on ITV1, and this was also the week that *Star Wars: Revenge of the Sith* premiered in cinemas, with all its attendant publicity. If anything, the surprise was that 'The Empty Child' performed so well that week. This is also true of the next episode, 'The Doctor Dances', which aired over a public holiday weekend at the beginning of a week-long school holiday in the UK, with lower viewing figures for television shows all round. Both the steady audience share figures and the immediate recovery for 'Boom Town' the next week provided the necessary confirmation that it was television in general – not *Doctor Who* alone – that was losing out against the sunshine and national events. One national event – a British tennis player being beaten at Wimbledon – managed ratings of a little over nine million the Saturday after *Doctor Who* finished its run. Much of the country was being rained on at the time; the second-highest

Wimbledon rating of the season to that point was a little under five million, and British players can't be relied on to lose on Saturdays. BBC1 seemed to have found its reliable Saturday evening champion – and it was not a tennis player.

Please note that, due to the wishes of the Broadcasters Audience Research Board (BARB), we are unable to provide the collected overnight ratings data in this book.

BBC THREE REPEATS

The BBC3 digital channel rebroadcast each episode of *Doctor Who* on the following Sunday evening at 7.00 pm. As of the fifth episode, 'World War Three', they also included an overnight repeat showing late Saturday night, and one episode, 'Bad Wolf', was also repeated the following Friday night. The following notes the final viewing figures for each repeat broadcast:

Episode	Late Night (Saturday) viewers	Sunday evening viewers	Friday night viewers
Rose	*	0.63m	*
The End of the World	*	0.47m	*
The Unquiet Dead	*	0.37m	*
Aliens of London	*	0.61m	*
World War Three	0.17m	0.55m	*
Dalek	0.18m	0.54m	*
The Long Game	0.16m	0.62m	*
Father's Day	0.16m	0.53m	*
The Empty Child	0.18m	0.79m	*
The Doctor Dances	0.24m	0.48m	*
Boom Town	0.17m	0.49m	*
Bad Wolf	0.25m	0.66m	0.24m
The Parting of the Ways	0.26m	0.74m	*
Series Average	0.20m	0.58m	0.24m

Source for viewing figures: Broadcasters Audience Research Board Ltd (BARB)
m: Millions of viewers

* No repeat broadcast

While these figures clearly show the seasonal decline towards the end of the series, the most dramatic figures are the leaps that occur in the figures for the BBC3 showings when ratings are depressed for the BBC1 premieres. Only 'The Doctor Dances' and 'Dalek' (in different ways) really buck this trend. Broadly, as can be seen in the figures for 'The Empty Child' and 'The Parting of the Ways' (shown on the hottest day of the year to that date), the lower the BBC1 overnight figure, the more people set their videos or caught the episode later on BBC3.

TOTAL VIEWERS PER EPISODE, RANKED

Combining the final BARB ratings of each episode along with the repeat showings on BBC3, one can complete a list of 'total viewers' for each episode, ranked as follows:

Episode	Total BARB consolidated + BBC3 figures
Rose	11.3m
Dalek	9.4m
The Unquiet Dead	9.2m
Father's Day	8.8m
The Long Game	8.7m
* Series average	8.6m
World War Three	8.6m
The End of the World	8.4m
Boom Town	8.3m
Aliens of London	8.2m
The Empty Child	8.0m
Bad Wolf	8.0m
The Parting of the Ways	7.9m
The Doctor Dances	7.6m

Source for viewing figures: Broadcasters Audience Research Board Ltd (BARB)
m: Millions of viewers

These figures are of necessity only very approximate, with BARB figures unavailable for BBC3 showings prior to Episode 9. They are possibly the clearest demonstration of how little the audiences varied across the series, with only Episode 1 significantly higher than the other twelve, and only Episode 10 noticeably lower.

DOCTOR WHO CONFIDENTIAL

The documentary series *Doctor Who Confidential* aired on the BBC3 network after each episode's broadcast was completed on BBC1, usually at 7.45 pm (though as with the broadcast of 'The Empty Child', that week's episode was half an hour early). With the broadcast of the third instalment, a Sunday evening rebroadcast was added; an additional over night airing, varying in time from late Saturday night to early Sunday morning, was added with the broadcast of the fourth episode. There was no Sunday night rebroadcast of the ninth episode of *Confidential*, while episode twelve had one additional repeat the following Friday night along with its counterpart *Doctor Who* episode, 'Bad Wolf'.

In addition, two documentaries produced by the same team as *Confidential* aired on BBC1: 'A New Dimension' was at 5.25 pm on 26 March, ninety-five minutes prior to the *Doctor Who* debut, while 'The Ultimate Guide' was shown at 6.15 pm on the final night of transmission, 18 June.

Note that some of the BBC3 repeats were retitled *Doctor Who Confidential: Cut Down* and significantly edited to fill a quarter-hour slot rather than the full half-hour. (The original Saturday night broadcasts remained unchanged.) The episodes reduced to *Cut Down* format in the Sunday repeat began with the sixth episode and (with the exception of episode nine) ran through to the end of the season.

Episode	Saturday viewers	Late night (Sat) viewers	Sunday viewers	Friday viewers
A New Dimension	4.02m **	*	*	*
1 Bringing Back the Doctor	0.87m	*	*	*
2 The Good, the Bad and the Ugly	0.37m	*	*	*
3 TARDIS Tales	0.55m	*	0.23m	*
4 I Get a Side-Kick out of You	0.52m	0.08m	0.41m	*
5 Why on Earth?	0.41m	0.09m	0.36m	*
6 Dalek	0.52m	0.11m	0.34m	*
7 The Dark Side	0.49m	0.10m	0.33m	*
8 Time Trouble	0.61m	0.09m	0.30m	*
9 Special Effects	0.43m	0.10m	*	*
10 Weird Science	0.40m	0.08m	0.26m	*
11 Unsung Heroes and Violent Death	0.54m	0.06m	0.32m	*
12 The World of Who	0.66m	0.15m	0.35m	0.20m
13 The Last Battle	0.69m	0.18m	0.42m	*
The Ultimate Guide	2.77m **	*	*	*

Source for viewing figures: Broadcasters Audience Research Board Ltd (BARB)
m: Millions of viewers

* No repeat broadcast
** Note: audience share for "A New Dimension" was 26%, "The Ultimate Guide" 23%; final share data on each episode of "Doctor Who Confidential" unavailable.

EPISODE POLLS

Members of the *Outpost Gallifrey* website forum participated in weekly discussions and rankings of each episode of the new series; each episode was given a ranking between one and five, with five being highest. With a large cross-section of *Doctor Who* fans participating – typically in the region of 2,500-3,000 people – they were a good indicator of fan reaction to the first series. The percentage rankings below have been calculated by adding together the total number of marks received by each episode (as of 12 July 2005) and dividing by the maximum that could have been achieved if everyone who voted had given the episode a five.

Dalek	93%
The Empty Child	91%
The Parting of the Ways	91%
The Doctor Dances	90%
Bad Wolf	89%
The Unquiet Dead	87%
Father's Day	86%
The End of the World	82%
Rose	79%
World War Three	75%
Aliens of London	72%
The Long Game	68%
Boom Town	68%

The top five fan-ranked episodes are also the top five rated episodes on the BBC's initial overnight Audience Appreciation Index (AI) figures. Of note, 'The Unquiet Dead' and 'The End of the World' rated quite differently in fan reaction (sixth and eighth, respectively) than they did on the overnight AI rankings (twelfth and thirteenth).

APPENDIX D:
CAST AND CREW INDEX

The following is a list of credited cast and crew associated with the first season of *Doctor Who*. The roles played by actors are in **boldface**, crew positions are *italicised*; the numerals match the episode number.

Adams, Christine: **Cathica** (107)

Adams, Jamie: *Assistant Editor* (109, 110)

Ahearne, Joe: *Director* (106, 108, 111-113)

Allan, Lucy: *Stunt Performer* (103)

Altena-Berk, Ailsa[1]: *Choreographer* (101-112)

Anscombe, Adrian: *Standby Props* (101-105); *Property Master* (106-113)

Any Effects: *Special Effects* (101-106, 109-113)

Armesto, Sebastian: **Broff** (112)

Armory, Beccy: **Raffalo** (102)

Arundel, Howard: *First Assistant Director* (111)

Badland, Annette: **Margaret Blaine** (104, 105, 111)

Baker, Matt: **Himself** (104)

Bannerman, Yasmin: **Jabe** (102)

Barrowman, John[2]: **Jack Harkness** (109-113)

Barton, Robert: **Registrar** (108)

Beckingham, Steven: **Polkowski** (106)

Begley, Patrick: *Property Master* (101-105)

Bellin, Eirlys: **Bev** (108)

Bennett, Peter: *First Assistant Director* (112, 113)

Bennett, Sara: *2D VFX Artist* (101-103, 108-109)

Benton, Mark: **Clive** (101)

Blackman, Kath: *A/Production Accountant* (101-113)

Boak, Keith: *Director* (101, 104, 105)

Bowers, Jenny: *Graphic Artist* (101-113)

Bowman, David: *2D VFX Artist* (101, 103-110, 112, 113)

Bradley, Jamie: **Strood** (112)

Briggs, Nicholas: **Nestene Voice** (101); **Dalek Voice** (106, 112, 113)

Brown, Marie: *Post Production Supervisor* (101-113)

Burgess, Dominic: **Agorax** (112)

Burton, Paul: *3D VFX Artist* (101, 102, 104, 105, 109, 112, 113)

Busser-Casas, Astrid: *2D VFX Artist* (102, 103, 107, 109-113)

Callis, Sam: **Security Guard** (112)

Callow, Simon: **Charles Dickens** (103)

Carl, Lachele: **Reporter** (104, 105)

Carpenter, Jana: **De Maggio** (106)

Carson, Silas: **Alien Voices** (102)

Cassey, Zoë: *On Line Editor* (109, 110)

Cater, Wayne: **Stage Manager** (103)

Chester, Peter: *Best Boy* (101-113)

Chowdhry, Navin: **Indra Ganesh** (104)

Chung, Basil: **Bau** (104)

Clarke, Matthew: *On Line Editor* (101-113)

Clarke, Noel[3]: **Mickey Smith** (101, 104, 105, 111, 113)

Clarke, Stuart: *Stunt Performer* (106, 112, 113)

Clayton, Sean: *Second Assistant Director* (106, 108)

Coduri, Camille: **Jackie Tyler** (101, 102, 104, 105, 108, 113)

Cohen, Will: *Visual FX Producer* (101-113)

Collinson, Phil: *Producer* (101-113)

Constantine, Susannah: **Voice of Zu-Zana** (112)

Cope, Martha: **Controller** (112)

Cornell, Paul: *Writer* (108)

Costelloe, Mike: *Camera Operator* (101-105)

Cottle, George: *Stunt Performer* (111)

David, Alan: **Gabriel Sneed** (103)

Davie, Linda: *Make-Up Supervisor* (101-113)

Davies, Russell T: *Executive Producer* (101-113); *Writer* (101, 102, 104, 105, 107, 111-113)

Day, Simon: **Steward** (102)

Deguara, Jean-Claude: *3D VFX Artist* (101, 104, 105, 107-109, 111-113)

Del Giudice, Liana: *Editor* (109, 110)

Dingwall, Shaun: **Pete Tyler** (108)

Doabe, Corey: **Spray Painter** (104, 105)

Doyle, Ceres: *Assistant Editor* (101-113)

Dundas, James: *Rights Executive* (106, 112, 113)

Dyer, Casey: **Young Mickey** (108)

Eccleston, Christopher: **Doctor Who** (101-113)

Edgell, Jamie: *Stunt Performer* (102); *Stunt Co-ordinator* (112, 113)

Edwards, Barnaby: **Dalek Operator** (106, 112, 113)

Lyn, Euros: *Director* (102, 103)

Marr, Andrew: **Himself** (104, 105)

Maskell, Tina: *Stunt Performer* (111)

Maxwell-Martin, Anna: **Suki** (107)

McCall, Davina: **Voice of Davinadroid** (112)

McCoy, Adam: **Clive's Son** (101)

McFadden, Paul: *Dialogue Editor* (101-113)

McGarrity, Kim: *Stunt Performer* (109-111)

McKinney, Matt: *3D VFX Artist* (102, 109-113)

Meire, Chad: *2D VFX Artist* (113)

Meire, Joel: *3D VFX Artist* (102, 111)

Meldrum, Debbie: *Production Runner* (113)

Mill, The: *Visual Effects* (101-113)

Millennium Effects: *Prosthetics* (101, 102, 104-107, 109-113)

Miller, Brandon: **Alf** (109)

Moffat, Steven: *Writer* (109, 110)

Montana, Joe: **Commander** (106)

Montanes, Alberto: *2D VFX Artist* (101-103, 107, 109)

Mori, Naoko: **Doctor Sato** (104)

Morison, David: *Standby Art Director* (111)

Morris, Steffan: *Second Assistant Director* (101-105, 107, 109-113)

Morus, Llyr: *Unit Manager* (106-108); *Location Manager* (109, 110, 112, 113)

MTFX: *Special Effects* (107)

Mumford, Dan: *Third Assistant Director* (102, 103, 106-113)

Murphy, Jordan: **Ernie** (109, 110)

Myles, Eve: **Gwyneth** (103)

Nation, Terry: *Daleks originally created by* (106, 112, 113)

Nayar, Nisha: **Female Programmer** (112, 113)

Nicholas, Stephen: *Supervising Art Director* (101-113)

Older, Jon: *First Assistant Director* (109, 110)

Otway, Helen: **Auton** (101)

Parry, Dafydd Rhys[7]: *Third Assistant Director* (101, 104, 105)

Peart-Smith, Yolanda: *Wardrobe Supervisor* (101-113)

Pedrick, Aled: **Idris Hopper** (111)

Peel, Bean: *Stunt Performer* (108)

Pegg, Nicholas: **Dalek Operator** (112, 113)

Pegg, Simon: **The Editor** (107)

Perrott, Porl[8]: *3D VFX Artist* (101, 102, 104, 105)

Perry, Dian: **Computer Voice** (109, 110)

Perry, Luke: **Timothy Lloyd** (110)

Petts, Chris: *3D VFX Artist* (101-110, 112, 113)

Piper, Billie: **Rose Tyler** (101-113)

Plowman, Anna-Louise: **Goddard** (106)

Potts, Eric: **Oliver Charles** (104)

Povey, Meic: **Driver** (103)

Pritchard, Claire: *Make-Up Artist* (103[9], 106-113)

Prockter, Colin: **Head Chef** (107)

Prosser, Sian: *Continuity* (101, 104, 105)

Pryor, Andy: *Casting Director* (101-113)

Pugsley, Richard: *Business Manager* (101-105); *Finance Manager* (106-113)

Raynor, Helen: *Script Editor* (103, 106, 109, 110, 112, 113)

Reid, Emma: *Unit Manager* (102, 103)

Rhys, Huw: **Redpath** (103)

Richards, John: *Editor* (102, 103, 107)

Richardson, Damian: *Boom Operator* (101-113)

Richardson, Ian: *Sound Recordist* (101-113)

Ricketts, Tim: *Dubbing Mixer* (101-105, 107-113)

Roberts, Richard: *2D VFX Artist* (113)

Robertson, Kirsty: *Casting Associate* (101-113)

Robinson, Anne: **Voice of Anne Droid** (112, 113)

Robinson, John: *Grip* (101-113)

Rogers, Seon: *Stunt Performer* (108)

Rowlands, Elwen: *Script Editor* (101, 102, 104, 105, 107, 108, 111)

Rozelaar-Green, Frank: **Sonny** (108)

Rumbelow, Joelle: *Production Buyer* (111)

Ruscoe, Alan: **Auton** (101); **Slitheen** (104, 105, 111); **Android** (112, 113)

Russell, Jenna: **Floor Manager** (112)

Samuel, Catherine: *Production Buyer* (101-110, 112, 113); *Set Decorator* (111)

Samuels, Damian: **Mr Lloyd** (109, 110)

Sant, David: **Auton** (101)

Schwab, John: **Bywater** (106)

Shearman, Robert: *Writer* (106)

Shellard, Phill: *Standby Props* (101-113)

Sheward, Lee: *Stunt Co-ordinator* (102, 103, 106-110, 111)

Simpson, Tracie: *Production Manager* (101-113)

Smith, Andrew: *Construction Manager* (101-113)

Speirs, Steve: **Strickland** (104, 105)

Stephens, Martin: *Camera Operator* (101-113)

Stewart, Sara: **Computer Voice** (102)

Stone Fewings, Jo: **Male Programmer** (112, 113)

1. Listed during broadcast for 101, but credit omitted on DVD release
2. Credited as Jack Harkness in 109, as Jack in 110, and as Captain Jack in 111-113
3. Credited as Mickey Smith in 101, 104, 105, and as Mickey in 111, 113
4. Credited as Michael Harison on broadcast for 102, corrected on DVD release
5. Credited as Nicolas Hernandes on 108
6. Credited as Tristan Howell on 106, 108
7. Credited as Dafydd Parry on 104
8. Credited as Paul Perrott in transmitted versions of 101, 102; corrected for DVD release
9. Listed during broadcast for 103, but credit omitted on DVD release

APPENDIX E:
FOR FURTHER INFORMATION ...

The extent of *Doctor Who* is not limited to thirteen forty-five-minute episodes each year, a documentary series and a handful of books ... There's a whole universe of *Doctor Who* waiting for you out there. The following is a quick guide to navigating *Doctor Who* beyond the television series; while it's by no means a complete list, it should get you started on your way!

ORGANISATIONS

A number of fan organisations exist across the globe; four major organisations act as national/international societies promoting *Doctor Who* in its many forms. The **Doctor Who Appreciation Society** is the world's largest fan club for the series, based in Britain with a local group network and worldwide membership. Established in 1976, the Society publishes a monthly print newsletter, *Celestial Toyroom*. The *DWAS* can be reached at PO Box 519, London, SW17 9XW, United Kingdom, or via the Internet at **dwas.drwho.org**.

Based in Canada, the **Doctor Who Information Network** (DWIN) is an international organisation founded in 1980. The longest running *Doctor Who* fan club in North America, DWIN publishes the bi-monthly *Enlightenment* magazine, *Myth Makers Doctor Who* fiction collections and is sponsor of occasional *Who Party* conventions and other events. You can reach DWIN at P.O.Box 912, Station F, Toronto, Ontario, Canada M4Y 2N9 or on the web at **www.dwin.org**.

The **Doctor Who Club of Australia** is that country's national fan organisation. They publish a bi-monthly periodical, *Data Extract*, and run a national convention, *Whovention*. You can contact the DWCA at GPO Box 2870, Sydney NSW 2001 Australia, or on the web at **www.doctorwhoaustralia.org**.

The **New Zealand Doctor Who Fan Club** (NZDWFC) is New Zealand's national group, based in Auckland. The NZDWFC publishes *Time Space Visualiser* (better known as *TSV*) , an outstanding periodical with a host of regular features, two to three times yearly. The organisation can be reached at PO Box 7061, Wellesley Street, Auckland, New Zealand or on the web at **www.doctorwho.org.nz**.

Scotland is also home to extensive *Doctor Who* fan activity, with groups in Edinburgh (**www.edinburghwho.co.uk**) and Glasgow (**zap.to/GlasgowWho**).

In additional to national and international groups, fan clubs exist the world over, from local groups to active mail organisations and even several autograph collectors' clubs. Local clubs not part of the main organisations spread out across these countries, some meeting on a regular or semi-regular basis.

Also, while there is no longer an active US-based national club, the US has many local groups active in such cities as: Los Angeles; New York; New Jersey; Chicago; Massachusetts; Indiana; Minneapolis/St Paul; St. Louis, Missouri; Des Moines, Iowa; Milwaukee, Wisconsin; Houston and Dallas, Texas; and central Florida. Many of these have websites that can be found online with ease ...

ON THE INTERNET

The World Wide Web is today's hotbed of *Doctor Who* fandom; the series is represented, at last count, by no fewer than 700 fan websites ... and a host of officially sanctioned ones, too! News and information, reference material, photos, fan fiction, illustration and chat – you can find it all on the Web, and it's easy to locate. Here's a quick guide to the most prominent parts of the Internet that involve the new *Doctor Who* series:

STARTING POINTS

Of course, any visit to the Internet for a *Doctor Who* fan should start with the official *Doctor Who* website (**www.bbc.co.uk/doctorwho**), which includes official news and information, video and audio clips, photos, webcasts and even games. (There are links there to their 'spinoff' sites such as *Who is Doctor Who?*, a *UNIT* site, a site for the fictional firm *Geocomtex*, and a primer on the Bad Wolf conspiracy.)

From there, fans usually head to *Outpost Gallifrey* (**www.gallifreyone.com**), the web's largest and most prominent *Doctor Who* fan site and community, which has extensive news sections, reviews, an updated events calendar, detailed reference guides and a popular discussion forum. *The Web Guide to Doctor Who* (**www.doctorwhowebguide.net**) features the most extensive *Doctor Who* links list to be found anywhere, and is a great starting point for any journey online. And the *Doctor Who Home Page* (**nitro9.earth.uni.edu/doctor/ homepage.html**) has long been considered an unofficial 'home' of online *Doctor Who* fandom, and still serves the community today.

NEWS AND INFORMATION

Besides the aforementioned, there are a number of other websites that provide quality *Doctor Who* news coverage. The *Doctor Who Cuttings Archive* (**www.cuttingsarchive.org.uk**) has in-depth coverage of *Doctor Who* in the media, with press clippings and news articles. *Planet Who* (**www.planetwho.co.uk**), *Gallifrey 5* (**www.gallifrey5.co.uk**) and *UNIT News* (**www.unitnews.org.uk**) are good, quick sources of news and information for the *Doctor Who* fan on the go. The website of the *Doctor Who* Appreciation Society (**dwas.drwho.org**) features updated news and information on the series including local flavour and appearances. *American Who* (**www.americanwho.net**) is an online *Doctor Who* 'radio' show featuring news and interviews with *Doctor Who* personalities. The BBC also maintains a *Doctor Who Locations Guide* (**www.bbc.co.uk/wales/southeast /sites/doctorwho/locationsguide.shtml**) which has information about where the show has been filmed in Wales, while BBC Radio 2 (**www.bbc.co.uk/radio2/events/doctorwho**) still has its webspace up that accompanied the *Project WHO* radio documentary. *This Week in Doctor Who* (**groups.yahoo.com/group/thisweekindoctorwho**) is a guide to every *Doctor Who* broadcast, webcast and viewing updated every Wednesday; it's the next best thing to having a *Doctor Who* TV guide of your very own. The free online encyclopedia *Wikipedia* has an entire section devoted to *Doctor Who* (**http://en.wikipedia.org/wiki/Doctor_Who**). And don't forget the *CBC Canada* TV website (**www.cbc.ca/doctorwho**), which has excellent resources about the series and its broadcast there.

APPENDIX E

REFERENCE AND REVIEW

The *Doctor Who Reference Guide* (**www.drwhoguide.com**) is an excellent resource for *Doctor Who* information, with extensive reference material and synopses. So is *A Brief History of Time Travel* (**go.to/drwho-history**), which looks at each episode from a behind-the-scenes perspective, compiling archives of *Doctor Who* episode material. *Timelash* (**www.timelash.com**) is an archive of *Doctor Who* books, audios, videos and periodicals that will prime any fan on what's out there, and what's left to complete the collection. *Whoniverse* (**www.whoniverse.org**) features information on each episode, book and audio, its references and messages, in a clear and concise fashion. And the *Doctor Who Ratings Guide* (**www.pagefillers.com/dwrg**) features an extensive set of reviews including the television series.

DISCUSSION COMMUNITIES

The Internet is teeming with many *Doctor Who* discussion communities, providing places for *Doctor Who* fans to congregate, share information or chat about everything from the series to sport to politics. *The Outpost Gallifrey Forum* is the largest (**www.doctorwhoforum.com**) and boasts an extensive selection of sections plus a variety of *Doctor Who* professionals (including several of the new series's writers) participating. The *Restoration Team Forum* (**www.rtforum.co.uk**) is a technical resource community for the folks behind the *Doctor Who* DVD releases, but also a fascinating place to talk about the video & DVD side of the show. So is *Roobarb's DVD Forum* (**www.zetaminor.com/roobarb**), a DVD discussion community with a very active *Doctor Who* section.

Several other online discussion communities include the *Loose Cannon* boards (**www.recons.com**), *Doctor Who World* (**www.doctorwhoworld.org.uk/forum**), the *DoctorWho2005* board (**s7.invisionfree.com/Doctor_Who_2005**), *Logopolis Metropolis* (**richietimelord.proboards21.com/index.cgi**) and even the *Tom Baker Forum* (**www.tombaker.tv/forum**), part of the former *Doctor Who* actor's official website but a very lively gang of new series aficionadoes reside there.

Meanwhile, *Yahoo!* hosts several large discussion communities. The most active include the *YaWho doctor_who* community (**groups.yahoo.com/group/doctor_who**) , the largest collection of fans on the *Yahoo!* service, featuring weekly discussions on episodes, news and reviews; the *Jade Pagoda* list (**groups.yahoo.com/group/jade_pagoda**), for discussions about *Doctor Who* books including the new TV series books; and the *gaywhovians* group (**groups.yahoo.com/group/gaywhovians**), welcoming gay and lesbian fans (and straight friends too) across *Doctor Who* fandom.

And finally, there's that old standby, the USENET newsgroups; check with your Internet provider to see if they have newsgroup access. Your best bet would be to access the **rec.arts.drwho.moderated** group to have lively discussions without being choked by spam or nonsense!

There are so many online communities that it would be impossible to list them all ... but these should start you off nicely.

BLOGS, JOURNALS AND FUN

The new series has brought a plethora of *Doctor Who* weblogs (also known simply as 'blogs') and online journals devoted to the new series. *Time and Chips* (**www.livejournal.com/community/time_and_chips**) is one such place, an immeasurably active *Doctor Who* LiveJournal community focusing primarily on the new series and its stars. LiveJournal's original *Doctor Who Community* (**www.livejournal.com/**

community/doctorwho) has been around for a while and its readers spend considerable time discussing all facets of the new show. *Behind the Sofa Again* (**tachyontv.typepad.com/waiting_for_christopher**) is a new series review blog from a variety of reviewers' differing points of view, while the *DoctorWhoBlog* (**www.doctorwhoblog.com**) from the DWIN in Canada is also kept updated. *TimeLord* (**www.timelord.co.uk**) is an enjoyable and creative site with fiction and fun. *Caption Who* (**www.glitterrock.org/capwhomain.html**) does exactly what it says ... captions pictures from each new *Doctor Who* episode, often with hilarious consequences. And there's *TachyonTV* (**tachyontv.typepad.com/tachyon**), a very funny satire blog where you'll find nothing but irreverence about the Davies era of the show (but all in good fun!) Plus, don't forget *Howe's Who*, (**www.howeswho.co.uk**), the blog of David J Howe of Telos Publising, publishers of this very book!

'SHIPPER' SITES

Shipper fandom – that is, fans of deep character relationships, such as that between the Doctor and Rose – has at last become part of the *Doctor Who* fan experience. *Better With Two* (**www.loony-archivist.com/who**) focuses on the Eccleston/Piper new series dynamic, as do *Abandon Innocence* (**www.abandon-innocence.com**) and *After Shock* (**serpensortia.org/shock**). *Captain Jack's Timeship* (**www.livejournal.com/ community/galactic_conman**) focuses on Captain Jack, while *Better With Three* (**www.livejournal.com/community/better_with_3**) celebrates the Eccleston/Piper/ Barrowman group. It's a relatively new, but very active, part of *Doctor Who* fandom on the Internet.

VISUALS

Two sites corner the online market on pictures and screengrabs of your favorite *Doctor Who* moments: the *Image Archive* (**www.shillpages.com/dw/dwia.htm**) and the *Tragical History Tour* (**drwhotht.phenominet.com**). They're usually all you need for good visual reference material.

PEOPLE

There are many sites devoted to the actors in the new series including several unofficial Christopher Eccleston sites (**christophereccleston.com, christophereccleston.info, www.freewebs.com/ceccleston** and **server11.web-mania.com/users/beyondtN/index2.html**), unofficial websites for David Tennant (**www.david-tennant.com** and **www.davidtennant.co.uk**) and official ones for John Barrowman (**www.johnbarrowman.com**) and Camille Coduri (**www.angelfire.com/film/camillecoduri**). There are also many Billie Piper tributes online, many of them about her days as a singer (and some that are a bit risqué; sorry, you'll have to find those on your own!)

CONVENTIONS AND EVENTS

onventions are a great way to meet fellow *Doctor Who* fans in a comfortable environment; most of the time, they're elaborate reasons to have a party with friends over a weekend. Actors, writers and production staff from the new *Doctor Who* series have recently started to attend these events, too! The following is a list of annual and other events:

UNITED KINGDOM

As the worldwide home of *Doctor Who*, the UK is home to many popular events. The *PanoptiCon* conventions (**www.dominitemporal.co.uk**) are held irregularly but have recently been sponsored by BBC Worldwide to celebrate events such as the series's fortieth anniversary. The *Tenth Planet* store in Barking (**www.tenthplanet.co.uk**) holds regular signings and special events such as the *Dimensions* and *Invasion* conventions. The *Doctor Who* Appreciation Society (**dwas.drwho.org**) holds its own semi-regular events including screenings. *Regenerations* (**www.regenerations.co.uk**) has just started up, with events bridging the classic and new series. *Cult TV* (**www.cult.tv**) holds a yearly science fiction gathering with *Doctor Who* and other series actors. The Edinburgh chapter of the DWAS (**www.edinburghwho.co.uk**) hosts its own semi-regular events. The *Doctor Who Autograph Collectors Club* (**www.angelfire.com/scifi2/dwaccevents**) features the occasional special signing event. *Cineffigy Events* (**www.doc-who.com**), *Vortex Events* (**www.vortex-events.freeserve.co.uk**), *Ascension Events* (**www.scifiheaven.net/main/ascensionevents**) and *SciFiCollector* (**www.scificollector.co.uk**) also hold occasional signings, open days and conferences geared toward the casual and active fan. And of course, one cannot forget the *Brighton Doctor Who Exhibition* (**www.doctorwhoexhibitions.co.uk**), where material on display from the series can be found.

UNITED STATES

The US has four regularly-scheduled *Doctor Who*-themed events that occur every year. *Gallifrey One* (**www.gallifreyone.com/gallifrey.php**) takes place every February in Los Angeles and attracts an international crowd of fans. *ChicagoTARDIS* (**www.chicagotardis.com**) takes place every Thanksgiving weekend in November. *United Fan Con* (**www.unitedfancon.com**) is a multimedia event with a special *Doctor Who* focus, taking place in Massachusetts in early November. And the *Sci-Fi Sea Cruise* (**www.scificruise.com**) is an annual excursion at sea with fans and guests setting sail from a variety of US ports at different times of the year.

AUSTRALIA

The nation's *Doctor Who* convention, *Whovention*, is hosted by the *Doctor Who Club of Australia* (**www.doctorwhoaustralia.org**). The DWCA also hosts several smaller annual events, usually gatherings with actors or production people from the series and special screenings.

CANADA

The *Doctor Who Information Network* (**www.dwin.org**) hosts a periodic gathering, *WhoParty*. Also, a large multimedia event, *Toronto Trek* (**www.icomm.ca/tcon**) has started to feature *Doctor Who* actors as well.

MAGAZINES

There are many magazines on the market that will aid you in your monthly *Doctor Who* fix. You can always start with *Doctor Who Magazine,* the officially-sanctioned monthly title from Panini Publishing; each issue is full of interviews and reviews and the latest production notes from Russell T Davies. Or try *SFX* Magazine from Future Publishing, which has terrific coverage including on-set photographs. Other magazines that have covered the series recently include *Dreamwatch, TV Zone, Cult Times* and *Starburst.* You can find any or all of them in your local bookshop or newsstand.

ACKNOWLEDGEMENTS

If I've learned anything while writing *Back to the Vortex*, it's that nothing like this ever happens in a vacuum. I'd therefore like to gratefully acknowledge the unprecedented support, encouragement and fellowship I have experienced from friends, colleagues, readers, and fellow participants in this vastness called *Doctor Who* fandom over the past twenty years, and especially during the lead up to and broadcast of this television series.

More specifically, I would like to offer my appreciation to the following individuals who made this possible:

To Steve Tribe and Paul Engelberg, who made *Back to the Vortex* a reality as much as I have. Largely because of Paul's tireless scouring of internet wires for articles and Steve's meticulous examination of source material and compiling of the ratings data (not to mention some email exchanges between the three of us that sometimes went well into the night), a good 90% of the reference material and information I required to be able to compile this book and to do it well reached my desk. Without them, this book would simply never have come to fruition, and I am eternally in their debt.

To the review team – Graeme Burk, Simon Catlow, Robert Franks, Sarah Hadley, Paul Hayes, Cameron Mason, Jon Preddle, Keith Topping and Scott Alan Woodard – who have all been instrumental in reading and contributing to the episode-by-episode section of this book. I've appreciated their enthusiasm for the project as much as their reviews, and they've kept a watchful eye on the reference material and made sure I didn't muck it up too much. Thank you all for being part of this and being so great to work with.

To Matt Dale, who went through each episode entry keeping an eye on the geography, British vs American dialects and other matters that cleaned up the data; he also contributed information about the series's music and the novels and comic strips, and easily helped complete the manuscript on time and with an impressive depth of detail in these areas.

To John Molyneux, who made it possible for me to be there alongside him and my other friends in the UK during the journey – or at least to make it seem that way.

To Philip Segal, whose generosity and friendship since we met in 1995 has been dearly appreciated, and whose participation in this book from the start meant a great deal to me.

To Rob Shearman, for listening, for great advice, for pointing out the obvious when it missed me entirely, and for keeping me focused.

To David J Howe and Stephen James Walker, who have not only been the models of professionalism but have made this process as easy as it could have been for me. I could not have asked for better editors and champions of this material, and it has been a pleasure to work with both of them.

To Arnold T Blumberg and Rosemary Howe, who have made sure the words look and sound good on paper. I appreciate all your hard work in putting this together.

To Gary Russell, Rob Shearman (again), Craig Hinton, Keith Topping (again) and Paul Cornell, whose friendship, support, and inspiration from their respective experiences as *Doctor Who* writers set a framework for me on this journey and helped me get there.

To a small group of friends who, along with the aforementioned, kept me going throughout this ordeal (because at some points it certainly seemed that way): Steve Hill, Greg McElhatton, Craig Byrne, Mike Doran, Jason Tucker, Trey Korte, Steve Traylen, Robert Smith?, Scott Clarke, Felicity Kusinitz, Nick Seidler, Jason Knight and Nick Johnson.

To the moderating staff of the *Outpost Gallifrey* forum, who over the years have helped bring fans together and have made my life easier in the process (especially when I desperately needed it while writing this book): Jennifer Kelley, Michael Zecca, Neil Chester, Matt Evenden, Garth Wilcox, Wil Cantrell, Mark Stevens, Raymond Sawaya, Jessie Loflin, Matthew Kopelke, Samantha Dings, Lindsay Johnson, Michael Blumenthal, Derek Kompare, Dave Whittam, Cavan Scott, Josiah Rowe, Dawn Livingston, Andy Frankham, James Bow and Karen Baldwin.

To the readers of *Outpost Gallifrey* and the denizens of the Forum, to the *Gallifrey One* convention committee, staff, volunteers and attendees who have been so supportive over the years, and to everyone else who has sent me news items and material over the years – you have all been instrumental in your contributions, suggestions, research and good wishes, and I am eternally grateful.

To Mark Phippen, because our work together on *Missing Pieces* prepared me for this in ways I never expected, and to Wilma Meier, who took a chance on me in 1989 and opened doors for me I never imagined possible.

To my parents and my brother Jeff for their love and support.

To the three people to whom this book is dedicated: my partner Chad Jones, for putting up with all this and for being my foundation; my friend Robert Franks (again), for sharing this experience with me and keeping my spirits high; and my mentor and friend Robbie Bourget, for helping me keep things in perspective, and for never letting me forget *why* it is that we do what we do.

I would also like to acknowledge the following individuals for specific contributions to this manuscript, whether it be reference material, resources, information, quotes, sage counsel or shared memories: Chuck Foster of the *Doctor Who* Appreciation Society, Andy Parish, John Bowman, Roger Anderson, Steve Manfred, Jamie Austin, Peter Weaver, Tom Beck, Andrew Pixley, Gillane Seaborne and Adam Page and everyone at *Doctor Who Confidential*, Malcolm Prince at BBC Radio 2, Clayton Hickman and Tom Spilsbury at *Doctor Who Magazine*, James Goss and Rob Francis of the official BBC *Doctor Who* website, Jason Haigh-Ellery, David McIntee, Jean-Marc and Randy Lofficier, Lisa Bowerman, Gene Smith, Benjamin Cook, Dave Owen (who reproduced his *Damaged Goods* review that I couldn't locate), Mark Gatiss, Steven Moffat, Simon Bishop, Nathan Baron, Lars Pearson, Rebecca Barber and Bruce Rowan, Dan Sandifer, Erik Engman, Suze Campagna, Scott Busman, Christian McGuire, Kathy Sullivan, Keith Hartman, Joe Cochran, Michael Donahue, Kenny Mittleider, Chris Newman, Mark Corsi, Geof Greenway, Bruce Aguilar, Tom Misiuraca, Clay Eichelberger, Tony & Jane Kenealy, Paul Taylor, Derek Hambly, Eric Hoffman, Jeff Ovik, Cary Woodward, Ben Brown, Lara Pascoe and everyone at *Time and Chips*, Rich Kirkpatrick, Peter Ware, Russ Merryman, Nick Salmond, Stephen Graves, Stuart Ian Burns, Ian Wheeler, Rod Mammitzsch, Steve O'Brien, Steve Freestone, Adam Kirk, Alex Wilcock, Andrew Harvey, Dan Garrett, Steve Berry, Ian Berriman, Daniel O'Malley, Martin Hearn, Darren Floyd, Eddie Brennan, Faiz Rehman, Mark Ayres, Richard Bignell, Graham Kibble-White, James Sellwood, Adam McGechan, Keith Armstrong, Timothy Farr, Paul Greaves, Shannon Patrick Sullivan, Jim Sangster, Paul Condon, Peter Anghelides, Stephen Gray, Dominic May, Joey Reynolds, Ben Keywood, Will Hadcroft, Nick Walters, Gareth Price, Mark Keeble, Lee Johnson, Chris Lane, Jonathan Knibbs, Paul Mount, Neil Jones, Mark Campbell, Andrew Wong, Peter Dickinson, Paul Waddington, Martin Hoscik, David Shaw, Anna Roberts, John Smith, William Owen,

ACKNOWLEDGEMENTS

Andrew Ford, Mark Coupe, Jez Connolly, John J Moran, Alex Willcox, John Campbell Rees and Benjamin Elliott. Plus a special shout out to everyone on the 2004 Sci Fi Sea Cruise, which served me well as a springboard for some of this book (and especially to Rob, Robert, Jason and Lisa, for some amazing moments ... and for keeping me sane).

Also, thanks to the following whose photographs were used in this book: Roger Anderson, Leon Hughes, Chuck Foster, Jason Stevens, Paul Mount, Dave Shuttleworth, Ian Golden, Rob Stradling, Tim Robins, Helena Drakakis, and Mark Davies (who took what has to be the best *Doctor Who* behind-the-scenes photograph ever ... the smoking Moxx of Balhoon).

And of course, special thanks to Special K. They know why.

Finally, I want to send a special note of thanks to Russell T Davies. Though we've never met in person, his warmth and sincerity during our brief exchanges have always been unfailingly supportive, and I appreciate his thoughtfulness. To Russell, to Julie Gardner, to Phil Collinson, and to everyone who worked on this wonderful first series ... congratulations on a great year, with the promise of many more to come.

Back To The Vortex was written in memory of Michael Mason (1960-2004): dear friend, confidante, ex-roommate, grief counsellor, convention buddy, IM chatter, Bistromathics wizard, kind-hearted soul ... and now a resident of that great iced tea heaven (no lemon) in the sky.

PHOTOGRAPHIC CREDITS

COLOUR SECTION 1:

1 – Recording outside Howells department store ('Rose') © 2004 Leon Hughes

2 – One of the first full shots of the TARDIS seen by the world, captured first by fans at the filming site ('Rose') © 2004 Roger Anderson

3 – An Auton hand is readied for action ('Rose') © 2004 Leon Hughes

4 – Chairs for the cast ... ('Rose') © 2004 Mark Davies

5 – Preparing to record on the banks of the Thames opposite the London Eye ('Rose') © 2004 Chuck Foster

6 – Christopher Eccleston and Billie Piper ('The End of the World') © 2004 Mark Davies

7 – Christopher Eccleston and Billie Piper ('The End of the World') © 2004 Ian Golden

8 – Jimmy Vee in partial costume as the Moxx of Balhoon ('The End of the World') © 2004 Mark Davies

9 – Two of the actors playing Platform One attendants ('The End of the World') © 2004 Mark Davies

10 – Christopher Eccleston and Simon Callow (centre and right) watch the action ('The Unquiet Dead') © 2004 Roger Anderson

11 – A Sneed and Company carriage ready for filming ('The Unquiet Dead') © 2004 Paul Mount

12 – Jennifer Hill, playing Mrs Peace, records the opening sequence where, possessed by the Gelth, she walks towards the camera ('The Unquiet Dead') © 2004 Jason Stevens

13 – One of the posters adorning the estate walls ('Aliens of London') © 2004 Chuck Foster

14 – The TARDIS ('Aliens of London') © 2004 Chuck Foster

15 – The Albion Hospital sign is erected outside the Cardiff Royal Infirmary ('Aliens of London') © 2004 Dave Shuttleworth

16 – One of the Army transport vehicles ('Aliens of London') © 2004 Rob Stradling

17 – Christopher Eccleston on the balcony ('Boom Town') © 2005 Tim Robins

18 – The TARDIS by the Millennium Stadium ('Boom Town') © 2005 Helena Drakakis

COLOUR SECTION 2: (All photographs © 2004/5 Wales News & Picture Service)

1 – The Dalek is ready for action ('Dalek')

2 – Rose (Billie Piper) ('Rose')

3 – The Autons emerge from the shopping centre ('Rose')

4 – Rose (Billie Piper) and friend record a scene ('Rose')

5 – Christopher Eccleston by his trailer ('Rose')

6 – Chaos in the high street. Recording the devastation ('Rose')

7 – An Auton ('Rose')

8 – One of the dead human bodies possessed by the Gelth ('The Unquiet Dead')

9 – The Doctor (Christopher Eccleston) and Rose (Billie Piper) in Cardiff 1869 ('The Unquiet Dead')

10 – Simon Callow as Charles Dickens ('The Unquiet Dead')

11 – A group of extras playing the Gelth-possessed humans ('The Unquiet Dead')

12 – The shadow of death approaches ('Dalek')

13 – A Dalek ('Dalek')

14 – Van Statten's troops try and keep the Dalek back ('Dalek')

15 – Another view of Van Statten's Metaltron ('Dalek')

16 – The Dalek prop with one of the remote control operators ('Dalek')

17 & 18 – John Barrowman, Christopher Eccleston, Noel Clarke and Billie Piper on location in Cardiff ('Boom Town')

ABOUT THE AUTHOR

Shaun Lyon has been involved in *Doctor Who* fandom for nearly twenty years, including as editor of the popular *Doctor Who* website *Outpost Gallifrey* (www.gallifreyone.com) and as co-founder, programme director and resident cheerleader of Gallifrey One, North America's longest-running annual *Doctor Who* convention. His previous published works include 'The Inquisitor's Story' in *Short Trips: Repercussions* and 'Goodwill Toward Men' in *Short Trips: A Christmas Treasury*, both licensed short fiction anthologies published by Big Finish Productions, as well as co-editing (with Mark Phippen) the bestselling *Doctor Who* charity fiction anthology *Missing Pieces*. He lives in Los Angeles, California, with his partner Chad Jones (who understands his *Doctor Who* passion) and two spoiled cats (who, quite obviously, don't).

ABOUT THE REVIEWERS

Graeme Burk is the editor of *Enlightenment*, the acclaimed fanzine of the *Doctor Who* Information Network. He was the first Canadian to contribute to *Doctor Who* professional fiction with two contributions to the *Short Trips* range of anthologies. In his spare time, he works as a freelance writer in Toronto. His guidebook to *Battlestar Galactica* will be published by Mad Norwegian Press in Spring 2006.

Simon Catlow was drawn into the versatile world of *Doctor Who* by its infinite possibilities, but his interest was maintained by the various forms it has evolved into following the conclusion of the original series. The audio dramas of Big Finish inspired him to create his website, *The Tertiary Console Room*, which he spends far too much time developing. He has contributed reviews and articles to *Outpost Gallifrey* and the fanzines *Shockeye's Kitchen* and *Whotopia*, and lives in the UK.

Robert Franks is considered one of *Doctor Who* fandom's experts on missing episodes and archive formats. He is the co-editor of the popular *Doctor Who* research and restoration fanzine *Nothing at the End of the Lane* and administers the *Doctor Who* DVD extras website *TimeRotor*. He lives in Minnesota.

Sarah Hadley has always been interested in the written word, contributing to such fiction anthologies as *Missing Pieces*, *Walking in Eternity*, and the collection she edited, *The 13 Crimes of Doctor Who*. She is a frequent reviewer for *Outpost Gallifrey*, and works as a freelance writer and post-production editor in her native state of Tennessee. The short film she wrote and produced, *Company*, is currently appearing in festivals across the US.

Paul Hayes was born in West Sussex, England in 1984. He has written articles on *Doctor Who* professionally for the *Stage* and the *Guardian* newspapers in the UK, and on an amateur basis for the DWAS's newsletter *Celestial Toyroom* and the Canadian fanzine *Whotopia*. He is also a regular contributor to the *Outpost Gallifrey* website, and was formerly one of those responsible for running a local group of the *Doctor Who* Appreciation Society in the Brighton area.

Cameron Mason was born in February 1983, just in time for Peter Davison's tour of his home nation of Australia. He is an avid viewer/reader/listener of the series in all its forms, and has a degree in secondary teaching (History/Geography). He is the author of 'Final Draft' in the short fiction spinoff anthology *Professor Bernice Summerfield: A Life Worth Living*.

Jon Preddle is a prominent figure in New Zealand fandom and a long-serving regular writer/researcher for the internationally highly respected fanzine, *TSV* (*Time Space Visualiser*). He also contributes to the online *Audio DiscContinuity Guide*, and authored *Timelink*, an unofficial guide to *Doctor Who* continuity. After seizing control of the family's VCR in 1982 (in time to record episode 4 of 'Logopolis'), Jon has never been quite the same since ...

Keith Topping is the UK-based author of several BBC *Doctor Who* novels including *Byzantium!* and *The King of Terror* and, with Martin Day, *The Hollow Men* and *The Devil Goblins of Neptune*, as well as the Telos novella *Ghost Ship* and many in-depth reference guides including *Slayer, Hollywood Vampire, Beyond the Gate, Inside Bartlett's White House* and, with Paul Cornell and Martin Day, the irreverent guide to *Doctor Who*, *The Discontinuity Guide*.

Scott Alan Woodard discovered *Doctor Who* in the mid '70s and his fascination with the series has never waned. He has been residing in Los Angeles since 1992 and while he currently makes a living promoting children's television, he previously worked in the physical special effects industry (as a fabricator and puppeteer). In February 2005, his first scripted *Doctor Who* audio, *The Juggernauts*, was released from Big Finish Productions.

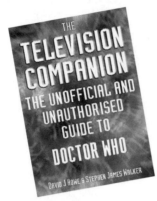

Other
Doctor Who
Telos Titles
Available

THE TELEVISION COMPANION: THE UNOFFICIAL AND UNAUTHORISED GUIDE TO DOCTOR WHO by DAVID J HOWE & STEPHEN JAMES WALKER
Complete episode guide to the popular TV show.
£14.99 (+ £4.75 UK p&p) Standard p/b ISBN: 1-903889-51-0

THE HANDBOOK: THE UNOFFICIAL AND UNAUTHORISED GUIDE TO THE PRODUCTION OF DOCTOR WHO by DAVID J HOWE, STEPHEN JAMES WALKER and MARK STAMMERS
Complete guide to the making of *Doctor Who*.
£14.99 (+ £4.75 UK p&p) Standard p/b ISBN: 1-903889-59-6
£30.00 (+ £4.75 UK p&p) Deluxe h/b ISBN: 1-903889-96-0

HOWE'S TRANSCENDENTAL TOYBOX: SECOND EDITION by DAVID J HOWE & ARNOLD T BLUMBERG
Complete guide to *Doctor Who* Merchandise.
£25.00 (+ £4.75 UK p&p) Standard p/b ISBN: 1-903889-56-1

HOWE'S TRANSCENDENTAL TOYBOX: UPDATE NO. 1: 2003 by DAVID J HOWE & ARNOLD T BLUMBERG
Complete guide to *Doctor Who* Merchandise released in 2003.
£7.99 (+ £1.50 UK p&p) Standard p/b ISBN: 1-903889-57-X

TIME HUNTER

A range of high-quality, original paperback and limited edition hardback novellas featuring the adventures in time of Honoré Lechasseur. Part mystery, part detective story, part dark fantasy, part science fiction … these books are guaranteed to enthral fans of good fiction everywhere, and are in the spirit of our acclaimed range of *Doctor Who* Novellas.

ALREADY AVAILABLE

THE WINNING SIDE by LANCE PARKIN
Emily is dead! Killed by an unknown assailant. Honoré and Emily find themselves caught up in a plot reaching from the future to their past, and with their very existence, not to mention the future of the entire world, at stake, can they unravel the mystery before it is too late?
An adventure in time and space.
£7.99 (+ £1.50 UK p&p) Standard p/b ISBN 1-903889-35-9 (pb)

THE TUNNEL AT THE END OF THE LIGHT by STEFAN PETRUCHA
In the heart of post-war London, a bomb is discovered lodged at a disused station between Green Park and Hyde Park Corner. The bomb detonates, and as the dust clears, it becomes apparent that *something* has been awakened. Strange half-human creatures attack the workers at the site, hungrily searching for anything containing sugar …
Meanwhile, Honoré and Emily are contacted by eccentric poet Randolph Crest, who believes himself to be the target of these subterranean creatures. The ensuing investigation brings Honoré and Emily up against a terrifying force from deep beneath the earth, and one which even with their combined powers, they may have trouble stopping.
An adventure in time and space.
£7.99 (+ £1.50 UK p&p) Standard p/b ISBN 1-903889-37-5 (pb)
£25.00 (+ £1.50 UK p&p) Deluxe h/b ISBN 1-903889-38-3 (hb)

THE CLOCKWORK WOMAN by CLAIRE BOTT
Honoré and Emily find themselves imprisoned in the 19th Century by a celebrated inventor … but help comes from an unexpected source – a humanoid automaton created by and to give pleasure to its owner. As the trio escape to London, they are unprepared for what awaits them, and at every turn it seems impossible to avert what fate may have in store for the Clockwork Woman.
An adventure in time and space.
£7.99 (+ £1.50 UK p&p) Standard p/b ISBN 1-903889-39-1 (pb)
£25.00 (+ £1.50 UK p&p) Deluxe h/b ISBN 1-903889-40-5 (hb)

KITSUNE by JOHN PAUL CATTON

In the year 2020, Honoré and Emily find themselves thrown into a mystery, as an ice spirit – *Yuki-Onna* – wreaks havoc during the Kyoto Festival, and a haunted funhouse proves to contain more than just paper lanterns and wax dummies. But what does all this have to do with the elegant owner of the Hide and Chic fashion chain … and to the legendary Chinese fox-spirits, the Kitsune?
An adventure in time and space.
£7.99 (+ £1.50 UK p&p) Standard p/b ISBN 1-903889-41-3 (pb)
£25.00 (+ £1.50 UK p&p) Deluxe h/b ISBN 1-903889-42-1 (hb)

THE SEVERED MAN by GEORGE MANN

What links a clutch of sinister murders in Victorian London, an angel appearing in a Staffordshire village in the 1920s and a small boy running loose around the capital in 1950? When Honoré and Emily encounter a man who appears to have been cut out of time, they think they have the answer. But soon enough they discover that the mystery is only just beginning and that nightmares can turn into reality.
An adventure in time and space.
£7.99 (+ £1.50 UK p&p) Standard p/b ISBN 1-903889-43-X (pb)
£25.00 (+ £1.50 UK p&p) Deluxe h/b ISBN 1-903889-44-8 (hb)

ECHOES by IAIN MCLAUGHLIN & CLAIRE BARTLETT

Echoes of the past … echoes of the future. Honoré Lechasseur can see the threads that bind the two together, however when he and Emily Blandish find themselves outside the imposing tower-block headquarters of Dragon Industry, both can sense something is wrong. There are ghosts in the building, and images and echoes of all times pervade the structure. But what is behind this massive contradiction in time, and can Honoré and Emily figure it out before they become trapped themselves …?
An adventure in time and space.
£7.99 (+ £1.50 UK p&p) Standard p/b ISBN 1-903889-45-6 (pb)
£25.00 (+ £1.50 UK p&p) Deluxe h/b ISBN 1-903889-46-4 (hb)

PECULIAR LIVES by PHILIP PURSER-HALLARD

Once a celebrated author of 'scientific romances', Erik Clevedon is an old man now. But his fiction conceals a dangerous truth, as Honoré Lechasseur and Emily Blandish discover after a chance encounter with a strangely gifted young pickpocket. Born between the Wars, the superhuman children known as 'the Peculiar' are reaching adulthood – and they believe that humanity is making a poor job of looking after the world they plan to inherit …
An adventure in time and space.
£7.99 (+ £1.50 UK p&p) Standard p/b ISBN 1-903889-47-2 (pb)
£25.00 (+ £1.50 UK p&p) Deluxe h/b ISBN 1-903889-48-0 (hb)

TIME HUNTER FILM

DAEMOS RISING by DAVID J HOWE, DIRECTED BY KEITH BARNFATHER

Daemos Rising is a sequel to both the *Doctor Who* adventure *The Daemons* and to *Downtime*, an earlier drama featuring the Yeti. It is also a prequel of sorts to Telos Publishing's *Time Hunter* series. It stars Miles Richardson as ex-UNIT operative Douglas Cavendish, and Beverley Cressman as Brigadier Lethbridge-Stewart's daughter Kate. Trapped in an isolated cottage, Cavendish thinks he is seeing ghosts. The only person who might understand and help is Kate Lethbridge-Stewart … but when she arrives, she realises that Cavendish is key in a plot to summon the Daemons back to the Earth. With time running out, Kate discovers that sometimes even the familiar can turn out to be your worst nightmare. Also starring Andrew Wisher, and featuring Ian Richardson as the Narrator.

An adventure in time and space.

£14.00 (+ £2.50 UK p&p) PAL format R4 DVD

Order direct from Reeltime Pictures, PO Box 23435, London SE26 5WU

HORROR/FANTASY

CAPE WRATH by PAUL FINCH

Death and horror on a deserted Scottish island as an ancient Viking warrior chief returns to life.

£8.00 (+ £1.50 UK p&p) Standard p/b ISBN: 1-903889-60-X

KING OF ALL THE DEAD by STEVE LOCKLEY & PAUL LEWIS

The king of all the dead will have what is his.

£8.00 (+ £1.50 UK p&p) Standard p/b ISBN: 1-903889-61-8

GUARDIAN ANGEL by STEPHANIE BEDWELL-GRIME

Devilish fun as Guardian Angel Porsche Winter loses a soul to the devil …

£9.99 (+ £2.50 UK p&p) Standard p/b ISBN: 1-903889-62-6

FALLEN ANGEL by STEPHANIE BEDWELL-GRIME

Porsche Winter battles she devils on Earth …

£9.99 (+ £2.50 UK p&p) Standard p/b ISBN: 1-903889-69-3

ASPECTS OF A PSYCHOPATH by ALISTAIR LANGSTON

Goes deeper than ever before into the twisted psyche of a serial killer. Horrific, graphic and gripping, this book is not for the squeamish.

£8.00 (+ £1.50 UK p&p) Standard p/b ISBN: 1-903889-63-4

SPECTRE by STEPHEN LAWS

The inseparable Byker Chapter: six boys, one girl, growing up together in the back streets of Newcastle. Now memories are all that Richard Eden has left, and one treasured photograph. But suddenly, inexplicably, the images of his companions start to fade, and as they vanish, so his friends are found dead and mutilated. Something is stalking the Chapter, picking them off one by one, something connected with their past, and with the girl they used to know.

£9.99 (+ £2.50 UK p&p) Standard p/b ISBN: 1-903889-72-3

THE HUMAN ABSTRACT by GEORGE MANN

A future tale of private detectives, AIs, Nanobots, love and death.

£7.99 (+ £1.50 UK p&p) Standard p/b ISBN: 1-903889-65-0

BREATHE by CHRISTOPHER FOWLER

The Office meets *Night of the Living Dead*.

£7.99 (+ £1.50 UK p&p) Standard p/b ISBN: 1-903889-67-7
£25.00 (+ £1.50 UK p&p) Deluxe h/b ISBN: 1-903889-68-5

HOUDINI'S LAST ILLUSION by STEVE SAVILE

Can master illusionist Harry Houdini outwit the dead shades of his past?

£7.99 (+ £1.50 UK p&p) Standard p/b ISBN: 1-903889-66-9

ALICE'S JOURNEY BEYOND THE MOON by R J CARTER

A sequel to the classic Lewis Carroll tales.

£6.99 (+ £1.50 UK p&p) Standard p/b ISBN: 1-903889-76-6
£30.00 (+ £1.50 UK p&p) Deluxe h/b ISBN: 1-903889-77-4

APPROACHING OMEGA by ERIC BROWN

A colonisation mission to Earth runs into problems.

£7.99 (+ £1.50 UK p&p) Standard p/b ISBN: 1-903889-98-7
£30.00 (+ £1.50 UK p&p) Deluxe h/b ISBN: 1-903889-99-5

VALLEY OF LIGHTS by STEPHEN GALLAGHER

A cop comes up against a body-hopping murderer …
£9.99 (+ £2.50 UK p&p) Standard p/b ISBN: 1-903889-74-X
£30.00 (+ £2.50 UK p&p) Deluxe h/b ISBN: 1-903889-75-8

TV/FILM GUIDES

A DAY IN THE LIFE: THE UNOFFICIAL AND UNAUTHORISED GUIDE TO 24 by KEITH TOPPING

Complete episode guide to the first season of the popular TV show.
£9.99 (+ £2.50 p&p) Standard p/b ISBN: 1-903889-53-7

THE TELEVISION COMPANION: THE UNOFFICIAL AND UNAUTHORISED GUIDE TO DOCTOR WHO by DAVID J HOWE & STEPHEN JAMES WALKER

Complete episode guide to the popular TV show.
£14.99 (+ £4.75 UK p&p) Standard p/b ISBN: 1-903889-51-0

LIBERATION: THE UNOFFICIAL AND UNAUTHORISED GUIDE TO BLAKE'S 7 by ALAN STEVENS & FIONA MOORE

Complete episode guide to the popular TV show.
Featuring a foreword by David Maloney
£9.99 (+ £2.50 UK p&p) Standard p/b ISBN: 1-903889-54-5

A VAULT OF HORROR by KEITH TOPPING

A Guide to 80 Classic (and not so classic) British Horror Films
£12.99 (+ £4.75 UK p&p) Standard p/b ISBN: 1-903889-58-8

BEAUTIFUL MONSTERS: THE UNOFFICIAL AND UNAUTHORISED GUIDE TO THE ALIEN AND PREDATOR FILMS by DAVID McINTEE

A Guide to the *Alien* and *Predator* Films
£9.99 (+ £2.50 UK p&p) Standard p/b ISBN: 1-903889-94-4

HANK JANSON

Classic pulp crime thrillers from the 1940s and 1950s.

TORMENT by HANK JANSON
£9.99 (+ £1.50 UK p&p) Standard p/b ISBN: 1-903889-80-4

WOMEN HATE TILL DEATH by HANK JANSON
£9.99 (+ £1.50 UK p&p) Standard p/b ISBN: 1-903889-81-2

SOME LOOK BETTER DEAD by HANK JANSON
£9.99 (+ £1.50 UK p&p) Standard p/b ISBN: 1-903889-82-0

SKIRTS BRING ME SORROW by HANK JANSON
£9.99 (+ £1.50 UK p&p) Standard p/b ISBN: 1-903889-83-9

WHEN DAMES GET TOUGH by HANK JANSON
£9.99 (+ £1.50 UK p&p) Standard p/b ISBN: 1-903889-85-5

ACCUSED by HANK JANSON
£9.99 (+ £1.50 UK p&p) Standard p/b ISBN: 1-903889-86-3

KILLER by HANK JANSON
£9.99 (+ £1.50 UK p&p) Standard p/b ISBN: 1-903889-87-1

FRAILS CAN BE SO TOUGH by HANK JANSON
£9.99 (+ £1.50 UK p&p) Standard p/b ISBN: 1-903889-88-X

BROADS DON'T SCARE EASY by HANK JANSON
£9.99 (+ £1.50 UK p&p) Standard p/b ISBN: 1-903889-89-8

KILL HER IF YOU CAN by HANK JANSON
£9.99 (+ £1.50 UK p&p) Standard p/b ISBN: 1-903889-90-1

Non-fiction:
THE TRIALS OF HANK JANSON by STEVE HOLLAND
£12.99 (+ £2.50 UK p&p) Standard p/b ISBN: 1-903889-84-7

The prices shown are correct at time of going to press. However, the publishers reserve the right to increase prices from those previously advertised without prior notice.

TELOS PUBLISHING
c/o Beech House, Chapel Lane, Moulton, Cheshire, CW9 8PQ, England
Email: orders@telos.co.uk
Web: www.telos.co.uk

To order copies of any Telos books, please visit our website where there are full details of all titles and facilities for worldwide credit card online ordering, or send a cheque or postal order (UK only) for the appropriate amount (including postage and packing), together with details of the book(s) you require, plus your name and address to the above address. Overseas readers please send two international reply coupons for details of prices and postage rates.